Case Studies in Contemporary Criticism

JAMES JOYCE

A Portrait of the Artist as a Young Man

WITHDRAWN

Case Studies in Contemporary Criticism
SERIES EDITOR: Ross C Murfin

Case Studies in Contemporary Criticism

SERIES EDITOR: Ross C Murfin, *Southern Methodist University*

JAMES JOYCE
A Portrait of the Artist as a Young Man

Complete, Authoritative Text with
Biographical, Historical, and Cultural Contexts,
Critical History, and Essays from
Contemporary Critical Perspectives

SECOND EDITION

EDITED BY
R. Brandon Kershner
University of Florida

Bedford/St. Martin's
BOSTON ◆ NEW YORK

For Bedford / St. Martin's

Executive Editor: Stephen A. Scipione
Editorial Assistants: Amy Hurd Gershman, Kaitlin Hannon
Senior Production Supervisor: Joe Ford
Production Associate: Christopher Gross
Project Management: DeMasi Design and Publishing Services
Cover Design: Donna Lee Dennison
Cover Art: Long Room, Trinity College, Dublin. © Michael St. Maur Sheil/
  CORBIS.
Composition: Stratford Publishing Services, Inc.
Printing and Binding: Haddon Craftsmen, an RR Donnelley & Sons
  Company

President: Joan E. Feinberg
Editorial Director: Denise B. Wydra
Editor in Chief: Karen S. Henry
Director of Marketing: Karen Melton Soeltz
Director of Editing, Design, and Production: Marcia Cohen
Manager, Publishing Services: Emily Berleth

For information, write: Bedford / St. Martin's,
75 Arlington Street, Boston, MA 02116   (617-399-4000)

ISBN: 0-312-40811-0
EAN: 978-0-312-40811-4

Acknowledgments

Acknowledgments and copyrights are continued at the back of the book on page
455, which constitutes an extension of the copyright page.

The text of *A Portrait of the Artist as a Young Man* is based on the version corrected
from the Dublin holograph by Chester G. Anderson, reviewed by Richard Ellmann, and
first published in the United States of America in 1964 by Viking Penguin Inc.

About the Series

Volumes in the *Case Studies in Contemporary Criticism* series introduce college students to the current critical and theoretical ferment in literary studies. Each volume reprints the complete text of a significant literary work, together with critical essays that approach the work from different theoretical perspectives and editorial matter that introduces both the literary work and the critics' theoretical perspectives.

The volume editor of each *Case Study* has selected and prepared an authoritative text of a classic work, written introductions (sometimes supplemented by cultural documents) that place the work in biographical and historical context, and surveyed the critical responses to the work since its original publication. Thus situated biographically, historically, and critically, the work is subsequently examined in several critical essays that have been prepared especially for students. The essays show theory in practice; whether written by established scholars or exceptional young critics, they demonstrate how current theoretical approaches can generate compelling readings of great literature.

As series editor, I have prepared introductions to the critical essays and to the theoretical approaches they entail. The introductions, accompanied by bibliographies, explain and historicize the principal concepts, major figures, and key works of particular theoretical approaches as a prelude to discussing how they pertain to the critical essays that follow. It is my hope that the introductions will reveal to students that

effective criticism — including their own — is informed by a set of coherent assumptions that can be not only articulated but also modified
and extended through comparison of different theoretical approaches.
Finally, I have included a glossary of key terms that recur in these volumes and in the discourse of contemporary theory and criticism.

I hope that the *Case Studies in Contemporary Criticism* series will
reaffirm the richness of its literary works, even as it presents invigorat-
ing new ways to mine their apparently inexhaustible wealth.

I would like to thank Supryia M. Ray, with whom I wrote *The Bedford Glossary of Critical and Literary Terms,* for her invaluable help in
revising introductions to the critical approaches represented in this
volume.

Ross C Murfin
Provost, Southern Methodist University
Series Editor

About This Volume

The text used in this edition of *A Portrait of the Artist as a Young Man* is based on that established by Chester G. Anderson with some modifications by Richard Ellmann; for this edition Professor Anderson has made a number of further changes to that edition, as he explains below ("About This Text"). The editing of Joyce's texts has become a surprisingly controversial topic over the past twenty years. Without attempting to join that debate, I will say that I believe Part One of this volume to be the best text of Joyce's novel currently available. I have added a number of brief explanatory notes for the text, mostly in cases where Joyce's use of words would cause confusion for the ordinary reader. Readers who wish further information about any of the numerous allusions in the book should check either standard references or specialized ones such as Don Gifford's *Joyce Annotated,* second edition (Berkeley: U of California P, 1982). I would also suggest that students first read the "Introduction: Biographical and Historical Contexts" in this volume, which identifies most of the major historical and cultural allusions in *Portrait.*

Part Two includes five critical essays exemplifying different current critical approaches to Joyce's *Portrait.* Choosing and commissioning these essays was a difficult task because of the wealth of material available. Joyceans have been among the earliest critics to adopt fresh critical approaches, and American Joyceans in particular have generally welcomed the variety of European critical perspectives that have developed since the 1960s. In part, no doubt, this is a consequence of the fact that Joyce is probably the most discussed modern writer, but in part I think it is due to the way in which his work in particular calls out for a wide variety of readings. As Cheryl Herr comments in her essay, "The language of *Portrait* . . . leads a reader . . . to [reach] out toward many schools of contemporary theory. Thinking about *Portrait* through cultural studies, colonial and postcolonial theory, feminism, and psychoanalysis helps us appreciate the complexity of Joyce's project as well as its grounding in everyday practical activity" (p. 417 in this volume).

All of the contributors featured here are well known for their work on Joyce. Sheldon Brivic's psychoanalytic essay is adapted from one in his book *Joyce Between Freud and Jung* (1980); he has since published *Joyce the Creator* (1985), *The Veil of Signs* (1991), and *Joyce's Waking Women* (1995). Suzette Henke, coeditor of the groundbreaking volume *Women in Joyce* (1982) and author of *James Joyce and the Politics of Desire* (1990), has provided a chapter condensed and adapted from her feminist discussions of *Portrait* in these two books. My own essay, written specially for this volume, is an attempt to view *Portrait* as an element in the cultural structures and tensions of its time. It touches on the economic and political situation of Dublin at the turn of the century as well as structures of authority, racial myths, popular scientific paradigms, and the ideology of genius. I regard this as a continuation and a considerable broadening of the mainly Bakhtinian reading of *Portrait* that I offered in *Joyce, Bakhtin, and Popular Literature* (1989).

Vincent Cheng's essay here is adapted from a chapter in his influential book *Joyce, Race, and Empire* (1995), and presents *Portrait* from a standpoint that pays particular attention to the political context: Stephen Dedalus is a citizen of a colonized country with a long tradition of colonial resistance that within six years of the book's publication would lead to a successful independence movement. Yet, as Cheng discusses, Joyce's own feelings about the Irish nationalist movement were complex and ambivalent. Cheryl Herr pays attention to this dimension of the text in her essay combining critical approaches, as well as to cultural studies approaches, feminism, and psychoanalytic modes of criticism. In addition to these, Herr frames her discussion in a mode that might be termed phenomenological. Known for her Marxist and semiotic readings of Joyce, especially in her groundbreaking book *Joyce's Anatomy of Culture* (1986) — itself an early example of the cultural studies approach — Herr in an essay that was commissioned especially for this volume touches on most of the critical approaches that have dominated the past twenty years, while still evoking a unique synthesis few other critics could have offered.

New to This Edition

The second edition of this *Case Study in Contemporary Criticism* includes a section of Cultural Documents and Illustrations — a wide variety of period photographs, maps, cartoons, illustrations, and records that bear on Joyce, his time, and his novel. Given the "turn toward history" of much contemporary criticism, it seems appropriate that some primary historical sources be provided for the student who wishes to think about *Portrait* in this context (as, for example, Vincent Cheng does in his essay). Cheng's essay is new in this edition, replacing an essay illustrating reader-response criticism. Here, the editors felt that the impact of (post-)colonial criticism on Joyce studies has been so marked that it would not fairly represent criticism of *Portrait* if such a reading were not included. In addition, Cheryl Herr's essay is new, replacing her essay exemplifying deconstructive criticism. The editors felt that since relatively few critical essays utilize a given critical approach in a pure state, it might be of more practical use to the student to present an essay that combines a variety of current approaches, as most published essays in fact do. My own essay, while it retains much of its content from the previous version intended to represent new historicism, has been substantially recast to represent cultural criticism. Suzette Henke and Sheldon Brivic have both made a number of minor changes in their essays from the first edition.

Acknowledgments

I first conceived this project after using Ross Murfin's fine edition of Joseph Conrad's *Heart of Darkness* in a graduate seminar and wishing that a similar edition were available for Joyce's *Portrait*. Once we had established the fact that such an edition would be possible, Ross Murfin's enthusiasm, efficiency, and expertise showed him to be the editor everyone hopes for but few find. At Bedford/St. Martin's, I thank those who initiated the project, Charles Christensen, Joan Feinberg, and Steve Scipione, and those who helped it toward completion, especially Emily Berleth, Anne Noyes, Amy Hurd Gershman, and Kaitlin Hannon.

Appreciation is also due to the instructors who responded to Bedford/St. Martin's questionnaire and made suggestions for revision of the original edition: Susan Blalock, School University of Alaska Fairbanks; Lesley Clement, Medicine Hat College; Angela DiPace, Sacred Heart University; Lia M. Hotchkiss, Central Connecticut State University; Jodi A. Johnson, Los Angeles Pierce College; Stanislaus J. Kozikowski, Bryant College; Perry Meisel, New York University; George O'Brien, Georgetown University; Trey Philpotts, Arkansas Tech University; Patricia L. Skarda, Smith College; Robin Visel, Furman University; David Walker, Oberlin College; and Deborah Wilson, Arkansas Tech University.

I would like to thank the contributors to this volume, who are friends as well as colleagues, for their permission to use their essays. Through their unselfish cooperation as well as the quality of their work, Sheldon Brivic, Suzette Henke, Vincent Cheng, and Cheryl Herr have showed me once again why Joyceans are especially fortunate in their fellows. Among Joyceans elsewhere, I am indebted for various sorts of help and encouragement to Zack Bowen, Bernard Benstock, Morris Beja, Walton Litz, Robert Spoo, and Margot Norris. I want to thank Dan Cottom for critical discussions in less than critical situations. I first read Joyce with Richard Macksey, and then with Ian Watt; I want to thank both for showing me what critical sophistication might look like. Over the years my students have probably influenced my thinking on Joyce more than has anyone else. Some of them, such as Garry Leonard, M. Keith Booker, and Eric Smith, have now joined the larger discussion of Joyce outside the walls of my classroom. I owe them all thanks for many ideas I now think of as my own. Finally, I want to offer my gratitude and dedication to Christina Carlton: as Bakhtin wrote, "the self is the gift of the other."

R. Brandon Kershner
University of Florida

About This Text

The text used here corrects the edition of *A Portrait* which I prepared as my doctoral dissertation at Columbia University and that was printed in 1964 and thereafter by the Viking Press, though with some changes vetoed by Richard Ellmann. That edition was based on Joyce's own fair copy holograph (now at the National Library of Ireland) and on corrections made by him to the *Egoist* serial and to the first edition. The rationale for the 1964 edition, which restored several hundred words and made many other corrections following Joyce's clear intention, can be found in *Neuphilologische Mitteilungen* (LXV, 2, Helsinki, 1964).

However, there were errors made in carrying out that rationale — most of them my own, though Mr. Ellmann's vetoes added to them substantially. With the help of Jill Whenmouth as my research assistant in 1971, I found these errors as best I could and corrected them. But even though Marshall Best, then the pleasant executive vice president at Viking, was willing to make the changes, Mr. Ellmann was not. When I visited him in New College, Oxford, in 1972, he scolded me with his usual cheeriness for not being Hans Walter Gabler (later to become well known as the textual editor of *Ulysses*), who had found some of the typescript pages made from the manuscript in Trieste in 1913 and 1914 and who would have other news about the text.

I corresponded with Professor Gabler in Munich that year and talked with him in Zurich in 1973. He then published two articles on the text: "Towards a Critical Text of *A Portrait* . . . ," in *Studies in Bibliography* 27 (1974) and "The Seven Lost Years of *A Portrait* . . . ," in *Approaches to Joyce's "Portrait": Ten Essays,* edited by Thomas E. Staley and Bernard Benstock (U of Pittsburgh P, 1976). He may one day fulfill the late Richard Ellmann's expectations and bring out a text more "scientific" than this one.

However that may be, I am most grateful to R. B. Kershner and Bedford / St. Martin's for enabling me to get these corrections into print for the first time — not least the most striking of them all, the change from *geen* to *green* in Stephen's song on the opening page.

Chester G. Anderson
Professor Emeritus of English
University of Minnesota

Contents

PART ONE

A Portrait of the Artist as a Young Man:
The Complete Text in Cultural Context

PART TWO

A Portrait of the Artist as a Young Man:
A Case Study in Contemporary Criticism

Case Studies in Contemporary Criticism

JAMES JOYCE

*A Portrait of the Artist
as a Young Man*

PART ONE

A Portrait of the Artist as a Young Man: The Complete Text in Cultural Context

Introduction:
Biographical and
Historical Contexts

James Augustine Aloysius Joyce was born on February 2, 1882, in Rathgar, a fairly prosperous southern suburb of Dublin, Ireland. His father, John Stanislaus Joyce, was from Cork, where the Joyce family had been merchants for some generations, and where they had married into the O'Connell family, who claimed a connection with the famous Irish nationalist, Daniel O'Connell, "the Liberator." The earliest Joyces were Norman but later established themselves in the west of Ireland near Galway, where a large area is known as "the Joyce Country." As the critic Edmund Epstein stresses (4–5), John Joyce insisted upon the family's noble descent, and indeed a Joyce coat of arms is registered, with the motto, *Mors aut honorabilis vita* ("An honorable life or death"). According to Colbert Kearney, who has researched the Cork background, family myth asserted that the gentlemanly Joyces of Cork, including John Joyce's father, James Augustine, were dragged down by the shopkeeping O'Connells.

Like all Irish Catholics, the Joyces inherited a tradition of legal and cultural repression. Having suffered invasions by Vikings and by Normans in medieval times, Ireland was more systematically conquered by the British, beginning in the Elizabethan period; successive waves of invasion and settlement established an "Anglo-Irish" aristocracy that controlled much of the land, while during the eighteenth century the "penal laws" effectively barred Catholics from social advancement. Even the Irish language spoken by Joyce's ancestors was prohibited. A series of reforms culminating in the Emancipation Act of 1829 allowed the growth of a Catholic middle class, but the hopes of the Catholic peasantry — and many of the middle class as well — remained firmly tied to the establishment of an independent Irish nation (Lyons).

When John Joyce moved from Cork to Dublin in his mid-twenties, he was a man of some means, including property in Cork; by the age of forty he had lost his final job as tax collector and was never again regularly employed. He was a man of considerable charm, a fine tenor and storyteller, but also an improvident spendthrift and drinker. A friend, Constantine Curran, described him as "a man of unparalleled vituperative power, a virtuoso in speech with unique control of the vernacular" (69). In many ways a disastrous parent, he nevertheless fathered eleven children, of whom eight survived to adulthood. Whatever strain this may have put on his resources, a pregnancy virtually every year following her marriage proved a far greater strain for May Joyce, who died at forty-four. James Joyce was the eldest surviving child; two of his siblings died of typhoid, a disease encouraged by the family's poverty.

But in 1888, when James Joyce was sent to board and study at Clongowes Wood College, most of these embarrassments and tragedies lay in the future. Clongowes, run by the influential Jesuit order, was perhaps the best preparatory school in Ireland (sons of the wealthier Anglo-Irish families were often sent to still better schools in England). Despite the repressive picture he paints of the school in *Portrait*, Joyce later spoke warmly of his experience there; unlike Stephen, whom we only see unjustly punished, Joyce received punishment that he admitted he deserved on several occasions, including once for bad language. Joyce was a good student at Clongowes despite his youth, and in some ways he never abandoned the habits of thought with which the Jesuits inculcated him. But public events in Ireland were equally important to him, at least as they reached him through the talk of his parents and their friends.

The two and a half years that Joyce attended Clongowes happened to coincide with the climax of the Parnell affair, which seized the young boy's imagination. (The scholar Malcolm Brown [326–47] has presented the story most vividly.) Charles Stewart Parnell, a Protestant landholder, entered the British House of Commons as an Irish member of Parliament in 1875. Along with the former Fenian, or Irish revolutionary, Michael Davitt, he founded the predominantly Catholic Land League to redistribute farmland. Gradually he became head of a political group that included nationalists of all sorts, from moderates to militant revolutionaries. By 1879 he had become leader of the Irish home rule movement, which insisted that the Irish be allowed a measure of self-government. He managed to unite the Irish vote in the House of Commons, and by threatening various tactics of parliamentary obstruction, he was able to bargain for the support of the prime minister, Gladstone, for home rule. His cause suffered a setback in 1882, when a radical group called the Invincibles assassinated two British officials in Phoenix Park, northwest of Dublin. Although Parnell publicly condemned the assassination, in 1887 the London *Times* ran a series of articles based on information supplied by a former Nationalist named Piggott, accusing Parnell of supporting the Invincibles. A trial showed that the letters supposedly written by Parnell were forgeries, but the ruthlessness of Parnell's conservative opposition was made clear. Then in 1890 Parnell was accused of adultery in a divorce suit brought by Captain William O'Shea, a former member of the Home Rule party, against his wife Katharine.

The trial made headlines. Parnell's ten-year liaison with Mrs. O'Shea, to which the captain had given tacit assent, was the stuff of scandal, and the intimate details that emerged were embarrassing for all concerned. For instance, Katharine and Parnell addressed one another as "King" and "Queen" in private. One of Parnell's code names in communicating with his lover, "Mr. Fox," became widely known, while Mrs. O'Shea was universally referred to as "Kitty," which was coincidentally a slang term for a prostitute. After a witness gave testimony that on one occasion Parnell had escaped from an upper-story window when Captain O'Shea had arrived home unexpectedly, vendors outside the courtroom produced and sold quantities of "Escaping Parnell" dolls that slid up and down tiny ladders (Mullin 87). Parnell was a man of enormous pride and rather cold, aristocratic demeanor. He refused to defend himself against the charge and wished simply to marry Mrs. O'Shea, who for ten years had remained legally married to her husband only in hopes of a legacy. Gladstone decided that his Liberal party's home rule policy could not withstand association with a man of such questionable moral character, and the Irish party, at the urging of Davitt and Parnell's former supporter, Tim Healy, removed Parnell from leadership. Parnell refused to capitulate, and the party split; he was denounced by Catholic churchmen, whose leaders hoped to regain influence over the Nationalist movement. Among his attackers was Archbishop William Walsh, whom Simon Dedalus characterizes as "Billy with the lip."

As his power diminished, Parnell was accused of outrageous things, such as embezzling the Land League's "Paris funds" to subsidize his love life. Following his marriage to Kitty, he continued, in weakening health, to take his campaign to the people. When he died in 1891, as many as one hundred and fifty thousand people accompanied his sealed coffin to Glasnevin cemetery, led by the radical Fenians who had supported him at the end. In a revulsion of popular feeling, Parnell gained a kind of mythic status even among those who had attacked him, and as it became clear that Irish nationalism was in disarray, he became the "dead king" who alone could have led Ireland to independence. Following Parnell's death, the nine-year-old Joyce wrote a bitter broadside poem against his betrayers entitled "Et tu Healy," which John Joyce had printed. Joyce came to see Parnell as a martyr, betrayed by his own people, in the mold of earlier nationalist heroes who had led aborted insurrections, such as Wolfe Tone and Robert Emmet. Like Joyce, Stephen Dedalus views himself as their potential successor, an artist-hero who may save his country not only from its enemies but from itself.

When he came to write *A Portrait of the Artist as a Young Man,* Joyce relied heavily on autobiography; in outline and in many details, the novel follows his own life from birth up to the age of twenty. His family and acquaintances often appear recognizably, with only a change of name, while schools, streets, businesses, hotels, and public figures generally appear under their real names — an unusual practice at the time and one that Joyce also followed in his book of short stories, *Dubliners,* causing him endless trouble when he tried to publish the book. But as Joyce's biographer Richard Ellmann clearly established, there are important differences between James Joyce and Stephen Dedalus. The timing of Stephen's attendance at Clongowes is altered so that Parnell's death occurs earlier. Although Joyce briefly attended a Christian Brothers' school after Clongowes, Stephen does not. Stephen avoids sports of all sorts, whereas Joyce was quite proud of winning a schoolboy race. Joyce in youth was called "Sunny Jim" by his family because of his cheerful disposition, while Stephen is more or less withdrawn and sullen. Joyce's relationship with his father appeared friendly to others, but Stephen's is increasingly bitter and tense. At parties Stephen is aloof; Joyce, who could indeed be distant in manner, was also known for his songs (he had a voice of professional quality), his impersonations, and his occasional manic, spidery dances.

Joyce's family fortunes continued to worsen, in part because his father had been a paid canvasser for Parnell. Joyce began attending the

Jesuit Belvedere College in Dublin in 1893. The following year, in a nationwide examination, he won one of the top prizes, or "exhibitions," worth twenty pounds. But by the age of 14 he began to patronize local prostitutes, who were easily come by in turn-of-the-century Dublin. Meanwhile, he was chosen prefect of the sodality of the Blessed Virgin Mary at school, an honor meant to recognize both his academic achievements and his moral character, and one that might well indicate that the boy was thought to have a vocation for the priesthood. A retreat sermon delivered by a priest from Clongowes in 1896 had a strong effect on Joyce, who was struggling with sexual guilt and self-hatred at the time; but during the following several years, his precocious reading of Byron and "dangerous" modern authors like Meredith, Hardy, Ibsen, and his countryman Yeats had an even more powerful cumulative effect. From these he began to acquire a critical attitude toward social institutions of bourgeois Ireland, including the Church itself, and from Yeats in particular he learned to see the world of art as an autonomous sphere removed from the pragmatic world of everyday experience and to see the figure of the artist as part prophet, part priest — the potential savior of his race. By the time he entered the Royal University in Dublin, also known as University College, he was permanently disaffected from Catholicism, much to the distress of his mother.

The critic Patrick Parrinder (17–40) stresses the importance of Joyce's university experience in forming his character and public image. University College had been founded by the famous convert John Henry Newman in 1854 to offer a liberal Catholic education alternative to the predominantly secular Trinity College, where the sons of the Protestant Ascendancy were educated. But Newman had failed to win independence from the bishops in making his appointments, and by the time Joyce entered it in 1898, the school, controlled by the Jesuits, offered a conservative and intellectually undemanding curriculum. Modern thought and modern art were condemned or ignored. When Joyce began to speak enthusiastically about the playwright Ibsen, who had been praised by the London intelligentsia for years, he gained a great deal of local notoriety as a dangerously radical thinker.

But if the instructors were relatively backward, the student body at University College was sensitive to the political and social turmoil of the time. Parnell's cause had not died with him, but after the apparent failure of parliamentary activism, more radical Nationalists came to the fore. A local branch of the Gaelic League, which encouraged the study of the Irish language and the playing of native Irish sports, was established by Joyce's friend George Clancy (Davin in *Portrait*). Somewhat less publicly, it organized military training for Nationalists who hoped for a popular insurrection (such as the one that indeed occurred in 1916); Davin, in *A Portrait,* is said to be practicing a military drill. But from Joyce's perspective, the most significant movement of the time was probably what later became known as the Irish Literary Revival or Irish Renaissance.

This movement, which was responsible for a period of immense literary productivity, lasted from roughly 1890 into the 1920s. It was spearheaded by William Butler Yeats, perhaps the greatest poet writing in English at that time. Yeats, seventeen years Joyce's senior, formed the notion of a national literature that would take its inspiration from Irish myth and folktale. Under the influence of his friend George Russell (who wrote under the mystic name "AE"), he imbued his work with a strong element of spiritualism, while under the influence of the Fenian John O'Leary and of Maud Gonne, the woman he loved, he also linked it to nationalist aspirations. The political and aesthetic dimensions of his work did not always coexist easily, however. In 1899 Yeats helped found the Irish Literary Theatre, where he presented his play *Countess Cathleen.* Although his later play *Kathleen Ni Houlihan* was enormously successful with Nationalists, *Countess Cathleen,* relying on an aristocratic figure who sells her soul to the devil in exchange for food for her starving people, caused riots protesting "a libel on Irish womanhood." In *Portrait* Stephen is portrayed as one of the few students at University College who refuses to sign a petition against the play, and in so doing he appears to choose art over politics. Later, he recites a verse from the play. These details are in fact autobiographical. Joyce knew many of Yeats's poems by heart, and he may have been drawn to specialize in prose because he feared he could not compete as a poet.

By the time he left University College, Joyce had met a number of figures prominent in the Revival, including Yeats, George Russell, and Yeats's patron and collaborator, Lady Augusta Gregory. On the strength of a few essays and verses he had begun to make a name for himself. But despite his enthusiasm for Yeats's work, Joyce from the beginning had serious reservations about the direction of Yeats's movement. For one thing, all the major figures were of the Protestant landholding class, and Yeats especially had an almost feudal respect for the "great families" like Lady Gregory's who were his models of aristocracy. For another thing, Yeats also romanticized the unlettered peasantry, whom he saw as a repository of folk wisdom and mystic insight. Joyce, a member of the urban poor with a very different notion of aristocracy, had little patience with this aspect of the Revival. And while he disliked British imperialism as strongly as Yeats's generation of writers, he was reluctant to join a movement such as the Gaelic League, which he saw as bigoted, backward-looking, and Church-dominated. With his friend George Clancy he briefly took Irish lessons from Padraic Pearse, a poet who was later executed after the 1916 insurrection, but objected to Pearse's disparagement of the English language. Also, like Stephen, he feared to commit himself wholly to a political movement in search of martyrs.

In his second year at university, Joyce distinguished himself by presenting a paper entitled "Drama and Life" at the school's Literary and Historical Society (Mason and Ellmann 38–46). In it he enthusiastically defended modern drama, as exemplified by Ibsen, against its attackers; art has a responsibility to represent life as it is actually lived rather than as convention dictates, he argued. Indeed, art has its own laws and logic as an expression of the artist that is nearly beyond judgment. More impressively, Joyce expanded upon his defense of Ibsen in an article that was published in the influential British *Fortnightly Review*. Ibsen himself responded with an appreciative note that his translator William Archer forwarded to Joyce, and Joyce set himself to learning Dano-Norwegian so as to read the Scandinavian master in the original.

From youth, Joyce had shown a talent for languages. The Jesuits had immediately set him to reading Latin, and at University College he studied Italian, German, and French. Yeats's enthusiasm for the native culture failed to win Joyce; he argued that "a nation which never advanced so far as a miracle play affords no literary model to the artist, and he must look abroad" (Mason and Ellmann 70). Gradually he was becoming convinced that he would have to escape Ireland. Europe he saw as a freer, more cosmopolitan world, and his languages would enable him to survive there. As it turned out, Joyce spent nearly the whole of his mature life in Europe, and his children were raised speaking Italian and French as easily as they did English.

Joyce, of course, was not the only artist or rebel at University College. His friend Francis Skeffington was a committed feminist and pacifist who argued that women should be admitted to Ireland's universities. Joyce and Skeffington, who appears rather unflatteringly as McCann in *Portrait*, published at their own expense a pamphlet containing an essay by Joyce attacking philistines entitled "The Day of the Rabblement" along with a feminist essay by his friend. Skeffington later married a friend of Joyce's and changed his name to Sheehy-Skeffington in her honor. He was murdered by a British officer during the 1916 insurrection after trying to stop British troops from looting.

This outrage caused consternation both among the British officer's family, which included the future Anglo-Irish novelist Elizabeth Bowen, and among Skeffington's British relatives, who changed their name in shame at his "treason" (Parrinder 20).

Other friends included John Francis Byrne, who appears as "Cranly" and who later published a book protesting Joyce's version of their relationship, and Vincent Cosgrave ("Lynch"), who caused Joyce pain several years later by falsely claiming to have slept with Joyce's lover, Nora. Cosgrave was to commit suicide, while Thomas Kettle, a talented scholar and writer, died in the Battle of the Somme, and George Clancy, who became mayor of Limerick, was shot by disguised Protestant irregulars in 1921. Joyce was often thought paranoid in later life because he refused to return to Ireland, but surprisingly few of his friends from college who remained in Ireland died a natural death.

Another acquaintance of this period who was to figure importantly in Joyce's writing was Oliver St. John Gogarty, son of a wealthy Anglo-Irish family. Gogarty was attending Trinity and, like many of Joyce's school friends, preparing for a career in medicine. He was a prolifically talented young man who became a protégé of Yeats, writing poems that appeared in several of Yeats's poetry anthologies. In later life he was a successful physician, an Irish senator, and a well-known public figure in Dublin. An athlete, scholar, writer, and general carouser, Gogarty "adopted" Joyce for a period, lending him clothing and money. For a week in 1904 the two shared quarters in a Martello tower south of Dublin. This period is immortalized in Joyce's *Ulysses,* where Gogarty appears as Stephen's companion, rival, and — for reasons that remain somewhat obscure — his betrayer, Buck Mulligan. Like several of Joyce's school friends, Gogarty was aware that Joyce was making notes on him, preparing to use him in a literary work. In *Ulysses* Stephen muses, "He fears the lancet of my art." Indeed, in later life Gogarty found himself protesting that he was *not* Buck Mulligan, but a real human being. Like Byrne, he published his own very different version of his relationship with Joyce. Like Joyce's brother Stanislaus, Gogarty appeared in an early version of *Portrait* (part of which has been published as *Stephen Hero*), but his absence from the final draft gives more prominence to Stephen.

For all their differences, Stephen and Joyce in this period shared what Joyce termed an "enigma of a manner" (Scholes and Kain 61), a rather formal and aloof persona with which to confront rival students, and a sometimes showy and pedantic way of speaking. Coupled with a certain reputation for debauchery — Stephen "confesses" some of his experiences with prostitutes to Davin — this manner helped establish his reputation as a young man to be reckoned with. His friend Eugene Sheehy observed that "Joyce, the schoolboy, was as icy, aloof, and imperturbable as . . . Joyce the man." Another friend described him delivering a paper before a debating society: "Joyce, thin and pale, stood erect, scarcely moving, cold and undisturbed by interruptions (and he had many), and seemed in passionless tones to wither the opposition by his air of indifferent disdain" (Scholes and Kain 141, 152). He might have been Yeats facing down the rioters at the Abbey Theatre ("You have disgraced yourselves again!"), or Parnell campaigning in his last years. Following the debate on Joyce's paper and his demolition of each of his critics, a student slapped his back and exclaimed, "Joyce, that was magnificent, but you're raving mad!" (Ellmann 73).

It should be noted that University College students of the time were a more rigorously selected group than those at the average American university today; also, typically they would have had training since childhood in Latin, perhaps Greek, and the classics. Competitiveness was instilled by nationwide examinations and cash prizes. Their primary and secondary education stressed memorization of passages and the preparation of essays modeled on those of the great rhetoricians, so that when Stephen attacks Lynch with his "dagger definitions," for instance, he is merely practicing the art for which he had been trained. The young Joyce's intellectual style was striking mainly because he chose to cite obscure ancients and embattled moderns rather than the accepted greats, and continental rather than English writers. Also, of course, he wrote very well. Still, Joyce's portrait gives Stephen more rigor and sophistication than he himself probably possessed at the time. Although Stephen considers himself a student of Aquinas and Aristotle — and garners intellectual status from this distinction — it appears from his notebooks that Joyce himself studied Aristotle intensely only after leaving the university.

Although Stephen has fixed his romantic yearnings since childhood upon the insubstantial "E—— C——," or "Emma," Joyce seems to have had no such abiding passion. His brother Stanislaus has suggested that he may have been infatuated for a time with a girl named Mary Sheehy, and certainly she, along with her bright and talented sister Hannah, served in part as a model for E—— C——. In *Stephen Hero* she appears more vigorously as Emma Clery, with whom Stephen is cautiously involved, and in that manuscript argues with him over the right of women to the same education as men receive. Stephen imperiously disagrees and later suggests that the two of them spend a single

night of wild passion, then part, never to see each other again. Not surprisingly, this generous offer fails to tempt her. A friend of Stephen's
observes that he could marry her, but Stephen thinks that price too
high; and like Joyce, he feels that the institution of marriage is an
unwarranted intrusion of state and Church into private relationships.
Like the Church, family, and nation, marriage is another "net" thrown
up to catch the artist's fledgling soul.

In 1902 Joyce graduated from University College with an undistinguished B.A., briefly enrolled as a medical student, and in December
left Dublin for Paris, armed with introductions from Yeats and others
and the possibility of supporting himself meagerly by writing book
reviews for newspapers. He left with George Russell a group of his unpublished verses. He also left with Russell what he called "epiphanies"
or "epicleti," short prose sketches that vary in character from lyrical,
dreamlike effusions to literal reportage of overheard vulgar conversations. Joyce struggled in Paris, returned home for money, then returned to Paris, where he stopped attending medical lectures and began
studying in the National Library. He met Yeats's protégé, the playwright John Millington Synge, whom he accused of being insufficiently
Aristotelian.

Then in April 1903, he was recalled home by a telegram announcing his mother's fatal illness. Her request that he pray with her brought
on another religious crisis, and during this time and following her
death, he drank heavily, especially with Gogarty. This behavior disgusted Stanislaus, his highly intelligent and more conventional younger
brother, whom he bullied, confided in, and depended upon for much
of his life. At the beginning of 1904, Joyce taught briefly in a school in
a Dublin suburb. Then, sometime around June 16, he met and, in the
Irish phrase, "walked out with" Nora Barnacle, a country girl from Galway who worked as a hotel chambermaid. She was to be in many ways
the central figure during the remainder of his life.

Joyce began writing in earnest now. He began with a lyrical, revolutionary, and rather obscure essay that Stanislaus entitled "A Portrait of
the Artist," which was to be the earliest version of the autobiographical
novel his friends had feared he was writing. He published a story entitled "The Sisters," which Russell had commissioned for his magazine
The Irish Homestead, under the pseudonym "Stephen Daedalus." Russell took two more stories and several of his poems. Joyce sent a collection of his poems entitled *Chamber Music* to the English publisher
Grant Richards. Then, in October 1904, he left Dublin with Nora,
without benefit of marriage, planning to teach English in a Berlitz

school in Zurich. Except for brief visits, he would never return to Ireland. Joyce wound up teaching in Trieste, Italy, and in 1905 completed nine more of the short stories that were to form the book *Dubliners.* He sent the whole collection to Richards, thus beginning a painful eight-year effort to publish the volume.

Stanislaus joined him in Trieste, and a son, George, or "Giorgio," was born to him and Nora. Two years later, his daughter, Lucia Ann was born. During this period Joyce was under considerable strain: although he had avoided the legal title of husband, he soon discovered that in practical terms he was both husband and father. Like his father he was generally improvident and given to bouts of drinking from which his constitution was never really strong enough to recover easily. At times, he doubted whether he should be with Nora. The responsibility of a family weighed upon him, especially as he never doubted that his primary responsibility should be to his art. Stanislaus often rescued the Joyces and tried to play the role of his brother's good conscience, a kindness that Joyce of course resented. After Joyce's death, Stanislaus wrote a book on James entitled *My Brother's Keeper* (1969).

By 1907 Joyce had added several stories to the *Dubliners* collection, including his masterpiece, "The Dead," and he had conceived the idea of a story involving a Dublin Jew that some fifteen years later was to become the monumental novel *Ulysses. Chamber Music* had been published. He was writing newspaper articles and delivering public lectures to the Trieste cultural community. Slowly he began to reshape the long, rambling, rather conventional autobiographical novel on which he had been working into a tight, elliptical, formally experimental work, although this process bore its greatest fruit only after 1913, when Ezra Pound began to encourage him.

Meanwhile, the effort to publish *Dubliners* was a continual frustration. Grant Richards, who had originally accepted the collection in 1906, demanded more and more changes. Joyce agreed to a few, refused others, and Richards finally rejected the book. After four other publishers had rejected it, Maunsel and Company accepted it in 1909. Under British law a printer as well as a publisher could be sued if a book were found libelous or obscene, and Maunsel's printer was timid. Finally, the galley sheets for the book were destroyed in 1912. Enraged, Joyce wrote a scurrilous and funny broadside poem about the publisher and printer entitled "Gas from a Burner" and had it distributed in Dublin. After more rejections by other publishers, Grant Richards reconsidered *Dubliners* in 1913 and printed it in the following year. No one sued or even objected publicly. Meanwhile, in an unsuccessful and uncharacteristic foray into business, in 1909 Joyce had helped establish the first cinema in Ireland.

Ezra Pound was probably as responsible as anyone other than Joyce for the appearance of *A Portrait of the Artist as a Young Man*. The American poet was not only a significant modernist writer in his own right, he was also an indefatigable discoverer and promoter of other artists. Yeats had sent him a lyric of Joyce's that he decided to include in his anthology *Des Imagistes*, and in response to his letter to Joyce, Pound received a revised first chapter of *Portrait* as well as a copy of *Dubliners*. Pound convinced a literary and philosophical journal called *The Egoist*, which was originally founded as a feminist organ, to serialize the novel. Meanwhile, war had broken out and Joyce had begun work on his only play, an Ibsenesque drama entitled *Exiles*. Generally considered his least interesting work, the play concerns an Irish writer who returns home after living in Europe with his common-law wife and son; he renews his acquaintance with a popular journalist and sensualist who attempts to seduce the woman. The writer has insisted that his relationship with his wife should be free and open, and in a sort of experiment asks her to encourage the other man's advances. After much suffering all around, the play ends ambiguously, with both writer and audience unsure whether his wife has been faithful to him, or even what faithfulness might mean. Joyce, always tormented but fascinated by his jealousy of Nora, was to use marital fidelity as an important theme in his later works.

Installments of *Portrait* began to appear in *The Egoist*. Perhaps more important, Harriet Shaw Weaver, the American who had taken over as editor, settled a trust on Joyce in 1919 that freed him from serious financial worries. Her personal as well as financial support was crucial during the remainder of his life. Meanwhile, after some unsuccessful attempts to publish the book in England, *Portrait* was published in New York by B. W. Huebsch in 1916, and Weaver's Egoist Press used the same plates for a British edition the following year. In 1917 Joyce had a serious attack of glaucoma, the beginning of the problems with his eyesight that were to grow increasingly acute until, in the last decade of his life, he was virtually blind. But his major interest during the war years was work on the book that was to become *Ulysses*, parts of which were serialized in the *Little Review* starting in 1918.

In some ways *Ulysses* begins where *Portrait* leaves off. It opens on June 16, 1904, with Stephen Dedalus sharing rooms in a Martello tower on the east coast of Ireland, south of Dublin, with Buck Mulligan and a visiting Englishman named Haines who is studying Irish culture. Stephen has returned from Paris, where he has had experiences much like Joyce's, and he is recovering from the death of his mother. But in the fourth chapter of the book we are introduced to a new character, a Jewish advertising canvasser named Leopold Bloom whose wife, Molly, is planning to commit adultery with a man named "Blazes" Boylan that afternoon. Bloom knows Stephen's father but has no obvious connection to the boy; nevertheless, the meeting of the two is as much of a dramatic climax as the book admits. The entirety of *Ulysses'* seven-hundred-odd pages takes place on the same day, during which we go deeply into the minds of both main characters and, finally, into the mind of Molly as well — and we meet a bewildering variety of subsidiary characters.

Perhaps the book's most striking feature is its narrative innovations. Starting around the ninth chapter, the narration, which had begun in a mode something like the last chapter of *Portrait* (although with more internal monologue), begins to vary wildly. There are interpolated episodes in play form, a chapter narrated by an unnamed barfly, one that is told as if it were a poorly written domestic romance, one told in ludicrously abstract question-and-answer form, and so forth. Perhaps the most noticeable shift in tone from *Portrait* is due to the humor of the book: it is crammed with jokes, from high intellectual verbal play to the most vulgar slapstick. On several occasions Joyce remarked that he wished reviewers, instead of worrying about the book's obscenity, would at least notice that it was funny.

While writing *Ulysses,* Joyce had returned to Trieste, and then in 1920 at the urging of Pound, the Joyces had gone to Paris for a week's excursion. They wound up staying twenty years. With the enthusiastic support of Pound, T. S. Eliot, and a Parisian bookstore owner named Sylvia Beach, Joyce soon gathered around him an admiring circle of friends, French literary luminaries, and aspiring young writers from England and America. When the *Little Review* editors were prosecuted for obscenity because of an episode of *Ulysses* that appeared in the magazine, the incident only added to Joyce's international fame. By the time Beach's bookstore, Shakespeare and Company, published the first edition of the complete book in 1922, Joyce was already the literary toast of Paris and had been acclaimed by many as the greatest modern writer of English prose.

Meanwhile, Joyce circulated among friends a chart showing in detail what the book's title had not made entirely clear: despite its surface naturalism, his novel contained an elaborate series of correspondences to Homer's *Odyssey*. Indeed, in 1930, after considerable help and occasional direction from Joyce, Stuart Gilbert published a book on *Ulysses* exploring these correspondences and many other subtle features of the novel. Critics now conventionally refer to the chapters of the book by the titles of the parallel episodes in the Odyssey, such as "Lestrygonians" or "Aeolus." Gilbert also helped with the French translation of *Ulysses*, which — again with Joyce's advice and encouragement — appeared in 1929, and had substantial impact upon French literature.

Despite the fact that it was banned from publication in the United States, *Ulysses* was frequently smuggled into the country, becoming one of the best-known banned books of all time. Still, it was not until 1934 that Random House, under the leadership of Bennett Cerf, won a landmark court battle and the right to publish *Ulysses* in the United States; two years later it was published in England as well. But in the meantime, starting in 1923, Joyce had begun work on his most radical and ambitious work of prose, parts of which were published as *Work in Progress* (among other provisional titles) but which finally emerged as the book *Finnegans Wake*. From its first fragment, published in Ford Madox Ford's *transatlantic review* in 1924, *Wake* caused trouble for Joyce. Many of his friends and supporters were dismayed. Pound confessed himself baffled, and even Harriet Weaver expressed disappointment, which hurt Joyce deeply. The book is written in a "nightlanguage" far removed from ordinary English, jammed with portmanteau words and multilingual puns. When a friend objected that some of the puns in the *Wake* were trivial, Joyce replied that some were indeed trivial, and some quadrivial. Worse, there are no fixed characters or events in the book — or, alternatively, there are too many for comfort.

Far more elaborately planned and embellished even than *Ulysses*, *Finnegans Wake* on one level concerns a publican in the Dublin suburb of Chapelizod named Humphrey Chimpden Earwicker, his wife, two sons, and daughter. But characters, time, and place seldom remain fixed for more than a sentence in this work; the ultimate male character appears in a wide variety of guises signaled by the initials "HCE," such as "Haveth Childers Everywhere" or "Here Comes Everybody," and in a great number of less easily identifiable ones as well, such as Adam, Humpty Dumpty, Parnell, or King Mark of the Tristan and Isolde legend. This figure merges into that of Tim Finnegan, hero of an Irish comic song about a man who arises at his own wake to share the drink, and with the mythic Irish hero Finn, who is also a mountain. The main female figure, usually called Anna Livia Plurabelle, or ALP, is most frequently identified with rivers, although she too has a variety of mythic and historical guises. The two embattled sons, Shem and Shaun, represent respectively the artistic personality — withdrawn, exiled, obsessed with sex and with excrement, a universal scapegoat — and the successful public personality — alternately postman, policeman, politician, and empire builder. The daughter, Issy, merges into virtually any young woman or splinters into groups of them.

But even this vague summary is far too explicitly literal: Joyce indicated his "characters" by "sigla," geometric symbols that seem to represent functions rather than anything we would ordinarily call "characters." In its own strange fashion the book reprises the history of Ireland, the author's life, and a selection of major myths from European culture. But more than any narrative line, *Wake*'s structure depends upon a conception by the eighteenth-century Italian philosopher Giambattista Vico, the idea that history progresses in a three-part cycle followed by a fourth part, the "ricorso" or return, that returns us to an initial stage after passing through theocratic, aristocratic, democratic, and chaotic phases. The book's three major chapters, followed by a briefer one, mirror this structure.

As with *Ulysses*, Joyce tried to orchestrate the reception of *Wake*. He encouraged twelve of his friends, including Stuart Gilbert and Samuel Beckett (who had informally apprenticed himself to Joyce), to produce a volume treating the book. This was published as *Our Examination round His Factification for Incamination of "Work in Progress"* in 1929. But events conspired against him. By the time the book was finally published, in 1939, the world was on the brink of war once again.

Joyce's own health and eyesight were failing during his last decade. Most painfully, his children, whom he had grown to cherish passionately, were in trouble. By 1929 it was becoming clear that his daughter, Lucia, a bright and talented girl, was mentally unstable. Joyce fought the realization as long as possible, arranging projects in which she could express her artistic impulses and encouraging her in everything. By 1932, however, when she conceived a hopeless passion for Samuel Beckett, even he had to seek treatment and finally institutionalization for her. Joyce's son, Giorgio, was unable to undertake a successful career, and his marriage was failing; in 1939 his wife had a breakdown and the two separated. In 1931, for various reasons including the wish to make a reconciliation with his dying father, Joyce took Nora to a London registry office to legalize their marriage. Perhaps the brightest spot in this period was the birth of Joyce's grandson, Stephen James Joyce, in 1932, less than two months after Joyce's father's death. "Ecce Puer"

("Behold the Child"), perhaps Joyce's most moving poem, commemorates these two events with stunning simplicity.

In 1940 the Joyces were forced to leave Paris for Vichy, where they stayed with a family friend while Joyce carried on protracted negotiations to be allowed to enter Switzerland. Meanwhile, he was assisting a number of Jewish friends to escape to neutral territory. He left only a few scattered comments about his ideas for his next book: that it would be a book of reawakening (after the dream world of *Wake*) and that it would be short and simple. In December 1940 the Joyces entered Switzerland and soon returned to Zurich. Less than a month later, Joyce was taken to the hospital with severe stomach cramps and was diagnosed as suffering from a perforated duodenal ulcer. Although an operation was apparently successful, he soon weakened, passed into a coma, and died on January 13, just before his fifty-ninth birthday. He was buried in the Fluntern cemetery above Zurich. Nora, out of respect for her husband's lifelong rebellion, refused the offer of Catholic rites.

R. Brandon Kershner

WORKS CITED

Brown, Malcolm. *The Politics of Irish Literature*. Seattle: U of Washington P, 1972.

Costello, Peter. *James Joyce: The Years of Growth, 1882–1915*. London: Kyle Cathie, 1992.

Curran, Constantine P. *James Joyce Remembered*. New York: Oxford UP, 1968.

Ellmann, Richard. *James Joyce*. Rev. ed. New York: Oxford UP, 1982. The standard biography of Joyce.

Epstein, Edmund. "James Augustine Aloysius Joyce." *A Companion to Joyce Studies*. Ed. Zack Bowen and James F. Carens. Westport: Greenwood, 1984. 3–38.

Jackson, John Wyse, and Peter Costello. *John Stanislaus Joyce: The Voluminous Life and Genius of James Joyce's Father*. London: Fourth Estate, 1997.

Joyce, Stanislaus. *My Brother's Keeper: James Joyce's Early Years*. Ed. Richard Ellmann. New York: Viking, 1969.

Kearney, Colbert. "The Joycead." *Coping with Joyce: Essays from the Copenhagen Symposium*. Ed. Morris Beja and Shari Benstock. Columbus: Ohio State UP, 1989. 55–72.

Lyons, F. S. L. *Ireland Since the Famine*. London: Collins, 1973.

Mason, Ellsworth, and Richard Ellmann, eds. *James Joyce: The Critical Writings*. New York: Viking, 1964.

Mullin, Katherine. *James Joyce, Sexuality and Social Purity*. Cambridge: Cambridge UP, 2003.

Parrinder, Patrick. *James Joyce*. Cambridge: Cambridge UP, 1984.

Scholes, Robert, and Richard M. Kain, eds. *The Workshop of Daedalus: James Joyce and the Raw Materials for "A Portrait of the Artist as a Young Man."* Evanston: Northwestern UP, 1965.

A Portrait of the Artist as a Young Man

Et ignotas animum dimittit in artes.°

— OVID, Metamorphoses, VIII, 188

I

Once upon a time and a very good time it was there was a moocow coming down along the road and this moocow that was coming down along the road met a nicens little boy named baby tuckoo. . . .

His father told him that story: his father looked at him through a glass:° he had a hairy face.

He was baby tuckoo. The moocow came down the road where Betty Byrne lived: she sold lemon platt.°

O, the wild rose blossoms
On the little green place.

He sang that song. That was his song.

O, the green wothe botheth.

When you wet the bed first it is warm then it gets cold. His mother put on the oilsheet. That had the queer smell.

His mother had a nicer smell than his father. She played on the piano the sailor's hornpipe for him to dance. He danced:

Tralala lala
Tralala tralaladdy
Tralala lala
Tralala lala.

Uncle Charles and Dante clapped. They were older than his father and mother but uncle Charles was older than Dante.

Dante had two brushes in her press.° The brush with the maroon velvet back was for Michael Davitt and the brush with the green velvet back was for Parnell. Dante gave him a cachou° every time he brought her a piece of tissue paper.

The Vances lived in number seven. They had a different father and mother. They were Eileen's father and mother. When they were grown up he was going to marry Eileen. He hid under the table. His mother said:

— O, Stephen will apologise.

Dante said:

— O, if not, the eagles will come and pull out his eyes.

Pull out his eyes,
Apologise,
Apologise,
Pull out his eyes.

Apologise,
Pull out his eyes,
Pull out his eyes,
Apologise.

*

*   *

The wide playgrounds were swarming with boys. All were shouting and the prefects° urged them on with strong cries. The evening air was pale and chilly and after every charge and thud of the footballers the greasy leather orb flew like a heavy bird through the grey light. He kept on the fringe of his line, out of sight of his prefect, out of the reach of the rude feet, feigning to run now and then. He felt his body small and weak amid the throng of players and his eyes were weak and watery. Rody Kickham was not like that: he would be captain of the third line° all the fellows said.

press: Closet.   *cachou:* A candy and breath freshener.   *prefects:* Teachers who work as housemasters and supervise outside activities.   *the third line:* Clongowes boys under thirteen.

Rody Kickham was a decent fellow but Nasty Roche was a stink. Rody Kickham had greaves in his number and a hamper in the refectory.° Nasty Roche had big hands. He called the Friday pudding dog in-the-blanket. And one day he had asked:

— What is your name?

Stephen had answered:

— Stephen Dedalus.°

Then Nasty Roche had said:

— What kind of a name is that?

And when Stephen had not been able to answer Nasty Roche had asked:

— What is your father?

Stephen had answered:

— A gentleman.

Then Nasty Roche had asked:

— Is he a magistrate?

He crept about from point to point on the fringe of his line, making little runs now and then. But his hands were bluish with cold. He kept his hands in the sidepockets of his belted grey suit. That was a belt round his pocket. And belt was also to give a fellow a belt. One day a fellow had said to Cantwell:

— I'd give you such a belt in a second.

Cantwell had answered:

— Go and fight your match. Give Cecil Thunder a belt. I'd like to see you. He'd give you a toe in the rump for yourself.

That was not a-nice expression. His mother had told him not to speak with the rough boys in the college. Nice mother! The first day in the hall of the castle when she had said goodbye she had put up her veil double to her nose to kiss him: and her nose and eyes were red. But he had pretended not to see that she was going to cry. She was a nice mother but she was not so nice when she cried. And his father had given him two fiveshilling pieces for pocket money. And his father had told him if he wanted anything to write home to him and, whatever he did, never to peach on° a fellow. Then at the door of the castle the rec-tor° had shaken hands with his father and mother, his soutane° flutter-

---

greaves in his number and a hamper in the refectory: Shinguards in his locker and a private supply of treats in the dining hall.   *Stephen Dedalus:* Stephen is the name of the first Christian martyr; Daedalus means "clever artificer" (artisan or inventor) in Greek. *peach on:* Tell on.   *rector:* Administrative head of the college.   *soutane:* Black gown with sleeves.

ing in the breeze, and the car had driven off with his father and mother on it. They had cried to him from the car, waving their hands:

— Goodbye, Stephen, goodbye!

— Goodbye, Stephen, goodbye!

He was caught in the whirl of a scrimmage and, fearful of the flashing eyes and muddy boots, bent down to look through the legs. The fellows were struggling and groaning and their legs were rubbing and kicking and stamping. Then Jack Lawton's yellow boots dodged out the ball and all the other boots and legs ran after. He ran after them a little way and then stopped. It was useless to run on. Soon they would be going home for the holidays. After supper in the studyhall he would change the number pasted up inside his desk from seventyseven to seventysix.

It would be better to be in the studyhall than out there in the cold. The sky was pale and cold but there were lights in the castle. He wondered from which window Hamilton Rowan had thrown his hat on the haha° and had there been flowerbeds at that time under the windows. One day when he had been called to the castle the butler had shown him the marks of the soldiers' slugs in the wood of the door and had given him a piece of shortbread that the community ate. It was nice and warm to see the lights in the castle. It was like something in a book. Perhaps Leicester Abbey was like that. And there were nice sentences in Doctor Cornwell's Spelling Book. They were like poetry but they were only sentences to learn the spelling from.

Wolsey died in Leicester Abbey
Where the abbots buried him.
Canker is a disease of plants,
Cancer one of animals.

It would be nice to lie on the hearthrug before the fire, leaning his head upon his hands, and think on those sentences. He shivered as if he had cold slimy water next his skin. That was mean of Wells to shoulder him into the square ditch° because he would not swop his little snuffbox for Wells's seasoned hacking chestnut,° the conqueror of forty. How cold and slimy the water had been! A fellow had once seen a big rat jump plop into the scum. He shivered and longed to cry. It would

Hamilton Rowan . . . haha: Patriot and friend of Wolfe Tone, who in 1794 supposedly took refuge from soldiers in the castle and threw his hat on a bank or dry moat as a decoy. *square ditch:* A running cesspool from the "square," or outdoor urinal. *hacking chestnut:* Dried chestnuts attached to strings and swung sharply against one another, the one that does not break being the winner.

be so nice to be at home. Mother was sitting at the fire with Dante wait-ing for Brigid to bring in the tea. She had her feet on the fender and her jewelly slippers were so hot and they had such a lovely warm smell! Dante knew a lot of things. She had taught him where the Mozam-bique Channel was and what was the longest river in America and what was the name of the highest mountain in the moon. Father Arnall knew more than Dante because he was a priest but both his father and uncle Charles said that Dante was a clever woman and a wellread woman. And when Dante made that noise after dinner and then put up her hand to her mouth: that was heartburn.

A voice cried far out on the playground:

— All in!

Then other voices cried from the lower and third lines:°

— All in! All in!

The players closed around, flushed and muddy, and he went among them, glad to go in. Rody Kickham held the ball by its greasy lace. A fellow asked him to give it one last: but he walked on without even answering the fellow. Simon Moonan told him not to because the pre-fect was looking. The fellow turned to Simon Moonan and said:

— We all know why you speak. You are McGlade's suck.°

Suck was a queer word. The fellow called Simon Moonan that name because Simon Moonan used to tie the prefect's false sleeves behind his back and the prefect used to let on to be angry. But the sound was ugly. Once he had washed his hands in the lavatory of the Wicklow Hotel and his father pulled the stopper up by the chain after and the dirty water went down through the hole in the basin. And when it had all gone down slowly the hole in the basin had made a sound like that: suck. Only louder.

To remember that and the white look of the lavatory made him feel cold and then hot. There were two cocks that you turned and water came out: cold and hot. He felt cold and then a little hot: and he could see the names printed on the cocks. That was a very queer thing.

And the air in the corridor chilled him too. It was queer and wet-tish. But soon the gas would be lit and in burning it made a light noise like a little song. Always the same: and when the fellows stopped talking in the playroom you could hear it.

It was the hour for sums. Father Arnall wrote a hard sum on the board and then he said:

---

lower . . . lines: See p. 21; boys from thirteen to fifteen.   *suck:* A sycophant, a boy who "sucks up" to a teacher.

— Now then, who will win? Go ahead, York! Go ahead, Lancaster!°

Stephen tried his best but the sum was too hard and he felt confused. The little silk badge with the white rose on it that was pinned on the breast of his jacket began to flutter. He was no good at sums but he tried his best so that York might not lose. Father Arnall's face looked very black but he was not in a wax:° he was laughing. Then Jack Lawton cracked his fingers and Father Arnall looked at his copybook and said:

— Right. Bravo Lancaster! The red rose wins. Come on now, York! Forge ahead!

Jack Lawton looked over from his side. The little silk badge with the red rose on it looked very rich because he had a blue sailor top on. Stephen felt his own face red too, thinking of all the bets about who would get first place in elements,° Jack Lawton or he. Some weeks Jack Lawton got the card for first and some weeks he got the card for first. His white silk badge fluttered and fluttered as he worked at the next sum and heard Father Arnall's voice. Then all his eagerness passed away and he felt his face quite cool. He thought his face must be white because it felt so cool. He could not get out the answer for the sum but it did not matter. White roses and red roses: those were beautiful colours to think of. And the cards for first place and second place and third place were beautiful colours too: pink and cream and lavender. Lavender and cream and pink roses were beautiful to think of. Perhaps a wild rose might be like those colours and he remembered the song about the wild rose blossoms on the little green place. But you could not have a green rose. But perhaps somewhere in the world you could.

The bell rang and then the classes began to file out of the rooms and along the corridors towards the refectory. He sat looking at the two prints of butter on his plate but could not eat the damp bread. The tablecloth was damp and limp. But he drank off the hot weak tea which the clumsy scullion, girt with a white apron, poured into his cup. He wondered whether the scullion's apron was damp too or whether all white things were cold and damp. Nasty Roche and Saurin drank cocoa that their people sent them in tins. They said they could not drink the tea; that it was hogwash. Their fathers were magistrates, the fellows said.

All the boys seemed to him very strange. They had all fathers and mothers and different clothes and voices. He longed to be at home and

---

York . . . Lancaster: The two English houses opposed in the War of the Roses.   **a wax:** A rage.   **elements:** English, math, geography, history, Latin.

lay his head on his mother's lap. But he could not: and so he longed for the play and study and prayers to be over and to be in bed.

He drank another cup of hot tea and Fleming said:

— What's up? Have you a pain or what's up with you?

— I don't know, Stephen said.

— Sick in your breadbasket, Fleming said, because your face looks white. It will go away.

— O yes, Stephen said.

But he was not sick there. He thought that he was sick in his heart if you could be sick in that place. Fleming was very decent to ask him. He wanted to cry. He leaned his elbows on the table and shut and opened the flaps of his ears. Then he heard the noise of the refectory every time he opened the flaps of his ears. It made a roar like a train at night. And when he closed the flaps the roar was shut off like a train going into a tunnel. That night at Dalkey the train had roared like that and then, when it went into the tunnel, the roar stopped. He closed his eyes and the train went on, roaring and then stopping; roaring again, stopping. It was nice to hear it roar and stop and then roar out of the tunnel again and then stop.

Then the higher line° fellows began to come down along the matting in the middle of the refectory, Paddy Rath and Jimmy Magee and the Spaniard who was allowed to smoke cigars and the little Portuguese who wore the woolly cap. And then the lower line tables and the tables of the third line. And every single fellow had a different way of walking.

He sat in a corner of the playroom pretending to watch a game of dominos and once or twice he was able to hear for an instant the little song of the gas. The prefect was at the door with some boys and Simon Moonan was knotting his false sleeves. He was telling them something about Tullabeg.

Then he went away from the door and Wells came over to Stephen and said:

— Tell us, Dedalus, do you kiss your mother every night before you go to bed?

Stephen answered:

— I do.

Wells turned to the other fellows and said:

— O, I say, here's a fellow says he kisses his mother every night before he goes to bed.

higher line: Boys from fifteen to eighteen.

The other fellows stopped their game and turned round, laughing. Stephen blushed under their eyes and said:

— I do not.

Wells said:

— O, I say, here's a fellow says he doesn't kiss his mother before he goes to bed.

They all laughed again. Stephen tried to laugh with them. He felt his whole body hot and confused in a moment. What was the right answer to the question? He had given two and still Wells laughed. But Wells must know the right answer for he was in third of grammar. He tried to think of Wells's mother but he did not dare to raise his eyes to Wells's face. He did not like Wells's face. It was Wells who had shouldered him into the square ditch the day before because he would not swop his little snuffbox for Wells's seasoned hacking chestnut, the conqueror of forty. It was a mean thing to do; all the fellows said it was. And how cold and slimy the water had been! And a fellow had once seen a big rat jump plop into the scum.

The cold slime of the ditch covered his whole body; and, when the bell rang for study and the lines filed out of the playrooms, he felt the cold air of the corridor and staircase inside his clothes. He still tried to think what was the right answer. Was it right to kiss his mother or wrong to kiss his mother? What did that mean, to kiss? You put your face up like that to say goodnight and then his mother put her face down. That was to kiss. His mother put her lips on his cheek; her lips were soft and they wetted his cheek; and they made a tiny little noise: kiss. Why did people do that with their two faces?

Sitting in the studyhall he opened the lid of his desk and changed the number pasted up inside from seventyseven to seventysix. But the Christmas vacation was very far away: but one time it would come because the earth moved round always.

There was a picture of the earth on the first page of his geography: a big ball in the middle of clouds. Fleming had a box of crayons and one night during free study he had coloured the earth green and the clouds maroon. That was like the two brushes in Dante's press, the brush with the green velvet back for Parnell and the brush with the maroon velvet back for Michael Davitt. But he had not told Fleming to colour them those colours. Fleming had done it himself.

He opened the geography to study the lesson; but he could not learn the names of places in America. Still they were all different places that had those different names. They were all in different countries and the countries were in continents and the continents were in the world and the world was in the universe.

He turned to the flyleaf of the geography and read what he had written there: himself, his name and where he was.

Stephen Dedalus
Class of Elements
Clongowes Wood College
Sallins
County Kildare
Ireland
Europe
The World
The Universe

That was in his writing: and Fleming one night for a cod° had written on the opposite page:

Stephen Dedalus is my name,
Ireland is my nation.
Clongowes is my dwellingplace
And heaven my expectation.

He read the verses backwards but then they were not poetry. Then he read the flyleaf from the bottom to the top till he came to his own name. That was he: and he read down the page again. What was after the universe? Nothing. But was there anything round the universe to show where it stopped before the nothing place began? It could not be a wall but there could be a thin thin line there all round everything. It was very big to think about everything and everywhere. Only God could do that. He tried to think what a big thought that must be but he could think only of God. God was God's name just as his name was Stephen. *Dieu* was the French for God and that was God's name too; and when anyone prayed to God and said *Dieu* then God knew at once that it was a French person that was praying. But though there were different names for God in all the different languages in the world and God understood what all the people who prayed said in their different languages still God remained always the same God and God's real name was God.

It made him very tired to think that way. It made him feel his head very big. He turned over the flyleaf and looked wearily at the green round earth in the middle of the maroon clouds. He wondered which was right, to be for the green or for the maroon, because Dante had

---

a cod: A joke or prank.

ripped the green velvet back off the brush that was for Parnell one day with her scissors and had told him that Parnell was a bad man. He wondered if they were arguing at home about that. That was called politics. There were two sides in it: Dante was on one side and his father and Mr Casey were on the other side but his mother and uncle Charles were on no side. Every day there was something in the paper about it.

It pained him that he did not know well what politics meant and that he did not know where the universe ended. He felt small and weak. When would he be like the fellows in poetry and rhetoric? They had big voices and big boots and they studied trigonometry. That was very far away. First came the vacation and then the next term and then vacation again and then again another term and then again the vacation. It was like a train going in and out of tunnels and that was like the noise of the boys eating in the refectory when you opened and closed the flaps of the ears. Term, vacation; tunnel, out; noise, stop. How far away it was! It was better to go to bed to sleep. Only prayers in the chapel and then bed. He shivered and yawned. It would be lovely in bed after the sheets got a bit hot. First they were so cold to get into. He shivered to think how cold they were first. But then they got hot and then he could sleep. It was lovely to be tired. He yawned again. Night prayers and then bed: he shivered and wanted to yawn. It would be lovely in a few minutes. He felt a warm glow creeping up from the cold shivering sheets, warmer and warmer till he felt warm all over, ever so warm; ever so warm and yet he shivered a little and still wanted to yawn.

The bell rang for night prayers and he filed out of the studyhall after the others and down the staircase and along the corridors to the chapel. The corridors were darkly lit and the chapel was darkly lit. Soon all would be dark and sleeping. There was cold night air in the chapel and the marbles were the colour the sea was at night. The sea was cold day and night: but it was colder at night. It was cold and dark under the sea-wall beside his father's house. But the kettle would be on the hob° to make punch.

The prefect of the chapel prayed above his head and his memory knew the responses:

O Lord, open our lips
And our mouth shall announce Thy praise.
Incline unto our aid, O God!
O Lord, make haste to help us!

hob: Shelf at back or side of a fireplace.

There was a cold night smell in the chapel. But it was a holy smell. It was not like the smell of the old peasants who knelt at the back of the chapel at Sunday mass. That was a smell of air and rain and turf° and corduroy. But they were very holy peasants. They breathed behind him on his neck and sighed as they prayed. They lived in Clane, a fellow said: there were little cottages there and he had seen a woman standing at the halfdoor of a cottage with a child in her arms, as the cars had come past from Sallins. It would be lovely to sleep for one night in that cottage before the fire of smoking turf, in the dark lit by the fire, in the warm dark, breathing the smell of the peasants, air and rain and turf and corduroy. But, O, the road there between the trees was dark! You would be lost in the dark. It made him afraid to think of how it was.

He heard the voice of the prefect of the chapel saying the last prayer. He prayed it too against the dark outside under the trees.

Visit, we beseech Thee, O Lord, this habitation and drive away from it all the snares of the enemy. May Thy holy angels dwell herein to preserve us in peace and may Thy blessing be always upon us through Christ, Our Lord. Amen.

His fingers trembled as he undressed himself in the dormitory. He told his fingers to hurry up. He had to undress and then kneel and say his own prayers and be in bed before the gas was lowered so that he might not go to hell when he died. He rolled his stockings off and put on his nightshirt quickly and knelt trembling at his bedside and repeated his prayers quickly quickly fearing that the gas would go down. He felt his shoulders shaking as he murmured:

God bless my father and my mother and spare them to me!
God bless my little brothers and sisters and spare them to me!
God bless Dante and uncle Charles and spare them to me!

He blessed himself and climbed quickly into bed and, tucking the end of the nightshirt under his feet, curled himself together under the cold white sheets, shaking and trembling. But he would not go to hell when he died; and the shaking would stop. A voice bade the boys in the dormitory goodnight. He peered out for an instant over the coverlet and saw the yellow curtains round and before his bed that shut him off on all sides. The light was lowered quietly.

The prefect's shoes went away. Where? Down the staircase and

---

turf: Aromatic kind of peat burned for warmth in rural Ireland.

along the corridors or to his room at the end? He saw the dark. Was it true about the black dog that walked there at night with eyes as big as carriagelamps? They said it was the ghost of a murderer. A long shiver of fear flowed over his body. He saw the dark entrance hall of the castle. Old servants in old dress were in the ironingroom° above the staircase. It was long ago. The old servants were quiet. There was a fire there but the hall was still dark. A figure came up the staircase from the hall. He wore the white cloak of a marshal;° his face was pale and strange; he held his hand pressed to his side. He looked out of strange eyes at the old servants. They looked at him and saw their master's face and cloak and knew that he had received his deathwound. But only the dark was where they looked: only dark silent air. Their master had received his deathwound on the battlefield of Prague far away over the sea. He was standing on the field; his hand was pressed to his side; his face was pale and strange and he wore the white cloak of a marshal.

O how cold and strange it was to think of that! All the dark was cold and strange. There were pale strange faces there, great eyes like carriagelamps. They were the ghosts of murderers, the figures of marshals who had received their deathwound on battlefields far away over the sea. What did they wish to say that their faces were so strange?

Visit, we beseech Thee, O Lord, this habitation and drive away from it all . . .

Going home for the holidays! That would be lovely: the fellows had told him. Getting up on the cars° in the early wintry morning outside the door of the castle. The cars were rolling on the gravel. Cheers for the rector!

Hurray! Hurray! Hurray!

The cars drove past the chapel and all caps were raised. They drove merrily along the country roads. The drivers pointed with their whips to Bodenstown. The fellows cheered. They passed the farmhouse of the Jolly Farmer. Cheer after cheer after cheer. Through Clane they drove, cheering and cheered. The peasant women stood at the halfdoors, the men stood here and there. The lovely smell there was in the wintry air: the smell of Clane: rain and wintry air and turf smouldering and corduroy.

---

ironingroom: Room where armor was formerly stored.   *cloak of a marshal:* The Browne family owned Clongowes Wood in the eighteenth century, and the Austrian-born son of an expatriate member was killed at the battle in 1757. His ghost is said to have appeared to the servants in the castle.   *cars:* Horse-drawn vehicles.

The train was full of fellows: a long long chocolate train with cream facings. The guards went to and fro opening, closing, locking, unlocking the doors. They were men in dark blue and silver; they had silvery whistles and their keys made a quick music: click, click: click, click.

And the train raced on over the flat lands and past the Hill of Allen. The telegraphpoles were passing, passing. The train went on and on. It knew. There were coloured lanterns in the hall of his father's house and ropes of green branches. There were holly and ivy round the pierglass and holly and ivy, green and red, twined round the chandeliers. There were red holly and green ivy round the old portraits on the walls. Holly and ivy for him and for Christmas.

Lovely . . .

All the people. Welcome home, Stephen! Noises of welcome. His mother kissed him. Was that right? His father was a marshal now: higher than a magistrate. Welcome home, Stephen!

Noises . . .

There was a noise of curtainrings running back along the rods, of water being splashed in the basins. There was a noise of rising and dressing and washing in the dormitory: a noise of clapping of hands as the prefect wet up and down telling the fellows to look sharp. A pale sunlight showed the yellow curtains drawn back, the tossed beds. His bed was very hot and his face and body were very hot.

He got up and sat on the side of his bed. He was weak. He tried to pull on his stocking. It had a horrid rough feel. The sunlight was queer and cold.

Fleming said:

— Are you not well?

He did not know; and Fleming said:

— Get back into bed. I'll tell McGlade you're not well.

— He's sick.

— Who is?

— Tell McGlade.

— Get back into bed.

— Is he sick?

A fellow held his arms while he loosened the stocking clinging to his foot and climbed back into the hot bed.

He crouched down between the sheets, glad of their tepid glow. He heard the fellows talk among themselves about him as they dressed for mass. It was a mean thing to do, to shoulder him into the square ditch, they were saying.

Then their voices ceased; they had gone. A voice at his bed said:

— Dedalus, don't spy on us, sure you won't?

Wells's face was there. He looked at it and saw that Wells was afraid.

— I didn't mean to. Sure you won't?

His father had told him, whatever he did, never to peach on a fellow. He shook his head and answered no and felt glad. Wells said:

— I didn't mean to, honour bright. It was only for cod. I'm sorry.

The face and the voice went away. Sorry because he was afraid. Afraid that it was some disease. Canker was a disease of plants and cancer one of animals: or another different. That was a long time ago then out on the playgrounds in the evening light, creeping from point to point on the fringe of his line, a heavy bird flying low through the grey light. Leicester Abbey lit up. Wolsey died there. The abbots buried him themselves.

It was not Wells's face, it was the prefect's. He was not foxing. No, no: he was sick really. He was not foxing. And he felt the prefect's hand on his forehead; and he felt his forehead warm and damp against the prefect's cold damp hand. That was the way a rat felt, slimy and damp and cold. Every rat had two eyes to look out of. Sleek shiny coats, little little feet tucked up to jump, black shiny eyes to look out of. They could understand how to jump. But the minds of rats could not understand trigonometry. When they were dead they lay on their sides. Their coats dried then. They were only dead things.

The prefect was there again and it was his voice that was saying that he was to get up, that Father Minister° had said he was to get up and dress and go to the infirmary. And while he was dressing himself as quickly as he could the prefect said:

— We must pack off to Brother Michael° because we have the collywobbles! Terrible thing to have the collywobbles! How we wobble when we have the collywobbles!

He was very decent to say that. That was all to make him laugh. But he could not laugh because his cheeks and lips were all shivery: and then the prefect had to laugh by himself.

The prefect cried:

— Quick march! Hayfoot! Strawfoot!

They went together down the staircase and along the corridor and past the bath. As he passed the door he remembered with a vague fear the warm turfcoloured bogwater, the warm moist air, the noise of plunges, the smell of the towels, like medicine.

Father Minister: The vice-rector.   *Brother Michael:* A man bound to the Jesuit order by vows but not educated as a priest would be; usually assigned housekeeping duties.

Brother Michael was standing at the door of the infirmary and from the door of the dark cabinet on his right came a smell like medicine. That came from the bottles on the shelves. The prefect spoke to Brother Michael and Brother Michael answered and called the prefect sir. He had reddish hair mixed with grey and a queer look. It was queer that he would always be a brother. It was queer too that you could not call him sir because he was a brother and had a different kind of look. Was he not holy enough or why could he not catch up on the others?

There were two beds in the room and in one bed there was a fellow: and when they went in he called out:

— Hello! It's young Dedalus! What's up?

— The sky is up, Brother Michael said.

He was a fellow out of third of grammar and, while Stephen was undressing, he asked Brother Michael to bring him a round of buttered toast.

— Ah, do! he said.

— Butter you up! said Brother Michael. You'll get your walking papers in the morning when the doctor comes.

— Will I? the fellow said. I'm not well yet.

Brother Michael repeated:

— You'll get your walking papers, I tell you.

He bent down to rake the fire. He had a long back like the long back of a tramhorse. He shook the poker gravely and nodded his head at the fellow out of third of grammar.

Then Brother Michael went away and after a while the fellow out of third of grammar turned in towards the wall and fell asleep.

That was the infirmary. He was sick then. Had they written home to tell his mother and father? But it would be quicker for one of the priests to go himself to tell them. Or he would write a letter for the priest to bring.

Dear Mother

I am sick. I want to go home. Please come and take me home. I am in the infirmary.

Your fond son,
Stephen

How far away they were! There was cold sunlight outside the window. He wondered if he would die. You could die just the same on a sunny day. He might die before his mother came. Then he would have a dead mass in the chapel like the way the fellows had told him it was when Little had died. All the fellows would be at the mass, dressed in black, all with sad faces. Wells too would be there but no fellow would look at him. The rector would be there in a cope of black and gold° and there would be tall yellow candles on the altar and round the catafalque.° And they would carry the coffin out of the chapel slowly and he would be buried in the little graveyard of the community off the main avenue of limes. And Wells would be sorry then for what he had done. And the bell would toll slowly.

He could hear the tolling. He said over to himself the song that Brigid had taught him.

> Dingdong! The castle bell!
> Farewell, my mother!
> Bury me in the old churchyard
> Beside my eldest brother.
> My coffin shall be black,
> Six angels at my back,
> Two to sing and two to pray
> And two to carry my soul away.

How beautiful and sad that was! How beautiful the words were where they said *Bury me in the old churchyard!* A tremor passed over his body. How sad and how beautiful! He wanted to cry quietly but not for himself: for the words, so beautiful and sad, like music. The bell! The bell! Farewell! O farewell!

The cold sunlight was weaker and Brother Michael was standing at his bedside with a bowl of beeftea. He was glad for his mouth was hot and dry. He could hear them playing on the playgrounds. It was after lunchtime. And the day was going on in the college just as if he were there.

Then Brother Michael was going away and the fellow out of third of grammar told him to be sure and come back and tell him all the news in the paper. He told Stephen that his name was Athy and that his father kept a lot of racehorses that were spiffing jumpers and that his father would give a good tip to Brother Michael any time he wanted it because Brother Michael was very decent and always told him the news out of the paper they got every day up in the castle. There was every kind of news in the paper: accidents, shipwrecks, sports and politics.

— Now it is all about politics in the paper, he said. Do your people talk about that too?

---

cope of black and gold: A long vestment in the colors appropriate for a funeral mass.
catafalque: Raised support for a coffin in a public funeral.

— Yes, Stephen said.

— Mine too, he said.

Then he thought for a moment and said:

— You have a queer name, Dedalus, and I have a queer name too, Athy. My name is the name of a town. Your name is like Latin.

Then he asked:

— Are you good at riddles?

Stephen answered:

— Not very good.

Then he said:

— Can you answer me this one? Why is the county Kildare like the leg of a fellow's breeches?

Stephen thought what could be the answer and then said:

— I give it up.

— Because there is a thigh in it, he said. Do you see the joke? Athy is the town in the county Kildare and a thigh is the other thigh.

— O, I see, Stephen said.

— That's an old riddle, he said.

After a moment he said:

— I say!

— What? asked Stephen.

— You know, he said, you can ask that riddle another way?

— Can you? said Stephen.

— The same riddle, he said. Do you know the other way to ask it?

— No, said Stephen.

— Can you not think of the other way? he said.

He looked at Stephen over the bedclothes as he spoke. Then he lay back on the pillow and said:

— There is another way but I won't tell you what it is.

Why did he not tell it? His father, who kept the racehorses, must be a magistrate too like Saurin's father and Nasty Roche's father. He thought of his own father, of how he sang songs while his mother played and of how he always gave him a shilling when he asked for six-pence and he felt sorry for him that he was not a magistrate like the other boys' fathers. Then why was he sent to that place with them? But his father had told him that he would be no stranger there because his granduncle had presented an address to the liberator° there fifty years before. You could know the people of that time by their old dress. It seemed to him a solemn time: and he wondered if that was the time

the liberator: Daniel O'Connell (1775–1847), political leader of Irish Catholics.

when the fellows in Clongowes wore blue coats with brass buttons and yellow waistcoats and caps of rabbitskin and drank beer like grownup people and kept greyhounds of their own to course the hares with.

He looked at the window and saw that the daylight had grown weaker. There would be cloudy grey light over the playgrounds. There was no noise on the playgrounds. The class must be doing the themes or perhaps Father Arnall was reading a legend out of the book.

It was queer that they had not given him any medicine. Perhaps Brother Michael would bring it back when he came. They said you got stinking stuff to drink when you were in the infirmary. But he felt better now than before. It would be nice getting better slowly. You could get a book then. There was a book in the library about Holland. There were lovely foreign names in it and pictures of strangelooking cities and ships. It made you feel so happy.

How pale the light was at the window! But that was nice. The fire rose and fell on the wall. It was like waves. Someone had put coal on and he heard voices. They were talking. It was the noise of the waves. Or the waves were talking among themselves as they rose and fell.

He saw the sea of waves, long dark waves rising and falling, dark under the moonless night. A tiny light twinkled at the pierhead where the ship was entering: and he saw a multitude of people gathered by the waters' edge to see the ship that was entering their harbour. A tall man stood on the deck, looking out towards the flat dark land: and by the light at the pierhead he saw his face, the sorrowful face of Brother Michael.

He saw him lift his hand towards the people and heard him say in a loud voice of sorrow over the waters:

— He is dead. We saw him lying upon the catafalque.

A wail of sorrow went up from the people.

— Parnell! Parnell! He is dead!°

They fell upon their knees, moaning in sorrow.

And he saw Dante in a maroon velvet dress and with a green velvet mantle hanging from her shoulders walking proudly and silently past the people who knelt by the waters' edge.

*

*   *

Parnell! He is dead: Parnell died in England and his body was brought by boat to Kingstown Harbor (now Dun Laoghaire) near Dublin, where it was met by a huge mourning crowd.

A great fire, banked high and red, flamed in the grate and under the ivytwined branches of the chandelier the Christmas table was spread. They had come home a little late and still dinner was not ready: but it would be ready in a jiffy, his mother had said. They were waiting for the door to open and for the servants to come in, holding the big dishes covered with their heavy metal covers.

All were waiting: uncle Charles, who sat far away in the shadow of the window, Dante and Mr Casey, who sat in the easychairs at either side of the hearth, Stephen, seated on a chair between them, his feet resting on the toasted boss.° Mr Dedalus looked at himself in the pierglass above the mantelpiece, waxed out his moustache-ends and then, parting his coattails, stood with his back to the glowing fire: and still, from time to time, he withdrew a hand from his coattail to wax out one of his moustache-ends. Mr Casey leaned his head to one side and, smiling, tapped the gland of his neck with his fingers. And Stephen smiled too for he knew now that it was not true that Mr Casey had a purse of silver in his throat. He smiled to think how the silvery noise which Mr Casey used to make had deceived him. And when he had tried to open Mr Casey's hand to see if the purse of silver was hidden there he had seen that the fingers could not be straightened out: and Mr Casey had told him that he had got those three cramped fingers making a birthday present for Queen Victoria.°

Mr Casey tapped the gland of his neck and smiled at Stephen with sleepy eyes: and Mr Dedalus said to him:

— Yes. Well now, that's all right. O, we had a good walk, hadn't we, John? Yes . . . I wonder if there's any likelihood of dinner this evening. Yes. . . . O, well now, we got a good breath of ozone round the Head° today. Ay, bedad.

He turned to Dante and said:

— You didn't stir out at all, Mrs Riordan?

Dante frowned and said shortly:

— No.

Mr Dedalus dropped his coattails and went over to the sideboard. He brought forth a great stone jar of whisky from the locker and filled the decanter slowly, bending now and then to see how much he had poured in. Then replacing the jar in the locker he poured out a little of

---

boss: A sort of hassock or footrest.   *a birthday present for Queen Victoria:* Probably the result of picking oakum as hard labor in prison for political activities.   *a good breath of ozone round the Head:* Fresh air from walking around the promontory Bray Head, just south of the Dedalus house, by one of the mountain paths.

the whisky into two glasses, added a little water and came back with them to the fireplace.

— A thimbleful, John, he said, just to whet your appetite.

Mr Casey took the glass, drank, and placed it near him on the mantelpiece. Then he said:

— Well, I can't help thinking of our friend Christopher manufacturing . . .

He broke into a fit of laughter and coughing and added:

—. . . manufacturing that champagne for those fellows.

Mr Dedalus laughed loudly.

— Is it Christy? he said. There's more cunning in one of those warts on his bald head than in a pack of jack foxes.°

He inclined his head, closed his eyes, and, licking his lips profusely, began to speak with the voice of the hotelkeeper.

— And he has such a soft mouth when he's speaking to you, don't you know. He's very moist and watery about the dewlaps, God bless him.

Mr Casey was still struggling through his fit of coughing and laughter. Stephen, seeing and hearing the hotelkeeper through his father's face and voice, laughed.

Mr Dedalus put up his eyeglass and, staring down at him, said quietly and kindly:

— What are you laughing at, you little puppy, you?

The servants entered and placed the dishes on the table. Mrs Dedalus followed and the places were arranged.

— Sit over, she said.

Mr Dedalus went to the end of the table and said:

— Now, Mrs Riordan, sit over. John, sit you down, my hearty.

He looked round to where uncle Charles sat and said:

— Now then, sir, there's a bird here waiting for you.

When all had taken their seats he laid his hand on the cover and then said quickly, withdrawing it:

— Now, Stephen.

Stephen stood up in his place to say the grace before meals:

Bless us, O Lord, and these Thy gifts which through Thy bounty we are about to receive through Christ Our Lord. Amen.

All blessed themselves and Mr Dedalus with a sigh of pleasure lifted from the dish the heavy cover pearled around the edge with glistening drops.

jack foxes: Male foxes.

Stephen looked at the plump turkey which had lain, trussed and skewered, on the kitchen table. He knew that his father had paid a guinea for it in Dunn's of D'Olier Street and that the man had prodded it often at the breastbone to show how good it was: and he remembered the man's voice when he had said:

— Take that one, sir. That's the real Ally Daly.°

Why did Mr Barrett in Clongowes call his pandybat° a turkey? But Clongowes was far away: and the warm heavy smell of turkey and ham and celery rose from the plates and dishes and the great fire was banked high and red in the grate and the green ivy and red holly made you feel so happy and when dinner was ended the big plumpudding would be carried in, studded with peeled almonds and sprigs of holly, with bluish fire running around it and a little green flag flying from the top.

It was his first Christmas dinner and he thought of his little brothers and sisters who were waiting in the nursery, as he had often waited, till the pudding came. The deep low collar and the Eton jacket made him feel queer and oldish: and that morning when his mother had brought him down to the parlour, dressed for mass, his father had cried. That was because he was thinking of his own father. And uncle Charles had said so too.

Mr Dedalus covered the dish and began to eat hungrily. Then he said:

— Poor old Christy, he's nearly lopsided now with roguery.

— Simon, said Mrs Dedalus, you haven't given Mrs Riordan any sauce.

Mr Dedalus seized the sauceboat.

— Haven't I? he cried. Mrs Riordan, pity the poor blind.

Dante covered her plate with her hands and said:

— No, thanks.

Mr Dedalus turned to uncle Charles.

— How are you off, sir?

— Right as the mail, Simon.

— You, John?

— I'm all right. Go on yourself.

— Mary? Here, Stephen, here's something to make your hair curl.

He poured sauce freely over Stephen's plate and set the boat again on the table. Then he asked uncle Charles was it tender. Uncle Charles could not speak because his mouth was full but he nodded that it was.

Ally Daly: The best.   *pandybat:* A stiff, reinforced leather strap.

— That was a good answer our friend made to the canon. What? said Mr Dedalus.

— I didn't think he had that much in him, said Mr Casey.

— *I'll pay you you dues, father, when you cease turning the house of God into a pollingbooth.*

— A nice answer, said Dante, for any man calling himself a catholic to give to his priest.

— They have only themselves to blame, said Mr Dedalus suavely. If they took a fool's advice they would confine their attention to religion.

— It is religion, Dante said. They are doing their duty in warning the people.

— We go to the house of God, Mr Casey said, in all humility to pray to our Maker and not to hear election addresses.

— It is religion, Dante said again. They are right. They must direct their flocks.

— And preach politics from the altar, is it? asked Mr Dedalus.

— Certainly, said Dante. It is a question of public morality. A priest would not be a priest if he did not tell his flock what is right and what is wrong.

Mrs Dedalus laid down her knife and fork, saying:

— For pity's sake and for pity sake let us have no political discussion on this day of all days in the year.

— Quite right, ma'am, said uncle Charles. Now, Simon, that's quite enough now. Not another word now.

— Yes, yes, said Mr Dedalus quickly.

He uncovered the dish boldly and said:

— Now then, who's for more turkey?

Nobody answered. Dante said:

— Nice language for any catholic to use!

— Mrs Riordan, I appeal to you, said Mrs Dedalus, to let the matter drop now.

Dante turned on her and said:

— And am I to sit here and listen to the pastors of my church being flouted?

— Nobody is saying a word against them, said Mr Dedalus, so long as they don't meddle in politics.

— The bishops and priests of Ireland have spoken, said Dante, and they must be obeyed.

— Let them leave politics alone, said Mr Casey, or the people may leave their church alone.

— You hear? said Dante turning to Mrs Dedalus.

— Mr Casey! Simon! said Mrs Dedalus. Let it end now.

— Too bad! Too bad! said uncle Charles.

— What? cried Mr Dedalus. Were we to desert him at the bidding of the English people?

— He was no longer worthy to lead, said Dante. He was a public sinner.

— We are all sinners and black sinners, said Mr Casey coldly.

— *Woe be to the man by whom the scandal cometh!* said Mrs Riordan. *It would be better for him that a millstone were tied about his neck and that he were cast into the depths of the sea rather than that he should scandalise one of these, my least little ones.* That is the language of the Holy Ghost.

— And very bad language if you ask me, said Mr Dedalus coolly.

— Simon! Simon! said uncle Charles. The boy.

— Yes, yes, said Mr Dedalus. I meant about the . . . I was thinking about the bad language of that railway porter. Well now, that's all right. Here, Stephen, show me your plate, old chap. Eat away now. Here.

He heaped up the food on Stephen's plate and served uncle Charles and Mr Casey to large pieces of turkey and splashes of sauce. Mrs Dedalus was eating little and Dante sat with her hands in her lap. She was red in the face. Mr Dedalus rooted with the carvers at the end of the dish and said:

— There's a tasty bit here we call the pope's nose.° If any lady or gentleman . . .

He held a piece of fowl up on the prong of the carvingfork. Nobody spoke. He put it on his own plate, saying:

— Well, you can't say but you were asked. I think I had better eat it myself because I'm not well in my health lately.

He winked at Stephen and, replacing the dishcover, began to eat again.

There was a silence while he ate. Then he said:

— Well now, the day kept up fine after all. There were plenty of strangers down too.

Nobody spoke. He said again:

— I think there were more strangers down than last Christmas.

He looked round at the others whose faces were bent towards their plates and, receiving no reply, waited for a moment and said bitterly:

— Well, my Christmas dinner has been spoiled anyhow.

pope's nose: Part of the turkey's rump.

— There could be neither luck nor grace, Dante said, in a house where there is no respect for the pastors of the church.

Mr Dedalus threw his knife and fork noisily on his plate.

— Respect! he said. Is it for Billy with the lip° or for the tub of guts up in Armagh?° Respect!

— Princes of the church, said Mr Casey with slow scorn.

— Lord Leitrim's coachman,° yes, said Mr Dedalus.

— They are the Lord's anointed, Dante said. They are an honour to their country.

— Tub of guts, said Mr Dedalus coarsely. He has a handsome face, mind you, in repose. You should see that fellow lapping up his bacon and cabbage of a cold winter's day. O Johnny!

He twisted his features into a grimace of heavy bestiality and made a lapping noise with his lips.

— Really, Simon, said Mrs Dedalus, you should not speak that way before Stephen. It's not right.

— O, he'll remember all this when he grows up, said Dante hotly — the language he heard against God and religion and priests in his own home.

— Let him remember too, cried Mr Casey to her from across the table, the language with which the priests and the priests' pawns broke Parnell's heart and hounded him into his grave. Let him remember that too when he grows up.

— Sons of bitches! cried Mr Dedalus. When he was down they turned on him to betray him and rend him like rats in a sewer. Lowlived dogs! And they look it! By Christ, they look it!

— They behaved rightly, cried Dante. They obeyed their bishops and their priests. Honour to them!

— Well, it is perfectly dreadful to say that not even for one day of the year, said Mrs Dedalus, can we be free from these dreadful disputes!

Uncle Charles raised his hands mildly and said:

— Come now, come now, come now! Can we not have our opinions whatever they are without this bad temper and this bad language? It is too bad surely.

Billy with the lip: Reverend William J. Walsh (1841–1921), archbishop of Dublin. *the tub of guts up in Armagh:* Reverend Michael Logue (1938–1924), archbishop of Armagh. *Lord Leitrim's coachman:* An oppressive landlord, Leitrim was assassinated in 1878 and his coachman tried to defend him, earning the contempt of radical nationalists.

Mrs Dedalus spoke to Dante in a low voice but Dante said loudly:

— I will not say nothing. I will defend my church and my religion when it is insulted and spit on by renegade catholics.

Mr Casey pushed his plate rudely into the middle of the table and, resting his elbows before him, said in a harsh voice to his host:

— Tell me, did I tell you that story about a very famous spit?

— You did not, John, said Mr Dedalus.

— Why then, said Mr Casey, it is a most instructive story. It happened not long ago in the county Wicklow where we are now.

He broke off and, turning towards Dante, said with quiet indignation:

— And I may tell you, ma'am, that I, if you mean me, am no renegade catholic. I am a catholic as my father was and his father before him and his father before him again when we gave up our lives rather than sell our faith.

— The more shame to you now, Dante said, to speak as you do.

— The story, John, said Mr Dedalus smiling. Let us have the story anyhow.

— Catholic indeed! repeated Dante ironically. The blackest protestant in the land would not speak the language I have heard this evening.

Mr Dedalus began to sway his head to and fro, crooning like a country singer.

— I am no protestant, I tell you again, said Mr Casey flushing.

Mr Dedalus, still crooning and swaying his head, began to sing in a grunting nasal tone:

O, come all you Roman catholics
That never went to mass.

He took up his knife and fork again in good humour and set to eating, saying to Mr Casey:

— Let us have the story, John. It will help us to digest.

Stephen looked with affection at Mr Casey's face which stared across the table over his joined hands. He liked to sit near him at the fire, looking up at his dark fierce face. But his dark eyes were never fierce and his slow voice was good to listen to. But why was he then against the priests? Because Dante must be right then. But he had heard his father say that she was a spoiled nun and that she had come out of the convent in the Alleghanies when her brother had got the money from the savages for the trinkets and the chainies.° Perhaps that made

chainies: Chinaware "seconds."

her severe against Parnell. And she did not like him to play with Eileen because Eileen was a protestant and when she was young she knew children that used to play with protestants and the protestants used to make fun of the litany of the Blessed Virgin. *Tower of Ivory,* they used to say, *House of Gold!*° How could a woman be a tower of ivory or a house of gold? Who was right then? And he remembered the evening in the infirmary in Clongowes, the dark waters, the light at the pierhead and the moan of sorrow from the people when they had heard.

Eileen had long white hands. One evening when playing tig° she had put her hands over his eyes: long and white and thin and cold and soft. That was ivory: a cold white thing. That was the meaning of *Tower of Ivory.*

— The story is very short and sweet, Mr Casey said. It was one day down in Arklow, a cold bitter day, not long before the chief died. May God have mercy on him!

He closed his eyes wearily and paused. Mr Dedalus took a bone from his plate and tore some meat from it with his teeth, saying:

— Before he was killed, you mean.

Mr Casey opened his eyes, sighed and went on:

— It was down in Arklow one day. We were down there at a meeting and after the meeting was over we had to make our way to the railway station through the crowd. Such booing and baaing, man, you never heard. They called us all the names in the world. Well there was one old lady, and a drunken old harridan she was surely, that paid all her attention to me. She kept dancing along beside me in the mud bawling and screaming into my face: *Priesthunter!*° *The Paris Funds! Mr Fox! Kitty O'Shea!*

— And what did you do, John? asked Mr Dedalus.

— I let her bawl away, said Mr Casey. It was a cold day and to keep up my heart I had (saving your presence, ma'am) a quid of Tullamore in my mouth and sure I couldn't say a word in any case because my mouth was full of tobacco juice.

— Well, John?

— Well. I let her bawl away, to her heart's content, *Kitty O'Shea* and the rest of it till at last she called that lady a name that I won't sully this Christmas board nor your ears, ma'am, nor my own lips by repeating.

Tower of Ivory . . . House of Gold: Epithets for the Blessed Virgin Mary from the Roman Catholic Litany of Our Lady.   *tig:* A game like hide-and-seek.   *Priesthunter:* Suggesting Parnell is like the paid informers in penal times who would turn in proscribed priests.

He paused. Mr Dedalus, lifting his head from the bone, asked:

— And what did you do, John?

— Do! said Mr Casey. She stuck her ugly old face up at me when she said it and I had my mouth full of the tobacco juice. I bent down to her and *Phth!* says I to her like that.

He turned aside and made the act of spitting.

— *Phth!* says I to her like that, right into her eye.

He clapped a hand to his eye and gave a hoarse scream of pain.

— *O Jesus, Mary and Joseph!* says she. *I'm blinded! I'm blinded and drownded!*

He stopped in a fit of coughing and laughter, repeating:

— *I'm blinded entirely.*

Mr Dedalus laughed loudly and lay back in his chair while uncle Charles swayed his head to and fro.

Dante looked terribly angry and repeated while they laughed:

— Very nice! Ha! Very nice!

It was not nice about the spit in the woman's eye. But what was the name the woman had called Kitty O'Shea that Mr Casey would not repeat? He thought of Mr Casey walking through the crowds of people and making speeches from a wagonette. That was what he had been in prison for and he remembered that one night Sergeant O'Neill had come to the house and had stood in the hall, talking in a low voice with his father and chewing nervously at the chinstrap of his cap. And that night Mr Casey had not gone to Dublin by train but a car had come to the door and he had heard his father say something about the Cabinteely road.

He was for Ireland and Parnell and so was his father: and so was Dante too for one night at the band on the esplanade she had hit a gentleman on the head with her umbrella because he had taken off his hat when the band played *God save the Queen* at the end.

Mr Dedalus gave a snort of contempt.

— Ah, John, he said. It is true for them. We are an unfortunate priestridden race and always were and always will be till the end of the chapter.

Uncle Charles shook his head, saying:

— A bad business! A bad business!

Mr Dedalus repeated:

— A priestridden Godforsaken race!

He pointed to the portrait of his grandfather on the wall to his right.

— Do you see that old chap up there, John? he said. He was a good Irishman when there was no money in the job. He was condemned to death as a whiteboy.° But he had a saying about our clerical friends, that he would never let one of them put his two feet under his mahogany.

Dante broke in angrily:

— If we are a priestridden race we ought to be proud of it! They are the apple of God's eye. *Touch them not, says Christ, for they are the apple of My eye.*

— And can we not love our country then? asked Mr Casey. Are we not to follow the man that was born to lead us?

— A traitor to his country! replied Dante. A traitor, an adulterer! The priests were right to abandon him. The priests were always the true friends of Ireland.

— Were they, faith? said Mr Casey.

He threw his fist on the table and, frowning angrily, protruded one finger after another.

— Didn't the bishops of Ireland betray us in the time of the union° when bishop Lanigan presented an address of loyalty to the Marquess Cornwallis?° Didn't the bishops and priests sell the aspirations of this country in 1829 in return for catholic emancipation?° Didn't they denounce the fenian movement° from the pulpit and in the confessionbox? And didn't they dishonour the ashes of Terence Bellew MacManus?°

His face was glowing with anger and Stephen felt the glow rise to his own cheek as the spoken words thrilled him. Mr Dedalus uttered a guffaw of coarse scorn.

— O, by God, he cried, I forgot little old Paul Cullen! Another apple of God's eye!

Dante bent across the table and cried to Mr Casey:

— Right! Right! They were always right! God and morality and religion come first.

Mrs Dedalus, seeing her excitement, said to her:

— Mrs Riordan, don't excite yourself answering them.

---

whiteboy: Member of a group working for land and tax reform, sometimes using terrorist means.   *time of the union:* The Act of Union in 1800 dissolved the separate parliament seated in Dublin.   *bishop Lanigan . . . Cornwallis:* James Lanigan, Bishop of Ossory, presented this address in 1799 to Cornwallis, then Lord Lieutenant of Ireland, in exchange for a promise of Catholic emancipation, a promise George III failed to honor. *catholic emancipation:* In 1829 the Catholic emancipation bill allowed Catholics to hold a variety of offices. Following this bill, which it had vigorously supported, the church was less energetic in working for repeal of the Union.   *fenian movement:* Name given the republican movement founded in 1858 in the U.S. along with the Irish Republican Brotherhood in Dublin.   *Terence Bellew MacManus:* (1823–1860), an Irish patriot and follower of O'Connell. Paul Cullen, first Irish cardinal and Church organizer, opposed clerical participation at the funeral.

— God and religion before everything! Dante cried. God and religion before the world!

Mr Casey raised his clenched fist and brought it down on the table with a crash.

— Very well, then, he shouted hoarsely, if it comes to that, no God for Ireland!

— John! John! cried Mr Dedalus, seizing his guest by the coatsleeve.

Dante stared across the table, her cheeks shaking. Mr Casey struggled up from his chair and bent across the table towards her, scraping the air from before his eyes with one hand as though he were tearing aside a cobweb.

— No God for Ireland! he cried. We have had too much God in Ireland. Away with God!

— Blasphemer! Devil! screamed Dante, starting to her feet and almost spitting in his face.

Uncle Charles and Mr Dedalus pulled Mr Casey back into his chair again, talking to him from both sides reasonably. He stared before him out of his dark flaming eyes, repeating:

— Away with God, I say!

Dante shoved her chair violently aside and left the table, upsetting her napkinring which rolled slowly along the carpet and came to rest against the foot of an easychair. Mrs Dedalus rose quickly and followed her towards the door. At the door Dante turned round violently and shouted down the room, her cheeks flushed and quivering with rage:

— Devil out of hell! We won! We crushed him to death! Fiend!

The door slammed behind her. Mr Casey, freeing his arms from his holders, suddenly bowed his head on his hands with a sob of pain.

— Poor Parnell! he cried loudly. My dead king!

He sobbed loudly and bitterly.

Stephen, raising his terrorstricken face, saw that his father's eyes were full of tears.

*
*   *

The fellows talked together in little groups.

One fellow said:

— They were caught near the Hill of Lyons.

— Who caught them?

— Mr Gleeson and the minister. They were on a car.

The same fellow added:

— A fellow in the higher line told me.

Fleming asked:

— But why did they run away, tell us?

— I know why, Cecil Thunder said. Because they had fecked° cash out of the rector's room.

— Who fecked it?

— Kickham's brother. And they all went shares in it.

But that was stealing. How could they have done that?

— A fat lot you know about it, Thunder! Wells said. I know why they scut.°

— Tell us why.

— I was told not to, Wells said.

— O, go on, Wells, all said. You might tell us. We won't let it out. Stephen bent forward his head to hear. Wells looked round to see if anyone was coming. Then he said secretly:

— You know the altar wine they keep in the press in the sacristy?

— Yes.

— Well, they drank that and it was found out who did it by the smell. And that's why they ran away, if you want to know.

And the fellow who had spoken first said:

— Yes, that's what I heard too from the fellow in the higher line.

The fellows were all silent. Stephen stood among them, afraid to speak, listening. A faint sickness of awe made him feel weak. How could they have done that? He thought of the dark silent sacristy. There were dark wooden presses there where the crimped surplices lay quietly folded. It was not the chapel but still you had to speak under your breath. It was a holy place. He remembered the summer evening he had been there to be dressed as boatbearer,° the evening of the procession to the little altar in the wood. A strange and holy place. The boy that held the censer° had swung it gently to and fro near the door with the silvery cap lifted by the middle chain to keep the coals lighting. That was called charcoal: and it had burned quietly as the fellow had swung it gently and had given off a weak sour smell. And then when all were vested he had stood holding out the boat to the rector and the rector had put a spoonful of incense in and it had hissed on the red coals.

The fellows were talking together in little groups here and there on the playground. The fellows seemed to him to have grown smaller: that was because a sprinter° had knocked him down the day before, a fellow out of second of grammar. He had been thrown by the fellow's

---

fecked: Stolen.   *scut:* Literally, tail of a rabbit; here, "turned tail and ran."   *boat-bearer:* One who carries the container of incense before it is lighted.   *censer:* Vessel in which incense is burned.   *sprinter:* Someone training in short-distance bicycle racing.

machine lightly on the cinderpath and his spectacles had been broken in three pieces and some of the grit of the cinders had gone into his mouth.

That was why the fellows seemed to him smaller and farther away and the goalposts so thin and far and the soft grey sky so high up. But there was no play on the football grounds for cricket was coming: and some said that Barnes would be the prof° and some said it would be Flowers. And all over the playgrounds they were playing rounders° and bowling twisters and lobs.° And from here and from there came the sounds of the cricketbats through the soft grey air. They said: pick, pack, pock, puck: like drops of water in a fountain slowly falling in the brimming bowl.

Athy, who had been silent, said quietly:

— You are all wrong.

All turned towards him eagerly.

— Why?

— Do you know?

— Who told you?

— Tell us, Athy.

Athy pointed across the playground to where Simon Moonan was walking by himself kicking a stone before him.

— Ask him, he said.

The fellows looked there and then said:

— Why him?

— Is he in it?

— Tell us, Athy. Go on. You might if you know.

Athy lowered his voice and said:

— Do you know why those fellows scut? I will tell you but you must not let on you know.

He paused for a moment and then said mysteriously:

— They were caught with Simon Moonan and Tusker Boyle in the square° one night.

The fellows looked at him and asked:

— Caught?

— What doing?

Athy said:

— Smugging.°

---

prof: Captain of cricket team.   *rounders:* British ball game.   *twisters and lobs:* Different kind of bowling in cricket.   *square:* The school latrine or urinal.   *Smugging:* Probably a mild sort of homosexual play.

All the fellows were silent: and Athy said:

— And that's why.

Stephen looked at the faces of the fellows but they were all looking across the playground. He wanted to ask somebody about it. What did that mean about the smugging in the square? Why did the five fellows out of the higher line run away for that? It was a joke, he thought. Simon Moonan had nice clothes and one night he had shown him a ball of creamy sweets that the fellows of the football fifteen had rolled down to him along the carpet in the middle of the refectory when he was at the door. It was the night of the match against the Bective Rangers and the ball was made just like a red and green apple only it opened and it was full of the creamy sweets. And one day Boyle had said that an elephant had two tuskers instead of two tusks and that was why he was called Tusker Boyle but some fellows called him Lady Boyle because he was always at his nails, paring them.

Eileen had long thin cool white hands too because she was a girl. They were like ivory; only soft. That was the meaning of *Tower of Ivory* but protestants could not understand it and made fun of it. One day he had stood beside her looking into the hotel grounds. A waiter was running up a trail of bunting on the flagstaff and a fox terrier was scampering to and fro on the sunny lawn. She had put her hand into his pocket where his hand was and he had felt how cool and thin and soft her hand was. She had said that pockets were funny things to have: and then all of a sudden she had broken away and had run laughing down the sloping curve of the path. Her fair hair had streamed out behind her like gold in the sun. *Tower of Ivory. House of Gold.* By thinking about things you could understand them.

But why in the square? You went there when you wanted to do something. It was all thick slabs of slate and water trickled all day out of tiny pinholes and there was a queer smell of stale water there. And behind the door of one of the closets there was a drawing in red pencil of a bearded man in a Roman dress with a brick in each hand and underneath was the name of the drawing:

Balbus was building a wall.

Some fellows had drawn it there for a cod. It had a funny face but it was very like a man with a beard. And on the wall of another closet there was written in backhand in beautiful writing:

Julius Cesar wrote The Calico Belly.°

The Calico Belly: Joke on Caesar's *Commentarii de Bello Gallico (Commentaries on the Gallic War)*.

Perhaps that was why they were there because it was a place where some fellows wrote things for cod. But all the same it was queer what Athy said and the way he said it. It was not a cod because they had run away. He looked with the others in silence across the playground and began to feel afraid.

At last Fleming said:

— And we are all to be punished for what other fellows did?

— I won't come back, see if I do, Cecil Thunder said. Three days' silence in the refectory and sending us up for six and eight° every minute.

— Yes, said Wells. And old Barrett has a new way of twisting the note so that you can't open it and fold it again to see how many ferulæ° you are to get. I won't come back too.

— Yes, said Cecil Thunder, and the prefect of studies° was in second of grammar this morning.

— Let us get up a rebellion, Fleming said. Will we?

All the fellows were silent. The air was very silent and you could hear the cricketbats but more slowly than before: pick, pock.

Wells asked:

— What is going to be done to them?

— Simon Moonan and Tusker are going to be flogged, Athy said, and the fellows in the higher line got their choice of flogging or being expelled.

— And which are they taking? asked the fellow who had spoken first.

— All are taking expulsion except Corrigan, Athy answered. He's going to be flogged by Mr Gleeson.

— Is it Corrigan that big fellow? said Fleming. Why, he'd be able for two of Gleeson!

— I know why, Cecil Thunder said. He is right and the other fellows are wrong because a flogging wears off after a bit but a fellow that has been expelled from college is known all his life on account of it. Besides Gleeson won't flog him hard.

— It's best of his play not to, Fleming said.

— I wouldn't like to be Simon Moonan and Tusker, Cecil Thunder said. But I don't believe they will be flogged. Perhaps they will be sent up for twice nine.°

---

six and eight: Number of blows with the strap given as punishment.   *ferula:* Strokes.
prefect of studies: Assistant to the rector in charge of academics.   *twice nine:* Nine strokes on each hand.

— No, no, said Athy. They'll both get it on the vital spot.
Wells rubbed himself and said in a crying voice:
— Please, sir, let me off!
Athy grinned and turned up the sleeves of his jacket, saying:

It can't be helped;
It must be done.
So down with your breeches
And out with your bum.

The fellows laughed; but he felt that they were a little afraid. In the silence of the soft grey air he heard the cricketbats from here and from there: pock. That was a sound to hear but if you were hit then you would feel a pain. The pandybat made a sound too but not like that. The fellows said it was made of whalebone and leather with lead inside: and he wondered what was the pain like. There were different kinds of pains for all the different kinds of sounds. A long thin cane would have a high whistling sound and he wondered what was that pain like. It made him shivery to think of it and cold: and what Athy said too. But what was there to laugh at in it? It made him shivery: but that was because you always felt like a shiver when you let down your trousers. It was the same in the bath when you undressed yourself. He wondered who had to let them down, the master or the boy himself. O how could they laugh about it that way?

He looked at Athy's rolledup sleeves and knuckly inky hands. He had rolled up his sleeves to show how Mr Gleeson would roll up his sleeves. But Mr Gleeson had round shiny cuffs and clean white wrists and fattish white hands and the nails of them were long and pointed. Perhaps he pared them too like Lady Boyle. But they were terribly long and pointed nails. So long and cruel they were though the white fattish hands were not cruel but gentle. And though he trembled with cold and fright to think of the cruel long nails and of the high whistling sound of the cane and of the chill you felt at the end of your shirt when you undressed yourself yet he felt a feeling of queer quiet pleasure inside him to think of the white fattish hands, clean and strong and gentle. And he thought of what Cecil Thunder had said; that Mr Gleeson would not flog Corrigan hard. And Fleming had said he would not because it was best of his play not to. But that was not why.

A voice from far out on the playgrounds cried:
— All in!
And other voices cried:
— All in! All in!

During the writing lesson he sat with his arms folded, listening to the slow scraping of the pens. Mr Harford went to and fro making little signs in red pencil and sometimes sitting beside the boy to show him how to hold the pen. He had tried to spell out the headline for himself though he knew already what it was for it was the last of the book. *Zeal without prudence is like a ship adrift*. But the lines of the letters were like fine invisible threads and it was only by closing his right eye tight tight and staring out of the left eye that he could make out the full curves of the capital.

But Mr Harford was very decent and never got into a wax. All the other masters got into dreadful waxes. But why were they to suffer for what fellows in the higher line did? Wells had said that they had drunk some of the altar wine out of the press in the sacristy and that it had been found out who had done it by the smell. Perhaps they had stolen a monstrance° to run away with it and sell it somewhere. That must have been a terrible sin, to go in there quietly at night, to open the dark press and steal the flashing gold thing into which God was put on the altar in the middle of flowers and candles at benediction while the incense went up in clouds at both sides as the fellow swung the censer and Dominic Kelly sang the first part by himself in the choir. But God was not in it of course when they stole it. But still it was a strange and a great sin even to touch it. He thought of it with deep awe; a terrible and strange sin: it thrilled him to think of it in the silence when the pens scraped lightly. But to drink the altar wine out of the press and be found out by the smell was a sin too: but it was not terrible and strange. It only made you feel a little sickish on account of the smell of the wine. Because on the day when he had made his first holy communion in the chapel he had shut his eyes and opened his mouth and put out his tongue a little: and when the rector had stooped down to give him the holy communion he had smelt a faint winy smell off the rector's breath after the wine of the mass. The word was beautiful: wine. It made you think of dark purple because the grapes were dark purple that grew in Greece outside houses like white temples. But the faint smell off the rector's breath had made him feel a sick feeling on the morning of his first communion. The day of your first communion was the happiest day of your life. And once a lot of generals had asked Napoleon what was the happiest day of his life. They thought he would say the day he won some great battle or the day he was made an emperor. But he said:

---

monstrance: Vessel of precious metal in which the host is displayed.

— Gentlemen, the happiest day of my life was the day on which I made my first holy communion.

Father Arnall came in and the Latin lesson began and he remained still, leaning on the desk with his arms folded. Father Arnall gave out the themebooks and he said that they were scandalous and that they were all to be written out again with the corrections at once. But the worst of all was Fleming's theme because the pages were stuck together by a blot: and Father Arnall held it up by a corner and said it was an insult to any master to send him up such a theme. Then he asked Jack Lawton to decline the noun *mare*° and Jack Lawton stopped at the ablative singular and could not go on with the plural.

— You should be ashamed of yourself, said Father Arnall sternly. You, the leader of the class!

Then he asked the next boy and the next and the next. Nobody knew. Father Arnall became very quiet, more and more quiet as each boy tried to answer and could not. But his face was blacklooking and his eyes were staring though his voice was so quiet. Then he asked Fleming and Fleming said that that word had no plural. Father Arnall suddenly shut the book and shouted at him:

— Kneel out there in the middle of the class. You are one of the idlest boys I ever met. Copy out your themes again the rest of you.

Fleming moved heavily out of his place and knelt between the two last benches. The other boys bent over their themebooks and began to write. A silence filled the classroom and Stephen, glancing timidly at Father Arnall's dark face, saw that it was a little red from the wax he was in.

Was that a sin for Father Arnall to be in a wax or was he allowed to get into a wax when the boys were idle because that made them study better or was he only letting on to be in a wax? It was because he was allowed because a priest would know what a sin was and would not do it. But if he did it one time by mistake what would he do to go to confession? Perhaps he would go to confession to the minister. And if the minister did it he would go to the rector: and the rector to the provincial: and the provincial to the general° of the jesuits. That was called the order: and he had heard his father say that they were all clever men. They could all have become highup people in the world if they had not

---

decline the noun mare: Latin for "sea," declined through its six grammatical cases, including the ablative singular and plural.   *provincial...general:* Highest Jesuit authority in Ireland; ultimate Jesuit authority in Rome.

become jesuits. And he wondered what Father Arnall and Paddy Barrett would have become and what Mr McGlade and Mr Gleeson would
have become if they had not become jesuits. It was hard to think what
because you would have to think of them in a different way with different coloured coats and trousers and with beards and moustaches and
different kinds of hats.

The door opened quietly and closed. A quick whisper ran through
the class: the prefect of studies. There was an instant of dead silence and
then the loud crack of a pandybat on the last desk. Stephen's heart leapt
up in fear.

— Any boys want flogging here, Father Arnall? cried the prefect of
studies. Any lazy idle loafers that want flogging in this class?

He came to the middle of the class and saw Fleming on his knees.

— Hoho! he cried. Who is this boy? Why is he on his knees? What is
your name, boy?

— Fleming, sir.

— Hoho, Fleming! An idler of course. I can see it in your eye. Why
is he on his knees, Father Arnall?

— He wrote a bad Latin theme, Father Arnall said, and he missed
all the questions in grammar.

— Of course he did! cried the prefect of studies. Of course he did!
A born idler! I can see it in the corner of his eye.

He banged his pandybat down on the desk and cried:

— Up, Fleming! Up, my boy!

Fleming stood up slowly.

— Hold out! cried the prefect of studies.

Fleming held out his hand. The pandybat came down on it with a
loud smacking sound: one, two, three, four, five, six.

— Other hand!

The pandybat came down again in six loud quick smacks.

— Kneel down! cried the prefect of studies.

Fleming knelt down squeezing his hands under his armpits, his face
contorted with pain, but Stephen knew how hard his hands were
because Fleming was always rubbing rosin into them. But perhaps he
was in great pain for the noise of the pandies was terrible. Stephen's
heart was beating and fluttering.

— At your work, all of you! shouted the prefect of studies. We want
no lazy idle loafers here, lazy idle little schemers. At your work, I tell
you. Father Dolan will be in to see you every day. Father Dolan will be
in tomorrow.

He poked one of the boys in the side with the pandybat, saying:

— You, boy! When will Father Dolan be in again?

— Tomorrow, sir, said Tom Furlong's voice.

— Tomorrow and tomorrow and tomorrow, said the prefect of studies. Make up your minds for that. Every day Father Dolan. Write away. You, boy, who are you?

Stephen's heart jumped suddenly.

— Dedalus, sir.

— Why are you not writing like the others?

— I . . . my . . .

He could not speak with fright.

— Why is he not writing, Father Arnall?

— He broke his glasses, said Father Arnall, and I exempted him from work.

— Broke? What is this I hear? What is this your name is? said the prefect of studies.

— Dedalus, sir.

— Out here, Dedalus. Lazy little schemer. I see schemer in your face. Where did you break your glasses?

Stephen stumbled into the middle of the class, blinded by fear and haste.

— Where did you break your glasses? repeated the prefect of studies.

— The cinderpath, sir.

— Hoho! The cinderpath! cried the prefect of studies. I know that trick.

Stephen lifted his eyes in wonder and saw for a moment Father Dolan's whitegrey not young face, his baldy whitegrey head with fluff at the sides of it, the steel rims of his spectacles and his nocoloured eyes looking through the glasses. Why did he say that he knew that trick?

— Lazy idle little loafer! cried the prefect of studies. Broke my glasses! An old schoolboy trick! Out with your hand this moment!

Stephen closed his eyes and held out in the air his trembling hand with the palm upwards. He felt the prefect of studies touch it for a moment at the fingers to straighten it and then the swish of the sleeve of the soutane as the pandybat was lifted to strike. A hot burning stinging tingling blow like the loud crack of a broken stick made his trembling hand crumple together like a leaf in the fire: and at the sound and the pain scalding tears were driven into his eyes. His whole body was shaking with fright, his arm was shaking and his crumpled burning livid hand shook like a loose leaf in the air. A cry sprang to his lips, a prayer to be let off. But though the tears scalded his eyes and his limbs quivered with pain and fright he held back the hot tears and the cry that scalded his throat.

— Other hand! shouted the prefect of studies.

Stephen drew back his maimed and quivering right arm and held out his left hand. The soutane sleeve swished again as the pandybat was lifted and a loud crashing sound and a fierce maddening tingling burning pain made his hand shrink together with the palms and fingers in a livid quivering mass. The scalding water burst forth from his eyes and, burning with shame and agony and fear, he drew back his shaking arm in terror and burst out into a whine of pain. His body shook with a palsy of fright and in shame and rage he felt the scalding cry come from his throat and the scalding tears falling out of his eyes and down his flaming cheeks.

— Kneel down! cried the prefect of studies.

Stephen knelt down quickly pressing his beaten hands to his sides. To think of them beaten and swollen with pain all in a moment made him feel so sorry for them as if they were not his hands but someone else's that he felt so sorry for. And as he knelt, calming the last sobs in his throat and feeling the burning tingling pain pressed in to his sides, he thought of the hands which he had held out in the air with the palms up and of the firm touch of the prefect of studies when he had steadied the shaking fingers and of the beaten swollen reddened mass of palm and fingers that shook helplessly in the air.

— Get at your work, all of you, cried the prefect of studies from the door. Father Dolan will be in every day to see if any boy, any lazy idle little loafer wants flogging. Every day. Every day.

The door closed behind him.

The hushed class continued to copy out the themes. Father Arnall rose from his seat and went among them, helping the boys with gentle words and telling them the mistakes they had made. His voice was very gentle and soft. Then he returned to his seat and said to Fleming and Stephen:

— You may return to your places, you two.

Fleming and Stephen rose and, walking to their seats, sat down. Stephen, scarlet with shame, opened a book quickly with one weak hand and bent down upon it, his face close to the page.

It was unfair and cruel because the doctor had told him not to read without glasses and he had written home to his father that morning to send him a new pair. And Father Arnall had said that he need not study till the new glasses came. Then to be called a schemer before the class and to be pandied when he always got the card for first or second and was the leader of the Yorkists! How could the prefect of studies know that it was a trick? He felt the touch of the prefect's fingers as they had steadied his hand and at first he had thought that he was going to shake hands with him because the fingers were soft and firm: but then in an instant he had heard the swish of the soutane sleeve and the crash. It was cruel and unfair to make him kneel in the middle of the class then: and Father Arnall had told them both that they might return to their places without making any difference between them. He listened to Father Arnall's low and gentle voice as he corrected the themes. Perhaps he was sorry now and wanted to be decent. But it was unfair and cruel. The prefect of studies was a priest but that was cruel and unfair. And his whitegrey face and the nocoloured eyes behind the steel-rimmed spectacles were cruel looking because he had steadied the hand first with his firm soft fingers and that was to hit it better and louder.

— It's a stinking mean thing, that's what it is, said Fleming in the corridor as the classes were passing out in file to the refectory, to pandy a fellow for what is not his fault.

— You really broke your glasses by accident, didn't you? Nasty Roche asked.

Stephen felt his heart filled by Fleming's words and did not answer.

— Of course he did! said Fleming. I wouldn't stand it. I'd go up and tell the rector on him.

— Yes, said Cecil Thunder eagerly, and I saw him lift the pandybat over his shoulder and he's not allowed to do that.

— Did they hurt much? Nasty Roche asked.

— Very much, Stephen said.

— I wouldn't stand it, Fleming repeated, from Baldyhead or any other Baldyhead. It's a stinking mean low trick, that's what it is. I'd go straight up to the rector and tell him about it after dinner.

— Yes, do. Yes, do, said Cecil Thunder.

— Yes, do. Yes, go up and tell the rector on him, Dedalus, said Nasty Roche, because he said that he'd come in tomorrow again to pandy you.

— Yes, yes. Tell the rector, all said.

And there were some fellows out of second of grammar listening and one of them said:

— The senate and the Roman people° declared that Dedalus had been wrongly punished.

---

the senate and the Roman people: Opening phrase of Roman Senatorial decrees.

It was wrong; it was unfair and cruel: and, as he sat in the refectory, he suffered time after time in memory the same humiliation until he began to wonder whether it might not really be that there was something in his face which made him look like a schemer and he wished he had a little mirror to see. But there could not be; and it was unjust and cruel and unfair.

He could not eat the blackish fish fritters they got on Wednesdays in Lent and one of his potatoes had the mark of the spade in it. Yes, he would do what the fellows had told him. He would go up and tell the rector that he had been wrongly punished. A thing like that had been done before by somebody in history, by some great person whose head was in the books of history. And the rector would declare that he had been wrongly punished because the senate and the Roman people always declared that the men who did that had been wrongly punished. Those were the great men whose names were in Richmal Magnall's Questions.° History was all about those men and what they did and that was what Peter Parley's Tales° about Greece and Rome were all about. Peter Parley himself was on the first page in a picture. There was a road over a heath with grass at the side and little bushes: and Peter Parley had a broad hat like a protestant minister and a big stick and he was walking fast along the road to Greece and Rome.

It was easy what he had to do. All he had to do was when the dinner was over and he came out in his turn to go on walking but not out to the corridor but up the staircase on the right that led to the castle. He had nothing to do but that: to turn to the right and walk fast up the staircase and in half a minute he would be in the low dark narrow corridor that led through the castle to the rector's room. And every fellow had said that it was unfair, even the fellow out of second of grammar who had said that about the senate and the Roman people.

What would happen? He heard the fellows of the higher line stand up at the top of the refectory and heard their steps as they came down the matting: Paddy Rath and Jimmy Magee and the Spaniard and the Portuguese and the fifth was big Corrigan who was going to be flogged by Mr Gleeson. That was why the prefect of studies had called him a schemer and pandied him for nothing: and, straining his weak eyes,

---

Richmal Magnall's Questions: *Historical and Miscellaneous Questions for the Use of Young People,* a textbook popular during the nineteenth century in question-and-answer format. **Peter Parley's Tales:** Authored by the American writer Samuel Griswold Goodrich (1793–1860). The *Tales about Ancient and Modern Greece* was published in 1832 and the *Tales about Ancient and Modern Rome* in 1833.

tired with the tears, he watched big Corrigan's broad shoulders and big hanging black head passing in the file. But he had done something and besides Mr Gleeson would not flog him hard: and he remembered how big Corrigan looked in the bath. He had skin the same colour as the turfcoloured bogwater in the shallow end of the bath and when he walked along the side his feet slapped loudly on the wet tiles and at every slap his thighs shook a little because he was fat.

The refectory was half empty and the fellows were still passing out in file. He could go up the staircase because there was never a priest or a prefect outside the refectory door. But he could not go. The rector would side with the prefect of studies and think it was a schoolboy trick and then the prefect of studies would come in every day the same only it would be worse because he would be dreadfully waxy at any fellow going up to the rector about him. The fellows had told him to go but they would not go themselves. They had forgotten all about it. No, it was best to forget all about it and perhaps the prefect of studies had only said he would come in. No, it was best to hide out of the way because when you were small and young you could often escape that way.

The fellows at his table stood up. He stood up and passed out among them in the file. He had to decide. He was coming near the door. If he went on with the fellows he could never go up to the rector because he could not leave the playground for that. And if he went and was pandied all the same all the fellows would make fun and talk about young Dedalus going up to the rector to tell on the prefect of studies.

He was walking down along the matting and he saw the door before him. It was impossible: he could not. He thought of the baldy head of the prefect of studies with the cruel nocoloured eyes looking at him and he heard the voice of the prefect of studies asking him twice what his name was. Why could he not remember the name when he was told the first time? Was he not listening the first time or was it to make fun out of the name? The great men in the history had names like that and nobody made fun of them. It was his own name that he should have made fun of if he wanted to make fun. Dolan: it was like the name of a woman that washed clothes.

He had reached the door and, turning quickly to the right, walked up the stairs and, before he could make up his mind to come back, he had entered the low dark narrow corridor that led to the castle. And as he crossed the threshold of the door of the corridor he saw, without turning his head to look, that all the fellows were looking after him as they went filing by.

He passed along the narrow dark corridor, passing little doors that were the doors of the rooms of the community. He peered in front of him and right and left through the gloom and thought that those must be portraits. It was dark and silent and his eyes were weak and tired with tears so that he could not see. But he thought they were the portraits of the saints and great men of the order who were looking down on him silently as he passed: saint Ignatius Loyola° holding an open book and pointing to the words *Ad Majorem Dei Gloriam*° in it, saint Francis Xavier pointing to his chest, Lorenzo Ricci with his berretta on his head like one of the prefects of the lines, the three patrons of holy youth, saint Stanislaus Kostka, saint Aloysius Gonzaga and blessed John Berchmans, all with young faces because they died when they were young, and Father Peter Kenny° sitting in a chair wrapped in a big cloak.

He came out on the landing above the entrance hall and looked about him. That was where Hamilton Rowan had passed and the marks of the soldiers' slugs were there. And it was there that the old servants had seen the ghost in the white cloak of a marshal.

An old servant was sweeping at the end of the landing. He asked him where was the rector's room and the old servant pointed to the door at the far end and looked after him as he went on to it and knocked.

There was no answer. He knocked again more loudly and his heart jumped when he heard a muffled voice say:

— Come in!

He turned the handle and opened the door and fumbled for the handle of the green baize door inside. He found it and pushed it open and went in.

He saw the rector sitting at a desk writing. There was a skull on the desk and a strange solemn smell in the room like the old leather of chairs.

His heart was beating fast on account of the solemn place he was in and the silence of the room: and he looked at the skull and at the rector's kindlooking face.

— Well, my little man, said the rector, what is it?

Stephen swallowed down the thing in his throat and said:

— I broke my glasses, sir.

---

saint Ignatius Loyola: (1491–1556), founder of Society of Jesus (Jesuit order).   *Ad Majorem Dei Gloriam:* For the Greater Glory of God, the Jesuit motto, which students in a Jesuit school might abbreviate to "A.M.D.G." and attach to their compositions.   *Father Peter Kenny:* Jesuit priest who founded Clongowes Wood College.

The rector opened his mouth and said:

— O!

Then he smiled and said:

— Well, if we broke our glasses we must write home for a new pair.

— I wrote home, sir, said Stephen, and Father Arnall said I am not to study till they come.

— Quite right! said the rector.

Stephen swallowed down the thing again and tried to keep his legs and his voice from shaking.

— But, sir . . .

— Yes?

— Father Dolan came in today and pandied me because I was not writing my theme.

The rector looked at him in silence and he could feel the blood rising to his face and the tears about to rise to his eyes.

The rector said:

— Your name is Dedalus, isn't it?

— Yes, sir.

— And where did you break your glasses?

— On the cinderpath, sir. A fellow was coming out of the bicycle house and I fell and they got broken. I don't know the fellow's name.

The rector looked at him again in silence. Then he smiled and said:

— O, well, it was a mistake. I am sure Father Dolan did not know.

— But I told him I broke them, sir, and he pandied me.

— Did you tell him that you had written home for a new pair? the rector asked.

— No, sir.

— O well then, said the rector, Father Dolan did not understand. You can say that I excuse you from your lessons for a few days.

Stephen said quickly for fear his trembling would prevent him:

— Yes, sir, but Father Dolan said he will come in tomorrow to pandy me again for it.

— Very well, the rector said, it is a mistake and I shall speak to Father Dolan myself. Will that do now?

Stephen felt the tears wetting his eyes and murmured:

— O yes, sir, thanks.

The rector held his hand across the side of the desk where the skull was and Stephen, placing his hand in it for a moment, felt a cool moist palm.

— Good day now, said the rector, withdrawing his hand and bowing.

— Good day, sir, said Stephen.

He bowed and walked quietly out of the room, closing the doors carefully and slowly.

But when he had passed the old servant on the landing and was again in the low narrow dark corridor he began to walk faster and faster. Faster and faster he hurried on through the gloom, excitedly. He bumped his elbow against the door at the end and, hurrying down the staircase, walked quickly through the two corridors and out into the air.

He could hear the cries of the fellows on the playgrounds. He broke into a run and, running quicker and quicker, ran across the cinderpath and reached the third line playground, panting.

The fellows had seen him running. They closed round him in a ring, pushing one against another to hear.

— Tell us! Tell us!

— What did he say?

— Did you go in?

— What did he say?

— Tell us! Tell us!

He told them what he had said and what the rector had said and, when he had told them, all the fellows flung their caps spinning up into the air and cried:

— Hurroo!

They caught their caps and sent them up again spinning skyhigh and cried again:

— Hurroo! Hurroo!

They made a cradle of their locked hands and hoisted him up among them and carried him along till he struggled to get free. And when he had escaped from them they broke away in all directions, flinging their caps again into the air and whistling as they went spinning up and crying:

— Hurroo!

And they gave three groans for Baldyhead Dolan and three cheers for Conmee and they said he was the decentest rector that was ever in Clongowes.

The cheers died away in the soft grey air. He was alone. He was happy and free: but he would not be anyway proud with Father Dolan. He would be very quiet and obedient: and he wished that he could do something kind for him to show him that he was not proud.

The air was soft and grey and mild and evening was coming. There was the smell of evening in the air, the smell of the fields in the country where they digged up turnips to peel them and eat them when they went out for a walk to Major Barton's, the smell there was in the little wood beyond the pavilion where the gallnuts° were.

The fellows were practising long shies° and bowling lobs and slow twisters. In the soft grey silence he could hear the bump of the balls: and from here and from there through the quiet air the sound of the cricketbats: pick, pack, pock, puck: like drops of water in a fountain falling softly in the brimming bowl.

II

Uncle Charles smoked such black twist° that at last his outspoken nephew suggested to him to enjoy his morning smoke in a little outhouse at the end of the garden.

— Very good, Simon. All serene, Simon, said the old man tranquilly. Anywhere you like. The outhouse will do me nicely: it will be more salubrious.

— Damn me, said Mr Dedalus frankly, if I know how you can smoke such villainous awful tobacco. It's like gunpowder, by God.

— It's very nice, Simon, replied the old man. Very cool and mollifying.

Every morning, therefore, uncle Charles repaired to his outhouse but not before he had creased and brushed scrupulously his back hair and brushed and put on his tall hat. While he smoked the brim of his tall hat and the bowl of his pipe were just visible beyond the jambs of the outhouse door. His arbour, as he called the reeking outhouse which he shared with the cat and the garden tools, served him also as a soundingbox: and every morning he hummed contentedly one of his favourite songs: *O, twine me a bower or Blue eyes and golden hair* or *The Groves of Blarney* while the grey and blue coils of smoke rose slowly from his pipe and vanished in the pure air.

During the first part of the summer in Blackrock° uncle Charles was Stephen's constant companion. Uncle Charles was a hale old man with a welltanned skin, rugged features and white side whiskers. On week days he did messages between the house in Carysfort Avenue and those shops in the main street of the town with which the family dealt.

---

gallnuts: Rounded growths on trees caused by insects.   *long shies:* Long hits by the batsman in cricket.   *black twist:* Strong tobacco twisted into a rope.   *Blackrock:* A suburb south of Dublin but closer than Bray.

Stephen was glad to go with him on these errands for uncle Charles helped him very liberally to handfuls of whatever was exposed in open boxes and barrels outside the counter. He would seize a handful of grapes and sawdust or three or four American apples and thrust them generously into his grandnephew's hand while the shopman smiled uneasily; and, on Stephen's feigning reluctance to take them, he would frown and say:

— Take them, sir. Do you hear me, sir? They're good for your bowels.

When the order list had been booked the two would go on to the park where an old friend of Stephen's father, Mike Flynn, would be found seated on a bench, waiting for them. Then would begin Stephen's run round the park. Mike Flynn would stand at the gate near the railway station, watch in hand, while Stephen ran round the track in the style Mike Flynn favoured, his head high lifted, his knees well lifted and his hands held straight down by his sides. When the morning practice was over the trainer would make his comments and sometimes illustrate them by shuffling along for a yard or so comically in an old pair of blue canvas shoes. A small ring of wonderstruck children and nursemaids would gather to watch him and linger even when he and uncle Charles had sat down again and were talking athletics and politics. Though he had heard his father say that Mike Flynn had put some of the best runners of modern times through his hands Stephen often glanced with mistrust at his trainer's flabby stubblecovered face, as it bent over the long stained fingers through which he rolled his cigarette, and with pity at the mild lustreless blue eyes which would look up suddenly from the task and gaze vaguely into the bluer distance while the long swollen fingers ceased their rolling and grains and fibres of tobacco fell back into the pouch.

On the way home uncle Charles would often pay a visit to the chapel and, as the font was above Stephen's reach, the old man would dip his hand and then sprinkle the water briskly about Stephen's clothes and on the floor of the porch. While he prayed he knelt on his red handkerchief and read above his breath from a thumbblackened prayerbook wherein catchwords were printed at the foot of every page. Stephen knelt at his side respecting, though he did not share, his piety. He often wondered what his granduncle prayed for so seriously. Perhaps he prayed for the souls in purgatory or for the grace of a happy death or perhaps he prayed that God might send him back a part of the big fortune he had squandered in Cork.

On Sundays Stephen with his father and his granduncle took their constitutional. The old man was a nimble walker in spite of his corns and often ten or twelve miles of the road were covered. The little village of Stillorgan was the parting of the ways. Either they went to the left towards the Dublin mountains or along the Goatstown road and thence into Dundrum, coming home by Sandyford. Trudging along the road or standing in some grimy wayside publichouse his elders spoke constantly of the subjects nearest their hearts, of Irish politics, of Munster and of the legends of their own family, to all of which Stephen lent an avid ear. Words which he did not understand he said over and over to himself till he had learned them by heart: and through them he had glimpses of the real world about him. The hour when he too would take his part in the life of that world seemed drawing near and in secret he began to make ready for the great part which he felt awaited him the nature of which he only dimly apprehended.

His evenings were his own; and he pored over a ragged translation of *The Count of Monte Cristo.*° The figure of that dark avenger stood forth in his mind for whatever he had heard or divined in childhood of the strange and terrible. At night he built up on the parlour table an image of the wonderful island cave out of transfers and paper flowers and coloured tissue paper and strips of the silver and golden paper in which chocolate is wrapped. When he had broken up this scenery, weary of its tinsel, there would come to his mind the bright picture of Marseilles, of sunny trellisses and of Mercedes. Outside Blackrock, on the road that led to the mountains, stood a small whitewashed house in the garden of which grew many rosebushes: and in this house, he told himself, another Mercedes lived. Both on the outward and on the homeward journey he measured distance by this landmark: and in his imagination he lived through a long train of adventures, marvellous as those in the book itself, towards the close of which there appeared an image of himself, grown older and sadder, standing in a moonlit garden with Mercedes who had so many years before slighted his love, and with a sadly proud gesture of refusal, saying:

— Madam, I never eat muscatel grapes.

He became the ally of a boy named Aubrey Mills and founded with him a gang of adventurers in the avenue. Aubrey carried a whistle

---

The Count of Monte Cristo: Adventure novel published in 1844 by Alexandre Dumas *père.* The hero, Edmond Dantes, is falsely convicted of treason and his fiancée Mercedes unwittingly marries one of his betrayers. When he attends a party of hers, in disguise as the Count, Dantes has refused all offers of food, leading her to offer at least a single grape.

dangling from his buttonhole and a bicycle lamp attached to his belt while the others had short sticks thrust daggerwise through theirs. Stephen, who had read of Napoleon's plain style of dress, chose to remain unadorned and thereby heightened for himself the pleasure of taking counsel with his lieutenant before giving orders. The gang made forays into the gardens of old maids or went down to the castle and fought a battle on the shaggy weedgrown rocks, coming home after it weary stragglers with the stale odours of the foreshore in their nostrils and the rank oils of the seawrack upon their hands and in their hair.

Aubrey and Stephen had a common milkman and often they drove out in the milkcar to Carrickmines where the cows were at grass. While the men were milking the boys would take turns in riding the tractable mare round the field. But when autumn came the cows were driven home from the grass: and the first sight of the filthy cowyard at Stradbrook with its foul green puddles and clots of liquid dung and steaming brantroughs sickened Stephen's heart. The cattle which had seemed so beautiful in the country on sunny days revolted him and he could not even look at the milk they yielded.

The coming of September did not trouble him this year for he knew he was not to be sent back to Clongowes. The practice in the park came to an end when Mike Flynn went into hospital. Aubrey was at school and had only an hour or two free in the evening. The gang fell asunder and there were no more nightly forays or battles on the rocks. Stephen sometimes went round with the car which delivered the evening milk: and these chilly drives blew away his memory of the filth of the cowyard and he felt no repugnance at seeing the cowhairs and hayseeds on the milkman's coat. Whenever the car drew up before a house he waited to catch a glimpse of a wellscrubbed kitchen or of a softly lighted hall and to see how the servant would hold the jug and how she would close the door. He thought it should be a pleasant life enough, driving along the roads every evening to deliver milk, if he had warm gloves and a fat bag of gingernuts in his pocket to eat from. But the same foreknowledge which had sickened his heart and made his limbs sag suddenly as he raced round the park, the same intuition which had made him glance with mistrust at his trainer's flabby stubblecovered face as it bent heavily over his long stained fingers, dissipated any vision of the future. In a vague way he understood that his father was in trouble and that this was the reason why he himself had not been sent back to Clongowes. For some time he had felt the slight changes in his house; and these changes in what he had deemed unchangeable were so many slight shocks to his boyish conception of the world. The ambition which he felt astir at times in the darkness of his soul sought no outlet. A dusk like that of the outer world obscured his mind as he heard the mare's hoofs clattering along the tramtrack on the Rock Road and the great can swaying and rattling behind him.

He returned to Mercedes and, as he brooded upon her image, a strange unrest crept into his blood. Sometimes a fever gathered within him and led him to rove alone in the evening along the quiet avenue. The peace of the gardens and the kindly lights in the windows poured a tender influence into his restless heart. The noise of children at play annoyed him and their silly voices made him feel, even more keenly than he had felt at Clongowes, that he was different from others. He did not want to play. He wanted to meet in the real world the unsubstantial image which his soul so constantly beheld. He did not know where to seek it or how: but a premonition which led him on told him that this image would, without any overt act of his, encounter him. They would meet quietly as if they had known each other and had made their tryst, perhaps at one of the gates or in some more secret place. They would be alone, surrounded by darkness and silence: and in that moment of supreme tenderness he would be transfigured. He would fade into something impalpable under her eyes and then, in a moment, he would be transfigured. Weakness and timidity and inexperience would fall from him in that magic moment.

*
*   *

Two great yellow caravans° had halted one morning before the door and men had come tramping into the house to dismantle it. The furniture had been hustled out through the front garden which was strewn with wisps of straw and rope ends and into the huge vans at the gate. When all had been safely stowed the vans had set off noisily down the avenue: and from the window of the railway carriage, in which he had sat with his redeyed mother, Stephen had seen them lumbering heavily along the Merrion Road.

The parlour fire would not draw that evening and Mr Dedalus rested the poker against the bars of the grate to attract the flame. Uncle Charles dozed in a corner of the half furnished uncarpeted room and near him the family portraits leaned against the wall. The lamp on the table shed a weak light over the boarded floor, muddied by the feet of the vanmen. Stephen sat on a footstool beside his father listening to a long and incoherent monologue. He understood little or nothing of it

---

caravans: Horse-drawn, covered carts or wagons.

at first but he became slowly aware that his father had enemies and that some fight was going to take place. He felt too that he was being enlisted for the fight, that some duty was being laid upon his shoulders. The sudden flight from the comfort and revery of Blackrock, the passage through the gloomy foggy city, the thought of the bare cheerless house in which they were now to live made his heart heavy: and again an intuition or foreknowledge of the future came to him. He understood also why the servants had often whispered together in the hall and why his father had often stood on the hearthrug, with his back to the fire, talking loudly to uncle Charles who urged him to sit down and eat his dinner.

— There's a crack of the whip left in me yet, Stephen, old chap, said Mr Dedalus, poking at the dull fire with fierce energy. We're not dead yet, sonny. No, by the Lord Jesus (God forgive me) nor half dead.

Dublin was a new and complex sensation. Uncle Charles had grown so witless that he could no longer be sent out on errands and the disorder in settling in the new house left Stephen freer than he had been in Blackrock. In the beginning he contented himself with circling timidly round the neighbouring square or, at most, going half way down one of the side streets: but when he had made a skeleton map of the city in his mind he followed boldly one of its central lines until he reached the customhouse. He passed unchallenged among the docks and along the quays wondering at the multitude of corks that lay bobbing on the surface of the water in a thick yellow scum, at the crowds of quay porters and the rumbling carts and the illdressed bearded policeman. The vastness and strangeness of the life suggested to him by the bales of merchandise stacked along the walls or swung aloft out of the holds of steamers wakened again in him the unrest which had sent him wandering in the evening from garden to garden in search of Mercedes. And amid this new bustling life he might have fancied himself in another Marseilles but that he missed the bright sky and the sunwarmed trellisses of the wineshops. A vague dissatisfaction grew up within him as he looked on the quays and on the river and on the lowering skies and yet he continued to wander up and down day after day as if he really sought someone that eluded him.

He went once or twice with his mother to visit their relatives: and, though they passed a jovial array of shops lit up and adorned for Christmas, his mood of embittered silence did not leave him. The causes of his embitterment were many, remote and near. He was angry with himself for being young and the prey of restless foolish impulses, angry also with the change of fortune which was reshaping the world about him into a vision of squalor and insincerity. Yet his anger lent nothing to the vision. He chronicled with patience what he saw, detaching himself from it and tasting its mortifying flavour in secret.

He was sitting on the backless chair in his aunt's kitchen. A lamp with a reflector hung on the japanned wall of the fireplace and by its light his aunt was reading the evening paper that lay on her knees. She looked a long time at a smiling picture that was set in it and said musingly:

— The beautiful Mabel Hunter!

A ringletted girl stood on tiptoe to peer at the picture and said softly:

— What is she in, mud?

— In the pantomime,° love.

The child leaned her ringletted head against her mother's sleeve, gazing on the picture, and murmured as if fascinated:

— The beautiful Mabel Hunter!

As if fascinated, her eyes rested long upon those demurely taunting eyes and she murmured again devotedly:

— Isn't she an exquisite creature?

And the boy who came in from the street, stamping crookedly under his stone° of coal, heard her words. He dropped his load promptly on the floor and hurried to her side to see. But she did not raise her easeful head to let him see. He mauled the edges of the paper with his reddened and blackened hands, shouldering her aside and complaining that he could not see.

He was sitting in the narrow breakfast room high up in the old darkwindowed house. The firelight flickered on the wall and beyond the window a spectral dusk was gathering upon the river. Before the fire an old woman was busy making tea and, as she bustled at her task, she told in a low voice of what the priest and the doctor had said. She told too of certain changes that she had seen in her of late and of her odd ways and sayings. He sat listening to the words and following the ways of adventure that lay open in the coals, arches and vaults and winding galleries and jagged caverns.

Suddenly he became aware of something in the doorway. A skull appeared suspended in the gloom of the doorway. A feeble creature like

---

pantomime: Popular show with song, dance, a loose story line, and local references.
stone: Fourteen pounds.

a monkey was there, drawn thither by the sound of voices at the fire. A whining voice came from the door, asking:

— Is that Josephine?

The old bustling woman answered cheerily from the fireplace:

— No, Ellen. It's Stephen.

— O . . . O, good evening, Stephen.

He answered the greeting and saw a silly smile break out over the face in the doorway.

— Do you want anything, Ellen? asked the old woman at the fire.

But she did not answer the question and said:

— I thought it was Josephine. I thought you were Josephine, Stephen.

And, repeating this several times, she fell to laughing feebly.

He was sitting in the midst of a children's party at Harold's Cross. His silent watchful manner had grown upon him and he took little part in the games. The children, wearing the spoils of their crackers,° danced and romped noisily and, though he tried to share their merriment, he felt himself a gloomy figure amid the gay cocked hats and sunbonnets.

But when he had sung his song and withdrawn into a snug corner of the room he began to taste the joy of his loneliness. The mirth, which in the beginning of the evening had seemed to him false and trivial, was like a soothing air to him, passing gaily by his senses, hiding from other eyes the feverish agitation of his blood while through the circling of the dancers and amid the music and laughter her glances travelled to his corner, flattering, taunting, searching, exciting his heart.

In the hall the children who had stayed latest were putting on their things: the party was over. She had thrown a shawl about her and, as they went together towards the tram,° sprays of her fresh warm breath flew gaily above her cowled head and her shoes tapped blithely on the glassy road.

It was the last tram. The lank brown horses knew it and shook their bells to the clear night in admonition. The conductor talked with the driver, both nodding often in the green light of the lamp. On the empty seats of the tram were scattered a few coloured tickets. No sound of footsteps came up or down the road. No sound broke the peace of the

---

crackers: Decorated noisemakers, often with small gifts inside.   *tram:* Means of public transport, during this period changing from horse-drawn vehicle to electric-powered streetcar.

night save when the lank brown horses rubbed their noses together and shook their bells.

They seemed to listen, he on the upper step and she on the lower. She came up to his step many times and went down to hers again between their phrases and once or twice stood close beside him for some moments on the upper step, forgetting to go down, and then went down. His heart danced upon her movements like a cork upon a tide. He heard what her eyes said to him from beneath their cowl and knew that in some dim past, whether in life or in revery, he had heard their tale before. He saw her urge her vanities, her fine dress and sash and long black stockings, and knew that he had yielded to them a thousand times. Yet a voice within him spoke above the noise of his dancing heart, asking him would he take her gift to which he had only to stretch out his hand. And he remembered the day when he and Eileen had stood looking into the hotel grounds, watching the waiters running up a trail of bunting on the flagstaff and the fox terrier scampering to and fro on the sunny lawn, and how, all of a sudden, she had broken out into a peal of laughter and had run down the sloping curve of the path. Now, as then, he stood listlessly in his place, seemingly a tranquil watcher of the scene before him.

— She too wants me to catch hold of her, he thought. That's why she came with me to the tram. I could easily catch hold of her when she comes up to my step: nobody is looking. I could hold her and kiss her.

But he did neither: and, when he was sitting alone in the deserted tram, he tore his ticket into shreds and stared gloomily at the corrugated footboard.

The next day he sat at his table in the bare upper room for many hours. Before him lay a new pen, a new bottle of ink and a new emerald exercise.° From force of habit he had written at the top of the first page the initial letters of the jesuit motto: A.M.D.G. On the first line of the page appeared the title of the verses he was trying to write: To E —— C ——. He knew it was right to begin so for he had seen similar titles in the collected poems of Lord Byron. When he had written this title and drawn an ornamental line underneath he fell into a daydream and began to draw diagrams on the cover of the book. He saw himself sitting at his table in Bray the morning after the discussion at the Christmas dinnertable, trying to write a poem about Parnell on the back of

---

emerald exercise: Patriotic green notebook for student work.

one of his father's second moiety notices.° But his brain had then refused to grapple with the theme and, desisting, he had covered the page with the names and addresses of certain of his classmates:

> Roderick Kickham
> John Lawton
> Anthony MacSwiney
> Simon Moonan

Now it seemed as if he would fail again but, by dint of brooding on the incident, he thought himself into confidence. During this process all those elements which he deemed common and insignificant fell out of the scene. There remained no trace of the tram itself nor of the trammen nor of the horses: nor did he and she appear vividly. The verses told only of the night and the balmy breeze and the maiden lustre of the moon. Some undefined sorrow was hidden in the hearts of the protagonists as they stood in silence beneath the leafless trees and when the moment of farewell had come the kiss, which had been withheld by one, was given by both. After this the letters L.D.S.° were written at the foot of the page and, having hidden the book, he went into his mother's bedroom and gazed at his face for a long time in the mirror of her dressingtable.

But his long spell of leisure and liberty was drawing to its end. One evening his father came home full of news which kept his tongue busy all through dinner. Stephen had been awaiting his father's return for there had been mutton hash that day and he knew that his father would make him dip his bread in the gravy. But he did not relish the hash for the mention of Clongowes had coated his palate with a scum of disgust.

— I walked bang into him, said Mr Dedalus for the fourth time, just at the corner of the square.

— Then I suppose, said Mrs Dedalus, he will be able to arrange it. I mean about Belvedere.

— Of course he will, said Mr Dedalus. Don't I tell you he's provincial of the order now?

— I never liked the idea of sending him to the christian brothers° myself, said Mrs Dedalus.

— Christian brothers be damned! said Mr Dedalus. Is it with Paddy Stink and Mickey Mud? No, let him stick to the jesuits in God's name

---

second moiety notices: Legal notices involving bankruptcy.   **L.D.S.:** *Laus Deo Semper* (Praise to the Lord Always), a Jesuit motto that might be appended to student work. *christian brothers:* Another order like the Jesuits, thought to be less prestigious.

since he began with them. They'll be of service to him in after years. Those are the fellows that can get you a position.

— And they're a very rich order, aren't they, Simon?

— Rather. They live well, I tell you. You saw their table at Clongowes. Fed up, by God, like gamecocks.

Mr Dedalus pushed his plate over to Stephen and bade him finish what was on it.

— Now then, Stephen, he said, you must put your shoulder to the wheel, old chap. You've had a fine long holiday.

— O, I'm sure he'll work very hard now, said Mrs Dedalus, especially when he has Maurice with him.

— O, Holy Paul, I forgot about Maurice, said Mr Dedalus. Here, Maurice! Come here, you thickheaded ruffian! Do you know I'm going to send you to a college where they'll teach you to spell c.a.t.: cat. And I'll buy you a nice little penny handkerchief to keep your nose dry. Won't that be grand fun.

Maurice grinned at his father and then at his brother. Mr Dedalus screwed his glass into his eye and stared hard at both his sons. Stephen mumbled his bread without answering his father's gaze.

— By the bye, said Mr Dedalus at length, the rector, or provincial, rather, was telling me that story about you and Father Dolan. You're an impudent thief, he said.

— O, he didn't, Simon!

— Not he! said Mr Dedalus. But he gave me a great account of the whole affair. We were chatting, you know, and one word borrowed another. And, by the way, who do you think he told me will get that job in the corporation?° But I'll tell you that after. Well, as I was saying, we were chatting away quite friendly and he asked me did our friend here wear glasses still and then he told me the whole story.

— And was he annoyed, Simon?

— Annoyed! Not he! *Manly little chap!* he said.

Mr Dedalus imitated the mincing nasal tone of the provincial.

— Father Dolan and I, when I told them all at dinner about it, Father Dolan and I had a great laugh over it. *You better mind yourself, Father Dolan,* said I, *or young Dedalus will send you up for twice nine.* We had a famous laugh together over it. Ha! Ha! Ha!

Mr Dedalus turned to his wife and interjected in his natural voice:

— Shows you the spirit in which they take the boys there. O, a jesuit for your life, for diplomacy!

the corporation: The Dublin Corporation, the city's administrative and legislative body.

He reassumed the provincial's voice and repeated:

— I told them all at dinner about it and Father Dolan and I and all of us we had a hearty laugh together over it. Ha! Ha! Ha!

*

*   *

The night of the Whitsuntide° play had come and Stephen from the window of the dressingroom looked out on the small grassplot across which lines of Chinese lanterns were stretched. He watched the visitors come down the steps from the house and pass into the theatre. Stewards° in evening dress, old Belvedereans, loitered in groups about the entrance to the theatre and ushered in the visitors with ceremony. Under the sudden glow of a lantern he could recognise the smiling face of a priest.

The Blessed Sacrament had been removed from the tabernacle and the first benches had been driven back so as to leave the dais of the altar and the space before it free. Against the walls stood companies of barbells and Indian clubs; the dumbbells were piled in one corner: and in the midst of countless hillocks of gymnasium shoes and sweaters and singlets in untidy brown parcels there stood the stout leatherjacketed vaulting horse waiting its turn to be carried up onto the stage. A large bronze shield, tipped with silver, leaned against the panel of the altar also waiting its turn to be carried up onto the stage and set in the middle of the winning team at the end of the gymnastic display.

Stephen, though in deference to his reputation for essay-writing he had been elected secretary to the gymnasium, had no part in the first section of the programme but in the play which formed the second section he had the chief part, that of a farcical pedagogue. He had been cast for it on account of his stature and grave manners for he was now at the end of his second year at Belvedere and in number two.

A score of the younger boys in white knickers and singlets came pattering down from the stage, through the vestry and into the chapel. The vestry and chapel were peopled with eager masters and boys. The plump bald sergeantmajor was testing with his foot the springboard of the vaulting horse. The lean young man in a long overcoat, who was to give a special display of intricate club swinging, stood near watching with interest, his silvercoated clubs peeping out of his deep sidepockets. The hollow rattle of the wooden dumbbells was heard as another team made ready to go up on the stage: and in another moment the excited

---

Whitsuntide: Week beginning with Pentecost, the seventh Sunday after Easter.   *Stewards:* Ushers.

prefect was hustling the boys through the vestry like a flock of geese, flapping the wings of his soutane nervously and crying to the laggards to make haste. A little troop of Neapolitan peasants were practising their steps at the end of the chapel, some circling their arms above their heads, some swaying their baskets of paper violets and curtseying. In a dark corner of the chapel at the gospel side of the altar a stout old lady knelt amid her copious black skirts. When she stood up a pinkdressed figure, wearing a curly golden wig and an oldfashioned straw sunbonnet, with black pencilled eyebrows and cheeks delicately rouged and powdered, was discovered. A low murmur of curiosity ran round the chapel at the discovery of this girlish figure. One of the prefects, smiling and nodding his head, approached the dark corner and, having bowed to the stout old lady, said pleasantly:

— Is this a beautiful young lady or a doll that you have here, Mrs Tallon?

Then, bending down to peer at the smiling painted face under the leaf of the bonnet, he exclaimed:

— No! Upon my word I believe it's little Bertie Tallon after all!

Stephen at his post by the window heard the old lady and the priest laugh together and heard the boys' murmur of admiration behind him as they pressed forward to see the little boy who had to dance the sunbonnet dance by himself. A movement of impatience escaped him. He let the edge of the blind fall and, stepping down from the bench on which he had been standing, walked out of the chapel.

He passed out of the schoolhouse and halted under the shed that flanked the garden. From the theatre opposite came the muffled noise of the audience and sudden brazen clashes of the soldiers' band. The light spread upwards from the glass roof making the theatre seem a festive ark, anchored amid the hulks of houses, her frail cables of lanterns looping her to her moorings. A sidedoor of the theatre opened suddenly and a shaft of light flew across the grassplots. A sudden burst of music issued from the ark, the prelude of a waltz: and when the sidedoor closed again the listener could hear the faint rhythm of the music. The sentiment of the opening bars, their languor and supple movement, evoked the incommunicable emotion which had been the cause of all his day's unrest and of his impatient movement of a moment before. His unrest issued from him like a wave of sound: and on the tide of flowing music the ark was journeying, trailing her cables of lanterns in her wake. Then a noise like dwarf artillery broke the movement. It was the clapping that greeted the entry of the dumbbell team on the stage.

At the far end of the shed near the street a speck of pink light showed in the darkness and as he walked towards it he became aware of a faint aromatic odour. Two boys were standing in the shelter of a doorway, smoking, and before he reached them he had recognised Heron by his voice.

— Here comes the noble Dedalus! cried a high throaty voice. Welcome to our trusty friend!

This welcome ended in a soft peal of mirthless laughter as Heron salaamed and then began to poke the ground with his cane.

— Here I am, said Stephen, halting and glancing from Heron to his friend.

The latter was a stranger to him but in the darkness, by the aid of the glowing cigarettetips, he could make out a pale dandyish face, over which a smile was travelling slowly, a tall overcoated figure and a hard hat. Heron did not trouble himself about an introduction but said instead:

— I was just telling my friend Wallis what a lark it would be tonight if you took off the rector in the part of the schoolmaster. It would be a ripping good joke.

Heron made a poor attempt to imitate for his friend Wallis the rector's pedantic bass and then, laughing at his failure, asked Stephen to do it.

— Go on, Dedalus, he urged, you can take him off rippingly. *He that will not hear the churcha let him be to theea as the heathena and the publicana.*

The imitation was prevented by a mild expression of anger from Wallis in whose mouthpiece the cigarette had become too tightly wedged.

— Damn this blankety blank holder, he said, taking it from his mouth and smiling and frowning upon it tolerantly. It's always getting stuck like that. Do you use a holder?

— I don't smoke, answered Stephen.

— No, said Heron, Dedalus is a model youth. He doesn't smoke and he doesn't go to bazaars and he doesn't flirt and he doesn't damn anything or damn all.

Stephen shook his head and smiled in his rival's flushed and mobile face, beaked like a bird's. He had often thought it strange that Vincent Heron had a bird's face as well as a bird's name. A shock of pale hair lay on the forehead like a ruffled crest: the forehead was narrow and bony and a thin hooked nose stood out between the closeset prominent eyes which were light and inexpressive. The rivals were school friends. They sat together in class, knelt together in the chapel, talked together after beads° over their lunches. As the fellows in number one were undistinguished dullards Stephen and Heron had been during the year the virtual heads of the school. It was they who went up to the rector together to ask for a free day or to get a fellow off.

— O by the way, said Heron suddenly, I saw your governor going in.

The smile waned on Stephen's face. Any allusion made to his father by a fellow or by a master put his calm to rout in a moment. He waited in timorous silence to hear what Heron might say next. Heron, however, nudged him expressively with his elbow and said:

— You're a sly dog, Dedalus!

— Why so? said Stephen.

— You'd think butter wouldn't melt in your mouth, said Heron. But I'm afraid you're a sly dog.

— Might I ask you what you are talking about? said Stephen urbanely.

— Indeed you might, answered Heron. We saw her, Wallis, didn't we? And deucedly pretty she is too. And so inquisitive! *And what part does Stephen take, Mr Dedalus? And will Stephen not sing Mr Dedalus?* Your governor was staring at her through that eyeglass of his for all he was worth so that I think the old man has found you out too. I wouldn't care a bit, by Jove. She's ripping, isn't she, Wallis?

— Not half bad, answered Wallis quietly as he placed his holder once more in a corner of his mouth.

A shaft of momentary anger flew through Stephen's mind at these indelicate allusions in the hearing of a stranger. For him there was nothing amusing in a girl's interest and regard. All day he had thought of nothing but their leavetaking on the steps of the tram at Harold's Cross, the stream of moody emotions it had made to course through him, and the poem he had written about it. All day he had imagined a new meeting with her for he knew that she was to come to the play. The old restless moodiness had again filled his breast as it had done on the night of the party but had not found an outlet in verse. The growth and knowledge of two years of boyhood stood between then and now, forbidding such an outlet: and all day the stream of gloomy tenderness within him had started forth and returned upon itself in dark courses and eddies, wearying him in the end until the pleasantry of the prefect and the painted little boy had drawn from him a movement of impatience.

beads: Saying of the rosary.

— So you may as well admit, Heron went on, that we've fairly found you out this time. You can't play the saint on me any more, that's one sure five.

A soft peal of mirthless laughter escaped from his lips and, bending down as before, he struck Stephen lightly across the calf of the leg with his cane, as if in jesting reproof.

Stephen's movement of anger had already passed. He was neither flattered nor confused but simply wished the banter to end. He scarcely resented what had seemed to him at first a silly indelicateness for he knew that the adventure in his mind stood in no danger from their words: and his face mirrored his rival's false smile.

— Admit! repeated Heron, striking him again with his cane across the calf of the leg.

The stroke was playful but not so lightly given as the first one had been. Stephen felt the skin tingle and glow slightly and almost painlessly; and bowing submissively, as if to meet his companion's jesting mood, began to recite the *Confiteor.*° The episode ended well for both Heron and Wallis laughed indulgently at the irreverence.

The confession came only from Stephen's lips and while they spoke the words, a sudden memory had carried him to another scene called up, as if by magic, at the moment when he had noted the faint cruel dimples at the corners of Heron's smiling lips and had felt the familiar stroke of the cane against his calf and heard the familiar word of admonition:

— Admit!

It was towards the close of his first term in the college when he was in number six. His sensitive nature was still smarting under the lashes of an undivined and squalid way of life. His soul was still disquieted and cast down by the dull phenomenon of Dublin. He had emerged from a two years' spell of revery to find himself in the midst of a new scene, every event and figure of which affected him intimately, disheartened him or allured him and, whether alluring or disheartening, filled him always with unrest and bitter thoughts. All the leisure that his school life left him was passed in the company of subversive writers whose gibes and violence of speech set up a ferment in his brain before they passed out of it into his crude writings.

The essay was for him the chief labour of his week and every Tuesday, as he marched from home to the school, he read his fate in the incidents of the way, pitting himself against some figure ahead of him and

Confiteor: Prayer in preparation for confession.

quickening his pace to outstrip it before a certain goal was reached or planting his steps scrupulously in the spaces of the patchwork of the footpath and telling himself that he would be first and not first in the weekly essay.

On a certain Tuesday the course of his triumphs was rudely broken. Mr Tate, the English master, pointed his finger at him and said bluntly:

— This fellow has heresy in his essay.

A hush fell on the class. Mr Tate did not break it but dug with his hand between his crossed thighs while his heavily starched linen creaked about his neck and wrists. Stephen did not look up. It was a raw spring morning and his eyes were still smarting and weak. He was conscious of failure and of detection, of the squalor of his own mind and home, and felt against his neck the raw edge of his turned and jagged collar.

A short loud laugh from Mr Tate set the class more at ease.

— Perhaps you didn't know that, he said.

— Where? asked Stephen.

Mr Tate withdrew his delving hand and spread out the essay.

— Here. It's about the Creator and the soul. Rrm . . . rrm . . . rrm. . . . Ah! *without a possibility of ever approaching nearer.* That's heresy.

Stephen murmured:

— I meant *without a possibility of ever reaching.*

It was a submission and Mr Tate, appeased, folded up the essay and passed it across to him, saying:

— O . . . Ah! *ever reaching.* That's another story.

But the class was not so soon appeased. Though nobody spoke to him of the affair after class he could feel about him a vague general malignant joy.

A few nights after this public chiding he was walking with a letter along the Drumcondra Road when he heard a voice cry:

— Halt!

He turned and saw three boys of his own class coming towards him in the dusk. It was Heron who had called out and, as he marched forward between his two attendants, he cleft the air before him with a thin cane, in time to their steps. Boland, his friend, marched beside him, a large grin on his face, while Nash came on a few steps behind, blowing from the pace and wagging his great red head.

As soon as the boys had turned into Clonliffe Road together they began to speak about books and writers, saying what books they were reading and how many books there were in their fathers' bookcases at home. Stephen listened to them in some wonderment for Boland was the dunce and Nash the idler of the class. In fact after some talk about their favourite writers Nash declared for Captain Marryat° who, he said, was the greatest writer.

— Fudge! said Heron. Ask Dedalus. Who is the greatest writer, Dedalus?

Stephen noted the mockery in the question and said:

— Of prose, do you mean?

— Yes.

— Newman, I think.

— Is it Cardinal Newman? asked Boland.

— Yes, answered Stephen.

The grin broadened on Nash's freckled face as he turned to Stephen and said:

— And do you like Cardinal Newman,° Dedalus?

— O many say that Newman has the best prose style, Heron said to the other two in explanation. Of course, he's not a poet.

— And who is the best poet, Heron? asked Boland.

— Lord Tennyson, of course, answered Heron.

— O, yes, Lord Tennyson, said Nash. We have all his poetry at home in a book.

At this Stephen forgot the silent vows he had been making and burst out:

— Tennyson a poet! Why, he's only a rhymester!

— O, get out! said Heron. Everyone knows that Tennyson is the greatest poet.

— And who do you think is the greatest poet? asked Boland, nudging his neighbour.

— Byron, of course, answered Stephen.

Heron gave the lead and all three joined in a scornful laugh.

— What are you laughing at? asked Stephen.

— You, said Heron. Byron the greatest poet! He's only a poet for uneducated people.

— He must be a fine poet! said Boland.

— You may keep your mouth shut, said Stephen, turning on him boldly. All you know about poetry is what you wrote up on the slates in the yard° and were going to be sent to the loft° for.

Captain Marryat: Frederick Marryat (1792–1848), author of popular adventure and sea stories.   **Cardinal Newman:** John Henry, Cardinal Newman (1801–1890), famous convert to Roman Catholicism, was involved in the founding of University College and was widely admired as a writer.   **slates in the yard:** On the walls of the urinal.   **the loft:** Place for punishment at Clongowes.

Boland, in fact, was said to have written on the slates in the yard a couplet about a classmate of his who often rode home from the college on a pony:

As Tyson was riding into Jerusalem
He fell and hurt his Alec Kafoozelum.

This thrust put the two lieutenants to silence but Heron went on:
— In any case Byron was a heretic and immoral too.
— I don't care what he was, cried Stephen hotly.
— You don't care whether he was a heretic or not? said Nash.
— What do you know about it? shouted Stephen. You never read a line of anything in your life except a trans° or Boland either.
— I know that Byron was a bad man, said Boland.
— Here, catch hold of this heretic, Heron called out.
In a moment Stephen was a prisoner.
— Tate made you buck up the other day, Heron went on, about the heresy in your essay.
— I'll tell him tomorrow, said Boland.
— Will you? said Stephen. You'd be afraid to open your lips.
— Afraid?
— Ay. Afraid of your life.
— Behave yourself! cried Heron, cutting at Stephen's legs with his cane.
It was the signal for their onset. Nash pinioned his arms behind while Boland seized a long cabbage stump which was lying in the gutter. Struggling and kicking under the cuts of the cane and the blows of the knotty stump Stephen was borne back against a barbed wire fence.
— Admit that Byron was no good.
— No.
— Admit.
— No.
— Admit.
— No. No.
At last after a fury of plunges he wrenched himself free. His tormentors set off towards Jones's Road, laughing and jeering at him, while he, torn and flushed and panting, stumbled after them half blinded with tears, clenching his fists madly and sobbing.
While he was still repeating the *Confiteor* amid the indulgent laughter of his hearers and while the scenes of that malignant episode were

trans: A translation (presumably a crib, to help him cheat at Latin).

still passing sharply and swiftly before his mind he wondered why he bore no malice now to those who had tormented him. He had not forgotten a whit of their cowardice and cruelty but the memory of it called forth no anger from him. All the descriptions of fierce love and hatred which he had met in books had seemed to him therefore unreal. Even that night as he stumbled homewards along Jones's Road he had felt that some power was divesting him of that suddenwoven anger as easily as a fruit is divested of its soft ripe peel.

He remained standing with his two companions at the end of the shed, listening idly to their talk or to the bursts of applause in the theatre. She was sitting there among the others perhaps waiting for him to appear. He tried to recall her appearance but could not. He could remember only that she had worn a shawl about her head like a cowl and that her dark eyes had invited and unnerved him. He wondered had he been in her thoughts as she had been in his. Then in the dark and unseen by the other two he rested the tips of the fingers of one hand upon the palm of the other hand, scarcely touching it and yet pressing upon it lightly. But the pressure of her fingers had been lighter and steadier: and suddenly the memory of their touch traversed his brain and body like an invisible warm wave.

A boy came towards them, running along under the shed. He was excited and breathless.

— O, Dedalus, he cried, Doyle is in a great bake° about you. You're to go in at once and get dressed for the play. Hurry up, you better.

— He's coming now, said Heron to the messenger with a haughty drawl, when he wants to.

The boy turned to Heron and repeated:

— But Doyle is in an awful bake.

— Will you tell Doyle with my best compliments that I damned his eyes? answered Heron.

— Well, I must go now, said Stephen, who cared little for such points of honour.

— I wouldn't, said Heron, damn me if I would. That's no way to send for one of the senior boys. In a bake, indeed! I think it's quite enough that you're taking a part in his bally old play.

This spirit of quarrelsome comradeship which he had observed lately in his rival had not seduced Stephen from his habits of quiet obedience. He mistrusted the turbulence and doubted the sincerity of such comradeship which seemed to him a sorry anticipation of manhood.

in a great bake: Angry or agitated.

The question of honour here raised was, like all such questions, trivial to him. While his mind had been pursuing its intangible phantoms and turning back in irresoluteness from such pursuit he had heard about him the constant voices of his father and of his masters, urging him to be a gentleman above all things and urging him to be a good catholic above all things. These voices had now come to be hollowsounding in his ears. When the gymnasium had been opened he had heard another voice urging him to be strong and manly and healthy and when the movement towards national revival had begun to be felt in the college yet another voice had bidden him be true to his country and help to raise up her fallen language and tradition. In the profane world, as he foresaw, a worldly voice would bid him raise up his father's fallen state by his labours and, meanwhile, the voice of his schoolcomrades urged him to be a decent fellow, to shield others from blame or to beg them off and to do his best to get free days for the school. And it was the din of all these hollowsounding voices that made him halt irresolutely in the pursuit of phantoms. He gave them ear only for a time but he was happy only when he was far from them, beyond their call, alone or in the company of phantasmal comrades.

In the vestry a plump freshfaced jesuit and an elderly man, in shabby blue clothes, were dabbling in a case of paints and chalks. The boys who had been painted walked about or stood still awkwardly, touching their faces in a gingerly fashion with their furtive fingertips. In the middle of the vestry a young jesuit, who was then on a visit to the college, stood rocking himself rhythmically from the tips of his toes to his heels and back again, his hands thrust well forward into his two side-pockets. His small head set off with glossy red curls and his newly shaven face agreed well with the spotless decency of his soutane and with his spotless shoes.

As he watched this swaying form and tried to read for himself the legend of the priest's mocking smile there came into Stephen's memory a saying which he had heard from his father before he had been sent to Clongowes, that you could always tell a jesuit by the style of his clothes. At the same moment he thought he saw a likeness between his father's mind and that of this smiling welldressed priest: and he was aware of some desecration of the priest's office or of the vestry itself, whose silence was now routed by loud talk and joking and its air pungent with the smells of the gasjets and the grease.

While his forehead was being wrinkled and his jaws painted black and blue by the elderly man he listened distractedly to the voice of the plump young jesuit which bade him speak up and make his points clearly. He could hear the band playing *The Lily of Killarney°* and knew that in a few moments the curtain would go up. He felt no stage fright but the thought of the part he had to play humiliated him. A remembrance of some of his lines made a sudden flush rise to his painted cheeks. He saw her serious alluring eyes watching him from among the audience and their image at once swept away his scruples, leaving his will compact. Another nature seemed to have been lent him: the infection of the excitement and youth about him entered into and transformed his moody mistrustfulness. For one rare moment he seemed to be clothed in the real apparel of boyhood: and, as he stood in the wings among the other players, he shared the common mirth amid which the drop scene was hauled upwards by two ablebodied priests with violent jerks and all awry.

A few moments after he found himself on the stage amid the garish gas and the dim scenery, acting before the innumerable faces of the void. It surprised him to see that the play which he had known at rehearsals for a disjointed lifeless thing had suddenly assumed a life of its own. It seemed now to play itself, he and his fellow actors aiding it with their parts. When the curtain fell on the last scene he heard the void filled with applause and, through a rift in the side scene, saw the simple body before which he had acted magically deformed, the void of faces breaking at all points and falling asunder into busy groups.

He left the stage quickly and rid himself of his mummery and passed out through the chapel into the college garden. Now that the play was over his nerves cried for some further adventure. He hurried onwards as if to overtake it. The doors of the theatre were all open and the audience had emptied out. On the lines which he had fancied the moorings of an ark a few lanterns swung in the night breeze, flickering cheerlessly. He mounted the steps from the garden in haste, eager that some prey should not elude him, and forced his way through the crowd in the hall and past the two jesuits who stood watching the exodus and bowing and shaking hands with the visitors. He pushed onward nervously feigning a still greater haste and faintly conscious of the smiles and stares and nudges which his powdered head left in its wake.

When he came out on the steps he saw his family waiting for him at the first lamp. In a glance he noted that every figure of the group was familiar and ran down the steps angrily.

The Lily of Killarney: 1862 opera by Sir Julius Benedict, based on Dion Boucicault's popular melodrama, *The Colleen Bawn* (1861).

— I have to leave a message down in George's Street, he said to his father quickly. I'll be home after you.

Without waiting for his father's questions he ran across the road and began to walk at breakneck speed down the hill. He hardly knew where he was walking. Pride and hope and desire like crushed herbs in his heart sent up vapours of maddening incense before the eyes of his mind. He strode down the hill amid the tumult of suddenrisen vapours of wounded pride and fallen hope and baffled desire. They streamed upwards before his anguished eyes in dense and maddening fumes and passed away above him till at last the air was clear and cold again.

A film still veiled his eyes but they burned no longer. A power, akin to that which had often made anger or resentment fall from him, brought his steps to rest. He stood still and gazed up at the sombre porch of the morgue and from that to the dark cobbled laneway at its side. He saw the word *Lotts* on the wall of the lane and breathed slowly the rank heavy air.

— That is horse piss and rotted straw, he thought. It is a good odour to breathe. It will calm my heart. My heart is quite calm now. I will go back.

*

*   *

Stephen was once again seated beside his father in the corner of a railway carriage at Kingsbridge. He was travelling with his father by the night mail to Cork. As the train steamed out of the station he recalled his childish wonder of years before and every event of his first day at Clongowes. But he felt no wonder now. He saw the darkening lands slipping past him, the silent telegraphpoles passing his window swiftly every four seconds, the little glimmering stations, manned by a few silent sentries, flung by the mail behind her and twinkling for a moment in the darkness like fiery grains flung backwards by a runner.

He listened without sympathy to his father's evocation of Cork and of scenes of his youth, a tale broken by sighs or draughts from his pocketflask whenever the image of some dead friend appeared in it or whenever the evoker remembered suddenly the purpose of his actual visit. Stephen heard but could feel no pity. The images of the dead were all strange to him save that of uncle Charles, an image which had lately been fading out of memory. He knew, however, that his father's property was going to be sold by auction and in the manner of his own dispossession he felt the world give the lie rudely to his phantasy.

At Maryborough he fell asleep. When he awoke the train had passed out of Mallow and his father was stretched asleep on the other seat. The cold light of the dawn lay over the country, over the unpeopled fields and the closed cottages. The terror of sleep fascinated his mind as he watched the silent country or heard from time to time his father's deep breath or sudden sleepy movement. The neighbourhood of unseen sleepers filled him with strange dread as though they could harm him; and he prayed that the day might come quickly. His prayer, addressed neither to God nor saint, began with a shiver, as the chilly morning breeze crept through the chink of the carriage door to his feet, and ended in a trail of foolish words which he made to fit the insistent rhythm of the train: and silently, at intervals of four seconds, the telegraphpoles held the galloping notes of the music between punctual bars. This furious music allayed his dread and, leaning against the windowledge, he let his eyelids close again.

They drove in a jingle° across Cork while it was still early morning and Stephen finished his sleep in a bedroom of the Victoria Hotel. The bright warm sunlight was streaming through the window and he could hear the din of traffic. His father was standing before the dressing-table, examining his hair and face and moustache with great care, craning his neck across the waterjug and drawing it back sideways to see the better. While he did so he sang softly to himself with quaint accent and phrasing:

> 'Tis youth and folly
> Makes young men marry,
> So here, my love, I'll
>   No longer stay.
> What can't be cured, sure,
> Must be injured, sure,
>   So I'll go
>   To Amerikay.

> My love she's handsome,
> My love she's bonny:
> She's like good whisky
>   When it is new;
> But when 'tis old
> And growing cold
> It fades and dies like
>   The mountain dew.

The consciousness of the warm sunny city outside his window and the tender tremors with which his father's voice festooned the strange sad-

---

jingle: A horse-drawn car.

happy air drove off all the mists of the night's illhumour from Stephen's brain. He got up quickly to dress and, when the song had ended, said
— That's much prettier than any of your other *come-all-yous.*°
— Do you think so? asked Mr Dedalus.
— I like it, said Stephen.
— It's a pretty old air, said Mr Dedalus, twirling the points of his moustache. Ah, but you should have heard Mick Lacy sing it! Poor Mick Lacy! He had little turns for it, gracenotes he used to put in that I haven't got. That was the boy could sing a *come-all-you,* if you like.

Mr Dedalus had ordered drisheens° for breakfast and during the meal he crossexamined the waiter for local news. For the most part they spoke at crosspurposes when a name was mentioned, the waiter having in mind the present holder and Mr Dedalus his father or perhaps his grandfather.
— Well, I hope they haven't moved the Queen's College anyhow, said Mr Dedalus, for I want to show it to this youngster of mine.

Along the Mardyke the trees were in bloom. They entered the grounds of the college and were led by the garrulous porter across the quadrangle. But their progress across the gravel was brought to a halt after every dozen or so paces by some reply of the porter's.
— Ah, do you tell me so? And is poor Pottlebelly dead?
— Yes, sir. Dead, sir.

During these halts Stephen stood awkwardly behind the two men, weary of the subject and waiting restlessly for the slow march to begin again. By the time they had crossed the quadrangle his restlessness had risen to fever. He wondered how his father, whom he knew for a shrewd suspicious man, could be duped by the servile manners of the porter: and the lively southern speech which had entertained him all the morning now irritated his ears.

They passed into the anatomy theatre where Mr Dedalus, the porter aiding him, searched the desks for his initials. Stephen remained in the background, depressed more than ever by the darkness and silence of the theatre and by the air it wore of jaded and formal study. On the desk before him he read the word *Fœtus* cut several times in the dark stained wood. The sudden legend startled his blood: he seemed to feel the absent students of the college about him and to shrink from their company. A vision of their life, which his father's words had been powerless to evoke, sprang up before him out of the word cut in the desk. A broadshouldered student with a moustache was cutting in the letters

---

come-all-yous: Street ballads.   *drisheens:* A sort of sweetbread, made with sheep's intestines.

with a jackknife, seriously. Other students stood or sat near him laughing at his handiwork. One jogged his elbow. The big student turned on him, frowning. He was dressed in loose grey clothes and had tan boots.

Stephen's name was called. He hurried down the steps of the theatre so as to be as far away from the vision as he could be and, peering closely at his father's initials, hid his flushed face.

But the word and the vision capered before his eyes as he walked back across the quadrangle and towards the college gate. It shocked him to find in the outer world a trace of what he had deemed till then a brutish and individual malady of his own mind. His recent monstrous reveries came thronging into his memory. They too had sprung up before him, suddenly and furiously, out of mere words. He had soon given in to them and allowed them to sweep across and abase his intellect, wondering always where they came from, from what den of monstrous images, and always weak and humble towards others, restless and sickened of himself when they had swept over him.

— Ay, bedad! And there's the Groceries° sure enough! cried Mr Dedalus. You often heard me speak of the Groceries, didn't you, Stephen. Many's the time we went down there when our names had been marked,° a crowd of us, Harry Peard and little Jack Mountain and Bob Dyas and Maurice Moriarty, the Frenchman, and Tom O'Grady and Mick Lacy that I told you of this morning and Joe Corbet and poor little good-hearted Johnny Keevers of the Tantiles.

The leaves of the trees along the Mardyke were astir and whispering in the sunlight. A team of cricketers passed, agile young men in flannels and blazers, one of them carrying the long green wicketbag. In a quiet bystreet a German band of five players in faded uniforms and with battered brass instruments was playing to an audience of street arabs° and leisurely messenger boys. A maid in a white cap and apron was watering a box of plants on a sill which shone like a slab of limestone in the warm glare. From another window open to the air came the sound of a piano, scale after scale rising into the treble.

Stephen walked on at his father's side, listening to stories he had heard before, hearing again the names of the scattered and dead revellers who had been the companions of his father's youth. And a faint sickness sighed in his heart. He recalled his own equivocal position in Belvedere, a free boy,° a leader afraid of his own authority, proud and

---

Groceries: A pub also selling provisions.   *our names had been marked:* Once they were marked as present at a lecture they would slip out.   *street arabs:* Poor or Gypsy children. *free boy:* Boy on a scholarship.

sensitive and suspicious, battling against the squalor of his life and against the riot of his mind. The letters cut in the stained wood of the desk stared upon him, mocking his bodily weakness and futile enthusiasms and making him loathe himself for his own mad and filthy orgies. The spittle in his throat grew bitter and foul to swallow and the faint sickness climbed to his brain so that for a moment he closed his eyes and walked on in darkness.

He could still hear his father's voice.

— When you kick out for yourself, Stephen — as I daresay you will one of those days — remember, whatever you do, to mix with gentlemen. When I was a young fellow I tell you I enjoyed myself. I mixed with fine decent fellows. Everyone of us could do something. One fellow had a good voice, another fellow was a good actor, another could sing a good comic song, another was a good oarsman or a good racket-player, another could tell a good story and so on. We kept the ball rolling anyhow and enjoyed ourselves and saw a bit of life and we were none the worse of it either. But we were all gentlemen, Stephen — at least I hope we were — and bloody good honest Irishmen too. That's the kind of fellows I want you to associate with, fellows of the right kidney. I'm talking to you as a friend, Stephen. I don't believe in playing the stern father. I don't believe a son should be afraid of his father. No, I treat you as your grandfather treated me when I was a young chap. We were more like brothers than father and son. I'll never forget the first day he caught me smoking. I was standing at the end of the South Terrace one day with some maneens° like myself and sure we thought we were grand fellows because we had pipes stuck in the corners of our mouths. Suddenly the governor passed. He didn't say a word or stop even. But the next day, Sunday, we were out for a walk together and when we were coming home he took out his cigar case and said: *By the bye, Simon, I didn't know you smoked:* or something like that. Of course I tried to carry it off as best I could. *If you want a good smoke,* he said, *try one of these cigars. An American captain made me a present of them last night in Queenstown.*

Stephen heard his father's voice break into a laugh which was almost a sob.

— He was the handsomest man in Cork at that time, by God he was! The women used to stand to look after him in the street.

He heard the sob passing loudly down his father's throat and opened his eyes with a nervous impulse. The sunlight breaking suddenly on his

maneens: Insulting term (little men).

sight turned the sky and clouds into a fantastic world of sombre masses with lakelike spaces of dark rosy light. His very brain was sick and powerless. He could scarcely interpret the letters of the signboards of the shops. By his monstrous way of life he seemed to have put himself beyond the limits of reality. Nothing moved him or spoke to him from the real world unless he heard in it an echo of the infuriated cries within him. He could respond to no earthly or human appeal, dumb and insensible to the call of summer and gladness and companionship, wearied and dejected by his father's voice. He could scarcely recognise as his his own thoughts: and repeated slowly to himself:

— I am Stephen Dedalus. I am walking beside my father whose name is Simon Dedalus. We are in Cork, in Ireland. Cork is a city. Our room is in the Victoria Hotel. Victoria and Stephen and Simon. Simon and Stephen and Victoria. Names.

The memory of his childhood suddenly grew dim. He tried to call forth some of its vivid moments but could not. He recalled only names: Dante, Parnell, Clane, Clongowes. A little boy had been taught geography by an old woman who kept two brushes in her wardrobe. Then he had been sent away from home to a college. In the college he had made his first communion and eaten slim jim° out of his cricketcap and watched the firelight leaping and dancing on the wall of a little bedroom in the infirmary and dreamed of being dead, of mass being said for him by the rector in a black and gold cope, of being buried then in the little graveyard of the community off the main avenue of limes. But he had not died then. Parnell had died. There had been no mass for the dead in the chapel and no procession. He had not died but he had faded out like a film in the sun. He had been lost or had wandered out of existence for he no longer existed. How strange to think of him passing out of existence in such a way, not by death but by fading out in the sun or by being lost and forgotten somewhere in the universe! It was strange to see his small body appear again for a moment: a little boy in a grey belted suit. His hands were in his sidepockets and his trousers were tucked in at the knees by elastic bands.

On the evening of the day on which the property was sold Stephen followed his father meekly about the city from bar to bar. To the sellers in the market, to the barmen and barmaids, to the beggars who importuned him for a lob° Mr Dedalus told the same tale, that he was an old Corkonian, that he had been trying for thirty years to get rid of his

---

slim jim: A long jelly candy.   *lob:* Some amount of money.

Cork accent up in Dublin and that Peter Pickackafax beside him was his eldest son but that he was only a Dublin jackeen.°

They had set out early in the morning from Newcombe's coffee-house where Mr Dedalus' cup had rattled noisily against its saucer and Stephen had tried to cover that shameful sign of his father's drinking-bout of the night before by moving his chair and coughing. One humiliation had succeeded another: the false smiles of the market sellers, the curvettings and oglings of the barmaids with whom his father flirted, the compliments and encouraging words of his father's friends. They had told him that he had a great look of his grandfather and Mr Dedalus had agreed that he was an ugly likeness. They had unearthed traces of a Cork accent in his speech and made him admit that the Lee was a much finer river than the Liffey. One of them in order to put his Latin to the proof had made him translate short passages from Dilectus° and asked him whether it was correct to say: *Tempora mutantur nos et mutamur in illis* or *Tempora mutantur et nos mutamur in illis.*° Another, a brisk old man, whom Mr Dedalus called Johnny Cashman, had covered him with confusion by asking him to say which were prettier, the Dublin girls or the Cork girls.

— He's not that way built, said Mr Dedalus. Leave him alone. He's a levelheaded thinking boy who doesn't bother his head about that kind of nonsense.

— Then he's not his father's son, said the little old man.

— I don't know, I'm sure, said Mr Dedalus, smiling complacently.

— Your father, said the little old man to Stephen, was the boldest flirt in the city of Cork in his day. Do you know that?

Stephen looked down and studied the tiled floor of the bar into which they had drifted.

— Now don't be putting ideas into his head, said Mr Dedalus. Leave him to his Maker.

— Yerra, sure I wouldn't put any ideas into his head. I'm old enough to be his grandfather. And I am a grandfather, said the little old man to Stephen. Do you know that?

— Are you? asked Stephen.

— Bedad I am, said the little old man. I have two bouncing grandchildren out at Sunday's Well. Now then! What age do you think I am?

---

jackeen: Arrogant, lower-class person.   ***Dilectus:*** A phrase book of Latin quotations. ***Tempora mutantur nos ... illis:*** Circumstances change and we change in them (in the second version, "with them"); both are grammatically correct, the second metrically correct.

And I remember seeing your grandfather in his red coat riding out to hounds. That was before you were born.

— Ay or thought of, said Mr Dedalus.

— Bedad I did! repeated the little old man. And more than that, I can remember even your greatgrandfather, old John Stephen Dedalus, and a fierce old fireeater he was. Now then! There's a memory for you!

— That's three generations — four generations, said another of the company. Why, Johnny Cashman, you must be nearing the century.

— Well, I'll tell you the truth, said the little old man. I'm just twenty-seven years of age.

— We're as old as we feel, Johnny, said Mr Dedalus. And just finish what you have there and we'll have another. Here, Tim or Tom or whatever your name is, give us the same again here. By God, I don't feel more than eighteen myself. There's that son of mine there not half my age and I'm a better man than he is any day of the week.

— Draw it mild now, Dedalus. I think it's time for you to take a back seat, said the gentleman who had spoken before.

— No, by God! asserted Mr Dedalus. I'll sing a tenor song against him or I'll vault a fivebarred gate against him or I'll run with him after the hounds across the country as I did thirty years ago along with the Kerry Boy and the best man for it.

— But he'll beat you here, said the little old man, tapping his forehead and raising his glass to drain it.

— Well, I hope he'll be as good a man as his father. That's all I can say, said Mr Dedalus.

— If he is, he'll do, said the little old man.

— And thanks be to God, Johnny, said Mr Dedalus, that we lived so long and did so little harm.

— But did so much good, Simon, said the little old man gravely. Thanks be to God we lived so long and did so much good.

Stephen watched the three glasses being raised from the counter as his father and his two cronies drank to the memory of their past. An abyss of fortune or of temperament sundered him from them. His mind seemed older than theirs: it shone coldly on their strifes and happiness and regrets like a moon upon a younger earth. No life or youth stirred in him as it had stirred in them. He had known neither the pleasure of companionship with others nor the vigour of rude male health nor filial piety. Nothing stirred within his soul but a cold and cruel and loveless lust. His childhood was dead or lost and with it his soul capable of simple joys: and he was drifting amid life like the barren shell of the moon.

Art thou pale for weariness°
Of climbing heaven and gazing on the earth,
Wandering companionless . . . ?

He repeated to himself the lines of Shelley's fragment. Its alternation of sad human ineffectualness with vast inhuman cycles of activity
chilled him: and he forgot his own human and ineffectual grieving.

*

*   *

Stephen's mother and his brother and one of his cousins waited at
the corner of quiet Foster Place while he and his father went up the
steps and along the colonnade where the highland sentry was parading.
When they had passed into the great hall and stood at the counter
Stephen drew forth his orders on the governor of the bank of Ireland
for thirty and three pounds, and these sums, the moneys of his exhibi-
tion° and essay prize, were paid over to him rapidly by the teller in notes
and in coin respectively. He bestowed them in his pockets with feigned
composure and suffered the friendly teller, to whom his father chatted,
to take his hand across the broad counter and wish him a brilliant career
in after life. He was impatient of their voices and could not keep his feet
at rest. But the teller still deferred the serving of others to say that he
was living in changed times and that there was nothing like giving a boy
the best education that money could buy. Mr Dedalus lingered in the
hall gazing about him and up at the roof and telling Stephen, who
urged him to come out, that they were standing in the house of commons of the old Irish parliament.

God help us! he said piously, to think of the men of those times,
Stephen, Hely Hutchinson and Flood and Henry Grattan and Charles
Kendal Bushe,° and the noblemen we have now, leaders of the Irish
people at home and abroad. Why, by God, they wouldn't be seen dead
in a tenacre field with them. No, Stephen, old chap, I'm sorry to say
that they are only as I roved out one fine May morning in the merry
month of sweet July.

A keen October wind was blowing round the bank. The three figures standing at the edge of the muddy path had pinched cheeks and
watery eyes. Stephen looked at his thinly clad mother and remembered

---

Art thou pale for weariness . . . : From "To the Moon," by Percy Bysshe Shelley
(1792–1822).   *exhibition:* Outstanding performance in one of the annual national
academic examinations.   *Hely Hutchinson . . . Bushe:* All famous Irish orators of the
eighteenth and early nineteenth centuries. Grattan and Bushe were leaders of the struggle
for legislative independence.

that a few days before he had seen a mantle priced at twenty guineas in the window of Barnardo's.

— Well that's done, said Mr Dedalus.

— We had better go to dinner, said Stephen. Where?

— Dinner? said Mr Dedalus. Well, I suppose we had better, what?

— Some place that's not too dear, said Mrs Dedalus.

— Underdone's?

— Yes. Some quiet place.

— Come along, said Stephen quickly. It doesn't matter about the dearness.

He walked on before them with short nervous steps, smiling. They tried to keep up with him, smiling also at his eagerness.

— Take it easy like a good young fellow, said his father. We're not out for the half mile, are we?

For a swift season of merrymaking the money of his prizes ran through Stephen's fingers. Great parcels of groceries and delicacies and dried fruits arrived from the city. Every day he drew up a bill of fare for the family and every night led a party of three or four to the theatre to see *Ingomar*° or *The Lady of Lyons*. In his coat pockets he carried squares of Vienna chocolate for his guests while his trousers' pockets bulged with masses of silver and copper coins. He bought presents for everyone, overhauled his room, wrote out resolutions, marshalled his books up and down their shelves, pored upon all kinds of price lists, drew up a form of commonwealth for the household by which every member of it held some office, opened a loan bank for his family and pressed loans on willing borrowers so that he might have the pleasure of making out receipts and reckoning the interests on the sums lent. When he could do no more he drove up and down the city in trams. Then the season of pleasure came to an end. The pot of pink enamel paint gave out and the wainscot of his bedroom remained with its unfinished and illplastered coat.

His household returned to its usual way of life. His mother had no further occasion to upbraid him for squandering his money. He too returned to his old life at school and all his novel enterprises fell to pieces. The commonwealth fell, the loan bank closed its coffers and its books on a sensible loss, the rules of life which he had drawn about himself fell into desuetude.

Ingomar: *Ingomar the Barbarian* (1851), play by Maria Lovell; *Lady of Lyons* (1838), play by Edward Bulwer-Lytton.

How foolish his aim had been! He had tried to build a breakwater of order and elegance against the sordid tide of life without him and to dam up, by rules of conduct and active interests and new filial relations, the powerful recurrence of the tides within him. Useless. From without as from within the water had flowed over his barriers: their tides began once more to jostle fiercely above the crumbled mole.

He saw clearly too his own futile isolation. He had not gone one step nearer the lives he had sought to approach nor bridged the restless shame and rancour that divided him from father and mother and brother and sister. He felt that he was hardly of the one blood with them but stood to them rather in the mystical kinship of fosterage, fosterchild and fosterbrother.

He burned to appease the fierce longings of his heart before which everything else was idle and alien. He cared little that he was in mortal sin, that his life had grown to be a tissue of subterfuges and falsehood. Beside the savage desire within him to realise the enormities which he brooded on nothing was sacred. He bore cynically with the shameful details of his secret riots in which he exulted to defile with patience whatever image had attracted his eyes. By day and by night he moved among distorted images of the outer world. A figure that had seemed to him by day demure and innocent came towards him by night through the winding darkness of sleep, her face transfigured by a lecherous cunning, her eyes bright with brutish joy. Only the morning pained him with its dim memory of dark orgiastic riot, its keen and humiliating sense of transgression.

He returned to his wanderings. The veiled autumnal evenings led him from street to street as they had led him years before along the quiet avenues of Blackrock. But no vision of trim front gardens or of kindly lights in the windows poured a tender influence upon him now. Only at times, in the pauses of his desire, when the luxury that was wasting him gave room to a softer languor, the image of Mercedes traversed the background of his memory. He saw again the small white house and the garden of rosebushes on the road that led to the mountains and he remembered the sadly proud gesture of refusal which he was to make there, standing with her in her moonlit garden after years of estrangement and adventure. At those moments the soft speeches of Claude Melnotte° rose to his lips and eased his unrest. A tender premonition touched him of the tryst he had then looked forward to and, in

Claude Melnotte: Hero of *The Lady of Lyons.*

spite of the horrible reality which lay between his hope of then and now, of the holy encounter he had then imagined at which weakness and timidity and inexperience were to fall from him.

Such moments passed and the wasting fires of lust sprang up again. The verses passed from his lips and the inarticulate cries and the unspoken brutal words rushed forth from his brain to force a passage. His blood was in revolt. He wandered up and down the dark slimy streets peering into the gloom of lanes and doorways, listening eagerly for any sound. He moaned to himself like some baffled prowling beast. He wanted to sin with another of his kind, to force another being to sin with him and to exult with her in sin. He felt some dark presence moving irresistibly upon him from the darkness, a presence subtle and murmurous as a flood filling him wholly with itself. Its murmur besieged his ears like the murmur of some multitude in sleep; its subtle streams penetrated his being. His hands clenched convulsively and his teeth set together as he suffered the agony of its penetration. He stretched out his arms in the street to hold fast the frail swooning form that eluded him and incited him: and the cry that he had strangled for so long in his throat issued from his lips. It broke from him like a wail of despair from a hell of sufferers and died in a wail of furious entreaty, a cry for an iniquitous abandonment, a cry which was but the echo of an obscene scrawl which he had read on the oozing wall of a urinal.

He had wandered into a maze of narrow and dirty streets. From the foul laneways he heard bursts of hoarse riot and wrangling and the drawling of drunken singers. He walked onward, undismayed, wondering whether he had strayed into the quarter of the jews. Women and girls dressed in long vivid gowns traversed the street from house to house. They were leisurely and perfumed. A trembling seized him and his eyes grew dim. The yellow gasflames arose before his troubled vision against the vapoury sky, burning as if before an altar. Before the doors and in the lighted halls groups were gathered arrayed as for some rite. He was in another world: he had awakened from a slumber of centuries.

He stood still in the middle of the roadway, his heart clamouring against his bosom in a tumult. A young woman dressed in a long pink gown laid her hand on his arm to detain him and gazed into his face. She said gaily:

— Good night, Willie dear!

Her room was warm and lightsome. A huge doll sat with her legs apart in the copious easychair beside the bed. He tried to bid his tongue speak that he might seem at ease, watching her as she undid her gown, noting the proud conscious movements of her perfumed head.

As he stood silent in the middle of the room she came over to him and embraced him gaily and gravely. Her round arms held him firmly to her and he, seeing her face lifted to him in serious calm and feeling the warm calm rise and fall of her breast, all but burst into hysterical weeping. Tears of joy and of relief shone in his delighted eyes and his lips parted though they would not speak.

She passed her tinkling hand through his hair, calling him a little rascal.

— Give me a kiss, she said.

His lips would not bend to kiss her. He wanted to be held firmly in her arms, to be caressed slowly, slowly, slowly. In her arms he felt that he had suddenly become strong and fearless and sure of himself. But his lips would not bend to kiss her.

With a sudden movement she bowed his head and joined her lips to his and he read the meaning of her movements in her frank uplifted eyes. It was too much for him. He closed his eyes, surrendering himself to her, body and mind, conscious of nothing in the world but the dark pressure of her softly parting lips. They pressed upon his brain as upon his lips as though they were the vehicle of a vague speech; and between them he felt an unknown and timid pressure, darker than the swoon of sin, softer than sound or odour.

III

The swift December dusk had come tumbling clownishly after its dull day and, as he stared through the dull square of the window of the schoolroom, he felt his belly crave for its food. He hoped there would be stew for dinner, turnips and carrots and bruised potatoes and fat mutton pieces to be ladled out in thick peppered flourfattened sauce. Stuff it into you, his belly counselled him.

It would be a gloomy secret night. After early nightfall the yellow lamps would light up, here and there, the squalid quarter of the brothels. He would follow a devious course up and down the streets, circling always nearer and nearer in a tremor of fear and joy, until his feet led him suddenly round a dark corner. The whores would be just coming out of their houses making ready for the night, yawning lazily after their sleep and settling the hairpins in their clusters of hair. He would pass by them calmly waiting for a sudden movement of his own will or a sudden call to his sinloving soul from their soft perfumed flesh. Yet as he prowled in quest of that call, his senses, stultified only by his desire, would note

keenly all that wounded or shamed them; his eyes, a ring of porter froth
on a clothless table or a photograph of two soldiers standing to attention or a gaudy playbill; his ears, the drawling jargon of greeting:

— Hello, Bertie, any good in your mind?

— Is that you, pigeon?

— Number ten. Fresh Nelly is waiting on you.

— Goodnight, husband! Coming in to have a short time?

The equation on the page of his scribbler began to spread out a
widening tail, eyed and starred like a peacock's: and when the eyes and
stars of its indices had been eliminated, began slowly to fold itself
together again. The indices appearing and disappearing were eyes opening and closing; the eyes opening and closing were stars being born and
being quenched. The vast cycle of starry life bore his weary mind outward to its verge and inward to its centre, a distant music accompany-
ing him outward and inward. What music? The music came nearer and
he recalled the words, the words of Shelley's fragment upon the moon
wandering companionless, pale for weariness. The stars began to crumble and a cloud of fine stardust fell through space.

The dull light fell more faintly upon the page whereon another
equation began to unfold itself slowly and to spread abroad its widening tail. It was his own soul going forth to experience, unfolding itself
sin by sin, spreading abroad the balefire° of its burning stars and folding
back upon itself, fading slowly, quenching its own lights and fires. They
were quenched: and the cold darkness filled chaos.

A cold lucid indifference reigned in his soul. At his first violent sin
he had felt a wave of vitality pass out of him and had feared to find his
body or his soul maimed by the excess. Instead the vital wave had carried him on its bosom out of himself and back again when it receded:
and no part of body or soul had been maimed but a dark peace had
been established between them. The chaos in which his ardour extinguished itself was a cold indifferent knowledge of himself. He had
sinned mortally not once but many times and he knew that, while he
stood in danger of eternal damnation for the first sin alone, by every
succeeding sin he multiplied his guilt and his punishment. His days and
works and thoughts could make no atonement for him, the fountains of
sanctifying grace having ceased to refresh his soul. At most by an alms
given to a beggar, whose blessing he fled from, he might hope wearily
to win for himself some measure of actual grace. Devotion had gone by
the board. What did it avail to pray when he knew that his soul lusted

balefire: Large fire in the open air.

after its own destruction? A certain pride, a certain awe, withheld him from offering to God even one prayer at night though he knew it was in God's power to take away his life while he slept and hurl his soul hellward ere he could beg for mercy. His pride in his own sin, his loveless awe of God, told him that his offence was too grievous to be atoned for in whole or in part by a false homage to the Allseeing and Allknowing.

— Well now, Ennis, I declare you have a head and so has my stick! Do you mean to say that you are not able to tell me what a surd° is?

The blundering answer stirred the embers of his contempt of his fellows. Towards others he felt neither shame nor fear. On Sunday mornings as he passed the churchdoor he glanced coldly at the worshippers who stood bareheaded, four deep, outside the church, morally present at the mass which they could neither see nor hear. Their dull piety and the sickly smell of the cheap hairoil with which they had anointed their heads repelled him from the altar they prayed at. He stooped to the evil of hypocrisy with others, sceptical of their innocence which he could cajole so easily.

On the wall of his bedroom hung an illuminated scroll, the certificate of his prefecture in the college of the sodality° of the Blessed Virgin Mary. On Saturday mornings when the sodality met in the chapel to recite the little office° his place was a cushioned kneelingdesk at the right of the altar from which he led his wing of boys through the responses. The falsehood of his position did not pain him. If at moments he felt an impulse to rise from his post of honour and, confessing before them all his unworthiness, to leave the chapel, a glance at their faces restrained him. The imagery of the psalms of prophecy soothed his barren pride. The glories of Mary held his soul captive: spikenard and myrrh and frankincense, symbolising the preciousness of God's gifts to her soul, rich garments, symbolising her royal lineage, her emblems, the lateflowering plant and lateblossoming tree, symbolising the agelong gradual growth of her cultus among men. When it fell to him to read the lesson towards the close of the office he read it in a veiled voice, lulling his conscience to its music.

Quasi cedrus exaltata sum in Libanon et quasi cupressus in monte Sion. Quasi palma exaltata sum in Gades et quasi plantatio rosae in Jericho. Quasi uliva speciosa in campis et quasi platanus exaltata

---

surd: In mathematics, an irrational number.   ***prefecture ... of the sodality:*** Leadership of an honorific student association.   ***the little office:*** A collection of psalms and lessons to be said on Saturday.

*sum juxta aquam in plateis. Sicut cinnamomum et balsamum
aromatizans odorem dedi et quasi myrrha electa dedi suavitatem
odoris.*°

His sin, which had covered him from the sight of God, had led him
nearer to the refuge of sinners. Her eyes seemed to regard him with
mild pity; her holiness, a strange light glowing faintly upon her frail
flesh, did not humiliate the sinner who approached her. If ever he was
impelled to cast sin from him and to repent the impulse that moved him
was the wish to be her knight. If ever his soul, reentering her dwelling
shyly after the frenzy of his body's lust had spent itself, was turned
towards her whose emblem is the morning star, *bright and musical,
telling of heaven and infusing peace,* it was when her names were murmured softly by lips whereon there still lingered foul and shameful
words, the savour itself of a lewd kiss.

That was strange. He tried to think how it could be but the dusk,
deepening in the schoolroom, covered over his thoughts. The bell
rang. The master marked the sums and cuts° to be done for the next
lesson and went out. Heron, beside Stephen, began to hum tunelessly.

My excellent friend Bombados.

Ennis, who had gone to the yard, came back, saying:
— The boy from the house is coming up for the rector.
A tall boy behind Stephen rubbed his hands and said:
— That's game ball.° We can scut° the whole hour. He won't be in
till after half two. Then you can ask him questions on the catechism,
Dedalus.

Stephen, leaning back and drawing idly on his scribbler, listened to
the talk about him which Heron checked from time to time by saying:
— Shut up, will you. Don't make such a bally racket!

It was strange too that he found an arid pleasure in following up to
the end the rigid lines of the doctrines of the church and penetrating
into obscure silences only to hear and feel the more deeply his own condemnation. The sentence of saint James which says that he who offends

---

Quasi cedrus . . . odoris: I was exalted like a cedar in Libanus [Lebanon], and as a cypress
tree in Mount Sion. I was exalted like a palm tree in Cades and as a rose plant in Jericho.
As a fair olive tree in the plains, and as a plane tree by the water in the streets was I
exalted. I gave forth a sweet smell like cinnamon and aromatic balm; I gave forth a sweet
odor like the best myrrh; from Ecclesiasticus 24, 13–15, a book of the Catholic Bible corresponding to what Protestants call the Apocrypha.   *sums and cuts:* Math problems,
generally based on Euclid.   *game ball:* Good luck.   *scut:* Skip.

against one commandment becomes guilty of all had seemed to him first a swollen phrase until he had begun to grope in the darkness of his own state. From the evil seed of lust all other deadly sins had sprung forth: pride in himself and contempt of others, covetousness in using money for the purchase of unlawful pleasure, envy of those whose vices he could not reach to and calumnious murmuring against the pious, gluttonous enjoyment of food, the dull glowering anger amid which he brooded upon his longing, the swamp of spiritual and bodily sloth in which his whole being had sunk.

As he sat in his bench gazing calmly at the rector's shrewd harsh face his mind wound itself in and out of the curious questions proposed to it. If a man had stolen a pound in his youth and had used that pound to amass a huge fortune how much was he obliged to give back, the pound he had stolen only or the pound together with the compound interest accruing upon it or all his huge fortune? If a layman in giving baptism pour the water before saying the words is the child baptised? Is baptism with a mineral water valid? How comes it that while the first beatitude promises the kingdom of heaven to the poor of heart the second beatitude° promises also to the meek that they shall possess the land? Why was the sacrament of the eucharist instituted under the two species of bread and wine if Jesus Christ be present body and blood, soul and divinity, in the bread alone and in the wine alone? Does a tiny particle of the consecrated bread contain all the body and blood of Jesus Christ or a part only of the body and blood? If the wine change into vinegar and the host crumble into corruption after they have been consecrated is Jesus Christ still present under their species as God and as man?

— Here he is! Here he is!

A boy from his post at the window had seen the rector come from the house. All the catechisms were opened and all heads bent upon them silently. The rector entered and took his seat on the dais. A gentle kick from the tall boy in the bench behind urged Stephen to ask a difficult question.

The rector did not ask for a catechism to hear the lesson from. He clasped his hands on the desk and said:

— The retreat will begin on Wednesday afternoon in honour of saint Francis Xavier whose feast day is Saturday. The retreat will go on

---

first beatitude . . . second beatitude: Being "poor in spirit" and "meek"; from the Sermon on the Mount in the Douay (Catholic) Bible version, Matthew 5.

from Wednesday to Friday. On Friday confessions will be heard all the afternoon after beads. If any boys have special confessors° perhaps it will be better for them not to change. Mass will be on Saturday morning at nine o'clock and general communion for the whole college. Saturday will be a free day. Sunday of course. But Saturday and Sunday being free days some boys might be inclined to think that Monday is a free day also. Beware of making that mistake. I think you, Lawless, are likely to make that mistake.

— I, sir? Why, sir?

A little wave of quiet mirth broke forth over the class of boys from the rector's grim smile. Stephen's heart began slowly to fold and fade with fear like a withering flower.

The rector went on gravely:

— You are all familiar with the story of the life of saint Francis Xavier, I suppose, the patron of your college. He came of an old and illustrious Spanish family and you remember that he was one of the first followers of saint Ignatius. They met in Paris where Francis Xavier was professor of philosophy at the university. This young and brilliant nobleman and man of letters entered heart and soul into the ideas of our glorious founder and you know that he, at his own desire, was sent by saint Ignatius to preach to the Indians. He is called, as you know, the apostle of the Indies. He went from country to country in the east, from Africa to India, from India to Japan, baptising the people. He is said to have baptised as many as ten thousand idolaters in one month. It is said that his right arm had grown powerless from having been raised so often over the heads of those whom he baptised. He wished then to go to China to win still more souls for God but he died of fever on the island of Sancian. A great saint, saint Francis Xavier! A great soldier of God!

The rector paused and then, shaking his clasped hands before him, went on:

— He had the faith in him that moves mountains. Ten thousand souls won for God in a single month! That is a true conqueror, true to the motto of our order: *ad majorem Dei gloriam!* A saint who has great power in heaven, remember: power to intercede for us in our grief, power to obtain whatever we pray for if it be for the good of our souls, power above all to obtain for us the grace to repent if we be in sin. A great saint, saint Francis Xavier! A great fisher of souls!

He ceased to shake his clasped hands and, resting them against his

special confessors: Priests to whom a penitent goes regularly.

forehead, looked right and left of them keenly at his listeners out of his dark stern eyes.

In the silence their dark fire kindled the dusk into a tawny glow. Stephen's heart had withered up like a flower of the desert that feels the simoom° coming from afar.

*

*   *

— *Remember only thy last things and thou shalt not sin for ever* — words taken, my dear little brothers in Christ, from the book of Ecclesiastes, seventh chapter, fortieth verse. In the name of the Father and of the Son and of the Holy Ghost. Amen.

Stephen sat in the front bench of the chapel. Father Arnall sat at a table to the left of the altar. He wore about his shoulders a heavy cloak; his pale face was drawn and his voice broken with rheum. The figure of his old master, so strangely rearisen, brought back to Stephen's mind his life at Clongowes: the wide playgrounds, swarming with boys, the square ditch, the little cemetery off the main avenue of limes where he had dreamed of being buried, the firelight on the wall of the infirmary where he lay sick, the sorrowful face of Brother Michael. His soul, as these memories came back to him, became again a child's soul.

— We are assembled here today, my dear little brothers in Christ, for one brief moment far away from the busy bustle of the outer world to celebrate and to honour one of the greatest of saints, the apostle of the Indies, the patron saint also of your college, saint Francis Xavier. Year after year for much longer than any of you, my dear little boys, can remember or than I can remember the boys of this college have met in this very chapel to make their annual retreat before the feast day of their patron saint. Time has gone on and brought with it its changes. Even in the last few years what changes can most of you not remember? Many of the boys who sat in those front benches a few short years ago are perhaps now in distant lands, in the burning tropics or immersed in professional duties or in seminaries or voyaging over the vast expanse of the deep or, it may be, already called by the great God to another life and to the rendering up of their stewardship. And still as the years roll by, bringing with them changes for good and bad, the memory of the great saint is honoured by the boys of his college who make every year their annual retreat on the days preceding the feast day set apart by our holy mother the church to transmit to all the ages the name and fame of one of the greatest sons of catholic Spain.

simoom: A hot wind, seasonal in some deserts.

— Now what is the meaning of this word *retreat* and why is it allowed on all hands to be a most salutary practice for all who desire to lead before God and in the eyes of men a truly christian life? A retreat, my dear boys, signifies a withdrawal for a while from the cares of our life, the cares of this workaday world, in order to examine the state of our conscience, to reflect on the mysteries of holy religion and to understand better why we are here in this world. During these few days I intend to put before you some thoughts concerning the four last things. They are, as you know from your catechism, death, judgment, hell and heaven. We shall try to understand them fully during these few days so that we may derive from the understanding of them a lasting benefit to our souls. And remember, my dear boys, that we have been sent into this world for one thing and for one thing alone: to do God's holy will and to save our immortal souls. All else is worthless. One thing alone is needful, the salvation of one's soul. What doth it profit a man to gain the whole world if he suffer the loss of his immortal soul? Ah, my dear boys, believe me there is nothing in this wretched world that can make up for such a loss.

— I will ask you therefore, my dear boys, to put away from your minds during these few days all worldly thoughts, whether of study or pleasure or ambition, and to give all your attention to the state of your souls. I need hardly remind you that during the days of the retreat all boys are expected to preserve a quiet and pious demeanour and to shun all loud unseemly pleasure. The elder boys, of course, will see that this custom is not infringed and I look especially to the prefects and officers of the sodality of Our Blessed Lady and of the sodality of the holy angels to set a good example to their fellowstudents.

— Let us try therefore to make this retreat in honour of saint Francis with our whole heart and our whole mind. God's blessing will then be upon all your year's studies. But, above and beyond all, let this retreat be one to which you can look back in after years when maybe you are far from this college and among very different surroundings, to which you can look back with joy and thankfulness and give thanks to God for having granted you this occasion of laying the first foundation of a pious honourable zealous christian life. And if, as may so happen, there be at this moment in these benches any poor soul which has had the unutterable misfortune to lose God's holy grace and to fall into grievous sin I fervently trust and pray that this retreat may be the turningpoint in the life of that soul. I pray to God through the merits of its zealous servant Francis Xavier that such a soul may be led to sincere repentance and that the holy communion on saint Francis' day of this year may be a lasting covenant between God and that soul. For just and unjust, for saint and sinner alike, may this retreat be a memorable one.

— Help me, my dear little brothers in Christ. Help me by your pious attention, by your own devotion, by your outward demeanour. Banish from your minds all worldly thoughts and think only of the last things, death, judgment, hell and heaven. He who remembers these things, says Ecclesiastes, shall not sin for ever. He who remembers the last things will act and think with them always before his eyes. He will live a good life and die a good death, believing and knowing that, if he has sacrificed much in this earthly life, it will be given to him a hundredfold and a thousandfold more in the life to come, in the kingdom without end — a blessing, my dear boys, which I wish you from my heart, one and all, in the name of the Father and of the Son and of the Holy Ghost. Amen.

As he walked home with silent companions a thick fog seemed to compass his mind. He waited in stupor of mind till it should lift and reveal what it had hidden. He ate his dinner with surly appetite and, when the meal was over and the greasestrewn plates lay abandoned on the table, he rose and went to the window, clearing the thick scum from his mouth with his tongue and licking it from his lips. So he had sunk to the state of a beast that licks his chaps after meat. This was the end: and a faint glimmer of fear began to pierce the fog of his mind. He pressed his face against the pane of the window and gazed out into the darkening street. Forms passed this way and that way through the dull light. And that was life. The letters of the name of Dublin lay heavily upon his mind, pushing one another surlily hither and thither with slow boorish insistence. His soul was fattening and congealing into a gross grease, plunging ever deeper in its dull fear into a sombre threatening dusk, while the body that was his stood, listless and dishonoured, gazing out of darkened eyes, helpless, perturbed and human for a bovine god to stare upon.

The next day brought death and judgment, stirring his soul slowly from its listless despair. The faint glimmer of fear became a terror of spirit as the hoarse voice of the preacher blew death into his soul. He suffered its agony. He felt the deathchill touch the extremities and creep onward towards the heart, the film of death veiling the eyes, the bright centres of the brain extinguished one by one like lamps, the last sweat oozing upon the skin, the powerlessness of the dying limbs, the speech thickening and wandering and failing, the heart throbbing faintly and more faintly, all but vanquished, the breath, the poor timid breath, the poor helpless human spirit, sobbing and sighing, gurgling and rattling in the throat. No help! No help! He, he himself, his body to which he had yielded was dying. Into the grave with it! Nail it down into a wooden box, the corpse. Carry it out of the house on the shoulders of hirelings. Thrust it out of men's sight into a long hole in the ground, into the grave, to rot, to feed the mass of its creeping worms and to be devoured by scuttling plumpbellied rats.

And while the friends were still standing in tears by the bedside the soul of the sinner was judged. At the last moment of consciousness the whole earthly life passed before the vision of the soul and, ere it had time to reflect, the body had died and the soul stood terrified before the judgmentseat. God, who had long been merciful, would then be just. He had long been patient, pleading with the sinful soul, giving it time to repent, sparing it yet awhile. But that time had gone. Time was to sin and to enjoy, time was to scoff at God and at the warnings of His holy church, time was to defy His majesty, to disobey His commands, to hoodwink one's fellow men, to commit sin after sin and sin after sin and to hide one's corruption from the sight of men. But that time was over. Now it was God's turn: and He was not to be hoodwinked or deceived. Every sin would then come forth from its lurkingplace, the most rebellious against the divine will and the most degrading to our poor corrupt nature, the tiniest imperfection and the most heinous atrocity. What did it avail then to have been a great emperor, a great general, a marvellous inventor, the most learned of the learned? All were as one before the judgmentseat of God. He would reward the good and punish the wicked. One single instant was enough for the trial of a man's soul. One single instant after the body's death, the soul had been weighed in the balance. The particular judgment was over and the soul had passed to the abode of bliss or to the prison of purgatory or had been hurled howling into hell.

Nor was that all. God's justice had still to be vindicated before men: after the particular there still remained the general judgment. The last day had come. Doomsday was at hand. The stars of heaven were falling upon the earth like the figs cast by the figtree which the wind has shaken. The sun, the great luminary of the universe, had become as sackcloth of hair. The moon was bloodred. The firmament was as a scroll rolled away. The archangel Michael, the prince of the heavenly host, appeared glorious and terrible against the sky. With one foot on the sea and one foot on the land he blew from the archangelical trumpet the brazen death of time. The three blasts of the angel filled all the universe. Time is, time was but time shall be no more. At the last blast the souls of universal humanity throng towards the valley of Jehoshaphat, rich and poor, gentle and simple, wise and foolish, good and wicked. The soul of every human being that has ever existed, the souls of all those who shall yet be born, all the sons and daughters of Adam, all are assembled on that supreme day. And lo the supreme judge is coming! No longer the lowly Lamb of God, no longer the meek Jesus of Nazareth, no longer the Man of Sorrows, no longer the Good Shepherd, He is seen now coming upon the clouds, in great power and majesty, attended by nine choirs of angels, angels and archangels, principalities, powers and virtues, thrones and dominations, cherubim and seraphim, God Omnipotent, God Everlasting. He speaks: and His voice is heard even at the farthest limits of space, even in the bottomless abyss. Supreme Judge, from His sentence there will be and can be no appeal. He calls the just to His side, bidding them enter into the kingdom, the eternity of bliss, prepared for them. The unjust He casts from Him, crying in His offended majesty: *Depart from me, ye cursed, into everlasting fire which was prepared for the devil and his angels.* O what agony then for the miserable sinners! Friend is torn apart from friend, children are torn from their parents, husbands from their wives. The poor sinner holds out his arms to those who were dear and near to him in this earthly world, to those whose simple piety perhaps he made a mock of, to those who counselled him and tried to lead him on the right path, to a kind brother, to a loving sister, to the mother and father who loved him so dearly. But it is too late: the just turn away from the wretched damned souls which now appear before the eyes of all in their hideous and evil character. O you hypocrites, O you whited sepulchres, O you who present a smooth smiling face to the world while your soul within is a foul swamp of sin, how will it fare with you in that terrible day?

And this day will come, shall come, must come; the day of death and the day of judgment. It is appointed unto man to die and after death the judgment. Death is certain. The time and manner are uncertain, whether from long disease or from some unexpected accident: the Son of God cometh at an hour when you little expect Him. Be therefore ready every moment, seeing that you may die at any moment. Death is the end of us all. Death and judgment, brought into the world by the sin of our first parents, are the dark portals that close our earthly existence, the portals that open into the unknown and the unseen, portals through which every soul must pass, alone, unaided save by its good works, without friend or brother or parent or master to help it, alone and trembling. Let that thought be ever before our minds and then we cannot sin. Death, a cause of terror to the sinner, is a blessed moment for him who has walked in the right path, fulfilling the duties of his station in life, attending to his morning and evening prayers, approaching the holy sacrament frequently and performing good and merciful works. For the pious and believing catholic, for the just man, death is no cause of terror. Was it not Addison, the great English writer, who, when on his deathbed, sent for the wicked young earl of Warwick to let him see how a christian can meet his end. He it is and he alone, the pious and believing christian, who can say in his heart:

> O grave, where is thy victory?
> O death, where is thy sting?°

Every word of it was for him. Against his sin, foul and secret, the whole wrath of God was aimed. The preacher's knife had probed deeply into his diseased conscience and he felt now that his soul was festering in sin. Yes, the preacher was right. God's turn had come. Like a beast in its lair his soul had lain down in its own filth but the blasts of the angel's trumpet had driven him forth from the darkness of sin into the light. The words of doom cried by the angel shattered in an instant his presumptuous peace. The wind of the last day blew through his mind; his sins, the jeweleyed harlots of his imagination, fled before the hurricane, squeaking like mice in their terror and huddled under a mane of hair.

As he crossed the square, walking homeward, the light laughter of a girl reached his burning ears. The frail gay sound smote his heart more strongly than a trumpetblast, and, not daring to lift his eyes, he turned aside and gazed, as he walked, into the shadows of the tangled shrubs. Shame rose from his smitten heart and flooded his whole being. The image of Emma appeared before him and, under her eyes, the flood of shame rushed forth anew from his heart. If she knew to what his mind had subjected her or how his brutelike lust had torn and trampled upon her innocence! Was that boyish love? Was that chivalry? Was that poetry? The sordid details of his orgies stank under his very nostrils: the sootcoated packet of pictures which he had hidden in the flue of the fireplace and in the presence of whose shameless or bashful wantonness he lay for hours sinning in thought and deed: his monstrous dreams, peopled by apelike creatures and by harlots with gleaming jewel eyes: the foul long letters he had written in the joy of guilty confession and carried secretly for days and days only to throw them under cover of night among the grass in the corner of a field or beneath some hingeless

---

O grave, where is thy victory . . . sting: Adapted by Alexander Pope from I Corinthians 15:55 in his poem "The Dying Christian to His Soul." Joseph Addison (1672–1719) supposedly sent for his stepson on his own deathbed and said to him, "See in what peace a Christian can die."

door or in some niche in the hedges where a girl might come upon them as she walked by and read them secretly. Mad! Mad! Was it possible he had done these things? A cold sweat broke out upon his forehead as the foul memories condensed within his brain.

When the agony of shame had passed from him he tried to raise his soul from its abject powerlessness. God and the Blessed Virgin were too far from him: God was too great and stern and the Blessed Virgin too pure and holy. But he imagined that he stood near Emma in a wide land and, humbly and in tears, bent and kissed the elbow of her sleeve.

In a wide land under a tender lucid evening sky, a cloud drifting westward amid a pale green sea of heaven, they stood together, children that had erred. Their error had offended deeply God's majesty though it was the error of two children, but it had not offended her whose beauty *is not like earthly beauty, dangerous to look upon, but like the morning star which is its emblem, bright and musical.* The eyes were not offended which she turned upon them nor reproachful. She placed their hands together, hand in hand, and said, speaking to their hearts:

— Take hands, Stephen and Emma. It is a beautiful evening now in heaven. You have erred but you are always my children. It is one heart that loves another heart. Take hands together, my dear children, and you will be happy together and your hearts will love each other.

The chapel was flooded by the dull scarlet light that filtered through the lowered blinds; and through the fissure between the last blind and the sash a shaft of wan light entered like a spear and touched the embossed brasses of the candlesticks upon the altar that gleamed like the battleworn mail armour of angels.

Rain was falling on the chapel, on the garden, on the college. It would rain for ever, noiselessly. The water would rise inch by inch, covering the grass and shrubs, covering the trees and houses, covering the monuments and the mountain tops. All life would be choked off, noiselessly: birds, men, elephants, pigs, children: noiselessly floating corpses amid the litter of the wreckage of the world. Forty days and forty nights the rain would fall till the waters had covered the face of the earth.

It might be. Why not?

— *Hell has enlarged its soul and opened its mouth without any limits* — words taken, my dear little brothers in Christ Jesus, from the book of Isaias, fifth chapter, fourteenth verse. In the name of the Father and of the Son and of the Holy Ghost. Amen.

The preacher took a chainless watch from a pocket within his soutane and, having considered its dial for a moment in silence, placed it silently before him on the table.

He began to speak in a quiet tone.

— Adam and Eve, my dear boys, were, as you know, our first parents and you will remember that they were created by God in order that the seats in heaven left vacant by the fall of Lucifer and his rebellious angels might be filled again. Lucifer, we are told, was a son of the morning, a radiant and mighty angel; yet he fell: he fell and there fell with him a third part of the host of heaven: he fell and was hurled with his rebellious angels into hell. What his sin was we cannot say. Theologians consider that it was the sin of pride, the sinful thought conceived in an instant: *non serviam:*° *I will not serve.* That instant was his ruin. He offended the majesty of God by the sinful thought of one instant and God cast him out of heaven into hell for ever.

— Adam and Eve were then created by God and placed in Eden, in the plain of Damascus, that lovely garden resplendent with sunlight and colour, teeming with luxuriant vegetation. The fruitful earth gave them her bounty: beasts and birds were their willing servants: they knew not the ills our flesh is heir to, disease and poverty and death: all that a great and generous God could do for them was done. But there was one condition imposed on them by God: obedience to His word. They were not to eat of the fruit of the forbidden tree.

— Alas, my dear little boys, they too fell. The devil, once a shining angel, a son of the morning, now a foul fiend, came to them in the shape of a serpent, the subtlest of all the beasts of the field. He envied them. He, the fallen great one, could not bear to think that man, a being of clay, should possess the inheritance which he by his sin had forfeited for ever. He came to the woman, the weaker vessel, and poured the poison of his eloquence into her ear, promising her — O, the blasphemy of that promise! — that if she and Adam ate of the forbidden fruit they would become as gods, nay as God Himself. Eve yielded to the wiles of the archtempter. She ate the apple and gave it also to Adam who had not the moral courage to resist her. The poison tongue of Satan had done its work. They fell.

— And then the voice of God was heard in that garden, calling His creature man to account: and Michael, prince of the heavenly host, with a sword of flame in his hand appeared before the guilty pair and drove them forth from Eden into the world, the world of sickness and striving, of cruelty and disappointment, of labour and hardship, to earn their bread in the sweat of their brow. But even then how merciful was

---

non serviam: Satan's defiant statement.

God! He took pity on our poor degraded first parents and promised that in the fulness of time He would send down from heaven One who would redeem them, make them once more children of God and heirs to the kingdom of heaven: and that One, that Redeemer of fallen man, was to be God's onlybegotten Son, the Second Person of the Most Blessed Trinity, the Eternal Word.

— He came. He was born of a virgin pure, Mary the virgin mother. He was born in a poor cowhouse in Judea and lived as a humble carpenter for thirty years until the hour of His mission had come. And then, filled with love for men, He went forth and called to men to hear the new gospel.

— Did they listen? Yes, they listened but would not hear. He was seized and bound like a common criminal, mocked at as a fool, set aside to give place to a public robber, scourged with five thousand lashes, crowned with a crown of thorns, hustled through the streets by the jewish rabble and the Roman soldiery, stripped of His garments and hanged upon a gibbet and His side was pierced with a lance and from the wounded body of Our Lord water and blood issued continually.

— Yet even then, in that hour of supreme agony, Our Merciful Redeemer had pity for mankind. Yet even there, on the hill of Calvary, He founded the holy catholic church against which, it is promised, the gates of hell shall not prevail. He founded it upon the rock of ages and endowed it with His grace, with sacraments and sacrifice, and promised that if men would obey the word of His church they would still enter into eternal life but if, after all that had been done for them, they still persisted in their wickedness there remained for them an eternity of torment: hell.

The preacher's voice sank. He paused, joined his palms for an instant, parted them. Then he resumed:

— Now let us try for a moment to realise, as far as we can, the nature of that abode of the damned which the justice of an offended God has called into existence for the eternal punishment of sinners. Hell is a strait and dark and foulsmelling prison, an abode of demons and lost souls, filled with fire and smoke. The straitness of this prison-house is expressly designed by God to punish those who refused to be bound by His laws. In earthly prisons the poor captive has at least some liberty of movement, were it only within the four walls of his cell or in the gloomy yard of his prison. Not so in hell. There, by reason of the great number of the damned, the prisoners are heaped together in their awful prison, the walls of which are said to be four thousand miles thick: and the damned are so utterly bound and helpless that, as a blessed saint, saint Anselm, writes in his book on similitudes, they are not even able to remove from the eye a worm that gnaws it.

— They lie in exterior darkness. For, remember, the fire of hell gives forth no light. As, at the command of God, the fire of the Babylonian furnace lost its heat but not its light so, at the command of God, the fire of hell, while retaining the intensity of its heat, burns eternally in darkness. It is a neverending storm of darkness, dark flames and dark smoke of burning brimstone, amid which the bodies are heaped one upon another without even a glimpse of air. Of all the plagues with which the land of the Pharaohs was smitten one plague alone, that of darkness, was called horrible. What name, then, shall we give to the darkness of hell which is to last not for three days alone but for all eternity?

— The horror of this strait and dark prison is increased by its awful stench. All the filth of the world, all the offal and scum of the world, we are told, shall run there as to a vast reeking sewer when the terrible conflagration of the last day has purged the world. The brimstone too which burns there in such prodigious quantity fills all hell with its intolerable stench; and the bodies of the damned themselves exhale such a pestilential odour that as saint Bonaventure says, one of them alone would suffice to infect the whole world. The very air of this world, that pure element, becomes foul and unbreathable when it has been long enclosed. Consider then what must be the foulness of the air of hell. Imagine some foul and putrid corpse that has lain rotting and decomposing in the grave, a jellylike mass of liquid corruption. Imagine such a corpse a prey to flames, devoured by the fire of burning brimstone and giving off dense choking fumes of nauseous loathsome decomposition. And then imagine this sickening stench multiplied a millionfold and a millionfold again from the millions upon millions of fetid carcasses massed together in the reeking darkness, a huge and rotting human fungus. Imagine all this and you will have some idea of the horror of the stench of hell.

— But this stench is not, horrible though it is, the greatest physical torment to which the damned are subjected. The torment of fire is the greatest torment to which the tyrant has ever subjected his fellowcreatures. Place your finger for a moment in the flame of a candle and you will feel the pain of fire. But our earthly fire was created by God for the benefit of man, to maintain in him the spark of life and to help him in the useful arts whereas the fire of hell is of another quality and was created by God to torture and punish the unrepentant sinner. Our earthly fire also consumes more or less rapidly according as the object which it attacks is more or less combustible so that human ingenuity has even succeeded in inventing chemical preparations to check or frustrate its action. But the sulphurous brimstone which burns in hell is a substance which is specially designed to burn for ever and for ever with unspeakable fury. Moreover our earthly fire destroys at the same time as it burns so that the more intense it is the shorter is its duration: but the fire of hell has this property that it preserves that which it burns and though it rages with incredible intensity it rages for ever.

— Our earthly fire again, no matter how fierce or widespread it may be, is always of a limited extent: but the lake of fire in hell is boundless, shoreless and bottomless. It is on record that the devil himself, when asked the question by a certain soldier, was obliged to confess that if a whole mountain were thrown into the burning ocean of hell it would be burned up in an instant like a piece of wax. And this terrible fire will not afflict the bodies of the damned only from without but each lost soul will be a hell unto itself, the boundless fire raging in its very vitals. O, how terrible is the lot of those wretched beings! The blood seethes and boils in the veins, the brains are boiling in the skull, the heart in the breast glowing and bursting, the bowels a redhot mass of burning pulp, the tender eyes flaming like molten balls.

— And yet what I have said as to the strength and quality and boundlessness of this fire is as nothing when compared to its intensity, an intensity which it has as being the instrument chosen by divine design for the punishment of soul and body alike. It is a fire which proceeds directly from the ire of God, working not of its own activity but as an instrument of divine vengeance. As the waters of baptism cleanse the soul with the body so do the fires of punishment torture the spirit with the flesh. Every sense of the flesh is tortured and every faculty of the soul therewith: the eyes with impenetrable utter darkness, the nose with noisome odours, the ears with yells and howls and execrations, the taste with foul matter, leprous corruption, nameless suffocating filth, the touch with redhot goads and spikes, with cruel tongues of flame. And through the several torments of the senses the immortal soul is tortured eternally in its very essence amid the leagues upon leagues of glowing fires kindled in the abyss by the offended majesty of the Omnipotent God and fanned into everlasting and ever increasing fury by the breath of the anger of the Godhead.

— Consider finally that the torment of this infernal prison is increased by the company of the damned themselves. Evil company on earth is so noxious that even the plants, as if by instinct, withdraw from the company of whatsoever is deadly or hurtful to them. In hell all laws are overturned: there is no thought of family or country, of ties or relationships.

The damned howl and scream at one another, their torture and rage intensified by the presence of beings tortured and raging like themselves. All sense of humanity is forgotten. The yells of the suffering sinners fill the remotest corners of the vast abyss. The mouths of the damned are full of blasphemies against God and of hatred for their fellowsufferers and of curses against those souls which were their accomplices in sin. In olden times it was the custom to punish the parricide, the man who had raised his murderous hand against his father, by casting him into the depths of the sea in a sack in which were placed a cock, a monkey and a serpent. The intention of those lawgivers who framed such a law, which seems cruel in our times, was to punish the criminal by the company of hateful and hurtful beasts. But what is the fury of those dumb beasts compared with the fury of execration which bursts from the parched lips and aching throats of the damned in hell when they behold in their companions in misery those who aided and abetted them in sin, those whose words sowed the first seeds of evil thinking and evil living in their minds, those whose immodest suggestions led them on to sin, those whose eyes tempted and allured them from the path of virtue. They turn upon those accomplices and upbraid them and curse them. But they are helpless and hopeless: it is too late now for repentance.

— Last of all consider the frightful torment to those damned souls, tempters and tempted alike, of the company of the devils. These devils will afflict the damned in two ways, by their presence and by their reproaches. We can have no idea of how horrible these devils are. Saint Catherine of Siena once saw a devil and she has written that, rather than look again for one single instant on such a frightful monster, she would prefer to walk until the end of her life along a track of red coals. These devils, who were once beautiful angels, have become as hideous and ugly as they once were beautiful. They mock and jeer at the lost souls whom they dragged down to ruin. It is they, the foul demons, who are made in hell the voices of conscience. Why did you sin? Why did you lend an ear to the temptings of fiends? Why did you turn aside from your pious practices and good works? Why did you not shun the occasions of sin? Why did you not leave that evil companion? Why did you not give up that lewd habit, that impure habit? Why did you not listen to the counsels of your confessor? Why did you not, even after you had fallen the first or the second or the third or the fourth or the hundredth time, repent of your evil ways and turn to God who only waited for your repentance to absolve you of your sins? Now the time for repentance has gone by. Time is, time was but time shall be no more! Time was to sin in secrecy, to indulge in that sloth and pride, to covet the unlawful, to yield to the promptings of your lower nature, to live like the beasts of the field, nay worse than the beasts of the field for they, at least, are but brutes and have not reason to guide them: time was but time shall be no more. God spoke to you by so many voices but you would not hear. You would not crush out that pride and anger in your heart, you would not restore those illgotten goods, you would not obey the precepts of your holy church nor attend to your religious duties, you would not abandon those wicked companions, you would not avoid those dangerous temptations. Such is the language of those fiendish tormentors, words of taunting and of reproach, of hatred and of disgust. Of disgust, yes! For even they, the very devils, when they sinned sinned by such a sin as alone was compatible with such angelical natures, a rebellion of the intellect: and they, even they, the foul devils must turn away, revolted and disgusted, from the contemplation of those unspeakable sins by which degraded man outrages and defiles the temple of the Holy Ghost, defiles and pollutes himself.

— O, my dear little brothers in Christ, may it never be our lot to hear that language! May it never be our lot, I say! In the last day of terrible reckoning I pray fervently to God that not a single soul of those who are in this chapel today may be found among those miserable beings whom the Great Judge shall command to depart for ever from His sight, that not one of us may ever hear ringing in his ears the awful sentence of rejection: *Depart from me, ye cursed, into everlasting fire which was prepared for the devil and his angels!*

He came down the aisle of the chapel, his legs shaking and the scalp of his head trembling as though it had been touched by ghostly fingers. He passed up the staircase and into the corridor along the walls of which the overcoats and waterproofs hung like gibbeted malefactors, headless and dripping and shapeless. And at every step he feared that he had already died, that his soul had been wrenched forth of the sheath of his body, that he was plunging headlong through space.

He could not grip the floor with his feet and sat heavily at his desk, opening one of his books at random and poring over it. Every word for him! It was true. God was almighty. God could call him now, call him as he sat at his desk, before he had time to be conscious of the summons. God had called him. Yes? What? Yes? His flesh shrank together as it felt the approach of the ravenous tongues of flames, dried up as it felt about it the swirl of stifling air. He had died. Yes. He was judged. A wave of fire swept through his body: the first. Again a wave. His brain began to glow. Another. His brain was simmering and bubbling within the cracking tenement of the skull. Flames burst forth from his skull like a corolla, shrieking like voices:

— Hell! Hell! Hell! Hell! Hell!

Voices spoke near him:

— On hell.

— I suppose he rubbed it into you well.

— You bet he did. He put us all into a blue funk.°

— That's what you fellows want: and plenty of it to make you work.

He leaned back weakly in his desk. He had not died. God had spared him still. He was still in the familiar world of the school. Mr Tate and Vincent Heron stood at the window, talking, jesting, gazing out at the bleak rain, moving their heads.

— I wish it would clear up. I had arranged to go for a spin on the bike with some fellows out by Malahide. But the roads must be kneedeep.

— It might clear up, sir.

The voices that he knew so well, the common words, the quiet of the classroom when the voices paused and the silence was filled by the sound of softly browsing cattle as the other boys munched their lunches tranquilly, lulled his aching soul.

There was still time. O Mary, refuge of sinners, intercede for him! O Virgin Undefiled, save him from the gulf of death!

The English lesson began with the hearing of the history. Royal persons, favourites, intriguers, bishops passed like mute phantoms behind their veil of names. All had died: all had been judged. What did it profit a man to gain the whole world if he lost his soul? At last he had understood: and human life lay around him, a plain of peace whereon ant-like men laboured in brotherhood, their dead sleeping under quiet mounds. The elbow of his companion touched him and his heart was touched: and when he spoke to answer a question of his master he heard his own voice full of the quietude of humility and contrition.

His soul sank back deeper into depths of contrite peace, no longer able to suffer the pain of dread, and sending forth, as she sank, a faint prayer. Ah yes, he would still be spared; he would repent in his heart and be forgiven: and then those above, those in heaven, would see what he would do to make up for the past: a whole life, every hour of life. Only wait.

— All, God! All, all!

A messenger came to the door to say that confessions were being

blue funk: Extreme depression and fear.

heard in the chapel. Four boys left the room; and he heard others passing down the corridor. A tremulous chill blew round his heart, no
stronger than a little wind, and yet, listening and suffering silently, he
seemed to have laid an ear against the muscle of his own heart, feeling it
close and quail, listening to the flutter of its ventricles.

No escape. He had to confess, to speak out in words what he had
done and thought, sin after sin. How? How?

— Father, I . . .

The thought slid like a cold shining rapier into his tender flesh: confession. But not there in the chapel of the college. He would confess all,
every sin of deed and thought, sincerely: but not there among his
school companions. Far away from there in some dark place he would
murmur out his own shame: and he besought God humbly not to be
offended with him if he did not dare to confess in the college chapel:
and in utter abjection of spirit he craved forgiveness mutely of the boyish hearts about him.

Time passed.

He sat again in the front bench of the chapel. The daylight without
was already failing and, as it fell slowly through the dull red blinds, it
seemed that the sun of the last day was going down and that all souls
were being gathered for the judgment.

— *I am cast away from the sight of Thine eyes:* words taken, my dear
little brothers in Christ, from the Book of Psalms, thirtieth chapter,
twentythird verse. In the name of the Father and of the Son and of the
Holy Ghost. Amen.

The preacher began to speak in a quiet friendly tone. His face was
kind and he joined gently the fingers of each hand, forming a frail cage
by the union of their tips.

— This morning we endeavoured, in our reflection upon hell, to
make what our holy founder calls in his book of spiritual exercises,
the composition of place.° We endeavoured, that is, to imagine with the
senses of the mind, in our imagination, the material character of that
awful place and of the physical torments which all who are in hell
endure. This evening we shall consider for a few moments the nature of
the spiritual torments of hell.

— Sin, remember, is a twofold enormity. It is a base consent to the
promptings of our corrupt nature to the lower instincts, to that which is
gross and beastlike; and it is also a turning away from the counsel of our

---

composition of place: St. Ignatius of Loyola suggests meditating on a physical, "corporeal" location as a means toward seeing a spiritual truth.

higher nature, from all that is pure and holy, from the Holy God Him-self. For this reason mortal sin is punished in hell by two different forms of punishment, physical and spiritual.

— Now of all these spiritual pains by far the greatest is the pain of loss, so great, in fact, that in itself it is a torment greater than all the oth-ers. Saint Thomas,° the greatest doctor of the church, the angelic doc-tor, as he is called, says that the worst damnation consists in this that the understanding of man is totally deprived of divine light and his affec-tion obstinately turned away from the goodness of God. God, remem-ber, is a being infinitely good and therefore the loss of such a being must be a loss infinitely painful. In this life we have not a very clear idea of what such a loss must be but the damned in hell, for their greater tor-ment, have a full understanding of that which they have lost and under-stand that they have lost it through their own sins and have lost it for ever. At the very instant of death the bonds of the flesh are broken asun-der and the soul at once flies towards God. The soul tends towards God as towards the centre of her existence. Remember, my dear little boys, our souls long to be with God. We come from God, we live by God, we belong to God: we are His, inalienably His. God loves with a divine love every human soul and every human soul lives in that love. How could it be otherwise? Every breath that we draw, every thought of our brain, every instant of life proceed from God's inexhaustible goodness. And if it be pain for a mother to be parted from her child, for a man to be exiled from hearth and home, for friend to be sundered from friend, O think what pain, what anguish, it must be for the poor soul to be spurned from the presence of the supremely good and loving Creator Who has called that soul into existence from nothingness and sustained it in life and loved it with an immeasurable love. This, then, to be sepa-rated for ever from its greatest good, from God, and to feel the anguish of that separation, knowing full well that it is unchangeable, this is the greatest torment which the created soul is capable of bearing, *pœna damni,*° the pain of loss.

— The second pain which will afflict the souls of the damned in hell is the pain of conscience. Just as in dead bodies worms are engendered by putrefaction so in the souls of the lost there arises a perpetual re-morse from the putrefaction of sin, the sting of conscience, the worm, as Pope Innocent the Third calls it, of the triple sting. The first sting inflicted by this cruel worm will be the memory of past pleasures. O

Saint Thomas: St. Thomas Aquinas (1225–1274), medieval theologian.   *pœna damni:* Torment of the damned (removal from God's sight).

what a dreadful memory will that be! In the lake of alldevouring flame
the proud king will remember the pomps of his court, the wise but
wicked man his libraries and instruments of research, the lover of artistic pleasures his marbles and pictures and other art treasures, he who
delighted in the pleasures of the table his gorgeous feasts, his dishes
prepared with such delicacy, his choice wines; the miser will remember
his hoard of gold, the robber his illgotten wealth, the angry and re-
vengeful and merciless murderers their deeds of blood and violence in
which they revelled, the impure and adulterous the unspeakable and
filthy pleasures in which they delighted. They will remember all this and
loathe themselves and their sins. For how miserable will all those pleasures seem to the soul condemned to suffer in hellfire for ages and ages.
How they will rage and fume to think that they have lost the bliss of
heaven for the dross of earth, for a few pieces of metal, for vain hon-
ours, for bodily comforts, for a tingling of the nerves. They will repent
indeed: and this is the second sting of the worm of conscience, a late
and fruitless sorrow for sins committed. Divine justice insists that the
understanding of those miserable wretches be fixed continually on the
sins of which they were guilty and, moreover, as saint Augustine points
out, God will impart to them His own knowledge of sin so that sin will
appear to them in ail its hideous malice as it appears to the eyes of God
Himself. They will behold their sins in ail their foulness and repent but
it will be too late and then they will bewail the good occasions which
they neglected. This is the last and deepest and most cruel sting of the
worm of conscience. The conscience will say: You had time and opportunity to repent and would not. You were brought up religiously by
your parents. You had the sacraments and graces and indulgences of the
church to aid you. You had the minister of God to preach to you, to call
you back when you had strayed, to forgive you your sins, no matter
how many, how abominable, if only you had confessed and repented.
No. You would not. You flouted the ministers of holy religion, you
turned your back on the confessional, you wallowed deeper and deeper
in the mire of sin. God appealed to you, threatened you, entreated you
to return to Him. O what shame, what misery! The Ruler of the universe entreated you, a creature of clay, to love Him Who made you and
to keep His law. No. You would not. And now, though you were to
flood all hell with your tears if you could still weep, all that sea of repentance would not gain for you what a single tear of true repentance shed
during your mortal life would have gained for you. You implore now a
moment of earthly life wherein to repent: in vain. That time is gone:
gone for ever.

— Such is the threefold sting of conscience, the viper which gnaws the very heart's core of the wretches in hell so that filled with hellish fury they curse themselves for their folly and curse the evil companions who have brought them to such ruin and curse the devils who tempted them in life and now mock them and torture them in eternity and even revile and curse the Supreme Being Whose goodness and patience they scorned and slighted but Whose justice and power they cannot evade.

— The next spiritual pain to which the damned are subjected is the pain of extension. Man, in this earthly life, though he be capable of many evils, is not capable of them all at once inasmuch as one evil corrects and counteracts another just as one poison frequently corrects another. In hell on the contrary one torment, instead of counteracting another, lends it still greater force: and moreover as the internal faculties are more perfect than the external senses so are they more capable of suffering. Just as every sense is afflicted with a fitting torment so is every spiritual faculty; the fancy with horrible images, the sensitive faculty with alternate longing and rage, the mind and understanding with an interior darkness more terrible even than the exterior darkness which reigns in that dreadful prison. The malice, impotent though it be, which possesses these demon souls is an evil of boundless extension, of limitless duration, a frightful state of wickedness which we can scarcely realise unless we bear in mind the enormity of sin and the hatred God bears to it.

— Opposed to this pain of extension and yet coexistent with it we have the pain of intensity. Hell is the centre of evils and, as you know, things are more intense at their centres than at their remotest points. There are no contraries or admixtures of any kind to temper or sotten in the least the pains of hell. Nay, things which are good in themselves become evil in hell. Company, elsewhere a source of comfort to the afflicted, will be there a continual torment: knowledge, so much longed for as the chief good of the intellect, will there be hatred worse than ignorance: light, so much coveted by all creatures from the lord of creation down to the humblest plant in the forest, will be loathed intensely. In this life our sorrows are either not very long or not very great because nature either overcomes them by habits or puts an end to them by sinking under their weight. But in hell the torments cannot be overcome by habit. For while they are of terrible intensity they are at the same time of continual variety, each pain, so to speak, taking fire from another and reendowing that which has enkindled it with a still fiercer flame. Nor can nature escape from these intense and various tortures by succumbing to them for the soul in hell is sustained and maintained in

evil so that its suffering may be the greater. Boundless extension of torment, incredible intensity of suffering, unceasing variety of torture —
this is what the divine majesty, so outraged by sinners, demands, this is
what the holiness of heaven, slighted and set aside for the lustful and
low pleasures of the corrupt flesh, requires, this is what the blood of the
innocent Lamb of God, shed for the redemption of sinners, trampled
upon by the vilest of the vile, insists upon.

— Last and crowning torture of all the tortures of that awful place
is the eternity of hell. Eternity! O, dread and dire word. Eternity! What
mind of man can understand it? And, remember, it is an eternity of
pain. Even though the pains of hell were not so terrible as they are yet
they would become infinite as they are destined to last for ever. But
while they are everlasting they are at the same time, as you know, intol-
erably intense, unbearably extensive. To bear even the sting of an insect
for all eternity would be a dreadful torment. What must it be, then, to
bear the manifold tortures of hell for ever! For ever! For all eternity!
Not for a year or for an age but for ever. Try to imagine the awful meaning of this. You have often seen the sand on the seashore. How fine are
its tiny grains! And how many of those tiny little grains go to make up
the small handful which a child grasps in its play. Now imagine a mountain of that sand, a million miles high, reaching from the earth to the
farthest heavens, and a million miles broad, extending to remotest
space, and a million miles in thickness: and imagine such an enormous
mass of countless particles of sand multiplied as often as there are leaves
in the forest, drops of water in the mighty ocean, feathers on birds,
scales on fish, hairs on animals, atoms in the vast expanse of the air: and
imagine that at the end of every million years a little bird came to that
mountain and carried away in its beak a tiny grain of that sand. How
many millions upon millions of centuries would pass before that bird
had carried away even a square foot of that mountain, how many eons
upon eons of ages before it had carried away all. Yet at the end of that
immense stretch of time not even one instant of eternity could be said
to have ended. At the end of all those billions and trillions of years eternity would have scarcely begun. And if that mountain rose again after it
had been all carried away and if the bird came again and carried it all
away again grain by grain: and if it so rose and sank as many times as
there are stars in the sky, atoms in the air, drops of water in the sea,
leaves on the trees, feathers upon birds, scales upon fish, hairs upon animals, at the end of all those innumerable risings and sinkings of that
immeasurably vast mountain not one single instant of eternity could be
said to have ended: even then, at the end of such a period, after that eon

of time the mere thought of which makes our very brain reel dizzily, eternity would have scarcely begun.

— A holy saint (one of our own fathers I believe it was) was once vouchsafed a vision of hell. It seemed to him that he stood in the midst of a great hall, dark and silent save for the ticking of a great clock. The ticking went on unceasingly; and it seemed to this saint that the sound of the ticking was the ceaseless repetition of the words: ever, never: ever, never. Ever to be in hell, never to be in heaven; ever to be shut off from the presence of God, never to enjoy the beatific vision; ever to be eaten with flames, gnawed by vermin, goaded with burning spikes, never to be free from those pains; ever to have the conscience upbraid one, the memory enrage, the mind filled with darkness and despair, never to escape; ever to curse and revile the foul demons who gloat fiendishly over the misery of their dupes, never to behold the shining raiment of the blessed spirits; ever to cry out of the abyss of fire to God for an instant, a single instant, of respite from such awful agony, never to receive, even for an instant, God's pardon; ever to suffer, never to enjoy; ever to be damned, never to be saved; ever, never; ever, never. O what a dreadful punishment! An eternity of endless agony, of endless bodily and spiritual torment, without one ray of hope, without one moment of cessation, of agony limitless in extent, limitless in intensity, of torment infinitely lasting, infinitely varied, of torture that sustains eternally that which it eternally devours, of anguish that everlastingly preys upon the spirit while it racks the flesh, an eternity, every instant of which is itself an eternity, and that eternity an eternity of woe. Such is the terrible punishment decreed for those who die in mortal sin by an almighty and a just God.

— Yes, a just God! Men, reasoning always as men, are astonished that God should mete out an everlasting and infinite punishment in the fires of hell for a single grievous sin. They reason thus because, blinded by the gross illusion of the flesh and the darkness of human understanding, they are unable to comprehend the hideous malice of mortal sin. They reason thus because they are unable to comprehend that even venial sin° is of such a foul and hideous nature that even if the omnipotent Creator could end all the evil and misery in the world, the wars, the diseases, the robberies, the crimes, the deaths, the murders, on condition that He allowed a single venial sin to pass unpunished, a single venial sin, a lie, an angry look, a moment of wilful sloth, He, the great

---

mortal sin ... venial sin: Mortal sin is soul-destroying, while venial sin merely damages the soul.

omnipotent God, could not do so because sin, be it in thought or deed, is a transgression of His law and God would not be God if He did not punish the transgressor.

— A sin, an instant of rebellious pride of the intellect, made Lucifer and a third part of the cohorts of angels fall from their glory. A sin, an instant of folly and weakness, drove Adam and Eve out of Eden and brought death and suffering into the world. To retrieve the consequences of that sin the onlybegotten Son of God came down to earth, lived and suffered and died a most painful death, hanging for three hours on the cross.

— O, my dear little brethren in Christ Jesus, will we then offend that good Redeemer and provoke His anger? Will we trample again upon that torn and mangled corpse? Will we spit upon that face so full of sorrow and love? Will we too, like the cruel jews and the brutal soldiers, mock that gentle and compassionate Saviour Who trod alone for our sake the awful winepress of sorrow? Every word of sin is a wound in His tender side. Every sinful act is a thorn piercing His head. Every impure thought, deliberately yielded to, is a keen lance transfixing that sacred and loving heart. No, no. It is impossible for any human being to do that which offends so deeply the divine majesty, that which is punished by an eternity of agony, that which crucifies again the Son of God and makes a mockery of Him.

— I pray to God that my poor words may have availed today to confirm in holiness those who are in a state of grace, to strengthen the wavering, to lead back to the state of grace the poor soul that has strayed if any such be among you. I pray to God, and do you pray with me, that we may repent of our sins. I will ask you now, all of you, to repeat after me the act of contrition,° kneeling here in this humble chapel in the presence of God. He is there in the tabernacle, burning with love for mankind, ready to comfort the afflicted. Be not afraid. No matter how many or how foul the sins if only you repent of them they will be forgiven you. Let no worldly shame hold you back. God is still the merciful Lord Who wishes not the eternal death of the sinner but rather that he be converted and live.

— He calls you to Him. You are His. He made you out of nothing. He loved you as only a God can love. His arms are open to receive you even though you have sinned against Him. Come to Him, poor sinner, poor vain and erring sinner. Now is the acceptable time. Now is the hour.

act of contrition: Formal prayer expressing remorse.

The priest rose and, turning towards the altar, knelt upon the step before the tabernacle in the fallen gloom. He waited till all in the chapel had knelt and every least noise was still. Then, raising his head, he repeated the act of contrition, phrase by phrase, with fervour. The boys answered him phrase by phrase. Stephen, his tongue cleaving to his palate, bowed his head, praying with his heart.

— O my God! —
— O my God! —
— I am heartily sorry —
— I am heartily sorry —
— for having offended Thee —
— for having offended Thee —
— and I detest my sins —
— and I detest my sins —
— above every other evil —
— above every other evil —
— because they displease Thee, my God —
— because they displease Thee my God —
— Who art so deserving —
— Who art so deserving —
— of all my love —
— of all my love —
— and I firmly purpose —
— and I firmly purpose —
— by Thy holy grace —
— by Thy holy grace —
— never more to offend Thee —
— never more to offend Thee —
— and to amend my life —
— and to amend my life —

*
*   *

He went up to his room after dinner in order to be alone with his soul: and at every step his soul seemed to sigh: at every step his soul mounted with his feet, sighing in the ascent, through a region of viscid gloom.

He halted on the landing before the door and then, grasping the porcelain knob, opened the door quickly. He waited in fear, his soul pining within him, praying silently that death might not touch his brow as he passed over the threshold, that the fiends that inhabit darkness might not be given power over him. He waited still at the threshold as at the entrance to some dark cave. Faces were there; eyes: they waited and watched.

— We knew perfectly well of course that although it was bound to come to the light he would find considerable difficulty in endeavouring to try to induce himself to try to endeavour to ascertain the spiritual plenipotentiary and so we knew of course perfectly well —

Murmuring faces waited and watched; murmurous voices filled the dark shell of the cave. He feared intensely in spirit and in flesh but, raising his head bravely, he strode into the room firmly. A doorway, a room, the same room, same window. He told himself calmly that those words had absolutely no sense which had seemed to rise murmurously from the dark. He told himself that it was simply his room with the door open.

He closed the door and, walking swiftly to the bed, knelt beside it and covered his face with his hands. His hands were cold and damp and his limbs ached with chill. Bodily unrest and chill and weariness beset him, routing his thoughts. Why was he kneeling there like a child saying his evening prayers? To be alone with his soul, to examine his conscience, to meet his sins face to face, to recall their times and manners and circumstances, to weep over them. He could not weep. He could not summon them to his memory. He felt only an ache of soul and body, his whole being, memory, will, understanding, flesh, benumbed and weary.

That was the work of devils, to scatter his thoughts and overcloud his conscience, assailing him at the gates of the cowardly and sincorrupted flesh: and, praying God timidly to forgive him his weakness, he crawled up on to the bed and, wrapping the blankets closely about him, covered his face again with his hands. He had sinned. He had sinned so deeply against heaven and before God that he was not worthy to be called God's child.

Could it be that he, Stephen Dedalus, had done those things? His conscience sighed in answer. Yes, he had done them, secretly, filthily, time after time, and, hardened in sinful impenitence, he had dared to wear the mask of holiness before the tabernacle itself while his soul within was a living mass of corruption. How came it that God had not struck him dead? The leprous company of his sins closed about him, breathing upon him, bending over him from all sides. He strove to forget them in act of prayer, huddling his limbs closer together and binding down his eyelids: but the senses of his soul would not be bound and, though his eyes were shut fast, he saw the places where he had sinned and, though his ears were tightly covered, he heard. He desired with all his will not to hear or see. He desired till his frame shook under the strain of his desire and until the senses of his soul closed. They closed for an instant and then opened. He saw.

A field of stiff weeds and thistles and tufted nettlebunches. Thick among the tufts of rank stiff growth lay battered canisters and clots and coils of solid excrement. A faint marshlight struggled upwards from all the ordure through the bristling greygreen weeds. An evil smell, faint and foul as the light, curled upwards sluggishly out of the canisters and from the stale crusted dung.

Creatures were in the field; one, three, six: creatures were moving in the field, hither and thither. Goatish creatures with human faces, hornybrowed, lightly bearded and grey as indiarubber. The malice of evil glittered in their hard eyes, as they moved hither and thither, trailing their long tails behind them. A rictus of cruel malignity lit up greyly their old bony faces. One was clasping about his ribs a torn flannel waistcoat, another complained monotonously as his beard stuck in the tufted weeds. Soft language issued from their spittleless lips as they swished in slow circles round and round the field, winding hither and thither through the weeds, dragging their long tails amid the rattling canisters. They moved in slow circles, circling closer and closer to enclose, to enclose, soft language issuing from their lips, their long swishing tails besmeared with stale shite, thrusting upwards their terrific faces . . .

Help!

He flung the blankets from him madly to free his face and neck. That was his hell. God had allowed him to see the hell reserved for his sins: stinking, bestial, malignant, a hell of lecherous goatish fiends. For him! For him!

He sprang from the bed, the reeking odour pouring down his throat, clogging and revolting his entrails. Air! The air of heaven! He stumbled towards the window, groaning and almost fainting with sickness. At the washstand a convulsion seized him within: and, clasping his cold forehead wildly, he vomited profusely in agony.

When the fit had spent itself he walked weakly to the window and, lifting the sash, sat in a corner of the embrasure and leaned his elbow upon the sill. The rain had drawn off; and amid the moving vapours from point to point of light the city was spinning about herself a soft cocoon of yellowish haze. Heaven was still and faintly luminous and the air sweet to breathe, as in a thicket drenched with showers: and amid peace and shimmering lights and quiet fragrances he made a covenant with his heart.

He prayed:

— He once had meant to come on earth in heavenly glory but we sinned: and then He could not safely visit us but with a shrouded majesty and a bedimmed radiance for He was God. So He came Himself in weakness not in power and He sent thee, a creature in His stead, with a creature's comeliness and lustre suited to our state. And now thy very face and form, dear mother, speak to us of the Eternal; not like earthly beauty, dangerous to look upon, but like the morning star which is thy emblem, bright and musical, breathing purity, telling of heaven and infusing peace. O harbinger of day! O light of the pilgrim! Lead us still as thou hast led. In the dark night, across the bleak wilderness guide us on to our Lord Jesus, guide us home.

His eyes were dimmed with tears and, looking humbly up to heaven, he wept for the innocence he had lost.

When evening had fallen he left the house and the first touch of the damp dark air and the noise of the door as it closed behind him made ache again his conscience, lulled by prayer and tears. Confess! Confess! It was not enough to lull the conscience with a tear and a prayer. He had to kneel before the minister of the Holy Ghost and tell over his hidden sins truly and repentantly. Before he heard again the footboard of the housedoor trail over the threshold as it opened to let him in, before he saw again the table in the kitchen set for supper he would have knelt and confessed. It was quite simple.

The ache of conscience ceased and he walked onward swiftly through the dark streets. There were so many flagstones on the footpath of that street and so many streets in that city and so many cities in the world. Yet eternity had no end. He was in mortal sin. Even once was a mortal sin. It could happen in an instant. But how so quickly? By seeing or by thinking of seeing. The eyes see the thing, without having wished first to see. Then in an instant it happens. But does that part of the body understand or what? The serpent, the most subtle beast of the field. It must understand when it desires in one instant and then prolongs its own desire instant after instant, sinfully. It feels and understands and desires. What a horrible thing! Who made it to be like that, a bestial part of the body able to understand bestially and desire bestially? Was that then he or an inhuman thing moved by a lower soul than his soul?

His soul sickened at the thought of a torpid snaky life feeding itself out of the tender marrow of his life and fattening upon the slime of lust. O why was that so? O why?

He cowered in the shadow of the thought, abasing himself in the awe of God Who had made all things and all men. Madness. Who could think such a thought? And, cowering in darkness and abject, he prayed mutely to his angel guardian to drive away with his sword the demon that was whispering to his brain.

The whisper ceased and he knew then clearly that his own soul had sinned in thought and word and deed wilfully through his own body. Confess! He had to confess every sin. How could he utter in words to the priest what he had done? Must, must. Or how could he explain without dying of shame? Or how could he have done such things without shame? A madman, a loathsome madman! Confess! O he would indeed to be free and sinless again! Perhaps the priest would know. O dear God!

He walked on and on through illlit streets, fearing to stand still for a moment lest it might seem that he held back from what awaited him, fearing to arrive at that towards which he still turned with longing. How beautiful must be a soul in the state of grace when God looked upon it with love!

Frowsy girls sat along the curbstones before their baskets of herrings. Their dank hair hung trailed over their brows. They were not beautiful to see as they crouched in the mire. But their souls were seen by God; and if their souls were in a state of grace they were radiant to see: and God loved them, seeing them.

A wasting breath of humiliation blew bleakly over his soul to think of how he had fallen, to feel that those souls were dearer to God than his. The wind blew over him and passed on to the myriads and myriads of other souls on whom God's favour shone now more and now less, stars now brighter and now dimmer, sustained and failing. And the glimmering souls passed away, sustained and failing, merged in a moving breath. One soul was lost; a tiny soul: his. It flickered once and went out, forgotten, lost. The end: black cold void waste.

Consciousness of place came ebbing back to him slowly over a vast tract of time, unlit, unfelt, unlived. The squalid scene composed itself around him; the common accents, the burning gasjets in the shops, odours of fish and spirits and wet sawdust, moving men and women. An old woman was about to cross the street, an oilcan in her hand. He bent down and asked her was there a chapel near.

— A chapel, sir? Yes, sir. Church Street chapel.

— Church?

She shifted the can to her other hand and directed him: and, as she held out her reeking withered right hand under its fringe of shawl, he bent lower towards her, saddened and soothed by her voice.

— Thank you.

— You are quite welcome, sir.

The candles on the high altar had been extinguished but the fragrance of incense still floated down the dim nave. Bearded workmen with pious faces were guiding a canopy° out through a sidedoor, the sacristan° aiding them with quiet gestures and words. A few of the faithful still lingered, praying before one of the sidealtars or kneeling in the benches near the confessionals. He approached timidly and knelt at the last bench in the body, thankful for the peace and silence and fragrant shadow of the church. The board on which he knelt was narrow and worn and those who knelt near him were humble followers of Jesus. Jesus too had been born in poverty and had worked in the shop of a carpenter, cutting boards and planing them, and had first spoken of the kingdom of God to poor fishermen, teaching all men to be meek and humble of heart.

He bowed his head upon his hands, bidding his heart be meek and humble that he might be like those who knelt beside him and his prayer as acceptable as theirs. He prayed beside them but it was hard. His soul was foul with sin and he dared not ask forgiveness with the simple trust of those whom Jesus, in the mysterious ways of God, had called first to His side, the carpenters, the fishermen, poor and simple people following a lowly trade, handling and shaping the wood of trees, mending their nets with patience.

A tall figure came down the aisle and the penitents stirred: and at the last moment, glancing up swiftly, he saw a long grey beard and the brown habit of a capuchin.° The priest entered the box and was hidden. Two penitents rose and entered the confessional at either side. The wooden slide was drawn back and the faint murmur of a voice troubled the silence.

His blood began to murmur in his veins, murmuring like a sinful city summoned from its sleep to hear its doom. Little flakes of fire fell and powdery ashes fell softly, alighting on the houses of men. They stirred, waking from sleep, troubled by the heated air.

---

a canopy: Carried over the priest bearing the sacrament in processions.   *sacristan:* An officer who is charged with the care of the sacristry (the room in which sacred vessels are kept), the church, and their contents.   *brown habit of a capuchin:* Belted robe worn by Capuchins, a branch of the Franciscan order of friars.

The slide was shot back. The penitent emerged from the side of the box. The farther slide was drawn. A woman entered quietly and deftly where the first penitent had knelt. The faint murmur began again.

He could still leave the chapel. He could stand up, put one foot before the other and walk out softly and then run, run, run swiftly through the dark streets. He could still escape from the shame. O what shame! His face was burning with shame. Had it been any terrible crime but that one sin! Had it been murder! Little fiery flakes fell and touched him at all points, shameful thoughts, shameful words, shameful acts. Shame covered him wholly like fine glowing ashes falling continually. To say it in words! His soul, stifling and helpless, would cease to be.

The slide was shot back. A penitent emerged from the farther side of the box. The near slide was drawn. A penitent entered where the other penitent had come out. A soft whispering noise floated in vaporous cloudlets out of the box. It was the woman: soft whispering cloudlets, soft whispering vapour, whispering and vanishing.

He beat his breast with his fist humbly, secretly under cover of the wooden armrest. He would be at one with others and with God. He would love his neighbour. He would love God Who had made and loved him. He would kneel and pray with others and be happy. God would look down on him and on them and would love them all.

It was easy to be good. God's yoke was sweet and light. It was better never to have sinned, to have remained always a child, for God loved little children and suffered them to come to Him. It was a terrible and a sad thing to sin. But God was merciful to poor sinners who were truly sorry. How true that was! That was indeed goodness.

The slide was shot to suddenly. The penitent came out. He was next. He stood up in terror and walked blindly into the box.

At last it had come. He knelt in the silent gloom and raised his eyes to the white crucifix suspended above him. God could see that he was sorry. He would tell all his sins. His confession would be long, long. Everybody in the chapel would know then what a sinner he had been. Let them know. It was true. But God had promised to forgive him if he was sorry. He was sorry. He clasped his hands and raised them towards the white form, praying with his darkened eyes, praying with all his trembling body, swaying his head to and fro like a lost creature, praying with whimpering lips.

— Sorry! Sorry! O sorry!

The slide clicked back and his heart bounded in his breast. The face of an old priest was at the grating, averted from him, leaning upon a hand. He made the sign of the cross and prayed of the priest to bless him for he had sinned. Then, bowing his head, he repeated the *Confiteor* in fright. At the words *my most grievous fault* he ceased, breathless.

— How long is it since your last confession, my child?

— A long time, father.

— A month, my child?

— Longer, father.

— Three months, my child?

— Longer, father.

— Six months?

— Eight months, father.

He had begun. The priest asked:

— And what do you remember since that time?

He began to confess his sins: masses missed, prayers not said, lies.

— Anything else, my child?

Sins of anger, envy of others, gluttony, vanity, disobedience.

— Anything else, my child?

— Sloth.

— Anything else, my child?

There was no help. He murmured:

— I . . . committed sins of impurity, father.

The priest did not turn his head.

— With yourself, my child?

— And . . . with others.

— With women, my child?

— Yes, father.

— Were they married women, my child?

He did not know. His sins trickled from his lips, one by one, trickled in shameful drops from his soul festering and oozing like a sore, a squalid stream of vice. The last sins oozed forth, sluggish, filthy. There was no more to tell. He bowed his head, overcome.

The priest was silent. Then he asked:

— How old are you, my child?

— Sixteen, father.

The priest passed his hand several times over his face. Then, resting his forehead against his hand, he leaned towards the grating and, with eyes still averted, spoke slowly. His voice was weary and old.

— You are very young, my child, he said, and let me implore of you to give up that sin. It is a terrible sin. It kills the body and it kills the soul. It is the cause of many crimes and misfortunes. Give it up, my child, for God's sake. It is dishonourable and unmanly. You cannot know where that wretched habit will lead you or where it will come against you. As long as you commit that sin, my poor child, you will never be worth one farthing to God. Pray to our mother Mary to help you. She will help you, my child. Pray to Our Blessed Lady when that sin comes into your mind. I am sure you will do that, will you not? You repent of all those sins. I am sure you do. And you will promise God now that by His holy grace you will never offend Him any more by that wicked sin. You will make that solemn promise to God, will you not?

— Yes, father.

The old and weary voice fell like sweet rain upon his quaking parching heart. How sweet and sad!

— Do so, my poor child. The devil has led you astray. Drive him back to hell when he tempts you to dishonour your body in that way — the foul spirit who hates Our Lord. Promise God now that you will give up that sin, that wretched wretched sin.

Blinded by his tears and by the light of God's mercifulness he bent his head and heard the grave words of absolution spoken and saw the priest's hand raised above him in token of forgiveness.

— God bless you, my child. Pray for me.

He knelt to say his penance, praying in a corner of the dark nave: and his prayers ascended to heaven from his purified heart like perfume streaming upwards from a heart of white rose.

The muddy streets were gay. He strode homeward, conscious of an invisible grace pervading and making light his limbs. In spite of all he had done it. He had confessed and God had pardoned him. His soul was made fair and holy once more, holy and happy.

It would be beautiful to die if God so willed. It was beautiful to live if God so willed, to live in grace a life of peace and virtue and forbearance with others.

He sat by the fire in the kitchen, not daring to speak for happiness. Till that moment he had not known how beautiful and peaceful life could be. The green square of paper pinned round the lamp cast down a tender shade. On the dresser was a plate of sausages and white pudding and on the shelf there were eggs. They would be for the breakfast in the morning after the communion in the college chapel. White pudding and eggs and sausages and cups of tea. How simple and beautiful was life after all! And life lay all before him.

In a dream he fell asleep. In a dream he rose and saw that it was morning. In a waking dream he went through the quiet morning towards the college.

The boys were all there, kneeling in their places. He knelt among them, happy and shy. The altar was heaped with fragrant masses of white flowers: and in the morning light the pale flames of the candles among the white flowers were clear and silent as his own soul.

He knelt before the altar with his classmates, holding the altarcloth with them over a living rail of hands. His hands were trembling: and his soul trembled as he heard the priest pass with the ciborium° from communicant to communicant.

— *Corpus Domini nostri.*°

Could it be? He knelt there sinless and timid: and he would hold upon his tongue the host and God would enter his purified body.

— *In vitam eternam.*° Amen.

Another life! A life of grace and virtue and happiness! It was true. It was not a dream from which he would wake. The past was past.

— *Corpus Domini nostri.*

The ciborium had come to him.

IV

Sunday was dedicated to the mystery of the Holy Trinity, Monday to the Holy Ghost, Tuesday to the Guardian Angels, Wednesday to Saint Joseph, Thursday to the Most Blessed Sacrament of the Altar, Friday to the Suffering Jesus, Saturday to the Blessed Virgin Mary.

Every morning he hallowed himself anew in the presence of some holy image or mystery. His day began with an heroic offering of its every moment of thought or action for the intentions of the sovereign pontiff and with an early mass. The raw morning air whetted his resolute piety; and often as he knelt among the few worshippers at the sidealtar, following with his interleaved prayerbook the murmur of the priest, he glanced up for an instant towards the vested figure standing in the gloom between the two candles which were the old and the new testaments and imagined that he was kneeling at mass in the catacombs.°

His daily life was laid out in devotional areas. By means of ejaculations° and prayers he stored up ungrudgingly for the souls in purgatory centuries of days and quarantines° and years; yet the spiritual triumph which he felt in achieving with ease so many fabulous ages of canonical penances did not wholly reward his zeal of prayer since he could never

---

ciborium: Vessel that holds the host during communion.   *Corpus Domini nostri:* The Body of Our Lord.   *In vitam eternam:* Unto everlasting life.   *catacombs:* Where early Christians under Roman persecution sometimes celebrated mass.   *ejaculations:* Brief outcries or prayers.   *quarantines:* Periods of forty days.

know how much temporal punishment he had remitted by way of suffrage for the agonising souls: and, fearful lest in the midst of the purgatorial fire, which differed from the infernal only in that it was not everlasting, his penance might avail no more than a drop of moisture, he drove his soul daily through an increasing circle of works of supererogation.°

Every part of his day, divided by what he regarded now as the duties of his station in life, circled about its own centre of spiritual energy. His life seemed to have drawn near to eternity; every thought, word and deed, every instant of consciousness could be made to revibrate radiantly in heaven: and at times his sense of such immediate repercussion was so lively that he seemed to feel his soul in devotion pressing like fingers the keyboard of a great cashregister and to see the amount of his purchase start forth immediately in heaven, not as a number but as a frail column of incense or as a slender flower.

The rosaries too which he said constantly — for he carried his beads loose in his trousers' pockets that he might tell them as he walked the streets — transformed themselves into coronals of flowers of such vague unearthly texture that they seemed to him as hueless and odourless as they were nameless. He offered up each of his three daily chaplets° that his soul might grow strong in each of the three theological virtues, in faith in the Father, in hope in the Son, in charity in the Holy Ghost, and as daily offerings of thanksgiving to the Father Who had created him, to the Son Who had redeemed him and to the Holy Ghost Who had sanctified him: and this thrice triple prayer he offered to the Three Persons through Mary in the name of her joyful and sorrowful and glorious mysteries.

On each of the seven days of the week he further prayed that one of the seven gifts of the Holy Ghost might descend upon his soul and drive out of it day by day the seven deadly sins which had defiled it in the past: and he prayed for each gift on its appointed day, confident that it would descend upon him, though it seemed to him strange at times that wisdom and understanding and knowledge were so distinct in their nature that each should be prayed for apart from the others. Yet he believed that at some future stage of his spiritual progress this difficulty would be removed when his sinful soul had been raised up from its weakness and enlightened by the Third Person of the Most Blessed

---

supererogation: Acts beyond the requirements of duty to establish a "reservoir of merit."   *chaplets:* The three divisions of the cycle of prayers called a rosary, each of which is subdivided into decades.

Trinity. He believed this all the more and with trepidation because of the divine gloom and silence wherein dwelt the unseen Paraclete,° Whose symbols were a dove and a mighty wind, to sin against Whom was a sin beyond forgiveness, the eternal, mysterious, secret Being to Whom, as God, the priests offered up mass once a year, robed in the scarlet of the tongues of fire.

The imagery through which the nature and kinship of the Three Persons of the Trinity were darkly shadowed forth in the books of devotion which he read — the Father contemplating from all eternity as in a mirror His Divine Perfections and thereby begetting eternally the Eternal Son and the Holy Spirit proceeding out of Father and Son from all eternity — were easier of acceptance by his mind by reason of their august incomprehensibility than was the simple fact that God had loved his soul from all eternity, for ages before he had been born into the world, for ages before the world itself had existed. He had heard the names of the passions of love and hate pronounced solemnly on the stage and in the pulpit, had found them set forth solemnly in books, and had wondered why his soul was unable to harbour them for any time or to force his lips to utter their names with conviction. A brief anger had often invested him but he had never been able to make it an abiding passion and had always felt himself passing out of it as if his very body were being divested with ease of some outer skin or peel. He had felt a subtle, dark and murmurous presence penetrate his being and fire him with a brief iniquitous lust: it too had slipped beyond his grasp leaving his mind lucid and indifferent. This, it seemed, was the only love and that the only hate his soul would harbour.

But he could no longer disbelieve in the reality of love since God Himself had loved his individual soul with divine love from all eternity. Gradually, as his soul was enriched with spiritual knowledge, he saw the whole world forming one vast symmetrical expression of God's power and love. Life became a divine gift for every moment and sensation of which, were it even the sight of a single leaf hanging on the twig of a tree, his soul should praise and thank the Giver. The world for all its solid substance and complexity no longer existed for his soul save as a theorem of divine power and love and universality. So entire and unquestionable was this sense of the divine meaning in all nature granted to his soul that he could scarcely understand why it was in any way necessary that he should continue to live. Yet that also was part of the divine purpose and he dared not question its use, he above all others

Paraclete: Term for the Holy Ghost.

who had sinned so deeply and so foully against the divine purpose. Meek and abased by this consciousness of the one eternal omnipresent perfect reality his soul took up again her burden of pieties, masses and prayers and sacraments and mortifications, and only then for the first time since he had brooded on the great mystery of love did he feel within him a warm movement like that of some newly born life or virtue of the soul itself. The attitude of rapture in sacred art, the raised and parted hands, the parted lips and eyes as of one about to swoon, became for him an image of the soul in prayer, humiliated and faint before her Creator.

But he had been forewarned of the dangers of spiritual exaltation and did not allow himself to desist from even the least or lowliest devotion, striving also by constant mortification to undo the sinful past rather than to achieve a saintliness fraught with peril. Each of his senses was brought under a rigorous discipline. In order to mortify the sense of sight he made it his rule to walk in the street with downcast eyes, glancing neither to right nor left and never behind him. His eyes shunned every encounter with the eyes of women. From time to time also he balked them by a sudden effort of the will, as by lifting them suddenly in the middle of an unfinished sentence and closing the book. To mortify his hearing he exerted no control over his voice which was then breaking, neither sang nor whistled and made no attempt to flee from noises which caused him painful nervous irritation such as the sharpening of knives on the knifeboard, the gathering of cinders on the fireshovel and the twigging° of the carpet. To mortify his smell was more difficult as he found in himself no instinctive repugnance to bad odours, whether they were the odours of the outdoor world such as those of dung and tar or the odours of his own person among which he had made many curious comparisons and experiments. He found in the end that the only odour against which his sense of smell revolted was a certain stale fishy stink like that of longstanding urine: and whenever it was possible he subjected himself to this unpleasant odour. To mortify the taste he practised strict habits at table, observed to the letter all the fasts of the church and sought by distraction to divert his mind from the savours of different foods. But it was to the mortification of touch that he brought the most assiduous ingenuity of inventiveness. He never consciously changed his position in bed, sat in the most uncomfortable positions, suffered patiently every itch and pain, kept away from the fire, remained on his knees all through the mass except at the

twigging: Brushing with a short broom.

gospels, left parts of his neck and face undried so that the ai
sting them and, whenever he was not saying his beads, carried hi
stiffly at his sides like a runner and never in his pockets or cl
behind him.

He had no temptations to sin mortally. It surprised him howeve
find that at the end of his course of intricate piety and selfrestraint
was so easily at the mercy of childish and unworthy imperfections. H
prayers and fasts availed him little for the suppression of anger at hear
ing his mother sneeze or at being disturbed in his devotions. It needed
an immense effort of his will to master the impulse which urged him to
give outlet to such irritation. Images of the outbursts of trivial anger
which he had often noted among his masters, their twitching mouths,
closeshut lips and flushed cheeks, recurred to his memory, discouraging
him, for all his practice of humility, by the comparison. To merge his life
in the common tide of other lives was harder for him than any fasting or
prayer, and it was his constant failure to do this to his own satisfaction
which caused in his soul at last a sensation of spiritual dryness together
with a growth of doubts and scruples. His soul traversed a period of
desolation in which the sacraments themselves seemed to have turned
into dried up sources. His confession became a channel for the escape
of scrupulous and unrepented imperfections. His actual reception of
the eucharist did not bring him the same dissolving moments of virginal
selfsurrender as did those spiritual communions made by him sometimes at the close of some visit to the Blessed Sacrament. The book
which he used for these visits was an old neglected book written by saint
Alphonsus Liguori,° with fading characters and sere foxpapered° leaves.
A faded world of fervent love and virginal responses seemed to be
evoked for his soul by the reading of its pages in which the imagery
of the canticles° was interwoven with the communicant's prayers. An
inaudible voice seemed to caress the soul, telling her names and glories, bidding her arise as for espousal and come away, bidding her look
forth, a spouse, from Amana and from the mountains of the leopards;
and the soul seemed to answer with the same inaudible voice, surrendering herself:

Inter ubera mea commorabitur.°

---

saint Alphonsus Liguori: (1696–1787), author of *Visits to the Most Blessed Sacrament.*
foxpapered: Having pages that are "foxed," or discolored.   **canticles:** The Song of
Songs or Song of Solomon in the Protestant Bible.   ***Inter ubera mea commorabitur:***
He shall lie between my breasts; from the Song of Solomon.

This idea of surrender had a perilous attraction for his mind now that he felt his soul beset once again by the insistent voices of the flesh which began to murmur to him again during his prayers and meditations. It gave him an intense sense of power to know that he could, by a single act of consent, in a moment of thought, undo all that he had done. He seemed to feel a flood slowly advancing towards his naked feet and to be waiting for the first faint timid noiseless wavelet to touch his fevered skin. Then, almost at the instant of that touch, almost at the verge of sinful consent, he found himself standing far away from the flood upon a dry shore, saved by a sudden act of the will or a sudden ejaculation: and, seeing the silver line of the flood far away and beginning again its slow advance towards his feet, a new thrill of power and satisfaction shook his soul to know that he had not yielded nor undone all.

When he had eluded the flood of temptation many times in this way he grew troubled and wondered whether the grace which he had refused to lose was not being filched from him little by little. The clear certitude of his own immunity grew dim and to it succeeded a vague fear that his soul had really fallen unawares. It was with difficulty that he won back his old consciousness of his state of grace by telling himself that he had prayed to God at every temptation and that the grace which he had prayed for must have been given to him inasmuch as God was obliged to give it. The very frequency and violence of temptations showed him at last the truth of what he had heard about the trials of the saints. Frequent and violent temptations were a proof that the citadel of the soul had not fallen and that the devil raged to make it fall.

Often when he had confessed his doubts and scruples, some momentary inattention at prayer, a movement of trivial anger in his soul or a subtle wilfulness in speech or act, he was bidden by his confessor to name some sin of his past life before absolution was given him. He named it with humility and shame and repented of it once more. It humiliated and shamed him to think that he would never be freed from it wholly, however holily he might live or whatever virtues or perfections he might attain. A restless feeling of guilt would always be present with him: he would confess and repent and be absolved, confess and repent again and be absolved again, fruitlessly. Perhaps that first hasty confession wrung from him by the fear of hell had not been good? Perhaps, concerned only for his imminent doom, he had not had sincere sorrow for his sin? But the surest sign that his confession had been good and that he had had sincere sorrow for his sin was, he knew, the amendment of his life.

— I have amended my life, have I not? he asked himself.

*

*   *

The director stood in the embrasure of the window, his back to the light, leaning an elbow on the brown crossblind and, as he spoke and smiled, slowly dangling and looping the cord of the other blind. Stephen stood before him, following for a moment with his eyes the waning of the long summer daylight above the roofs or the slow deft movements of the priestly fingers. The priest's face was in total shadow. but the waning daylight from behind him touched the deeply grooved temples and the curves of the skull. Stephen followed also with his ears the accents and intervals of the priest's voice as he spoke gravely and cordially of indifferent themes, the vacation which had just ended, the colleges of the order abroad, the transference of masters. The grave and cordial voice went on easily with its tale and in the pauses Stephen felt bound to set it on again with respectful questions. He knew that the tale was a prelude and his mind waited for the sequel. Ever since the message of summons had come for him from the director his mind had struggled to find the meaning of the message; and during the long restless time he had sat in the college parlour waiting for the director to come in his eyes had wandered from one sober picture to another around the walls and his mind had wandered from one guess to another until the meaning of the summons had almost become clear. Then, just as he was wishing that some unforeseen cause might prevent the director from coming, he had heard the handle of the door turning and the swish of a soutane.

The director had begun to speak of the dominican° and franciscan° orders and of the friendship between saint Thomas and saint Bonaventure. The capuchin dress, he thought, was rather too . . .

Stephen's face gave back the priest's indulgent smile and, not being anxious to give an opinion, he made a slight dubitative movement with his lips.

— I believe, continued the director, that there is some talk now among the capuchins themselves of doing away with it and following the example of the other franciscans.

— I suppose they would retain it in the cloister, said Stephen.

— O, certainly, said the director. For the cloister it is all right but for the street I really think it would be better to do away with it, don't you?

— It must be troublesome, I imagine.

---

dominican: Order founded by St. Dominic.   **franciscan:** Order founded by St. Francis of Assisi.

— Of course it is: of course. Just imagine, when I was in Belgium I used to see them out cycling in all kinds of weather with this thing up about their knees! It was really ridiculous. *Les jupes,*° they call them in Belgium.

The vowel was so modified as to be indistinct.

— What do they call them?

— *Les jupes.*

— O.

Stephen smiled again in answer to the smile which he could not see on the priest's shadowed face, its image or spectre only passing rapidly across his mind as the low discreet accent fell upon his ear. He gazed calmly before him at the waning sky, glad of the cool of the evening and of the faint yellow glow which hid the tiny flame kindling upon his cheek.

The names of articles of dress worn by women or of certain soft and delicate stuffs used in their making brought always to his mind a delicate and sinful perfume. As a boy he had imagined the reins by which horses are driven as slender silken bands and it shocked him to feel at Stradbrook the greasy leather of harness. It had shocked him too when he had felt for the first time beneath his tremulous fingers the brittle texture of a woman's stocking for, retaining nothing of all he read save that which seemed to him an echo or a prophecy of his own state, it was only amid softworded phrases or within rosesoft stuffs that he dared to conceive of the soul or body of a woman moving with tender life.

But the phrase on the priest's lips was disingenuous for he knew that a priest should not speak lightly on that theme. The phrase had been spoken lightly with design and he felt that his face was being searched by the eyes in the shadow. Whatever he had heard or read of the craft of jesuits he had put aside frankly as not borne out by his own experience. His masters, even when they had not attracted him, had seemed to him always intelligent and serious priests, athletic and high-spirited prefects. He thought of them as men who washed their bodies briskly with cold water and wore clean cold linen. During all the years he had lived among them in Clongowes and in Belvedere he had received only two pandies and, though these had been dealt him in the wrong, he knew that he had often escaped punishment. During all those years he had never heard from any of his masters a flippant word: it was they who had taught him christian doctrine and urged him to live a good life and, when he had fallen into grievous sin, it was they who had led him back

Les jupes: Skirts (French).

to grace. Their presence had made him diffident of himself when he was a muff° in Clongowes and it had made him diffident of himself also while he had held his equivocal position in Belvedere. A constant sense of this had remained with him up to the last year of his school life. He had never once disobeyed or allowed turbulent companions to seduce him from his habit of quiet obedience: and, even when he doubted some statement of a master, he had never presumed to doubt openly. Lately some of their judgments had sounded a little childish in his ears and had made him feel a regret and pity as though he were slowly passing out of an accustomed world and were hearing its language for the last time. One day when some boys had gathered round a priest under the shed near the chapel, he had heard the priest say:

— I believe that Lord Macaulay° was a man who probably never committed a mortal sin in his life, that is to say, a deliberate mortal sin.

Some of the boys had then asked the priest if Victor Hugo° were not the greatest French writer. The priest had answered that Victor Hugo had never written half so well when he had turned against the church as he had written when he was a catholic.

— But there are many eminent French critics, said the priest, who consider that even Victor Hugo, great as he certainly was, had not so pure a French style as Louis Veuillot.°

The tiny flame which the priest's allusion had kindled upon Stephen's cheek had sunk down again and his eyes were still fixed calmly on the colorless sky. But an unresting doubt flew hither and thither before his mind. Masked memories passed quickly before him: he recognised scenes and persons yet he was conscious that he had failed to perceive some vital circumstance in them. He saw himself walking about the grounds watching the sports in Clongowes and eating slim jim out of his cricketcap. Some jesuits were walking round the cycletrack in the company of ladies. The echoes of certain expressions used in Clongowes sounded in remote caves of his mind.

His ears were listening to these distant echoes amid the silence of the parlour when he became aware that the priest was addressing him in a different voice.

— I sent for you today, Stephen, because I wished to speak to you on a very important subject.

---

muff: A bungler, novice, or outsider.   ***Lord Macaulay:*** Thomas Babington Macaulay (1800–1859), the English historian, was not particularly notable for an ethical life. ***Victor Hugo:*** (1802–1885), French Romantic novelist and poet.   ***Louis Veuillot:*** (1813–1883), French writer notable for defending Roman Catholicism.

— Yes, sir.

— Have you ever felt that you had a vocation?°

Stephen parted his lips to answer yes and then withheld the word suddenly. The priest waited for the answer and added:

— I mean have you ever felt within yourself, in your soul, a desire to join the order. Think.

— I have sometimes thought of it, said Stephen.

The priest let the blindcord fall to one side and, uniting his hands, leaned his chin gravely upon them, communing with himself.

— In a college like this, he said at length, there is one boy or perhaps two or three boys whom God calls to the religious life. Such a boy is marked off from his companions by his piety, by the good example he shows to others. He is looked up to by them; he is chosen perhaps as prefect by his fellow sodalists. And you, Stephen, have been such a boy in this college, prefect of Our Blessed Lady's sodality. Perhaps you are the boy in this college whom God designs to call to Himself.

A strong note of pride reinforcing the gravity of the priest's voice made Stephen's heart quicken in response.

— To receive that call, Stephen, said the priest, is the greatest honour that the Almighty God can bestow upon a man. No king or emperor on this earth has the power of the priest of God. No angel or archangel in heaven, no saint, not even the Blessed Virgin herself has the power of a priest of God: the power of the keys, the power to bind and to loose from sin, the power of exorcism, the power to cast out from the creatures of God the evil spirits that have power over them, the power, the authority, to make the great God of Heaven come down upon the altar and take the form of bread and wine. What an awful power, Stephen!

A flame began to flutter again on Stephen's cheek as he heard in this proud address an echo of his own proud musings. How often had he seen himself as a priest wielding calmly and humbly the awful power of which angels and saints stood in reverence! His soul had loved to muse in secret on this desire. He had seen himself, a young and silent-mannered priest, entering a confessional swiftly, ascending the altar-steps, incensing, genuflecting, accomplishing the vague acts of the priesthood which pleased him by reason of their semblance of reality and of their distance from it. In that dim life which he had lived through in his musings he had assumed the voices and gestures which he had noted with various priests. He had bent his knee sideways like such a one, he had

a vocation: A "calling" for the priesthood.

shaken the thurible° only slightly like such a one, his chasuble° had swung open like that of such another as he had turned to the altar again after having blessed the people. And above all it had pleased him to fill the second place in those dim scenes of his imagining. He shrank from the dignity of celebrant because it displeased him to imagine that all the vague pomp should end in his own person or that the ritual should assign to him so clear and final an office. He longed for the minor sacred offices, to be vested with the tunicle of subdeacon° at high mass, to stand aloof from the altar, forgotten by the people, his shoulders covered with a humeral veil,° holding the paten° within its folds, or, when the sacrifice had been accomplished, to stand as deacon in a dalmatic° of cloth of gold on the step below the celebrant, his hands joined and his face towards the people, and sing the chant *Ite, missa est*.° If ever he had seen himself celebrant it was as in the pictures of the mass in his child's massbook, in a church without worshippers, save for the angel of the sacrifice, at a bare altar and served by an acolyte scarcely more boyish than himself. In vague sacrificial or sacramental acts alone his will seemed drawn to go forth to encounter reality: and it was partly the absence of an appointed rite which had always constrained him to inaction whether he had allowed silence to cover his anger or pride or had suffered only an embrace he longed to give.

He listened in reverent silence now to the priest's appeal and through the words he heard even more distinctly a voice bidding him approach, offering him secret knowledge and secret power. He would know then what was the sin of Simon Magus° and what the sin against the Holy Ghost for which there was no forgiveness. He would know obscure things, hidden from others, from those who were conceived and born children of wrath. He would know the sins, the sinful longings and sinful thoughts and sinful acts, of others, hearing them murmured into his ear in the confessional under the shame of a darkened chapel by the lips of women and of girls: but rendered immune mysteriously at his ordination by the imposition of hands his soul would pass again uncontaminated to the white peace of the altar. No touch of sin would linger upon the hands with which he would elevate and break

---

thurible: Censer, in which incense is burned.   *chasuble:* Long outer vestment worn by a priest celebrating the mass.   *tunicle of subdeacon:* Wide-sleeved vestment worn by the person who prepares the sacred vessels during the celebration of the Mass. *humeral veil:* Veil covering the shoulders.   *paten:* Plate on which the eucharistic bread is placed.   *dalmatic:* Wide-sleeved vestment worn during celebration of High Mass by the deacon, the person ranked second to the celebrant himself.   *Ite, missa est:* Go, the Mass is completed.   *sin of Simon Magus:* Simony, the sale of spiritual power.

the host; no touch of sin would linger on his lips in prayer to make him eat and drink damnation to himself, not discerning the body of the Lord. He would hold his secret knowledge and secret power, being as sinless as the innocent: and he would be a priest for ever according to the order of Melchisedec.°

— I will offer up my mass tomorrow morning, said the director, that Almighty God may reveal to you His holy will. And let you, Stephen, make a novena° to your holy patron saint,° the first martyr, who is very powerful with God, that God may enlighten your mind. But you must be quite sure, Stephen, that you have a vocation because it would be terrible if you found afterwards that you had none. Once a priest always a priest, remember. Your catechism tells you that the sacrament of Holy Orders is one of those which can be received only once because it imprints on the soul an indelible spiritual mark which can never be effaced. It is before you must weigh well, not after. It is a solemn question, Stephen, because on it may depend the salvation of your eternal soul. But we will pray to God together.

He held open the heavy halldoor and gave his hand as if already to a companion in the spiritual life. Stephen passed out on to the wide platform above the steps and was conscious of the caress of mild evening air. Towards Findlater's Church a quartet of young men were striding along with linked arms, swaying their heads and stepping to the agile melody of their leader's concertina. The music passed in an instant, as the first bars of sudden music always did, over the fantastic fabrics of his mind, dissolving them painlessly and noiselessly as a sudden wave dissolves the sandbuilt turrets of children. Smiling at the trivial air he raised his eyes to the priest's face and, seeing in it a mirthless reflection of the sunken day, detached his hand slowly which had acquiesced faintly in that companionship.

As he descended the steps the impression which effaced his troubled selfcommunion was that of a mirthless mask reflecting a sunken day from the threshold of the college. The shadow, then, of the life of the college passed gravely over his consciousness. It was a grave and ordered and passionless life that awaited him, a life without material cares. He wondered how he would pass the first night in the novitiate° and with what dismay he would wake the first morning in the dormitory. The troubling odour of the long corridors of Clongowes came back to him and he heard the discreet murmur of the burning gasflames. At once from every part of his being unrest began to irradiate. A feverish quickening of his pulses followed and a din of meaningless words drove his reasoned thoughts hither and thither confusedly. His lungs dilated and sank as if he were inhaling a warm moist unsustaining air and he smelt again the warm moist air which hung in the bath in Clongowes above the sluggish turfcoloured water.

Some instinct, waking at these memories, stronger than education or piety, quickened within him at every near approach to that life, an instinct subtle and hostile, and armed him against acquiescence. The chill and order of the life repelled him. He saw himself rising in the cold of the morning and filing down with the others to early mass and trying vainly to struggle with his prayers against the fainting sickness of his stomach. He saw himself sitting at dinner with the community of a college. What, then, had become of that deeprooted shyness of his which had made him loth to eat or drink under a strange roof? What had come of the pride of his spirit which had always made him conceive himself as a being apart in every order?

The Reverend Stephen Dedalus, S.J.°

His name in that new life leaped into characters before his eyes and to it there followed a mental sensation of an undefined face or colour of a face. The colour faded and became strong like a changing glow of pallid brick red. Was it the raw reddish glow he had so often seen on wintry mornings on the shaven gills of the priests? The face was eyeless and sourfavoured and devout, shot with pink tinges of suffocated anger. Was it not a mental spectre of the face of one of the jesuits whom some of the boys called Lantern Jaws and others Foxy Campbell?

He was passing at that moment before the jesuit house in Gardiner Street and wondered vaguely which window would be his if he ever joined the order. Then he wondered at the vagueness of his wonder, at the remoteness of his soul from what he had hitherto imagined her sanctuary, at the frail hold which so many years of order and obedience had of him when once a definite and irrevocable act of his threatened to end for ever, in time and in eternity, his freedom. The voice of the director urging upon him the proud claims of the church and the mystery and power of the priestly office repeated itself idly in his memory. His soul was not there to hear and greet it and he knew now that the exhortation he had listened to had already fallen into an idle formal tale. He would never swing the thurible before the tabernacle as priest.

S.J.: Society of Jesus (the Jesuit order).

His destiny was to be elusive of social or religious orders. The wisdom of the priest's appeal did not touch him to the quick. He was destined to learn his own wisdom apart from others or to learn the wisdom of others himself wandering among the snares of the world.

The snares of the world were its ways of sin. He would fall. He had not yet fallen but he would fall silently, in an instant. Not to fall was too hard, too hard: and he felt the silent lapse of his soul, as it would be at some instant to come, falling, falling but not yet fallen, still unfallen but about to fall.

He crossed the bridge over the stream of the Tolka and turned his eyes coldly for an instant towards the faded blue shrine of the Blessed Virgin which stood fowlwise on a pole in the middle of a hamshaped encampment of poor cottages. Then, bending to the left, he followed the lane which led up to his house. The faint sour stink of rotted cabbages came towards him from the kitchengardens on the rising ground above the river. He smiled to think that it was this disorder, the misrule and confusion of his father's house and the stagnation of vegetable life, which was to win the day in his soul. Then a short laugh broke from his lips as he thought of that solitary farmhand in the kitchengardens behind their house whom they had nicknamed the man with the hat. A second laugh, taking rise from the first after a pause, broke from him involuntarily as he thought of how the man with the hat worked, considering in turn the four points of the sky and then regretfully plunging his spade in the earth.

He pushed open the latchless door of the porch and passed through the naked hallway into the kitchen. A group of his brothers and sisters was sitting round the table. Tea was nearly over and only the last of the second watered tea remained in the bottoms of the small glassjars and jampots which did service for teacups. Discarded crusts and lumps of sugared bread, turned brown by the tea which had been poured over them, lay scattered on the table. Little wells of tea lay here and there on the board and a knife with a broken ivory handle was stuck through the pith of a ravaged turnover.

The sad quiet greyblue glow of the dying day came through the window and the open door, covering over and allaying quietly a sudden instinct of remorse in Stephen's heart. All that had been denied them had been freely given to him, the eldest: but the quiet glow of evening showed him in their faces no sign of rancour.

He sat near them at the table and asked where his father and mother were. One answered:

— Goneboro toboro lookboro atboro aboro houseboro.

Still another removal! A boy named Fallon in Belevedere had often asked him with a silly laugh why they moved so often. A frown of scorn darkened quickly his forehead as he heard again the silly laugh of the questioner.

He asked:

— Why are we on the move again, if it's a fair question?

The same sister answered:

— Becauseboro theboro landboro lordboro willboro putboro usboro outboro.

The voice of his youngest brother from the farther side of the fireplace began to sing the air *Oft in the Stilly Night.*° One by one the others took up the air until a full choir of voices was singing. They would sing so for hours, melody after melody, glee after glee, till the last pale light died down on the horizon, till the first dark nightclouds came forth and night fell.

He waited for some moments, listening, before he too took up the air with them. He was listening with pain of spirit to the overtone of weariness behind their frail fresh innocent voices. Even before they set out on life's journey they seemed weary already of the way.

He heard the choir of voices in the kitchen echoed and multiplied through an endless reverberation of the choirs of endless generations of children: and heard in all the echoes an echo also of the recurring note of weariness and pain. All seemed weary of life even before entering upon it. And he remembered that Newman had heard this note also in the broken lines of Virgil *giving utterance, like the voice of Nature herself, to that pain and weariness yet hope of better things which has been the experience of her children in every time.*°

*
*   *

He could wait no longer.

From the door of Byron's publichouse to the gate of Clontarf Chapel, from the gate of Clontarf Chapel to the door of Byron's publichouse and then back again to the chapel and then back again to the publichouse he had paced slowly at first, planting his steps scrupulously in the spaces of the patchwork of the footpath, then timing their fall to the fall of verses. A full hour had passed since his father had gone in with Dan Crosby, the tutor, to find out for him something about the

Oft in the Stilly Night: Song from a poem by Thomas Moore (1779–1852), popular "national poet of Ireland." *giving utterance . . . time:* From Newman's *An Essay in Aid of a Grammar of Assent* (1881).

university. For a full hour he had paced up and down, waiting: but he could wait no longer.

He set off abruptly for the Bull,° walking rapidly lest his father's shrill whistle might call him back; and in a few moments he had rounded the curve at the police barrack and was safe.

Yes, his mother was hostile to the idea, as he had read from her listless silence. Yet her mistrust pricked him more keenly than his father's pride and he thought coldly how he had watched the faith which was fading down in his soul aging and strengthening in her eyes. A dim antagonism gathered force within him and darkened his mind as a cloud against her disloyalty: and when it passed, cloudlike, leaving his mind serene and dutiful towards her again, he was made aware dimly and without regret of a first noiseless sundering of their lives.

The university! So he had passed beyond the challenge of the sentries who had stood as guardians of his boyhood and had sought to keep him among them that he might be subject to them and serve their ends. Pride after satisfaction uplifted him like long slow waves. The end he had been born to serve yet did not see had led him to escape by an unseen path: and now it beckoned to him once more and a new adventure was about to be opened to him. It seemed to him that he heard notes of fitful music leaping upwards a tone and downwards a diminished fourth, upwards a tone and downwards a major third, like triple-branching flames leaping fitfully, flame after flame, out of a midnight wood. It was an elfin prelude, endless and formless: and, as it grew wilder and faster, the flames leaping out of time, he seemed to hear from under the boughs and grasses wild creatures racing, their feet pattering like rain upon the leaves. Their feet passed in pattering tumult over his mind, the feet of hares and rabbits, the feet of hinds and harts and antelopes, until he heard them no more and remembered only a proud cadence from Newman: *Whose feet are as the feet of harts and underneath the everlasting arms.*°

The pride of that dim image brought back to his mind the dignity of the office he had refused. All through his boyhood he had mused upon that which he had so often thought to be his destiny and when the moment had come for him to obey the call he had turned aside, obeying a wayward instinct. Now time lay between: the oils of ordination would never anoint his body. He had refused. Why?

He turned seaward from the road at Dollymount and as he passed on to the thin wooden bridge he felt the planks shaking with the tramp of heavily shod feet. A squad of christian brothers was on its way back from the Bull and had begun to pass, two by two, across the bridge. Soon the whole bridge was trembling and resounding. The uncouth faces passed him two by two, stained yellow or red or livid by the sea, and, as he strove to look at them with ease and indifference, a faint stain of personal shame and commiseration rose to his own face. Angry with himself he tried to hide his face from their eyes by gazing down sideways into the shallow swirling water under the bridge but he still saw a reflection therein of their topheavy silk hats and humble tapelike collars and loosely hanging clerical clothes.

— Brother Hickey.

Brother Quaid.

Brother MacArdle.

Brother Keogh.

Their piety would be like their names, like their faces, like their clothes: and it was idle for him to tell himself that their humble and contrite hearts, it might be, paid a far richer tribute of devotion than his had ever been, a gift tenfold more acceptable than his elaborate adoration. It was idle for him to move himself to be generous towards them, to tell himself that if he ever came to their gates, stripped of his pride, beaten and in beggar's weeds, that they would be generous towards him, loving him as themselves. Idle and embittering, finally, to argue, against his own dispassionate certitude, that the commandment of love bade us not to love our neighbour as ourselves with the same amount and intensity of love but to love him as ourselves with the same kind of love.

He drew forth a phrase from his treasure and spoke it softly to himself:

— A day of dappled seaborne clouds.°

The phrase and the day and the scene harmonised in a chord. Words. Was it their colours? He allowed them to glow and fade, hue after hue: sunrise gold, the russet and green of apple orchards, azure of waves, the greyfringed fleece of clouds. No, it was not their colours: it was the poise and balance of the period itself. Did he then love the rhythmic rise and fall of words better than their associations of legend and colour? Or was it that, being as weak of sight as he was shy of mind, he drew less pleasure from the reflection of the glowing sensible world

A day ... clouds: Misquoted slightly from Hugh Miller's *The Testimony of the Rocks* (1857).

through the prism of a language manycoloured and richly storied than from the contemplation of an inner world of individual emotions mirrored perfectly in a lucid supple periodic prose?

He passed from the trembling bridge on to firm land again. At that instant, as it seemed to him, the air was chilled and looking askance towards the water he saw a flying squall darkening and crisping suddenly the tide. A faint click at his heart, a faint throb in his throat told him once more of how his flesh dreaded the cold infrahuman odour of the sea: yet he did not strike across the downs on his left but held straight on along the spine of rocks that pointed against the river's mouth.

A veiled sunlight lit up faintly the grey sheet of water where the river was embayed. In the distance along the course of the slowflowing Liffey slender masts flecked the sky and, more distant still, the dim fabric of the city lay prone in haze. Like a scene on some vague arras, old as man's weariness, the image of the seventh city of christendom was visible to him across the timeless air, no older nor more weary nor less patient of subjection than in the days of the thingmote.°

Disheartened, he raised his eyes towards the slowdrifting clouds, dappled and seaborne. They were voyaging across the deserts of the sky, a host of nomads on the march, voyaging high over Ireland, westward bound. The Europe they had come from lay out there beyond the Irish Sea, Europe of strange tongues and valleyed and woodbegirt and citadelled and of entrenched and marshalled races. He heard a confused music within him as of memories and names which he was almost conscious of but could not capture even for an instant; then the music seemed to recede, to recede, to recede: and from each receding trail of nebulous music there fell always one longdrawn calling note, piercing like a star the dusk of silence. Again! Again! Again! Again! A voice from beyond the world was calling.

— Hello, Stephanos!°

— Here comes The Dedalus!

— Ao! . . . Eh, give it over, Dwyer, I'm telling you or I'll give you a stuff in the kisser for yourself. . . . Ao!

— Good man, Towser! Duck him!

— Come along, Dedalus! Bous Stephanoumenos! Bous Stephaneforos!°

— Duck him! Guzzle him now, Towser!

---

thingmote: Place where Danes held council of law when they ruled Dublin in medieval times.   **Stephanos:** Greek for crown, wreath, or garland.   **Bous Stephanoumenos! Bous Stephaneforos:** Greek variants for "ox bearing wreaths" (i.e., being led for sacrifice).

— Help! Help! . . . Ao!

He recognised their speech collectively before he distinguished their faces. The mere sight of that medley of wet nakedness chilled him to the bone. Their bodies, corpsewhite or suffused with a pallid golden light or rawly tanned by the suns, gleamed with the wet of the sea. Their divingstone, poised on its rude supports and rocking under their plunges, and the roughhewn stones of the sloping breakwater over which they scrambled in their horseplay gleamed with cold wet lustre. The towels with which they smacked their bodies were heavy with cold seawater: and drenched with cold brine was their matted hair.

He stood still in deference to their calls and parried their banter with easy words. How characterless they looked: Shuley without his deep unbuttoned collar, Ennis without his scarlet belt with the snaky clasp and Connolly without his Norfolk coat with the flapless sidepockets! It was a pain to see them and a swordlike pain to see the signs of adolescence that made repellent their pitiable nakedness. Perhaps they had taken refuge in number and noise from the secret dread in their souls. But he, apart from them and in silence, remembered in what dread he stood of the mystery of his own body.

— Stephanos Dedalos! Bous Stephanoumenos! Bous Stephaneforos!

Their banter was not new to him and now, as always, it flattered his mild proud sovereignty. Now, as never before, his strange name seemed to him a prophecy. So timeless seemed the grey warm air, so fluid and impersonal his own mood, that all ages were as one to him. A moment before the ghost of the ancient kingdom of the Danes had looked forth through the vesture of the hazewrapped city. Now, at the name of the fabulous artificer,° he seemed to hear the noise of dim waves and to see a winged form flying above the waves and slowly climbing the air. What did it mean? Was it a quaint device opening a page of some medieval book of prophecies and symbols, a hawklike man flying sunward above the sea, a prophecy of the end he had been born to serve and had been following through the mists of childhood and boyhood, a symbol of the artist forging anew in his workshop out of the sluggish matter of the earth a new soaring impalpable imperishable being?

His heart trembled; his breath came faster and a wild spirit passed over his limbs as though he were soaring sunward. His heart trembled in an ecstasy of fear and his soul was in flight. His soul was soaring in an air beyond the world and the body he knew was purified in a breath and

artificer: Inventor or craftsman (i.e., Daedalus).

delivered of incertitude and made radiant and commingled with the element of the spirit. An ecstasy of flight made radiant his eyes and wild his breath and tremulous and wild and radiant his windswept limbs.

— One! Two! . . . Look out!

— O, cripes, I'm drownded!

— One! Two! Three and away!

— Me next! Me next!

— One! . . . Uk!

— Stephaneforos!

His throat ached with a desire to cry aloud, the cry of a hawk or eagle on high, to cry piercingly of his deliverance to the winds. This was the call of life to his soul not the dull gross voice of the world of duties and despair, not the inhuman voice that had called him to the pale service of the altar. An instant of wild flight had delivered him and the cry of triumph which his lips withheld cleft his brain.

— Stephaneforos!

What were they now but the cerements° shaken from the body of death — the fear he had walked in night and day, the incertitude that had ringed him round, the shame that had abased him within and without — cerements, the linens of the grave?

His soul had arisen from the grave of boyhood, spurning her graveclothes. Yes! Yes! Yes! He would create proudly out of the freedom and power of his soul, as the great artificer whose name he bore, a living thing, new and soaring and beautiful, impalpable, imperishable.

He started up nervously from the stoneblock° for he could no longer quench the flame in his blood. He felt his cheeks aflame and his throat throbbing with song. There was a lust of wandering in his feet that burned to set out for the ends of the earth. On! On! his heart seemed to cry. Evening would deepen above the sea, night fall upon the plains, dawn glimmer before the wanderer and show him strange fields and hills and faces. Where?

He looked northward towards Howth. The sea had fallen below the line of seawrack on the shallow side of the breakwater and already the tide was running out fast along the foreshore. Already one long oval bank of sand lay warm and dry amid the wavelets. Here and there warm isles of sand gleamed above the shallow tide: and about the isles and around the long bank and amid the shallow currents of the beach were lightclad gayclad figures, wading and delving.

---

cerements: Burial clothes.   **the stoneblock:** Term for a group of rocks on the side of Bull Wall suitable for diving.

In a few moments he was barefoot, his stockings folded in his pockets and his canvas shoes dangling by their knotted laces over his shoulders: and, picking a pointed salteaten stick out of the jetsam among the rocks, he clambered down the slope of the breakwater.

There was a long rivulet in the strand: and, as he waded slowly up its course, he wondered at the endless drift of seaweed. Emerald and black and russet and olive, it moved beneath the current, swaying and turning. The water of the rivulet was dark with endless drift and mirrored the highdrifting clouds. The clouds were drifting above him silently and silently the seatangle was drifting below him; and the grey warm air was still: and a new wild life was singing in his veins.

Where was his boyhood now? Where was the soul that had hung back from her destiny, to brood alone upon the shame of her wounds and in her house of squalor and subterfuge to queen it in faded cerements and in wreaths that withered at the touch? Or where was he?

He was alone. He was unheeded, happy and near to the wild heart of life. He was alone and young and wilful and wildhearted, alone amid a waste of wild air and brackish waters and the seaharvest of shells and tangle and veiled grey sunlight and gayclad lightclad figures, of children and girls and voices childish and girlish in the air.

A girl stood before him in midstream: alone and still, gazing out to sea. She seemed like one whom magic had changed into the likeness of a strange and beautiful seabird. Her long slender bare legs were delicate as a crane's and pure save where an emerald trail of seaweed had fashioned itself as a sign upon the flesh. Her thighs, fuller and soft-hued as ivory, were bared almost to the hips where the white fringes of her drawers were like featherings of soft white down. Her slateblue skirts were kilted boldly about her waist and dovetailed behind her. Her bosom was as a bird's, soft and slight; slight and soft as the breast of some darkplumaged dove. But her long fair hair was girlish; and girlish and touched with the wonder of mortal beauty, her face.

She was alone and still, gazing out to sea; and when she felt his presence and the worship of his eyes her eyes turned to him in quiet sufferance of his gaze, without shame or wantonness. Long, long she suffered his gaze and then quietly withdrew her eyes from his and bent them towards the stream, gently stirring the water with her foot hither and thither. The first faint noise of gently moving water broke the silence, low and faint and whispering, faint as the bells of sleep; hither and thither, hither and thither: and a faint flame trembled on her cheek.

— Heavenly God! cried Stephen's soul, in an outburst of profane joy.

He turned away from her suddenly and set off across the strand. His cheeks were aflame; his body was aglow; his limbs were trembling. On and on and on and on he strode, far out over the sands, singing wildly to the sea, crying to greet the advent of the life that had cried to him.

Her image had passed into his soul for ever and no word had broken the holy silence of his ecstasy. Her eyes had called him and his soul had leaped at the call. To live, to err, to fall, to triumph, to recreate life out of life! A wild angel had appeared to him, the angel of mortal youth and beauty, an envoy from the fair courts of life, to throw open before him in an instant of ecstasy the gates of all the ways of error and glory. On and on and on and on!

He halted suddenly and heard his heart in the silence. How far had he walked? What hour was it?

There was no human figure near him nor any sound borne to him over the air. But the tide was near the turn and already the day was on the wane. He turned landward and ran towards the shore and, running up the sloping beach, reckless of the sharp shingle, found a sandy nook amid a ring of tufted sandknolls and lay down there that the peace and silence of the evening might still the riot of his blood.

He felt above him the vast indifferent dome and the calm processes of the heavenly bodies: and the earth beneath him, the earth that had borne him, had taken him to her breast.

He closed his eyes in the languor of sleep. His eyelids trembled as if they felt the vast cyclic movement of the earth and her watchers, trembled as if they felt the strange light of some new world. His soul was swooning into some new world, fantastic, dim, uncertain as under sea, traversed by cloudy shapes and beings. A world, a glimmer or a flower? Glimmering and trembling, trembling and unfolding, a breaking light, an opening flower, it spread in endless succession to itself, breaking in full crimson and unfolding and fading to palest rose, leaf by leaf and wave of light by wave of light, flooding all the heavens with its soft flushes, every flush deeper than other.

Evening had fallen when he woke and the sand and arid grasses of his bed glowed no longer. He rose slowly and, recalling the rapture of his sleep, sighed at its joy.

He climbed to the crest of the sandhill and gazed about him. Evening had fallen. A rim of the young moon cleft the pale waste of sky like the rim of a silver hoop embedded in grey sand: and the tide was flowing in fast to the land with a low whisper of her waves, islanding a few last figures in distant pools.

V

He drained his third cup of watery tea to the dregs and set to chewing the crusts of fried bread that were scattered near him, staring into the dark pool of the jar. The yellow dripping had been scooped out like a boghole and the pool under it brought back to his memory the dark turfcoloured water of the bath in Clongowes. The box of pawntickets at his elbow had just been rifled and he took up idly one after another in his greasy fingers the blue and white dockets, scrawled and sanded and creased and bearing the name of the pledger as Daly or MacEvoy.

1 Pair Buskins.°
1 D. Coat
3 Articles and White.
1 Man's Pants.

Then he put them aside and gazed thoughtfully at the lid of the box, speckled with lousemarks, and asked vaguely:

— How much is the clock fast now?

His mother straightened the battered alarmclock that was lying on its side in the middle of the kitchen mantelpiece until its dial showed a quarter to twelve and then laid it once more on its side.

— An hour and twentyfive minutes, she said. The right time now is twenty past ten. The dear knows you might try to be in time for your lectures.

— Fill out the place for me to wash, said Stephen.

— Katey, fill out the place for Stephen to wash.

— Boody, fill out the place for Stephen to wash.

— I can't, I'm going for blue.° Fill it out, you, Maggie.

When the enamelled basin had been fitted into the well of the sink and the old washingglove flung on the side of it he allowed his mother to scrub his neck and root into the folds of his ears and into the interstices at the wings of his nose.

— Well, it's a poor case, she said, when a university student is so dirty that his mother has to wash him.

— But it gives you pleasure, said Stephen calmly.

An earsplitting whistle was heard from upstairs and his mother thrust a damp overall into his hands, saying:

— Dry yourself and hurry out for the love of goodness.

Buskins: Ceremonial stockings of silk worn by the celebrant of a mass.   *going for blue:* Working as hard as possible (alternatively, "bluing" is used in washing clothes).

A second shrill whistle, prolonged angrily, brought one of the girls to the foot of the staircase.

— Yes, father?

— Is your lazy bitch of a brother gone out yet?

— Yes, father.

— Sure?

— Yes, father.

— Hm!

The girl came back making signs to him to be quick and go out quietly by the back. Stephen laughed and said:

— He has a curious idea of genders if he thinks a bitch is masculine.

— Ah, it's a scandalous shame for you, Stephen, said his mother, and you'll live to rue the day you set your foot in that place. I know how it has changed you.

— Good morning, everybody, said Stephen, smiling and kissing the tips of his fingers in adieu.

The lane behind the terrace was waterlogged and as he went down it slowly, choosing his steps amid heaps of wet rubbish, he heard a mad nun screeching in the nuns' madhouse beyond the wall.

— Jesus! O Jesus! Jesus!

He shook the sound out of his ears by an angry toss of his head and hurried on, stumbling through the mouldering offal, his heart already bitten by an ache of loathing and bitterness. His father's whistle, his mother's mutterings, the screech of an unseen maniac were to him now so many voices offending and threatening to humble the pride of his youth. He drove their echoes even out of his heart with an execration: but, as he walked down the avenue and felt the grey morning light falling about him through the dripping trees and smelt the strange wild smell of the wet leaves and bark, his soul was loosed of her miseries.

The rainladen trees of the avenue evoked in him, as always, memories of the girls and women in the plays of Gerhart Hauptmann:° and the memory of their pale sorrows and the fragrance falling from the wet branches mingled in a mood of quiet joy. His morning walk across the city had begun: and he foreknew that as he passed the sloblands° of Fairview he would think of the cloistral silverveined prose of Newman, that as he walked along the North Strand Road, glancing idly at the windows of the provision shops, he would recall the dark humour of

---

Gerhart Hauptmann: (1862–1946), German writer. His women characters are often delicate and tragic.   *sloblands:* Local term for a particular trashy area of tidal flatland.

Guido Cavalcanti° and smile, that as he went by Baird's stonecutting works in Talbot Place the spirit of Ibsen° would blow through him like a keen wind, a spirit of wayward boyish beauty, and that passing a grimy marinedealer's shop beyond the Liffey he would repeat the song by Ben Jonson° which begins:

I was not wearier where I lay.

His mind, when wearied of its search for the essence of beauty amid the spectral words of Aristotle or Aquinas, turned often for its pleasure to the dainty songs of the Elizabethans. His mind, in the vesture of a doubting monk, stood often in shadow under the windows of that age, to hear the grave and mocking music of the lutenists or the frank laughter of waistcoateers° until a laugh too low, a phrase, tarnished by time, of chambering° and false honour, stung his monkish pride and drove him on from his lurkingplace.

The lore which he was believed to pass his days brooding upon so that it had rapt him from the companionships of youth was only a garner of slender sentences from Aristotle's poetics and psychology and a *Synopsis Philosophiæ Scholasticæ ad mentem divi Thomæ.°* His thinking was a dusk of doubt and selfmistrust lit up at moments by the lightnings of intuition, but lightnings of so clear a splendour that in those moments the world perished about his feet as if it had been fireconsumed: and thereafter his tongue grew heavy and he met the eyes of others with unanswering eyes for he felt that the spirit of beauty had folded him round like a mantle and that in revery at least he had been acquainted with nobility. But, when this brief pride of silence upheld him no longer, he was glad to find himself still in the midst of common lives, passing on his way amid the squalor and noise and sloth of the city fearlessly and with a light heart.

Near the hoardings° on the canal he met the consumptive man with the doll's face and the brimless hat coming towards him down the slope of the bridge with little steps, tightly buttoned into his chocolate overcoat and holding his furled umbrella a span or two from him like a

***

Guido Cavalcanti: (1259–1300), Italian poet whose style derived from troubadour lyrics.   **Ibsen:** (1828–1906), Henrik Ibsen, Norwegian dramatist, hero of the young Joyce.   **Ben Jonson:** (1572–1637), English poet and dramatist contemporary with Shakespeare. This line is from *The Vision of Delight* (1617).   **waistcoateers:** Prostitutes (Elizabethan term).   **chambering:** Wanton sexual indulgence (Elizabethan term). **Synopsis Philosophiæ . . . :** *A Synopsis of Scholastic Philosophy for the Understanding of St. Thomas* (Aquinas).   **hoardings:** Billboards.

diviningrod. It must be eleven, he thought, and peered into a dairy to see the time. The clock in the dairy told him that it was five minutes to five but, as he turned away, he heard a clock somewhere near him but unseen beating eleven strokes in swift precision. He laughed as he heard it for it made him think of MacCann, and he saw him a squat figure in a shooting jacket and breeches and with a fair goatee, standing in the wind at Hopkins' corner, and heard him say:

— Dedalus, you're an antisocial being, wrapped up in yourself. I'm not. I'm a democrat: and I'll work and act for social liberty and equality among all classes and sexes in the United States of the Europe of the future.

Eleven! Then he was late for that lecture too. What day of the week was it? He stopped at a newsagent's to read the headline of a placard. Thursday. Ten to eleven, English; eleven to twelve, French; twelve to one, physics. He fancied to himself the English lecture and felt, even at that distance, restless and helpless. He saw the heads of his classmates meekly bent as they wrote in their notebooks the points they were bidden to note, nominal definitions, essential definitions and examples or dates of birth or death, chief works, a favourable and an unfavourable criticism side by side. His own head was unbent for his thoughts wandered abroad and whether he looked around the little class of students or out of the window across the desolate gardens of the green an odour assailed him of cheerless cellardamp and decay. Another head than his, right before him in the first benches, was poised squarely above its bending fellows like the head of a priest appealing without humility to the tabernacle for the humble worshippers about him. Why was it that when he thought of Cranly he could never raise before his mind the entire image of his body but only the image of the head and face? Even now against the grey curtain of the morning he saw it before him like the phantom of a dream, the face of a severed head or deathmask, crowned on the brows by its stiff black upright hair as by an iron crown. It was a priestlike face, priestlike in its pallor, in the widewinged nose, in the shadowings below the eyes and along the jaws, priestlike in the lips that were long and bloodless and faintly smiling: and Stephen, remembering swiftly how he had told Cranly of all the tumults and unrest and longings in his soul, day after day and night by night, only to be answered by his friend's listening silence, would have told himself that it was the face of a guilty priest who heard confessions of those whom he had not power to absolve but that he felt again in memory the gaze of its dark womanish eyes.

Through this image he had a glimpse of a strange dark cavern of speculation but at once turned away from it, feeling that it was not yet the hour to enter it. But the nightshade of his friend's listlessness seemed to be diffusing in the air around him a tenuous and deadly exhalation and he found himself glancing from one casual word to another on his right or left in stolid wonder that they had been so silently emptied of instantaneous sense until every mean shop legend bound his mind like the words of a spell and his soul shrivelled up, sighing with age as he walked on in a lane among heaps of dead language. His own consciousness of language was ebbing from his brain and trickling into the very words themselves which set to band and disband themselves in wayward rhythms:

> The ivy whines upon the wall
> And whines and twines upon the wall
> The ivy whines upon the wall
> The yellow ivy on the wall
> Ivy, ivy up the wall.

Did any one ever hear such drivel? Lord Almighty! Who ever heard of ivy whining on a wall? Yellow ivy: that was all right. Yellow ivory also. And what about ivory ivy?

The word now shone in his brain, clearer and brighter than any ivory sawn from the mottled tusks of elephants. *Ivory, ivoire, avorio, ebur.*° One of the first examples that he had learnt in Latin had run: *India mittit ebur;*° and he recalled the shrewd northern face of the rector who had taught him to construe the Metamorphoses of Ovid° in a courtly English, made whimsical by the mention of porkers and potsherds and chines of bacon. He had learnt what little he knew of the laws of Latin verse from a ragged book written by a Portuguese priest.

Contrahit orator, variant in carmine vates.°

The crises and victories and secessions in Roman history were handed on to him in the trite words *in tanto discrimine*° and he had tried to peer into the social life of the city of cities through the words *implere ollam denariorum*° which the rector had rendered sonorously as the filling of a pot with denaries. The pages of his timeworn Horace° never

---

Ivory, ivoire, avorio, ebur: The same word in English, French, Italian, and Latin. *India mittit ebur:* India sends (or produces) ivory.   *Metamorphoses of Ovid:* Publius Ovidius Naso (43 B.C.–A.D. 18), poetic narratives centering on marvelous transformations.   *Contrahit orator . . . vates:* The orator summarizes; the poet (or prophet) amplifies (or transforms).   *in tanto discrimine:* In such a crisis.   *implere ollam denariorum:* To fill the jar with denarii (Roman silver coins).   *Horace:* Quintus Horatius Flaccus (56–8 B.C.), Roman poet.

felt cold to the touch even when his own fingers were cold: they were human pages: and fifty years before they had been turned by the human fingers of John Duncan Inverarity and by his brother William Malcolm Inverarity. Yes, those were noble names on the dusky flyleaf and, even for so poor a Latinist as he, the dusky verses were as fragrant as though they had lain all those years in myrtle and lavender and vervain: but yet it wounded him to think that he would never be but a shy guest at the feast of the world's culture and that the monkish learning, in terms of which he was striving to forge out an esthetic philosophy, was held no higher by the age he lived in than the subtle and curious jargons of heraldry and falconry.

The grey block of Trinity on his left, set heavily in the city's ignorance like a great dull stone set in a cumbrous ring, pulled his mind downward: and while he was striving this way and that to free his feet from the fetters of the reformed conscience he came upon the droll statue of the national poet of Ireland.°

He looked at it without anger: for, though sloth of the body and of the soul crept over it like unseen vermin, over the shuffling feet and up the folds of the cloak and around the servile head, it seemed humbly conscious of its indignity. It was a Firbolg in the borrowed cloak of a Milesian,° and he thought of his friend Davin, the peasant student. It was a jesting name between them but the young peasant bore with it lightly saying:

— Go on, Stevie. I have a hard head, you tell me. Call me what you will.

The homely version of his christian name on the lips of his friend had touched Stephen pleasantly when first heard for he was as formal in speech with others as they were with him. Often, as he sat in Davin's rooms in Grantham Street, wondering at his friend's wellmade boots that flanked the wall pair by pair and repeating for his friend's simple ear the verses and cadences of others which were the veils of his own longing and dejection, the rude Firbolg mind of his listener had drawn his mind towards it and flung it back again, drawing it by a quiet inbred courtesy of attention or by a quaint turn of old English speech or by the force of its delight in rude bodily skill — for Davin had sat at the feet of Michael Cusack,° the Gael° — repelling swiftly and suddenly by a

---

national poet of Ireland: Thomas Moore.   *Firbolg . . . Milesian:* Firbolgs were thought to be the original small, dark inhabitants of Ireland, Milesians later, taller and more cultivated invaders.   *Michael Cusack:* (1847–1907), Founder of the Gaelic Athletic Association, an active nationalist.   *Gael:* Irishman or Celt.

grossness of intelligence or by a bluntness of feeling or by a dull stare of terror in the eyes, the terror of soul of a starving Irish village in which the curfew was still a nightly fear.

Side by side with his memory of the deeds of prowess of his uncle Mat Davin, the athlete, the young peasant worshipped the sorrowful legend of Ireland. The gossip of his fellowstudents which strove to render the flat life of the college significant at any cost loved to think of him as a young fenian. His nurse had taught him Irish and shaped his rude imagination by the broken lights of Irish myth. He stood towards this myth upon which no individual mind had ever drawn out a line of beauty and to its unwieldy tales that divided against themselves as they moved down the cycles° in the same attitude as towards the Roman catholic religion, the attitude of a dullwitted loyal serf. Whatsoever of thought or of feeling came to him from England or by way of English culture his mind stood armed against in obedience to a password: and of the world that lay beyond England he knew only the foreign legion of France in which he spoke of serving.

Coupling this ambition with the young man's diffident humour Stephen had often called him one of the tame geese:° and there was even a point of irritation in the name pointed against that very reluctance of speech and deed in his friend which seemed so often to stand between Stephen's mind, eager of speculation, and the hidden ways of Irish life.

One night the young peasant, his spirit stung by the violent or luxurious language in which Stephen escaped from the cold silence of intellectual revolt, had called up before Stephen's mind a strange vision. The two were walking slowly towards Davin's room through the dark narrow streets of the poorer jews.

— A thing happened to myself, Stevie, last autumn, coming on winter, and I never told it to a living soul and you are the first person now I ever told it to. I disremember if it was October or November. It was October because it was before I came up here to join the matriculation class.

Stephen had turned his smiling eyes towards his friend's face, flattered by his confidence and won over to sympathy by the speaker's simple accent.

— I was away all that day from my own place over in Buttevant — I don't know if you know where that is — at a hurling match° between

---

cycles: Related groups of Irish myths and legends.   *tame geese:* Joke on "the wild geese," a term for Irish who went into exile.   *hurling match:* Irish game, a sort of field hockey.

the Croke's Own Boys and the Fearless Thurles and by God, Stevie, that was the hard fight. My first cousin, Fonsy Davin, was stripped to his buff° that day minding cool° for the Limericks but he was up with the forwards half the time and shouting like mad. I never will forget that day. One of the Crokes made a woeful wipe° at him one time with his camaun° and I declare to God he was within an aim's ace° of getting it at the side of the temple. O, honest to God, if the crook of it caught him that time he was done for.

— I am glad he escaped, Stephen had said with a laugh, but surely that's not the strange thing that happened to you?

— Well, I suppose that doesn't interest you but leastways there was such noise after the match that I missed the train home and I couldn't get any kind of a yoke° to give me a lift for, as luck would have it, there was a mass meeting that same day over in Castletownroche and all the cars in the country were there. So there was nothing for it only to stay the night or to foot it out. Well, I started to walk and on I went and it was coming on night when I got into the Ballyhoura hills; that's better than ten miles from Kilmallock and there's a long lonely road after that. You wouldn't see the sign of a christian house along the road or hear a sound. It was pitch dark almost. Once or twice I stopped by the way under a bush to redden my pipe and only for the dew was thick I'd have stretched out there and slept. At last, after a bend of the road, I spied a little cottage with a light in the window. I went up and knocked at the door. A voice asked who was there and I answered I was over at the match in Buttevant and was walking back and that I'd be thankful for a glass of water. After a while a young woman opened the door and brought me out a big mug of milk. She was half undressed as if she was going to bed when I knocked and she had her hair hanging: and I thought by her figure and by something in the look of her eyes that she must be carrying a child. She kept me in talk a long while at the door and I thought it strange because her breast and her shoulders were bare. She asked me was I tired and would I like to stop the night there. She said she was all alone in the house and that her husband had gone that morning to Queenstown with his sister to see her off. And all the time she was talking, Stevie, she had her eyes fixed on my face and she stood so close to me I could hear her breathing. When I handed her back the mug at last she took my hand to draw me in over the threshold

---

buff: Skin.   *minding cool*: Playing safety defender.   *woeful wipe*: Huge blow to the ball.   *camaun*: Curved stick used in hurling.   *aim's ace*: Very small amount or distance.   *yoke*: Idiomatic Irish expression for "thing" (any artifact).

and said: *Come in and stay the night here. You've no call to be frightened. There's no-one in it but ourselves.* . . . I didn't go in, Stevie. I thanked her and went on my way again, all in a fever. At the first bend of the road I looked back and she was standing in the door.

The last words of Davin's story sang in his memory and the figure of the woman in the story stood forth reflected in other figures of the peasant women whom he had seen standing in the doorways at Clane as the college cars drove by, as a type of her race and his own, a batlike soul waking to the consciousness of itself in darkness and secrecy and loneliness and, through the eyes and voice and gesture of a woman without guile, calling the stranger to her bed.

A hand was laid on his arm and a young voice cried:

— Ah, gentleman, your own girl, sir! The first handsel° today, gentleman. Buy that lovely bunch. Will you, gentleman?

The blue flowers which she lifted towards him and her young blue eyes seemed to him at that instant images of guilelessness: and he halted till the image had vanished and he saw only her ragged dress and damp coarse hair and hoydenish face.

— Do, gentleman! Don't forget your own girl, sir!

— I have no money, said Stephen.

— Buy them lovely ones, will you, sir? Only a penny.

— Did you hear what I said? asked Stephen, bending towards her. I told you I had no money. I tell you again now.

— Well, sure, you will some day, sir, please God, the girl answered after an instant.

— Possibly, said Stephen, but I don't think it likely.

He left her quickly fearing that her intimacy might turn to gibing and wishing to be out of the way before she offered her ware to another, a tourist from England or a student of Trinity. Grafton Street along which he walked prolonged that moment of discouraged poverty. In the roadway at the head of the street a slab was set to the memory of Wolfe Tone and he remembered having been present with his father at its laying. He remembered with bitterness that scene of tawdry tribute. There were four French delegates in a brake° and one, a plump smiling young man, held, wedged on a stick, a card on which were printed the words: *Vive l'Irlande!*°

But the trees in Stephen's Green were fragrant of rain and the rain-sodden earth gave forth its mortal odour, a faint incense rising upward

---

handsel: Good-luck omen or gift; also money, as in a tip.   **brake:** Scaffold.   **Vive l'Irlande:** Long live Ireland!

through the mould from many hearts. The soul of the gallant venal city which his elders had told him of had shrunk with time to a faint mortal odour rising from the earth and he knew that in a moment when he entered the sombre college he would be conscious of a corruption other than that of Buck Egan and Burnchapel Whaley.°

It was too late to go upstairs to the French class. He crossed the hall and took the corridor to the left which led to the physics theatre. The corridor was dark and silent but not unwatchful. Why did he feel that it was not unwatchful? Was it because he had heard that in Buck Whaley's time there was a secret staircase there? Or was the jesuit house extraterritorial and was he walking among aliens? The Ireland of Tone and of Parnell seemed to have receded in space.

He opened the door of the theatre and halted in the chilly grey light that struggled through the dusty windows. A figure was crouching before the large grate and by its leanness and greyness he knew that it was the dean of studies lighting the fire. Stephen closed the door quietly and approached the fireplace.

— Good morning, sir! Can I help you?

The priest looked up quickly and said:

— One moment now, Mr Dedalus, and you will see. There is an art in lighting a fire. We have the liberal arts and we have the useful arts. This is one of the useful arts.

— I will try to learn it, said Stephen.

— Not too much coal, said the dean, working briskly at his task, that is one of the secrets.

He produced four candlebutts from the sidepockets of his soutane and placed them deftly among the coals and twisted papers. Stephen watched him in silence. Kneeling thus on the flagstone to kindle the fire and busied with the disposition of his wisps of paper and candlebutts he seemed more than ever a humble server making ready the place of sacrifice in an empty temple, a levite° of the Lord. Like a levite's robe of plain linen the faded worn soutane draped the kneeling figure of one whom the canonicals° or the bellbordered ephod° would irk and trouble. His very body had waxed old in lowly service of the Lord — in tending the fire upon the altar, in bearing tidings secretly, in waiting upon worldlings, in striking swiftly when bidden — and yet had remained ungraced

---

Buck Egan and Burnchapel Whaley: John Egan (ca. 1750–1810), a politician; Richard Whaley (ca. 1700–1769), a Protestant opponent of the Roman Catholic Church. Both could be described as "bucks," high-living members of the Ascendancy class.   **levite:** Subordinate priest.   **canonicals:** Prescribed vestments.   **ephod:** Old Testament religious garment.

by aught of saintly or of prelatic beauty. Nay, his very soul had waxed old in that service without growing towards light and beauty or spreading abroad a sweet odour of her sanctity — a mortified will no more responsive to the thrill of its obedience than was to the thrill of love or combat his aging body, spare and sinewy, greyed with a silverpointed down.

The dean rested back on his hunkers and watched the sticks catch. Stephen, to fill the silence, said:

— I am sure I could not light a fire.

— You are an artist, are you not, Mr Dedalus, said the dean, glancing up and blinking his pale eyes. The object of the artist is the creation of the beautiful. What the beautiful is is another question.

He rubbed his hands slowly and drily over the difficulty.

— Can you solve that question now? he asked.

— Aquinas, answered Stephen, says *Pulcra sunt quæ visa placent.*°

— This fire before us, said the dean, will be pleasing to the eye. Will it therefore be beautiful?

— In so far as it is apprehended by the sight, which I suppose means here esthetic intellection, it will be beautiful. But Aquinas also says *Bonum est in quod tendit appetitus.*° In so far as it satisfies the animal craving for warmth fire is a good. In hell however it is an evil.

— Quite so, said the dean, you have certainly hit the nail on the head.

He rose nimbly and went towards the door, set it ajar and said:

— A draught is said to be a help in these matters.

As he came back to the hearth, limping slightly but with a brisk step, Stephen saw the silent soul of a jesuit look out at him from the pale loveless eyes. Like Ignatius he was lame but in his eyes burned no spark of Ignatius' enthusiasm. Even the legendary craft of the company, a craft subtler and more secret than its fabled books of secret subtle wisdom, had not fired his soul with the energy of apostleship. It seemed as if he used the shifts and lore and cunning of the world, as bidden to do, for the greater glory of God, without joy in their handling or hatred of that in them which was evil but turning them, with a firm gesture of obedience, back upon themselves: and for all this silent service it seemed as if he loved not at all the master and little, if at all, the ends he served. *Similiter atque senis baculus,*° he was, as the founder would have had him, like a staff in an old man's hand, to be left in a corner, to be

---

Pulcra sunt quæ visa placent: That is beautiful which gives pleasure to the eye.   **Bonum est in quod tendit appetitus:** That is good toward which the appetite is moved (or which is desired).   ***Similiter atque senis baculus:*** Like an old man's walking stick.

leaned on in the road at nightfall or in stress of weather, to lie with a lady's nosegay on a garden seat, to be raised in menace.

The dean returned to the hearth and began to stroke his chin.

— When may we expect to have something from you on the esthetic question? he asked.

— From me! said Stephen in astonishment. I stumble on an idea once a fortnight if I am lucky.

— These questions are very profound, Mr Dedalus, said the dean. It is like looking down from the cliffs of Moher into the depths. Many go down into the depths and never come up. Only the trained diver can go down into those depths and explore them and come to the surface again.

— If you mean speculation, sir, said Stephen, I also am sure that there is no such thing as free thinking inasmuch as all thinking must be bound by its own laws.

— Ha!

— For my purpose I can work on at present by the light of one or two ideas of Aristotle and Aquinas.

— I see. I quite see your point.

— I need them only for my own use and guidance until I have done something for myself by their light. If the lamp smokes or smells I shall try to trim it. If it does not give light enough I shall sell it and buy or borrow another.

— Epictetus° also had a lamp, said the dean, which was sold for a fancy price after his death. It was the lamp he wrote his philosophical dissertations by. You know Epictetus?

— An old gentleman, said Stephen coarsely, who said that the soul is very like a bucketful of water.

— He tells us in his homely way, the dean went on, that he put an iron lamp before a statue of one of the gods and that a thief stole the lamp. What did the philosopher do? He reflected that it was the character of a thief to steal and determined to buy an earthen lamp next day instead of the iron lamp.

A smell of molten tallow came up from the dean's candlebutts and fused itself in Stephen's consciousness with the jingle of the words, bucket and lamp and lamp and bucket. The priest's voice too had a hard jingling tone. Stephen's mind halted by instinct, checked by the strange tone and the imagery and by the priest's face which seemed like an unlit

---

Epictetus: Stoic philosopher, b. ca. 50 A.D., who believed men should wish only freedom and contentment.

lamp or a reflector hung in a false focus. What lay behind it or within it? A dull torpor of the soul or the dullness of the thundercloud, charged with intellection and capable of the gloom of God?

— I meant a different kind of lamp, sir, said Stephen.

— Undoubtedly, said the dean.

— One difficulty, said Stephen, in esthetic discussion is to know whether words are being used according to the literary tradition or according to the tradition of the marketplace. I remember a sentence of Newman's in which he says of the Blessed Virgin that she was detained in the full company of the saints. The use of the word in the marketplace is quite different. *I hope I am not detaining you.*

— Not in the least, said the dean politely.

— No, no, said Stephen, smiling, I mean . . .

— Yes, yes: I see, said the dean quickly, I quite catch the point: *detain.*

He thrust forward his under jaw and uttered a dry short cough.

— To return to the lamp, he said, the feeding of it is also a nice problem. You must choose the pure oil and you must be careful when you pour it in not to overflow it, not to pour in more than the funnel can hold.

— What funnel? asked Stephen.

— The funnel through which you pour the oil into your lamp.

— That? said Stephen. Is that called a funnel? Is it not a tundish?°

— What is a tundish?

— That. The . . . the funnel.

— Is that called a tundish in Ireland? asked the dean. I never heard the word in my life.

— It is called a tundish in Lower Drumcondra, said Stephen laughing, where they speak the best English.

— A tundish, said the dean reflectively. That is a most interesting word. I must look that word up. Upon my word I must.

His courtesy of manner rang a little false and Stephen looked at the English convert with the same eyes as the elder brother in the parable may have turned on the prodigal. A humble follower in the wake of clamorous conversions, a poor Englishman in Ireland, he seemed to have entered on the stage of jesuit history when that strange play of intrigue and suffering and envy and struggle and indignity had been all but given through — a latecomer, a tardy spirit. From what had he set out? Perhaps he had been born and bred among serious dissenters, see-

tundish: Archaic English (not Irish) word for a funnel.

ing salvation in Jesus only and abhorring the vain pomps of the establishment. Had he felt the need of an implicit faith amid the welter of
sectarianism and the jargon of its turbulent schisms, six principle men,
peculiar people, seed and snake baptists, supralapsarian dogmatists?°
Had he found the true church all of a sudden in winding up to the end
like a reel of cotton some finespun line of reasoning upon insufflation°
or the imposition of hands or the procession of the Holy Ghost? Or had
Lord Christ touched him and bidden him follow, like that disciple who
had sat at the receipt of custom, as he sat by the door of some zin-
croofed chapel, yawning and telling over his church pence?

The dean repeated the word yet again.

— Tundish! Well now, that is interesting!

— The question you asked me a moment ago seems to me more
interesting. What is that beauty which the artist struggles to express
from lumps of earth, said Stephen coldly.

The little word seemed to have turned a rapier point of his sensitiveness against this courteous and vigilant foe. He felt with a smart of
dejection that the man to whom he was speaking was a countryman of
Ben Jonson. He thought:

— The language in which we are speaking is his before it is mine.
How different are the words *home, Christ, ale, master* on his lips and on
mine! I cannot speak or write these words without unrest of spirit. His
language, so familiar and so foreign, will always be for me an acquired
speech. I have not made or accepted its words. My voice holds them at
bay. My soul frets in the shadow of his language.

— And to distinguish between the beautiful and the sublime, the
dean added. To distinguish between moral beauty and material beauty.
And to inquire what kind of beauty is proper to each of the various arts.
These are some interesting points we might take up.

Stephen, disheartened suddenly by the dean's firm dry tone, was
silent. The dean also was silent: and through the silence a distant noise
of many boots and confused voices came up the staircase.

— In pursuing these speculations, said the dean conclusively, there
is however the danger of perishing of inanition. First you must take your
degree. Set that before you as your first aim. Then, little by little, you
will see your way. I mean in every sense, your way in life and in think-

---

Six principle men . . . dogmatists: Most of these are nineteenth-century American Baptist sects. Supralapsarianism is the belief that God before man's fall had already chosen
some to receive eternal life, rejecting all others. Human effort is irrelevant to the bestow-
ing of God's grace, in this view.   **insufflation:** Breathing on someone or something to
symbolize the coming of the Holy Ghost and the banishing of evil spirits.

ing. It may be uphill pedalling at first. Take Mr Moonan. He was a long time before he got to the top. But he got there.

— I may not have his talent, said Stephen quietly.

— You never know, said the dean brightly. We never can say what is in us. I most certainly should not be despondent. *Per aspera ad astra.*°

He left the hearth quickly and went towards the landing to oversee the arrival of the first arts' class.

Leaning against the fireplace Stephen heard him greet briskly and impartially every student of the class and could almost see the frank smiles of the coarser students. A desolating pity began to fall like a dew upon his easily embittered heart for this faithful servingman of the knightly Loyola, for this halfbrother of the clergy, more venal than they in speech, more steadfast of soul than they, one whom he would never call his ghostly father: and he thought how this man and his companions had earned the name of worldlings at the hands not of the unworldly only but of the worldly also for having pleaded, during all their history, at the bar of God's justice for the souls of the lax and the lukewarm and the prudent.

The entry of the professor was signalled by a few rounds of Kentish fire° from the heavy boots of those students who sat on the highest tier of the gloomy theatre under the grey cobwebbed windows. The calling of the roll began and the responses to the names were given out in all tones until the name of Peter Byrne was reached.

— Here!

A deep bass note in response came from the upper tier, followed by coughs of protest along the other benches.

The professor paused in his reading and called the next name:

— Cranly!

No answer.

— Mr Cranly!

A smile flew across Stephen's face as he thought of his friend's studies.

— Try Leopardstown! said a voice from the bench behind.

Stephen glanced up quickly but Moynihan's snoutish face outlined on the grey light was impassive. A formula was given out. Amid the rustling of the notebooks Stephen turned back again and said:

— Give me some paper for God's sake.

— Are you as bad as that? asked Moynihan with a broad grin.

Per aspera ad astra: By rough ways to the stars (a cliché).   *Kentish fire:* Prolonged stamping or clapping to show impatience or disapproval.

He tore a sheet from his scribbler and passed it down, whispering:

— In case of necessity any layman or woman can do it.

The formula which he wrote obediently on the sheet of paper, the coiling and uncoiling calculations of the professor, the spectrelike symbols of force and velocity fascinated and jaded Stephen's mind. He had heard some say that the old professor was an atheist freemason. O the grey dull day! It seemed a limbo of painless patient consciousness through which souls of mathematicians might wander, projecting long slender fabrics from plane to plane of ever rarer and paler twilight, radiating swift eddies to the last verges of a universe ever vaster, farther and more impalpable.

— So we must distinguish between elliptical and ellipsoidal. Perhaps some of you gentlemen may be familiar with the works of Mr W. S. Gilbert. In one of his songs he speaks of the billiard sharp who is condemned to play:

> On a cloth untrue
> With a twisted cue
> And elliptical billiard balls°

He means a ball having the form of the ellipsoid of the principal axes of which I spoke a moment ago.

Moynihan leaned down towards Stephen's ear and murmured:

— What price ellipsoidal balls! Chase me, ladies, I'm in the cavalry!

His fellowstudent's rude humour ran like a gust through the cloister of Stephen's mind, shaking into gay life limp priestly vestments that hung upon the walls, setting them to sway and caper in a sabbath of misrule. The forms of the community emerged from the gustblown vestments, the dean of studies, the portly florid bursar with his cap of grey hair, the president, the little priest with feathery hair who wrote devout verses, the squat peasant form of the professor of economics, the tall form of the young professor of mental science discussing on the landing a case of conscience with his class like a giraffe cropping high leafage among a herd of antelopes, the grave troubled prefect of the sodality, the plump roundheaded professor of Italian with his rogue's eyes. They came ambling and stumbling, tumbling and capering, kilting their gowns for leap frog, holding one another back, shaken with deep false laughter, smacking one another behind and laughing at their rude malice, calling to one another by familiar nicknames, protesting

On a cloth . . . balls: From *The Mikado*'s last act (1885).

with sudden dignity at some rough usage, whispering two and two behind their hands.

The professor had gone to the glass cases on the sidewall from a shelf of which he took down a set of coils, blew away the dust from many points and, bearing it carefully to the table, held a finger on it while he proceeded with his lecture. He explained that the wires in modern coils were of a compound called platinoid lately discovered by F. W. Martino.°

He spoke clearly the initials and surname of the discoverer. Moynihan whispered from behind:

— Good old Fresh Water Martin!

— Ask him, Stephen whispered back with weary humour, if he wants a subject for electrocution. He can have me.

Moynihan, seeing the professor bend over the coils, rose in his bench and, clacking noiselessly the fingers of his right hand, began to call with the voice of a slobbering urchin:

— Please, teacher! Please, teacher! This boy is after saying a bad word, teacher.

— Platinoid, the professor said solemnly, is preferred to German silver because it has a lower coefficient of resistance variation by changes of temperature. The platinoid wire is insulated and the covering of silk that insulates it is wound double on the ebonite bobbins just where my finger is. If it were wound single an extra current would be induced in the coils. The bobbins are saturated in hot paraffin wax . . .

A sharp Ulster voice said from the bench below Stephen:

— Are we likely to be asked questions on applied science?

The professor began to juggle gravely with the terms pure science and applied science. A heavybuilt student wearing gold spectacles stared with some wonder at the questioner. Moynihan murmured from behind in his natural voice:

— Isn't MacAlister a devil for his pound of flesh?

Stephen looked down coldly on the oblong skull beneath him overgrown with tangled twinecoloured hair. The voice, the accent, the mind of the questioner offended him and he allowed the offence to carry him towards wilful unkindness, bidding his mind think that the student's father would have done better had he sent his son to Belfast to study and have saved something on the trainfare by so doing.

F. W. Martino: Fernando Wood Martin was an American chemist who published on platinum.

The oblong skull beneath did not turn to meet this shaft of thought and yet the shaft came back to its bowstring: for he saw in a moment the student's wheypale face.

— That thought is not mine, he said to himself quickly. It came from the comic Irishman in the bench behind. Patience. Can you say with certitude by whom the soul of your race was bartered and its elect betrayed — by the questioner or by the mocker? Patience. Remember Epictetus. It is probably in his character to ask such a question at such a moment in such a tone and to pronounce the word *science* as a monosyllable.

The droning voice of the professor continued to wind itself slowly round and round the coils it spoke of, doubling, trebling, quadrupling its somnolent energy as the coil multiplied its ohms of resistance.

Moynihan's voice called from behind in echo to a distant bell:

— Closing time, gents!°

The entrance hall was crowded and loud with talk. On a table near the door were two photographs in frames and between them a long roll of paper bearing an irregular tail of signatures. MacCann went briskly to and fro among the students, talking rapidly, answering rebuffs and leading one after another to the table. In the inner hall the dean of studies stood talking to a young professor, stroking his chin gravely and nodding his head.

Stephen, checked by the crowd at the door, halted irresolutely. From under the wide falling leaf of a soft hat Cranly's dark eyes were watching him.

— Have you signed? Stephen asked.

Cranly closed his long thinlipped mouth, communed with himself an instant and answered:

— *Ego habeo.*°

— What is it for?

— *Quod?*°

— What is it for?

Cranly turned his pale face to Stephen and said blandly and bitterly:

— *Per pax universalis.*°

Stephen pointed to the Czar's photograph° and said:

— He has the face of a besotted Christ.

Closing time, gents: How the end of legal drinking hours might be announced at a pub. *Ego habeo:* I have, in "dog Latin," a humorous schoolboy imitation of Latin that translates English words literally and is scattered throughout the following conversations. *Quod:* What?   *Per pax universalis:* For universal peace.   *Czar's photograph:* Tsar Nicholas II of Russia issued a "Peace Rescript" in 1898.

The scorn and anger in his voice brought Cranly's eyes back from a calm survey of the walls of the hall.

— Are you annoyed? he asked.

— No, answered Stephen.

— Are you in bad humour?

— No.

— *Credo ut vos sanguinarius mendax estis,* said Cranly, *quia facies vostra monstrat ut vos in damno malo humore estis.*°

Moynihan, on his way to the table, said in Stephen's ear:

— MacCann is in tiptop form. Ready to shed the last drop. Brand-new world. No stimulants and votes for the bitches.

Stephen smiled at the manner of this confidence and, when Moynihan had passed, turned again to meet Cranly's eyes.

— Perhaps you can tell me, he said, why he pours his soul so freely into my ear. Can you?

A dull scowl appeared on Cranly's forehead. He stared at the table where Moynihan had bent to write his name on the roll, and then said flatly:

— A sugar!

— *Quis est in malo humore,* said Stephen, *ego aut vos?*°

Cranly did not take up the taunt. He brooded sourly on his judgment and repeated with the same flat force:

— A flaming bloody sugar, that's what he is!

It was his epitaph for all dead friendships and Stephen wondered whether it would ever be spoken in the same tone over his memory. The heavy lumpish phrase sank slowly out of hearing like a stone through a quagmire. Stephen saw it sink as he had seen many an other, feeling its heaviness depress his heart. Cranly's speech, unlike that of Davin, had neither rare phrases of Elizabethan English nor quaintly turned versions of Irish idioms. Its drawl was an echo of the quays of Dublin given back by a bleak decaying seaport, its energy an echo of the sacred eloquence of Dublin given back flatly by a Wicklow pulpit.

The heavy scowl faded from Cranly's face as MacCann marched briskly towards them from the other side of the hall.

— Here you are! said MacCann cheerily.

— Here I am! said Stephen.

— Late as usual. Can you not combine the progressive tendency with a respect for punctuality?

Credo ut vos . . . estis: I think you are a bloody liar, because your face shows you are in a damned bad humor.   *Quis est . . . vos:* Who is in a bad humor, you or I?

— That question is out of order, said Stephen. Next business.

His smiling eyes were fixed on a silverwrapped tablet of milk chocolate which peeped out of the propagandist's breastpocket. A little ring of listeners closed round to hear the war of wits. A lean student with olive skin and lank black hair thrust his face between the two, glancing from one to the other at each phrase and seeming to try to catch each flying phrase in his open moist mouth. Cranly took a small grey handball from his pocket and began to examine it closely, turning it over and over.

— Next business? said MacCann. Hom!

He gave a loud cough of laughter, smiled broadly and tugged twice at the strawcoloured goatee which hung from his blunt chin.

— The next business is to sign the testimonial.

— Will you pay me anything if I sign? asked Stephen.

— I thought you were an idealist, said MacCann.

The gipsylike student looked about him and addressed the onlookers in an indistinct bleating voice.

— By hell, that's a queer notion. I consider that notion to be a mercenary notion.

His voice faded into silence. No heed was paid to his words. He turned his olive face, equine in expression, towards Stephen, inviting him to speak again.

MacCann began to speak with fluent energy of the Czar's rescript,° of Stead,° of general disarmament, arbitration in cases of international disputes, of the signs of the times, of the new humanity and the new gospel of life which would make it the business of the community to secure as cheaply as possible the greatest possible happiness of the greatest possible number.

The gipsy student responded to the close of the period by crying:

— Three cheers for universal brotherhood!

— Go on, Temple, said a stout ruddy student near him. I'll stand you a pint after.

— I'm a believer in universal brotherhood, said Temple, glancing about him out of his dark, oval eyes. Marx is only a bloody cod.°

Cranly gripped his arm tightly to check his tongue, smiling uneasily, and repeated:

— Easy, easy, easy!

rescript: Originally, an epistle issued by the pope regarding some question referred to him.   ***Stead:*** William Thomas Stead (1849–1912), crusading journalist and publisher. ***cod:*** A joker or fool.

Temple struggled to free his arm but continued, his mouth flecked by a thin foam:

— Socialism was founded by an Irishman and the first man in Europe who preached the freedom of thought was Collins. Two hundred years ago. He denounced priestcraft, the philosopher of Middlesex. Three cheers for John Anthony Collins!°

A thin voice from the verge of the ring replied:

— Pip! pip!

Moynihan murmured beside Stephen's ear:

— And what about John Anthony's poor little sister:

Lottie Collins lost her drawers;
Won't you kindly lend her yours?

Stephen laughed and Moynihan, pleased with the result, murmured again:

— We'll have five bob each way on John Anthony Collins.

— I am waiting for your answer, said MacCann briefly.

— The affair doesn't interest me in the least, said Stephen wearily. You know that well. Why do you make a scene about it?

— Good! said MacCann, smacking his lips. You are a reactionary then?

— Do you think you impress me, Stephen asked, when you flourish your wooden sword?

— Metaphors! said MacCann bluntly. Come to facts.

Stephen blushed and turned aside. MacCann stood his ground and said with hostile humour:

— Minor poets, I suppose, are above such trivial questions as the question of universal peace.

Cranly raised his head and held the handball between the two students by way of a peaceoffering, saying:

— *Pax super totum sanguinarium globum.*°

Stephen, moving away the bystanders, jerked his shoulder angrily in the direction of the Czar's image, saying:

— Keep your icon. If we must have a Jesus, let us have a legitimate Jesus.

— By hell, that's a good one! said the gipsy student to those about him. That's a fine expression. I like that expression immensely.

He gulped down the spittle in his throat as if he were gulping down

---

John Anthony Collins: (1676–1729), deist and author of *Discourse of Free-Thinking* (1713).   *Pax super . . . globum:* Peace over the whole bloody world.

the phrase and, fumbling at the peak of his tweed cap, turned to Stephen, saying:

— Excuse me, sir, what do you mean by that expression you uttered just now?

Feeling himself jostled by the students near him, he said to them:

— I am curious to know now what he meant by that expression.

He turned again to Stephen and said in a whisper:

— Do you believe in Jesus? I believe in man. Of course, I don't know if you believe in man. I admire you, sir. I admire the mind of man independent of all religions. Is that your opinion about the mind of Jesus?

— Go on, Temple, said the stout ruddy student, returning, as was his wont, to his first idea, that pint is waiting for you.

— He thinks I'm an imbecile, Temple explained to Stephen, because I'm a believer in the power of mind.

Cranly linked his arms into those of Stephen and his admirer and said:

— *Nos ad manum ballum jocabimus.°*

Stephen, in the act of being led away, caught sight of MacCann's flushed bluntfeatured face.

— My signature is of no account, he said politely. You are right to go your way. Leave me to go mine.

— Dedalus, said MacCann crisply, I believe you're a good fellow but you have yet to learn the dignity of altruism and the responsibility of the human individual.

A voice said:

— Intellectual crankery is better out of this movement than in it.

Stephen, recognising the harsh tone of MacAlister's voice, did not turn in the direction of the voice. Cranly pushed solemnly through the throng of students, linking Stephen and Temple like a celebrant attended by his ministers on his way to the altar.

Temple bent eagerly across Cranly's breast and said:

— Did you hear MacAlister what he said? That youth is jealous of you. Did you see that? I bet Cranly didn't see that. By hell, I saw that at once.

As they crossed the inner hall the dean of studies was in the act of escaping from the student with whom he had been conversing. He stood at the foot of the staircase, a foot on the lowest step, his threadbare soutane gathered about him for the ascent with womanish care, nodding his head often and repeating:

— Not a doubt of it, Mr Hackett! Very fine! Not a doubt of it!

Nos ad . . . jocabimus: Let's go play handball.

In the middle of the hall the prefect of the college sodality was speaking earnestly, in a soft querulous voice, with a boarder. As he spoke he wrinkled a little his freckled brow and bit, between his phrases, at a tiny bone pencil.

— I hope the matric men will all come. The first arts men are pretty sure. Second arts° too. We must make sure of the newcomers.

Temple bent again across Cranly, as they were passing through the doorway, and said in a swift whisper:

— Do you know that he is a married man? He was a married man before they converted him. He has a wife and children somewhere. By hell, I think that's the queerest notion I ever heard! Eh?

His whisper trailed off into sly cackling laughter. The moment they were through the doorway Cranly seized him rudely by the neck and shook him, saying:

— You flaming floundering fool! I'll take my dying bible there isn't a bigger bloody ape, do you know, than you in the whole flaming bloody world!

Temple wriggled in his grip, laughing still with sly content, while Cranly repeated flatly at every rude shake:

— A flaming flaring bloody idiot!

They crossed the weedy garden together. The president, wrapped in a heavy loose cloak, was coming towards them along one of the walks, reading his office. At the end of the walk he halted before turning and raised his eyes. The students saluted, Temple fumbling as before at the peak of his cap. They walked forward in silence. As they neared the alley Stephen could hear the thuds of the players' hands and the wet smacks of the ball and Davin's voice crying out excitedly at each stroke.

The three students halted round the box on which Davin sat to follow the game. Temple, after a few moments, sidled across to Stephen and said:

— Excuse me, I wanted to ask you do you believe that Jean Jacques Rousseau° was a sincere man.

Stephen laughed outright. Cranly, picking up the broken stave of a cask from the grass at his foot, turned swiftly and said sternly:

— Temple, I declare to the living God if you say another word, do you know, to anybody on any subject I'll kill you *super spottum*.°

---

matric men ... Second arts: Referring to a set of four examinations to be passed before a degree is granted. *Jean Jacques Rousseau:* (1712–1778), Swiss political philosopher and Romantic, famous for his *Confessions* and the concept of the "noble savage." *super spottum:* On the spot.

— He was like you, I fancy, said Stephen, an emotional man.

— Blast him, curse him! said Cranly broadly. Don't talk to him at all. Sure, you might as well be talking, do you know, to a flaming chamber-pot as talking to Temple. Go home, Temple. For God's sake, go home.

— I don't care a damn about you, Cranly, answered Temple, moving out of reach of the uplifted stave and pointing at Stephen. He's the only man I see in this institution that has an individual mind.

— Institution! Individual! cried Cranly. Go home, blast you, for you're a hopeless bloody man.

— I'm an emotional man, said Temple. That's quite rightly expressed. And I'm proud that I'm an emotionalist.

He sidled out of the alley, smiling slily. Cranly watched him with a blank expressionless face.

— Look at him! he said. Did you ever see such a go-by-the-wall?

His phrase was greeted by a strange laugh from a student who lounged against the wall, his peaked cap down on his eyes. The laugh, pitched in a high key and coming from a so muscular frame, seemed like the whinny of an elephant. The student's body shook all over and, to ease his mirth, he rubbed both his hands delightedly, over his groins.

— Lynch is awake, said Cranly.

Lynch, for answer, straightened himself and thrust forward his chest.

— Lynch puts out his chest, said Stephen, as a criticism of life.

Lynch smote himself sonorously on the chest and said:

— Who has anything to say about my girth?

Cranly took him at the word and the two began to tussle. When their faces had flushed with the struggle they drew apart, panting. Stephen bent down towards Davin who, intent on the game, had paid no heed to the talk of the others.

— And how is my little tame goose? he asked. Did he sign too?

Davin nodded and said:

— And you, Stevie?

Stephen shook his head.

— You're a terrible man, Stevie, said Davin, taking the short pipe from his mouth. Always alone.

— Now that you have signed the petition for universal peace, said Stephen, I suppose you will burn that little copybook I saw in your room.

As Davin did not answer Stephen began to quote:

— Long pace, fianna!° Right incline, fianna! Fianna, by numbers, salute, one, two!

fianna: Irish (Gaelic) for Fenians.

— That's a different question, said Davin. I'm an Irish nationalist, first and foremost. But that's you all out. You're a born sneerer, Stevie.

— When you make the next rebellion with hurleysticks,° said Stephen, and want the indispensable informer tell me. I can find you a few in this college.

— I can't understand you, said Davin. One time I hear you talk against English literature. Now you talk against the Irish informers. What with your name and your ideas . . . Are you Irish at all?

— Come with me now to the office of arms and I will show you the tree of my family, said Stephen.

— Then be one of us, said Davin. Why don't you learn Irish? Why did you drop out of the league class° after the first lesson?

— You know one reason why, answered Stephen.

Davin tossed his head and laughed.

— O, come now, he said. Is it on account of that certain young lady and Father Moran? But that's all in your own mind, Stevie. They were only talking and laughing.

Stephen paused and laid a friendly hand upon Davin's shoulder.

— Do you remember, he said, when we knew each other first? The first morning we met you asked me to show you the way to the matriculation class, putting a very strong stress on the first syllable. You remember? Then you used to address the jesuits as father. You remember? I ask myself about you: *Is he as innocent as his speech?*

— I'm a simple person, said Davin. You know that. When you told me that night in Harcourt Street those things about your private life, honest to God, Stevie, I was not able to eat my dinner. I was quite bad. I was awake a long time that night. Why did you tell me those things?

— Thanks, said Stephen. You mean I am a monster.

— No, said Davin, but I wish you had not told me.

A tide began to surge beneath the calm surface of Stephen's friendliness.

— This race and this country and this life produced me, he said. I shall express myself as I am.

— Try to be one of us, repeated Davin. In your heart you are an Irishman but your pride is too powerful.

— My ancestors threw off their language and took on another, Stephen said. They allowed a handful of foreigners to subject them. Do you fancy I am going to pay in my own life and person debts they made? What for?

---

hurleysticks: Used in the Irish game hurley, a kind of field hockey.   *league class:* Class in Irish language sponsored by the Gaelic League.

— For our freedom, said Davin.

— No honourable and sincere man, said Stephen, has given up to you his life and his youth and his affections from the days of Tone to those of Parnell but you sold him to the enemy or failed him in need or reviled him and left him for another. And you invite me to be one of you. I'd see you damned first.

— They died for their ideals, Stevie, said Davin. Our day will come yet, believe me.

Stephen, following his own thought, was silent for an instant.

— The soul is born, he said vaguely, first in those moments I told you of. It has a slow and dark birth, more mysterious than the birth of the body. When the soul of a man is born in this country there are nets flung at it to hold it back from flight. You talk to me of nationality, language, religion. I shall try to fly by those nets.

Davin knocked the ashes from his pipe.

— Too deep for me, Stevie, he said. But a man's country comes first. Ireland first, Stevie. You can be a poet or a mystic after.

— Do you know what Ireland is? asked Stephen with cold violence. Ireland is the old sow that eats her farrow.

Davin rose from his box and went towards the players, shaking his head sadly. But in a moment his sadness left him and he was hotly disputing with Cranly and the two players who had finished their game. A match of four was arranged, Cranly insisting, however, that his ball should be used. He let it rebound twice or thrice to his hand and struck it strongly and swiftly towards the base of the alley, exclaiming in answer to its thud:

— Your soul!

Stephen stood with Lynch till the score began to rise. Then he plucked him by the sleeve to come away. Lynch obeyed, saying:

— Let us eke° go, as Cranly has it.

Stephen smiled at this sidethrust. They passed back through the garden and out through the hall where the doddering porter was pinning up a notice in the frame. At the foot of the steps they halted and Stephen took a packet of cigarettes from his pocket and offered it to his companion.

— I know you are poor, he said.

— Damn your yellow insolence, answered Lynch.

This second proof of Lynch's culture made Stephen smile again.

---

eke: Archaic for "also" (Cranly probably means to say "e'en").

— It was a great day for European culture, he said, when you made up your mind to swear in yellow.

They lit their cigarettes and turned to the right. After a pause Stephen began:

— Aristotle has not defined pity and terror. I have. I say . . .

Lynch halted and said bluntly:

— Stop! I won't listen! I am sick. I was out last night on a yellow drunk with Horan and Goggins.

Stephen went on:

— Pity is the feeling which arrests the mind in the presence of whatsoever is grave and constant in human sufferings and unites it with the human sufferer. Terror is the feeling which arrests the mind in the presence of whatsoever is grave and constant in human sufferings and unites it with the secret cause.

— Repeat, said Lynch.

Stephen repeated the definitions slowly.

— A girl got into a hansom a few days ago, he went on, in London. She was on her way to meet her mother whom she had not seen for many years. At the corner of a street the shaft of a lorry shivered the window of the hansom in the shape of a star. A long, fine needle of the shivered glass pierced her heart. She died on the instant. The reporter called it a tragic death. It is not. It is remote from terror and pity according to the terms of my definitions.

— The tragic emotion, in fact, is a face looking two ways, towards terror and towards pity, both of which are phases of it. You see I use the word *arrest*. I mean that the tragic emotion is static. Or rather the dramatic emotion is. The feelings excited by improper art are kinetic, desire or loathing. Desire urges us to possess, to go to something; loathing urges us to abandon, to go from something. These are kinetic emotions. The arts which excite them, pornographical or didactic, are therefore improper arts. The esthetic emotion (I use the general term) is therefore static. The mind is arrested and raised above desire and loathing.

— You say that art must not excite desire, said Lynch. I told you that one day I wrote my name in pencil on the backside of the Venus of Praxiteles in the Museum. Was that not desire?

— I speak of normal natures, said Stephen. You also told me that when you were a boy in that charming carmelite° school you ate pieces of dried cowdung.

carmelite: Order of nuns.

Lynch broke again into a whinny of laughter and again rubbed both his hands over his groins but without taking them from his pockets.

— O I did! I did! he cried.

Stephen turned towards his companion and looked at him for a moment boldly in the eyes. Lynch, recovering from his laughter, answered his look from his humbled eyes. The long slender flattened skull beneath the long pointed cap brought before Stephen's mind the image of a hooded reptile. The eyes, too, were reptilelike in glint and gaze. Yet at that instant, humbled and alert in their look, they were lit by one tiny human point, the window of a shrivelled soul, poignant and selfembittered.

— As for that, Stephen said in polite parenthesis, we are all animals. I also am an animal.

— You are, said Lynch.

— But we are just now in a mental world, Stephen continued. The desire and loathing excited by improper esthetic means are really unesthetic emotions not only because they are kinetic in character but also because they are not more than physical. Our flesh shrinks from what it dreads and responds to the stimulus of what it desires by a purely reflex action of the nervous system. Our eyelid closes before we are aware that the fly is about to enter our eye.

— Not always, said Lynch critically.

— In the same way, said Stephen, your flesh responded to the stimulus of a naked statue but it was, I say, simply a reflex action of the nerves. Beauty expressed by the artist cannot awaken in us an emotion which is kinetic or a sensation which is purely physical. It awakens, or ought to awaken, or induces, or ought to induce, an esthetic stasis, an ideal pity or an idea, terror, a stasis called forth, prolonged and at last dissolved by what I call the rhythm of beauty.

— What is that exactly? asked Lynch.

— Rhythm, said Stephen, is the first forma, esthetic relation of part to part in any esthetic whole or of an esthetic whole to its part or parts or of any part to the esthetic whole of which it is a part.

— If that is rhythm, said Lynch, let me hear what you call beauty: and, please remember, though I did eat a cake of cowdung once, that I admire only beauty.

Stephen raised his cap as if in greeting. Then, blushing slightly, he laid his hand on Lynch's thick tweed sleeve.

— We are right, he said, and the others are wrong. To speak of these things and to try to understand their nature and, having understood it, to try slowly and humbly and constantly to express, to press out again, from the gross earth or what it brings forth, from sound and shape and colour which are the prison gates of our soul, an image of the beauty we have come to understand — that is art.

They had reached the canal bridge and, turning from their course, went on by the trees. A crude grey light, mirrored in the sluggish water, and a smell of wet branches over their heads seemed to war against the course of Stephen's thought.

— But you have not answered my question, said Lynch. What is art? What is the beauty it expresses?

— That was the first definition I gave you, you sleepyheaded wretch, said Stephen, when I began to try to think out the matter for myself. Do you remember the night? Cranly lost his temper and began to talk about Wicklow bacon.

— I remember, said Lynch. He told us about them flaming fat devils of pigs.

— Art, said Stephen, is the human disposition of sensible or intelligible matter for an esthetic end. You remember the pigs and forget that. You are a distressing pair, you and Cranly.

Lynch made a grimace at the raw grey sky and said:

— If I am to listen to your esthetic philosophy give me at least another cigarette. I don't care about it. I don't even care about women. Damn you and damn everything. I want a job of five hundred a year. You can't get me one.

Stephen handed him the packet of cigarettes. Lynch took the last one that remained, saying simply:

— Proceed!

— Aquinas, said Stephen, says that is beautiful the apprehension of which pleases.

Lynch nodded.

— I remember that, he said. *Pulcra sunt quæ visa placent.*°

— He uses the word *visa*, said Stephen, to cover esthetic apprehension of all kinds, whether through sight or hearing or through any other avenue of apprehension. This word, though it is vague, is clear enough to keep away good and evil which excite desire and loathing. It means certainly a stasis and not a kinesis. How about the true? It produces also a stasis of the mind. You would not write your name in pencil across the hypothenuse of a rightangled triangle.

— No, said Lynch, give me the hypothenuse of the Venus of Praxiteles.

Pulcra sunt . . . placent: See p. 167.

— Static therefore, said Stephen. Plato, I believe, said that beauty is the splendour of truth. I don't think that it has a meaning but the true and the beautiful are akin. Truth is beheld by the intellect which is appeased by the most satisfying relations of the intelligible: beauty is beheld by the imagination which is appeased by the most satisfying relations of the sensible. The first step in the direction of truth is to understand the frame and scope of the intellect itself, to comprehend the act itself of intellection. Aristotle's entire system of philosophy rests upon his book of psychology and that, I think, rests on his statement that the same attribute cannot at the same time and in the same connection belong to and not belong to the same subject. The first step in the direction of beauty is to understand the frame and scope of the imagination, to comprehend the act itself of esthetic apprehension. Is that clear?

— But what is beauty? asked Lynch impatiently. Out with another definition. Something we see and like! Is that the best you and Aquinas can do?

— Let us take woman, said Stephen.

— Let us take her! said Lynch fervently.

— The Greek, the Turk, the Chinese, the Copt, the Hottentot, said Stephen, all admire a different type of female beauty. That seems to be a maze out of which we cannot escape. I see however two ways out. One is this hypothesis: that every physical quality admired by men in women is in direct connection with the manifold functions of women for the propagation of the species. It may be so. The world, it seems, is drearier than even you, Lynch, imagined. For my part I dislike that way out. It leads to eugenics rather than to esthetic. It leads you out of the maze into a new gaudy lectureroom where MacCann, with one hand on *The Origin of Species°* and the other hand on the new testament, tells you that you admired the great flanks of Venus because you felt that she would bear you burly offspring and admired her great breasts because you felt that she would give good milk to her children and yours.

— Then MacCann is a sulphuryellow liar, said Lynch energetically.

— There remains another way out, said Stephen, laughing.

— To wit? said Lynch.

— This hypothesis, Stephen began.

A long dray laden with old iron came round the corner of sir Patrick Dun's hospital covering the end of Stephen's speech with the harsh roar of jangled and rattling metal. Lynch closed his ears and gave out oath

---

Origin of Species: Charles Darwin's 1859 book *On the Origin of Species by Means of Natural Selection.*

after oath till the dray had passed. Then he turned on his heel rudely. Stephen turned also and waited for a few moments till his companion's illhumour had had its vent.

— This hypothesis, Stephen repeated, is the other way out: that, though the same object may not seem beautiful to all people, all people who admire a beautiful object find in it certain relations which satisfy and coincide with the stages themselves of all esthetic apprehension. These relations of the sensible, visible to you through one form and to me through another, must be therefore the necessary qualities of beauty. Now, we can return to our old friend saint Thomas for another pennyworth of wisdom.

Lynch laughed.

— It amuses me vastly, he said, to hear you quoting him time after time like a jolly round friar. Are you laughing in your sleeve?

— MacAlister, answered Stephen, would call my esthetic theory applied Aquinas. So far as this side of esthetic philosophy extends Aquinas will carry me all along the line. When we come to the phenomena of artistic conception, artistic gestation and artistic reproduction I require a new terminology and a new personal experience.

— Of course, said Lynch. After all Aquinas, in spite of his intellect, was exactly a good round friar. But you will tell me about the new personal experience and new terminology some other day. Hurry up and finish the first part.

— Who knows? said Stephen, smiling. Perhaps Aquinas would understand me better than you. He was a poet himself. He wrote a hymn for Maundy Thursday.° It begins with the words *Pange lingua gloriosi.*° They say it is the highest glory of the hymnal. It is an intricate and soothing hymn. I like it: but there is no hymn that can be put beside that mournful and majestic processional song, the *Vexilla Regis*° of Venantius Fortunatus.

Lynch began to sing softly and solemnly in a deep bass voice:

Impleta sunt quæ concinit
David fideli carmine
Dicendo nationibus
Regnavit a ligno Deus.°

Maundy Thursday: The Thursday before Good Friday.   ***Pange lingua gloriosi:*** Tell, my tongue, in glorious . . . ; part of the opening line of a hymn by Aquinas.   ***Vexilla Regis:*** From "Vexilla Regis Prodeunt," "The Banners of the King Advance."   ***Impleta sunt . . . Deus:*** Fulfilled is all that David told / In true prophetic song of old: / Amidst the nations, God, saith he, / Hath reigned and triumphed from the Tree.

— That's great! he said, well pleased. Great music!

They turned into Lower Mount Street. A few steps from the corner a fat young man, wearing a silk neckcloth, saluted them and stopped.

— Did you hear the results of the exams? he asked. Griffin was plucked.° Halpin and O'Flynn are through the home civil. Moonan got fifth place in the Indian. O'Shaughnessy got fourteenth. The Irish fellows in Clarke's gave them a feed last night. They all ate curry.

His pallid bloated face expressed benevolent malice and, as he had advanced through his tidings of success, his small fatencircled eyes vanished out of sight and his weak wheezing voice out of hearing.

In reply to a question of Stephen's his eyes and his voice came forth again from their lurkingplaces.

— Yes, MacCullagh and I, he said. He's taking pure mathematics and I'm taking constitutional history. There are twenty subjects. I'm taking botany too. You know I'm a member of the field club.

He drew back from the other two in a stately fashion and placed a plump woollengloved hand on his breast from which muttered wheezing laughter at once broke forth.

— Bring us a few turnips and onions the next time you go out, said Stephen drily, to make a stew.

The fat student laughed indulgently and said:

— We are all highly respectable people in the field club. Last Saturday we went out to Glenmalure, seven of us.

— With women, Donovan? said Lynch.

Donovan again laid his hand on his chest and said:

— Our end is the acquisition of knowledge.

Then he said quickly:

— I hear you are writing some essay about esthetics.

Stephen made a vague gesture of denial.

— Goethe and Lessing,° said Donovan, have written a lot on that subject, the classical school and the romantic school and all that. The *Laocoon* interested me very much when I read it. Of course it is idealistic, German, ultraprofound.

Neither of the others spoke. Donovan took leave of them urbanely.

— I must go, he said softly and benevolently. I have a strong suspicion, amounting almost to a conviction, that my sister intended to make pancakes today for the dinner of the Donovan family.

---

was plucked: Flunked.   ***Goethe and Lessing:*** Johann Wolfgang von Goethe (1749–1832) and Gotthold Ephraim Lessing (1729–1781). The latter was author of the essay *Laocoon* (1766), discussing the difference beween the verbal and plastic arts.

— Goodbye, Stephen said in his wake. Don't forget the turnips for me and my mate.

Lynch gazed after him, his lip curling in slow scorn till his face resembled a devil's mask:

— To think that that yellow pancakeeating excrement can get a good job, he said at length, and I have to smoke cheap cigarettes!

They turned their faces towards Merrion Square and went on for a little in silence.

— To finish what I was saying about beauty, said Stephen, the most satisfying relations of the sensible must therefore correspond to the necessary phases of artistic apprehension. Find these and you find the qualities of universal beauty. Aquinas says: *ad pulcritudinem tria requiruntur, integritas, consonantia, claritas.* I translate it so: *Three things are needed for beauty, wholeness, harmony and radiance.* Do these correspond to the phases of apprehension? Are you following?

— Of course, I am, said Lynch. If you think I have an excrementitious intelligence run after Donovan and ask him to listen to you.

Stephen pointed to a basket which a butcher's boy had slung inverted on his head.

— Look at that basket, he said.

— I see it, said Lynch.

— In order to see that basket, said Stephen, your mind first of all separates the basket from the rest of the visible universe which is not the basket. The first phase of apprehension is a bounding line drawn about the object to be apprehended. An esthetic image is presented to us either in space or in time. What is audible is presented in time, what is visible is presented in space. But, temporal or spatial, the esthetic image is first luminously apprehended as selfbounded and selfcontained upon the immeasurable background of space or time which is not it. You apprehend it as *one* thing. You see it as one whole. You apprehend its wholeness. That is *integritas.*

— Bull's eye! said Lynch, laughing. Go on.

— Then, said Stephen, you pass from point to point, led by its formal lines; you apprehend it as balanced part against part within its limits; you feel the rhythm of its structure. In other words the synthesis of immediate perception is followed by the analysis of apprehension. Having first felt that it is *one* thing you feel now that it is a *thing.* You apprehend it as complex, multiple, divisible, separable, made up of its parts, the result of its parts and their sum, harmonious. That is *consonantia.*

— Bull's eye again! said Lynch wittily. Tell me now what is *claritas* and you win the cigar.

— The connotation of the word, Stephen said, is rather vague. Aquinas uses a term which seems to be inexact. It baffled me for a long time. It would lead you to believe that he had in mind symbolism or idealism, the supreme quality of beauty being a light from some other world, the idea of which the matter is but the shadow, the reality of which it is but the symbol. I thought he might mean that *claritas* is the artistic discovery and representation of the divine purpose in anything or a force of generalisation which would make the esthetic image a universal one, make it outshine its proper conditions. But that is literary talk. I understand it so. When you have apprehended that basket as one thing and have then analysed it according to its form and apprehended it as a thing you make the only synthesis which is logically and esthetically permissible. You see that it is that thing which it is and no other thing. The radiance of which he speaks is the scholastic *quidditas,* the *whatness* of a thing. This supreme quality is felt by the artist when the esthetic image is first conceived in his imagination. The mind in that mysterious instant Shelley° likened beautifully to a fading coal. The instant wherein that supreme quality of beauty, the clear radiance of the esthetic image, is apprehended luminously by the mind which has been arrested by its wholeness and fascinated by its harmony is the luminous silent stasis of esthetic pleasure, a spiritual state very like to that cardiac condition which the Italian physiologist Luigi Galvani,° using a phrase almost as beautiful as Shelley's, called the enchantment of the heart.

Stephen paused and, though his companion did not speak, felt that his words had called up around them a thoughtenchanted silence.

— What I have said, he began again, refers to beauty in the wider sense of the word, in the sense which the word has in the literary tradition. In the marketplace it has another sense. When we speak of beauty in the second sense of the term our judgment is influenced in the first place by the art itself and by the form of that art. The image, it is clear, must be set between the mind or senses of the artist himself and the mind or senses of others. If you bear this in memory you will see that art necessarily divides itself into three forms progressing from one to the next. These forms are: the lyrical form, the form wherein the artist presents his image in immediate relation to himself; the epical form, the form wherein he presents his image in mediate relation to himself and to others; the dramatic form, the form wherein he presents his image in immediate relation to others.

Shelley: In *A Defence of Poetry* (1821).   **Luigi Galvani:** (1737–1798), Italian physicist, describing the temporary stoppage of a frog's heartbeat.

— That you told me a few nights ago, said Lynch, and we began the famous discussion.

— I have a book at home, said Stephen, in which I have written down questions which are more amusing than yours were. In finding the answers to them I found the theory of esthetic which I am trying to explain. Here are some questions I set myself: *Is a chair finely made tragic or comic? Is the portrait of Mona Lisa good if I desire to see it? Is the bust of Sir Philip Crampton° lyrical, epical or dramatic? Can excrement or a child or a louse be a work of art? If not, why not?*

— Why not, indeed? said Lynch, laughing.

— *If a man hacking in fury at a block of wood,* Stephen continued, *make there an image of a cow is that image a work of art? If not, why not?*

— That's a lovely one, said Lynch, laughing again. That has the true scholastic stink.

— Lessing, said Stephen, should not have taken a group of statues to write of. The art, being inferior, does not present the forms I spoke of distinguished clearly one from another. Even in literature, the highest and most spiritual art, the forms are often confused. The lyrical form is in fact the simplest verbal vesture of an instant of emotion, a rhythmical cry such as ages ago cheered on the man who pulled at the oar or dragged stones up a slope. He who utters it is more conscious of the instant of emotion than of himself as feeling emotion. The simplest epical form is seen emerging out of lyrical literature when the artist prolongs and broods upon himself as the centre of an epical event and this form progresses till the centre of emotional gravity is equidistant from the artist himself and from others. The narrative is no longer purely personal. The personality of the artist passes into the narration itself, flowing round and round the persons and the action like a vital sea. This progress you will see easily in that old English ballad *Turpin Hero* which begins in the first person and ends in the third person. The dramatic form is reached when the vitality which has flowed and eddied round each person fills every person with such vital force that he or she assumes a proper and intangible esthetic life. The personality of the artist, at first a cry or a cadence or a mood and then a fluid and lambent narrative, finally refines itself out of existence, impersonalises itself, so to speak. The esthetic image in the dramatic form is life purified in and reprojected from the human imagination. The mystery of esthetic like that of material creation is accomplished. The artist, like the God of the creation, remains within or behind or beyond or above

Sir Philip Crampton: (1777–1858), Dublin surgeon.

his handiwork, invisible, refined out of existence, indifferent, paring his fingernails.

— Trying to refine them also out of existence, said Lynch.

A fine rain began to fall from the high veiled sky and they turned into the duke's lawn, to reach the national library before the shower came.

— What do you mean, Lynch asked surlily, by prating about beauty and the imagination in this miserable Godforsaken island? No wonder the artist retired within or behind his handiwork after having perpetrated this country.

The rain fell faster. When they passed through the passage beside the royal Irish academy they found many students sheltering under the arcade of the library. Cranly, leaning against a pillar, was picking his teeth with a sharpened match, listening to some companions. Some girls stood near the entrance door. Lynch whispered to Stephen:

— Your beloved is here.

Stephen took his place silently on the step below the group of students, heedless of the rain which fell fast, turning his eyes towards her from time to time. She too stood silently among her companions. She has no priest to flirt with, he thought with conscious bitterness, remembering how he had seen her last. Lynch was right. His mind, emptied of theory and courage, lapsed back into a listless peace.

He heard the students talking among themselves. They spoke of two friends who had passed the final medical examination, of the chances of getting places on ocean liners, of poor and rich practices.

— That's all a bubble. An Irish country practice is better.

— Hynes was two years in Liverpool and he says the same. A frightful hole he said it was. Nothing but midwifery cases. Half a crown cases.

— Do you mean to say it is better to have a job here in the country than in a rich city like that? I know a fellow . . .

— Hynes has no brains. He got through by stewing,° pure stewing.

— Don't mind him. There's plenty of money to be made in a big commercial city.

— Depends on the practice.

— *Ego credo ut vita pauperum est simpliciter atrox, simpliciter sanguinarius atrox, in Liverpoolio.*°

Their voices reached his ears as if from a distance in interrupted pulsation. She was preparing to go away with her companions.

The quick light shower had drawn off, tarrying in clusters of dia-

---

stewing: Unintelligent, grinding study.   ***Ego credo . . . Liverpoolio:*** I believe that the life of the poor is simply awful, simply bloody awful, in Liverpool (dog Latin).

monds among the shrubs of the quadrangle where an exhalation was breathed forth by the blackened earth. Their trim boots prattled as they stood on the steps of the colonnade talking quietly and gaily, glancing at the clouds, holding their umbrellas at cunning angles against the few last raindrops, closing them again, holding their skirts demurely.

And if he had judged her harshly? If her life were a simple rosary of hours, her life simple and strange as a bird's life, gay in the morning, restless all day, tired at sundown? Her heart simple and wilful as a bird's heart?

*

*   *

Towards dawn he awoke. O what sweet music! His soul was all dewy wet. Over his limbs in sleep pale cool waves of light had passed. He lay still, as if his soul lay amid cool waters, conscious of faint sweet music. His mind was waking slowly to a tremulous morning knowledge, a morning inspiration. A spirit filled him, pure as the purest water, sweet as dew, moving as music. But how faintly it was inbreathed, how passionlessly, as if the seraphim° themselves were breathing upon him! His soul was waking slowly, fearing to awake wholly. It was that windless hour of dawn when madness wakes and strange plants open to the light and the moth flies forth silently.

An enchantment of the heart! The night had been enchanted. In dream or vision he had known the ecstasy of seraphic life. Was it an instant of enchantment only or long hours and days and years and ages?

The instant of inspiration seemed now to be reflected from all sides at once from a multitude of cloudy circumstance of what had happened or of what might have happened. The instant flashed forth like a point of light and now from cloud on cloud of vague circumstance confused form was veiling softly its afterglow. O! In the virgin womb of the imagination the word was made flesh. Gabriel the seraph had come to the virgin's chamber. An afterglow deepened within his spirit, whence the white flame had passed, deepening to a rose and ardent light. That rose and ardent light was her strange wilful heart, strange that no man had known or would know, wilful from before the beginning of the world: and lured by that ardent roselike glow the choirs of the seraphim were falling from heaven.

> Are you not weary of ardent ways,
> Lure of the fallen seraphim?
> Tell no more of enchanted days.

seraphim: The highest order of angels.

The verses passed from his mind to his lips and, murmuring them over, he felt the rhythmic movement of a villanelle° pass through them. The roselike glow sent forth its rays of rhyme; ways, days, blaze, praise, raise. Its rays burned up the world, consumed the hearts of men and angels: the rays from the rose that was her wilful heart.

> Your eyes have set man's heart ablaze
> And you have had your will of him.
> Are you not weary of ardent ways?

And then? The rhythm died away, ceased, began again to move and beat. And then? Smoke, incense ascending from the altar of the world.

> Above the flame the smoke of praise
> Goes up from ocean rim to rim.
> Tell no more of enchanted days.

Smoke went up from the whole earth, from the vapoury oceans, smoke of her praise. The earth was like a swinging swaying smoking censer, a ball of incense, an ellipsoidal ball. The rhythm died out at once; the cry of his heart was broken. His lips began to murmur the first verses over and over; then went on stumbling through half verses, stammering and baffled; then stopped. The heart's cry was broken.

The veiled windless hour had passed and behind the panes of the naked window the morning light was gathering. A bell beat faintly very far away. A bird twittered; two birds, three. The bell and the bird ceased: and the dull white light spread itself east and west, covering the world, covering the roselight in his heart.

Fearing to lose all he raised himself suddenly on his elbow to look for paper and pencil. There was neither on the table; only the soupplate he had eaten the rice from for supper and the candlestick with its tendrils of tallow and its paper socket, singed by the last flame. He stretched his arm wearily towards the foot of the bed, groping with his hand in the pockets of the coat that hung there. His fingers found a pencil and then a cigarette packet. He lay back and, tearing open the packet, placed the last cigarette on the windowledge and began to write out the stanzas of the villanelle in small neat letters on the rough cardboard surface.

Having written them out he lay back on the lumpy pillow, murmuring them again. The lumps of knotted flock under his head reminded

---

villanelle: Nineteen-line poem using only two rhymes, with rhymes and lines repeated according to a set pattern.

him of the lumps of knotted horsehair in the sofa of her parlour on
which he used to sit, smiling or serious, asking himself why he had
come, displeased with her and with himself, confounded by the print
of the Sacred Heart above the untenanted sideboard. He saw her approach him in a lull of the talk and beg him to sing one of his curious
songs. Then he saw himself sitting at the old piano, striking chords
softly from its speckled keys and singing, amid the talk which had risen
again in the room, to her who leaned beside the mantelpiece a dainty
song of the Elizabethans, a sad and sweet loth to depart, the victory
chant of Agincourt,° the happy air of Greensleeves. While he sang and
she listened, or feigned to listen, his heart was at rest but when the
quaint old songs had ended and he heard again the voices in the room
he remembered his own sarcasm: the house where young men are
called by their christian names a little too soon.

At certain instants her eyes seemed about to trust him but he had
waited in vain. She passed now dancing lightly across his memory as she
had been that night at the carnival ball, her white dress a little lifted, a
white spray nodding in her hair. She danced lightly in the round. She
was dancing towards him and, as she came, her eyes were a little averted
and a faint glow was on her cheek. At the pause in the chain of hands
her hand had lain in his an instant, a soft merchandise.

— You are a great stranger now.
— Yes. I was born to be a monk.
— I am afraid you are a heretic.
— Are you much afraid?

For answer she had danced away from him along the chain of
hands, dancing lightly and discreetly, giving herself to none. The white
spray nodded to her dancing and when she was in shadow the glow was
deeper on her cheek.

A monk! His own image started forth a profaner of the cloister, a
heretic franciscan, willing and willing not to serve, spinning like Gher-
ardino da Borgo San Donnino° a lithe web of sophistry and whispering
in her ear.

No, it was not his image. It was the image of the young priest in
whose company he had seen her last, looking at him out of dove's eyes,
toying with the pages of her Irish phrasebook.

— Yes, yes, the ladies are coming round to us. I can see it every day.
The ladies are with us. The best helpers the language has.

Agincourt: English victory over the French, 1415.   *da Borgo San Donnino:* Leader
of a reform group of Franciscans, died condemned as a heretic in 1276.

— And the church, Father Moran?

— The church too. Coming round too. The work is going ahead there too. Don't fret about the church.

Bah! he had done well to leave the room in disdain. He had done well not to salute her on the steps of the library. He had done well to leave her to flirt with her priest, to toy with a church which was the scullerymaid of christendom.

Rude brutal anger routed the last lingering instant of ecstasy from his soul. It broke up violently her fair image and flung the fragments on all sides. On all sides distorted reflections of her image started from his memory: the flowergirl in the ragged dress with damp coarse hair and a hoyden's face who had called herself his own girl and begged his handsel, the kitchengirl in the next house who sang over the clatter of her plates with the drawl of a country singer the first bars of *By Killarney's Lakes and Fells,* a girl who had laughed gaily to see him stumble when the iron grating in the footpath near Cork Hill had caught the broken sole of his shoe, a girl he had glanced at, attracted by her small ripe mouth as she passed out of Jacob's biscuit factory, who had cried to him over her shoulder:

— Do you like what you seen of me, straight hair and curly eyebrows?

And yet he felt that, however he might revile and mock her image, his anger was also a form of homage. He had left the classroom in disdain that was not wholly sincere, feeling that perhaps the secret of her race lay behind those dark eyes upon which her long lashes flung a quick shadow. He had told himself bitterly as he walked through the streets that she was a figure of the womanhood of her country, a batlike soul waking to the consciousness of itself in darkness and secrecy and loneliness, tarrying awhile, loveless and sinless, with her mild lover and leaving him to whisper of innocent transgressions in the latticed ear of a priest. His anger against her found vent in coarse railing at her paramour, whose name and voice and features offended his baffled pride: a priested peasant, with a brother a policeman in Dublin and a brother a potboy° in Moycullen. To him she would unveil her soul's shy nakedness, to one who was but schooled in the discharging of a formal rite rather than to him, a priest of the eternal imagination, transmuting the daily bread of experience into the radiant body of everliving life.

The radiant image of the eucharist united again in an instant his bitter and despairing thoughts, their cries arising unbroken in a hymn of thanksgiving.

---

potboy: Waiter who serves beer or ale.

Our broken cries and mournful lays
Rise in one eucharistic hymn.
Are you not weary of ardent ways?

While sacrificing hands upraise
The chalice flowing to the brim,
Tell no more of enchanted days.

He spoke the verses aloud from the first lines till the music and
rhythm suffused his mind, turning it to quiet indulgence; then copied
them painfully to feel them the better by seeing them; then lay back on
his bolster.

The full morning light had come. No sound was to be heard: but he
knew that all around him life was about to awaken in common noises,
hoarse voices, sleepy prayers. Shrinking from that life he turned towards
the wall, making a cowl of the blanket and staring at the great overblown scarlet flowers of the tattered wallpaper. He tried to warm his
perishing joy in their scarlet glow, imagining a roseway from where he
lay upwards to heaven, all strewn with scarlet flowers. Weary! Weary!
He too was weary of ardent ways.

A gradual warmth, a languorous weariness passed over him, descend-
ing along his spine from his closely cowled head. He felt it descend and,
seeing himself as he lay, smiled. Soon he would sleep.

He had written verses for her again after ten years. Ten years before
she had worn her shawl cowlwise about her head, sending sprays of her
warm breath into the night air, tapping her foot upon the glassy road. It
was the last tram; the lank brown horses knew it and shook their bells to
the clear night in admonition. The conductor talked with the driver,
both nodding often in the green light of the lamp. They stood on the
steps of the tram, he on the upper, she on the lower. She came up to his
step many times between their phrases and went down again and once
or twice remained beside him forgetting to go down and then went
down. Let be! Let be!

Ten years from that wisdom of children to his folly. If he sent her
the verses? They would be read out at breakfast amid the tapping of
eggshells. Folly indeed! The brothers would laugh and try to wrest the
page from each other with their strong hard fingers. The suave priest,
her uncle, seated in his armchair, would hold the page at arm's length,
read it smiling and approve of the literary form.

No, no: that was folly. Even if he sent her the verses she would not
show them to others. No, no: she could not.

He began to feel that he had wronged her. A sense of her innocence moved him almost to pity her, an innocence he had never understood till he had come to the knowledge of it through sin, an innocence which she too had not understood while she was innocent or before the strange humiliation of her nature had first come upon her. Then first her soul had begun to live as his soul had when he had first sinned: and a tender compassion filled his heart as he remembered her frail pallor and her eyes, humbled and saddened by the dark shame of womanhood.

While his soul had passed from ecstasy to languor where had she been? Might it be, in the mysterious ways of spiritual life, that her soul at those same moments had been conscious of his homage? It might be.

A glow of desire kindled again his soul and fired and fulfilled all his body. Conscious of his desire she was waking from odorous sleep, the temptress of his villanelle. Her eyes, dark and with a look of languor, were opening to his eyes. Her nakedness yielded to him, radiant, warm, odorous and lavishlimbed, enfolded him like a shining cloud, enfolded him like water with a liquid life: and like a cloud of vapour or like waters circumfluent in space the liquid letters of speech, symbols of the element of mystery, flowed forth over his brain.

Are you not weary of ardent ways,
Lure of the fallen seraphim?
Tell no more of enchanted days.

Your eyes have set man's heart ablaze
And you have had your will of him.
Are you not weary of ardent ways?

Above the flame the smoke of praise
Goes up from ocean rim to rim.
Tell no more of enchanted days.

Our broken cries and mournful lays
Rise in one eucharistic hymn.
Are you not weary of ardent ways?

While sacrificing hands upraise
The chalice flowing to the brim,
Tell no more of enchanted days.

And still you hold our longing gaze
With languorous look and lavish limb!
Are you not weary of ardent ways?
Tell no more of enchanted days.

*
*   *

What birds were they? He stood on the steps of the library to look at them, leaning wearily on his ashplant.° They flew round and round the jutting shoulder of a house in Molesworth Street. The air of the late March evening made clear their flight, their dark darting quivering bodies flying clearly against the sky as against a limphung cloth of smoky tenuous blue.

He watched their flight: bird after bird: a dark flash, a swerve, a flash again, a dart aside, a curve, a flutter of wings. He tried to count them before all their darting quivering bodies passed: six, ten, eleven: and wondered were they odd or even in number. Twelve, thirteen: for two came wheeling down from the upper sky. They were flying high and low but ever round and round in straight and curving lines and ever flying from left to right, circling about a temple of air.

He listened to the cries: like the squeak of mice behind the wainscot: a shrill twofold note. But the notes were long and shrill and whirring, unlike the cry of vermin, falling a third or a fourth and trilled as the flying beaks clove the air. Their cry was shrill and clear and fine and falling like threads of silken light unwound from whirring spools.

The inhuman clamour soothed his ears in which his mother's sobs and reproaches murmured insistently and the dark frail quivering bodies wheeling and fluttering and swerving round an airy temple of the tenuous sky soothed his eyes which still saw the image of his mother's face.

Why was he gazing upwards from the steps of the porch, hearing their shrill twofold cry, watching their flight? For an augury of good or evil? A phrase of Cornelius Agrippa° flew through his mind and then there flew hither and thither shapeless thoughts from Swedenborg on the correspondence of birds to things of the intellect and of how the creatures of the air have their knowledge and know their times and seasons because they, unlike man, are in the order of their life and have not perverted that order by reason.

And for ages men had gazed upward as he was gazing at birds in flight. The colonnade above him made him think vaguely of an ancient temple and the ashplant on which he leaned wearily of the curved stick of an augur.° A sense of fear of the unknown moved in the heart of his weariness, a fear of symbols and portents, of the hawklike man whose name he bore soaring out of his captivity on osierwoven wings, of Thoth,

---

ashplant: Joyce's term for a staff made of ash.   *Cornelius Agrippa:* Heinrich Cornelius Agrippa von Nettesheim (1486–1535), German philosopher known for his occult works.   *augur:* Roman professional prophet.

the god of writers, writing with a reed upon a tablet and bearing on his narrow ibis head the cusped moon.

He smiled as he thought of the god's image for it made him think of a bottlenosed judge in a wig, putting commas into a document which he held at arm's length and he knew that he would not have remembered the god's name but that it was like an Irish oath. It was folly. But was it for this folly that he was about to leave for ever the house of prayer and prudence into which he had been born and the order of life out of which he had come?

They came back with shrill cries over the jutting shoulder of the house, flying darkly against the fading air. What birds were they? He thought that they must be swallows who had come back from the south. Then he was to go away for they were birds ever going and coming, building ever an unlasting home under the eaves of men's houses and ever leaving the homes they had built to wander.

Bend down your faces,° Oona and Aleel.
I gaze upon them as the swallow gazes
Upon the nest under the eave before
He wander the loud waters.

A soft liquid joy like the noise of many waters flowed over his memory and he felt in his heart the soft peace of silent spaces of fading tenuous sky above the waters, of oceanic silence, of swallows flying through the seadusk over the flowing waters.

A soft liquid joy flowed through the words where the soft long vowels hurtled noiselessly and fell away, lapping and flowing back and ever shaking the white bells of their waves in mute chime and mute peal and soft low swooning cry: and he felt that the augury he had sought in the wheeling darting birds and in the pale space of sky above him had come forth from his heart like a bird from a turret quietly and swiftly.

Symbol of departure or of loneliness? The verses crooned in the ear of his memory composed slowly before his remembering eyes the scene of the hall on the night of the opening of the national theatre.° He was alone at the side of the balcony, looking out of jaded eyes at the culture of Dublin in the stalls and at the tawdry scenecloths and human dolls framed by the garish lamps of the stage. A burly policeman sweated behind him and seemed at every moment about to act. The catcalls and

---

Bend down your faces . . . : Beginning of Countess Cathleen's death speech in Yeats's play (1892).   *opening of the national theatre:* May 8, 1899, was the first production of the Irish Literary Theatre, the first performance of *Countess Cathleen,* which drew vigorous protests.

hisses and mocking cries ran in rude gusts round the hall from his scattered fellowstudents.

— A libel on Ireland!

— Made in Germany!

— Blasphemy!

— We never sold our faith!

— No Irish woman ever did it!

— We want no amateur atheists.

— We want no budding buddhists.

A sudden swift hiss fell from the windows above him and he knew that the electric lamps had been switched on in the reader's room. He turned into the pillared hall, now calmly lit, went up the staircase and passed in through the clicking turnstile.

Cranly was sitting over near the dictionaries. A thick book, opened at the frontispiece, lay before him on the wooden rest. He leaned back in his chair, inclining his ear like that of a confessor to the face of the medical student who was reading to him a problem from the chess page of a journal. Stephen sat down at his right and the priest at the other side of the table closed his copy of *The Tablet*° with an angry snap and stood up.

Cranly gazed after him blandly and vaguely. The medical student went on in a softer voice:

— Pawn to king's fourth.

— We had better go, Dixon, said Stephen in warning. He has gone to complain.

Dixon folded the journal and rose with dignity, saying:

— Our men retired in good order.

— With guns and cattle, added Stephen, pointing to the titlepage of Cranly's book on which was printed *Diseases of the Ox*.

As they passed through a lane of the tables Stephen said:

— Cranly, I want to speak to you.

Cranly did not answer or turn. He laid his book on the counter and passed out, his wellshod feet sounding flatly on the floor. On the staircase he paused and gazing absently at Dixon repeated:

— Pawn to king's bloody fourth.

— Put it that way if you like, Dixon said.

He had a quiet toneless voice and urbane manners and on a finger of his plump clean hand he displayed at moments a signet ring.

As they crossed the hall a man of dwarfish stature came towards

The Tablet: Conservative Roman Catholic weekly.

them. Under the dome of his tiny hat his unshaven face began to smile with pleasure and he was heard to murmur. The eyes were melancholy as those of a monkey.

— Good evening, captain, said Cranly, halting.

— Good evening, gentlemen, said the stubblegrown monkeyish face.

— Warm weather for March, said Cranly. They have the windows open upstairs.

Dixon smiled and turned his ring. The blackish monkey-puckered face pursed its human mouth with gentle pleasure: and its voice purred:

— Delightful weather for March. Simply delightful.

— There are two nice young ladies upstairs, captain, tired of waiting, Dixon said.

Cranly smiled and said kindly:

— The captain has only one love: sir Walter Scott. Isn't that so, captain?

— What are you reading now, captain? Dixon asked. *The Bride of Lammermoor?*°

— I love old Scott, the flexible lips said. I think he writes something lovely. There is no writer can touch sir Walter Scott.

He moved a thin shrunken brown hand gently in the air in time to his praise and his thin quick eyelids beat often over his sad eyes.

Sadder to Stephen's ear was his speech: a genteel accent, low and moist, marred by errors: and listening to it he wondered was the story true and was the thin blood that flowed in his shrunken frame noble and come of an incestuous love.

The park trees were heavy with rain and rain fell still and ever in the lake, lying grey like a shield. A game of swans° flew there and the water and the shore beneath were fouled with their greenwhite slime. They embraced softly, impelled by the grey rainy light, the wet silent trees, the shieldlike witnessing lake, the swans. They embraced without joy or passion, his arm about his sister's neck. A grey woolen cloak was wrapped athwart her from her shoulder to her waist: and her fair head was bent in willing shame. He had loose redbrown hair and tender shapely strong freckled hands. Face. There was no face seen. The brother's face was bent upon her fair rainfragrant hair. The hand freckled and strong and shapely and caressing was Davin's hand.

He frowned angrily upon his thought and on the shrivelled mannikin

The Bride of Lammermoor: (1819), novel by Sir Walter Scott.   *game of swans:* A flock of domestic swans.

who had called it forth. His father's gibes at the Bantry gang° leaped
out of his memory. He held them at a distance and brooded uneasily on
his own thought again. Why were they not Cranly's hands? Had
Davin's simplicity and innocence stung him more secretly?

He walked on across the hall with Dixon, leaving Cranly to take
leave elaborately of the dwarf.

Under the colonnade Temple was standing in the midst of a little
group of students. One of them cried:

— Dixon, come over till you hear. Temple is in grand form.

Temple turned on him his dark gipsy eyes.

— You're a hypocrite, O'Keeffe, he said, and Dixon's a smiler. By
hell, I think that's a good literary expression.

He laughed slily, looking in Stephen's face, repeating:

— By hell, I'm delighted with that name. A smiler.

A stout student who stood below them on the steps said:

— Come back to the mistress, Temple. We want to hear about that.

— He had, faith, Temple said. And he was a married man too. And
all the priests used to be dining there. By hell, I think they all had a
touch.°

— We shall call it riding a hack to spare the hunter,° said Dixon.

— Tell us, Temple, O'Keeffe said, how many quarts of porter have
you in you?

— All your intellectual soul° is in that phrase, O'Keeffe, said Temple
with open scorn.

He moved with a shambling gait round the group and spoke to
Stephen.

— Did you know that the Forsters are the kings of Belgium? he
asked.

Cranly came out through the door of the entrance hall, his hat
thrust back on the nape of his neck and picking his teeth with care.

— And here's the wiseacre, said Temple. Do you know that about
the Forsters?

He paused for an answer. Cranly dislodged a figseed from his teeth
on the point of his rude toothpick and gazed at it intently.

— The Forster family, Temple said, is descended from Baldwin the

---

Bantry gang: A group of politicians who turned against Parnell, notably Timothy Sullivan and Timothy Healy.   **a touch:** Sexual play or intercourse.   **hack . . . hunter:**
Ordinary horse . . . prize horse.   **intellectual soul:** Aristotle distinguishes among the
vegetable, animal, and intellectual souls in humans.

First, king of Flanders. He was called the Forester. Forester and Forster are the same name. A descendant of Baldwin the First, captain Francis Forster, settled in Ireland and married the daughter of the last chieftain of Clanbrassil. Then there are the Blake Forsters. That's a different branch.

— From Baldhead, king of Flanders, Cranly repeated, rooting again deliberately at his gleaming uncovered teeth.

— Where did you pick up all that history? O'Keeffe asked.

— I know all the history of your family too, Temple said, turning to Stephen. Do you know what Giraldus Cambrensis° says about your family?

— Is he descended from Baldwin too? asked a tall consumptive student with dark eyes.

— Baldhead, Cranly repeated, sucking at a crevice in his teeth.

— *Pernobilis et pervetusta familia,*° Temple said to Stephen.

The stout student who stood below them on the steps farted briefly. Dixon turned towards him saying in a soft voice:

— Did an angel speak?

Cranly turned also and said vehemently but without anger:

— Goggins, you're the flamingest dirty devil I ever met, do you know.

— I had it on my mind to say that, Goggins answered firmly. It did no-one any harm, did it?

— We hope, Dixon said suavely, that it was not of the kind known to science as a *paulo post futurum.*°

— Didn't I tell you he was a smiler? said Temple, turning right and left. Didn't I give him that name?

— You did. We're not deaf, said the tall consumptive.

Cranly still frowned at the stout student below him. Then, with a snort of disgust, he shoved him violently down the steps.

— Go away from here, he said rudely. Go away, you stinkpot. And you are a stinkpot.

Goggins skipped down on to the gravel and at once returned to his place with good humour. Temple turned back to Stephen and asked:

— Do you believe in the law of heredity?

— Are you drunk or what are you or what are you trying to say? asked Cranly, facing round on him with an expression of wonder.

Giraldus Cambrensis: (ca. 1146–1220), Welsh churchman and early chronicler of Ireland.   *Pernobilis et pervetusta familia:* Of a noble and venerable family.   ***paulo post futurum:*** Grammatical term referring to the verb form used for an event about to happen.

— The most profound sentence ever written, Temple said with enthusiasm, is the sentence at the end of the zoology. Reproduction is the beginning of death.

He touched Stephen timidly at the elbow and said eagerly:

— Do you feel how profound that is because you are a poet?

Cranly pointed his long forefinger.

— Look at him! he said with scorn to the others. Look at Ireland's hope!

They laughed at his words and gesture. Temple turned on him bravely, saying:

— Cranly, you're always sneering at me. I can see that. But I am as good as you are any day. Do you know what I think about you now as compared with myself?

— My dear man, said Cranly urbanely, you are incapable, do you know, absolutely incapable of thinking.

— But do you know, Temple went on, what I think of you and of myself compared together?

— Out with it, Temple! the stout student cried from the steps. Get it out in bits!

Temple turned right and left, making sudden feeble gestures as he spoke.

— I'm a ballocks,° he said, shaking his head in despair. I am. And I know I am. And I admit it that I am.

Dixon patted him lightly on the shoulder and said mildly:

— And it does you every credit, Temple.

— But he, Temple said, pointing to Cranly. He is a ballocks too like me. Only he doesn't know it. And that's the only difference I see.

A burst of laughter covered his words. But he turned again to Stephen and said with a sudden eagerness:

— That word is a most interesting word. That's the only English dual number.° Did you know?

— Is it? Stephen said vaguely.

He was watching Cranly's firmfeatured suffering face, lit up now by a smile of false patience. The gross name had passed over it like foul water poured over an old stone image, patient of injuries: and, as he watched him, he saw him raise his hat in salute and uncover the black hair that stood up stiffly from his forehead like an iron crown.

She passed out from the porch of the library and bowed across

ballocks: Set of testicles (figuratively, a clumsy oaf or a mess).   *dual number:* Obsolete grammatical form for nouns indicating a pair.

Stephen in reply to Cranly's greeting. He also? Was there not a slight flush on Cranly's cheek? Or had it come forth at Temple's words? The light had waned. He could not see.

Did that explain his friend's listless silence, his harsh comments, the sudden intrusions of rude speech with which he had shattered so often Stephen's ardent wayward confessions? Stephen had forgiven freely for he had found this rudeness also in himself towards himself. And he remembered an evening when he had dismounted from a borrowed creaking bicycle to pray to God in a wood near Malahide. He had lifted up his arms and spoken in ecstasy to the sombre nave of the trees, knowing that he stood on holy ground and in a holy hour. And when two constabularymen had come into sight round a bend in the gloomy road he had broken off his prayer to whistle loudly an air from the last pantomime.

He began to beat the frayed end of his ashplant against the base of a pillar. Had Cranly not heard him? Yet he could wait. The talk about him ceased for a moment: and a soft hiss fell again from a window above. But no other sound was in the air and the swallows whose flight he had followed with idle eyes were sleeping.

She had passed through the dusk. And therefore the air was silent save for one soft hiss that fell. And therefore the tongues about him had ceased their babble. Darkness was falling.

Darkness falls from the air.°

A trembling joy, lambent as a faint light, played like a fairy host around him. But why? Her passage through the darkening air or the verse with its black vowels and its opening sound, rich and lutelike?

He walked away slowly towards the deeper shadows at the end of the colonnade; beating the stone softly with his stick to hide his revery from the students whom he had left: and allowed his mind to summon back to itself the age of Dowland° and Byrd and Nash.

Eyes, opening from the darkness of desire, eyes that dimmed the breaking east. What was their languid grace but the softness of chambering? And what was their shimmer but the shimmer of the scum that mantled the cesspool of the court of a slobbering Stuart. And he tasted in the language of memory ambered wines, dying fallings of sweet airs, the proud pavan:° and saw with the eyes of memory kind gentlewomen

---

Darkness falls from the air: Misquotation of "brightness falls from the air," a line from "A Litany in Time of Plague" (1592) by English poet Thomas Nashe.   *age of Dowland:* Elizabethan age (1558–1603), famous for lyricism.   *pavan:* A formal kind of Elizabethan dance.

in Covent Garden wooing from their balconies with sucking mouths and the poxfouled wenches of the taverns and young wives that, gaily yielding to their ravishers, clipped° and clipped again.

The images he had summoned gave him no pleasure. They were secret and enflaming but her image was not entangled by them. That was not the way to think of her. It was not even the way in which he thought of her. Could his mind then not trust itself? Old phrases, sweet only with a disinterred sweetness like the figseeds Cranly rooted out of his gleaming teeth.

It was not thought nor vision though he knew vaguely that her figure was passing homeward through the city. Vaguely first and then more sharply he smelt her body. A conscious unrest seethed in his blood. Yes, it was her body that he smelt: a wild and languid smell: the tepid limbs over which his music had flowed desirously and the secret soft linen upon which her flesh distilled odour and a dew.

A louse crawled over the nape of his neck and, putting his thumb and forefinger deftly beneath his loose collar, he caught it. He rolled its body, tender yet brittle as a grain of rice, between thumb and finger for an instant before he let it fall from him and wondered would it live or die. There came to his mind a curious phrase from Cornelius a Lapide° which said that the lice born of human sweat were not created by God with the other animals on the sixth day. But the tickling of the skin of his neck made his mind raw and red. The life of his body, illclad, illfed, louseeaten, made him close his eyelids in a sudden spasm of despair: and in the darkness he saw the brittle bright bodies of lice falling from the air and turning often as they fell. Yes: and it was not darkness that fell from the air. It was brightness.

Brightness falls from the air.

He had not even remembered rightly Nash's line. All the images it had awakened were false. His mind bred vermin. His thoughts were lice born of the sweat of sloth.

He came back quickly along the colonnade towards the group of students. Well then let her go and be damned to her. She could love some clean athlete who washed himself every morning to the waist and had black hair on his chest. Let her.

Cranly had taken another dried fig from the supply in his pocket

---

clipped: Embraced.   *Cornelius a Lapide:* (1567–1637), Flemish Jesuit author of *The Great Commentary on the Bible,* published posthumously in 1681, which includes this assertion.

and was eating it slowly and noisily. Temple sat on the pediment of a pillar, leaning back, his cap pulled down on his sleepy eyes. A squat young man came out of the porch, a leather portfolio tucked under his armpit. He marched towards the group, striking the flags with the heels of his boots and with the ferule of his heavy umbrella. Then, raising the umbrella in salute, he said to all:

— Good evening, sirs.

He struck the flags again and tittered while his head trembled with a slight nervous movement. The tall consumptive student and Dixon and O'Keeffe were speaking in Irish and did not answer him. Then, turning to Cranly, he said:

— Good evening, particularly to you.

He moved the umbrella in indication and tittered again. Cranly, who was still chewing the fig, answered with loud movements of his jaws.

— Good? Yes. It is a good evening.

The squat student looked at him seriously and shook his umbrella gently and reprovingly.

— I can see, he said, that you are about to make obvious remarks.

— Um, Cranly answered, holding out what remained of the half-chewed fig and jerking it towards the squat student's mouth in sign that he should eat.

The squat student did not eat it but, indulging his special humour, said gravely, still tittering and prodding his phrase with his umbrella:

— Do you intend that . . .

He broke off, pointed bluntly to the munched pulp of the fig and said loudly:

— I allude to that.

— Um, Cranly said as before.

— Do you intend that now, the squat student said, as *ipso facto* or, let us say, as so to speak?

Dixon turned aside from his group, saying:

— Goggins was waiting for you, Glynn. He has gone round to the Adelphi to look for you and Moynihan. What have you there? he asked, tapping the portfolio under Glynn's arm.

— Examination papers, Glynn answered. I give them monthly examinations to see that they are profiting by my tuition.

He also tapped the portfolio and coughed gently and smiled.

— Tuition! said Cranly rudely. I suppose you mean the barefooted children that are taught by a bloody ape like you. God help them!

He bit off the rest of the fig and flung away the butt.

— I suffer little children to come unto me, Glynn said amiably.

— A bloody ape, Cranly repeated with emphasis, and a blasphemous bloody ape!

Temple stood up and, pushing past Cranly, addressed Glynn:

— That phrase you said now, he said, is from the new testament about suffer the children to come to me.

— Go to sleep again, Temple, said O'Keeffe.

— Very well, then, Temple continued, still addressing Glynn, and if Jesus suffered the children to come why does the church send them all to hell if they die unbaptised? Why is that?

— Were you baptised yourself, Temple? the consumptive student asked.

— But why are they sent to hell if Jesus said they were all to come? Temple said, his eyes searching in Glynn's eyes.

Glynn coughed and said gently, holding back with difficulty the nervous titter in his voice and moving his umbrella at every word:

— And, as you remark, if it is thus I ask emphatically whence comes this thusness.

— Because the church is cruel like all old sinners, Temple said.

— Are you quite orthodox on that point, Temple? Dixon said suavely.

— Saint Augustine says that about unbaptised children going to hell, Temple answered, because he was a cruel old sinner too.

— I bow to you, Dixon said, but I had the impression that limbo existed for such cases.

— Don't argue with him, Dixon, Cranly said brutally. Don't talk to him or look at him. Lead him home with a sugan° the way you'd lead a bleating goat.

— Limbo! Temple cried. That's a fine invention too. Like hell.

— But with the unpleasantness left out, Dixon said.

He turned smiling to the others and said:

— I think I am voicing the opinions of all present in saying so much.

— You are, Glynn said in a firm tone. On that point Ireland is united.

He struck the ferule of his umbrella on the stone floor of the colonnade.

— Hell, Temple said. I can respect that invention of the grey spouse of Satan. Hell is Roman, like the walls of the Romans, strong and ugly. But what is limbo?

— Put him back into the perambulator, Cranly, O'Keeffe called out.

sugan: Rope made of straw (Irish).

Cranly made a swift step towards Temple, halted, stamping his foot and crying as if to a fowl:

— Hoosh!

Temple moved away nimbly.

— Do you know what limbo is? he cried. Do you know what we call a notion like that in Roscommon?

— Hoosh! Blast you! Cranly cried, clapping his hands.

— Neither my arse nor my elbow! Temple cried out scornfully. And that's what I call limbo.

— Give us that stick here, Cranly said.

He snatched the ashplant roughly from Stephen's hand and sprang down the steps: but Temple, hearing him move in pursuit, fled through the dusk like a wild creature, nimble and fleetfooted. Cranly's heavy boots were heard loudly charging across the quadrangle and then returning heavily, foiled and spurning the gravel at each step.

His step was angry and with an angry abrupt gesture he thrust the stick back into Stephen's hand. Stephen felt that his anger had another cause but, feigning patience, touched his arm slightly and said quietly:

— Cranly, I told you I wanted to speak to you. Come away.

Cranly looked at him for a few moments and asked:

— Now?

— Yes, now, Stephen said. We can't speak here. Come away.

They crossed the quadrangle together without speaking. The birdcall from *Siegfried°* whistled softly followed them from the steps of the porch. Cranly turned: and Dixon, who had whistled, called out:

— Where are you fellows off to? What about that game, Cranly?

They parleyed in shouts across the still air about a game of billiards to be played in the Adelphi hotel. Stephen walked on alone and out into the quiet of Kildare Street. Opposite Maple's hotel he stood to wait, patient again. The name of the hotel, a colourless polished wood, and its colourless quiet front stung him like a glance of polite disdain. He stared angrily back at the softly lit drawingroom of the hotel in which he imagined the sleek lives of the patricians of Ireland housed in calm. They thought of army commissions and land agents: peasants greeted them along the roads in the country: they knew the names of certain French dishes and gave orders to jarvies° in highpitched provincial voices which pierced through their skintight accents.

How could he hit their conscience or how cast his shadow over the

---

birdcall from **Siegfried:** Series of passages from Richard Wagner's opera *Siegfried*, a part of the *Ring of the Nibelungs.*   **jarvies:** Horse-cab drivers.

imaginations of their daughters, before their squires begat upon them, that they might breed a race less ignoble than their own? And under the deepened dusk he felt the thoughts and desires of the race to which he belonged flitting like bats across the dark country lanes, under trees by the edges of streams and near the poolmottled bogs. A woman had waited in the doorway as Davin had passed by at night and, offering him a cup of milk, had all but wooed him to her bed: for Davin had the mild eyes of one who could be secret. But him no woman's eyes had wooed.

His arm was taken in a strong grip and Cranly's voice said:

— Let us eke go.

They walked southward in silence. Then Cranly said:

— That blithering idiot Temple! I swear to Moses, do you know, that I'll be the death of that fellow one time.

But his voice was no longer angry and Stephen wondered was he thinking of her greeting to him under the porch.

They turned to the left and walked on as before. When they had gone on so for some time Stephen said:

— Cranly, I had an unpleasant quarrel this evening.

— With your people? Cranly asked.

— With my mother.

— About religion?

— Yes, Stephen answered.

After a pause Cranly asked:

— What age is your mother?

— Not old, Stephen said. She wishes me to make my easter duty.°

— And will you?

— I will not, Stephen said.

— Why not? Cranly said.

— I will not serve, answered Stephen.

— That remark was made before, Cranly said calmly.

— It is made behind now, said Stephen hotly.

Cranly pressed Stephen's arm, saying:

— Go easy, my dear man. You're an excitable bloody man, do you know.

He laughed nervously as he spoke and, looking up into Stephen's face with moved and friendly eyes, said:

— Do you know that you are an excitable man?

— I daresay I am, said Stephen, laughing also.

easter duty: Going to communion service on Easter.

Their minds, lately estranged, seemed suddenly to have been drawn closer, one to the other.

— Do you believe in the eucharist? Cranly asked.

— I do not, Stephen said.

— Do you disbelieve then?

— I neither believe in it nor disbelieve in it, Stephen answered.

— Many persons have doubts, even religious persons, yet they overcome them or put them aside, Cranly said. Are your doubts on that point too strong?

— I do not wish to overcome them, Stephen answered.

Cranly, embarrassed for a moment, took another fig from his pocket and was about to eat it when Stephen said:

— Don't, please. You cannot discuss this question with your mouth full of chewed fig.

Cranly examined the fig by the light of a lamp under which he halted. Then he smelt it with both nostrils, bit a tiny piece, spat it out and threw the fig rudely into the gutter. Addressing it as it lay, he said:

— Depart from me, ye cursed, into everlasting fire!

Taking Stephen's arm, he went on again and said:

— Do you not fear that those words may be spoken to you on the day of judgment?

— What is offered me on the other hand? Stephen asked. An eternity of bliss in the company of the dean of studies?

— Remember, Cranly said, that he would be glorified.

— Ay, Stephen said somewhat bitterly, bright, agile, impassible and, above all, subtle.

— It is a curious thing, do you know, Cranly said dispassionately, how your mind is supersaturated with the religion in which you say you disbelieve. Did you believe in it when you were at school? I bet you did.

— I did, Stephen answered.

— And were you happier then? Cranly asked softly. Happier than you are now, for instance?

— Often happy, Stephen said, and often unhappy. I was someone else then.

— How someone else? What do you mean by that statement?

— I mean, said Stephen, that I was not myself as I am now, as I had to become.

— Not as you are now, not as you had to become, Cranly repeated. Let me ask you a question. Do you love your mother?

Stephen shook his head slowly.

— I don't know what your words mean, he said simply.

— Have you never loved anyone? Cranly asked.

— Do you mean women?

— I am not speaking of that, Cranly said in a colder tone. I ask you if you ever felt love towards anyone or anything.

Stephen walked on beside his friend, staring gloomily at the footpath.

— I tried to love God, he said at length. It seems now I failed. It is very difficult. I tried to unite my will with the will of God instant by instant. In that I did not always fail. I could perhaps do that still . . .

Cranly cut him short by asking:

— Has your mother had a happy life?

— How do I know? Stephen said.

— How many children had she?

— Nine or ten, Stephen answered. Some died.

— Was your father. . . . Cranly interrupted himself for an instant: and then said: I don't want to pry into your family affairs. But was your father what is called well-to-do? I mean when you were growing up?

— Yes, Stephen said.

— What was he? Cranly asked after a pause.

Stephen began to enumerate glibly his father's attributes.

— A medical student, an oarsman, a tenor, an amateur actor, a shouting politician, a small landlord, a small investor, a drinker, a good fellow, a storyteller, somebody's secretary, something in a distillery, a taxgatherer, a bankrupt and at present a praiser of his own past.

Cranly laughed, tightening his grip on Stephen's arm, and said:

— The distillery is damn good.

— Is there anything else you want to know? Stephen asked.

— Are you in good circumstances at present?

— Do I look it? Stephen asked bluntly.

— So then, Cranly went on musingly, you were born in the lap of luxury.

He used the phrase broadly and loudly as he often used technical expressions as if he wished his hearer to understand that they were used by him without conviction.

— Your mother must have gone through a good deal of suffering, he said then. Would you not try to save her from suffering more even if . . . or would you?

— If I could, Stephen said. That would cost me very little.

— Then do so, Cranly said. Do as she wishes you to do. What is it for you? You disbelieve in it. It is a form: nothing else. And you will set her mind at rest.

He ceased and, as Stephen did not reply, remained silent. Then, as if giving utterance to the process of his own thought, he said:

— Whatever else is unsure in this stinking dunghill of a world a mother's love is not. Your mother brings you into the world, carries you first in her body. What do we know about what she feels? But whatever she feels, it, at least, must be real. It must be. What are our ideas or ambitions? Play. Ideas! Why, that bloody bleating goat Temple has ideas. MacCann has ideas too. Every jackass going the roads thinks he has ideas.

Stephen, who had been listening to the unspoken speech behind the words, said with assumed carelessness:

— Pascal,° if I remember rightly, would not suffer his mother to kiss him as he feared the contact of her sex.

— Pascal was a pig, said Cranly.

— Aloysius Gonzaga, I think, was of the same mind, Stephen said.

— And he was another pig then, said Cranly.

— The church calls him a saint, Stephen objected.

— I don't care a flaming damn what anyone calls him, Cranly said rudely and flatly. I call him a pig.

Stephen, preparing the words neatly in his mind, continued:

— Jesus too seems to have treated his mother with scant courtesy in public but Suarez,° a jesuit theologian and Spanish gentleman, has apologised for him.

— Did the idea ever occur to you, Cranly asked, that Jesus was not what he pretended to be?

— The first person to whom that idea occurred, Stephen answered, was Jesus himself.

— I mean, Cranly said, hardening in his speech, did the idea ever occur to you that he was himself a conscious hypocrite, what he called the jews of his time, a whited sepulchre? Or, to put it more plainly, that he was a blackguard?

— That idea never occurred to me, Stephen answered. But I am curious to know are you trying to make a convert of me or a pervert of yourself?

He turned towards his friend's face and saw there a raw smile which some force of will strove to make finely significant.

Cranly asked suddenly in a plain sensible tone:

Pascal: Blaise Pascal (1623–1662), French philosopher, defender of conservative Catholic doctrine. The story about his mother is not factual.   *Suarez:* Francisco Suarez (1548–1617), Spanish Jesuit.

— Tell me the truth. Were you at all shocked by what I said?

— Somewhat, Stephen said.

— And why were you shocked, Cranly pressed on in the same tone, if you feel sure that our religion is false and that Jesus was not the son of God?

— I am not at all sure of it, Stephen said. He is more like a son of God than a son of Mary.

— And is that why you will not communicate, Cranly asked, because you are not sure of that too, because you feel that the host too may be the body and blood of the son of God and not a wafer of bread? And because you fear that it may be?

— Yes, Stephen said quietly. I feel that and I also fear it.

— I see, Cranly said.

Stephen, struck by his tone of closure, reopened the discussion at once by saying:

— I fear many things: dogs, horses, firearms, the sea, thunderstorms, machinery, the country roads at night.

— But why do you fear a bit of bread?

— I imagine, Stephen said, that there is a malevolent reality behind those things I say I fear.

— Do you fear then, Cranly asked, that the God of the Roman catholics would strike you dead and damn you if you made a sacrilegious communion?

— The God of the Roman catholics could do that now, Stephen said. I fear more than that the chemical action which would be set up in my soul by a false homage to a symbol behind which are massed twenty centuries of authority and veneration.

— Would you, Cranly asked, in extreme danger commit that particular sacrilege? For instance, if you lived in the penal days?°

— I cannot answer for the past, Stephen replied. Possibly not.

— Then, said Cranly, you do not intend to become a protestant?

— I said that I had lost the faith, Stephen answered, but not that I had lost selfrespect. What kind of liberation would that be to forsake an absurdity which is logical and coherent and to embrace one which is illogical and incoherent?

They had walked on towards the township of Pembroke and now, as they went on slowly along the avenues, the trees and the scattered lights in the villas soothed their minds. The air of wealth and repose

penal days: Period (mostly in the eighteenth century) when especially repressive "penal laws" against Irish Catholics were enforced.

diffused about them seemed to comfort their neediness. Behind a hedge of laurel a light glimmered in the window of a kitchen and the voice of a servant was heard singing as she sharpened knives. She sang, in short broken bars, *Rosie O'Grady.*

Cranly stopped to listen, saying:

— *Mulier cantat.*°

The soft beauty of the Latin word touched with an enchanting touch the dark of the evening, with a touch fainter and more persuading than the touch of music or of a woman's hand. The strife of their minds was quelled. The figure of woman as she appears in the liturgy of the church passed silently through the darkness: a whiterobed figure, small and slender as a boy and with a falling girdle. Her voice, frail and high as a boy's, was heard intoning from a distant choir the first words of a woman which pierce the gloom and clamour of the first chanting of the passion:

— *Et tu cum Jesu Galilæo eras.*°

And all hearts were touched and turned to her voice, shining like a young star, shining clearer as the voice intoned the proparoxyton° and more faintly as the cadence died.

The singing ceased. They went on together, Cranly repeating in strongly stressed rhythm the end of the refrain:

And when we are married,
O, how happy we'll be
For I love sweet Rosie O'Grady
And Rosie O'Grady loves me.

— There's real poetry for you, he said. There's real love.

He glanced sideways at Stephen with a strange smile and said:

— Do you consider that poetry? Or do you know what the words mean?

— I want to see Rosie first, said Stephen.

— She's easy to find, Cranly said.

His hat had come down on his forehead. He shoved it back: and in the shadow of the trees Stephen saw his pale face, framed by the dark, and his large dark eyes. Yes. His face was handsome: and his body was strong and hard. He had spoken of a mother's love. He felt then the sufferings of women, the weaknesses of their bodies and souls: and

---

Mulier cantat: The [or a] woman sings.   *Et tu cum Jesu Galilæo eras:* And you were with Jesus of Galilee.   *proparoxyton:* Rhetorical term for a (Latin) word having the acute accent on the next to last syllable.

would shield them with a strong and resolute arm and bow his mind to them.

Away then: it is time to go. A voice spoke softly to Stephen's lonely heart, bidding him go and telling him that his friendship was coming to an end. Yes, he would go. He could not strive against another. He knew his part.

— Probably I shall go away, he said.

— Where? Cranly asked.

— Where I can, Stephen said.

— Yes, Cranly said. It might be difficult for you to live here now. But is it that that makes you go?

— I have to go, Stephen answered.

— Because, Cranly continued, you need not look upon yourself as driven away if you do not wish to go or as a heretic or an outlaw. There are many good believers who think as you do. Would that surprise you? The church is not the stone building nor even the clergy and their dogmas. It is the whole mass of those born into it. I don't know what you wish to do in life. Is it what you told me the night we were standing outside Harcourt Street station?

— Yes, Stephen said, smiling in spite of himself at Cranly's way of remembering thoughts in connection with places. The night you spent half an hour wrangling with Doherty about the shortest way from Sallygap to Larras.

— Pothead! Cranly said with calm contempt. What does he know about the way from Sallygap to Larras? Or what does he know about anything for that matter? And the big slobbering washingpot head of him!

He broke out into a loud long laugh.

— Well? Stephen said. Do you remember the rest?

— What you said, is it? Cranly asked. Yes, I remember it. To discover the mode of life or of art whereby your spirit could express itself in unfettered freedom.

Stephen raised his hat in acknowledgment.

— Freedom! Cranly repeated. But you are not free enough yet to commit a sacrilege. Tell me, would you rob?

— I would beg first, Stephen said.

— And if you got nothing, would you rob?

— You wish me to say, Stephen answered, that the rights of property are provisional and that in certain circumstances it is not unlawful to rob. Everyone would act in that belief. So I will not make you that answer. Apply to the jesuit theologian Juan Mariana de Talavera° who will also explain to you in what circumstances you may lawfully kill your king and whether you had better hand him his poison in a goblet or smear it for him upon his robe or his saddlebow. Ask me rather would I suffer others to rob me or, if they did, would I call down upon them what I believe is called the chastisement of the secular arm?

— And would you?

— I think, Stephen said, it would pain me as much to do so as to be robbed.

— I see, Cranly said.

He produced his match and began to clean the crevice between two teeth. Then he said carelessly:

— Tell me, for example, would you deflower a virgin?

— Excuse me, Stephen said politely, is that not the ambition of most young gentlemen?

— What then is your point of view? Cranly asked.

His last phrase, soursmelling as the smoke of charcoal and disheartening, excited Stephen's brain, over which its fumes seemed to brood.

— Look here, Cranly, he said. You have asked me what I would do and what I would not do. I will tell you what I will do and what I will not do. I will not serve that in which I no longer believe whether it call itself my home, my fatherland or my church: and I will try to express myself in some mode of life or art as freely as I can and as wholly as I can, using for my defence the only arms I allow myself to use, silence, exile, and cunning.

Cranly seized his arm and steered him round so as to head back towards Leeson Park. He laughed almost slily and pressed Stephen's arm with an elder's affection.

— Cunning indeed! he said. Is it you? You poor poet, you!

— And you made me confess to you, Stephen said, thrilled by his touch, as I have confessed to you so many other things, have I not?

— Yes, my child, Cranly said, still gaily.

— You made me confess the fears that I have. But I will tell you also what I do not fear. I do not fear to be alone or to be spurned for another or to leave whatever I have to leave. And I am not afraid to make a mistake, even a great mistake, a lifelong mistake and perhaps as long as eternity too.

Cranly, now grave again, slowed his pace and said:

— Alone, quite alone. You have no fear of that. And you know what

---

Talavera: Juan Mariana de Talavera (1536–1623), Spanish theologian.

that word means? Not only to be separate from all others but to have not even one friend.

— I will take the risk, said Stephen.

— And not to have any one person, Cranly said, who would be more than a friend, more even than the noblest and truest friend a man ever had.

His words seemed to have struck some deep chord in his own nature. Had he spoken of himself, of himself as he was or wished to be? Stephen watched his face for some moments in silence. A cold sadness was there. He had spoken of himself, of his own loneliness which he feared.

— Of whom are you speaking? Stephen asked at length.

Cranly did not answer.

*

*   *

20 *March:* Long talk with Cranly on the subject of my revolt. He had his grand manner on. I supple and suave. Attacked me on the score of love for one's mother. Tried to imagine his mother: cannot. Told me once, in a moment of thoughtlessness, his father was sixtyone when he was born. Can see him. Strong farmer type. Pepper and salt suit. Square feet. Unkempt grizzled beard. Probably attends coursing-matches.° Pays his dues regularly but not plentifully to Father Dwyer of Larras. Sometimes talks to girls after nightfall. But his mother? Very young or very old? Hardly the first. If so, Cranly would not have spoken as he did. Old then. Probably, and neglected. Hence Cranly's despair of soul: the child of exhausted loins.

21 *March, morning:* Thought this in bed last night but was too lazy and free to add it. Free, yes. The exhausted loins are those of Elisabeth and Zachary.° Then is he the precursor. Item:° he eats chiefly belly bacon and dried figs. Read locusts and wild honey. Also, when thinking of him, saw always a stern severed head or deathmask as if outlined on a grey curtain or veronica.° Decollation they call it in the fold. Puzzled for the moment by saint John at the Latin gate. What do I see? A decollated° precursor trying to pick the lock.

21 *March, night:* Free. Soulfree and fancyfree. Let the dead bury the dead. Ay. And let the dead marry the dead.

---

coursing-matches: In which greyhounds chase hares.   *Elisabeth and Zachary:* Parents of John the Baptist (known as "the precursor"), both elderly at his birth.   *Item:* Term used in wills in enumerating bequests.   *veronica:* A cloth bearing the image of Jesus' face.   *decollated:* Beheaded.

22 *March:* In company with Lynch followed a sizable hospital nurse. Lynch's idea. Dislike it. Two lean hungry greyhounds walking after a heifer.

23 *March:* Have not seen her since that night. Unwell? Sits at the fire perhaps with mamma's shawl on her shoulders. But not peevish. A nice bowl of gruel? Won't you now?

24 *March:* Began with a discussion with my mother. Subject: B.V.M.° Handicapped by my sex and youth. To escape held up relations between Jesus and Papa against those between Mary and her Son. Said religion was not a lying-in hospital. Mother indulgent. Said I have a queer mind and have read too much. Not true. Have read little and understood less. Then she said I would come back to faith because I had a restless mind. This means to leave church by backdoor of sin and reenter through the skylight of repentance. Cannot repent. Told her so and asked for sixpence. Got threepence.

Then went to college. Other wrangle with little roundhead rogue's-eye Ghezzi. This time about Bruno the Nolan.° Began in Italian and ended in pidgin English. He said Bruno was a terrible heretic. I said he was terribly burned. He agreed to this with some sorrow. Then gave me recipe for what he calls *risotto alla bergamasca*.° When he pronounces a soft *o* he protrudes his full carnal lips as if he kissed the vowel. Has he? And could he repent? Yes, he could: and cry two round rogue's tears, one from each eye.

Crossing Stephen's, that is, my green, remembered that his countrymen and not mine had invented what Cranly the other night called our religion. A quartet of them, soldiers of the ninetyseventh infantry regiment, sat at the foot of the cross and tossed up dice for the overcoat of the crucified.

Went to library. Tried to read three reviews. Useless. She is not out yet. Am I alarmed? About what? That she will never be out again.

Blake wrote:

I wonder if William Bond will die
For assuredly he is very ill.°

Alas, poor William!

B.V.M.: Blessed Virgin Mary.   ***Bruno the Nolan:*** Giordano Bruno of Nola (1548–1600), a philosopher and theologian, was burned at the stake during the Inquisition. **risotto alla bergamasca:** A rice dish made as in Belgamo (Italy).   *I wonder if William Bond . . . ill:* From the poem "William Bond" by William Blake (1757–1827).

I was once at a diorama in Rotunda.° At the end were pictures of big nobs. Among them William Ewart Gladstone,° just then dead. Orchestra played *O, Willie, we have missed you.*

A race of clodhoppers!

25 *March, morning:* A troubled night of dreams. Want to get them off my chest.

A long curving gallery. From the floor ascend pillars of dark vapours. It is peopled by the images of fabulous kings, set in stone. Their hands are folded upon their knees in token of weariness and their eyes are darkened for the errors of men go up before them for ever as dark vapours.

Strange figures advance from a cave. They are not as tall as men. One does not seem to stand quite apart from another. Their faces are phosphorescent, with darker streaks. They peer at me and their eyes seem to ask me something. They do not speak.

30 *March:* This evening Cranly was in the porch of the library, proposing a problem to Dixon and her brother. A mother let her child fall into the Nile. Still harping on the mother. A crocodile seized the child. Mother asked it back. Crocodile said all right if she told him what he was going to do with the child, eat it or not eat it.

This mentality, Lepidus° would say, is indeed bred out of your mud by the operation of your sun.

And mine? Is it not too? Then into Nilemud with it!

1 *April:* Disapprove of this last phrase.

2 *April:* Saw her drinking tea and eating cakes in Johnston, Mooney and O'Brien's. Rather, lynxeyed Lynch saw her as we passed. He tells me Cranly was invited there by brother. Did he bring his crocodile? Is he the shining light now? Well, I discovered him. I protest I did. Shining quietly behind a bushel of Wicklow bran.

3 *April:* Met Davin at the cigar shop opposite Findlater's church. He was in a black sweater and had a hurleystick. Asked me was it true I was going away and why. Told him the shortest way to Tara was *via* Holyhead.° Just then my father came up. Introduction. Father, polite

---

diorama in Rotunda: A precursor of the cinema, in the Rotunda, a large, round building that also housed a maternity hospital at the north end of what was then Sackville Street.   **William Ewart Gladstone:** (1808–1898), British prime minister who turned against Parnell.   **Lepidus:** Character in Shakespeare's *Antony and Cleopatra* whom Stephen paraphrases (II, vii 29–31).   **Tara ... Holyhead:** Tara is the traditional Irish seat of kings, Holyhead a Welsh port commonly used by Irish leaving the country.

and observant. Asked Davin if he might offer him some refreshment. Davin could not, was going to a meeting. When we came away father told me he had a good honest eye. Asked me why I did not join a rowingclub. I pretended to think it over. Told me then how he broke Pennyfeather's heart.° Wants me to read law. Says I was cut out for that. More mud, more crocodiles.

5 *April:* Wild spring. Scudding clouds. O life! Dark stream of swirling bogwater on which appletrees have cast down their delicate flowers. Eyes of girls among the leaves. Girls demure and romping. All fair or auburn: no dark ones. They blush better. Houp-la!

6 *April:* Certainly she remembers the past. Lynch says all women do. Then she remembers the time of her childhood — and mine if I was ever a child. The past is consumed in the present and the present is living only because it brings forth the future. Statues of women, if Lynch be right, should always be fully draped, one hand of the woman feeling regretfully her own hinder parts.

6 *April, later:* Michael Robartes° remembers forgotten beauty and, when his arms wrap her round, he presses in his arms the loveliness which has long faded from the world. Not this. Not at all. I desire to press in my arms the loveliness which has not yet come into the world.

10 *April:* Faintly, under the heavy night, through the silence of the city which has turned from dreams to dreamless sleep as a weary lover whom no caresses move, the sound of hoofs upon the road. Not so faintly now as they come near the bridge: and in a moment as they pass the darkened windows the silence is cloven by alarm as by an arrow. They are heard now far away, hoofs that shine amid the heavy night as gems, hurrying beyond the sleeping fields to what journey's end — what heart? — bearing what tidings?

11 *April:* Read what I wrote last night. Vague words for a vague emotion. Would she like it? I think so. Then I should have to like it also.

13 *April:* That tundish has been on my mind for a long time. I looked it up and find it is English and good old blunt English too. Damn the dean of studies and his funnel! What did he come here for to teach us his own language or to learn it from us? Damn him one way or the other!

---

broke Pennyfeather's heart: A stock phrase for disappointment in love, origin unknown.
Michael Robartes: Paraphrased from William Butler Yeats's poem "Michael Robartes Remembers Forgotten Beauty" (1899).

14 *April:* John Alphonsus Mulrennan has just returned from the west of Ireland. (European and Asiatic papers please copy.) He told us he met an old man there in a mountain cabin. Old man had red eyes and short pipe. Old man spoke Irish. Mulrennan spoke Irish. Then old man and Mulrennan spoke English. Mulrennan spoke to him about universe and stars. Old man sat, listened, smoked, spat. Then said:

— Ah, there must be terrible queer creatures at the latter end of the world.

I fear him. I fear his redrimmed horny eyes. It is with him I must struggle all through this night till day come, till he or I lie dead, gripping him by the sinewy throat till . . . Till what? Till he yield to me? No. I mean him no harm.

15 *April:* Met her today pointblank in Grafton Street. The crowd brought us together. We both stopped. She asked me why I never came, said she had heard all sorts of stories about me. This was only to gain time. Asked me was I writing poems? About whom? I asked her. This confused her more and I felt sorry and mean. Turned off that valve at once and opened the spiritual-heroic refrigerating apparatus, invented and patented in all countries by Dante Alighieri. Talked rapidly of myself and my plans. In the midst of it unluckily I made a sudden gesture of a revolutionary nature. I must have looked like a fellow throwing a handful of peas up into the air. People began to look at us. She shook hands a moment after and, in going away, said she hoped I would do what I said.

Now I call that friendly, don't you?

Yes, I liked her today. A little or much? Don't know. I liked her and it seems a new feeling to me. Then, in that case, all the rest, all that I thought I thought and all that I felt I felt, all the rest before now, in fact . . . O, give it up, old chap! Sleep it off!

16 *April:* Away! Away!

The spell of arms and voices: the white arms of roads, their promise of close embraces and the black arms of tall ships that stand against the moon, their tale of distant nations. They are held out to say: We are alone. Come. And the voices say with them: We are your kinsmen. And the air is thick with their company as they call to me, their kinsman, making ready to go, shaking the wings of their exultant and terrible youth.

26 *April:* Mother is putting my new secondhand clothes in order. She prays now, she says, that I may learn in my own life and away from home and friends what the heart is and what it feels. Amen. So be it.

Welcome, O life! I go to encounter for the millionth time the reality of experience and to forge in the smithy of my soul the uncreated conscience of my race.

    27 April: Old father, old artificer, stand me now and ever in good stead.

Dublin 1904
Trieste 1914

Cultural Documents
and Illustrations

James Joyce's novel *A Portrait of the Artist as a Young Man* is a complex, densely patterned, labyrinthine book whose patterns of word, motif, and imagery have a structural beauty that even the casual reader can sense and that becomes more rich and meaningful on rereading. No wonder Joyce thought his work akin to the illuminations of the medieval Irish Book of Kells (p. 226), saying, "you can compare much of my work to [its] intricate illustrations" (Ellmann 545). But in addition, *A Portrait* is both autobiographical and realistic in some unprecedented ways. This means that Joycean critics are accustomed to moving back and forth between details of the life of Stephen Dedalus and those of the life of Joyce himself, sometimes complicating the process with items drawn from *Stephen Hero,* the first-draft manuscript of *A Portrait.* There are obvious dangers to this slippage, since Stephen Dedalus and James Joyce are very different in many ways, and certain details of Joyce's life have been altered or omitted in the fictional version. For example, we do not see Stephen attend a Christian Brothers school between his attendance at Clongowes and Belvedere College, although Joyce did so. Stephen is punished only once, unjustly, at Clongowes, while the "Punishment Book" at the real college shows several occasions on which the young Joyce was punished for "bad language."

It is difficult not to interpolate facts and circumstances from Joyce's life into our reading of the novel when they seem entirely appropriate:

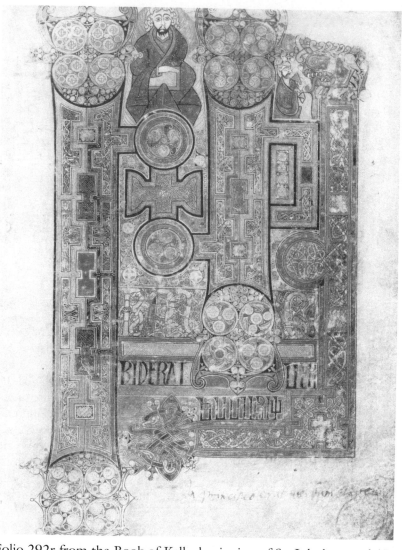

Folio 292r from the Book of Kells, beginning of St. John's gospel (*In principio erat verbum* — In the beginning was the Word). This typical illumination from the Book of Kells, a manuscript codex of the gospels, was probably created in the early ninth century. The complexity of the graphic design, including the "Irish knots," circles, and labyrinthine patterns, reminded Joyce of aspects of his own writing.

Reprinted by permission of The Board of Trinity College Dublin.

Stephen has the part of a "farcical pedagogue" (p. 76 in this volume) in his school play, but the title of the play is not specifically identified. The play in which James Joyce took that part at Belvedere was *Vice-Versa*, by F. Anstey, a popular school comedy in which a stuffy Victorian father who insists that his son's school days are happy and fulfilling is magically transposed into the body of the boy, where he learns his error. The play is the basis of four or five recent movies, and is a strikingly apposite intertext to *Portrait*, in which Simon Dedalus wants to play the child while Stephen is asked to take on adult responsibilities. I mention the play merely as a demonstration that at times material from Joyce's life can lend unexpected insights into the novel, even if we must be careful always to honor the distinction between the fictional Stephen Dedalus and the historical James Joyce.

Be that as it may, I think that period photographs both of Joyce and of turn-of-the-century Dublin capture a background for the novel that Joyce does not always represent, but which both he and Irish readers of his time would have assumed. Because the narration is so centered on Stephen, little is explained or described that Stephen does not consciously notice or think about, and so we have no way of knowing, for example, that no adult man would ever appear outdoors without a hat, a fact made clear by numerous photographs of the time. The photograph of Joyce at six years old sitting in front of his Class of Elements like a class mascot (p. 228) makes clear as few other documents could just how small and young he was; no wonder he "kept on the fringe of his line . . . out of reach of the rude feet" (p. 21)   Stephen is not simply unathletic and timid, but would stand no chance against the much bigger boys. Academically, though, he could excel, as his examination results at the age of thirteen show (p. 229). Later he was to lose much of his interest in academic achievement.

The Cultural Documents section contains maps of Dublin and the surrounding area because, perhaps to a greater degree than any previous novel, *Portrait* is about walking in a modern city. Dublin is still a remarkably walkable city for a capital, and after all Stephen is too poor to engage in many other amusements — even sitting in a café costs something. But walking for Stephen seems to take on some quality of ritual. He even comes to associate walking in certain places with particular literary passages: "he foreknew that as he passed the sloblands of Fairview he would think of the cloistral silverveined prose of Newman, that as he walked along the North Strand Road . . . he would recall the dark humour of Guido Cavalcante and smile" (pp. 158–59). The streets of Dublin have two Daedalian functions: they form a labyrinth, a

The elements class at Clongowes Wood College, 1888–1889, with class master Father William Power (Fr Arnall). Joyce is front and center in a light suit, and at the age of "half past six" is easily the youngest pupil. In the back row, Rody Kickham is sixth from the left, Christopher "Nasty" Roche fifth from the right. In the front row, Wells is second from the right.

Courtesy of Father Bruce Bradley, S.J.

"maze of narrow and dirty streets" (p. 98) from which Stephen must escape, but they also come to suggest runways for Stephen the aspiring "hawklike man" (p. 153), where he can prepare for flight as he circles farther and farther from home. Joyce identifies many streets, shops, newspapers, and public personages by name, a practice that got him into trouble when he was trying to publish *Dubliners*, and it is a useful exercise for the student to try to trace some of the young man's wanderings through and outside the city (p. 230 and pp. 232–33). Some period photographs show what remained of the handsome eighteenth-century city laid out with broad avenues and long vistas (p. 234). The fictional Stephen Dedalus particularly enjoys the large, central park that is still called St. Stephen's Green (p. 235), and affectionately refers to it as "my green" (p. 220). Readers interested in pursuing such matters might consult Bruce Bidwell and Linda Heffer, *The Joycean Way: A Topographic Guide to "Dubliners" and "A Portrait of the Artist as a Young Man"* (Baltimore: Johns Hopkins UP, 1982).

The two most significant public events from Joyce's point of view during his youth were probably the fall of Parnell, which occurred when Joyce was still a boy, and the public outcry over Yeats's play *The Countess Cathleen*, while Joyce was attending University College Dub-

Examination Number	STUDENT'S NAME AND ADDRESS	Greek	Latin	English	Grammar / English	French	Italian	Celtic	Arithmetic	Book-keeping	Euclid	Algebra	Natural Philosophy	Chemistry	Drawing	Shorthand	Total under marks 55	Examination Number
MAXIMUM		1200	1200	1200	600	700		500	600	200	600	600	500	500	900	900		
3821	Jones, Christopher F., Merchant Taylors' Sch., Wellington qy., Dublin	×	294	395	35	343	×	×	310	×	185	150	×	×	120	190	2022	3821
3822	[Failed]	×	×	7	×	3	×	f	f	×	f	f	×	×	80	×	90	3822
3823	Jones, James E., Educational Institution, Dundalk	×	f	255	20	568	×	×	330	×	220	10	130	50	170	×	1859	3823
3824	Jones, Sidney A., Avoca School, Blackrock	299	150	200	×	254	×	×	10	×	165	5	×	×	f	×	1092	3824
3825	Jones, Webb B., Portora Royal School, Enniskillen	×	f	185	×	65	×	×	175	×	350	275	×	×	35	×	1085	3825
3826	[Failed]	×	×	50	×	f	×	×	20	P	f	×	×	×	85	×	155	3826
3827	[Failed]	×	×	f	f	×	21	×	×	145	×	245	30	f	×	25	×	466	3827
3828	Jordan, Hugh, Christian Schools, Newry [P Ex.'94]	×	×	225	×	219	94	142	150	×	165	60	100	60	135	×	1442	3828
3829	Joyce, James A., Belvedere College (s.i.), Dublin [P.Ex.'94]	×	636	540	×	410	223	×	250	×	175	175	190	100	×	×	2699	3829
3830	[Failed]	×	×	27	×	f	×	×	f	15	f	f	×	×	×	×	42	3830
3831	[Failed]	×	×	15	×	f	×	×	205	f	×	50	f	×	55	f	325	3831
3832	[Failed]	×	f	25	×	f	×	×	f	×	135	×	×	×	×	×	160	3832
3833	Judge, Maurice J., Blackrock College, co. Dublin	×	f	180	×	57	×	×	10	×	105	f	×	×	×	×	352	3833
3834	Judge, Thomas M., Rockwell College, Cashel	×	174	60	×	221	×	f	110	×	155	f	×	×	×	×	720	3834
3835	Kane, John J., Christian Schools, Tipperary	226	40	240	×	200	×	f	22	×	0.	×	×	160	×	f	×	1136	3835
3836	[Failed]												×	×	f	×	×	3836
3837	Kavanagh, Jeremiah M., Christian												P	f	f	×	65	×	1512	3837
3838	Kavanagh, John J., Christian Sch												×	×	f	×	684	3838
3839	Kavanagh, Patrick, Christian Scho												×	×	5	×	276	3839
3840	Kavanagh, Patrick J., Christian S												×	×	170	25	1276	3840
3841	[Not Examined]												×	×	×	×	×	3841
3842	[Failed]												×	×	15	×	253	3842
3843	Kavanagh, William, Rockwell Coll												×	×	×	×	2051	3843
3844	Kealy, Michael, Christian Schools,												×	×	30	365	3844
3845	[Failed]												×	×	×	5	3845
3846	Kean, William F., Christian Schoc									210	115	115	×	×	×	2335	3846
3847	Keane, Daniel, Christian Schools,									250	400	185	×	×	×	3174	3847
3848	[Failed]									×	×	f	f	×	×	3848
3849	Keane, William, Christian Schools									×	×	30	×	479	3849
3850	Keany, Matthew J., St. Patrick's C	1	3338							45	×	f	×	774	3850
3851	[Failed]	2	3313							×	×	×	103	3851
3852	Kearney, John, Presentation Colle	3	4115							×	140	×	1179	3852
3853	[Failed]	4	4135							×	105	×	390	3853
3854	[Failed]	5	2676							×	35	×	35	3854
3855	[Failed]	6	4746							×	×	f	275	3855
3856	[Failed]	163	4896							×	f	f	60	3856
3857	[Failed]	164	3829							×	×	f	190	3857
3858	Keeffe, Michael, Christian Schools									30	×	30	×	223	3858

Intermediate Education Board for Ireland.   [Boys,   Examinations, 1895

Intermediate Education Board for Ireland.

JUNIOR GRADE

TABLE I.—EXHIBITIONS, value £20 a-year each, tenable for Three Years, have been awarded to the following Students:—

Order of Merit	Examination Number	STUDENTS NAME AND ADDRESS	Net Total of Marks under Rule 22
1	3338	Farrell, James A., Presentation Coll., Queenstown [P Ex '94]	5212
2	3313	Houston, Robert M., Academical Institution, Coleraine	5016
3	4115	MacMahon, Bernard, Rockwell College, Cashel [P.Ex.'94]	4795
4	4135	M'Cabe, Robert W., Clongowes Wood College (s.i.), Sallins	4614
5	2676	Boyland, Albert H., St. Macarten's Seminary, Monaghan	4583
6	4746	O'Neill, John, Rockwell College, Cashel	4450
...	...	Hutchinson, John, Clongowes Wood College (s.i.), Sallins	4343
163	4896	Richardson, John J., St. Mel's College, Longford	2701
164	3829	Joyce, James A., Belvedere College (s.i.), Dublin [P.Ex.'94]	2699

Examination results of the Intermediate Education Board showing Joyce's marks at the age of thirteen. The 20 pounds per year Joyce won represented the rental of a respectable middle class flat in Dublin around the turn of the century.

Courtesy of the National Library of Ireland.

lin. The cartoon of Parnell as "Crowbar King" (p. 236) captures some of the British animosity felt toward the Irish parliamentary leader who demonstrated his "impudence" in the House of Commons by demanding support for Home Rule from Gladstone's Liberal party in exchange for the block vote of the Irish MPs in other items on the Liberal agenda. As president of the Land League, Parnell, a Protestant landholder, was seen as a traitor to his class by many British and some Anglo-Irish citizens. Because the Land League was a popular movement, which could evoke the threat of mass violence without directly employing it, Parnell was seen by his enemies as at least potentially a man of violence — and Irish party politics indeed did at times degenerate into fisticuffs.

The nineteenth century was a great age for political cartooning, and the work of that period often has a force and frank brutality that we seldom encounter in these more "politically correct" times. The cartoon labeled "Two Forces" (p. 237) shows Britannia — whose features are

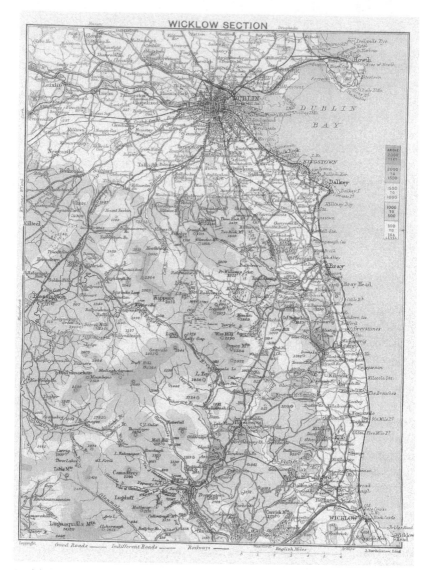

Dublin area map drawn by J. Bartholomew, Edinburgh, ca. 1890. The Dedalus family lives in Bray and then Blackrock, both coastal towns, before being forced into cheaper lodgings in Dublin itself. Stephen's friend Cranly is from Wicklow.

From the private collection of R. B. Kershner.

clean-cut and suggest Greek and Roman prototypes — in opposition to an Irish male labeled "Anarchy," whose features are blunt and rather simian and who threatens a swooning female figure supported by Britannia. Clearly this is no political difference among equals, but the atavistic impulse for destruction of a biologically primitive force attacking weakness (the female figure of Ireland), only held at bay by the more highly developed figure representing the British Empire. The effect of such cartoons with their simplistic melodrama and their perversion of Darwinian ideas was to dismiss any possibility of negotiation or reasoned discussion of the political issues; after all, there is no need to bargain with inferior and evil beings. "The King of A-Shantee" (p. 238) is a straightforward exercise in contempt for the Irish, portraying them as at home in their natural squalor and casting their facial features as either simian or Negroid. The cartoon is given some ironic force by the fact that living conditions for many poor Irish during this period were indeed worse than even that of the peasantry in Eastern Europe, although from our perspective this may seem more a reproach to the British economic system of colonization than it is evidence of any inherent primitivism of the Irish.

Meanwhile, the Phoenix Park murders heightened the British fear of armed revolt. These political assassinations were carried out by a terrorist group called "The Invincibles," who stabbed to death the chief secretary for Ireland and an undersecretary in 1882, near the viceregal lodge. The Piggott forgeries, letters seemingly sent by Parnell that seemed to prove that he secretly approved of the Phoenix Park assassinations, did him great damage. But he was finally destroyed by a divorce trial (1889–1890), during which Captain William O'Shea's wife Katherine became known to the general public as "Kitty" and the most intimate details of her adulterous virtual marriage to Parnell were brought to public scrutiny. Pressure from Gladstone and a coalition of clergy, politicians, and business leaders effectively ended Parnell's leadership. Just a few months after marrying Katherine, his health broken by the strain of the trial and his political battles, Parnell collapsed and died. Perhaps because neither Parnell nor Katherine participated in the trial and because of the hatred for Parnell among his enemies, the newspaper coverage was more extensive and personal than it had been in previous such cases. Contemporary readers will probably be struck by the thoroughness of the trial coverage, a sample of which is included in this section (p. 239).

Joyce attended the premiere of William Butler Yeats's play *The Countess Cathleen* at the National Literary Theatre on May 8, 1899,

Dublin city map drawn by J. Bartholomew ca. 1890. Many of the features Stephen encounters can be located, including Stephen's Green, Trinity College, and the university he attends, University College Dublin (then called "Catholic University College" and affiliated with the Royal University). The main route across the Liffey going north, Sackville Street, is now called O'Connell Street.

From the private collection of R. B. Kershner.

View of Sackville Street and Nelson's Pillar, ca. 1890. The pillar, which figures in Joyce's *Ulysses,* was dynamited by Irish nationalists in the 1960s and has now been replaced by the "Millennium Spire." Note the horse-drawn tram; by 1904 all the trams were electric. Note also the remarkably broad avenue, laid out in the eighteenth century.

Courtesy of Antique Prints, South Anne Street, Dublin.

where he witnessed the disturbance caused by protesting university students. In Yeats's play, set in some vague medieval period, famine has stricken the land, and the devil is buying up the souls of the peasantry in exchange for food. On hearing this, Countess Cathleen determines to save her people by sacrificing her own soul. She does so, but at the last minute God intervenes to save her soul because the "Lord of Lights looks only on the motive / Not the deed." Although the nominally Protestant Yeats had obtained the approval of some Catholic dignitaries, the common people and the general run of the clergy were apt to see the play as a libel on the noble, pious peasantry; they also saw selling one's soul to the devil as simply evil, whatever the motive. Besides, Yeats's well-known fascination with Theosophy and with Eastern mysticism in general was viewed with great suspicion by many Dubliners; as one of Stephen's classmates yells at the theater, "We want no budding buddhists" (p. 201). But the letter I have included written by the students (p. 240) gives a much deeper picture of the motives of the pro-

View of Stephen's Green, ca. 1900. Royal 4413.
Courtesy of the National Library of Ireland.

testers than does Stephen's brief, scornful memory of the incident in
Portrait. Joyce, who memorized many of Yeats's poems and some of his
stories, refused to sign the protest, although he came to have reservations about the National Literary Theatre, which he viewed as all too
nationalist. Nonetheless, the *Countess Cathleen* incident was one of the
first where he was forced to see the cause of art as, at least sometimes,
opposed to nationalism; here he saw clearly where his greater loyalty lay.

Cartoon of Parnell as "The Crowbar King" by Tom Merry, from *St. Stephen's Review,* December 27, 1890. A torn copy of *United Ireland* is under his right foot, and mounted on his throne are the skulls of some famous victims of violence during the 1880s. Cavendish, the chief secretary for Ireland, and his undersecretary Burke were the victims of the Phoenix Park Murders. Miles Joyce (no relation), a Gaelic speaker unable to comprehend his trial proceedings, was falsely convicted of murder in County Mayo in 1882.

Courtesy of David Pierce.

"Two Forces": Britannia vs. Anarchy, an illustration by John Tenniel from *Punch*, October 29, 1881. Ireland, in the guise of a frightened girl, is protected from the savage, primitive Irish male representing anarchy by a rather androgynous Britannia who wields the sword of the Law and crushes the banner of the Land League under her sandal. Note the simian appearance of Paddy, the stereotypical Irishman.

Reproduced with Permission of Punch Ltd.

The King of A-Shantee, cartoon by Frederick B. Opper from *Puck*, February 15, 1882: 378. The stereotyped Irish couple with their squalid "shanty" is connected to the African "Äshanti" through the pun.

Reproduced with Permission of Punch Ltd.

THE O'SHEA DIVORCE SUIT.

SUMMING UP AND VERDICT.

(BY TELEGRAPH.)

(FROM OUR CORRESPONDENT.)

LONDON, MONDAY EVENING.

Again to-day there was little or no stir outside the adjourned divorce suit of "O'Shea v. O'Shea and Parnell." There was naturally a warm demand for sittings within the court, all of which had, as a matter of fact, been allotted days ago, and when the ushers had repeatedly informed the besiegers that there was not a vacant seat, they were begged to "try and squeeze me in somewhere."

Reporters, barristers, jurymen, and a very small number of outsiders occupied the few dozen seats, and even then the crush was remarkably inconvenient for the members of the Press. It was of no use protesting or to dart angry looks at the intruders themselves on the edges of the benches, in the gangways, and elsewhere, was not only more than sufficient to provoke irritation, but to induce strong language far stronger than a whether. However, there they were. The intruders stuck—literally glued to such seats as they could nod on by serenely oblivious of contiguous dissatisfaction. Amongst them was a woman—whether she came as "a lady journalist" or whether she read upon the strength of woman's proverbial traits—mere curiosity—was not definitely known.

At the solicitors' table, which is in the well of the court, were Captain O'Shea, General Sir Evelyn Wood, V.C., his sister, Mrs. Steele, wife of General Steele; her sister, (Mrs.) Leonard, Madame Van———, young Gerard O'Shea, who without thinking on with his work, lady in close scrutiny to which he was subjected, and Mr. Mulqueeny, who will be remembered as one of the Times witnesses before the Special Commission. The fog which was thick outside had to some extent penetrated the court, and the brilliancy of the electric light dissipated to a great extent the murky gloom, and discovered the ladies to be very quietly attired in black. The dinner Bar, which had no business in court, is said to be highly indignant at being excluded from its interior in favour of the Press, a course which, while somewhat galling to their amour propre, undoubtedly the best on from the point of view of the public interest, which, after all, is of slightly more importance than the personal wishes of the "Jun on" It may be consoling to them to know that even all the reporters and "specials" did not get in.

The Judge did not take his seat until 11 o'clock. The Solicitor-General (immediately on the Clerk calling out in the most commonplace manner—"O'Shea v. O'Shea and Parnell,") rose from his seat and shouted "Jane Glenister." Whilst the ushers were searching for this young woman, the Judge (Mr. Justice Butt) intimated to the Solicitor-General that it was not by any means to be assumed that he was satisfied that the identity of Mr. Parnell had been conclusively established by the photographs produced on Saturday, it being the practice of the court never in such cases to act upon photographic evidence alone. The Solicitor-General intimated his familiarity with this practice, and created a mild sensation by announcing that he had subpoenaed Mr. Parnell, and would call him if necessary, but, he added, he thought he had ample evidence of identity to dispense with Mr. Parnell. This satisfied the judge.

The evidence to-day was quite as prosaic as that of Saturday, servants from Eltham and others being called to bear out the opening statement of the Solicitor-General as to the studious cumulativeness attending Mr. Parnell's visits, and the indistinctness betrayed into many scenes of mirth. There was an outbreak of laughter however, at the expense of the first witness, who was amusingly innocent. This was Jane Glenister, a young and well-possessed and somewhat sullen woman, who spoke of Mr. Parnell's visits to Mrs. O'Shea at Eltham and Brighton from October, 1880, to October, 1882, during which time Jane was in Mrs. O'Shea's service. The witness said that Mr. Parnell slept in a room separated from Mrs. O'Shea's by a dressing-room, which communicated with both apartments. Only on one occasion did she find the door locked, and Mrs. O'Shea explained that such incidents as happened in this matter, for there was a secret society about, and she may be necessary for the door to be locked. Further, she was told by Mrs. O'Shea to say to any body who asked for Mr. Parnell that he was not there. Jane Chapman, a waitress in Mrs. O'Shea's service in July and August, 1885, said Mr. Parnell was with Mrs. O'Shea the whole of the time that they were at times; in a room with the door locked, and that they often stayed out late. A coachman—Richard Wise—with Mrs. O'Shea from the spring of 1885 to the aster part of 1888; also spoke to Mr. Parnell's visits, and the collision with his brougham on the 21st May, 1886. Thomas Partridge, a relative of the last witness, gave corroborative evidence. Their testimony was uninteresting, having exclusive reference to Mr. Parnell's visits, and disclosing nothing that was novel. A page boy named Thomas Partridge, who has since enlisted, and who happened to be in court in a cavalry uniform, and a number of other witnesses spoke in particular to the stay of Mrs. O'Shea and Mr. Parnell at Eastbourne in 1886.

In addition to the evidence of the servants, which, in view of the attitude taken by the respondent and co-respondent, was not of an exhaustive character, several house agents were called, and some amusement was caused by this Mrs. O'Shea and the who had taken the house at Eastbourne just used Mr. Parnell as a reference as to her character. It also transpired that, in addition to his many aliases, Mr. Parnell was known to the servants at Regent's Park as "Mr. O'Shea." The whole of the ten witnesses were examined within an hour and a half.

The intelligent juryman, however, had yet to be reckoned with. He was most aggressively intelligent this time, and rose to demand from the judge some satisfaction as to his doubts as to the change of neglect made by the respondent in her pleadings against the petitioner. Mr. Justice Butt pointed out to him that the respondent had made no attempt to substantiate the charges which were entirely unsupported. One juryman, however, was not satisfied. He would have Captain O'Shea back in the box to be cross-examined. The Court deferred to his wish of the study objection, and another lawyer, who had Strayed into the dozen of good men, and true cross-examined the witness in the correct "breaking" method, being particularly desirous to know why the Captain should have chambers at Westminster whilst his wife and family lived within an hour's journey of London. In vain did the petitioner point out that he was in Parliament, where his duties detained him late at night, that he frequently visited his wife, was always in communication with her, and had shown himself a kind and affectionate husband and father. The juror had got firmly fixed in his modicum of mind the good old British doctrine of domesticity, that it is the first duty of a husband to sleep nightly in the bosom of his family. It was on this principle, upon the visible insistence of the court and the humorous amazement of the witness eventually wore him down, and he subsided. After this another juryman had a short question to put, and then the judge entered upon his charge to the jury. This was clear, concise, and forcible, and terminated with the putting of two issues to the jury. (1) Had the adultery alleged between the respondent and the co-respondent been committed; and (2) had the petitioner connived at such adultery. Without a moment's hesitation the jury returned with a verdict in the affirmative, which meant that Captain O'Shea had not connived at it, and the judge pronounced the decree nisi, which marks the penultimate chapter in the history of the case O'Shea v. O'Shea and Parnell.

THE CASE.

The hearing of the petition of Captain O'Shea for a divorce from his wife, with Mr. Parnell, M.P. as co-respondent, was concluded to-day in the Divorce Court before Mr. Justice Butt and a special jury. Captain O'Shea was represented by the Solicitor-General (Sir E. Clarke), Mr. Inderwick, Q.C., and Mr. L. Coward. Mrs. O'Shea by Mr. Lockwood, Q.C., while (Mr. McCall watched the case for Mrs. Steele (Mrs. O'Shea's sister).

On the Judge taking his seat he said:—Mr. Solicitor-General, on Saturday there were one or two photographs produced which the co-respondent put in, and they were produced in the regular way. You mentioned the matter to me, I think, after assuming that they would be a satisfactory way of proving the identification, but I did not intend to assent to such a proposition.

The Solicitor-General—Oh, no, my lord.

The Judge—Because, you know, we never rely on photographs in these cases.

The Solicitor-General—We have subpoenaed Mr. Parnell for the purposes of this case for Saturday and to-day, and certainly I have no doubt it would be possible to bring him into court for identification, but I do not desire to do that if we can prove identification without it.

AT WONERSH LODGE.

Jane Glenister was then called and examined by the Solicitor-General, who asked—Did you go into the service of Mr. Parnell, Mrs. O'Shea at Wonersh Lodge in October, 1880? Yes, sir.

And remained in the service until October, 1882? Yes, sir.

How soon after entering the service did you see Mr. Parnell at Eltham? Either in November or December of 1880.

Did he at that time remain in the house for any time? Yes, sir, he remained a few days, and slept in the house.

Then, I think, Mrs. O'Shea in the early part of 1881 went to Brighton? Yes, sir.

Was Captain O'Shea stopping there when Mr. Parnell first came to Wonersh Lodge? Yes, I believe, Captain O'Shea was there?

The Judge—The whole of the time? Yes.

Examination continued—In the early part of 1881 we went to Brighton. We came back to Wonersh Lodge about April, 1881. From May of that year and during the remainder of the year Mr. Parnell was at the Lodge a great deal. He occupied the spare bedroom. There was between this and Mrs. O'Shea's room a dressing-room with doors communicating in both rooms, so that anyone could pass from one room to the other without going out on the landing. Mr. Parnell occupied the bedroom all O'Shea was there and occupied the bedroom all the time. After breakfast he would go into the drawing-room, and remain there with Mrs. O'Shea until he went to Parliament.

THE "SECRET SOCIETY."

The Solicitor-General—Have you known Mr. Parnell and Mrs. O'Shea to be in that room with the door locked? Only on one occasion.

What happened? I did not take much notice of it, because Mrs. O'Shea told me the "secret society" was about, and it was necessary to have the door locked.

What was the "secret society" was the door was locked? Yes.

The Judge—Does she mean the door of the house or of the room?

The witness—The door of the drawing-room.

And when it was locked were Mr. Parnell and Mrs. O'Shea in it together? Yes.

When you came back from Brighton did you hear anything of a door being broken? Yes, the schoolroom door. The other narrative tells me about it. Mrs. O'Shea told me that Mr. Parnell got through between one and two o'clock in the morning.

The O'Shea Divorce Suit: Summing Up and Verdict, from *The Irish Times*, November 18, 1890. Courtesy of *The Irish Times*.

MR. YEATS'S "COUNTESS CATHLEEN.

LETTER FROM UNIVERSITY STUDENTS.

To the Editor of the "Freeman's Journal."

Antient Concert Rooms,
Monday, May 8th.

Sir—Mr William Butler Yeats, as the most prominent among the founders of the Irish Literary Theatre, has at length fulfilled to his own satisfaction the contract concluded with the Irish public some months ago. By the terms of that contract Mr Yeats promised, if sufficiently supported, to "put on the stage plays dealing with Irish subjects or reflecting Irish ideas and sentiments." The drama in which Mr Yeats claims to have satisfied at least one of these alternatives. "The Countess Cathleen," has by this time acquired some notoriety. Two criticisms of the work, supported by extracts, have been generally circulated, that of Mr O'Donnell and that of the "Irish Daily Nation." In replying to these criticisms on Saturday Mr Yeats wisely confined himself to abstract platitudes, and sheltered himself behind an objection, which is in general valid, that a work cannot be fairly judged from mere quotations of words used by personages who figure in that work. Your readers may test the validity of this objection in this particular instance, and the truth of our interpretation of the play, by studying it in the Kildare street Library (without expense).

Let us sum briefly the results of our examination. The subject is not Irish. It has been shown that the plot is founded on a German legend. The characters are ludicrous travesties of the Irish Catholic Celt. The purpose of Mr Yeats's drama is apparently to show the sublimity of self-sacrifice. The questionable nature of that self-sacrifice forces Mr Yeats to adopt still more questionable means to produce an occasion for it. He represents the Irish peasant as a crooning barbarian, crazed with morbid superstition, who, having added the Catholic faith to his store of superstition, sells that faith for gold or bread in the proving of famine. Is Mr Yeats prepared to justify this view of our national character, by putting his finger on historical famines in the 16th century, or any other century, in which the Irish peasants generally exchanged life eternal for a full maw? Has he read or heard from living lips the story of the famine of this century?

Has Mr Yeats thoroughly considered the probable effect of presenting this slanderous caricature of the Irish peasant, to an average English or Continental audience, unread in Irish history? We do not seek the goodwill of England, but we object to be made the butt of her bitter contempt.

Have the Irish public and the Irish Press thoroughly considered what their approval of Mr Yeats's picture means from a national and historical handpoint? Why, if this be a true portrait of Irish Catholic character, every effort of England to stamp out our religion, and incidentally our nationality, is not merely to be justified, but to be applauded. If this be a true portrait, the spoiling of our monasteries, the banning of our priests, the oppression of our people, fire, sword, the rope, become instruments of the Christian indignation—the Penal Laws are a salutary code. Carew is a saint, and Castlereagh a martyr.

Do the Irish people intend to accept the picture as true?

Is it too much to expect ome pronouncement from each of the Nationalist and Catholic leaders whose names have been lent to support this drama? If they are not prepared to repudiate this distortion of the character of their countrymen, this negation of the most cherished Irish ideas and sentiments, let them confess themselves hypocrites, fighting for a contemptible cause.

We are not opposed to a movement for the reform of the stage in Ireland. We should be most ardent supporters of a healthy genuine movement in that direction. But we object to be compromised by plays such as "The Countess Cathleen."

We have no personal quarrel with Mr Yeats, we know him only from his books. We recognise him as a fine literary artist. We recognise him, further, as one endowed with the rare gift of extending an infinitesimal quantity of the gold of thought in a seemingly infinite area of the tinsel of melodiously meaningless verse. As long as the reading-public treated Mr William Butler Yeats as Mr William Butler Yeats, and was content to accompany him through the clouds with occasional descents and ascents, we were not concerned in the matter. But when Mr William Butler Yeats is apparently treated as the leader, the pattern, and the despair of the modern Irish intellectual movement, as a reliable painter of Irish life and an accurate analyst of Irish character, then, despite the "sober follies of the wise and great" who countenance his work in these aspects, we feel it our duty, in the name and for the honour of Dublin Catholic students of the Royal University to protest against an art, even a dispassionate art, which offers as a type of our people a loathsome brood of apostates.

(Signed) P J Merriman, B A ; D J M'Grath, B A ; J J Power, Thos M Kettle, J C SKeffington, J O'Toole. Sch ; P J Dwyer, J Houliban, Sch ; E B Healy, John Francis Byrne, P Kent, Sch ; P J O'Brien, Patrick J Dwyer, G Clancy, Arthur Harrison, Wm Fallon, J Clandillon, C E O'Brien, R G Moore, R J D Sheehy, E Clarke, G Madden, Louis J Walsh, J Clarke, Aodh Kennedy, G M Collins, Patrick J Hefferman, Wm Nunan, Alphonsus J Farrelly, F M'Donald, Peter Walsh, James A Murnaghan, Conor J Byrne.

LETTER FROM MR. T. W. ROLLESTON

To the Editor of the "Freeman's Journal."

Sir—It happens that I was sitting close to the "dozen disorderly boys" referred to by your correspondent in his account of the performance of Monday night, and with your permission I should like to say a word or two on this subject. It appeared to me that their expressions of disapproval were not exactly "disorderly." There is unquestionably much in the play that must put a strain on the patriotic and religious feelings of any audience not accustomed to look at dramatic literature from a purely artistic standpoint, and paradoxical as it may seem, it is only very unlettered or very highly cultivated audiences that are capable of doing that. An audience, or any members of it, have a right to express disapproval as well as to applaud. It would be the death of the drama to abrogate this right, as Goethe sought to do at Weimar, with the natural result that the audiences at Weimar ultimately swept "Iphigenie" and "Egmont" from the stage, and went wild over the performances of an accomplished poodle. The young men (there were about 20 of them) who hissed and hooted at certain passages last night appeared to me to be probably Royal University students. They expressed their sentiments with vigour, but in a perfectly gentlemanlike manner. They flung no insults at the author or the company; they made no attempt to seriously interfere with the performance, and they applauded as vigorously as anyone, nay, they even led the applause, at some of the fine and touching passages in the play. Undoubtedly the ferocious attacks and incitements to violence made from certain quarters during the last few days had much to do with the warm demonstrations of sympathy made by the audience. But they did not inspire the opposition in the theatre. The impression left on my mind by the whole affair was that a representative Dublin audience had splendidly vindicated, in the teeth of bitter prejudice and hostility, an author's right to a fair hearing for his work, and also that the hostile element in the audience had expressed itself in a manner, which, if one is permitted to be hostile at all, had no trace of malice or stupid violence.—Yours truly,

T W ROLLESTON.

Opposite and Above: Letter from University College Dublin students regarding Yeats's *Countess Cathleen;* letter from T. W. Rolleston on the audience's behavior. *Freeman's Journal and National Press,* May 10, 1899. Among the signatories, Thomas Kettle became a well-known writer and politician before his untimely death in the war. J. C. Skeffington (later Sheehy-Skeffington) was a radical pacifist and advocate of women's rights; Joyce thought him the cleverest man in UC apart from himself, although he is portrayed unflatteringly as McCann in *Portrait.* John Francis Byrne is the model for Cranly, and George Clancy for Davin; Byrne became a physician and wrote a memoir of Joyce, while Clancy was killed by the Black and Tans, a British army auxiliary group, while serving as Lord Mayor of Limerick. T. W. Rolleston, author of the appended letter, was a minor poet and editor of the *Dublin University Review.*

Courtesy of *The Irish Times.*

PART TWO

A Portrait of the Artist as a Young Man: A Case Study in Contemporary Criticism

A Critical History of
A Portrait of the Artist
as a Young Man

Joyce is arguably the most influential modern writer in the Western world. His influence on the fictional technique of twentieth-century writers, from traditional realists to the most wildly experimental post-modernists, has been decisive. Although Joyce's *Ulysses* has evoked a far greater amount of critical discussion, there is no doubt that *A Portrait of the Artist as a Young Man* is Joyce's most widely read work. *Portrait* is among the most frequently taught novels in modern university curricula, but it is also a novel undergraduates often discover on their own. Despite its surface difficulties, young people still respond to the book's eerily convincing portrayal of a sensitive youth who is harrowed by religious and sexual guilt and transfigured by an idea of beauty. Stephen's remarkable self-involvement and his frustration under the authority of church, state, and parents rings especially true for undergraduate readers today, however different the specifics of circumstance.

So well established is *Portrait* as a modern classic that it is difficult to imagine the situation of the book's early reviewers, faced with writing of a sort they had not encountered before. Spotting literary greatness on its first appearance is an almost impossible task; Ezra Pound did it with Joyce, and so did T. S. Eliot, but even as perceptive a reader as Edward Garnett, who had encouraged Joseph Conrad, Ford Madox Ford, and D. H. Lawrence, balked at Joyce. In a reader's report for the publisher Duckworth and Company, collected with many other early reviews in Robert Deming's two-volume *James Joyce: The Critical Heritage,* Garnett admitted that the book was "ably written" but suggested that it needed revision because it was too "discursive, formless, unrestrained, and ugly things, ugly words, are too prominent." The novel was too "unconventional," Garnett asserted, and "unless the author will use restraint and proportion he will not gain readers" (Deming 81). Given this sort of misjudgment by a usually sensitive reader, it is all the more surprising that so many of the initial reviews of *Portrait* hailed it as a major achievement, even a work of "genius."

Ezra Pound's review in *The Egoist,* where the book had appeared in installments, stressed that it was well written — and tried to suggest just how rare that was among novels in English. Indeed, "Joyce produces the nearest thing to Flaubertian prose that we now have in English." Aside from that, "I doubt if a comparison of Mr. Joyce to other English writers or Irish writers would help much to define him." Pound stressed Joyce's realism and the book's value as "diagnosis," but otherwise said virtually nothing about the novel's content (Deming 83). Others were more struck by what they saw as the book's unpleasantness. A review in *Everyman* entitled "A Study in Garbage" called it "an astonishingly powerful and extraordinary dirty study of the upbringing of a young man by Jesuits" and suggested that at the end of the book Stephen goes mad (Deming 85). Similarly, H. G. Wells, in a rather awestruck essay comparing Joyce with Swift, Sterne, and Conrad, nevertheless complained about Joyce's "cloacal obsession" (Deming 86–88). The *Times* protested the "occasional improprieties," the *Literary World* complained of "the brutal probing of the depths of uncleanness," and the *Manchester Guardian* of the novel's "astounding bad manners" (Deming 89, Deming 92, Deming 93).

Like other reviewers, the *Guardian*'s essayist found in Stephen "a passion for foul-smelling things" (Deming 93), confusing Joyce's unusual technique of documenting odors and textures with his protagonist's tastes. Irish reviewers were, if anything, more offended than British ones. The *Freeman's Journal* claimed that "Mr. Joyce plunges and drags his readers after him into the slime of foul sewers" (Deming 98). These critics' stress on *Portrait*'s unpleasantness is likely to be somewhat baffling to modern readers until we realize that the "impropriety" found on the book's "very first page" (Deming 89) can only be the reference to bed-wetting; at this point we understand what a large part of human existence in 1916 was held to be inappropriate for mention in literature. One theme not picked up in later criticism is the concern over whether Stephen and his companions are representative of

Irish youth in their ideas. Wells noted that "every human being" in the book "accepts as a matter of course . . . that the English are to be hated," and adds that he thinks that picture is "only too true" (Deming 88). The *Freeman's Journal,* on the other hand, protested that "English critics, with a complacency that makes one despair of their intelligence, are already hailing the author as a typical Irishman, and his book as a faithful picture of Irish life." It would be just as accurate to see De Quincy's *Confessions of an English Opium-Eater* as a typical picture of British youth, the reviewer asserted (Deming 99).

Still, Joyce's technique was so convincing that the reviewers had to admit that something beyond conventional realism was at work. A. Clutton Brock said that "[Joyce] can make anything happen that he chooses" in his writing, and that "no living writer is better at conversations" (Deming 89). J. C. Squire agreed that the dialogue "is as close to the dialogue of life as anything I have ever come across" (Deming 101). Virtually all reviewers praised the writing, and some were swept away despite themselves, protesting all the while. The *Guardian*'s writer began, "When one recognizes genius in a book one can perhaps best leave criticism alone," and then went on to give his reservations. Interestingly, he continued, "Not for its apparent formlessness should the book be condemned. A subtle sense of art has worked amidst the chaos, making this hither-and-thither record of a young mind and soul . . . a complete and ordered thing" (Deming 92). In noting this he is unusual, for nearly all the early reviewers complained of the book's formlessness, its abrupt transitions, its lack of plot, and its unusual demands upon the reader. Just as the term "naturalism" was used to evoke the "gutter realism" of the notorious Emile Zola, the term "impressionism" occurred frequently to suggest an aesthetic combination of shapelessness and sensitivity in both protagonist and book.

But reaction to the novel did not develop in a vacuum, because within two years installments of Joyce's even more challenging *Ulysses* began to appear in *The Little Review.* In a now-famous essay entitled "Modern Novels" that appeared in 1919, Virginia Woolf hailed Joyce's writing as an example of a revolutionary sort of fiction that does away with outmoded conventions. "Let us record the atoms as they fall upon the mind in the order in which they fall, let us trace the pattern, however disconnected and incoherent in appearance, which each sight or incident scores upon the consciousness," she urged. In doing this — in shifting the focus inward, toward momentary perceptions and a "spiritual" dimension of consciousness — Woolf felt the artist would produce something closer to "life itself" (Deming 125–26). Gradually it began to be realized that a group of writers — including Eliot, Pound, Joyce, and (somewhat later) Woolf herself — was engaged in similar challenges to literary conventions, and that the art of such writers demanded evaluation on its own terms rather than censure for departing from the norms of Victorian prose and verse. This development had two effects: first, published commentary on writers like Joyce tended to become either exclusively laudatory or exclusively derogatory, depending on which position the reviewer took in the politics of art. And further, as comments by Joyce's increasing circle of admirers appeared, those critics who took him seriously began to devote their energies to explicating his work rather than evaluating it.

The advent of *Ulysses* in 1922 helped draw the battle lines more clearly than *Portrait* had done. Stuart Gilbert's 1930 book, *James Joyce's "Ulysses,"* written with the help of Joyce, revealed to an uninformed public the complexity of Joyce's mythic structure in that book, as well as the richness and variety of his stylistic and narrative effects. One implication was that *Portrait* and even the earlier story collection *Dubliners* might well have formal complexities of their own that — as with *Ulysses* — had gone unnoticed. Gilbert also put some stress on Joyce's use of symbolism, a characteristic of his prose that his early reviewers, obsessed by his use of naturalistic detail, had slighted. This cut little ice with reviewers on the political left who, especially during the reign of "socialist realism" in the 1930s, dismissed Joyce as obscure, bourgeois, and apolitical. A Russian essay translated in *New Masses* (1933) saw the stream-of-consciousness method of *Ulysses* as "too closely connected with the ultrasubjectivism of the parasitic, rentier bourgeoisie, and entirely unadaptable to the art of one who is building socialist society." The naturalism of *Portrait* might at first seem more promising, since it exposes the material evils of capitalism, but it has its roots in "a morbid, defeatist delight in the ugly and repulsive" and in "an aesthetico-proprietary desire for the possession of 'things'" (Deming 591–92). As for the portions of *Work in Progress* (the temporary title of *Finnegans Wake*) that had so far appeared in journals, the Marxist reviewer (like mainstream reviewers throughout Europe and America) dismissed them as nonsense.

Meanwhile, another artistic trend was on Joyce's side. Increasingly during the twentieth century, Anglophone writers became aware of the Continental literary tradition; indeed, in the 1920s both British and American writers migrated to Paris, often to sit at the feet of Joyce or Gertrude Stein, the great expatriates. Since Joyce's literary models were generally European rather than British or Irish, his work was more intelligible and less frighteningly original when seen in this context. Indeed, *Ulysses* was probably the first important work of English literature to be explicated and celebrated first by French critics. During the 1930s and 1940s a generation of American critics who were conversant with European literature naturally named Joyce among the great contemporary writers. Most notably, Edmund Wilson in his 1931 book, *Axel's Castle: A Study in the Imaginative Literature of 1870–1930,* placed Joyce in the literary tradition of the French Symbolist poets of 1870–90.

The first serious study of Joyce's writing as a whole, apart from early biographical studies and the writing of Joyce's friends, was Harry Levin's pioneering *James Joyce: A Critical Introduction* (1941). This remarkable book, much of it written when only portions of *Finnegans Wake* had appeared, is still one of the better introductions to Joyce's work. Levin treats *Portrait* as autobiography and sees little irony in Joyce's treatment of Stephen. Levin presents *Portrait* as a late example of the *Bildungsroman,* or "novel of development," such as Stendhal's *The Red and the Black* or Flaubert's *A Sentimental Education.* He briefly discusses Stephen's aesthetic theory, and suggests that the progression from "lyric" to "epic" to "dramatic" forms characterizes Joyce's work as a whole. Levin presents Joyce as heir to the two apparently opposed late nineteenth-century strains of naturalism and symbolism, and he argues that in Joyce, as in Flaubert, the two "come to terms" (Levin 4). In a rather general way he discusses the structural balance of *Portrait*'s five chapters. Although most of his discussion in the book concerns *Ulysses* and the *Wake,* Levin does point out the dominant symbolic motif of flight and the role of the mythical Daedalus, the "fabulous artificer," in *Portrait.*

A number of other introductory works on Joyce were published during the 1940s, none of Levin's quality. One general study from the 1950s that is still useful is Richard Kain and Marvin Magalaner's *Joyce: The Man, the Work, the Reputation* (1956). Surveying both the early reviews and the serious criticism available up to then, Kain and Magalaner intelligently discuss the problem of Joyce's biography, quoting from then-unpublished letters. Their treatment of *Portrait* is particularly interesting. They compare *Portrait* with its first-draft version, published as *Stephen Hero* (1955), stress the revision's condensation, abrupt transitions, and impressionist technique, and explore some of the references to obscure or popular works such as Bulwer-Lytton's play *The Lady of Lyons* and Dumas's *The Count of Monte Cristo.* Most of their discussion centers on motifs such as apology, names, and blindness, and

upon the idea of the epiphany and its function in the book. Kain and
Magalaner also highlight for discussion the single most influential essay
on *Portrait* of the time, Hugh Kenner's "The *Portrait* in Perspective,"
first published in 1948 and revised in his book *Dublin's Joyce* (1956).

Kenner's essay reads *Portrait* in the light of *Ulysses* and *Wake* and
finds in the earlier book similar complexities of implication. Where "the
two major works strive toward an inclusive mythopoeic vision embracing in an archetypal pattern of fall, struggle, and redemption every
mode of human activity," *Portrait* does this only on the level of individual human action, suggesting "other possible levels of analogy" by implication (1948, 142). By pursuing these implications, Kenner shows
how the book's first two pages "enact the entire action in microcosm"
(137). He pursues the "verbal leitmotif" linking whiteness, cold, and
damp as a repellent complex and shows how words with their tricky
meanings and associations illustrate stages in Stephen's development.
Kenner argues that Stephen's "epiphanies," which arrest and embody
artistic meaning in a single moment, are not Joyce's method; instead, in
each chapter of the book Joyce repeats the same pattern of showing
Stephen embracing a dream in contempt of reality and then seeing the
dream destroyed. "The movement of the book is dialectical; each chapter closes with a synthesis of triumph which in turn feeds the sausage-
machine set up in the next chapter" (169). Most important, Kenner
argues that "Stephen's flight into adolescent 'freedom' is not meant to
be the 'message' of the book" (153). Stephen, in Kenner's view an
"indigestibly Byronic" figure, is regarded ironically throughout. His
rather Neoplatonic aesthetic is not Joyce's; his Romanticism is scorned
by the more classically minded Joyce; and instead of becoming the
author of *Portrait* and *Ulysses,* Stephen will become a "parlor esthete"
(157), priggish, horrified by the sensual world, and egotistically self-
involved.

Although Kenner qualified his argument in later books and articles,
his essay sets the terms for the arguments of other critics. The question
is that of Joyce's ironic distance from his protagonist, and since the narrative voice itself changes greatly in the course of *Portrait,* the answer
is not easy to determine. In his critical edition of *Portrait* (1968),
Chester G. Anderson summarizes the debate (446–54) and includes
relevant essays by Wayne C. Booth and Robert Scholes. Booth's essay,
which originally appeared in his *Rhetoric of Fiction,* contends that the
degree of Joyce's irony — his "authorial distance"— cannot be established with any certainty because Joyce at times clearly admires Stephen
and at times clearly satirizes him. As Booth points out, the problem is

epitomized by Stephen's poem, the "Villanelle of the Temptress"; it is unclear to many readers whether we are to take the poem as a success or as a failure. For Booth the problem is that Joyce was never certain of his own attitude toward his protagonist, although when Stephen appears in *Ulysses* with his wings clipped, it seems likely that we are to assume that the boy was self-deluded in his more grandiose moments. The problem, according to Booth, is a flaw in *Portrait* itself. In response, Robert Scholes points out that the villanelle was written by Joyce long before the novel and argues that it is "a far richer poem" than may first appear (472). Similarly, Scholes implies, Stephen is far more of an artist than Kenner allows or than Booth will admit. This argument is by no means settled, and echoes down to the present day in the debate over whether Stephen's misogyny is also Joyce's or is being ironically displayed by a Joyce sympathetic to feminism.

Meanwhile, many critics were less concerned with Joyce's moral stance toward his hero than with the internal complexities of his work. William York Tindall wrote three influential studies during the 1950s — *James Joyce: His Way of Interpreting the Modern World* (1950), *A Reader's Guide to James Joyce* (1959), and *The Joyce Country* (1960) — all of which mingled Tindall's flair for close, "New Critical" textual explication with his interest in literary symbolism and in Freud. In his *Reader's Guide* Tindall begins by asserting that Stephen may not be Joyce, but he is indeed the artist-hero-rebel. True to the formalist assumptions of the New Critics, Tindall looks at the four sections of chapters one, two, and five and the three sections of chapters three and four, and asserts that while he is unsure of the function of each part, "I am sure from what I know of Joyce that no part could be omitted or placed elsewhere without injuring the great design" (62). Such a declaration strikes contemporary critics as closer to religious faith in the principle of organic unity than to objective analysis. As is appropriate given the New Critical valuation of irony, Tindall continues by cataloguing some of the ironic juxtapositions and echoes in the novel.

Like other formalists, Tindall is passionately interested in symbolism as well as structure, and so he spends a number of pages on the wings and labyrinth built by the mythical Daedalus (echoed by Stephen's imaginative "flights" and the maze of Dublin streets), not to mention the sexual contrivance he made for Queen Pasiphaë and the "robot" Talus he fashioned to protect Crete (neither of which, unfortunately, does Tindall find present in *Portrait*). Tindall explores Stephen's less sweeping identifications with Jesus Christ (with Cranly playing John the Baptist, the "precursor"), Napoleon, Parnell, the Count of Monte

Cristo, Dante, and St. Stephen (the first Christian martyr) before lingering for a while on Lucifer ("bearer of light"), who like Stephen
declares, "I will not serve" and like Prometheus brings mankind the
forbidden fire of knowledge.

Less significant than symbols but also helping to unify the work,
motifs greatly interest Tindall. He finds on the opening pages *road, cow,
water, woman, flower,* and *bird,* all of which will recur meaningfully
and musically (86). Other motifs, such as *dogs, darkness* and *light,* and
the related *blindness* and *sight,* work similarly. Tindall "unpacks" a few
of these images, showing how birds can be threatening (Heron, the
eagles), images of escape (the birds above the library), or images of
beauty (the wading "bird-girl" of Stephen's epiphany in chapter four).
Birds also, of course, relate to the Daedalus myth. Similarly, the flower,
a Neoplatonic symbol for the woman who exemplifies transcendent
beauty and thus the poet's path to the divine world, is complicated by
Stephen's invocation of an artificial "green rose." The green rose relates
also to the red-green opposition throughout the book: green suggests
the imagination, fertility, Ireland, while red suggests British authority,
the church, hellfire, and so forth.

Not all of these insights were unique to Tindall, of course, but aside
from his own contributions he conveniently and wittily synthesized the
work of many scholars for a generation of readers. Among other studies
exploring aspects of the book on which Tindall touches, Chester Anderson's "The Sacrificial Butter" (Connolly 124–36) discusses specifically images that Joyce draws from Roman Catholic iconography, while
David Hayman's "Daedalian Imagery in *A Portrait*" (1964) further
explores Joyce's use of that myth and Bernard Benstock's "A Light
from Some Other World" (Staley and Benstock, 185–212) shows how
many image patterns contribute to the book's meaning. Studies of the
novel's structure include Lee T. Lemon's *"Portrait of the Artist as a
Young Man:* Motif as Motivation and Structure" (1966), an analysis
inspired by the Russian Formalists, and Sidney Feshbach's "A Slow and
Dark Birth: A Study of the Organization of *A Portrait of the Artist as a
Young Man*" (1967), which is more psychological in orientation. Other
essays representative of work done in the 1950s and 1960s can be
found in the collections of essays on *Portrait* edited by Connolly (1962),
Morris and Nault (1962), Anderson (1968), and Schutte (1968).

But New Critical studies of the book as a self-contained structure
unified by symbols and motifs were not the only work done during this
period — or even, in some respects, the most important work. The nat-

ural course of Joyce criticism was altered forever by the publication of Richard Ellmann's magisterial biography *James Joyce* in 1959. Trained as a New Critic, Ellmann nonetheless "read" Joyce's life as if it were a literary text. Given a writer whose life and work were as intimately intertwined as they were in the case of Joyce, this proved to be extremely convincing, especially as Ellmann skillfully interwove literary interpretation with biography throughout. Stuart Gilbert had edited a collection of Joyce's letters in 1957; in 1966 Ellmann reedited that volume and produced two additional volumes. The sheer mass of information about Joyce, some of it quite intimate, was enough to make some critics forget the dangers of the "biographical fallacy." Meanwhile, Robert Scholes and Richard Kain's *The Workshop of Daedalus* (1965) made available Joyce's unpublished "epiphanies" along with various working notebooks and manuscript fragments and a considerable amount of biographical information, all of which spurred interest in Joyce's composition process and his artistic development generally. For instance, the most influential essay treating Joyce's actual composition process in writing *Portrait* is Hans Walter Gabler's "The Seven Lost Years of *A Portrait of the Artist as a Young Man*."

The 1970s saw the impact in American and British criticism of a variety of Continental critical approaches, most of which had been strenuously resisted during the previous decades. The so-called phenomenological criticism of the Geneva School, whose best American practitioner was the early J. Hillis Miller, was reflected in Suzette Henke's *Joyce's Moraculous Sindbook* (1978), which deals with *Ulysses*, and by R. B. Kershner's "Time and Language in Joyce's *Portrait of the Artist*" (1976), a study of the interiority of Stephen's time-sense and the ways in which subjectivity and objectivity are unified in his experience. *The Exile of James Joyce* (1972) by Hélène Cixous — who later would be best known as a major French feminist — combines a psychological approach to Joyce's whole work with themes such as absence and silence or art as transgression that were of particular interest to structuralists and poststructuralists.

A renewed interest in Marxist criticism, especially as adapted by the Frankfurt School (and in socially and politically based criticism in general), led to a new critical distance from the society of which both Stephen and Joyce were a part; issues such as Joyce's sexual tastes now seemed less important in themselves and more significant as markers of social development at a given historical moment. James Naremore's "Consciousness and Society in *A Portrait*" (1976) discusses "some of the ways that Stephen Dedalus's ideas, language, and art have been affected by his economic status and his Catholic upbringing" (114), and also reveals Joyce's fictional technique as a variety of realism that betrays the author's defensive reaction against his own "excremental vision." The Godlike impersonality that Stephen claimed for the artist, and that New Critics claimed for Joyce, was wearing thin. While Naremore had asserted that Joyce was a more politically aware writer than most earlier critics had thought, Richard Ellmann's *The Consciousness of Joyce* (1977) provided evidence for the writer's interest in politics from Joyce's own library. Joyce had early termed himself a socialist and had referred to the change in the relationship between men and women as the most important social change of his time; Ellmann demonstrated that Joyce's political awareness was not simply a fashion of his youth. Dominic Manganiello's full-scale study *Joyce's Politics* (1980) broadened the argument, presenting Joyce as — unlike other major modernists such as Yeats, Eliot, or Pound — a social progressive.

During the 1970s and 1980s a host of varieties of historically responsive criticism evolved, and with them a broad spectrum of interests that might once have seemed peripheral to Joyce's art. Richard Brown's *James Joyce and Sexuality* (1985) showed how the sexual rebelliousness, oddity, or experimentation of Joyce's characters occurred within a political context in which, for instance, assenting to a conventional marriage could be seen as ceding control of one's sexuality to the state. Cheryl Herr's groundbreaking study *Joyce's Anatomy of Culture* (1986) set Joyce's work within the context of the popular press, the popular theater, and the tradition of popular religious oratory, arguing that Joyce's use of these materials produced a powerful social critique. Three years later, R. B. Kershner's *Joyce, Bakhtin, and Popular Literature,* which treated Joyce's early writing, made a similar argument from an analysis of Joyce's sources in popular writing of the late nineteenth century, and included an extended discussion of *Portrait.*

Meanwhile, structuralism, deconstruction, and poststructuralism began to have a major impact on Joyce studies. Relatively few of the Continental critics and their followers addressed *Portrait* directly though, preferring to use *Ulysses* and especially the *Wake* to exemplify the ways in which language itself formed complex structures independent of signification or (alternately) undermined itself. Starting in the 1970s, essays on Joyce by Roland Barthes and Jacques Derrida began appearing in Joyce conference volumes, and books and articles devoted to Joyce took on a new theoretical rigor. Following Barthes's announcement of the "death of the author" in modern literature, the new work paid increased attention to style and structure in Joyce's work — and especially to the linguistic and philosophical implications of these — and once again shunned the biographical. Derrida's critique of structuralism in many ways exaggerated these tendencies.

The book that best exemplifies these trends, and applies them to *Portrait* as well, is Colin MacCabe's poststructuralist *James Joyce and the Revolution of the Word* (1979, 2003). Summary is difficult for a book such as this, especially as MacCabe refuses to "interpret" Joyce in any conventional sense: "Instead of constructing a meaning, Joyce's texts concern themselves with the position of the subject in language" (4). While MacCabe also refuses to "psychologize" Joyce in any ordinary way, he does rely heavily on the work of Jacques Lacan, the revisionist Freudian who redirected attention to language as the primary material of the psychoanalytic method. Further, MacCabe insists that his reading of Joyce is radically political, because Joyce's revolutionary politics are inherent in his *language* and its new relationship to representation, rather than residing in any particular statements in his texts.

MacCabe sees in the movement from *Stephen Hero* to *Portrait* a change from the ordered world of the "classic realist text," in which meaning is guaranteed by a "Father" and resolution is implied by the very narrative, to a new world in which all meanings are provisory, in which third and first person blend, and in which sound carries more weight than sense. Although the language of the artist threatens to establish a "meta-language" (66) that will enable us to evaluate the other languages represented in the book, even this possibility is frustrated by the book's discontinuities. The technical problems that for critics like Booth had marked flaws in *Portrait* are precisely those Mac-Cabe celebrates as liberating us from the epistemology of bourgeois humanism.

The general trend of criticism during the 1970s and 1980s was away from the New Critical presumption of organic unity in Joyce's works, away from symbolic interpretation, and in some ways away from biography; the stress was upon close analysis of style, a reexamination of the social and political context of Joyce's work, an intense theoretical examination of the implications of Joyce's writing project, and a questioning of previous interpretations of the entire modernist movement. An excellent article that exemplifies some of these points (although it foregrounds critical theory far less than many others) is Michael Levenson's "Stephen's Diary in Joyce's *Portrait* — the Shape of Life" (1985). Levenson's reading shows traces of the critical movement known as the reader-response school, an approach developed in different ways by

Norman Holland, Wolfgang Iser, and Stanley Fish, and applied to Joyce by, among others, Iser and Brook Thomas. Throughout the period important works on Joyce appeared under the stimulus of Continental approaches, and the fact that both Derrida and Lacan championed Joyce has encouraged a great deal of work in deconstructive and other post-structuralist modes. It is fair to say, however, that *Ulysses* and *Finnegans Wake* have been the object of critical attention of this sort far more than has *Portrait*. At least until recently, the work of two of the most distinguished Joyceans to have been inspired by the work of Derrida — Derek Attridge and Margot Norris — has fallen into this category.

The 1990s and the opening years of the new millennium have entertained a variety of critical approaches, as various critical orthodoxies have begun to break up, but probably the dominant issue has been the turn toward history. This turn has taken several forms, implicating the attendant criticism in several different contexts. There has been a relatively untheorized interest in the embedding of Joyce and his texts in history, whether early-twentieth-century European or specifically Irish; here the critical approach simply assumes that the historical perspective benefits from the waning of the New Criticism and that for all Joyce's unique genius, we can learn much from an examination of his historical and cultural milieu. An example of this sort of work might be John McCourt's *The Years of Bloom: James Joyce in Trieste, 1904–1920* (2000). Works with more ambitious theoretical backgrounds include James Fairhall's *James Joyce and the Question of History* (1993) and Robert Spoo's *James Joyce and the Language of History: Dedalus's Nightmare* (1994). A second category of historical criticism is still closely bound to (or invigorated by) deconstructive strategies of reading, and sometimes to Lacanian psychology as well. Such critics attempt to combine this with a more sophisticated sense of the impact of history upon writing. Here we might look to books by Christine van Boheemen-Saaf and Patrick McGee, as well as recent work by Margot Norris and Derek Attridge. A third category of historical Joycean criticism, of course, is that broadly designated as postcolonial criticism, although in Joyce's case much of it is actually the investigation of a colonial situation (or, in Derek Attridge's term taken from *Wake,* a "semicolonial" one). These are discussed at more length in the introduction to the chapter on this subject later in this volume. We might note in addition that a number of significant studies combining interest in current theory with the specifics of Joyce's works might fall under the category of new historicism. This approach, which was given an entire chapter in an earlier edition of this book, has by consensus now more or less merged into the broader category of cultural studies, although it is somewhat anomalous there because of the frequent assumption by cultural studies practitioners that the field applies strictly to contemporary culture.

Finally we might note two books from the past decade devoted exclusively to *A Portrait*. The first of these is *The Antimodernism of Joyce's Portrait of the Artist as a Young Man*, by Weldon Thornton (1994). Thornton makes a rather radical argument in claiming that while Stephen is portrayed as having a characteristically modernist concern with the relation of inner and outer worlds and the related issue of individualism, Joyce as author is concerned to show the limits of such dichotomies. Thornton's work has interesting affinities to other recent work discussing the issue of modernism and postmodernism in Joyce, especially as the entire question of modernism comes under closer examination. *Joyce's Comic Portrait* by Roy Gottfried (2000) argues that criticism has always tended to read the book as either serious or ironic, but never as strictly comic. Unlike irony, which is characteristically modernist and serves as a corrective to advance the telic purpose of the narrative, the comic in *Portrait* is nonpurposive, circular, indirect, and diffuse: again, parallels to descriptions of the postmodern suggest themselves.

The collection of politically oriented contemporary critical approaches loosely grouped together as "cultural critique" or "cultural studies" and the allied approach known as new historicism have both had an impact. The most important intellectual event of the past twenty years, the rise of feminist criticism, has been reflected in a wide variety of feminist approaches to Joyce as well. Most of these developments are discussed and exemplified in the essays and introductions that follow.

WORKS CITED

Anderson, Chester G., ed. *A Portrait of the Artist as a Young Man: Text, Criticism, and Notes.* New York: Viking, 1968.

Attridge, Derek. *Joyce Effects: On Language, Theory, and History.* Cambridge: Cambridge UP, 2000.

Boheemen-Saaf, Christine van. *Joyce, Derrida, Lacan, and the Trauma of History: Reading, Narration, and Postcolonialism.* Cambridge: Cambridge UP, 1999.

Booth, Wayne. "The Problem of Distance in *A Portrait.*" *The Rhetoric of Fiction.* Chicago: U of Chicago P, 1961. 323–36.

Brown, Richard. *James Joyce and Sexuality.* Cambridge: Cambridge UP, 1985.

Cixous, Hélène. *The Exile of James Joyce.* Trans. Sally A. J. Purcell. New York: Lewis, 1972.

Connolly, Thomas, ed. *Joyce's "Portrait": Criticisms and Critiques.* New York: Appleton, 1962.

Deming, Robert H., ed. *James Joyce: The Critical Heritage.* 2 vols. London: Routledge, 1970.

Ellmann, Richard. *The Consciousness of Joyce.* New York: Oxford UP, 1977.

——, ed. *Letters of James Joyce.* Volumes 2 and 3. New York: Viking, 1966.

——. *James Joyce.* New York: Oxford UP, 1959. Rev. ed. 1982.

Fairhall, James. *James Joyce and the Question of History.* Cambridge: Cambridge UP, 1993.

Feshbach, Sidney. "A Slow and Dark Birth: A Study of the Organization of *A Portrait of the Artist as a Young Man.*" *James Joyce Quarterly* 4 (Summer 1967): 289–300.

Gabler, Hans Walter. "The Seven Lost Years of *A Portrait of the Artist as a Young Man.*" *Approaches to Joyce's "Portrait."* Ed. Thomas Staley and Bernard Benstock. Pittsburgh: U of Pittsburgh P, 1976. 25–60.

Gilbert, Stuart, ed. *Letters of James Joyce.* Volume 1. New York: Viking, 1957.

Gottfried, Roy. *Joyce's Comic Portrait.* Gainesville: UP of Florida, 2000.

Hayman, David. "Daedalian Imagery in *A Portrait.*" *Hereditas: Seven Essays on the Modern Experience of the Classical.* Ed. Frederick Will. Austin: U of Texas P, 1964. 31–54.

Henke, Suzette. *Joyce's Moraculous Sindbook: A Study of "Ulysses."* Columbus: Ohio State UP, 1978.

Herr, Cheryl. *Joyce's Anatomy of Culture.* Urbana: U of Illinois P, 1986.

Kain, Richard M., and Marvin Magalaner. *James Joyce: The Man, the Work, the Reputation.* New York: New York UP, 1956.

Kenner, Hugh. *Dublin's Joyce.* Bloomington: Indiana UP, 1956.

——. "The *Portrait* in Perspective." *James Joyce: Two Decades of Criticism.* Ed. Seon Givens. New York: Vanguard, 1948. 132–74.

Kershner, R. B. *Joyce, Bakhtin, and Popular Literature*. Chapel Hill: U of North Carolina P, 1989.

———. "Time and Language in Joyce's *Portrait of the Artist*." *ELH* 43 (1976): 604–19.

Lemon, Lee T. "*Portrait of the Artist as a Young Man:* Motif as Motivation and Structure." *Modern Fiction Studies* 12 (Winter 1966/67): 430–50.

Levenson, Michael. "Stephen's Diary in Joyce's *Portrait* — The Shape of Life." *ELH* 52 (1985): 1017–35.

Levin, Harry. *James Joyce: A Critical Introduction*. 1941. Rev. ed. New York: New Directions, 1960.

MacCabe, Colin. *James Joyce and the Revolution of the Word*. New York: Barnes and Noble, 1979, Houndsmill, UK; New York: Palgrave, 2003.

Manganiello, Dominic. *Joyce's Politics*. London: Routledge, 1980.

McCourt, John. *The Years of Bloom: James Joyce in Trieste, 1904–1920*. Madison: U of Wisconsin P, 2000.

McGee, Patrick. *Joyce Beyond Marx: History and Desire in "Ulysses" and "Finnegans Wake."* Gainesville: U of Florida P, 2001.

Morris, William, and Clifford Nault, eds. *Portraits of an Artist: A Casebook for James Joyce's "A Portrait."* New York: Odyssey, 1962.

Naremore, James. "Consciousness and Society in *A Portrait*." *Approaches to Joyce's "Portrait": Ten Essays*. Eds. Thomas F. Staley and Bernard Benstock. Pittsburgh: U of Pittsburgh P, 1976. 113–34.

Norris, Margot. *Suspicious Readings of Joyce's "Dubliners."* Philadelphia: U of Pennsylvania P, 2003.

Scholes, Robert, and Richard M. Kain, eds. *The Workshop of Daedalus: James Joyce and the Raw Materials for "A Portrait of the Artist as a Young Man."* Evanston, IL: Northwestern UP, 1965.

Schutte, William, ed. *Twentieth-Century Interpretations of "A Portrait of the Artist as a Young Man."* Englewood Cliffs, NJ: Prentice-Hall, 1968.

Spoo, Robert. *James Joyce and the Language of History: Dedalus's Nightmare*. Oxford: Oxford UP, 1994.

Staley, Thomas F., and Bernard Benstock, eds. *Approaches to Joyce's "Portrait": Ten Essays*. Pittsburgh: U of Pittsburgh P, 1976.

Thornton, Weldon. *The Antimodernism of Joyce's "A Portrait of the Artist as a Young Man."* Syracuse, NY: Syracuse UP, 1994.

Tindall, William York. *James Joyce: His Way of Interpreting the Modern World.* New York: Scribner's, 1950.

———. *The Joyce Country.* University Park: Pennsylvania State UP, 1960.

———. *A Reader's Guide to James Joyce.* New York: Noonday-Farrar, 1959.

Wilson, Edmund. *Axel's Castle: A Study of Imaginative Literature of 1870–1930.* New York: Scribner's, 1931.

Psychoanalytic Criticism
and *A Portrait of the Artist*
as a Young Man

WHAT IS PSYCHOANALYTIC CRITICISM?

It seems natural to think about novels in terms of dreams. Like dreams, literary works are fictions, inventions of the mind that, although based on reality, are by definition not literally true. Like a literary work, a dream may have some truth to tell, but, like a literary work, it may need to be interpreted before that truth can be grasped. We can live vicariously through romantic fictions, much as we can through daydreams. Terrifying novels and nightmares affect us in much the same way, plunging us into an atmosphere that continues to cling, even after the last chapter has been read — or the alarm clock has sounded.

The notion that dreams allow such psychic explorations, of course, like the analogy between literary works and dreams, owes a great deal to the thinking of Sigmund Freud, the famous Austrian psychoanalyst who in 1900 published a seminal essay, *The Interpretation of Dreams*. But is the reader who feels that Emily Brontë's *Wuthering Heights* is dreamlike — who feels that Mary Shelley's *Frankenstein* is nightmarish — necessarily a Freudian literary critic? To some extent the answer has to be yes. We are all Freudians, really, whether or not we have read a single work by Freud. At one time or another, most of us have referred to ego, libido, complexes, unconscious desires, and sexual repression. The premises of Freud's thought have changed the way the

Western world thinks about itself. Psychoanalytic criticism has influenced the teachers our teachers studied with, the works of scholarship and criticism they read, and the critical and creative writers *we* read as well.

What Freud did was develop a language that described, a model that explained, a theory that encompassed human psychology. Many of the elements of psychology he sought to describe and explain are present in the literary works of various ages and cultures, from Sophocles' *Oedipus Rex* to Shakespeare's *Hamlet* to works being written in our own day. When the great novel of the twenty-first century is written, many of these same elements of psychology will probably inform its discourse as well. If, by understanding human psychology according to Freud, we can appreciate literature on a new level, then we should acquaint ourselves with his insights.

Freud's theories are either directly or indirectly concerned with the nature of the unconscious mind. Freud didn't invent the notion of the unconscious; others before him had suggested that even the supposedly "sane" human mind was conscious and rational only at times, and even then at possibly only one level. But Freud went further, suggesting that the powers motivating men and women are *mainly* and *normally* unconscious.

Freud, then, powerfully developed an old idea: that the human mind is essentially dual in nature. He called the predominantly passional, irrational, unknown, and unconscious part of the psyche the *id,* or "it." The *ego,* or "I," was his term for the predominantly rational, logical, orderly, conscious part. Another aspect of the psyche, which he called the *superego,* is really a projection of the ego. The superego almost seems to be outside of the self, making moral judgments, telling us to make sacrifices for good causes even though self-sacrifice may not be quite logical or rational. And, in a sense, the superego *is* "outside," since much of what it tells us to do or think we have learned from our parents, our schools, or our religious institutions.

What the ego and superego tell us *not* to do or think is repressed, forced into the unconscious mind. One of Freud's most important contributions to the study of the psyche, the theory of repression, goes something like this: much of what lies in the unconscious mind has been put there by consciousness, which acts as a censor, driving underground unconscious or conscious thoughts or instincts that it deems unacceptable. Censored materials often involve infantile sexual desires, Freud postulated. Repressed to an unconscious state, they emerge only in disguised forms: in dreams, in language (so-called Freudian slips), in creative activity that may produce art (including literature), and in neurotic behavior.

According to Freud, all of us have repressed wishes and fears; we all have dreams in which repressed feelings and memories emerge disguised, and thus we are all potential candidates for dream analysis. One of the unconscious desires most commonly repressed is the childhood wish to displace the parent of our own sex and take his or her place in the affections of the parent of the opposite sex. This desire really involves a number of different but related wishes and fears. (A boy — and it should be remarked in passing that Freud here concerns himself mainly with the male — may fear that his father will castrate him, and he may wish that his mother would return to nursing him.) Freud referred to the whole complex of feelings by the word *oedipal*, naming the complex after the Greek tragic hero Oedipus, who unwittingly killed his father and married his mother.

Why are oedipal wishes and fears repressed by the conscious side of the mind? And what happens to them after they have been censored? As Roy P. Basler puts it in *Sex, Symbolism, and Psychology in Literature* (1975), "from the beginning of recorded history such wishes have been restrained by the most powerful religious and social taboos, and as a result have come to be regarded as 'unnatural,'" even though "Freud found that such wishes are more or less characteristic of normal human development":

> In dreams, particularly, Freud found ample evidence that such wishes persisted. . . . Hence he conceived that natural urges, when identified as "wrong," may be repressed but not obliterated. . . .
> In the unconscious, these urges take on symbolic garb, regarded as nonsense by the waking mind that does not recognize their significance. (14)

Freud's belief in the significance of dreams, of course, was no more original than his belief that there is an unconscious side to the psyche. Again, it was the extent to which he developed a theory of how dreams work — and the extent to which that theory helped him, by analogy, to understand far more than just dreams — that made him unusual, important, and influential beyond the perimeters of medical schools and psychiatrists' offices.

The psychoanalytic approach to literature not only rests on the theories of Freud; it may even be said to have *begun* with Freud, who was interested in writers, especially those who relied heavily on symbols.

Such writers regularly cloak or mystify ideas in figures that make sense only when interpreted, much as the unconscious mind of a neurotic disguises secret thoughts in dream stories or bizarre actions that need to be interpreted by an analyst. Freud's interest in literary artists led him to make some unfortunate generalizations about creativity; for example, in the twenty-third lecture in *Introductory Lectures on Psycho-Analysis* (1922), he defined the artist as "one urged on by instinctive needs that are too clamorous" (314). But it also led him to write creative literary criticism of his own, including an influential essay on "The Relation of a Poet to Daydreaming" (1908) and "The Uncanny" (1919), a provocative psychoanalytic reading of E. T. A. Hoffman's supernatural tale "The Sandman."

Freud's application of psychoanalytic theory to literature quickly caught on. In 1909, only a year after Freud had published "The Relation of a Poet to Daydreaming," the psychoanalyst Otto Rank published *The Myth of the Birth of the Hero*. In that work, Rank subscribes to the notion that the artist turns a powerful, secret wish into a literary fantasy, and he uses Freud's notion about the "oedipal" complex to explain why the popular stories of so many heroes in literature are so similar. A year after Rank had published his psychoanalytic account of heroic texts, Ernest Jones, Freud's student and eventual biographer, turned his attention to a tragic text: Shakespeare's *Hamlet*. In an essay first published in the *American Journal of Psychology*, Jones, like Rank, makes use of the oedipal concept: he suggests that Hamlet is a victim of strong feelings toward his mother, the queen.

Between 1909 and 1949, numerous other critics decided that psychological and psychoanalytic theory could assist in the understanding of literature. I. A. Richards, Kenneth Burke, and Edmund Wilson were among the most influential to become interested in the new approach. Not all of the early critics were committed to the approach; neither were all of them Freudians. Some followed Alfred Adler, who believed that writers wrote out of inferiority complexes, and others applied the ideas of Carl Gustav Jung, who had broken with Freud over Freud's emphasis on sex and who had developed a theory of the *collective* unconscious. According to Jungian theory, a great work of literature is not a disguised expression of its author's personal, repressed wishes; rather, it is a manifestation of desires once held by the whole human race but now repressed because of the advent of civilization.

It is important to point out that among those who relied on Freud's models were a number of critics who were poets and novelists as well. Conrad Aiken wrote a Freudian study of American literature, and poets such as Robert Graves and W. H. Auden applied Freudian insights when writing critical prose. William Faulkner, Henry James, James Joyce, D. H. Lawrence, Marcel Proust, and Toni Morrison are only a few of the novelists who have either written criticism influenced by Freud or who have written novels that conceive of character, conflict, and creative writing itself in Freudian terms. The poet H. D. (Hilda Doolittle) was actually a patient of Freud's and provided an account of her analysis in her book *Tribute to Freud*. By giving Freudian theory credibility among students of literature that only they could bestow, such writers helped to endow earlier psychoanalytic criticism with a largely Freudian orientation that has begun to be challenged only in the last two decades.

The willingness, even eagerness, of writers to use Freudian models in producing literature and criticism of their own consummated a relationship that, to Freud and other pioneering psychoanalytic theorists, had seemed fated from the beginning; after all, therapy involves the close analysis of language. René Wellek and Austin Warren included "psychological" criticism as one of the five "extrinsic" approaches to literature described in their influential book *Theory of Literature* (1942). Psychological criticism, they suggest, typically attempts to do at least one of the following: provide a psychological study of an individual writer; explore the nature of the creative process; generalize about "types and laws present within works of literature"; or theorize about the psychological "effects of literature upon its readers" (81). Entire books on psychoanalytic criticism began to appear, such as Frederick J. Hoffman's *Freudianism and the Literary Mind* (1945).

Probably because of Freud's characterization of the creative mind as "clamorous" if not ill, psychoanalytic criticism written before 1950 tended to psychoanalyze the individual author. Poems were read as fantasies that allowed authors to indulge repressed wishes, to protect themselves from deep-seated anxieties, or both. A perfect example of author analysis would be Marie Bonaparte's 1933 study of Edgar Allan Poe. Bonaparte found Poe to be so fixated on his mother that his repressed longing emerges in his stories in images such as the white spot on a black cat's breast, said to represent mother's milk.

A later generation of psychoanalytic critics often paused to analyze the characters in novels and plays before proceeding to their authors. But not for long, since characters, both evil and good, tended to be seen by these critics as the author's potential selves, or projections of various repressed aspects of his or her psyche. For instance, in *A Psychoanalytic Study of the Double in Literature* (1970), Robert Rogers begins with the view that human beings are double or multiple in nature. Using this assumption, along with the psychoanalytic concept of "dissociation" (best known by its result, the dual or multiple personality), Rogers concludes that writers reveal instinctual or repressed selves in their books, often without realizing that they have done so.

In the view of critics attempting to arrive at more psychological insights into an author than biographical materials can provide, a work of literature is a fantasy or a dream — or at least so analogous to daydream or dream that Freudian analysis can help explain the nature of the mind that produced it. The author's purpose in writing is to gratify secretly some forbidden wish, in particular an infantile wish or desire that has been repressed into the unconscious mind. To discover what the wish is, the psychoanalytic critic employs many of the terms and procedures developed by Freud to analyze dreams.

The literal surface of a work is sometimes spoken of as its "manifest content" and treated as a "manifest dream" or "dream story" would be treated by a Freudian analyst. Just as the analyst tries to figure out the "dream thought" behind the dream story — that is, the latent or hidden content of the manifest dream — so the psychoanalytic literary critic tries to expose the latent, underlying content of a work. Freud used the words *condensation* and *displacement* to explain two of the mental processes whereby the mind disguises its wishes and fears in dream stories. In condensation, several thoughts or persons may be condensed into a single manifestation or image in a dream story; in displacement, an anxiety, a wish, or a person may be displaced onto the image of another, with which or whom it is loosely connected through a string of associations that only an analyst can untangle. Psychoanalytic critics treat metaphors as if they were dream condensations; they treat metonyms — figures of speech based on extremely loose, arbitrary associations — as if they were dream displacements. Thus figurative literary language in general is treated as something that evolves as the writer's conscious mind resists what the unconscious tells it to picture or describe. A symbol is, in Daniel Weiss's words, "a meaningful concealment of truth as the truth promises to emerge as some frightening or forbidden idea" (20).

In a 1970 article entitled "The 'Unconscious' of Literature," Norman Holland, a literary critic trained in psychoanalysis, succinctly sums up the attitudes held by critics who would psychoanalyze authors, but without quite saying that it is the *author* who is being analyzed by the psychoanalytic critic. "When one looks at a poem psychoanalytically," he writes, "one considers it as though it were a dream or as though some ideal patient [were speaking] from the couch in iambic pentameter." One "looks for the general level or levels of fantasy associated with the language. By level I mean the familiar stages of childhood development — oral [when desires for nourishment and infantile sexual desires overlap], anal [when infants receive their primary pleasure from defecation], urethral [when urinary functions are the locus of sexual pleasure], phallic [when the penis or, in girls, some penis substitute is of primary interest], oedipal." Holland continues by analyzing not Robert Frost but Frost's poem "Mending Wall" as a specifically oral fantasy that is not unique to its author. "Mending Wall" is "about breaking down the wall which marks the separated or individuated self so as to return to a state of closeness to some Other"— including and perhaps essentially the nursing mother ("'Unconscious'" 136, 139).

While not denying the idea that the unconscious plays a role in creativity, psychoanalytic critics such as Holland began to focus more on the ways in which authors create works that appeal to *our* repressed wishes and fantasies. Consequently, they shifted their focus away from the psyche of the author and toward the psychology of the reader and the text. Holland's theories, which have concerned themselves more with the reader than with the text, have helped to establish another school of critical theory: reader-response criticism. Elizabeth Wright explains Holland's brand of modern psychoanalytic criticism in this way: "What draws us as readers to a text is the secret expression of what we desire to hear, much as we protest we do not. The disguise must be good enough to fool the censor into thinking that the text is respectable, but bad enough to allow the unconscious to glimpse the unrespectable" (117).

Holland is one of dozens of critics who have revised Freud significantly in the process of revitalizing psychoanalytic criticism. Another such critic is R. D. Laing, whose controversial and often poetical writings about personality, repression, masks, and the double or "schizoid" self have (re)blurred the boundary between creative writing and psychoanalytic discourse. Yet another is D. W. Winnicott, an "object relations" theorist who has had a significant impact on literary criticism. Critics influenced by Winnicott and his school have questioned the tendency to see reader/text as an either/or construct; instead, they have seen reader and text (or audience and play) in terms of a *relationship* taking place in what Winnicott calls a "transitional" or "potential" space — space in which binary terms such as *real* and *illusory*, *objective* and *subjective*, have little or no meaning.

Psychoanalytic theorists influenced by Winnicott see the transitional or potential reader/text (or audience/play) space as being *like* the space entered into by psychoanalyst and patient. More important, they also see it as being similar to the space between mother and infant: a space characterized by trust in which categorizing terms such as *knowing* and *feeling* mix and merge and have little meaning apart from one another.

Whereas Freud saw the mother-son relationship in terms of the son and his repressed oedipal complex (and saw the analyst-patient relationship in terms of the patient and the repressed "truth" that the analyst could scientifically extract), object-relations analysts see both relationships as *dyadic* — that is, as being dynamic in both directions. Consequently, they don't depersonalize analysis or their analyses. It is hardly surprising, therefore, that contemporary literary critics who apply object-relations theory to the texts they discuss don't depersonalize critics or categorize their interpretations as "truthful," at least not in any objective or scientific sense. In the view of such critics, interpretations are made of language — itself a transitional object — and are themselves the mediating terms or transitional objects of a relationship.

Like critics of the Winnicottian school, the French structuralist theorist Jacques Lacan focused on language and language-related issues. He treated the unconscious *as* a language and, consequently, viewed the dream not as Freud did (that is, as a form and symptom of repression) but rather as a form of discourse. Thus we may study dreams psychoanalytically to learn about literature, even as we may study literature to learn more about the unconscious. In Lacan's seminar on Poe's "The Purloined Letter," a pattern of repetition like that used by psychoanalysts in their analyses is used to arrive at a reading of the story. Elizabeth Wright, in an essay on "Modern Psychoanalytic Criticism" (1982), explains that "the new psychoanalytic structural approach to literature" employs "analogies from psychoanalysis . . . to explain the workings of the text as distinct from the workings of a particular author's, character's, or even reader's mind" (125).

Lacan, however, did far more than extend Freud's theory of dreams, literature, and the interpretation of both. More significantly, he took Freud's whole theory of psyche and gender and added to it a crucial third term — that of language. In the process, he both used and significantly developed Freud's ideas about the oedipal stage and complex.

Lacan pointed out that the pre-oedipal stage, in which the child at first does not even recognize its independence from its mother, is also a pre*verbal* stage, one in which the child communicates without the medium of language, or — if we insist on calling the child's communications a language — in a language that can only be called *literal*. ("Coos," certainly, cannot be said to be figurative or symbolic.) Then, while still in the pre-oedipal stage, the child enters the *mirror* stage.

During the mirror period, the child comes to view itself and its mother, later other people as well, *as* independent selves. This is the stage in which the child is first able to fear the aggressions of another, to desire what is recognizably beyond the self (initially the mother), and, finally, to want to compete with another for the same desired object. This is also the stage at which the child first becomes able to feel sympathy with another being who is being hurt by a third, to cry when another cries. All of these developments, of course, involve projecting beyond the self and, by extension, constructing one's own self (or "ego" or "I") as others view one — that is, as *another*. Such constructions, according to Lacan, are just that: constructs, products, artifacts — fictions of coherence that in fact hide what Lacan called the "absence" or "lack" of being.

The mirror stage, which Lacan also referred to as the *imaginary* stage, is fairly quickly succeeded by the oedipal stage. As in Freud, this stage begins when the child, having come to view itself as self and the father and mother as separate selves, perceives gender and gender differences between its parents and between itself and one of its parents. For boys, gender awareness involves another, more powerful recognition, for the recognition of the father's phallus as the mark of his difference from the mother involves, at the same time, the recognition that his older and more powerful father is also his rival. That, in turn, leads to the understanding that what once seemed wholly his and even indistinguishable from himself is in fact someone else's: something properly desired only at a distance and in the form of socially acceptable *substitutes*.

The fact that the oedipal stage roughly coincides with the entry of the child into language is extremely important for Lacan. For the linguistic order is essentially a figurative or "Symbolic" order; words are not the things they stand for but are, rather stand-ins or substitutes for those things. Hence boys, who in the most critical period of their development have had to submit to what Lacan called the "Law of the Father"— a law that prohibits direct desire for and communicative intimacy with what has been the boy's whole world — enter more easily into the realm of language and the Symbolic order than do girls, who have never really had to renounce that which once seemed continuous with the self: the mother. The gap that has been opened up for boys, which includes the gap between signs and what they substitute — the gap marked by the phallus and encoded with the boy's sense of his maleness — has not opened up for girls, or has not opened up in the same way, to the same degree.

For Lacan, the father need not be present to trigger the oedipal stage; nor does his phallus have to be seen to catalyze the boy's (easier) transition into the Symbolic order. Rather, Lacan argued, a child's recognition of its gender is intricately tied up with a growing recognition of the system of names and naming, part of the larger system of substitutions we call language. A child has little doubt about who its mother is, but who is its father, and how would one know? The father's claim rests on the mother's *word* that he is in fact the father; the father's relationship to the child is thus established through language and a system of marriage and kinship — names — that in turn is basic to rules of everything from property to law. The name of the father (*nom du père*, which in French sounds like *non du père*) involves, in a sense, nothing of the father — nothing, that is, except his word or name.

Lacan's development of Freud has had several important results. First, his sexist-seeming association of maleness with the Symbolic order, together with his claim that women cannot therefore enter easily into the order, has prompted feminists not to reject his theory out of hand but, rather, to look more closely at the relation between language and gender, language and women's inequality. Some feminists have gone so far as to suggest that the social and political relationships between male and female will not be fundamentally altered until language itself has been radically changed. (That change might begin dialectically, with the development of some kind of "feminine language" grounded in the presymbolic, literal-to-imaginary communication between mother and child.)

Second, Lacan's theory has proved of interest to deconstructors and other poststructuralists, in part because it holds that the ego (which in Freud's view is as necessary as it is natural) is a product or construct. The ego-artifact, produced during the mirror stage, *seems* at once unified, consistent, and organized around a determinate center. But the unified self, or ego, is a fiction, according to Lacan. The yoking together of fragments and destructively dissimilar elements takes its psychic toll, and it is the job of the Lacanian psychoanalyst to "deconstruct," as it were, the ego, to show its continuities to be contradictions as well.

In the pages that follow, Sheldon Brivic focuses on Stephen Dedalus's gradual alienation from family, church, and nation. He grounds the process of self-isolation in early, unconscious fantasies and fears.

Specifically, Brivic traces Stephen's adolescent and adult behavior patterns back to an oedipal desire for the mother, arguing that the romantic fantasies and feelings of guilt attendant upon the oedipal complex explain everything from Stephen's "minor relationship with Eileen" (p. 281 in this volume) to his fears of castration, violence, and homosexuality. Brivic finds evidence of the oedipal complex in Stephen's longings (to lay his head on his mother's lap, for instance) and dreams, the latter of which are populated by dead, wounded, or wounding father figures.

As the discussion of Stephen's dreams reminds us, the oedipal complex involves fear of the father (and of threatening males in general) as fully as it involves desire for the mother (and for inferior, inadequate mother substitutes). Brivic focuses consideration on Stephen's preoccupation with threats of male violence, discussing the pandying scene and the consequent scene in the rector's office in terms of oedipal fear and resistance. The church fathers, in other words, come to be replacements for the biological father in the novel's oedipal drama.

Brivic focuses on the novel's substitutes as well as on its patriarchal representations. He discusses Emma Clery, whom Stephen "spiritualizes," (p. 287) the prostitute Stephen turns to in desperation, and the "sheltering arms" (p. 288) of the Virgin in terms of oedipal desire and guilt. Finally, and most significantly, he views the girl on the beach, Stephen's imaginative reconfiguration of her, and the subsequent pursuit of transcendental art in terms of a mother transfigured and a typical oedipal longing for phallic sexuality, power, control. "For Stephen," Brivic writes, "the artist's stance *is* the relation of son to mother (p. 285).

Building on other critics' observations about the parallel form of *Portrait* — an Irish muse replaces the Virgin who replaces the prostitute who replaces E—— C—— who replaces the mother as Feminine Ideal — Brivic sees these repetitions in terms of compulsive behavior, in which people become locked in cyclical patterns of frustration and failure. Stephen's feeling that he is destined to become an artist is viewed as just another myth "generated by" his "neurotic need" (p. 292) to alienate himself again and again from that which he feels he cannot have. It is little wonder, Brivic comments, that "his parental attachments and anxieties return in the fifth chapter" (p. 293).

Brivic's essay functions on at least three levels. At the most obvious, it tells us that "Joyce knew about Freud" (p. 279) and illustrated Freud's theories novelistically in the process of writing *Portrait*. At another level, Brivic provides a psychoanalytic analysis of a literary character, Stephen, and shows that the goals and struggles of his life are grounded in unconscious complexes and motivations. At its deepest level, however, the subject of Brivic's analysis is not Stephen but *Portrait* itself, a "structure" whose "motivation" is said to be "unconscious," (p. 279) an artifact that contains and describes dreams and at the same time functions something *like* a dream, revealing what its author (and reader) might not otherwise confront. Like the power of unacknowledged desires, like the power of dream stories whose underlying dream thoughts are unclear or even conflicting, "much of the power of *Portrait*," in Brivic's words, "comes from what is not resolved. . . . Balance"— including the patterns and parallels placed in the text by the author or apprehended by critics and readers — "is there to be unbalanced" (p. 294).

Ross C Murfin

PSYCHOANALYTIC CRITICISM:
A SELECTED BIBLIOGRAPHY

Some Short Introductions to
Psychological and Psychoanalytic Criticism

Holland, Norman. "The 'Unconscious' of Literature." *Contemporary Criticism*. Ed. Norman Bradbury and David Palmer. Stratford-upon-Avon Series 12. New York: St. Martin's, 1970. 131–54.

Natoli, Joseph, and Frederik L. Rusch, comps. *Psychocriticism: An Annotated Bibliography*. Westport: Greenwood, 1984.

Rogers, Robert A. *A Psychoanalytic Study of the Double in Literature*. Detroit: Wayne State UP, 1970.

Scott, Wilbur. *Five Approaches to Literary Criticism*. London: Collier-Macmillan, 1962. See the essays by Burke and Gorer as well as Scott's introduction to the section "The Psychological Approach: Literature in the Light of Psychological Theory."

Weiss, Daniel. *The Critic Agonistes: Psychology, Myth, and the Art of Fiction*. Ed. Stephen Arkin and Eric Solomon. Seattle: U of Washington P, 1985.

Wellek, René, and Austin Warren. *Theory of Literature*. New York: Harcourt, 1942. See the chapter "Literature and Psychology" in pt. 3, "The Extrinsic Approach to the Study of Literature."

Wright, Elizabeth, "Modern Psychoanalytic Criticism." *Modern Literary Theory: A Comparative Introduction*. Ed. Ann Jefferson and David Robey. Totowa: Barnes, 1982. 113–33.

Freud, Lacan, and Their Influence

Althusser, Louis. *Writings on Psychoanalysis: Freud and Lacan*. Ed. Olivier Corpet and Francois Matheron. Trans. Jeffrey Mehlman. New York: Columbia UP, 1996.

Basler, Roy P. *Sex, Symbolism, and Psychology in Literature*. New York: Octagon, 1975. See especially 13–19.

Bowie, Malcolm. *Lacan*. Cambridge: Harvard UP, 1991.

Clement, Catherine. *The Lives and Legends of Jacques Lacan*. Trans. Arthur Goldhammer. New York: Columbia UP, 1983.

Copjec, Joan. *Read My Desire: Lacan Against the Historicists*. Cambridge: MIT P, 1994.

Feldstein, Richard, Bruce Fink, and Maire Jaanus, eds. *Reading Seminar XI: Lacan's Four Fundamental Concepts of Psychoanalysis*. Albany: State U of New York P, 1995.

Fink, Bruce. *The Lacanian Subject: Between Language and Jouissance*. Princeton: Princeton UP, 1995.

Freud, Sigmund. *The Interpretation of Dreams*. Trans. James Strachey. New York: Avon, 1965.

———. *Introductory Lectures on Psycho-Analysis*. Trans. Joan Riviere. London: Allen, 1922.

Hill, Philip. *Lacan for Beginners*. New York: Writers and Readers, 1997.

Hoffman, Frederick J. *Freudianism and the Literary Mind*. Baton Rouge: Louisiana State UP, 1945.

Lacan, Jacques. *Ecrits: A Selection*. Trans. Alan Sheridan. New York: Norton, 1977.

———. *The Ego in Freud's Theory and in the Technique of Psychoanalysis 1954–1955*. Ed. Jacques-Alain Miller. Trans. Sylvana Tomaselli. The Seminar of Jacques Lacan Book II. New York: Norton, 1988.

———. *The Ethics of Psychoanalysis: 1959–1960*. Ed. Jacques-Alain Miller. Trans. Dennis Porter. The Seminar of Jacques Lacan Book VII. New York: Norton, 1992.

————. *Feminine Sexuality: Lacan and the ecole freudienne.* Ed. Juliet Mitchell and Jacqueline Rose. Trans. Rose. New York: Norton, 1982.

————. *The Four Fundamental Concepts of Psychoanalysis.* Trans. Alan Sheridan. London: Penguin, 1980.

————. *Freud's Papers on Technique 1953–1954.* Ed. Jacques-Alain Miller. Trans. John Forrester. The Seminar of Jacques Lacan Book I. New York: Norton, 1988.

————. *On Feminine Sexuality: The Limits of Love and Knowledge.* Ed. Jacques-Alain Miller. Trans. Bruce Fink. The Seminar of Jacques Lacan Book XX: Encore 1972–1973. New York: Norton, 1998.

————. *The Seminar of Jacques Lacan: Book VII: The Ethics of Psychoanalysis, 1959–1960.* Ed. Jacques-Alain Miller. Trans. Dennis Porter. New York: Norton, 1992.

————. *The Seminar of Jacques Lacan: Book XX Encore: On Feminine Sexuality, The Limits of Love and Knowledge, 1972–1973.* Ed. Jacques-Alain Miller. Trans. Bruce Fink. New York: Norton, 1998.

Lee, Jonathan Scott. *Jacques Lacan.* Boston: Twayne, 1990.

Rabaté, Jean-Michel, ed. *The Cambridge Companion to Lacan.* Cambridge: Cambridge UP, 2003.

Ragland-Sullivan, Ellie. *Essays on the Pleasures of Death: From Freud to Lacan.* New York: Routledge, 1995.

Roudinesco, Elisabeth. *Jacques Lacan.* Trans. Barbara Bray. New York: Columbia UP, 1997.

Schneiderman, Stuart. *Jacques Lacan: The Death of an Intellectual Hero.* Cambridge: Harvard UP, 1983.

Winnicott, Donald W. *Playing and Reality.* Harmondsworth: Penguin, 1974.

Zizek, Slavoj. *Enjoy Your Symptom: Jacques Lacan in Hollywood and Out.* New York: Routledge, 1992.

————. *Looking Awry: An Introduction to Jacques Lacan through Popular Culture.* Cambridge, MA: MIT, 1991.

————. *The Metastases of Enjoyment: Six Essays on Woman and Causality.* New York: Verso, 1994.

————. *The Sublime Object of Ideology.* New York: Verso, 1989.

Psychoanalysis, Feminism, and Literature

Barr, Marleen S., and Richard Feldstein. *Discontented Discourses: Feminism/Textual Intervention/Psychoanalysis.* Urbana: U of Illinois P, 1989.

Benjamin, Jessica. *The Bonds of Love: Psychoanalysis, Feminism and the Problem of Domination.* New York: Pantheon, 1988.

Bernheimer, Charles, and Claire Kahane, eds. *In Dora's Case: Freud-Hysteria-Feminism.* New York: Columbia UP, 1985.

Butler, Judith. *Gender Trouble: Feminism and the Subversion of Identity.* New York: Routledge, 1990.

———. *Bodies That Matter: On the Discursive Limits of "Sex."* New York: Routledge, 1993.

de Lauretis, Teresa. *The Practice of Love: Lesbian Sexuality and Perverse Desire.* Bloomington: Indiana UP, 1994.

Elliott, Patricia. *From Mastery to Analysis: Theories of Gender in Psychoanalytic Criticism.* Ithaca: Cornell UP, 1991.

Felman, Shoshana. *What Does a Woman Want? Reading and Sexual Difference.* Baltimore: Johns Hopkins UP, 1993.

Gallop, Jane. *The Daughter's Seduction: Feminism and Psychoanalysis.* Ithaca: Cornell UP, 1982.

———. *Thinking Through the Body.* New York: Columbia UP, 1988.

Garner, Shirley Nelson, Claire Kahane, and Madelon Sprengnether. *The (M)other Tongue: Essays in Feminist Psychoanalytic Interpretation.* Ithaca: Cornell UP, 1985.

Grosz, Elizabeth. *Jacques Lacan: A Feminist Introduction.* New York: Routledge, 1990.

Irigaray, Luce. *This Sex Which Is Not One.* Trans. Catherine Porter. Ithaca: Cornell UP, 1985.

———. *Speculum of the Other Woman.* Trans. Gillian C. Gill. Ithaca: Cornell UP, 1985.

Jacobus, Mary. "Is There a Woman in This Text?" *New Literary History* 14 (1982): 117–41.

Kristeva, Julia. *The Kristeva Reader.* Ed. Toril Moi. New York: Columbia UP, 1986. See especially the selection from *Revolution in Poetic Language* 89–136.

MacCannell, Juliet Flower. *The Regime of the Brother: After the Patriarchy.* New York: Routledge, 1991.

Mitchell, Juliet. *Psychoanalysis and Feminism.* New York: Random, 1974.

Mitchell, Juliet, and Jacqueline Rose. Introduction I and Introduction II. Lacan, *Feminine Sexuality: Jacques Lacan and the ecole freudienne.* New York: Pantheon, 1982. 1–26, 27–57.

Rose, Jacqueline. *Sexuality in the Field of Vision.* New York: Verso, 1986.

Sprengnether, Madelon. *The Spectral Mother: Freud, Feminism, and Psychoanalysis.* Ithaca: Cornell UP, 1990.

Psychological and Psychoanalytic Studies of Literature, Culture, and the Arts

Apollon, Willy, and Richard Feldstein, eds. *Lacan. Politics, Aesthetics.* Albany: State U of New York P, 1996.

Bersani, Leo. *Baudelaire and Freud.* Berkeley: U of California P, 1977.

———. *The Freudian Body: Psychoanalysis and Art.* New York: Columbia UP, 1986.

Bettelheim, Bruno. *The Uses of Enchantment: The Meaning and Importance of Fairy Tales.* New York: Knopf, 1976.

Bracher, Mark. *Lacan, Discourse, and Social Change: A Psychoanalytic Cultural Criticism.* Ithaca: Cornell UP, 1993.

Grosz, Elizabeth. *Space, Time, and Perversion: Essays on the Politics of Bodies.* New York: Routledge, 1995.

Hartman, Geoffrey, ed. *Psychoanalysis and the Question of the Text.* Baltimore: Johns Hopkins UP, 1978.

Hertz, Neil. *The End of the Line: Essays on Psychoanalysis and the Sublime.* New York: Columbia UP, 1985.

Jacobus, Mary. *First Things: The Maternal Imaginary in Literature, Art, and Psychoanalysis.* New York: Routledge, 1995.

Krauss, Rosalind. *The Optical Unconscious.* Cambridge: MIT P, 1994.

Poizat, Michel. *The Angel's Cry: Beyond the Pleasure Principle in Opera.* Trans. Arthur Denner. Ithaca: Cornell UP, 1992.

Salecl, Renata, and Slavoj Zizek, eds. *Gaze and Voice as Love Objects.* Durham: Duke UP, 1996.

Silverman, Kaja. *The Threshold of the Visible World.* New York: Routledge, 1996.

Wright, Elizabeth. *Psychoanalytic Criticism: A Reappraisal.* 2nd ed. New York: Routledge, 1998.

Lacanian Psychoanalytic Studies of Literature

Booker, M. Keith. "Notes Toward a Lacanian Reading of Wallace Stevens." *Journal of Modern Literature* 16 (1990): 493–509.

Davis, Robert Con, ed. *The Fictional Father: Lacanian Readings of the Text.* Amherst: U of Massachusetts P, 1981.

———. *Lacan and Narration: The Psychoanalytic Difference in Narrative Theory.* Baltimore: Johns Hopkins UP, 1984.

Devlin, Kim. "Castration and Its Discontents: A Lacanian Approach to *Ulysses.*" *James Joyce Quarterly* 29 (1991): 117–44.

Felman, Shoshana, ed. *Literature and Psychoanalysis: The Question of Reading: Otherwise*. Baltimore: Johns Hopkins UP, 1982. Includes Lacan's seminar on Shakespeare's *Hamlet*.

Homans, Margaret. *Bearing the Word: Language and Female Experience in Nineteenth-Century Women's Writing*. Chicago: U of Chicago P, 1986.

Lacan, Jacques. "The Essence of Tragedy: A Commentary on Sophocles's *Antigone*." Lacan, *The Ethics of Psychoanalysis*. New York: Norton, 1997. 243–87.

Mellard, James M. *Using Lacan, Reading Fiction*. Urbana: U of Illinois P, 1991.

Miller, David Lee. "Writing the Specular Son: Jonson, Freud, Lacan, and the (K)not of Masculinity." *Desire in the Renaissance: Psychoanalysis and Literature*. Ed. Valeria Finucci and Regina Schwartz. Princeton: Princeton UP, 1994. 233–60.

Muller, John P., and William J. Richardson, eds. *The Purloined Poe: Lacan, Derrida. and Psychoanalytic Reading*. Baltimore: Johns Hopkins UP, 1988. Includes Lacan's seminar on Poe's "The Purloined Letter."

Netto, Jeffrey A. "Dickens with Kant and Sade." *Style* 29 (1995): 441–58.

Rabaté, Jean-Michel. *Jacques Lacan: Psychoanalysis and the Subject of Literature*. New York: Palgrave, 2001.

Rapaport, Herman. *Between the Sign & the Gaze*. Ithaca: Cornell UP, 1994.

Schad, John. " 'No One Dreams': Hopkins, Lacan, and the Unconscious." *Victorian Poetry* 32 (1994): 141–56.

Psychoanalytic Approaches to Joyce

Anderson, Chester G. "Baby Tuckoo: Joyce's 'Features of Infancy,' " *Approaches to Joyce's "Portrait": Ten Essays*. Ed. Thomas F. Staley and Bernard Benstock. Pittsburgh: U of Pittsburgh P, 1976. 135–169.

Boheemen, Christine van. *The Novel as Family Romance: Language, Gender, and Authority from Fielding to Joyce*. Ithaca: Cornell UP, 1987, passim.

Brivic, Sheldon. "Gender Dissonance, Hysteria, and History in James Joyce's *A Portrait* . . ." *James Joyce Quarterly* 39 (Spring 2002): 457–76.

———. *Joyce the Creator*. Madison and London: U of Wisconsin P, 1985.

————. *Joyce between Freud and Jung.* Port Washington, NY, and London: Kennikat, 1980.

————. *Joyce's Waking Women: An Introduction to "Finnegans Wake."* Madison: U of Wisconsin P, 1995.

————. *The Veil of Signs: Joyce, Lacan, and Perception.* Champaign: U of Illinois P, 1991.

Devlin, Kimberly J. *Joycean Fraudstuff.* Gainesville: UP of Florida, 2002.

Ellmann, Maud. "The Name and the Scar: Identity in *The Odyssey* and *A Portrait . . ."* *James Joyce's "A Portrait of the Artist as a Young Man": A Casebook.* Ed. Mark A Wollaeger. Oxford: Oxford UP, 2003.

Fenichel, Robert. "A Portrait of the Artist as a Young Orphan." *Literature and Psychology* 9 (Spring 1959): 19–22.

Harari, Roberto. *How James Joyce Made His Name: A Reading of the Final Lacan.* Trans. Luke Thurston. New York: Other P, 2002.

Henke, Suzette. *James Joyce and the Politics of Desire.* New York: Routledge, 1990.

Hoffman, Frederick C. "Infroyce." *Freudianism and the Literary Mind.* Baton Rouge: Louisiana State UP, 1945.

James Joyce Quarterly 13 (Spring 1976). "Joyce and Modern Psychology" issue.

James Joyce Quarterly 29 (Fall 1991). "Joyce between Genders: Lacanian Views" issue.

Kimball, Jean. "Freud, Leonardo, and Joyce: The Dimensions of a Childhood Memory." *The Seventh of Joyce.* Ed. Bernard Benstock. Bloomington: Indiana UP, 1982. 57–73.

————. *Joyce and the Early Freudians.* Gainesville: UP of Florida, 2003.

Lamos, Colleen. *Deviant Modernism: Sexual and Textual Errancy in T. S. Eliot, James Joyce, and Marcel Proust.* Cambridge: Cambridge UP, 1998.

Leonard, Garry. *Reading "Dubliners" Again: A Lacanian Perspective.* Syracuse, NY: Syracuse UP, 1993.

O'Brien, Darcy. "Some Psychological Determinants of Joyce's View of Love and Sex." *New Light on Joyce from the Dublin Symposium.* Ed. Fritz Senn. Bloomington: Indiana UP, 1970. 137–55.

Rabaté, Jean-Michel. *James Joyce and the Politics of Egoism.* Cambridge: Cambridge UP, 2001.

Rea, Joanne E. "Joyce's 'Beastly' Bitch Motif: Sadic Castration Threat and Separation Anxiety." *Journal of Evolutionary Psychology* 7 (March 1986): 28–33.

Schwaber, Paul. *The Cast of Characters: A Reading of "Ulysses."* New Haven: Yale UP, 1999.

Sheckner, Mark. *Joyce in Nightown: A Psychoanalytic Inquiry into "Ulysses."* Berkeley: U of California P, 1974.

Thurston, Luke, ed. *Re-inventing the Symptom: Essays on the Final Lacan.* New York: Other P, 2002.

Valente, Joseph. *James Joyce and the Problem of Justice: Negotiating Sexual and Colonial Difference.* Cambridge: Cambridge UP, 1995.

Wasson, Richard. "Stephen Dedalus and the Imagery of Sight: A Psychological Approach." *Literature and Psychology* 15 (Fall 1965): 195–209.

A PSYCHOANALYTIC PERSPECTIVE

SHELDON BRIVIC

The Disjunctive Structure of Joyce's *Portrait*[1]

Psychoanalysis shows how the images that weave through *Portrait* are linked by unconscious motivation to form a dynamic structure. Within this structure Stephen Dedalus develops his thinking around a central principle of connecting with the world through alienation. And the conflicts and transformations in the structure enact opposing views by which Joyce both supports and condemns Stephen. Joyce knew about Freud during the last years of his work on *Portrait*,[2] so many patterns I will trace may have been consciously designed. But most of the novel's motivation was unconscious and sprang from Joyce's personal vision of his youthful development: he usually stuck close to the facts,

---

[1] The 1993 version of this essay has been preserved, but it is supplemented by new material. The new edition of Lacan's *Écrits* is cited.

[2] Richard Ellmann (54) reports that Joyce bought three psychoanalytic works by Freud, Ernest Jones, and C. G. Jung around the time they were published in 1909–1911. Hans Walter Gabler (34) believes that Joyce revised the first three chapters of *Portrait* extensively after 1911.

only occasionally altering them for artistic purposes. According to the theory that the subject is made up of opposing agencies, an idea of Freud's that was expanded by Lacan (281–312), the different sides of Stephen in *Portrait* express different intentions of Joyce's. The interaction of these opposed intentions makes up the rhythm of Stephen's mental life.

The action of *Portrait* consists of Stephen's sundering of himself from his society, his parents, his church, his beloved E—— C——, and his nation. The book justifies these alienations by its critical portrayal of institutions and its presentation of ideas about freedom, personal development, and aesthetics. These ideas have great validity, but the root of Stephen's alienation, while it is shaped by social systems, is already planted in his unconscious before he can criticize society.

Stephen's first six years are represented in the section that takes up the first page and a half of *Portrait,* introducing many key images, including his looming, hairy father and the "nicer smell" (p. 21 in this volume) of mother. Central to this section is Stephen's first writing. Like all of his writing, and Joyce's, it is addressed to mother, and is a shameful, incomprehensible self-expression that starts changing its nature as soon as it is inscribed: "When you wet the bed first it is warm then it gets cold" (p. 20). My daughter once told me that her infant son just loved to be changed, especially to have his genitals cleaned. Stephen has here passed beyond being changed, but he wants to return to it. So his effusion forces his mother to wipe off his parts in an action that is omitted, but inevitable. She would not change his sheet and leave him wet.[3]

---

[3]Urination, and being wiped off, absorbed, or interpreted, remains as a basic model for writing and sexuality through *Finnegans Wake,* which describes Shem as making ink out of his urine (185). Stephen and May are so absorbed in such wiping that they cannot help repeating variations on it long after they know they should not, for a dozen or more years:

> When the enamelled basin had been fitted . . . and the old washingglove flung on the side of it he allowed his mother to scrub his neck and root into the folds of his ears and into the interstices at the wings of his nose.
> — Well, it's a poor case, she said, when a university student is so dirty that his mother has to wash him.
> — But it gives you pleasure, said Stephen calmly. (p. 157)

The extensive history behind this ritual is indicated by the age of the glove. He still needs to think that she enjoys the embarrassment of wiping off his excretory organs (ears and nose) and rooting into the outlines of his protuberances. This delineates him in Lacanian terms as a signifier with roots and "interstices" (271–78). The winged nasal phallus is ground into with a rough, wet expertise by the mother — who has probably done it every day, so she knows Stephen's reactions.

The conclusion of this section, based on an early incident in Joyce's life recorded in his *Epiphanies* (Anderson 267–68), poses a threat that echoes through *Portrait:*

> When they were grown up he was going to marry Eileen. He hid under the table. His mother said:
> — O, Stephen will apologise.
> Dante said:
> — O, if not, the eagles will come and pull out his eyes.
> *Pull out his eyes,*
> *Apologise,*
> *Apologise,*
> *Pull out his eyes.* (p. 21)

The loss of eyes is an image of castration, having been established by Oedipus himself. Freud says that the idea of castration starts to be important for children during the phallic or ocdipal stage, around ages four and five, which seems to be the time of Stephen's "Eagle" epiphany. The child at this stage develops a strong desire for genital contact with the parent of the opposite gender, desire that is forced out of consciousness by the fear of castration, bringing on years of latency (Freud 19: 174–76). In this scene from *Portrait* the oedipal content is naturally disguised, but Stephen is being punished for wanting to play the role of the father: "When they were grown up he was going to marry Eileen." That the minor relationship with Eileen serves as a screen for a deeper love for mother is suggested by its importance in establishing basic patterns for the novel. As Hélène Cixous points out, Stephen already practices here the silence, exile, and cunning that he will advocate later (278). He deals with his threat by turning it into poetry, focusing on the formal qualities of language, the common rhythm of "pull out his eyes" and "apologise."

Images of inadequacy pervade the following football scene: ". . . the greasy leather orb flew like a heavy bird. . . . He kept . . . out of the reach of the rude feet. . . . felt his body small and weak amid the throng . . . and his eyes were weak and watery" (p. 21). The inability to rise and the sense of smallness or weakness define a feeling of bodily negation that is based on genital negation. As the game goes on, Stephen remains "fearful of the [other boys'] flashing eyes and muddy boots" (p. 23). His dread of being unmanned or reduced to femininity makes him sensitive to suggestions of violence or homosexuality. Such a suggestion propels him into a mental flight along paths of association that lead to the main source of his comfort and object of his desire. One of Joyce's key innovations is to follow these paths by reproducing the movement of the mind beneath its superstructure of logic. The Joycean stream of consciousness often parallels Freud's free association:

> Cantwell had answered [to another boy]:
> . . . Give Cecil Thunder a belt. I'd like to see you. He'd give you a toe in the rump for yourself.
> That was not a nice expression. His mother had told him not to speak with the rough boys in the college. Nice mother! . . . when she had said goodbye she had put up her veil double to her nose to kiss him: and her nose and eyes were red. (p. 22)

The emotionally charged memory of the parting kiss, with its overtones of moist, pink exposure, is soon followed by escape into a revery of mother that expands and clarifies a prevailing contrast between a cold paternal threat and a warm maternal haven, using a hearth as womb:

> It would be nice to lie on the hearthrug before the fire . . . and think on those sentences. He shivered as if he had cold slimy water next his skin. That was mean of Wells to shoulder him into the square ditch. . . . Mother was sitting at the fire. . . . She had her feet on the fender and her jewelly slippers were so hot and they had such a lovely warm smell! (pp. 23–24)

The bully Wells embodies the threat visited on Stephen for thoughts of the "hearth" and so is called to mind by them. Wells initiates a series of father figures who knock Stephen down by degrading or dispossessing him in each chapter. The presentation of the mother in terms of feet and jewelly slippers is fetishistic. Freud says that the child's discovery that his mother does not have a penis is shocking because it suggests his own castration. This shock may lead to fetishism, in which a woman must bear a phallic symbol in order to be attractive (21: 152–57). Fetishism prevails in Joyce and defines gender roles as ambivalent by showing how woman wields phallic power.

A few pages later the masculine competition of Clongowes again forces Stephen to yearn for the womb: "He longed to . . . lay his head on his mother's lap" (pp. 25–26). Stephen is separated from the other boys by a sense of guilt that makes him feel threatened by them, and the source of this guilt is touched when Wells asks, "Tell us, Dedalus, do you kiss your mother every night before you go to bed?" (p. 26). This refers not to Stephen being at home with his mother but to an imaginary mother Stephen kisses in the present. Whether Stephen answers yes or no, Wells mocks him and the other boys laugh: "Stephen blushed under their eyes . . ." (p. 27). As Richard Wasson first pointed out, eyes, male or female, have phallic value throughout the novel, generally being either aggressive and piercing or defeated and downcast. The idea of kissing mother is given great weight here and seems to stand for more than kissing. Reminded of his guilt, Stephen is reduced to impotence and does "not dare to raise his eyes" (p. 27). He now punishes himself by reviewing the square ditch incident in detail, but then turns again from these unpleasant images to meditate on "motherkiss" in an abstract way that represses the feelings involved: "Was it right to kiss his mother or wrong to kiss his mother? . . . Why did people do that with their two faces?" (p. 27).

When the characteristic combination of longing for the mother and the resultant fear of castration next recurs, the womb again appears as a hearth, and the vagina is a half-door:

> . . . he had seen a woman standing at the halfdoor of a cottage with a child in her arms. . . . It would be lovely to sleep for one night in tat cottage before the fire of smoking turf, in the dark lit by the fire, in the warm dark. . . . But, O, the road there between the trees was dark! You would be lost in the dark. It made him afraid to think of how it was. (p. 30)

Stephen's fear of the dark is related to repressed patricidal impulses. He is preoccupied by the ghost of a mortally wounded marshal who is said to have haunted Clongowes. Stephen fears this image but is fascinated by it. Its appeal as an image of wounded, mature, male authority is confirmed by the long dream he has immediately after brooding on the marshal. This is the dream's climax: "Welcome home, Stephen! . . . His mother kissed him. Was that right? His father was a marshal now: higher than a magistrate" (p. 32). Evert Sprinchorn points out that while Stephen seems to be doing his father a favor by making him a marshal, the latent content involves killing him because the marshal is associated with death (Sprinchorn 17–18). This is the oedipal combination of loving mother and killing father, and Stephen's dream of a ship bearing Parnell's body may also evoke patricide (p. 37). But more prominent in Stephen's experience is a pattern in which attacking the father is transformed by guilt into fear of being injured by him.

Stephen's anxiety may be reflected in the illness he develops in this part of the novel, for he feels that he is "sick in his heart" (p. 26). The prospect of the infirmary appeals to Stephen because there he can be safely alone with a book (p. 37). Because his mind generates the paternal threat whenever it approaches the maternal goal, Stephen cannot sustain the active male role. Such an emphasis on the inseparability of satisfaction from guilt is linked by Freud to compulsion neurosis. Compulsives tend to forgo action in favor of controlling and rationalizing their feelings. They focus on language as a controllable substitute for reality; and they regress from the genital to the anal stage, which is bisexual or ambivalent (Freud 20: 113–23). The pattern is illustrated in *Portrait* by a math competition in which Stephen stops competing when he hears the voice of the father: ". . . he worked at the next sum and heard Father Arnall's voice. Then all his eagerness passed away and he felt his face quite cool" (p. 25). Stephen gives up the real rose of victory and starts theorizing about imaginary roses in aesthetic colors. The roots of his art and intellectual life lie in defenses against conflict.

The compulsive seesaw brings out sexual ambivalence, and indeed Stephen enacts Freud's idea that all people contain both genders. His anxiety about homosexuality is strongly developed as he meditates on the word *suck*, which is linked here to the terms *cock* and *queer,* and to the ambivalence of "cold and hot": all of these terms get repeated within a page (p. 24). An indication of why Stephen has difficulty claiming manhood appears in the Christmas dinner scene, where he sees his father's manhood broken: "Stephen, raising his terrorstricken face, saw that his father's eyes were full of tears" (p. 48). The destruction of the father here is a product of colonialism and religion, which emasculate Simon Dedalus by cutting off his great leader, Parnell.

Following this breaking of the father, Stephen is intensely preoccupied with threats of male violence. We return to Stephen at school to find that a "sprinter" has knocked him down and broken his glasses, putting his eyes out of commission (pp. 49–50). Now his mind dwells on a mysterious crime he hears called "smugging," and although he doesn't seem to realize the fact, the term refers to homosexual petting. Smugging leads to thoughts of flogging:

> And though he trembled with cold and fright to think of [Mr. Gleeson's] cruel long nails and of the high whistling sound of the cane and of the chill you felt at the end of your shirt when you undressed yourself yet he felt a feeling of queer quiet pleasure inside him to think of the white fattish hands, clean and strong and gentle. (p. 53)

Stephen's mind swarms with unconsciously perverse fantasies for a time, but when he is finally beaten by Father Dolan, he experiences the pandying as a terrifyingly direct breakage: "A hot burning stinging tingling blow like the loud crack of a broken stick made his trembling hand crumple together like a leaf in the fire . . ." (p. 57). The acuteness of the sense of castration involved in the actual experience negates the pleasurable aspect of the fantasies and causes a reaction against the idea of submission. The pandying aggravates anxieties instead of placating them.

Stephen now affirms his manhood by striking out from his peers and going to the rector. In doing so, he uses literary sources (making reference, for instance, to heroes of antiquity [p. 60]) to overcome a system that Joyce saw as designed to break his manhood by abusing him within an all-male environment. His trip to the rector's office, as an assertion of masculinity, is described repeatedly as an entrance into the female: ". . . he would be in the low dark narrow corridor that led . . . to the rector's room . . . had entered the low dark narrow corridor . . . passed along the narrow dark corridor . . ." (p. 60). After this channel, Stephen passes through a pair of doors to be hailed by the rector as "my little man" (p. 62). The chapter ends in victory for his masculinity, but he is disillusioned when he finds at the beginning of the second chapter that his father and the rector were amused by his protest (p. 75). His compulsive alternation of submission and assertion will continue.

The first chapter establishes a fundamental model for all of *Portrait* and, with modification, for *Ulysses*. The desire for mother is clear here and the paternal threat is physical. Later, these elements grow sublimated and disguised as the original sources of Stephen's attitudes are denied and isolated from feeling. Yet a longing for a distant mother and a causally related fear of a father remain as the ground plan for all of Stephen's experience.

When the threat of the church fathers grew intolerable in chapter one, Stephen diverged in a new direction. In the second chapter the masculine threat is represented paradoxically by the collapse of Stephen's actual father, whose failure and aging are emphasized throughout: "There's a crack of the whip left in me yet, Stephen, old chap, said Mr Dedalus, poking at the dull fire with fierce energy. We're not dead yet . . ." (p. 70). This paternal defeat stirs guilt and anxiety in Stephen. He now wanders around Blackrock, repeating the divergence of the first chapter:

> . . . he was different from others. He did not want to play. He wanted to meet in the real world the unsubstantial image which his soul so constantly beheld. He did not know where to seek it or how: but a premonition . . . told him that this image would, without any overt act of his, encounter him. They would meet quietly as if they had known each other and had made their tryst, perhaps

at one of the gates or in some more secret place. They would be alone, surrounded by darkness and silence: and in that moment of supreme tenderness he would be transfigured. . . . Weakness and timidity and inexperience would fall from him in that magic moment. (p. 69)

He does "not know where to seek" this "unsubstantial image," and on the next page, when he has moved to Dublin, "a vague dissatisfaction" has grown in him and he continues "to wander up and down day after day as if he really sought someone that eluded him" (p. 70). If this does not seem odd, it may be because all adolescents are subject to such vague longings; but it is absurd to yearn for something without knowing what one yearns for. Psychoanalysis explains that the object of such desire is repressed. But if Stephen does not know what he seeks, he indicates by details the nature of this object. He will meet it "perhaps at one of the gates or in some more secret place . . . surrounded by darkness." This associates his image with the womb, and he associates it too with tenderness and security. He also says, "They would meet quietly as if they had known each other. . . ," and later, when he feels tempted by E—— C——, he thinks, "He heard what her eyes said to him . . . and knew that in some dim past, whether in life or in revery, he had heard their tale before" (p. 73). Freud's theory shows us why Stephen projects his complex onto the girl. Both in his vague state of "unsubstantial" desire and in the later stage in which he focuses on E—— C——, he senses that the object of desire is one with which he has somehow been familiar for a long time, one he knew in the "dim past." It is his mother. But the idea of mother has now been sublimated into a spiritual ideal associated with transfiguration. Stephen soon finds that his mind wants to pursue "intangible phantoms," but the voices of his father, his masters, and his (male) peers interrupt this pursuit to urge him to accept responsibility (p. 85). Mother fixation has now become intellectual opposition to the norms of society and the expected roles of son and man.

Stephen's interest in Emma Clery is a more concrete aspect of his now-splintered pursuit of his mother. He is first drawn to Emma immediately after an epiphany in which he is mistaken for a woman (p. 72), showing that he asserts his masculinity primarily in order to deny his femininity. His scene with Emma on the tram emphasizes his sense of having known her before: seeing her temptations, he "knew that he had yielded to them a thousand times" (p. 73). He wants to "catch hold" of her and believes she wants him to, yet he stands "listlessly in his place, seemingly a tranquil watcher of the scene before him" (p. 73). His unexplained passivity suggests not only the artist's stance, but the relation of son to mother, with its powerful inhibition. For Stephen, the artist's stance *is* the relation of son to mother. Nothing of E——— C——— is described but her clothing and her eyes; these details represent her fetishistically, but they also serve another function. By reducing Emma to eyes and apparel, just as he also abstracts her name, Stephen eliminates her body and thus spiritualizes her. Though he regards her as a calculating temptress, he cannot touch her; and when he writes a poem about her, it is set between Jesuit mottoes and colored by "the maiden lustre of the moon" (p. 74). The poem concludes with a parting kiss — a prominent image in chapter one — and after writing it, Stephen gazes at his face in the mirror of his mother's dressing table. In Lacanian terms, this is the mirror of his mother (see *Écrits* 3–7).

The two aspects of woman as temptress and virgin, a commonplace of Joycean criticism, are evident here. We can understand this Joycean dichotomy through Freud's essay "On the Universal Tendency to Debasement in the Sphere of Love" (11: 177–90). Here Freud describes how many boys cultivate ideal, desexualized visions of their mothers. A boy reaches adolescence hearing that sex is nasty and refusing to admit that his mother engages in it. As a man, he separates women into two types, one of which is idealized and loved but cannot be defiled by sex, while the other is sexually approachable but can never be respected. Stephen sees both sides in Emma, but the idealizing tendency is clearly dominant, for it dictates his actions to her, while the temptress finds expression only in his fantasies.

In chapter two, as the Dedaluses move to poorer quarters and adolescence advances, Stephen repeatedly feels disturbed by a conjunction of tides of filth inside and outside him (pp. 68, 71, 91). Unconsciously blaming the external disorder on his dirty thoughts, he strives to control "the squalor of his own mind and home" (p. 81). But the compulsive "breakwater of order" that he has erected "against the sordid tide" (p. 97) is finally overwhelmed, and he is driven to seek release in vice. Joyce emphasizes Stephen's feminine relation to paternal power by imaging the desire that drives him to lose his virginity as an incubus that penetrates his body (p. 98).

At the end of the second chapter Stephen finds his transfiguration in the maternal arms of a prostitute. He wants to be "held firmly" and "caressed slowly": "In her arms he felt that he had suddenly become

strong and fearless and sure of himself" (p. 99).[4] But as he achieves contact with the mother through prostitution in the third chapter, the paternal threat arises, and soon Stephen feels himself pierced by the phallic
force of the words of Father Arnall: "The preacher's knife had probed
deeply into his diseased conscience . . ." (p. 110); "The thought slid
like a cold shining rapier into his tender flesh: confession" (p. 119). As he
wandered then in search of a prostitute, Stephen now wanders in search
of a confessional, and he seeks the sheltering arms of the Virgin whose
name is that of his mother. But in his religious life in chapter four, he
comes to feel threatened because the submissive attitude he adopts
toward God the Father is felt as a reduction to femininity. This threat is
indicated by repeated references to Stephen's soul (*anima*) as female:
"His soul sank . . . into depths of contrite peace . . . sending forth, as
she sank, a faint prayer" (p. 118); ". . . his soul took up again her burden of pieties . . . humiliated and faint before her Creator" (p. 138).

Freud described parallels between the rituals practiced by compulsives and those of religion (9: 115–28); and during his religious phase,
Stephen focuses on ascetic rituals that help to control his feelings. He is
having difficulty maintaining this retentive control when his interview
with the Jesuit director brings matters to a head. The looped cord of
the blind that the director dangles before Stephen represents hanging
and also castration. *Les jupes,* the skirts worn by Capuchins that the
director mentions to test Stephen (p. 142), suggest that the priestly
role offered to Stephen here is feminine.

Having left the church, Stephen wanders once more, once more
uncertain about what he seeks: "He had refused. Why? He turned seaward . . ." (p. 150). What he is looking for is indicated by the value
he places on words: "He drew forth a phrase from his treasure . . ."
(p. 151). What is this value?

> . . . was it that, being as weak of sight as he was shy of mind, he
> drew less pleasure from the reflection of the glowing sensible world
> through the prism of a language manycoloured and richly storied
> than from the contemplation of an inner world of individual
> emotions mirrored perfectly in a lucid supple periodic prose?
> (pp. 151–52)

He indicates here that his use of words is subjective, that he writes
primarily to mirror the inner world; but the statement is expressed in

---

[4]As I wrote in 1980, "It is because heterosexuality is a reaction to homosexuality in
our artist that it is held so intensely" (47).

language that is circuitous and distorted. The subordination of the important but vague "shy of mind" to the less important "weak of sight," the fancy, indistinct adjectives, and the general emphasis on sound over sense tend to obscure the meaning of the words. This language is typical of the beach scene and of what is called the "purple prose" of *Portrait*. This sort of writing represents strong ideas and emotions so ornately that they are submerged by virtuosity, and in the following chapter Stephen constructs an aesthetic theory that, among other things, serves to deny that he uses art to express his emotions.[5]

The "treasure" image shows that Stephen is now compulsively accumulating words, as he accumulated penances at the start of this chapter, or money for vice at the start of the previous one. His words express desire and aggression without exposing him to action. In chapter two, when Simon boasts that he is stronger and more of a man than Stephen, a friend of Simon's, "tapping his forehead," says, "But he'll beat you here" (p. 94). Soon after this, Stephen uses money he wins by his writing to temporarily take over his family, dumbfounding his father (p. 96). Words are Stephen's major weapon, and he frequently uses the "rapier point of his sensitiveness" (p. 170) to thrust and parry in the dialogues of the final chapter.

On the beach, Stephen's sense of the power of art inspires a vision of Daedalus aflight. Freud says in his study of da Vinci, which Joyce bought around the time it came out in 1910 (Ellmann 54), that the common dream image of flying usually represents erection and phallic sexuality. Here the image is spiritualized and dissociated from its physical basis: "His soul was soaring in an air beyond the world and the body he knew was purified in a breath and delivered of incertitude and made radiant and commingled with the element of the spirit" (pp. 153–54). This description parallels Stephen's earlier adolescent sexual longings: "He would fade into something impalpable under her eyes and then, in a moment, he would be transfigured. Weakness and timidity and inexperience would fall from him . . ." (p. 69). This passage is echoed when Stephen meets the prostitute (pp. 98–99), and at his conversion, when his soul is raised and made fair and holy. These recurrent transfigurations are all based on a lost original dream of union with mother. And they repeat the material image of being changed by her.

Stephen pursues his phantom of transcendence through many fields: schoolwork, rebellion, debauchery, religion, and now words. Whenever he

---

[5]The emotional level of *Portrait* was recently brought out by Christine van Boheemen-Saaf (42–73) in terms of Stephen's trauma at being colonized.

settles in an area close to some maternal surrogate, senses of dissatisfaction and emasculation arise linked to a father figure in league with established authority. This threat forces him to wander off, expanding his horizons, in search of a new goal. Each chapter ends with a triumphant sense of uplift as he finds his goal, which is portrayed with an image of nurture, either maternal or oral. But soon this new goal begins to disappoint and to evoke the paternal threat in the following chapter. Parallel form in the chapters of *Portrait* was first pointed out by Hugh Kenner (129), but psychoanalysis allows us to diagram this structure in greater causal detail (Table 1). The first stage at the top of this diagram in all five chapters refers to a new world that will soon be superseded. In each chapter, Stephen has his eyes on a definite maternal goal that motivates him in an economy of saving up units that are meant to bring him closer to "her." I have already referred to treasures saved up. . . . Early in chapter one, his mind returns to counting the days before Christmas break (pp. 23, 29). His eagerness is remarkable here, for the number of days is seventy-six! In chapter two, the business of "saving up" involves that of chronicling short scenes of everyday life that end focused on a mysterious significance. In *Stephen Hero,* such scenes are called epiphanies (Anderson 286–89). The first three all start with "He was sitting" and all lead toward the image of woman (pp. 71–72). This goal also involves replacing his father — as the Count of Monte Cristo takes on in effect the role of God — a Byronic act both revolutionary and demonic. The saving up aims at realizing oneself through uniting with one's mother by becoming one's own father — both acts being Satanic and impossible.

The theories Stephen saves up in chapter five depend on the talent for abstraction that the Church developed in him in chapter four, as well as on a new interest in subverting scholastic texts. This indicates how each phase contributes to the next one even though they contradict each other. After he is shaken loose from his prior mother by the paternal reality principle, he enters a world of naturalistic disorder, the mother's body without form. When he realizes his new idea of mother as freedom at the end, he reconsolidates his focus onto images that are microscopically close, intensely desired.

There is more than one way to read the table, and I will sketch an opposition between two of its main aspects. In the Freudian terms on which I have based it, the diagram emphasizes how the pattern of Stephen's experience repeats. Otto Fenichel says of compulsives, "The patients enter an ever-growing cycle: remorse, penitence, new transgressions, new remorse" (294). Stephen can develop significantly insofar as

Table 1. Cyclical Structure of *A Portrait*

	Chapter I	*Chapter II*	*Chapter III*	*Chapter IV*	*Chapter V*
New world	School	Family homes	Nighttown	Church	College
Saving up	Days, spoken words	Epiphanies	Money for sex	Grace	Theories, written words
Maternal goal	Mother (and alma mater)	E—— C—— as ideal	Prostitutes	Virgin	Irish muse
Paternal threat	Wells and Dolan	Heron and father's collapse	Arnall's sermon	Director's offer	Cranly (as conventional Ireland)
Wandering	To rector	To whore	To confession	To beach	To Europe
Disorder	Shock of beating	Maze of streets	Maze of streets	Naked bathers	Dublin decay
Triumph	Lifted by boys	Kiss	Eucharist	Vocation	Flight
Micro focus	Drops of water	Lips	Ciborium	Eyelids (p. 156)	Diary
Nursing image	"the brimming bowl" (p. 65)	Kiss	Taking wafer	"the earth that had borne him . . . to her breast" (p. 156)	"The white arms of roads, their promise of close embraces" (p. 223)

he recognizes and accepts this cycle, and doing so is a sort of self-analysis. But there is another element in his development, which is indicated on the beach when he thinks, "The end he had been born to serve yet did not see had led him to escape by an unseen path . . ." (p. 150). Once Stephen assumes that he is destined to be an artist, all of his alienation and conflict turn out to serve a positive purpose. This destiny is not a fact, but a myth generated by Stephen's neurotic need. His belief in it, however, is powerfully productive, and this is why Jung's theories of the spiritual power of the unconscious have a place. In mythic terms, each chapter involves a ritual sacrifice, and from each death Stephen is reborn stronger, with a more ambitious aim, and freed from his compulsions. A Lacanian view of the diagram might see Stephen as identifying with a certain signifier or definite identity at the start of each chapter and growing aware of an otherness outside this role as the chapter proceeds. The threat that arises in the middle of the chapter defines the limits of his perception. And the wandering that this authorial reality principle drives him into leads him toward new connections that form a new signifier with an enhanced sense of reality; but this reality is a changing one that consists of a chain of signifiers rather than any point in the network. The source of growth, as with Freud, is seeing the structure.[6] Lacan says that the effects of the spirit may be produced by the letter (150), and the expansion of Stephen's subject can be linguistically described without Jung's mythology. Stephen's positive development should be recognized, for we cannot rule out the possibility that he may be the artist as a young man on his way to conquering for Ireland the literary world of the twentieth century. His focus on his weakness allows him to spiral toward a breathtaking scope.

On the beach, Stephen tells himself that he has risen from the repressive "grave of boyhood" and that he will create out of freedom (p. 154). He uses the birdlike girl he sees to project his new freedom of seeing reality without idealizing or condemning it, for he claims that her beauty is "without shame or wantonness" (p. 155). Nevertheless, details of her appearance suggest that in fact she is *not* without shame, for "a faint flame trembled on her cheek," and she can hardly be "without wantonness" if at the turn of the century her "skirts were kilted boldly about her waist" (p. 155).[7] Stephen's myth of transcendence is

---

[6]For a Lacanian reading of this diagram, see my *Veil of Signs* 37–60.

[7]Thomas Flanagan has suggested in conversation that the girl's position and the "noise of gently moving water" that issues from her probably indicate that she is urinating. The stream of her urine could constitute a phallic symbol and so add to the fetishism of the scene.

not an escape from his neurosis but a product of it, and his parental attachments and anxieties return in the fifth chapter. His fantasies of transcendence are contained in a framework that shows them to be illusions, but without them Stephen could not build his vision. The presence of both opposing vectors in the diagram, repetition and transcendence, is what allows the structure to embody the vitality of Stephen's mind.

Inspired by his vision on the beach, Stephen devotes himself to art and begins to formulate his system of aesthetics. These theories fashion art into a means of protection and a means of escape from entrapment by the past and by crippling fixations. Stephen is anxious to prove that art can be isolated from intense personal feelings. To this compulsive end he seizes on Aquinas's statement that art satisfies the mind, not the body, and expands it into his idea of stasis. The statement that in art "the mind is arrested and raised above desire and loathing" (p. 183) has some truth, although as Lynch suggests there may be exceptions. But Stephen's explanation of this stasis is false. He claims that art operates on an entirely different level from kinetic emotions:

> Our flesh shrinks from what it dreads and responds to . . . what it desires by a purely reflex action of the nervous system. . . . [But] Beauty expressed by the artist cannot awaken in us an emotion which is kinetic or a sensation which is purely physical. It awakens . . . an esthetic stasis, an ideal pity or an ideal terror, a stasis called forth, prolonged and at last dissolved by what I call the rhythm of beauty. (p. 184)

It is not true that desire and loathing are purely physical reflexes. Stephen is trying to divide mental activity, which mixes reason with feeling, into two exclusive levels. Even as he does so, however, his ideas are dictated by his desires, for he is trying to build an intellectual edifice to shelter him from neurotic anxiety, an art to fulfill a maternal function.

Nor is it true that art "cannot awaken . . . an emotion which is kinetic": there is no such thing as nonkinetic emotion, only emotion whose kinesis is relatively weak or indirect. Art is built on the same drives, conscious and unconscious, that operate in life. But in art these drives are so manipulated by sublimation, construction, and disguise that the reader who participates in the feelings involved controls tension and achieves gratification (Lesser 59–144). The peace of stasis is arrived at by balancing opposed psychic forces in a pleasing way. If this balance is not achieved and drives obtrude in such a way that they violate truth, morality, or some other function of psychic balance, the work is dismissed as pornographic or didactic, cheap or prohibitive, untrue or unhealthy. *Portrait* appeals to people partly by enacting the conflicts of youth, and the stasis it achieves is suspended in a balance between desire of mother and fear of father, between ideal and reality — a stasis of conflict between opposing values. In fact, much of the power of *Portrait* comes from what is not resolved, what continues to question itself. Balance is there to be unbalanced.

Stephen senses the dynamic nature of this stasis when he speaks of "the rhythm of beauty." And although his explanation of beauty in terms of three stages of perception — wholeness, harmony, and radiance — elevates formal considerations at the expense of content, it does focus on a process of interaction with the object. Formalistic as it is, Stephen's aesthetics still contains hints that for him art is fundamentally a sexual activity. The object he uses as his main example in discussion with Lynch is a beautiful woman; and the final stage of apprehension — *claritas,* or radiance — is described as a luminous state of mind like a fading coal (p. 190). This description suggests orgasm, which Joyce represents through fading fireworks in the "Nausicaa" episode of *Ulysses.* The phases following this aesthetic consummation are described as "artistic conception, artistic gestation and artistic reproduction" (p. 187). I surmise that on an important level the sexual union involved in Stephen's idea of art is union with mother. The villanelle he composes in the following section is addressed to a female figure who seems to be E—— C——. But she combines elements of the Blessed Virgin with the idea of the temptress, and her heart is "wilful from before the beginning of the world" (p. 193). She was there before he was, and these are signs of Stephen's maternal fixation.

When the villanelle concludes, *"Are you not weary of ardent ways? / Tell no more of enchanted days"* (p. 193), it is calling on women to give up their traditional role of temptress and free themselves to face reality. Stephen's art, like Joyce's, aims primarily at a female audience. He strives to influence the "daughters" of Ireland to "breed a race less ignoble" (p. 211). Here he feels that effects that seem genetic can be transformed through art primarily by transforming women. He assumes that women are more transformable than men, and this may lead him to resent women who take a definite stance, which he sees as their subservience to the paternal principle. His progressive critique of women is hard to separate from the fear of them described by Suzette Henke in her essay in this volume (see pp. 317–36).

While Stephen is preparing to strive for union through art with an idealization of the mother, in the last third of the novel he is renouncing his real mother and her surrogates in life. In chapter four he begins to have a growing feeling that his mother is betraying him by her devotion to the Church: "A dim antagonism . . . darkened his mind as a cloud against her disloyalty: and when it passed . . . he was made aware dimly and without regret of a first noiseless sundering of their lives" (p. 150). Stephen's "dim" feeling that his mother has betrayed him follows what Freud sees as a universal tendency of adolescents to blame their mothers for infidelity because their mothers have given themselves to their fathers (11: 165–75).

Stephen's vision of a defiled, treacherous mother expands in the last chapter to include all of Ireland. He thinks of his country as a "venal" woman who has given herself over to domination by England and Rome. He sees images of decay and corruption all about him as he walks the streets "amid heaps of wet rubbish . . . stumbling through the mouldering offal" (p. 158). Whether he looks at his class or out the window, "an odour assailed him of cheerless cellardamp and decay" (p. 160). A lane is filled with "heaps of dead language" (p. 161), and "sloth of the body and of the soul" creeps over a statue of Thomas Moore "like unseen vermin" (p. 162). In Stephen's nostrils the soul of Dublin "had shrunk with time to a faint mortal odour rising from the earth and he knew that in a moment when he entered the sombre college he would be conscious of a corruption . . ." (p. 166).

Likewise he dwells on thoughts of morally questionable women, such as a flower girl whom he sees as selling not only her blue flowers but her blue eyes (p. 165) and a factory girl who calls to him (p. 196). Stephen sees the peasant woman who offered herself to his friend Davin as "a type of her race and his own, a batlike soul waking to the consciousness of itself in darkness and secrecy . . . a woman without guile, calling the stranger to her bed" (p. 165). Irish womanhood gives itself away because the Irish "allowed a handful of foreigners to subject them" (p. 181).

Stephen's obsession with the idea of the unfaithful mother assimilates E—— C——, whom he links to two father figures, Father Moran and Cranly. When Cranly is angry, Stephen sees his anger as a sign that he is thinking of Emma (pp. 205–06), and when Cranly's anger goes away, Stephen again believes he is thinking of her (p. 211). No matter what the evidence, Stephen will put the woman he loves in the position of his mother by finding her attached to another man. Cranly's recommendation that Stephen compromise is quite reasonable and considerate, which is why it represents the ultimate threat that would cut

Stephen off from development by keeping him from disaster. Cranly's very attractiveness and considerateness make Stephen see him as bound to take Emma away (p. 217), thus confirming his own decision to leave.

With friendship as with love, Stephen cannot approach satisfaction without feeling a threat. The compulsive link between gratification and anxiety makes Stephen a wanderer endlessly compelled to shift toward new goals. This pattern is powerful in Joyce's work, in which each book not only differs in form from every other one but also changes its nature and increases in complexity between its inception and its conclusion. Stephen's neurosis here feeds his creativity, as it does through his compulsive preoccupation with words. At each stage of the structure of *Portrait*, Stephen could not make progress if he did not entrap himself.

In chapter five Stephen blames or projects his problems onto Irish society. One must be alienated to attack one's own world, and Stephen could not criticize his society so strongly if he did not have a transcendent aim and a psychosexual motivation. Joyce insists on the transcendent and sexual elements in the book's structure because he believes that the idea that one can criticize society objectively is the most dangerous delusion. In Stephen's debates with the radical MacCann, the nationalist Davin, and the conformist Cranly, Joyce allows Stephen's opponents to be partly right so that Stephen knows he cannot be sure of his position, which is dialogical in the sense of being suspended between living alternatives.

Those who dismiss Stephen for having the wrong ideology overlook his irony about himself and his involvement in change (as well as the deadness of a character with correct ideology). Far from validating his own views, Stephen, who denies his own Shakespeare theory in *Ulysses*, sees his thinking as "a dusk of doubt and selfmistrust" (*Portrait* p. 159) and recognizes that "his mind bred vermin" (p. 207). He repeatedly retracts his condemnation of E—— C—— for her conventionality (pp. 197, 207, 223), having a strong realization within a page of the end that he has been all wrong about her. This climactic denial of sexism is especially penetrating because Stephen realizes that his whole history of attitudes toward women has been imposed on him: "I liked her and it seems a new feeling to me. Then, in that case. All the rest, all that I thought I thought and all that I felt I felt, all the rest before now, in fact . . . O, give it up, old chap!" (p. 223). Earlier it had occurred to him that a debased fantasy he had about Emma "was not even the way in which he thought of her" (p. 207); and now he sees that his thoughts about women were not his thoughts, that his misogyny is something alien and phantasmatic that has been implanted in him by a pernicious social order.

Stephen's commitment "to live, to err, to fall, to triumph, to recreate life out of life!" (p. 156) makes him aware that any position he takes is only a stage in a process of reversals. From the 1904 sketch "A Portrait of the Artist," Joyce conceived of his portrait as "the development of an entity of which our actual present is a phase only . . . individuating rhythm . . . not an identificative paper but rather the curve of an emotion" (Anderson 257–58). This rhythmic curve, reflected in my diagram, indicates that Stephen's personality consists of ongoing opposition. He senses the cycle of his life well enough to suspect that his triumph at the end, as he sets out to encounter reality "for the millionth time" (p. 224), must be followed by a fall; and having passed through childhood, vice, and religion before art, he knows his views must change radically. It is by seeing how he repeats that he prepares for change.

Stephen has a powerful relationship to history. Although he is a socialist, he knows that joining a contemporary Irish leftist movement will endanger his life while yet leaving him under the dominance of the church. He correctly realizes that by far the most valuable historical role he can play is "to forge in the smithy of my soul the uncreated conscience of my race" (p. 224). He aims to re-form human consciousness by bringing a new awareness of the mind through self-exploration. He succeeds to the extent that *Portrait* — together with Lawrence's *The Rainbow* (chapter 11), also written in 1915 — vividly establishes the idea that every person is entitled to define his or her self apart from church, state, and family (p. 182). Once this idea has spread, with *Portrait* inspiring writers as diverse as Ralph Ellison and Yukio Mishima, human freedom has advanced in a way that may be critical and lasting.

WORKS CITED

Anderson, Chester G., ed. *James Joyce, "A Portrait of the Artist as a Young Man": Text, Criticism, and Notes.* New York: Viking, 1968.

Boheemen-Saaf, Christine. *Joyce, Derrida, Lacan, and the Trauma of History: Reading, Narrative, and Postcolonialism.* Cambridge: Cambridge UP, 1999.

Brivic, Sheldon R. *Joyce between Freud and Jung.* Port Washington, NY, and London: Kennikat, 1980.

————. *The Veil of Signs: Joyce, Lacan, and Perception.* Urbana: U of Illinois P, 1991.

Cixous, Hélène. *The Exile of James Joyce.* Trans. Sally A. J. Purcell. New York: David Lewis, 1972.

Ellmann, Richard. *The Consciousness of Joyce.* New York: Oxford UP, 1977.

Fenichel, Otto. *The Psychoanalytic Theory of Neurosis.* New York: Norton, 1945.

Freud, Sigmund. *The Standard Edition of the Complete Psychological Works of Sigmund Freud.* Ed. James Strachey. 24 vols. London: Hogarth, 1953–74.

Gabler, Hans Walter. "The Seven Lost Years of *A Portrait . . .*" *Approaches to Joyce's "Portrait": Ten Essays.* Ed. Thomas F. Staley and Bernard Benstock. Pittsburgh: U of Pittsburgh P, 1976.

Joyce, James. *Finnegans Wake.* New York: Penguin, 1999.

Kenner, Hugh. *Dublin's Joyce.* Boston: Beacon, 1962.

Lacan, Jacques. *Écrits: A Selection.* Trans. Bruce Fink in collaboration with Heloise Fink and Russell Grigg. New York: Norton, 2002.

Lesser, Simon O. *Fiction and the Unconscious.* New York: Vintage, 1962.

Sprinchorn, Evert. "A Portrait of the Artist as Achilles." *Approaches to the Twentieth-Century Novel.* Ed. John E. Unterecker. New York: Crowell, 1965.

Wasson, Richard. "Stephen Dedalus and the Imagery of Sight: A Psychological Approach." *Literature and Psychology* 15 (1965): 195–209.

Feminist Criticism
and
A Portrait of the Artist
as a Young Man

WHAT IS FEMINIST CRITICISM?

Feminist criticism comes in many forms, and feminist critics have a variety of goals. Some have been interested in rediscovering the works of women writers overlooked by a masculine-dominated culture. Others have revisited books by male authors and reviewed them from a woman's point of view to understand how they both reflect and shape the attitudes that have held women back. A number of contemporary feminists have turned to topics as various as women in postcolonial societies, women's autobiographical writings, lesbians and literature, womanliness as masquerade, and the role of film and other popular media in the construction of the feminine gender.

Until a few years ago, however, feminist thought tended to be classified not according to topic but, rather, according to country of origin. This practice reflected the fact that, during the 1970s and early 1980s, French, American, and British feminists wrote from somewhat different perspectives.

French feminists tended to focus their attention on language, analyzing the ways in which meaning is produced. They concluded that language as we commonly think of it is a decidedly male realm. Drawing on the ideas of the psychoanalytic philosopher Jacques Lacan, they reminded us that language is a realm of public discourse. A child enters the linguistic realm just as it comes to grasp its separateness from its mother, just about the time that boys identify with their father, the family representative of culture. The language learned reflects a binary logic that opposes such terms as active/passive, masculine/feminine, sun/moon, father/mother, head/heart, son/daughter, intelligent/sensitive, brother/sister, form/matter, phallus/vagina, reason/emotion. Because this logic tends to group with masculinity such qualities as light, thought, and activity, French feminists said that the structure of language is phallocentric: it privileges the phallus and, more generally, masculinity by associating them with things and values more appreciated by the (masculine-dominated) culture. Moreover, French feminists suggested, "masculine desire dominates speech and posits woman as an idealized fantasy-fulfillment for the incurable emotional lack caused by separation from the mother" (Jones, "Inscribing" 83).

French feminists associated language with separation from the mother. Its distinctions, they argued, represent the world from the male point of view. Language systematically forces women to choose: either they can imagine and represent themselves as men imagine and represent them (in which case they may speak, but will speak as men) or they can choose "silence," becoming in the process "the invisible and unheard sex" (Jones, "Inscribing" 83).

But some influential French feminists maintained that language only *seems* to give women such a narrow range of choices. There is another possibility, namely, that women can develop a *feminine* language. In various ways, early French feminists such as Annie Leclerc, Xavière Gauthier, and Marguerite Duras suggested that there is something that may be called *l'écriture féminine:* women's writing. More recently, Julia Kristeva has said that feminine language is "semiotic," not "symbolic." Rather than rigidly opposing and ranking elements of reality, rather than symbolizing one thing but not another in terms of a third, feminine language is rhythmic and unifying. If from the male perspective it seems fluid to the point of being chaotic, that is a fault of the male perspective.

According to Kristeva, feminine language is derived from the preoedipal period of fusion between mother and child. Associated with the maternal, feminine language is not only a threat to culture, which is patriarchal, but also a medium through which women may be creative in new ways. But Kristeva paired her central, liberating claim — that truly feminist innovation in all fields requires an understanding of the relation between maternity and feminine creation — with a warning. A feminist language that refuses to participate in "masculine" discourse, that places its future entirely in a feminine, semiotic discourse, risks being politically marginalized by men. That is to say, it risks being relegated to the outskirts (pun intended) of what is considered socially and politically significant.

Kristeva, who associated feminine writing with the female body, was joined in her views by other leading French feminists. Hélène Cixous, for instance, also posited an essential connection between the woman's body, whose sexual pleasure has been repressed and denied expression, and women's writing. "Write your self. Your body must be heard," Cixous urged; once they learn to write their bodies, women will not only realize their sexuality but enter history and move toward a future based on a "feminine" economy of giving rather than the "masculine" economy of hoarding (Cixous 880). For Luce Irigaray, women's sexual pleasure (*jouissance*) cannot be expressed by the dominant, ordered, "logical," masculine language. Irigaray explored the connection between women's sexuality and women's language through the following analogy: as women's *jouissance* is more multiple than men's unitary, phallic pleasure ("woman has sex organs just about everywhere"), so "feminine" language is more diffusive than its "masculine" counterpart. ("That is undoubtedly the reason . . . her language . . . goes off in all directions and . . . he is unable to discern the coherence," Irigaray writes [*This Sex* 101–03].)

Cixous's and Irigaray's emphasis on feminine writing as an expression of the female body drew criticism from other French feminists. Many argued that an emphasis on the body either reduces "the feminine" to a biological essence or elevates it in a way that shifts the valuation of masculine and feminine but retains the binary categories. For Christine Fauré, Irigaray's celebration of women's difference failed to address the issue of masculine dominance, and a Marxist-feminist, Catherine Clément, warned that "poetic" descriptions of what constitutes the feminine will not challenge that dominance in the realm of production. The boys will still make the toys, and decide who gets to use them. In her effort to redefine women as political rather than as sexual beings, Monique Wittig called for the abolition of the sexual categories that Cixous and Irigaray retained and revalued as they celebrated women's writing.

American feminist critics of the 1970s and early 1980s shared with French critics both an interest in and a cautious distrust of the concept of feminine writing. Annette Kolodny, for instance, worried that the "richness and variety of women's writing" will be missed if we see in it only its "feminine mode" or "style" ("Some Notes" 78). And yet Kolodny herself proceeded, in the same essay, to point out that women *have* had their own style, which includes reflexive constructions ("she found herself crying") and particular, recurring themes (clothing and self-fashioning are mentioned by Kolodny; other American feminists have focused on madness, disease, and the demonic).

Interested as they became in the "French" subject of feminine style, American feminist critics began by analyzing literary texts rather than philosophizing abstractly about language. Many reviewed the great works by male writers, embarking on a revisionist rereading of literary tradition. These critics examined the portrayals of women characters, exposing the patriarchal ideology implicit in such works and showing how clearly this tradition of systematic masculine dominance is inscribed in our literary tradition. Kate Millett, Carolyn Heilbrun, and Judith Fetterley, among many others, created this model for American feminist criticism, a model that Elaine Showalter came to call "the feminist critique" of "male-constructed literary history" ("Poetics" 128).

Meanwhile another group of critics including Sandra Gilbert, Susan Gubar, Patricia Meyer Spacks, and Showalter herself created a somewhat different model. Whereas feminists writing "feminist critique" analyzed works by men, practitioners of what Showalter used to refer to as "gynocriticism" studied the writings of those women who, against all odds, produced what she calls "a literature of their own." In *The Female Imagination* (1975), Spacks examined the female literary tradition to find out how great women writers across the ages have felt, perceived themselves, and imagined reality. Gilbert and Gubar, in *The Madwoman in the Attic* (1979), concerned themselves with well-known women writers of the nineteenth century, but they too found that general concerns, images, and themes recur, because the authors that they wrote about lived "in a culture whose fundamental definitions of literary authority" were "both overtly and covertly patriarchal" (45–46).

If one of the purposes of gynocriticism was to (re)study well-known women authors, another was to rediscover women's history and culture, particularly women's communities that nurtured female creativity. Still another related purpose was to discover neglected or forgotten women writers and thus to forge an alternative literary tradition, a canon that better represents the female perspective by better representing the literary works that have been written by women. Showalter, in *A Literature of Their Own* (1977), admirably began to fulfill this purpose, providing a remarkably comprehensive overview of women's writing through three of its phases. She defined these as the "Feminine,

Feminist, and Female" phases, phases during which women first imitated a masculine tradition (1840–80), then protested against its standards and values (1880–1920), and finally advocated their own autonomous, female perspective (1920 to the present).

With the recovery of a body of women's texts, attention returned to a question raised in 1978 by Lillian Robinson: Shouldn't feminist criticism need to formulate a theory of its own practice? Won't reliance on theoretical assumptions, categories, and strategies developed by men and associated with nonfeminist schools of thought prevent feminism from being accepted as equivalent to these other critical discourses? Not all American feminists came to believe that a special or unifying theory of feminist practice was urgently needed; Showalter's historical approach to women's culture allowed a feminist critic to use theories based on nonfeminist disciplines. Kolodny advocated a "playful pluralism" that encompasses a variety of critical schools and methods. But Jane Marcus and others responded that if feminists adopt too wide a range of approaches, they may relax the tensions between feminists and the educational establishment necessary for political activism.

The question of whether feminism weakens or fortifies itself by emphasizing its separateness — and by developing unity through separateness — was one of several areas of debate within American feminism during the 1970s and early 1980s. Another area of disagreement touched on earlier, between feminists who stress universal feminine attributes (the feminine imagination, feminine writing) and those who focus on the political conditions experienced by certain groups of women at certain times in history, paralleled a larger distinction between American feminist critics and their British counterparts.

While it gradually became customary to refer to an Anglo-American tradition of feminist criticism, British feminists tended to distinguish themselves from what they saw as an American overemphasis on texts linking women across boundaries and decades and an underemphasis on popular art and culture. They regarded their own critical practice as more political than that of North American feminists, whom they sometimes faulted for being uninterested in historical detail. They joined such American critics as Myra Jehlen in suggesting that a continuing preoccupation with women writers may bring about the dangerous result of placing women's texts outside the history that conditions them.

British feminists felt that the American opposition to male stereotypes that denigrate women often leads to counterstereotypes of feminine virtue that ignore real differences of race, class, and culture among women. In addition, they argued that American celebrations of individual heroines falsely suggest that powerful individuals may be immune to repressive conditions and may even imply that *any* individual can go through life unconditioned by the culture and ideology in which she or he lives.

Similarly, the American endeavor to recover women's history — for example, by emphasizing that women developed their own strategies to gain power within their sphere — was seen by British feminists like Judith Newton and Deborah Rosenfelt as an endeavor that "mystifies" male oppression, disguising it as something that has created for women a special world of opportunities. More important from the British standpoint, the universalizing and "essentializing" tendencies in both American practice and French theory disguise women's oppression by highlighting sexual difference, suggesting that a dominant system is impervious to political change. By contrast, British feminist theory emphasized an engagement with historical process in order to promote social change.

By now the French, American, and British approaches have so thoroughly critiqued, influenced, and assimilated one another that the work of most Western practitioners is no longer easily identifiable along national boundary lines. Instead, it tends to be characterized according to whether the category of *woman* is the major focus in the exploration of gender and gender oppression or, alternatively, whether the interest in sexual difference encompasses an interest in other differences that also define identity. The latter paradigm encompasses the work of feminists of color, Third World (preferably called postcolonial) feminists, and lesbian feminists, many of whom have asked whether the universal category of woman constructed by certain French and North American predecessors is appropriate to describe women in minority groups or non-Western cultures.

These feminists stress that, while all women are female, they are something else as well (such as African American, lesbian, Muslim Pakistani). This "something else" is precisely what makes them, their problems, and their goals different from those of other women. As Armit Wilson has pointed out, Asian women living in Britain are expected by their families and communities to preserve Asian cultural traditions; thus, the expression of personal identity through clothing involves a much more serious infraction of cultural rules than it does for a Western woman. Gloria Anzaldúa has spoken personally and eloquently about the experience of many women on the margins of Eurocentric North

American culture. "I am a border woman," she writes in *Borderlands: La Frontera = The New Mestiza* (1987). "I grew up between two cultures, the Mexican (with a heavy Indian influence) and the Anglo. . . . Living on the borders and in margins, keeping intact one's shifting and multiple identity and integrity is like trying to swim in a new element, an 'alien' element" (i).

Instead of being divisive and isolating, this evolution of feminism into femin*isms* has fostered a more inclusive, global perspective. The era of recovering women's texts — especially texts by white Western women — has been succeeded by a new era in which the goal is to recover entire cultures of women. Two important figures of this new era are Trinh T. Minh-ha and Gayatri Spivak. Spivak, in works such as *In Other Worlds: Essays in Cultural Politics* (1987) and *Outside in the Teaching Machine* (1993), has shown how political independence (generally looked upon by metropolitan Westerners as a simple and beneficial historical and political reversal) has complex implications for "subaltern" or subproletarian women.

The understanding of woman not as a single, deterministic category but rather as the nexus of diverse experiences has led some white, Western, "majority" feminists like Jane Tompkins and Nancy K. Miller to advocate and practice "personal" or "autobiographical" criticism. Once reluctant to inject themselves into their analyses for fear of being labeled idiosyncratic, impressionistic, and subjective by men, some feminists are now openly skeptical of the claims to reason, logic, and objectivity that have been made in the past by male critics. With the advent of more personal feminist critical styles has come a powerful new interest in women's autobiographical writings.

Shari Benstock, who has written personal criticism in her book *Textualizing the Feminine* (1991), was one of the first feminists to argue that traditional autobiography is a gendered, "masculinist" genre. Its established conventions, feminists have recently pointed out, call for a life-plot that turns on action, triumph through conflict, intellectual self-discovery, and often public renown. The body, reproduction, children, and intimate interpersonal relationships are generally well in the background and often absent. Arguing that the lived experiences of women and men differ — women's lives, for instance, are often characterized by interruption and deferral — Leigh Gilmore has developed a theory of women's self-representation in her book *Autobiographics: A Feminist Theory of Self-Representation* (1994).

Autobiographics and personal criticism are only two of a number of recent developments in contemporary feminist criticism. Others alluded to in the first paragraph of this introduction — lesbian studies, performance or "masquerade" theory, and studies of the role played by film and various other "technologies" in shaping gender today — are prominent in contemporary *gender* criticism. Although there are several differences between the feminist and the newer gender approaches, the fact of this overlap should remind us that categories obscure similarities even as they help us make distinctions. Feminist criticism is, after all, a form of gender criticism, and contemporary gender criticism could never have developed without feminist criticism.

Suzette Henke begins the feminist encounter with *Portrait* that follows this introduction by examining the images of women in Stephen Dedalus's consciousness. She points out that Stephen's conception of women exists within a framework of dichotomies (flesh and spirit, politics and religion, Davitt and Parnell). In general, women are aligned in Stephen's mind with the realm of the physical, toward which Stephen is deeply ambivalent. Grounding her argument in the psychoanalytic theories of Freud and Lacan, Henke suggests that Stephen's divided attitude toward the world of the senses is rooted in what Freud referred to as the Oedipus complex. (A boy's passion for his mother generates feelings of desire and pleasure but also of guilt and fear.)

Having suggested that Stephen's consciousness generally connects women with physicality, Henke goes on to show that, within that general association, more destructive dichotomies exist. The realm of the physical, after all, includes the warmth of a protective mother's slippers as well as the very different warmth of a prostitute's embrace. Stephen's all too typical, nineteenth-century tendency to see women as one or the other — as virgins or whores — is as limited and limiting as his tendency to see them in terms of the physical. Henke relates Stephen's conception of women not only to an earlier, psychological complex but also to the voices and images of his education; the novels he reads, as well as popular entertainments of his culture, project the same images of women, with few variations.

The poetry Stephen writes is, in Henke's view, an attempted compensation for the relationships with women that he cannot achieve. Like his experience with the prostitute, it only seems to promise release and relief from frustration and failure. Stephen's response to these repeated cycles of frustration, hope, and failure is, according to Henke, a panicky retreat into the security of Catholic law and patriarchal protection. In the Church — and in the Church alone, it seems to Stephen — is to be found a safe and satisfactory image of women: that of a Virgin who is also a mother, that of a female at once physical and sinless. Although he eventually rejects the calling of the priesthood for an artistic vocation, he does so in an epiphanic moment in which he imaginatively transfigures a girl on a beach into a "profane virgin" (p. 330 in this volume), another masculine version of woman at once "mortal and angelic, sensuous and serene" (p. 329).

The novel ends with Stephen "once again accosted by ubiquitous reminders of Mother Church and Mother Ireland" (p. 329). But Stephen repudiates both and repudiates his mother as well, refusing to take communion at Easter. "Unlike his companion Cranly, who glorifies mother love, Stephen resolves to detach himself from 'the sufferings of women, the weaknesses of their bodies and souls.' In casting off matriarchy, he asserts his manhood in filial collusion with Daedalus, his classical mentor (p. 331).

Henke views Stephen, finally, as one who has relentlessly attempted to achieve mastery over the outer world by adopting a male model of creation. She sees *Portrait* as an ironic or even satiric novel, calling it at one point "Joyce's satirical rendering of Stephen's logocentric paradigm" (p. 334). The "conclusion of [the] text," she writes, "seems to imply that the developing artist's notorious misogyny will prove to be still another dimension (and limitation) of his youthful priggishness" (p. 335). In taking this tack, Henke proves to be neither the kind of feminist whose project is to expose the chauvinism of phallocentric male writers nor the kind who would eschew such authors in favor of women writers whose visions offer a feminist critique of patriarchal ideology and masculine-dominated culture.

Rather, against the background of psychoanalytic theorists from Jung to Freud to Lacan — and with the help of several French and American feminists — she finds vestiges of a feminist critique in a male writer's fiction, arguing that, as a result of Joyce's novelistic strategies, "Woman" proves to be what Luce Irigaray would identify as the "blind spot" in Stephen's discourse. Furthermore, in Henke's view, Joyce makes clear to his audience that Stephen's fear of what he does not adequately see and his resulting rejection of women and contempt for sensuous life are among the many inhibitions that stifle his budding creativity.

Ross C Murfin

FEMINIST CRITICISM:
A SELECTED BIBLIOGRAPHY

French Feminist Theory

Cixous, Hélène. "The Laugh of the Medusa." Trans. Keith Cohen and Paula Cohen. *Signs* 1 (1976): 875–94.

Cixous, Hélène, and Catherine Clément. *The Newly Born Woman.* Trans. Betsy Wing. Minneapolis: U of Minnesota P, 1986.

Feminist Readings: French Texts/American Contexts. Special issue of *Yale French Studies* 62 (1981).

French Feminist Theory. Special issue of *Signs* 7.1 (1981).

Irigaray, Luce. *An Ethics of Sexual Difference.* Trans. Carolyn Burke and Gillian C. Gill. Ithaca: Cornell UP, 1993.

———. *This Sex Which Is Not One.* Trans. Catherine Porter. Ithaca: Cornell UP, 1985.

Jardine, Alice A. *Gynesis: Configurations of Woman and Modernity.* Ithaca: Cornell UP, 1985.

Jenson, Deborah, ed. *"Coming to Writing" and Other Essays* (essays by Hélène Cixous). Trans. Sarah Cornell. Cambridge: Harvard UP, 1991.

Jones, Ann Rosalind. "Inscribing Femininity: French Theories of the Feminine." *Making a Difference: Feminist Literary Criticism.* Ed. Gayle Green and Coppélia Kahn. London: Methuen, 1985. 80–112.

———. "Writing the Body: Toward an Understanding of *L'Écriture féminine*." Showalter, *New Feminist Criticism.* New York: Pantheon, 1985. 361–77.

Kristeva, Julia. *Desire in Language: A Semiotic Approach to Literature and Art.* Ed. Leon S. Roudiez. Trans. Thomas Gora, Alice Jardine, and Leon S. Roudiez. New York: Columbia UP, 1980.

———. *Revolution in Poetic Language.* New York: Columbia UP, 1984.

Marks, Elaine, and Isabelle de Courtivron, eds. *New French Feminisms: An Anthology.* Amherst: U of Massachusetts P, 1980.

Moi, Toril, ed. *French Feminist Thought: A Reader.* Oxford: Basil Blackwell, 1987.

Spivak, Gayatri Chakravorty. "French Feminism in an International Frame." *Yale French Studies* 62 (1981): 154–84.

Stanton, Donna C. "Language and Revolution: The Franco-American Dis-Connection." *The Future of Difference.* Ed. Hester Eisenstein and Alice Jardine. Boston: G. K. Hall, 1980. 73–87.

Wittig, Monique. *Les Guérillères.* 1969. Trans. David Le Vay. New York: Avon, 1973.

British and American Feminist Theories

Benhabib, Seyla, and Drucilla Cornell, eds. *Feminism as Critique: On the Politics of Gender.* Minneapolis: U of Minnesota P, 1987.

Butler, Judith. *Bodies That Matter.* New York: Routledge, 1993.

———. *Gender Trouble.* New York: Routledge, 1990.

de Lauretis, Teresa. *The Practice of Love.* Bloomington: Indiana UP, 1994.

Farwell, Marilyn. *Heterosexual Plots and Lesbian Narratives.* New York: New York UP, 1996.

Feminist Readings: French Texts/American Contexts. Special issue. *Yale French Studies* 62 (1982). Essays by Jardine and Spivak.

Gilbert, Sandra M., and Susan Gubar. *No Man's Land: The Place of the Woman Writer in the Twentieth Century.* 3 vols. New Haven: Yale UP, 1988–96.

Grosz, Elizabeth. *Sexual Subversions.* London: Allen & Unwin, 1989.

———. *Volatile Bodies: Toward a Corporeal Feminism.* Bloomington: Indiana UP, 1994.

The Lesbian Issue. Special issue. *Signs* 9 (Summer 1984).

The Feminist Critique

Daly, Mary. *Gyn/Ecology.* Boston: Beacon, 1978.

Scott, Bonnie Kime, ed. *The Gender of Modernism.* Bloomington: Indiana UP, 1990.

———. *The Gender Complex of Modernism.* Urbana & Chicago: U of Illinois P, forthcoming.

Woolf, Virginia. *Three Guineas.* New York: Harcourt, 1938.

Feminist Theory: Classic Texts, General Approaches, Collections

Abel, Elizabeth, and Emily K. Abel, eds. *The "Signs" Reader: Women, Gender, and Scholarship.* Chicago: U of Chicago P, 1983.

Barrett, Michèle, and Anne Phillips. *Destabilizing Theory: Contemporary Feminist Debates.* Stanford: Stanford UP, 1992.

Beauvoir, Simone de. *The Second Sex.* 1949. Trans. and ed. H. M. Parshley. New York: Vintage, 1974.

Benstock, Shari, ed. *Feminist Issues in Literary Scholarship.* Bloomington: Indiana UP, 1987.

de Lauretis, Teresa, ed. *Feminist Studies/Critical Studies.* Bloomington: Indiana UP, 1986.

Fetterley, Judith. *The Resisting Reader: A Feminist Approach to American Fiction.* Bloomington: Indiana UP, 1978.

Fuss, Diana. *Essentially Speaking: Feminism, Nature and Difference.* New York: Routledge, 1989.

Gallop, Jane. *Around 1981: Academic Feminist Critical Theory.* New York: Routledge, 1992.

Greer, Germaine. *The Female Eunuch.* New York: McGraw, 1971.

Herndl, Diana Price, and Robyn Warhol, eds. *Feminisms: An Anthology of Literary Theory and Criticism.* New Brunswick: Rutgers UP, 1991.

hooks, bell. *Feminist Theory: From Margin to Center.* Boston: South End, 1984.

Keohane, Nannerl O., Michelle Z. Rosaldo, and Barbara C. Gelpi, eds. *Feminist Theory: A Critique of Ideology.* Chicago: U of Chicago P, 1982.

Kolodny, Annette. "Dancing through the Minefield: Some Observations on the Theory, Practice, and Politics of a Feminist Literary Criticism." Showalter, *New Feminist Criticism.* New York: Pantheon, 1985. 144–67.

———. "Some Notes on Defining a 'Feminist Literary Criticism.'" *Critical Inquiry* 2 (1975): 75–92.

Lovell, Terry, ed. *British Feminist Thought: A Reader.* Oxford: Basil Blackwell, 1990.

Malson, Micheline, et al., eds. *Feminist Theory in Practice and Process.* Chicago: U of Chicago P, 1986.

Meese, Elizabeth. *Crossing the Double-Cross: The Practice of Feminist Criticism.* Chapel Hill: U of North Carolina P, 1986.

Millett, Kate. *Sexual Politics.* Garden City: Doubleday, 1970.

Rich, Adrienne. *On Lies, Secrets, and Silence: Selected Prose, 1966–1979.* New York: Norton, 1979.

Showalter, Elaine, ed. *The New Feminist Criticism: Essays on Women, Literature, and Theory.* New York: Pantheon, 1985.

————. "Toward a Feminist Poetics." *The New Feminist Criticism* 125–43.

————. "Women's Time, Women's Space: Writing the History of Feminist Criticism." *Tulsa Studies in Women's Literature* 3 (1984): 29–43. Rpt. in Benstock, *Feminist Issues in Literary Scholarship*. 30–44.

Stimpson, Catherine R. "Feminist Criticism." *Redrawing the Boundaries: The Transformation of English and American Literary Studies*. Ed. Stephen Greenblatt and Giles Gunn. New York: MLA, 1992. 251–70.

————. *Where the Meanings Are: Feminism and Cultural Spaces*. New York: Methuen, 1988.

Weed, Elizabeth, ed. *Coming to Terms: Feminism, Theory, Politics*. New York: Routledge, 1989.

Woolf, Virginia. *A Room of One's Own*. New York: Harcourt, 1929.

Women's Writing and Creativity

Abel, Elizabeth, ed. *Writing and Sexual Difference*. Chicago: U of Chicago P, 1982.

Abel, Elizabeth, Marianne Hirsch, and Elizabeth Langland, eds. *The Voyage In: Fictions of Female Development*. Hanover: UP of New England, 1983.

Auerbach, Nina. *Communities of Women: An Idea in Fiction*. Cambridge: Harvard UP, 1978.

Benstock, Shari. "Reading the Signs of Women's Writing." *Tulsa Studies in Women's Literature* 4 (1985): 5–15.

Diehl, Joanne Feit. "Come Slowly Eden: An Exploration of Women Writers and Their Muse." *Signs* 3 (1978): 572–87.

DuPlessis, Rachel Blau. *The Pink Guitar: Writing as Feminist Practice*. New York: Routledge, 1990.

Finke, Laurie. *Feminist Theory, Women's Writing*. Ithaca: Cornell UP, 1992.

Gilbert, Sandra M., and Susan Gubar. *The Madwoman in the Attic: The Woman Writer and the Nineteenth-Century Literary Imagination*. New Haven: Yale UP, 1979.

Homans, Margaret. *Bearing the Word: Language and Female Experience in Nineteenth-Century Women's Writing*. Chicago: U of Chicago P, 1986.

Jacobus, Mary, ed. *Women Writing and Writing about Women*. New York: Barnes, 1979.

Miller, Nancy K., ed. *The Poetics of Gender.* New York: Columbia UP, 1986.

———. *Subject to Change: Reading Feminist Writing.* New York: Columbia UP, 1988.

Montefiore, Janet. "Feminine Identity and the Poetic Tradition." *Feminist Review* 13 (1983): 69–94.

Newton, Judith Lowder. *Women, Power and Subversion: Social Strategies in British Fiction, 1778–1860.* Athens: U of Georgia P, 1981.

Poovey, Mary. *The Proper Lady and the Woman Writer: Ideology as Style in the Works of Mary Wollstonecraft, Mary Shelley, and Jane Austen.* Chicago: U of Chicago P, 1984.

Showalter, Elaine. *Daughters of Decadence: Women Writers of the Fin de Siècle.* New Brunswick: Rutgers UP, 1993.

———. *A Literature of Their Own: British Women Novelists from Brontë to Lessing.* Princeton: Princeton UP, 1977.

———. "Women Who Write Are Women." *New York Times Book Review* I (December 16, 1984): 31–33.

Women's History/Women's Studies

Bridenthal, Renate, et al., ed. *Becoming Visible: Women in European History.* Rev. ed. Boston: Houghton Mifflin, 1998.

Donovan, Josephine. "Feminism and Aesthetics." *Critical Inquiry* 3 (1977): 605–8.

Farnham, Christie, ed. *The Impact of Feminist Research in the Academy.* Bloomington: Indiana UP, 1987.

Kelly, Joan. *Women, History & Theory: The Essays of Joan Kelly.* Chicago: U of Chicago P, 1984.

McConnell-Ginet, Sally, et al., eds. *Woman and Language in Literature and Society.* New York: Praeger, 1980.

Mitchell, Juliet, and Ann Oakley, eds. *The Rights and Wrongs of Women.* London: Penguin, 1976.

Riley, Denise. *"Am I That Name?": Feminism and the Category of "Women" in History.* Minneapolis: U of Minnesota P, 1988.

Rowbotham, Sheila. *Woman's Consciousness, Man's World.* Harmondsworth, UK: Penguin, 1973.

Spacks, Patricia Meyer. *The Female Imagination.* New York: Knopf, 1975.

Feminisms and Sexualities

Snitow, Ann, Christine Stansell, and Sharon Thompson, eds. *Powers of Desire: The Politics of Sexuality.* New York: Monthly Review P, 1983.

Vance, Carole S., ed. *Pleasure and Danger: Exploring Female Sexuality.* Boston: Routledge, 1984.

Feminism, Race, Class, and Nationality

Anzaldúa, Gloria. *Borderlands: La Frontera = The New Mestiza.* San Francisco: Spinsters/Aunt Lute, 1987.

Christian, Barbara. *Black Feminist Criticism: Perspectives on Black Women Writers.* New York: Pergamon, 1985.

Collins, Patricia Hill. *Black Feminist Thought: Knowledge, Consciousness, and the Politics of Empowerment.* Boston: Hyman, 1990.

hooks, bell. *Ain't I a Woman?: Black Women and Feminism.* Boston: South End, 1981.

———. *Black Looks: Race and Representation.* Boston: South End, 1992.

Mitchell, Juliet. *Woman's Estate.* New York: Pantheon, 1971.

Moraga, Cherrie, and Gloria Anzaldúa, eds. *This Bridge Called My Back: Writings by Radical Women of Color.* New York: Kitchen Table, 1981.

Newton, Judith, and Deborah Rosenfelt, eds. *Feminist Criticism and Social Change: Sex, Class, and Race in Literature and Culture.* New York: Methuen, 1985.

Newton, Judith L., et al., eds. *Sex and Class in Women's History.* London: Routledge, 1983.

Pryse, Marjorie, and Hortense Spillers, eds. *Conjuring: Black Women, Fiction, and Literary Tradition.* Bloomington: Indiana UP, 1985.

Robinson, Lillian S. *Sex, Class, and Culture.* 1978. New York: Methuen, 1986.

Smith, Barbara. "Towards a Black Feminist Criticism." Showalter, *New Feminist Criticism.* New York: Pantheon, 1985. 168–85.

Feminism and Postcoloniality

Emberley, Julia. *Thresholds of Difference: Feminist Critique, Native Women's Writings, Postcolonial Theory.* Toronto: U of Toronto P, 1993.

Minh-ha, Trinh T. *Woman, Native, Other: Writing Postcoloniality and Feminism.* Bloomington: Indiana UP, 1989.

Mohanty, Chandra Talpade, Ann Russo, and Lourdes Torres, eds. *Third World Women and the Politics of Feminism.* Bloomington: Indiana UP, 1991.

Schipper, Mineke, ed. *Unheard Words: Women and Literature in Africa, the Arab World, Asia, the Caribbean, and Latin America.* London: Allison, 1985.

Spivak, Gayatri Chakravorty. *In Other Worlds: Essays in Cultural Politics.* New York: Methuen, 1987.

———. *Outside in the Teaching Machine.* New York: Routledge, 1993.

Wilson, Armit. *Finding a Voice: Asian Women in Britain.* 1979. London: Virago, 1980.

Women's Self-Representation and Personal Criticism

Benstock, Shari, ed. *The Private Self: Theory and Practice of Women's Autobiographical Writings.* Chapel Hill: U of North Carolina P, 1988.

Brodski, Bella, and Celeste Schenck, eds. *Life/Lines: Theorizing Women's Autobiography.* Ithaca: Cornell UP, 1988.

Gilmore, Leigh. *Autobiographics: A Feminist Theory of Self-Representation.* Ithaca: Cornell UP, 1994.

Miller, Nancy K. *Getting Personal: Feminist Occasions and Other Autobiographical Acts.* New York: Routledge, 1991.

Feminism and Other Critical Approaches

Armstrong, Nancy, ed. *Literature as Women's History I.* Spec. issue of *Genre* 19–20 (1986–87).

Barrett, Michèle. *Women's Oppression Today: Problems in Marxist Feminist Analysis.* London: Verso, 1980.

Belsey, Catherine, and Jane Moore, eds. *The Feminist Reader: Essays in Gender and the Politics of Literary Criticism.* New York: Basil Blackwell, 1989.

Benjamin, Jessica. *The Bonds of Love: Psychoanalysis, Feminism, and the Problem of Domination.* New York: Pantheon, 1988.

Benstock, Shari. *Textualizing the Feminine: On the Limits of Genre.* Norman: U of Oklahoma P, 1991.

Butler, Judith, and Joan W. Scott, eds. *Feminists Theorize the Political.*
    New York: Routledge, 1992.

de Lauretis, Teresa. *Alice Doesn't: Feminism, Semiotics, Cinema.*
    Bloomington: Indiana UP, 1986.

de Lauretis, Teresa, and Stephen Heath. *The Cinematic Apparatus.*
    London: Macmillan, 1980.

Delphy, Christine. *Close to Home: A Materialist Analysis of Women's
    Oppression.* Trans. and ed. Diana Leonard. Amherst: U of
    Massachusetts P, 1984.

Dimock, Wai-chee. "Feminism, New Historicism, and the Reader."
    American Literature 63 (1991): 601–22.

Doane, Mary Ann. *Re-vision: Essays in Feminist Film Criticism.*
    Frederick: U Publications of America, 1984.

Felman, Shoshana, ed. *Literature and Psychoanalysis: The Questions of
    Reading: Otherwise.* Baltimore: Johns Hopkins UP, 1982.

———. "Women and Madness: The Critical Fallacy." *Diacritics* 5
    (1975): 2–10.

Feminist Studies. Special issue on feminism and deconstruction, 14
    (1988).

Gallop, Jane. *The Daughter's Seduction: Feminism and Psychoanalysis.*
    Ithaca: Cornell UP, 1982.

Gilligan, Carol. *In a Different Voice: Psychological Theory and Women's
    Development.* Cambridge: Harvard UP, 1982.

Hartsock, Nancy C. M. *Money, Sex, and Power: Toward a Feminist
    Historical Materialism.* Boston: Northeastern UP, 1985.

Hirsch, Marianne. *The Mother/Daughter Plot: Narrative,
    Psychoanalysis, Feminism.* Bloomington: Indiana UP, 1989.

Kaplan, Cora. *Sea Changes: Essays on Culture and Feminism.* London:
    Verso, 1986.

Meese, Elizabeth, and Alice Parker, eds. *The Difference Within:
    Feminism and Critical Theory.* Philadelphia: John Benjamins, 1989.

Modleski, Tania. *Feminism without Women: Culture and Criticism in
    a "Postfeminist" Age.* New York: Routledge, 1991.

Mulvey, Laura. *Visual and Other Pleasures.* Bloomington: Indiana UP,
    1989.

Newton, Judith Lowder. "History as Usual? Feminism and the New
    Historicism." *The New Historicism.* Ed. H. Aram Veeser. New
    York: Routledge, 1989. 152–67.

Nicholson, Linda J., ed. *Feminism/Postmodernism.* New York:
    Routledge, 1990.

Penley, Constance, ed. *Feminism and Film Theory*. New York: Routledge, 1988.

Riviere, Joan. "Womanliness as a Masquerade." *The International Journal of Psycho-Analysis* 10 (1929): 303–13. Rpt. in *Formations of Fantasy*. Ed. Victor Burgin, James Donald, and Cora Kaplan. New York: Methuen, 1986. 35–44.

Rose, Jacqueline. Introduction II. *Feminine Sexuality: Jacques Lacan and the Ecole Freudienne*. Ed. Juliet Mitchell and Rose. Trans. Rose. New York: Norton, 1983.

Rudnytsky, Peter L., and Andrew M. Gordon, eds. *Psychoanalyses/ Feminisms*. Albany and Buffalo: State U of New York P, 2000.

Sargent, Lydia, ed. *Women and Revolution: A Discussion of the Unhappy Marriage of Marxism and Feminism*. Montreal: Black Rose, 1981.

Weedon, Chris. *Feminist Practice and Poststructuralist Theory*. New York: Basil Blackwell, 1987.

Feminist Approaches to Joyce

Benstock, Shari. "City Spaces and Women's Places in Joyce's Dublin." *James Joyce: The Augmented Ninth*. Ed. Bernard Benstock. Syracuse: Syracuse UP, 1988. 293–307.

———. *Women of the Left Bank*. Austin: U of Texas P, 1986.

Church, Margaret. "The Adolescent Point of View toward Women in Joyce's *Portrait*." *Irish Renaissance Annual* 2 (1981): 158–65.

Cixous, Hélène. "Joyce: The (r)use of writing." *Post-Structuralist Joyce*. Ed. Derek Attridge and Daniel Ferrer. Cambridge: Cambridge UP, 1984. 15–30.

Devlin, Kimberly J. "The Female Eye: Joyce's Voyeuristic Narcissists." *New Alliances in Joyce Studies*. Ed. Bonnie Kime Scott. Newark: U of Delaware P, 1988. 135–43.

———. *James Joyce's "Fraudstuff."* Gainesville: UP of Florida, 2002.

Devlin, Kimberly J., and Marilyn Reizbaum. *"Ulysses": En-Gendered Perspectives*. Columbia: U of South Carolina P, 1999.

French, Marilyn. *The Book as World*. Cambridge: Harvard UP, 1975.

———. "Women in Joyce's Dublin." *James Joyce: The Augmented Ninth*. Ed. Bernard Benstock. Syracuse: Syracuse UP, 1988. 267–72.

Henke, Suzette. *James Joyce and the Politics of Desire*. New York: Routledge, 1990.

Henke, Suzette, and Elaine Unkeless, eds. *Women in Joyce*. Urbana: U of Illinois P, 1982.

Lawrence, Karen. "Joyce and Feminism." *The Cambridge Companion to James Joyce.* Ed. Derek Attridge. Cambridge: Cambridge UP, 1990.

Mahaffey, Vicki. *Reauthorizing Joyce.* Gainesville: UP of Florida, 1995.

Modern Fiction Studies 35 (Autumn 1989). "Feminist Readings of Joyce" issue.

Norris, Margot. *The Decentered Universe of "Finnegans Wake."* Baltimore: Johns Hopkins UP, 1974.

———. *Joyce's Web: The Social Unraveling of Modernism.* Austin: U of Texas P, 1988.

———. "Portraits of the Artist as a Young Lover." *New Alliances in Joyce Studies.* Ed. Bonnie Kime Scott. Newark: U of Delaware P, 1988. 144–52.

Scott, Bonnie Kime. *James Joyce.* Feminist Readings Series. Brighton, UK: Harvester P; Atlantic Highlands: Humanities P Intl., 1987.

———. *Joyce and Feminism.* Bloomington: Indiana UP, 1984.

Wawrzycka, Jolanta, and Marlena G. Corcoran, eds. *Gender in Joyce.* Gainesville: UP of Florida, 1997.

A FEMINIST PERSPECTIVE

SUZETTE HENKE

Stephen Dedalus and Women: A Feminist Reading of *Portrait*

I. MOTHER AND CHILD

Female characters are present everywhere and nowhere in *A Portrait of the Artist as a Young Man.* They pervade the novel, yet remain elusive. Their sensuous figures haunt the developing consciousness of Stephen Dedalus and provide a foil against which he defines himself as both man and artist. Like everything else in *A Portrait,* women are portrayed almost exclusively from Stephen's point of view. Seen through his eyes and colored by his fantasies, they often appear as one-dimensional projections of a narcissistic imagination. Demonized by Stephen's childhood sense of abjection, women emerge as powerful emblems of the flesh — frightening reminders of sex, generation, and bodily decay.

At the dawn of infantile consciousness, Stephen interprets the external world in terms of complementary pairs: male and female, father and mother, politics and religion, Davitt and Parnell. Baby Stephen's cosmos is organized in binary structures that set the stage for a dialectic of personal development. He perceives his father as a primordial storyteller who inaugurates the linguistic apprenticeship that inscribes the boy into the symbolic order of patriarchal authority. Simon Dedalus is a bearer of the law and the word, twin instruments of the will that promise psychological mastery over a hostile material environment. The male parent appeals to Stephen's imagination, awakening him to a sense of individual identity at the moment when language necessarily establishes a gap between subjective desire and self-representation: "He was baby tuckoo. . . . He sang that song. That was his song" (p. 20 in this volume). By virtue of receiving a forename, Stephen is able to enunciate himself as a subject of discourse and to gain access to narrative representation. Inscribed into the linguistic circuit of exchange, he identifies himself in terms of the dominant culture's signifying practices.

At the psychological juncture between pre-oedipal attachment and oedipal separation, Stephen first sees his mother as a powerful and beneficent source of physical pleasure. She ministers to her son's corporal needs, changes the oilsheet, and encourages his artistic expression by playing the piano. This sweet-smelling guardian is more directly responsive to the boy's infantile emotional demands and more closely associated with sensuous comfort and bodily joy. It is the "nice" mother, however, whom Stephen recognizes as one of the women principally responsible for introducing him to a hostile external world and to the repressive strictures of middle-class morality. The first of the many imperatives that thwart his ego, "apologise," is associated in his mind and vivid imagination with matriarchal threats.

Dante and Mrs. Dedalus both represent the inhibitions of an ominous reality principle that begins, at this point, to take precedence over the polymorphously perverse gratifications of infantile narcissism. As Dorothy Dinnerstein explains in *The Mermaid and the Minotaur*, it is usually a woman who serves as

> every infant's first love, first witness and first boss. . . . The initial experience of dependence on a largely uncontrollable outside source of good is focused on a woman, and so is the earliest experience of vulnerability to disappointment and pain. (28)

Nancy Chodorow, in her work on object relations, observes that this
pre-oedipal mother,

> simply as a result of her omnipotence and activity, causes a 'narcis-
> sistic wound.'. . . . Children of both sexes . . . will maintain a fear-
> some unconscious maternal image as a result of projecting upon it
> the hostility derived from their own feelings of impotence. (122)

As Simone de Beauvoir explains in *The Second Sex,* the male child, in
particular, has a tendency to associate the maternal figure with viscosity
and immanence — with a chaotic, uncontrollable world of physicality,
process, and unsatisfied desire. He develops a conviction that women
are bound by the generative demands of the species, and the presence
of his own mother becomes a reminder of contingency, the shame of his
animal nature and the threat of personal extinction.

> The uncleanness of birth is reflected upon the mother. . . . And if
> the little boy remains in early childhood sensually attached to the
> maternal flesh, when he grows older, becomes socialized, and
> takes note of his individual existence, this same flesh frightens
> him . . . calls him back to those realms of immanence whence he
> would fly. (136)

"Reproduction is the beginning of death" (p. 205), argued Hegel,
and so argues Stephen's friend Temple. The Manichean dichotomy between flesh and spirit, body and mind, has long been allied in the writings of male philosophers with a fantasized polarity between the sexes
and the linguistic construction of sexual difference. Stephen extends the
tradition of Nietzsche and Schopenhauer when, in *Stephen Hero,* he proposes a misogynist "theory of dualism which would symbolise the twin
eternities of spirit and nature in the twin eternities of male and female"
(*Stephen Hero* 210). According to Simone de Beauvoir, man's symbolic
association of woman with the flesh reflects an embedded infantile disdain for corporality and anarchic libidinal drives. The male identifies
himself as spirit by virtue of his own subjective consciousness; he then
perceives the female as "the Other, who limits and denies him" (129).

The sexual antagonism that pervades Irish society is impressed on
Stephen at an early age. He loathes his mother's feminine vulnerability
and thinks that she is "not nice" when she bursts into tears. Armed with
ten shillings and his father's injunction toward a code of masculine loyalty, he enters the competitive joust of life at Clongowes determined to
adopt an ethic of manly stoicism: "his father had told him . . . whatever
he did, never to peach on a fellow" (p. 22).

In a world of social Darwinism where only the ruthless survive, Stephen defines himself as both literally and figuratively marginal. Small, frail, and feeling very much like an outsider in this thundering herd of pugnacious schoolboys, he mentally takes refuge in artistic evocations of the family hearth protected by beneficent female spirits. As he relives the horror of being shouldered into a rat-infested urinal ditch by the bully Wells, Stephen projects himself beyond the vermin and the scum to an apparently dissociated reverie of his mother sitting by the fire in hot "jewelly slippers" that exude a "lovely warm smell" (p. 24). Alienated from a brutal male environment, Stephen longs to return to this female figure of security and comfort, "to be at home and lay his head on his mother's lap" (pp. 25–26).

As the growing boy moves in the direction of manhood, he feels increasingly compelled to cast off the shackles of female influence. His childhood educator Dante, "a clever woman and a wellread woman" who teaches him geography and lunar lore, is supplanted by male instructors: "Father Arnall knew more than Dante because he was a priest" (p. 24). The Jesuit masters at Clongowes invite Stephen to ponder the mysteries of religion, death, canker, and cancer. They introduce him to a system of male authority and discipline, to a pedagogical regimen that will ensure his correct training and proper socialization. Through examinations that pit red roses against white, Yorks against Lancastrians, they make education an aggressive game of simulated warfare in which students, like soldiers, are depersonalized through institutional surveillance.

By the time Stephen is old enough to join his parents' table at Christmas, his mother can no longer protect him from the world of masculine aggression or the turbulence of Irish politics. At the holiday meal, the impressionable child assimilates the knowledge that rabid women like Dante Riordan support ecclesiastical authority in the name of moral righteousness. Like the Irish sow devouring her farrow, Dante is willing to sacrifice Parnell as a political scapegoat to the prelates of Irish Catholicism. In the face of Mr. Casey's Fenianism and Simon's contemptuous snorting, she labels the Catholic clergy "the apple of God's eye" (p. 47). "*Touch them not,* says Christ, *for they are the apple of My eye*" (p. 47). As Ireland's perverted Eve, Dante defends this ecclesiastical apple against an adulterous Nationalist leader, a scandalous sinner crushed by an irate populace. Her impassioned ravings, bred of puritanical self-righteousness, suggest a formidable alliance between the Catholic church and the ideals of bourgeois morality guarded by a horde of pious women. "God and morality and religion come first," shrieks Dante (p. 47), and Mr. Casey counters with his own incendiary slogan.

In the battle between male and female, Mother Church emerges as a bastion of sexual repression. Dante's own credibility is socially diminished by her age, gender, and involuntary celibacy. Stephen "had heard his father say that she was a spoiled nun and that she had come out of the convent in the Alleghanies when her brother had got the money from the savages for the trinkets and the chainies" (p. 44). Stephen's own role models, Simon Dedalus and John Casey, boldly assert masculine prowess through republican fervor directed against dissenting countrymen rather than their imperial masters. In this mock scenario of political self-assertion, women and children prove fair game. Hence Casey's braggadocio in recounting his triumph over the hag who screamed "whore": "I had my mouth full of the tobacco juice. I bent down to her and *Phth!* says I to her like that . . . right into her eye" (p. 46).

When Stephen returns to Clongowes, he realizes that his peacemaking mother, a mollifying agent of social arbitration, has failed to offer a viable sanctuary from the male-dominated power structure that controls the outer world. He must learn to survive in a society that protects bullies like Wells and sadists like Father Dolan, condones brutality, and takes advantage of the weak and the helpless. The pandybat incident at the end of chapter one symbolically reinforces the rites of objectification characteristic of Jesuit training. Stephen is being socialized into what Philip Slater identifies in *The Glory of Hera* as a culture of male narcissism. According to Slater, single-sex education and the separation of young boys from maternal nurturance promotes misogyny, narcissism, and a residual terror of the female. Little boys suffer from an "unconscious fear of being feminine, which leads to 'protest masculinity,' exaggeration of the difference between men and women" (Slater 416). Once the child is deprived of his mother's affection, he "seeks compensation through self-aggrandizement — renouncing love for admiration. . . . He becomes vain, hypersensitive, invidious, ambitious, . . . boastful, and exhibitionistic" (439).

Stephen's brash appeal to Father Conmee at the end of the episode is motivated not only by optimistic faith in a male-controlled world but by personal vanity and a tendency toward exhibitionism. "The prefect of studies was a priest but that was cruel and unfair," he insists (p. 59). With an absurdly Panglossian view of the world, he feels certain of ethical exoneration from Conmee. Having rebelled against Father Dolan's totalitarian power, Stephen is unanimously acclaimed a revolutionary hero by his jubilant peers. But the child, apparently triumphant, later discovers an ironic sequel to his ostensible victory: Dolan and Conmee, in smug condescension, treat the incident as a riproaring joke. Stephen has unwittingly played the fool at the court of his Jesuit masters and, in a bold attempt to assert his budding manhood, has merely served as an object of wry patriarchal amusement.

II. VIRGIN AND WHORE

In chapter five of *Portrait*, Cranly asks Stephen if he would deflower a virgin. His companion replies by posing another half-mocking query: "Excuse me, . . . is that not the ambition of most young gentlemen?" (p. 218). Figuratively, it is Stephen's ambition throughout the novel to deflower the Blessed Virgin of Catholicism and supplant the Italian Madonna with a profane surrogate — a voluptuous Irish muse rooted in sensuous reality.

With the Count of Monte Cristo as his model, Stephen conjures up adolescent fantasies of a beautiful Mercedes whom he stalks in the suburbs of Blackrock. He envisages a scene of beatific transformation in a moonlit garden when the romantic heroine, meeting her erstwhile lover, blesses him with nothing less than the power of refusal. In spiritualizing his life, she paradoxically endows him with sufficient grace to conquer libidinal temptation. When Stephen dreams of himself as Edmond Dantes, he identifies with a man betrayed by his friends and his mistress, unjustly exiled and imprisoned, but eventually able to wreak vengeance on those who failed him. Monte Cristo's adventures culminate in a "sadly proud gesture of refusal": "Madam, I never eat muscatel grapes" (p. 67). As a nascent artist, Stephen admires the self-sufficiency of Dantes, an isolated hero who eventually conquers the woman he loves through a complex process of amorous sublimation.

In a different, more realistic setting, the Dublin family menage provides an unsalubrious atmosphere for those smiling soubrettes whose delicate features grace the evening papers and capture the attention of Stephen's aunt and cousins. "The beautiful Mabel Hunter" of pantomime fame stares from a newspaper photograph with "demurely taunting eyes" (p. 71). This "exquisite creature" intrudes on the squalor of Irish life to provide a popular though elusive model of seductive femininity. Stephen's ringleted cousin admires the music-hall artist with a kind of religious devotion. The popular press has constructed an icon of girlish charm, a figure of the female body as a desirable and coyly inaccessible market commodity. The price of such fetishistic com-modification of women is reflected in the aggressive behavior of Stephen's unidentified male relative, a boy growing up in an atmo-sphere of boorish insensitivity. Like a voracious animal, he mauls the edges of the paper and roughly pushes his sister aside to get a glimpse of Mabel's photograph. Greedy and whining, he appropriates this pretty pinup for his own lascivious enjoyment.

Unmoved by such popular representations of feminine charm, Stephen seeks refuge from reality in the priesthood of art: he longs to confront the beauty and mystery of creation while tasting the joy of loneliness. Before the tantalizing face of Emma cowled in nun's veiling, he forces himself to remain calm and controlled, repressing "the fever-ish agitation of his blood" (p. 72). He characteristically projects his own erotic vulnerability onto the girl he believes to be "flattering, taunting, searching, exciting his heart" (p. 72). Emma appears in the guise of Kathleen Ni Houlihan, a Celtic figure inviting Stephen to romantic initiation in the peaceful stillness of a moonlit evening. Deper-sonalized and seen through the haze of mythic reverie, she emerges as a shadowy emblem out of the unconscious — Mercedes in Dublin garb, Eve in nun's habit.

> He saw her urge her vanities, her fine dress and sash and long black stockings, and knew that he had yielded to them a thousand times. Yet a voice within him spoke above the noise of his dancing heart, asking him would he take her gift to which he had only to stretch out his hand. (p. 73)

In this self-indulgent exercise, Stephen gains symbolic mastery over Emma's erratic movements by assuming that he can, at will, catch hold of her darting figure. Focusing on fetishes of stockings and dress, he casts her in the incongruous role of Irish temptress and refuses her gift of an adolescent kiss. On the verge of losing emotional composure, Stephen refuses to yield to this purported temptation. Like the Count of Monte Cristo, he turns away from Emma in proud abnegation, determined to possess his mistress wholly through art.

Blurring the figures of himself and his beloved in the womb of his artistic imagination, Stephen is able to give cathartic expression to the pain of loss associated with unacted desire. Byronic verses written to E—— C—— consummate the memory of romantic intimacy, as Stephen imagines that "the kiss, which had been withheld by one, was given by both" (p. 74). Poetry offers aesthetic compensation for frus-trated physical desire, and the stirrings of adolescent sexuality are deftly sublimated through an exercise in lyrical fulfillment. The artist's mind is cold, chaste, and detached, like that of the virginal muse Diana, as his disciplined verses statically embalm the experience of romantic epiphany. The scene has been purged of reality and naturalistic detail, the participants vaguely depersonalized. Emotional mutuality has been restricted to art: Stephen feels fulfilled, but Emma is left to pine in her nunlike cowl. Her desires are safely crystallized in Byronic verses framed by two Jesuit mottoes.

Refusing to communicate his passion, Stephen mediates libidinal desire through the literary language of courtly love and nineteenth-century romantic convention. Taking Daddy Byron as master, he succeeds in mastering the young woman who would otherwise be mistress of his heart. The poem that he pens provides an emotional circuit of substitution that short-circuits libidinal drive and sublimates Eros to the symbolic order of Daedalus/Byron/Stephen/Father/Joyce.

The night of the Whitsuntide play two years later, Stephen remembers the touch of Emma's hand and the sight of dark eyes that "had invited and unnerved him" (p. 84). "All day he had thought of nothing but their leavetaking on the steps of the tram at Harold's Cross" (p. 79). Despite the lapse in time, he continues to feel tormented by the stream of moody emotions that hurt him into poetry, as he imagines a tender reunion and a chance to rewrite the scene with a different ending. Clothing his frustration in a tapestry of lyrical effects, Stephen is able to defuse the seminal eruptions of repressed physicality through psychological strategies of erotic displacement.

Dashing to an alley behind the Dublin morgue, he soberly takes comfort in the "good odour" of "horse piss and rotted straw" (p. 87), mortifying the flesh in a repulsive atmosphere chosen to vent his residual contempt for female physiology. Urine and ordure symbolically cling to the archaic memory of an inaccessible maternal body always lost to the ego's field of insatiable demands. Stephen's morbid sentiments are Thomistic and medieval, reminiscent of religious triptychs that portray a woman first at the height of vanity and sensuous beauty, then aged and wrinkled, and finally as a skeleton draped in richly embroidered grave-clothes. Accosted by the immanence of his carnal connection with the world, Stephen, like the fathers of the Church, rebels against mortality by renouncing the fires of lust. As Saint Augustine wryly noted, *"Inter faeces et urinam nascimur"* (we are born between feces and urine). Joyce's artist is well on his way to developing a similar excremental vision of sex.

Stephen no longer seeks to emulate the Count of Monte Cristo when the transfiguration he once sought through Mercedes is consummated in the embrace of a Dublin whore. He finds himself stalking a prostitute in the manner of a savage, predatory animal. "His blood was in revolt. . . . He moaned to himself like some baffled prowling beast" (p. 98). His search is motivated by a perverse desire for temporary communion, as he seeks release from his own imprisoned ego: "He wanted to sin with another of his kind, to force another being to sin with him and to exult with her in sin" (p. 98). The sexual imagery at the end of chapter two is ironically inverted. As Stephen feels the shadow of a streetwalker "moving irresistibly upon him" in penumbrous alleyways, he figuratively suffers the "agony of its penetration" and surrenders to a murmurous flood of physical excitation (p. 98). The fusion of erotic and romantic imagery degenerates into a vague rite of sexual initiation that reverses traditional symbolism. Stephen envisages himself in the role of deflowered virgin, raped by a phallic figure and flooded with seminal streams. His "cry for an iniquitous abandonment" again evokes an excremental vision of sex, as his moans reverberate with "the echo of an obscene scrawl which he had read on the oozing wall of a urinal" (p. 98).

When Stephen/Icarus, wandering through a Daedalian maze of narrow and dirty streets, steps before a phantasmal altar illumined by yellow gasflames, he resembles both a sacrificial victim and a child about to burst into hysterical weeping. The perfumed female who takes him in her arms recalls his nice-smelling mother at the same time that she functions as high priestess or Vestal virgin in a contemporary phallic cult. Clothed in a long pink gown, she leads the boy into a womblike chamber, tousles his hair, calls him "little rascal," and embraces him with a vaguely maternal caress. Soothed like a baby or a fetus by the "warm calm rise and fall of her breast," Stephen momentarily retrieves an illusion of infant satiety: "He closed his eyes, surrendering himself to her, body and mind, conscious of nothing in the world but the dark pressure of her softly parting lips" (p. 99).

In this oral-regressive encounter, the prostitute becomes mistress of Stephen's lips and, through a lingual kiss that inaugurates a fantasy of pre-oedipal bliss, temporarily appropriates the highly guarded powers of artistic speech. Inarticulate and swooning, the boy feels reduced to a lavish, infantile dependency that leaves him childlike and passive, penetrated by a foreign tongue, but gloriously centered in the mystified presence of an imaginary figure of wholeness and coherence. Stephen feels that he has at last realized spiritual transfiguration: "He was in another world: he had awakened from a slumber of centuries" into a sybaritic, pagan sanctuary (p. 98).

III. THE CATHOLIC VIRGIN

At the outset of chapter three, Stephen approaches the forbidden pleasures of the Dublin red-light district almost ritualistically, pursuing a devious course among back streets and alleys until surprised by the joy of soft, perfumed flesh. Wallowing in the pleasures of a physicality that has always tormented him, Stephen delights in a riot of sensuality. His defiant sexual practices mesmerize consciousness until, watched by a thousand flickering heavenly eyes, his weary mind is transported into a "vast cycle of starry life" (p. 100).

As prefect of the sodality of the Blessed Virgin, Stephen chants Mary's praises in an act of proud dissimulation. "His sin, which had covered him from the sight of God, had led him nearer to the refuge of sinners" (p. 102). The Catholic Virgin becomes a figure of courtly devotion, whose holiness radiates a hypnotic, translucent glow. Desirous of serving as her knight and courtier, Stephen prostrates himself in sacerdotal obeisance before his vision of the adored female. He worships the flesh of an icon that seems an object of both veneration and desire. A sanctuary of heavenly peace after the fervor of sexual frenzy, the Virgin becomes a postcoital Madonna offering refuge from the turmoil of hormonal agitation. The self-conscious sinner takes perverse satisfaction in befouling her image by reciting the Holy Office with "lips whereon there still lingered foul and shameful words, the savour itself of a lewd kiss" (p. 102). Later in the episode, Stephen will offer a panicked prayer to Mary, whom he invokes in the guise of a beneficent mother. Repentant of his fall from grace, he no longer imagines her as a frail-fleshed virgin but appeals to the powerful *magna mater,* whose beauty is *"not like earthly beauty, dangerous to look upon, but like the morning star"* (p. 129).

As the "jeweleyed harlots" of lascivious transgression dance before the boy's fevered imagination, he feels horrified by the realization that he has besmirched the icon of his beloved Emma by making her the object of masturbatory fantasy: "The image of Emma appeared before him and, under her eyes, the flood of shame rushed forth anew from his heart. If she knew to what his mind had subjected her or how his brutelike lust had torn and trampled upon her innocence!" (p. 110).

He feels that he has violated both Emma's honor and his own code of chivalry, not to mention the rigorous ethic of purity enforced by Irish Catholicism.

Without the innocent Emma to serve as a surrogate Beatrice, Stephen feels as "helpless and hopeless" as the souls of the damned in Dante's hell (p. 116) and hallucinates a vision of the libidinous inferno prepared especially for him, "a hell of lecherous goatish fiends" (p. 128). These "goatish creatures with human faces, hornybrowed, lightly bearded and grey as indiarubber" (p. 128) are demonic satyrs who mimic the goat-god Pan but whose dry, spittleless lips are incapable of communicative utterance. They embody the artist's most terrible nightmare: a hell in which language has been deracinated from meaning, articulation is torturous, and spoken sounds echo in waves of vacuous gibberish.

Stephen's Catholic training forces him simultaneously to renounce Satan, the female, and his own genitalia in an act of psychological castration. Haunted by fantasies of sexual alienation, he feels compelled to assert moral superiority over an antagonistic penis that seems to operate with a will of its own: "His soul sickened at the thought of a torpid snaky life feeding itself out of the tender marrow of his life and fattening upon the slime of lust" (p. 130). Like the confused adolescent boy described by Simone de Beauvoir in *The Second Sex*, Stephen feels "possessed by a magic not of himself. . . . That organ by which he thought to assert himself does not obey him; heavy with unsatisfied desires, unexpectedly becoming erect, . . . it manifests a suspicious and capricious vitality" (150–51).

In order to confess his sins against the sixth and ninth commandments, Stephen must self-consciously revert to a state of childhood innocence and amend his life for the sake of atonement with the Christian community. Echoing the inaugural words of catechismal instruction and droning a litany of religious clichés, he determines to repress budding sexual urges by renouncing the one sin that shames him even more than murder. The temptress has reduced his soul to a syphilitic chancre "festering and oozing like a sore, a squalid stream of vice" (p. 133). Repelled by the lurid imagery of venereal disease, Stephen humbles himself before the old and weary voice of a father-priest-confessor, who counsels a "life of grace and virtue and happiness" (p. 135) and invokes the Virgin Mary as moral guardian of Christian manliness.

As penitential prefect of Our Blessed Lady's sodality, Stephen scrupulously disciplines his senses to the point of masochistic self-abuse. He obsessively attempts to recapture, through puritanical self-mortification, the prepubescent calm of juvenile innocence. Fervently invoking the Virgin to *"guide us home"* (p. 129), he fails to realize the futility of such a project. One cannot go home again to the lost womb of sexual latency.

IV. THE BIRD-GIRL: AESTHETIC MUSE

In his return to ritualistic devotion, Stephen becomes involved in an aesthetic love affair with his own soul. The *anima,* the feminine aspect of the psyche, has won his passion and holds him enthralled. Like Narcissus, Stephen has fallen in love with his projected self-image clothed in female garb.

> The attitude of rapture in sacred art, the raised and parted hands, the parted lips and eves as of one about to swoon, became for him an image of the soul in prayer, humiliated and faint before her Creator. (p. 138)

In the glorified female, says Simone de Beauvoir, "man also perceives his mysterious double; man's soul is Psyche, a woman" (166–67). The feminine side of Stephen's identity, personified as the soul, swoons in erotic ecstasy before her Creator, just as the young man earlier swooned in the arms of a Dublin prostitute.

The Catholic priesthood offers Stephen a chance to consummate this narcissistic love affair with his psyche. It bestows on the soul the magical power of transubstantiation, and it promises a rite of passage into male-guarded mysteries that successfully counteract female authority: "No angel or archangel in heaven, no saint, not even the Blessed Virgin herself has the power of a priest of God" (p. 144). A Jesuit vocation would guarantee Stephen ascendancy over the Catholic Madonna. By virtue of the secret knowledge promised by an exclusively masculine fraternity, he would be admitted to the inner sanctum of patriarchal privilege.

The price, however, of this "awful power of which angels and saints stood in reverence" is an irrevocable act that would destroy his freedom and condemn him to the "grave and ordered and passionless life" of Jesuit conformity (pp. 144–46). Still painting himself in the images of Lord Byron and Edmond Dantes, Stephen passionately embraces the marginal stance of aesthetic outlaw. He chooses the misrule and confusion of his father's house, the messiness and chaos of sensuous experience, over a "mirthless reflection of the sunken day" (p. 146) evinced by his Jesuit counselor's spectral visage. Turning away from this symbolic death's head, Stephen instinctively rejects the selfless, unquestioning obedience demanded by a Catholic life of religious celibacy. He will commit himself, instead, to the pagan priesthood of that fabulous artificer, old Father Daedalus. Like the solitary farmhand, he will cast his gaze toward an ethereal ideal, then plunge the spade of art into solid, terrestrial, and mundane matter.

Stephen's implicit choice of an artistic vocation seems emotionally confirmed by his climactic encounter with a profane virgin emblematic of earthly beauty — a wading girl "whom magic had changed into the likeness of a strange and beautiful seabird" (p. 155). Her epiphanic figure amalgamates a plethora of images from pagan, Christian, and Celtic iconography. She is at once mortal and angelic, sensuous and serene. Her softhued, ivory thighs recall Eileen's ivory hands as well as the Catholic Virgin, Tower of Ivory. Her avian transformation harks back to the Greek myth of Leda and the swan. And because her bosom, like "the breast of some darkplumaged dove" (p. 155), suggests the Holy Ghost of Catholicism, Stephen, as purveyor of the word, imaginatively begets a surrogate Holy Spirit.

The irony of this romantic moment is subtle but implicit. If Stephen feels sexual arousal in the presence of exposed female thighs, he quickly sublimates erotic agitation beneath effusions of purple prose. Confronted with an attractive nubile form, he immediately detaches himself from participation in the scene. His reaction is self-consciously static, theoretically purged of desire or loathing. Once again, his leap into aesthetic fantasy quenches an initial impulse to approach the girl, to reach out and touch her, or to risk social intercourse.

As the girl rises out of the sea, she is reminiscent of Venus, the goddess of love born of the ocean foam. She is pure and virginal, yet an emerald trail of seaweed functions as a sign of mortality stamped upon her flesh. She belongs to the mundane world of decay and corruption, and the vegetation clinging to her ankle suggests a fetishistic image of emotional entrapment. The woman appears as an "angel of mortal youth and beauty, an envoy from the fair courts of life" (p. 156). But like an Irish Circe, she has the potential to drag Stephen down into the emerald green nets of Dublin paralysis.

In sociological terms this attractive young woman, approached and courted, might well threaten Stephen with the kind of domestic entrapment associated with Catholic marriage. The aspiring poet knows that he may look but not touch, admire but not speak. He glorifies the wading girl as angelic muse but never actually approaches her in the teeming ocean waters. Communication has been safely limited to narcissistic projection: "Her image had passed into his soul for ever and no word had broken the holy silence of his ecstasy" (p. 156). Afraid of the "waters circumfluent in space" (p. 198) that symbolize the fluidity of female desire, Stephen is determined to control the world of physiological process by freezing life in the sacrament of art. His "spiritual-heroic refrigerating apparatus" (p. 223) has already begun to implement this psychological flight from woman. His response to the girl is exclusively specular, as he takes refuge in a masculine, visual, sexual economy and sublimates tactile and olfactory drives that would move him toward sensuous contact. The mimesis of romantic passion offers a successfully mediated and comfortably mastered form of sexual gratification.

For Joyce's young man, an exercise in scopophilia (love of looking) masquerades as aesthetic delight. If, as Freud suggests, the specular gaze is anal and obsessive, an unconscious expression of a sadistic will to power, then Stephen's cold, pellucid *regard* penetrates its object through a strategy of phallocentric framing and claims it as a fetishistic trophy to grace the scene of writing. The bird-girl functions as an imaginary symbol of beauty and coherence, of desire playfully, masterfully, and joyously deferred through an endless dissemination of creative pleasure. Woman proves to be what Luce Irigaray would identify as the "blind spot" in Stephen's discourse. The bird-girl is represented as a fantasized paradigm of psychic cohesion, the Other whose realistic fragmentation would threaten the poet's idealized aesthetic project. Because this female icon remains a mute, fetishized, and perpetually mediated object of desire, her difference assures psychological stability to the speaking/seeing subject, the authorial I/eye who frames and appropriates her figure.

At nightfall, the exhausted poet feels his soul "swooning into some new world, fantastic, dim, uncertain as under sea, traversed by cloudy shapes and beings. A world, a glimmer, or a flower?" (p. 156). His spirit seems to embark on an archetypal journey toward the multifoliate rose of Dante's beatific vision. The bird-girl has imaginatively served as Stephen's profane virgin, a Beatrice who ushers him into paradisal experience. The Dantesque underworld may symbolize the artistic unconscious, but the pre-Raphaelite rose imagery casts satirical light on Stephen's romantic reverie. As the young man attempts to "still the riot of his blood," he swoons in languorous ecstasy. He moodily contemplates an opening flower "breaking in full crimson and unfolding and fading to palest rose, . . . flooding all the heavens with its soft flushes"

(p. 156). Sublimating the sexual component of his experience, Stephen vividly imagines a metaphorical rose engulfing the heavens, and his language of flowers suggests a psychoanalytic exercise in erotic mimesis. The boy's fantasy re-creates a repressed vision of female genitalia spreading in luxuriant, rose pink petals before his aroused phallic consciousness. His active libido summons veiled images of a woman's body revealing its vulvular mysteries and palpitating with the crimson flush of physical stimulation. Florid prose imitates the orgasmic rhythms of sexual excitement, as tension mounts "leaf by leaf and wave of light by wave of light" until the dream suddenly climaxes in a flood of soft flushes. Stephen may want to believe that he has purified his sensuous encounter by making it into a mimetic replication of spiritual transcendence, but even his Dantesque beatitude is founded on sexual passion thinly disguised by the language of Freudian displacement.

V. FLIGHT FROM THE MOTHER

Although the gates of salvation open at the end of chapter four, Stephen finds himself, at the beginning of chapter five, exiled from the Garden of Eden. Chewing crusts of fried bread, he remembers the "turfcoloured" water in the bath at Clongowes — a spectral image that resonates with associations of death, drowning, and spiritual claustrophobia. As the nascent artist tries to escape the sordid reality of Dublin by taking shelter in a world of words, he continues to struggle for liberation from the nets of a cloying family life, the demands of Irish nationality, and the stultifying authority of the Catholic church.

Proudly proclaiming that he "will not serve," Stephen nevertheless relies on his mother's service for physical nurturance and psychological support. Mary Dedalus washes her son's face and ears, enjoins him to receive the Eucharist, and packs his secondhand clothes in preparation for his exodus to France. Having magically transmuted the power of the female into a static object of aesthetic contemplation, Stephen is once again accosted by ubiquitous reminders of Mother Church and Mother Ireland. He feels compelled simultaneously to reject all three mothers — biological, ecclesiastical, and political. His refusal to take communion at Easter is as much a gesture of rebellion against a pleading Mary Dedalus as it is a rejection of Catholic authority. The image of woman metonymically absorbs all the paralyzing nets that constrain the potential artist. Unlike his companion Cranly, who glorifies mother love, Stephen resolves to detach himself from "the sufferings of women, the weaknesses of their bodies and souls" (p. 216). In casting off the yoke of matriarchy, he asserts his manhood in filial collusion with Daedalus, his classical mentor.

It is not enough, however, to repudiate the female: the artist must successfully usurp her procreative powers. Stephen seems to consider the aesthetic endeavor a kind of symbolic couvade, a rite of psychological compensation for the male inability to give birth. He describes the act of aesthetic postcreation in metaphors of parturition, explaining to Lynch: "When we come to the phenomena of artistic conception, artistic gestation and artistic reproduction I require a new terminology and a new personal experience" (p. 187).

After awakening from what seems to have been a wet dream, Stephen feels inspired to compose a lyrical aubade to a fantasized temptress. The poet welters in a confused haze of light and beauty, but the instant of inspiration is climactic: "In the virgin womb of the imagination the word was made flesh" (p. 193). The moment of mental conception simulates a sexual process culminating in erotic ecstasy. In a strange instance of mental transsexuality, Stephen envisions his own aesthetic impregnation by the Holy Spirit, an experience modeled on the Virgin Mary's biblical gestation of the word of God. As the artist falls into a vision of rapturous enchantment, he conflates the ingenuous Emma with Mercedes and the bird-girl, then re-creates this female figure in the awesome, uncanny form of eternal temptress — a seductive Lilith luring the seraphim from heaven. His courtly villanelle is inspired by a shudder in the loins that engenders not Yeats's Leda or a burning Troy, but a handful of precious verses.

The enchantment of the heart that Stephen and Shelley both praise for its radiance now bursts forth into fire and flame. The metaphor of smoky praise issuing from a chivalric heart seems puerile at best, part of an ecclesiastical rite complete with "swaying censer" and ellipsoidal incense balls. With decadent weariness, Stephen gropes for his tablets and finds, instead, an abandoned cigarette packet. The smoke from the censer of the world is recorded on the cardboard remnant of a package of smokes, all smoked but one. Stephen longs to immerse himself in a Dantesque ambiance of secret roses reminiscent of the multifoliate flower of paradise, but he is forced to fashion a phantasmal, rose-strewn path to heaven from the "great overblown scarlet flowers of the tattered wallpaper" that plaster his dingy room in Dublin (p. 197).

Unable to win the young and fickle heart of Emma, Stephen re-creates her in baleful, aesthetic guise. Her figure is kaleidoscopically reflected in memories of lower-class peasant women: a flowergirl, a kitchengirl "with the drawl of a country singer," a girl who mocked him, and a vamp whose "small ripe mouth" made her good enough to eat (p. 196). Seeing Emma on the steps of the National Library, Stephen wonders if her life might be as "simple and strange as a bird's life" and her heart as "simple and wilful as a bird's" (p. 193). But the bird, an emblem of simplicity and trust, quickly melds with the iconography of the inscrutable bat, a creature whose enigmatic flight and dark habitation makes it a symbol of mystery and cunning. "Bat," too, is an Irish slang term for "prostitute," an association implicit in the multiple bat references that pepper the final pages of *Portrait*. Stephen condescends to think of Emma as a younger incarnation of the pregnant woman who tried to seduce Davin in the Ballyhoura Hills and who emerges as a symbol of Mother Ireland, a nurturant and guileless female ingenuously bedding the stranger. Emma, too, becomes "a figure of the womanhood of her country, a batlike soul waking to the consciousness of itself in darkness and secrecy and loneliness" (p. 196).

By purging Emma of naturalistic dross, by abstracting her from an Irish domestic scene of horsehair and flirtation and celebrating her as archetypal temptress, Stephen, "a priest of the eternal imagination, transmuting the daily bread of experience into the radiant body of ever-living life" (p. 196), metaphorically consumes her body in the sacramental act of aesthetic communion. Erotic union gives way to a spiritual Eucharist, as the poet raises the sacred chalice of devotion before the altar of the muse. Emma figuratively surrenders herself to the artist who conquers her voluptuous form: "Her nakedness yielded to him, radiant, warm, odorous and lavishlimbed" (p. 198).

Stephen paradoxically composes the villanelle out of the same pornographic urgency that his Thomistic theory earlier censured. The fires of lust inspire his aubade, a poetic explosion that conceals lascivious motives: "A glow of desire kindled again his soul and fired . . . his body" (p. 198). Weary of the ardent ways of frustrated passion, he cools his blazing heart through a masturbatory ritual that explodes in both aesthetic and physical ecstasy. By raising Emma to heights of Circean power that pique her erotic desirability, Stephen magically defuses her flirtatious spell and reduces her to a mystified figure controlled by his priestly imagination.

The formal, highly wrought verses of the villanelle ingeniously subdue the seductress whose *"eyes have set man's heart ablaze"* from the beginning of time. Against overwhelming enchantment, Stephen arrays the forces of aesthetic transformation. As poet-priest, he transubstantiates the eternal feminine into a disembodied muse that, once out of nature, ceases to threaten. Consigned to the Yeatsian realm of Byzantium, the Circean figure can no longer arouse animal lust or sensuous desire.

Throughout the novel, Stephen seeks the evacuation of affect from language and a reinscription of his filial self into the symbolic order and law of the father. By replicating himself in a discursive process of substitutability, he acquires a male aesthetic signature and triumphantly appropriates the female body/text. Inscribing himself into an august company of paternal authority figures (Daedalus, Edmond Dantes, Lord Byron, Father Conmee, Father Arnall, Dante Alighieri, Simon Dedalus, and Cranly), he fabricates an authorial persona purged of unsettling libidinal drives. The eternal temptress he celebrates is a disguised replica of the phallic mother who tantalizes with nurturant pleasure, then obstinately withholds satisfaction. Incestuous attraction to the body of the mother is repressed and displaced onto a radiant icon of female beauty. Emma provides a substitute for the mother (both consubstantial and Catholic Madonna) whose image, in turn, is reproduced in the specular icon of a wading bird-girl, then lyrically transformed into an enchantress idealized out of existence and consigned to the icy realm of Platonic stasis.

Throughout *Portrait,* Stephen manifests a psychological horror of woman as a figure of immanence, a symbol of unsettling sexual difference, and a perpetual reminder of bodily abjection. At the conclusion of chapter five, he prepares to flee from all the women who have served as catalysts in his own adolescent development. His journey into exile will release him from what he perceives as a cloying matriarchal authority. He must blot from his ears "his mother's sobs and reproaches" and strike from his eyes the insistent "image of his mother's face" (p. 199). Alone and proud, isolated and free, Stephen proclaims joyful allegiance to the masculine fraternity of Daedalus, his priest and patron: "Welcome, O life! I go to encounter for the millionth time the reality of experience and to forge in the smithy of my soul the uncreated conscience of my race" (p. 224).

The hyperbolic resonance of Stephen's invocation leads us to suspect that his fate will prove Icarian rather than Daedalian. Insofar as women are concerned, he goes to encounter the reality of experience not for the millionth time but for the first. Much of the irony in *Portrait* results from Joyce's satirical rendering of Stephen's logocentric paradigm. The sociopathic hero, pompous and aloof, passionately gathers phrases for his word hoard without infusing his "capful of light odes" (*Ulysses* 14:1119) with the generative spark of human sympathy.

Certainly, the reader may feel baffled or uneasy about the degree of irony implicit in Joyce's portrait of the artist as a young narcissist. Stephen/Icarus has flown from one youthful illusion to another, first trusting the rectitude of his Clongowes masters and emulating the Count of Monte Cristo, then sliding into illicit sexual exultation in an initiation ritual immediately undercut by scenes of debased sensuality and emotional self-hatred. As the body, in turn, is disciplined and mortified, a devotion to the priesthood of art displaces the young man's Catholic asceticism. Embracing his newfound mission with all the exuberance of an aesthetic convert, Stephen is left exhausted and swooning before the sanctified icon of a wading girl transformed in his imagination into a mystical muse. Incapable of sustaining this romantic fantasy in the hostile environment of Dublin, he takes psychological refuge in vaguely erotic verses generated by a wet dream and/or by masturbatory excitation. Toward the end of the novel, Stephen adopts a Wildean pose of triumphant perversity as he proclaims revolutionary freedom and projects a vision of liberating flight "across the kathartic ocean" (*Finnegans Wake* 185.6) to the haunts of bohemian Paris. Emotionally static and incapable of meaningful connection with other human beings, the aspiring poet is poised in a stance of Icarian impotence. His final diary entries suggest imminent emigration, but they delineate neither flight nor failure.

The conclusion of Joyce's text seems to imply that the artist's notorious misogyny will prove to be still another dimension (and limitation) of his youthful priggishness. The pervasive irony that tinges the hero's scrupulous devotions and gives his aesthetic theory that "true scholastic stink" surely informs his relations with women — from his mother and Dante Riordan to Emma and the unnamed bird-girl he transfigures on the beach. In a tone of gentle mockery, Joyce makes clear to his audience that Stephen's fear of women and his contempt for sensuous life are among the many inhibitions that stifle his creativity. Before he can become a true priest of the eternal imagination, Stephen must first divest himself of "the spiritual-heroic refrigerating apparatus" that characterizes the egocentric aesthete. Narcissism and misogyny are adolescent traits he has to outgrow on the path to artistic maturity. Not until the epic *Ulysses* will a new model begin to emerge, one that recognizes the need for the intellectual artist to make peace with the mother/lover of his dreams and to incorporate into his masterful work those mysterious breaks, flows, gaps, and ruptures associated with the repressed and sublimated flow of male-female desire.

WORKS CITED

Beauvoir, Simone de. *The Second Sex*. 1953. Trans. and ed. H. M. Parshley. New York: Bantam, 1961.

Chodorow, Nancy. *The Reproduction of Mothering*. Berkeley: U of California P, 1978.

Dinnerstein, Dorothy. *The Mermaid and the Minotaur: Sexual Arrangements and Human Malaise*. New York: Harper, 1976.

Joyce, James. *Finnegans Wake*. New York: Viking, 1939.

———. *Stephen Hero*. Ed. John J. Slocum and Herbert Cahoon. New York: New Directions, 1963.

———. *Ulysses*. Ed. Hans Walter Gabler, et al. New York: Random, 1986.

Slater, Philip E. *The Glory of Hera*. 1968. Rpt. Boston: Beacon, 1971.

Cultural Criticism
and
A Portrait of the Artist as a Young Man

WHAT IS CULTURAL CRITICISM?

What do you think of when you think of culture? The opera or ballet? A performance of a Mozart symphony at Lincoln Center or a Rembrandt show at the De Young Museum in San Francisco? Does the phrase "cultural event" conjure up images of young people in jeans and T-shirts — or of people in their sixties dressed formally? Most people hear "culture" and think "high culture." Consequently, when they first hear of cultural criticism, most people assume it is more formal than, well, say, formalism. They suspect it is "highbrow," in both subject and style.

Nothing could be further from the truth. Cultural critics oppose the view that culture refers exclusively to high culture, Culture with a capital C. Cultural critics want to make the term refer to popular, folk, urban, and mass (mass-produced, -disseminated, -mediated, and -consumed) culture, as well as to that culture we associate with the so-called classics. Raymond Williams, an early British cultural critic whose ideas will later be described at greater length, suggested that "art and culture are ordinary"; he did so not to "pull art down" but rather to point out that there is "creativity in all our living. . . . We create our human world as we have thought of art being created" (*Revolution* 37).

Cultural critics have consequently placed a great deal of emphasis on what Michel de Certeau has called "the practice of everyday life." Rather than approaching literature in the elitist way that academic literary critics have traditionally approached it, cultural critics view it more as an anthropologist would. They ask how it emerges from and competes with other forms of discourse within a given culture (science, for instance, or television). They seek to understand the social contexts in which a given text was written, and under what conditions it was — and is — produced, disseminated, read, and used.

Contemporary cultural critics are as willing to write about *Star Trek* as they are to analyze James Joyce's *Ulysses,* a modern literary classic full of allusions to Homer's *Odyssey.* And when they write about *Ulysses,* they are likely to view it as a collage reflecting and representing cultural forms common to Joyce's Dublin, such as advertising, journalism, film, and pub life. Cultural critics typically show how the boundary we tend to envision between high and low forms of culture — forms thought of as important on one hand and relatively trivial on the other — is transgressed in all sorts of exciting ways within works on both sides of the putative cultural divide.

A cultural critic writing about a revered classic might contrast it with a movie, or even a comic-strip version produced during a later period. Alternatively, the literary classic might be seen in a variety of other ways: in light of some more common form of reading material (a novel by Jane Austen might be viewed in light of Gothic romances or ladies' conduct manuals); as the reflection of some common cultural myths or concerns (*Adventures of Huckleberry Finn* might be shown to reflect and shape American myths about race and concerns about juvenile delinquency); or as an example of how texts move back and forth across the alleged boundary between "low" and "high" culture. For instance, one group of cultural critics has pointed out that although Shakespeare's history plays probably started off as popular works enjoyed by working people, they were later considered "highbrow" plays that only the privileged and educated could appreciate. That view of them changed, however, due to film productions geared toward a national audience. A film version of *Henry V* produced during World War II, for example, made a powerful, popular, patriotic statement about England's greatness during wartime (Humm, Stigant, and Widdowson 6–7). More recently, cultural critics have analyzed the "cultural work" accomplished cooperatively by Shakespeare and Kenneth Branagh in the latter's 1992 film production of *Henry V.*

In combating old definitions of what constitutes culture, of course, cultural critics sometimes end up contesting old definitions of what constitutes the literary canon, that is, the once-agreed-upon honor roll of Great Books. They tend to do so, however, neither by adding books (and movies and television sitcoms) *to* the old list of texts that every "culturally literate" person should supposedly know nor by substituting some kind of counterculture canon. Instead, they tend to critique the very *idea* of canon.

Cultural critics want to get us away from thinking about certain works as the "best" ones produced by a given culture. They seek to be more descriptive and less evaluative, more interested in relating than in rating cultural products and events. They also aim to discover the (often political) reasons *why* a certain kind of aesthetic or cultural product is more valued than others. This is particularly true when the product in question is one produced since 1945, for most cultural critics follow Jean Baudrillard (*Simulations,* 1981) and Andreas Huyssen (*After the Great Divide,* 1986) in thinking that any distinctions that may once have existed between high, popular, and mass culture collapsed after the end of World War II. Their discoveries have led them beyond the literary canon, prompting them to interrogate many other value hierarchies. For instance, Pierre Bourdieu in *Distinction: A Social Critique of the Judgment of Taste* (1984) and Dick Hebdige in *Hiding the Light: On Images and Things* (1988) have argued that definitions of "good taste"— which are instrumental in fostering and reinforcing cultural discrimination — tell us at least as much about prevailing social, economic, and political conditions as they do about artistic quality and value.

In an article entitled "The Need for Cultural Studies," four groundbreaking cultural critics have written that "Cultural Studies should . . . abandon the goal of giving students access to that which represents a culture." A literary work, they go on to suggest, should be seen in relation to other works, to economic conditions, or to broad social discourses (about childbirth, women's education, rural decay, and so on) within whose contexts it makes sense. Perhaps most important, critics practicing cultural studies should counter the prevalent notion of culture as some preformed whole. Rather than being static or monolithic, culture is really a set of interactive *cultures,* alive and changing, and cultural critics should be present- and even future-oriented. They should be "resisting intellectuals," and cultural studies should be "an emancipatory project" (Giroux et al. 478–80).

The paragraphs above are peppered with words like *oppose, counter, deny, resist, combat, abandon,* and *emancipatory.* What such words quite accurately suggest is that a number of cultural critics view themselves in political, even oppositional, terms. Not only are they likely to take on the literary canon, they are also likely to oppose the institution of the university, for that is where the old definitions of culture as high culture (and as something formed, finished, and canonized) have been most vigorously preserved, defended, and reinforced.

Cultural critics have been especially critical of the departmental structure of universities, which, perhaps more than anything else, has kept the study of the "arts" relatively distinct from the study of history, not to mention from the study of such things as television, film, advertising, journalism, popular photography, folklore, current affairs, shoptalk, and gossip. By maintaining artificial boundaries, universities have tended to reassert the high/low culture distinction, implying that all the latter subjects are best left to historians, sociologists, anthropologists, and communication theorists. Cultural critics have taken issue with this implication, arguing that the way of thinking reinforced by the departmentalized structure of universities keeps us from seeing the aesthetics of an advertisement as well as the propagandistic elements of a work of literature. Cultural critics have consequently mixed and matched the analytical procedures developed in a variety of disciplines. They have formed — and encouraged other scholars to form — networks and centers, often outside of those enforced departmentally.

Some initially loose interdisciplinary networks have, over time, solidified to become cultural studies programs and majors. As this has happened, a significant if subtle danger has arisen. Richard Johnson, who along with Hebdige, Stuart Hall, and Richard Hoggart was instrumental in developing the Center for Contemporary Cultural Studies at Birmingham University in England, has warned that cultural studies must not be allowed to turn into yet another traditional academic discipline — one in which students encounter a canon replete with soap operas and cartoons, one in which belief in the importance of such popular forms has become an "orthodoxy" (39). The only principles that critics doing cultural studies can doctrinally espouse, Johnson suggests, are the two that have thus far been introduced: the principle that "culture" has been an "inegalitarian" concept, a "tool" of "condescension," and the belief that a new, "interdisciplinary (and even antidisciplinary)" approach to *true* culture (that is, to the forms in which culture currently lives) is required now that history, art, and the communications media are so complex and interrelated (42).

The object of cultural study should not be a body of works assumed to comprise or reflect a given culture. Rather, it should be human consciousness, and the goal of that critical analysis should be to understand and show how that consciousness is itself forged and formed, to a great extent, by cultural forces. "Subjectivities," as Johnson has put it, are "produced, not given, and are . . . objects of inquiry" inevitably related to "social practices," whether those involve factory rules, supermarket behavior patterns, reading habits, advertisements, myths, or languages and other signs to which people are exposed (44–45).

Although the United States has probably contributed more than any other nation to the *media* through which culture is currently expressed, and although many if not most contemporary practitioners of cultural criticism are North American, the evolution of cultural criticism and, more broadly, cultural studies has to a great extent been influenced by theories developed in Great Britain and on the European continent.

Among the Continental thinkers whose work allowed for the development of cultural studies are those whose writings we associate with structuralism and poststructuralism. Using the linguistic theory of Ferdinand de Saussure, structuralists suggested that the structures of language lie behind all human organization. They attempted to create a *semiology* — a science of signs — that would give humankind at once a scientific and holistic way of studying the world and its human inhabitants. Roland Barthes, a structuralist who later shifted toward poststructuralism, attempted to recover literary language from the isolation in which it had been studied and to show that the laws that govern it govern all signs, from road signs to articles of clothing. Claude Lévi-Strauss, an anthropologist who studied the structures of everything from cuisine to villages to myths, looked for and found recurring, common elements that transcended the differences within and between cultures.

Of the structuralist and poststructuralist thinkers who have had an impact on the evolution of cultural studies, Jacques Lacan is one of three whose work has been particularly influential. A structuralist psychoanalytic theorist, Lacan posited that the human unconscious is structured like a language and treated dreams not as revealing symptoms of repression but, rather, as forms of discourse. Lacan also argued that the ego, subject, or self that we think of as being natural (our individual human nature) is in fact a product of the social order and its symbolic systems (especially, but not exclusively, language). Lacan's thought has served as the theoretical underpinning for cultural critics seeking to show the way in which subjectivities are produced by social discourses and practices.

Jacques Derrida, a French philosopher whose name has become synonymous with poststructuralism, has had an influence on cultural criticism at least as great as that of Lacan. The linguistic focus of structuralist thought has by no means been abandoned by poststructuralists, despite their opposition to structuralism's tendency to find universal patterns instead of textual and cultural contradictions. Indeed, Derrida has provocatively asserted that *"there is nothing outside the text"* (158), by which he means something like the following: we come to know the world through language, and even our most worldly actions and practices (the Gulf War, the wearing of condoms) are dependent upon discourses (even if they deliberately contravene those discourses). Derrida's "deconstruction" of the world/text distinction, like his deconstruction of so many of the hierarchical oppositions we habitually use to interpret and evaluate reality, has allowed cultural critics to erase the boundaries between high and low culture, classic and popular literary texts, and literature and other cultural discourses that, following Derrida, may be seen as manifestations of the same textuality.

Michel Foucault is the third Continental thinker associated with structuralism and/or poststructuralism who has had a particularly powerful impact on the evolution of cultural studies — and perhaps *the* strongest influence on American cultural criticism and the so-called new historicism, an interdisciplinary form of cultural criticism whose evolution has often paralleled that of cultural criticism. Although Foucault broke with Marxism after the French student uprisings of 1968, he was influenced enough by Marxist thought to study cultures in terms of power relationships. Unlike Marxists, however, Foucault refused to see power as something exercised by a dominant class over a subservient class. Indeed, he emphasized that power is not just repressive power, that is, a tool of conspiracy by one individual or institution against another. Power, rather, is a whole complex of forces; it is that which produces what happens.

Thus even a tyrannical aristocrat does not simply wield power but is empowered by "discourses"— accepted ways of thinking, writing, and speaking — and practices that embody, exercise, and amount to power. Foucault tried to view all things, from punishment to sexuality, in terms of the widest possible variety of discourses. As a result, he traced what he called the "genealogy" of topics he studied through texts that more traditional historians and literary critics would have overlooked, examining (in Lynn Hunt's words) "memoirs of deviants, diaries, political treatises, architectural blueprints, court records, doctors' reports — appl[ying] consistent principles of analysis in search of moments of reversal in discourse, in search of events as loci of the conflict where social practices were transformed" (39). Foucault tended not only to build interdisciplinary bridges but also, in the process, to bring into the study of culture the "histories of women, homosexuals, and minorities"— groups seldom studied by those interested in Culture with a capital C (Hunt 45).

Of the British influences on cultural studies and criticism, two stand out prominently. One, the Marxist historian E. P. Thompson, revolutionized the study of the industrial revolution by writing about its impact on human attitudes, even consciousness. He showed how a shared cultural view, specifically that of what constitutes a fair or just price, influenced crowd behavior and caused such things as the "food riots" of the eighteenth and nineteenth centuries (during which the women of Nottingham repriced breads in the shops of local bakers, paid for the goods they needed, and carried them away). The other, even more important early British influence on contemporary cultural criticism and cultural studies was Raymond Williams, who coined the phrase "culture is ordinary." In works like *Culture and Society, 1780–1950* (1958) and *The Long Revolution* (1961) Williams demonstrated that culture is not fixed and finished but, rather, living and evolving. One of the changes he called for was the development of a common socialist culture.

Although Williams dissociated himself from Marxism during the period 1945–58, he always followed the Marxist practice of viewing culture in relation to ideologies, which he defined as the "residual," "dominant," or "emerging" ways of viewing the world held by classes or individuals holding power in a given social group. He avoided dwelling on class conflict and class oppression, however, tending instead to focus on people as people, on how they experience the conditions in which they find themselves and creatively respond to those conditions through their social practices. A believer in the resiliency of the individual, Williams produced a body of criticism notable for what Stuart Hall has called its "humanism" (63).

As is clearly suggested in several of the preceding paragraphs, Marxism is the background to the background of cultural criticism. What isn't as clear is that some contemporary cultural critics consider themselves Marxist critics as well. It is important, therefore, to have some familiarity with certain Marxist concepts — those that would have been familiar to Foucault, Thompson, and Williams, plus those espoused by contemporary cultural critics who self-identify with Marxism. That familiarity can be gained from an introduction to the works of four important Marxist thinkers: Mikhail Bakhtin, Walter Benjamin, Antonio Gramsci, and Louis Althusser.

Bakhtin was a Russian, later a Soviet, critic so original in his thinking and wide-ranging in his influence that some would say he was never a Marxist at all. He viewed literary works in terms of discourses and dialogues *between* discourses. The narrative of a novel written in a society in flux, for instance, may include an official, legitimate discourse, plus others that challenge its viewpoint and even its authority. In a 1929 book on Dostoyevsky and the 1940 study *Rabelais and His World,* Bakhtin examined what he calls "polyphonic" novels, each characterized by a multiplicity of voices or discourses. In Dostoyevsky the independent status of a given character is marked by the difference of his or her language from that of the narrator. (The narrator's language may itself involve a dialogue between opposed points of view.) In works by Rabelais, Bakhtin finds that the (profane) languages of Carnival and of other popular festivities play against and parody the more official discourses of the magistrates and the church. Bakhtin's relevance to cultural criticism lies in his suggestion that the dialogue involving high and low culture takes place not only between classic and popular texts but also between the "dialogic" voices that exist within all great books.

Walter Benjamin was a German Marxist who, during roughly the same period, attacked fascism and questioned the superior value placed on certain traditional literary forms that he felt conveyed a stultifying "aura" of culture. He took this position in part because so many previous Marxist critics (and, in his own day, Georg Lukács) had seemed to prefer nineteenth-century realistic novels to the modernist works of their own time. Benjamin not only praised modernist movements, such as dadaism, but also saw as promising the development of new art forms utilizing mechanical production and reproduction. These forms, including photography, radio, and film, promised that the arts would become a more democratic, less exclusive, domain. Anticipating by decades the work of those cultural critics interested in mass-produced, mass-mediated, and mass-consumed culture, Benjamin analyzed the meanings and (defensive) motivations behind words like *unique* and *authentic* when used in conjunction with mechanically reproduced art.

Antonio Gramsci, an Italian Marxist best known for his *Prison Notebooks* (first published in 1947), critiqued the very concept of literature and, beyond that, of culture in the old sense, stressing the importance of culture more broadly defined and the need for nurturing and developing proletarian, or working-class, culture. He argued that all intellectual or cultural work is fundamentally political and expressed the need for what he called "radical organic" intellectuals. Today's cultural critics urging colleagues to "legitimate the notion of writing reviews and books for the general public," to "become involved in the political reading of popular culture," and more generally to "repoliticize" scholarship have viewed Gramsci as an early precursor (Giroux et al. 482).

Gramsci related literature to the ideologies — the prevailing ideas, beliefs, values, and prejudices — of the culture in which it was produced. He developed the concept of "hegemony," which refers at once to the process of consensus formation and to the authority of the ideologies so formed, that is to say, their power to shape the way things look, what they would seem to mean, and, therefore, what reality *is* for the majority of people. But Gramsci did not see people, even poor people, as the helpless victims of hegemony, as ideology's pathetic robots. Rather, he believed that people have the freedom and power to struggle against and shape ideology, to alter hegemony, to break out of the weblike system of prevailing assumptions and to form a new consensus. As Patrick Brantlinger has suggested in *Crusoe's Footprints: Cultural Studies in Britain and America* (1990), Gramsci rejected the "intellectual arrogance that views the vast majority of people as deluded zombies, the victims or creatures of ideology" (100).

Of those Marxists who, after Gramsci, explored the complex relationship between literature and ideology, the French Marxist Louis Althusser had a significant impact on cultural criticism. Unlike Gramsci, Althusser tended to portray ideology as being in control of people, and not vice versa. He argued that the main function of ideology is to reproduce the society's existing relations of production, and that that function is even carried out in literary texts. In many ways, though, Althusser is as good an example of how Marxism and cultural criticism part company as he is of how cultural criticism is indebted to Marxists and their ideas. For although Althusser did argue that literature is relatively autonomous — more independent of ideology than, say, church, press, or state — he meant literature in the high cultural sense, certainly not the variety of works that present-day cultural critics routinely examine alongside those of Tolstoy and Joyce, Eliot and Brecht. Popular fictions, Althusser assumed, were mere packhorses designed (however unconsciously) to carry the baggage of a culture's ideology, or mere brood mares destined to reproduce it.

Thus, while a number of cultural critics would agree both with Althusser's notion that works of literature reflect certain ideological formations and with his notion that, at the same time, literary works may be relatively distant from or even resistant to ideology, they have rejected the narrow limits within which Althusser and some other Marxists (such as Georg Lukács) have defined literature. In "Marxism and Popular Fiction" (1986), Tony Bennett uses *Monty Python's Flying Circus* and another British television show, *Not the 9 O'clock News*, to argue that the Althusserian notion that all forms of culture belong "among [all those] many material forms which ideology takes . . . under capitalism" is "simply not true." The "entire field" of "popular fiction"— which Bennett takes to include films and television shows as well as books — is said to be "replete with instances" of works that do what Bennett calls the "work" of "distancing." That is, they have the effect of separating the audience from, not rebinding the audience to, prevailing ideologies (249).

Although Marxist cultural critics exist (Bennett himself is one, carrying on through his writings what may be described as a lovers' quarrel with Marxism), most cultural critics are not Marxists in any strict sense. Anne Beezer, in writing about such things as advertisements and women's magazines, contests the "Althusserian view of ideology as the construction of the subject" (qtd. in Punter 103). That is, she gives both the media she is concerned with and their audiences more credit than Althusserian Marxists presumably would. Whereas they might argue that such media make people what they are, she points out that the same magazines that, admittedly, tell women how to please their men may, at the same time, offer liberating advice to women about how to preserve their independence by not getting too serious romantically. And, she suggests, many advertisements advertise their status as ads, just as many people who view or read them see advertising as advertising and interpret it accordingly.

The complex sort of analysis that Beezer has brought to bear on women's magazines and advertisements has been focused on paperback romance novels by Tania Modleski and Janice A. Radway in *Loving with a Vengeance* (1982) and *Reading the Romance* (1984), respectively. Radway, a feminist cultural critic who uses but ultimately goes beyond Marxism, points out that many women who read romances do so in order to carve out a time and space that is wholly their own, not to be intruded upon by husbands or children. Although many such novels end in marriage, the marriage is usually between a feisty and independent heroine and a powerful man she has "tamed," that is, made sensitive and caring. And why do so many of these stories involve such heroines and end as they do? Because, as Radway demonstrates through painstaking research into publishing houses, bookstores, and reading communities, their consumers *want* them to. They don't buy or, if they buy they don't recommend — romances in which, for example, a heroine is raped: thus, in time, fewer and fewer such plots find their way onto the racks by the supermarket checkout.

Radway's reading is typical of feminist cultural criticism in that it is *political*, but not exclusively about oppression. The subjectivities of women may be "produced" by romances — the thinking of romance readers may be governed by what is read — but the same women also govern, to a great extent, what gets written or produced, thus performing "cultural work" of their own. Rather than seeing all forms of popular culture as manifestations of ideology, soon to be remanifested in the minds of victimized audiences, cultural critics tend to see a sometimes disheartening but always dynamic synergy between cultural forms and the culture's consumers. Their observations have increasingly led to an analysis of consumerism, from a feminist but also from a more general point of view. This analysis owes a great deal to the work of de Certeau, Hall, and, especially, Hebdige, whose 1979 book *Subculture: The Meaning of Style* paved the way for critics like John Fiske (*Television Culture*, 1987), Greil Marcus (*Dead Elvis*, 1991), and Rachel Bowlby (*Shopping with Freud*, 1993). These latter critics have analyzed everything from the resistance tactics employed by television audiences to the influence of consumers on rock music styles to the psychology of consumer choice.

The overlap between feminist and cultural criticism is hardly surprising, especially given the recent evolution of feminism into various femin*isms*, some of which remain focused on "majority" women of European descent, others of which have focused instead on the lives and writings of minority women in Western culture and of women living in Third World (now preferably called postcolonial) societies. The culturalist analysis of value hierarchies within and between cultures has inevitably focused on categories that include class, race, national origin, gender, and sexualities; the terms of its critique have proved useful to contemporary feminists, many of whom differ from their predecessors insofar as they see *woman* not as a universal category but, rather, as one of several that play a role in identity- or subject-formation. The influence of cultural criticism (and, in some cases, Marxist class analysis) can be seen in the work of contemporary feminist critics such as Gayatri Spivak, Trinh T. Minh-ha, and Gloria Anzaldúa, each of whom has stressed that while all women are female, they are something else as well (such as working-class, lesbian, Native American, Muslim, Pakistani), and that that something else must be taken into account when their writings are read and studied.

The expansion of feminism and feminist literary criticism to include multicultural analysis, of course, parallels a transformation of education in general. On college campuses across North America, the field of African-American studies has grown and flourished. African-American critics have been influenced by and have contributed to the cultural approach by pointing out that the white cultural elite of North America has tended to view the oral-musical traditions of African Americans (traditions that include jazz, the blues, sermons, and folktales) as entertaining, but nonetheless inferior. Black writers, in order not to be similarly marginalized, have produced texts that, as Henry Louis Gates has pointed out, fuse the language and traditions of the white Western canon with a black vernacular and traditions derived from African and Caribbean cultures. The resulting "hybridity" (to use Homi K. Bhabha's word), although deplored by a handful of black separatist critics, has proved both rich and complex — fertile ground for many cultural critics practicing African-American criticism.

Interest in race and ethnicity at home has gone hand in hand with a new, interdisciplinary focus on colonial and postcolonial societies abroad, in which issues of race, class, and ethnicity also loom large. Edward Said's book *Orientalism* (1978) is generally said to have inaugurated postcolonial studies, which in Bhabha's words "bears witness to the unequal and uneven forces of cultural representation involved in the contest for political and social authority within the modern world order" ("Postcolonial Criticism" 437). *Orientalism* showed how Eastern and Middle Eastern peoples have for centuries been systematically stereotyped by the West, and how that stereotyping facilitated the colonization of vast areas of the East and Middle East by Westerners. Said's more recent books, along with postcolonial studies by Bhabha and Patrick Brantlinger, are among the most widely read and discussed works of literary scholarship. Brantlinger focuses on British literature of the Victorian period, examining representations of the colonies in works written during an era of imperialist expansion. Bhabha complements Brantlinger by suggesting that modern Western culture is best understood from the postcolonial perspective.

Thanks to the work of scholars like Brantlinger, Bhabha, Said, Gates, Anzaldúa, and Spivak, education in general and literary study in particular are becoming more democratic, decentered (less patriarchal and Eurocentric), and multicultural. The future of literary criticism will owe a great deal indeed to those early cultural critics who demonstrated that the boundaries between high and low culture are at once repressive and permeable, that culture is common and therefore includes all forms of popular culture, that cultural definitions are inevitably political, and that the world we see is seen through society's ideology. In a very real sense, the future of education *is* cultural studies.

In "The Culture of Dedalus: Urban Circulation, Degeneration, and the Panopticon," the essay that follows this introduction, cultural critic R. Brandon Kershner views Joyce's novel in terms of its "social, political, and economic contexts." At the time in which *Portrait* is set, Dublin was a city "gripped" by an "economic decline" (p. 358 in this volume). The societal manifestations of that downturn included a "public health . . . crisis" (p. 359) spawned by an inadequate and deteriorating sewage system, "widespread prostitution" and resulting "venereal disease" (which "some commentators believe that both Joyce and his father suffered from"), and "alcoholism (such as Simon Dedalus suffers from)" (p. 360).

The city's economic decline, Kershner points out, was "highly unusual for major cities during the industrializing nineteenth century"— especially cities with a growing middle class. Then again, Kershner reminds us, Dublin was an unusual European city in many respects, having been "deposed as a capital city with the Act of Union in 1800, making Ireland a part of the British empire" (p. 358). Indeed, Dublin was "unique" in being a "first-world colonial city"— a "deposed capital" (p. 358), in the words of Mary Daly, a noted social historian. As for Dublin's emerging middle class, Kershner quotes Daly as saying that "the new Catholic middle class was frequently accused of having betrayed its origins" (p. 358).

Kershner's contextualization of the novel in light of economic and class struggle is typical of what we might call classical cultural criticism and cultural theory, as are his later, related references to Marx and citations of later Marxist theorists such as Walter Benjamin. Equally representative of contemporary cultural theory and criticism is Kershner's open indebtedness to theorist Michel Foucault and resulting interest in another cultural context prevalent at the time Joyce wrote *Portrait,* namely, ideas about surveillance that were prevalent at the time the novel was written.

Kershner begins his discussion of surveillance by citing Foucault's reference, in *Discipline and Punish,* to the " 'Panopticon'— an architectural model for a prison in which a central, unseen observer can watch each prisoner at will" (p. 361). Foucault used the Panopticon "as his own model for the technologies of regulation that arose after the eighteenth century in Europe" (p. 361); for Kershner, it serves as a model for what Church and state — and society in general — seem to the young Stephen we meet at the beginning of *Portrait.* Power and power relationships have become faceless, "disindividualized" (p. 362), in the late nineteenth-century Ireland in which Stephen struggles to grow up. Such power tends to have, in Foucault's words, "its principle not so much in a person as in a certain concerted distribution of bodies, surfaces, lights, gazes" (p. 362).

So powerful is the sense of being watched in Stephen's — and Joyce's — historical time and place that Stephen's very habits of thought are governed by the principles and discourses of observation. At first thinking that his sin has "covered him from the sight of God," he quickly reverts to the opinion that in all he does he is watched:

> But after the first retreat sermon he imagines that he has merely exchanged God's gaze for one more demonic; he sees himself as a beastly body "gazing out of darkened eyes, helpless, perturbed and human for a bovine god to stare upon." (p. 362)

Kershner, following Foucault, explores the seemingly paradoxical connection between surveillance and discipline and the rise of "the ideology of individualism" (p. 363). He finds the apparent contradiction illustrated in Stephen's confession, an act of revealing "the secret thoughts and actions that [Stephen] believes have made him uniquely damned" (p. 363), an act that at the same time proves the weakness of the individual and the complementary power of authority. Stephen's various attempts at self-liberation are consequently viewed by Kershner as what Michel de Certeau has called the "practices" and "tactics" (p. 363) whereby people attempt to resist the totalizing tendencies of modern culture.

Among Stephen's tactics is his attempt to fashion himself into a Celtic artist-aristocrat, an Irish genius beyond the reach of his culture's fixing, deadening gaze. The trouble is, as Kershner points out, the very concept of "class"— let alone aristocracy — has become deeply suspect to the Irish way of thinking. Furthermore, the nineteenth-century concept of genius informing Stephen's thinking is: (1) a "racialist" one associating the people of Ireland (among others) with the very *opposite* of genius, and (2) tightly intertwined with the oppressive idea of the priesthood. Thus, Kershner suggests, Stephen's decision to attempt to disentangle and distinguish himself by becoming an Irish artistic genius is virtually doomed from the start.

Kershner goes on to place all of these ideas in a still wider cultural context of fearful, late-nineteenth-century discourses about familial and racial degeneration, but to summarize these in detail would be to spoil the experience of following the essay's unfolding argument. Suffice it to say here that Kershner elucidates ideas such as "Stephen's guilt and terror at his sexual self-indulgence" (p. 369) by tracing them back not only to their religious and ethical sources but also to prevailing cultural views. (In this case, he refers to attitudes toward masturbation, which was connected in the popular mind with the decline of genius and the devolution of the race.) The result is a dense critical canvas, one that situates Joyce's text vis-à-vis those nonliterary contexts forming what Michel de Certeau — whom Kershner quotes — refers to as "the practice of everyday life" (p. 363). Yet another distinguishing feature of Kershner's critical canvas is the way it also identifies the frame around the picture it presents, thereby acknowledging that it, too, is historically and culturally grounded in our own world—and ways of reading.

Ross C Murfin

CULTURAL CRITICISM:
A SELECTED BIBLIOGRAPHY

General Introductions to
Cultural Criticism, Cultural Studies

Bathrick, David. "Cultural Studies." *Introduction to Scholarship in Modern Languages and Literatures.* Ed. Joseph Gibaldi. New York: MLA, 1992. 320–40.

Brantlinger, Patrick. *Crusoe's Footprints: Cultural Studies in Britain and America.* New York: Routledge, 1990.

———. "Cultural Studies vs. the New Historicism." *English Studies/Cultural Studies: Institutionalizing Dissent.* Ed. Isaiah Smithson and Nancy Ruff. Urbana: U of Illinois P, 1994. 43–58.

Brantlinger, Patrick, and James Naremore, eds. *Modernity and Mass Culture*. Bloomington: Indiana UP, 1991.

Brummett, Barry. *Rhetoric in Popular Culture*. New York: St. Martin's, 1994.

Desan, Philippe, Priscilla Parkhurst Ferguson, and Wendy Griswold. "Editors' Introduction: Mirrors, Frames, and Demons: Reflections on the Sociology of Literature." *Literature and Social Practice*. Ed. Desan, Ferguson, and Griswold. Chicago: U of Chicago P, 1989. 1–10.

During, Simon, ed. *The Cultural Studies Reader.* New York: Routledge, 1993.

Eagleton, Terry. "Two Approaches in the Sociology of Literature." *Critical Inquiry* 14 (1988): 469–76.

Easthope, Antony. *Literary into Cultural Studies*. New York: Routledge, 1991.

Fisher, Philip. "American Literary and Cultural Studies since the Civil War." *Redrawing the Boundaries: The Transformation of English and American Literary Studies*. Ed. Stephen Greenblatt and Giles Gunn. New York: MLA, 1992. 232–50.

Giroux, Henry, David Shumway, Paul Smith, and James Sosnoski. "The Need for Cultural Studies: Resisting Intellectuals and Oppositional Public Spheres." *Dalhousie Review* 64.2 (1984): 472–86.

Graff, Gerald, and Bruce Robbins. "Cultural Criticism." *Redrawing the Boundaries: The Transformation of English and American Literary Studies*. Ed. Stephen Greenblatt and Giles Gunn. New York: MLA, 1992. 419–36.

Grossberg, Lawrence, Cary Nelson, and Paula A. Treichler, eds. *Cultural Studies*. New York: Routledge, 1992.

Gunn, Giles. *The Culture of Criticism and the Criticism of Culture*. New York: Oxford UP, 1987.

Hall, Stuart. "Cultural Studies: Two Paradigms." *Media, Culture and Society* 2 (1980): 57–72.

Humm, Peter, Paul Stigant, and Peter Widdowson, eds. *Popular Fictions: Essays in Literature and History*. New York: Methuen, 1986.

Hunt, Lynn, ed. *The New Cultural History: Essays*. Berkeley: U of California P, 1989.

Johnson, Richard. "What Is Cultural Studies Anyway?" *Social Text* 16 (1986–87): 38–80.

Pfister, Joel. "The Americanization of Cultural Studies." *Yale Journal of Criticism* 4 (1991): 199–229.

Punter, David, ed. *Introduction to Contemporary Critical Studies.* New York: Longman, 1986. See especially Punter's "Introduction: Culture and Change" 1–18, Tony Dunn's "The Evolution of Cultural Studies" 71–91, and the essay "Methods for Cultural Studies Students" by Anne Beezer, Jean Grimshaw, and Martin Barker 95–118.

Storey, John. *An Introductory Guide to Cultural Theory and Popular Culture.* Athens: U of Georgia P, 1993.

Turner, Graeme. *British Cultural Studies: An Introduction.* Boston: Unwin Hyman, 1990.

Cultural Studies:
Some Early British Examples

Hoggart, Richard. *Speaking to Each Other.* 2 vols. London: Chatto, 1970.

———. *The Uses of Literacy: Changing Patterns in English Mass Culture.* Boston: Beacon, 1961.

Thompson, E. P. *The Making of the English Working Class.* New York: Harper, 1958.

———. *William Morris: Romantic to Revolutionary.* New York: Pantheon, 1977.

Williams, Raymond. *Culture and Society, 1780–1950.* New York: Harper, 1966.

———. *The Long Revolution.* New York: Columbia UP, 1961.

Cultural Studies:
Continental and Marxist Influences

Althusser, Louis. *For Marx.* Trans. Ben Brewster. New York: Pantheon, 1969.

———. "Ideology and Ideological State Apparatuses." *Lenin and Philosophy.* Trans. Ben Brewster. New York: Monthly Review P, 1971. 127–86.

Althusser, Louis, and Étienne Balibar. *Reading Capital.* Trans. Ben Brewster. New York: Pantheon, 1971.

Bakhtin, Mikhail. *The Dialogic Imagination: Four Essays.* Ed. Michael Holquist. Trans. Caryl Emerson. Austin: U of Texas P, 1981.

———. *Rabelais and His World.* Trans. Hélène Iswolsky. Cambridge: MIT P, 1968.

Baudrillard, Jean. *Simulations.* Trans. Paul Foss, Paul Patton, and Philip Beitchnan. 1981. New York: Semiotext(e), 1983.

Benjamin, Walter. *Illuminations.* Ed. with intro. by Hannah Arendt. Trans. H. Zohn. New York: Harcourt, 1968.

Bennett, Tony. "Marxism and Popular Fiction." Humm, Stigant, and Widdowson 237–65.

Bourdieu, Pierre. *Distinction: A Social Critique of the Judgment of Taste.* Trans. Richard Nice. Cambridge: Harvard UP, 1984.

de Certeau, Michel. *The Practice of Everyday Life.* Trans. Steven F. Rendall. Berkeley: U of California P, 1984.

Derrida, Jacques. *Of Grammatology.* 1969. Trans. Gayatri C. Spivak. Baltimore: Johns Hopkins UP, 1976.

Foucault, Michel. *Discipline and Punish: The Birth of the Prison.* Trans. Alan Sheridan. New York: Pantheon, 1978.

———. *The History of Sexuality.* Trans. Robert Hurley. Vol. 1. New York: Pantheon, 1978.

Gramsci, Antonio. *Selections from the Prison Notebooks.* Ed. Quintin Hoare and Geoffrey Nowell Smith. New York: International, 1971.

Modern Cultural Studies:
Selected British and American Examples

Bagdikian, Ben H. *The Media Monopoly.* Boston: Beacon, 1983.

Bowlby, Rachel. *Shopping with Freud.* New York: Routledge, 1993.

Chambers, Iain. *Popular Culture: The Metropolitan Experience.* New York: Methuen, 1986.

Colls, Robert, and Philip Dodd, eds. *Englishness: Politics and Culture, 1880–1920.* London: Croom Helm, 1986.

Denning, Michael. *Mechanic Accents: Dime Novels and Working-Class Culture in America.* New York: Verso, 1987.

Fiske, John. "British Cultural Studies and Television." *Channels of Discourse: Television and Contemporary Criticism.* Ed. Robert C. Allen. Chapel Hill: U of North Carolina P, 1987.

———. *Television Culture.* New York: Methuen, 1987.

Hebdige, Dick. *Hiding the Light: On Images and Things.* New York: Routledge, 1988.

———. *Subculture: The Meaning of Style.* London: Methuen, 1979.

Huyssen, Andreas. *After the Great Divide: Modernism, Mass Culture, Postmodernism.* Bloomington: Indiana UP, 1986.

Marcus, Greil. *Dead Elvis: A Chronicle of a Cultural Obsession.* New York: Doubleday, 1991.

———. *Lipstick Traces: A Secret History of the Twentieth Century.* Cambridge: Harvard UP, 1989.

Modleski, Tania. *Loving with a Vengeance: Mass-Produced Fantasies for Women.* Hamden: Archon, 1982.

Poovey, Mary. *Uneven Developments: The Ideological Work of Gender in Mid-Victorian England.* Chicago: U of Chicago P, 1988.

Radway, Janice A. *Reading the Romance: Women, Patriarchy, and Popular Literature.* Chapel Hill: U of North Carolina P, 1984.

Reed, T. V. *Fifteen Jugglers, Five Believers: Literary Politics and the Poetics of American Social Movements.* Berkeley: U of California P, 1992.

Ethnic and Minority Criticism: Postcolonial Studies

Anzaldúa, Gloria. *Borderlands: La Frontera = The New Mestiza.* San Francisco: Spinsters/Aunt Lute, 1987.

Baker, Houston. *Blues, Ideology, and Afro-American Literature: A Vernacular Theory.* Chicago: U of Chicago P, 1984.

———. *The Journey Back: Issues in Black Literature and Criticism.* Chicago: U of Chicago P, 1980.

Bhabha, Homi K. *The Location of Culture.* New York: Routledge, 1994.

———, ed. *Nation and Narration.* New York: Routledge, 1990.

———. "Postcolonial Criticism." *Redrawing the Boundaries: The Transformation of English and American Literary Studies.* Ed. Stephen Greenblatt and Giles Gunn. New York: MLA, 1992. 437–65.

Brantlinger, Patrick. *Rule of Darkness: British Literature and Imperialism, 1830–1914.* Ithaca: Cornell UP, 1988.

Gates, Henry Louis, Jr. *Black Literature and Literary Theory.* New York: Methuen, 1984.

———, ed. *"Race," Writing, and Difference.* Chicago: U of Chicago P, 1986.

Gayle, Addison. *The Black Aesthetic.* Garden City: Doubleday, 1971.

———. *The Way of the New World: The Black Novel in America.* Garden City: Doubleday, 1975.

JanMohamed, Abdul. *Manichean Aesthetics: The Politics of Literature in Colonial Africa.* Amherst: U of Massachusetts P, 1983.

JanMohamed, Abdul, and David Lloyd, eds. *The Nature and Context of Minority Discourse.* New York: Oxford UP, 1991.

Kaplan, Amy, and Donald E. Pease, eds. *Cultures of United States Imperialism*. Durham: Duke UP, 1983.

Min-ha, Trinh T. *Woman, Native, Other: Writing Postcoloniality and Feminism*. Bloomington: Indiana UP, 1989.

Neocolonialism. Special issue of *Oxford Literary Review* 13 (1991).

Said, Edward. *After the Last Sky: Palestinian Lives*. New York: Pantheon, 1986.

———. *Culture and Imperialism*. New York: Knopf, 1993.

———. *Orientalism*. New York: Pantheon, 1978.

———. *The World, the Text, and the Critic*. Cambridge: Harvard UP, 1983.

Spivak, Gayatri Chakravorty. *In Other Worlds: Essays in Cultural Politics*. New York: Methuen, 1987.

Stepto, Robert B. *From Behind the Veil: A Study of Afro-American Narrative*. Urbana: U of Illinois P, 1979.

Young, Robert. *White Mythologies: Writing, History, and the West*. London: Routledge, 1990.

Cultural Criticism Relating to
A Portrait of the Artist as a Young Man

Bauerle, Ruth, ed. *Picking Up Airs: Hearing the Music in Joyce's Text*. Urbana: U of Illinois P, 1993.

Bowen, Zack. *Musical Allusions in the Works of James Joyce: Early Poetry through "Ulysses."* Albany: State U of New York P, 1974.

Brown, Richard. *James Joyce and Sexuality*. Cambridge: Cambridge UP, 1985.

Fiedler, Leslie. "To Whom Does Joyce Belong? *Ulysses* as Parody, Pop and Porn." *Light Rays: James Joyce and Modernism*. Ed. Heyward Ehrlich. New York: New Horizon, 1984. 26–30.

Herr, Cheryl. *Joyce's Anatomy of Culture*. Urbana: U of Illinois P, 1986.

Kelly, Joseph. *Our Joyce: From Outcast to Icon*. Austin: U of Texas P, 1998.

Kershner, R. Brandon, ed. *Cultural Studies of Joyce*. Amsterdam: Rodopi, 2003.

———. *Joyce, Bakhtin, and Popular Literature: Chronicles of Disorder*. Chapel Hill: U of North Carolina P, 1989.

———, ed. *Joyce and Popular Culture*. Gainesville: UP of Florida, 1996.

Lamos, Colleen. *Deviant Modernism: Sexual and Textual Errancy in T. S. Eliot, James Joyce, and Marcel Proust.* Cambridge: Cambridge UP, 1998.

Leonard, Garry. *Advertising and Commodity Culture in Joyce.* Gainesville: UP of Florida, 1998.

Leonard, Garry, and Jennifer Wicke, eds. *Joyce and Advertising.* Special issue of *James Joyce Quarterly* 30.4/31.1 (1993).

Lowe-Evans, Mary. *Crimes against Fecundity: Joyce and Population Control.* Syracuse: Syracuse UP, 1989.

Mullin, Katherine. *James Joyce, Sexuality and Social Purity.* Cambridge: Cambridge UP, 2003.

Rainey, Lawrence. *Institutions of Modernism: Literary Elites and Public Culture.* New Haven: Yale UP, 1998.

Saint-Amour, Paul K. *The Copywrights: Intellectual Property and Literary Imagination.* Ithaca: Cornell UP, 2003.

Valente, Joseph, ed. *Quare Joyce.* Ann Arbor: U of Michigan P, 1998.

Watt, Stephen. *Joyce, O'Casey, and the Irish Popular Theatre.* Syracuse: Syracuse UP, 1991.

Wicke, Jennifer. *Advertising Fictions: Literature, Advertisement, and Social Reading.* New York: Columbia UP, 1988.

A CULTURAL PERSPECTIVE

R. BRANDON KERSHNER

The Culture of Dedalus: Urban Circulation, Degeneration, and the Panopticon

Genius is the ability to recall your childhood at will.
                                                                        —Baudelaire

Our experience of Stephen Dedalus's youth is a complicated and heavily mediated affair. Joyce raises but fails to answer directly a host of historical and sociological questions regarding the immediate world of Stephen's experience, and Joyce's readers — most of them now over a century removed from that time and immeasurably distant from that place — have no obvious way of reconstructing for themselves the material culture, the quality of the life-world that invisibly surrounds, forms, and informs Joyce's self-absorbed protagonist. For instance, unless we have studied pictures of Dublin at the end of the nineteenth century it will not occur to us that no adult male would appear in public without a hat, and that this fact is linked to a dense set of assumptions shared by both bourgeois and working-class Dubliners regarding "gentility" and "respectability." Without study we cannot be expected to know that the gradual decline of the Dedalus family, partly attributable to Simon's incompetence and alcoholism, is also the result of an economic crisis that gripped this unique first-world colonial city, a city that social historian Mary Daly has memorably characterized as "the deposed capital."

Dublin was deposed as a capital city with the Act of Union in 1800, making Ireland a part of the British Empire and removing even the limited sort of self-regulation it had formerly possessed. Dublin's ceasing to function as a seat of government, while remaining a sort of "default capital," produced a set of social contradictions that plagued and paralyzed the citizenry throughout the nineteenth century. Dublin Castle functioned as a center of bureaucratic regulation and even, as Joyce makes clear in "Ivy Day in the Committee Room" and in *Ulysses*, as a center of covert and overt surveillance; and yet it did so only as it were by proxy, through appointed representatives of the true metropolitan center of power in London. Further, as Daly observes, "the focus of power in Dublin shifted from the Protestant ascendancy as Catholics gradually took control of local politics, and to a lesser degree of the city's businesses and professions . . . yet . . . the new Catholic middle class was frequently accused of having betrayed its origins, dismissed by phrases such as 'Castle Catholic,' or D. P. Moran's vituperative 'West Briton'" (1). A Catholic of the middle class such as Simon Dedalus might well feel that he is owed deference as a gentleman (by birth) and a true Irishman (i.e., a Catholic), even as he tries to come to terms with his increasing poverty; he might also feel betrayed by his former companions, the "upstarts" of the rising Catholic middle class who seem to have abandoned him as they take up their positions of apparent power; and finally, he might console himself with the realization that for all their petty bickering and political maneuvering, none of them holds any real power — nothing that could change the lives of Ireland's British subjects.

Meanwhile, the city's economic decline — highly unusual for major cities during the industrializing nineteenth century — continued. The local decline was exacerbated by the refusal of English manufacturing interests — especially textiles and woolens, which had been the city's only manufacturing base — to share profits with their easily defeated Irish counterparts. The two main exceptions to this rule were breweries and distilleries on the one hand and publishing and newspapers on the other — alcohol and the production of verbiage both being Irish clichés. Meanwhile, with the help of the famine of the 1840s and its aftermath, Dublin went from being the second largest city in the British Isles and among the ten largest in Europe to ranking second even among Irish cities, overtaken by Belfast (Daly 2). Although its population increased in absolute terms, from 182,000 to 260,000, in the context of the century's giant population expansion this was the equivalent of a precipitous decline.

Some large part of the relative decline was due to emigration in search of jobs. Irish unemployment was the highest in Great Britain, and a 1906 article claimed that "Distress in Dublin due to unemployment is not as it is in some more favourable cities, sporadic and occasional, but endemic and permanent" (qtd. in Daly 64). Joseph O'Brien refers to a "crisis of unemployment" between 1904 and 1912 (213), and we should recall that Stephen's heroic and romantic-seeming self-exile to Europe reflected James Joyce's successful search for gainful employment in another country. Although most of his countrymen chose America or other parts of the British Empire over Europe, Joyce in this regard was part of a sizeable minority. Stephen rather convincingly appears before us bathed in an aura of uniqueness — as if he were himself that traditional, singular work of art that, as Walter Benjamin points out, "withers in the age of mechanical reproduction" (221). But we should remind ourselves that this is an effect of his own internal mythologies. Just as the real Joyce had a number of talented and rebellious peers at University College, all of whom seem to have been erased from *A Portrait,* so Dedalus is one of a cohort of struggling, intelligent, frustrated young Irishmen and Irishwomen grappling with the contradictions of modernity in a "semicolonial" country.

After his father's economic decline — a decline that is all too characteristic of the Irish of his class — Stephen's major battle is with grinding poverty, something only hinted at in the stale crusts and watered tea of *Portrait.* Although comparing degrees of misery is always fruitless, the Dublin poor were surely among the most benighted of Europe, and visiting commentators frequently looked to Bombay and Calcutta for parallels. Roughly a quarter of the Dublin population was classified as in "serious poverty." Public health was in crisis. The system of "drains" or sewage at the turn of the century was antiquated, and much of the effluent simply poured into the Liffey (O'Brien 19).

Plans for reform launched by the Dublin Corporation were frequently abandoned as the economic situation failed to yield sufficient disposable funds (Daly 57). Dublin had the highest rate of mortality among the cities of Great Britain, and in 1898 the mortality rate for children under five years old was 290 out of 1,000 (O'Brien 21). We might note that a harrowing episode in *Stephen Hero* recounts the rather mysterious death of one of Stephen's brothers, while in *Ulysses* the Blooms have a child mortality rate of 50 percent. Stephen is famously averse to bathing, but it should be remembered that in any case very few homes had indoor facilities for washing, and there were few public baths. Although objective statistics are hard to come by, alcoholism (such as Simon Dedalus suffers from) certainly contributed to the ills of many families; so did venereal disease, which at least in the army was rampant, despite the public denials of Irish spokesmen. Some commentators believe that both Joyce and his father suffered from this disease at various points in their lives.

Meanwhile, effective social action seemed to be impossible; the authorities like everyone else in the city appeared to be in the grip of what Joyce characterized as "paralysis." When Joyce's one-time friend Oliver St. John Gogarty, as a public health officer, made progressive proposals for dealing with widespread prostitution in Dublin, Dubliners preferred to turn their heads and pretend that prostitution was strictly a British or a French problem. When the physical degeneration of Dubliners was noted by medical authorities — an effect easily explainable by poor-quality and inadequate food and sanitation — the Bishop of Ross preferred to explain it as the effect of Jews selling adulterated tea (O'Brien 162). The myths and paradigms through which Stephen structures the world of his experience are less noxious than this, but perhaps no less strange.

Stephen's apparent uniqueness and his aesthetic elevation are not disembodied artistic phenomena; they both reflect and contest broader historical currents in Joyce's society and in ours as well. In approaching such problems, a number of possible social and historical contexts present themselves: the situation of Joyce as a colonial writer in the waning years of the British Empire; the situation of Stephen as a young, artistically inclined intellectual at the time of the greatest prestige of positivistic science; the situation of the book as an example of "high culture" literary production during a period when "popular literature" had developed fully but was not yet transmuted into an aspect of "mass culture." But for now, I would like to explore some of *Portrait*'s social and historical resonances by concentrating on two major patterns:

Stephen's attempt to move from observed to observing subject and his deployment of the popular myth of the Genius, linked to images of the superhuman and the subhuman, in his effort to alter his social positioning.

I

In *Discipline and Punish: The Birth of the Prison,* Michel Foucault adapts the eighteenth-century philosopher Jeremy Bentham's invention of the "Panopticon"— an architectural model for a prison in which a central, unseen observer can watch each prisoner at will — as his own model for the technologies of regulation that arose after the eighteenth century in Europe. Before this time, punishment was public and somewhat random; afterward, the idea of ritualistic punishment was gradually replaced by the concept of individual rehabilitation, a process that would be continuously monitored. As Foucault notes, the Panopticon model applies not only to prisons but to schools, hospitals, factories, sanatoriums, and by extension, to the whole of European society as it becomes increasingly bureaucratic. Without itself embodying power, it models the pathways through which power must flow. The effects upon the participants, Foucault suggests, are basic: "The Panopticon is a machine for dissociating the see/being seen dyad: in the peripheral ring, one is totally seen, without ever seeing; in the central tower, one sees everything without being seen" (201–02).

At the beginning of *Portrait* all sources of authority blend together for Stephen — his family, other adults, the church, the state, books, even older children, all of whom seem to know the rules of which he is ignorant. Gradually, he learns to distinguish among these sources and their varying ideologies. For instance, the state rather paradoxically combines Britain's colonial administration with local "nationalist" authorities who both represent and contest Britain's power (Parnell is the prime example here). Similarly, while the church formally claims no temporal power, in popular mythology it is associated with the independence movement; this is the tradition to which Dante appeals when she asserts that "[t]he priests were always the true friends of Ireland" (p. 47 in this volume). At the same time, popular wisdom notes that it now appears intimately involved with the colonial administration. As Simon Dedalus says of the Jesuits, "Those are the fellows that can get you a position" (p. 75).

But while Stephen comes to master these distinctions intellectually, on a more fundamental level he is coming to realize that what constantly observes him is no individual or group of individuals, but a faceless "They" whose identities, motivations, and sources of authority are finally irrelevant. Foucault notes that the mechanism of the Panopticon "automatizes and disindividualizes power. Power has its principle not so much in a person as in a certain concerted distribution of bodies, surfaces, lights, gazes." Finally, the observation is internalized by the one observed, who "inscribes in himself the power relation in which he simultaneously plays both roles; he becomes the principle of his own subjection" (Foucault 202–03). As Stephen announces much later in *Ulysses,* tapping his brow, "In here it is I must kill the priest and the king" (15: 4436–37).

An observing but somehow distant or disembodied eye haunts Stephen throughout *Portrait.* First is his father, who "looked at him through a glass" (p. 20), immediately followed by the sharp-eyed eagles who threaten to "pull out his eyes" if he does not apologize for his (unconscious) error of wishing to marry a Protestant girl. The peculiar turn that the mechanism of observation and discipline takes in *Portrait* is that it is often Stephen's own sight that is threatened or brought into question. As he grows more conscious of the watching authorities he is correspondingly more aware that "his eyes were weak and watery" (p. 21). When Father Dolan arrives in the classroom the students are displayed in organized rows, all easily visible from his position of authority. He knows that particular boys deserve punishment not only because he can immediately see that they are not doing their lesson but because, as he warns a child, "I can see it in your eye" (p. 56). The eye of authority sees, while Stephen's eye only betrays. Dolan's "nocoloured eyes behind the steelrimmed spectacles" (p. 57) are invulnerable, but after his punishment, myopic Stephen is further blinded by tears.

As Stephen grows, his sins become more substantial: first masturbation, then consorting with prostitutes. His initial reaction is disengagement, as he sees that no immediate retribution has come. Indeed, he thinks that his sin has "covered him from the sight of God" (p. 102), whose cosmic, sleepless eye has superseded all others. But after the first retreat sermon he imagines that he has merely exchanged God's gaze for one more demonic; he sees himself as a beastly body, "gazing out of darkened eyes, helpless, perturbed and human for a bovine god to stare upon" (p. 107). And the text of the final sermon, *"I am cast away from the sight of Thine eyes"* (Psalms 30:23; p. 119) makes it clear to him that to be removed from God's sight means to cease to exist in any familiar sense. He will be cast into utter darkness, "not even able to remove from the eye a worm that gnaws it" (p. 114). Unseen by God — or by His representative, the church — the sinner no longer exists as human. Or will he be unseen? The hellfire sermon's whole point is to visually display the sufferings sinners like Stephen will undergo; in it, Father Arnall creates an eye — the "eye of the narrative"— that sadistically notes every nuance of the pain of the damned.

From the emphasis on sight, it might seem that what is in question here is the transgressor's actions, or even appearance, but this is not so. As Foucault makes clear, the Panopticon model is a technology of self-hood: "It is no longer the body, but the soul" that is addressed by authority (101). Foucault articulates a central paradox of modern societies: that the ideology of individualism, which purports to assign value to people "in themselves," is an effect of the Panopticon model of surveillance and discipline. The individual must be known — in effect, socially created in distinction to others — in order to be educated, policed, healed, and generally categorized. The confessional to which Stephen resorts neatly embodies this contradiction, because here Stephen will confess the secret thoughts and actions that he believes have made him uniquely damned, and here the priest will assign him to the proper category of sinners and set him the approved penance for his case. Here, as Marxist critics argue is generally the case, the ideology of individualism is easily appropriated by authority.

As is usual in Romantic novels — and *Portrait* shares many characteristics with the Romantic variety of *Bildungsroman* — the protagonist's response to the totalizing power of social institutions is not to abandon the ideology of individualism on which those institutions rest but to assert even more forcefully his unique selfhood. Nor is this necessarily entirely ineffectual. Michel de Certeau has discussed ways in which people in modern societies are able to resist their cultures' totalizing tendencies through what he calls "practices" or "tactics":

> A way of using imposed systems constitutes the resistance to the historical law of a state of affairs and its dogmatic legitimations. A practice of the order constructed by others redistributes its space; it creates at least a certain play in that order, a space for maneuvers of unequal forces and for utopian points of reference. (18)

Popular culture, de Certeau asserts, can be one such practice. Unlike Theodor Adorno, who sees modern mass culture as merely a repressive part of the ideological state apparatus, de Certeau sees ways in which examples of mass culture can be liberating.

Certainly this is the way in which Stephen attempts to use his reading of Alexandre Dumas's *The Count of Monte Cristo*. The hero of the novel, Edmond Dantes, is betrayed by his friends on the day he was to wed the beautiful Mercedes, and is unjustly thrown into an island prison; there, with the help of a fellow prisoner, he transforms himself into a master of all arts and sciences. After his escape he retrieves the lost treasure of the Borgias, whose location his fellow prisoner has entrusted to him, and returns to France, unrecognizable, as the Count of Monte Cristo. There, shrouded in mystery, with almost superhuman powers and endless wealth, he takes his revenge on his former friends. He also coldly rejects Mercedes, who abandoned hope of his return too soon for Dantes's liking, with the words, "Madam, I never eat muscatel grapes" (p. 67). The count's weapons throughout are those that Stephen claims: silence, exile, and cunning (Kershner, *Joyce* 204).

As Dantes himself explains in an extended speech, the real source of his power is the fact that he belongs to no country; indeed, he has no identity. We might say he has stepped outside the Panopticon, or has discovered an invisible location within it. Throughout the book he adopts different disguises and sets a variety of elaborate plots in motion, then quite literally sits back and watches their denouement like a spectator at a drama. His mastery of the social forms — for example, his cold politeness — masks the fact that he no longer belongs to French society and is immune to its claims upon him. Although he and his Oriental slave girl are a spectacle in Paris, in a fundamental sense he cannot be seen by others and has usurped the position of author-observer. Indeed, all the literary figures with whom Stephen identifies in the second chapter, such as Claude Melnotte (from Bulwer-Lytton's *Lady of Lyons*) or Ingomar (from Maria Lovell's *Ingomar the Barbarian*) are disguised outsiders who gain power by virtue of that fact (Kershner, *Joyce* 221–27).

II

But what is actually happening when Stephen attempts to construct himself as subject with the aid of such fantasies? And what are their roots and implications? I would argue that these are important questions for the book, because the "aristocracy of art" (Harper 6) to which Stephen lays claim, the particular language in which he expresses his sense of superiority, the imagery with which he portrays those around him, and even his final decision to conjoin exile with authorship are all aspects of his attempt at social self-definition (Joyceans more usually refer to Stephen's attempt to "father himself"). I want to suggest that Stephen's defensive tactic, his ascent to the sphere of art, is entangled with a number of formations in the nineteenth-century popular mind, many of which have their genesis in scientific conceptions of the period. It should not be overlooked that the methodology of positivistic science is itself a mode of subject formation, in that it places the scientist-observer at the center of his own Panopticon. Indeed, nineteenth-century medical scientists and psychologists, with their clinical studies and pathological taxonomies, are major contributors to Foucault's conception. Yet on the other hand, each scientist or pseudoscientist, insofar as he feels able to "step outside" his society in order to view humanity with detachment, can make some weak claim to having regained the center of the universe.

Many scientific approaches to humanity in the late nineteenth century, for all their vaunted objectivity, seem from our contemporary perspective to be rather transparently structured by exactly those social norms from which they declare their independence. Most versions of sociology and anthropology, for instance, were heavily "racialist" (we would say, pejoratively, "racist") in their foundations. Beginning with de Gobineau's influential *Essay on the Inequality of the Human Races* (1853–55), which proposed the idea of an Aryan race, a host of books elaborated the idea of a spectrum of races, which was in fact a disguised hierarchy, each with different "essential" qualities. Following Darwin, the idea that different races represent different biological stages in the development of modern man soon gained general acceptance, with the Anglo-Saxon race, at least in British books, often placed at the summit. Otherwise, the crown was usually awarded to de Gobineau's synthetic "Aryan race," which unsurprisingly happened to include strains from most politically dominant European nations.

Even so firm a believer in the determining force of culture as Matthew Arnold adopted a racial rhetoric when he codified the characteristics of the Celtic and English peoples in his 1867 *Study of Celtic Literature.* In the essay, Seamus Deane observes, "Of course, every virtue of the Celt was matched by a vice of the British bourgeoisie; everything the philistine middle classes of England needed, the Celt could supply. (The reverse was also true.)" (25). Arnold's binary opposition, which George Bernard Shaw parodically reversed in his 1907 play *John Bull's Other Island,* pictured the Celt as dreamy, imaginative, and ineffectual, full of primitive vigor and sensuality, while presenting the Anglo-Saxon as pragmatic, hardworking but anemic and overcivilized, yet filled with the virtues of intellectual force and organization. Less sympathetic English portraitists, enraged by the increasing political agitation of the late nineteenth century in Ireland, filled the Sunday press with cartoons of barely civilized, apelike Irishmen. No wonder Stephen fears that the peasant woman he once saw in a doorway, a "batlike soul," is "a type of her race and his own" (pp. 165). He knows that "[t]his race . . . produced me" (p. 181) and can only hope that by superhuman effort and some miraculous personal transformation he may be able to "forge in the smithy of [his] soul the uncreated conscience of [his] race" (p. 224).

But race was a particularly vexed question in late-nineteenth-century Ireland, where indigenous racial myths collided with political realities. When Stephen describes the statue of the Irish national poet Thomas Moore as "a Firbolg in the borrowed cloak of a Milesian," he refers to an Irish belief that the original rude, dwarfish inhabitants of Ireland, called Firbolgs, intermixed with a tall, "aristocratic" race that originated in Spain. From the condescension he shows his peasant friend Davin, whom he calls "Firbolg" (p. 162), there is no doubt that Stephen considers himself the true Milesian. When Davin questions whether he is Irish at all, Stephen offers to show his friend the Dedalus family crest and family tree in the office of arms (p. 181). Indeed, one of the first things we hear him tell a schoolfellow is that his father is "[a] gentleman" (p. 22). In reality, of course, from the perspective of any recognized aristocracy Simon Dedalus could at best consider himself a member of the bourgeoisie fallen on hard times.

Racial myths aside, the social structure of Ireland at the time virtually guaranteed that claims to true social distinction were reserved for members of the Protestant "Anglo-Irish Ascendancy" who made up the great bulk of the landholding class as well as dominating the professions (O'Brien 5), rather than Catholic families like the Dedaluses (or the Joyces, for that matter). Still, aristocracy was a slippery concept at the turn of the century, when commoners could earn British peerages by conspicuous merit, or even indirectly purchase them. The originally Celtic Irish, whose traditional systems of class distinction had been destroyed, by default considered themselves "all kings' sons," somewhat as Americans came to consider descent from Mayflower families a kind of de facto claim to aristocracy. The fact that many of the Irish national leaders such as Parnell were from old Protestant Anglo-Irish families was tactfully ignored by middle-class Catholics. The conflicting claims of political and racial nationalism further complicated the issue. In the 1870s the Irish parliamentary leader Isaac Butt and the radical nationalist John Mitchel had both argued for greater Irish self-determination on the grounds that the Irish should join the British in administering the empire of "lesser breeds"; fifteen years later, Parnell and others were speaking out for the rights of Irish, Indians, Chinese, and other victims of British oppression (Brasted). The shift in political identification entailed a change in the contextualizing of racial identity as well, underlining the fact that the concept of race had always had an unacknowledged political element.

Stephen's growing sense of his own aristocracy is paradoxical, confused, and heavily overdetermined; that is, it has a multitude of contributing causes. On the level of personal psychology, Stephen is engaged in what Freud identified as a fantasy shared by many prepubescent children of the period that they were not really the children of their own parents but actually the offspring of nobility, for unknown reasons being raised in ordinary households. On a social level, his confused sense of election reflects a general confusion about what could constitute aristocracy in modern Ireland. Stephen invokes his family's ancient lineage in Ireland, but then so could the Murphys and Dolans whom he scorns. Formal titles of aristocracy were mostly reserved for the Anglo-Irish families who had been imported into the country starting in the Tudor period, and though many of these families considered themselves as Irish as any Celt, their titles were a function of empire, and thus (for Stephen) were tainted. The old aristocracy of lineage was gradually giving way during the nineteenth century to an aristocracy of capital; and indeed during the brief period when his family is better off than his neighbors Stephen is happy enough to consider this a sign of election. When the Dedaluses fall on hard times, however, he decides that they are still noble, but distressed.

III

But overriding these conflicting paradigms of racial and personal distinction was the doctrine of racial and familial degeneration, which by the turn of the century had blossomed from a hypothesis suggested by a few clinical psychologists and anthropologists into an article of popular faith and a cause for general alarm throughout Great Britain and Europe (Gilman; Kershner 1986). In his 1857 *Treatise on the Physical, Intellectual, and Moral Degeneration on the Human Species,* the French physician B. A. Morel hypothesized that an organism's necessary but costly adaptation to pathological circumstances could include dangerous modifications that would be exaggerated in later generations, leading to sterility and death. Valentin Magnan's *The Degenerates* (1895) extended this idea, arguing that a weakening of the "psychophysical resistance" of certain species, or indeed human families or inbred groups, would be progressive. Since most scientists up through the turn of the century were Lamarckian — that is, they believed that acquired characteristics in an organism would be passed on to later generations — this process was seen as more rapid and unopposed than would be the case with the slower modifications produced by Darwinian selection. Social commentators, such as Max Nordau in his highly influential book *Degeneration,* translated in 1895, extended the idea to the realms of politics and art: everything of which Nordau disapproved in modern society — from Impressionist painting, Wagnerism, and Ibsenism to Marxism and women's education — was for him a sign of physical and mental degeneration. Impressionist paintings were fuzzy, he asserted, because the painters were victims of "nystagmus," a trembling of the eyeball. Feminists were really masculine females, Ibsenites hysterics, and so on through his personal list of modern evils.

Nordau, a physician, claimed that his argument was neither political nor aesthetic but merely a scientific diagnosis. Meanwhile, Darwin's demonstration that humanity had evolved from animal species lent a nightmarish coloration to the popularization of the idea of degeneration: under primitive conditions, or indeed under the pathological conditions of lower-class urban life, might not humans physically regress, becoming increasingly animal? The general tendency of late-nineteenth-century scientific and sociological thinking was to look for overt physical signs of "bestiality" that would mirror an individual's degenerate inner state. One of the most honored scientists of the time, Cesare Lombroso, published a book in 1878 that purported to distinguish subhuman criminal types from the population as a whole on the basis of facial and bodily appearance. What he called the born criminal was an atavism, a reversion to fierce primitive ancestors and even beasts, especially the apes.

British and European thinkers around the turn of the century were increasingly worried by various forms of the idea of degeneration. The British in particular feared the urban underclass, then called the "residuum," whose members lived in conditions that liberal reformers called "subhuman"; it was an easy step even for liberals like Lombroso to see the people themselves as less than human, through no fault of their own. The dubious performance by the British army in the Boer War and the disturbing statistics on physical fitness that emerged from the army's examinations of potential recruits fed popular fears that the empire was in a decline that was not only spiritual but biological. Racism fed these fears, inasmuch as the expansion of the British Empire had led to a certain amount of miscegenation, and mixing of races was widely held to lead to degeneration. The distinguished biologist Louis Agassiz argued that "interbreeding" was catastrophic: "Let anyone who doubts the evil of this mixture of races . . . come to Brazil. He cannot deny the deterioration consequent upon the amalgamation of races" (qtd. in Holmes 248–49).

Another focus of the fears of degeneration was sexual license, especially masturbation, which was thought to be a clear sign of degeneracy. J. H. Kellogg, a physician and director of the American cereal company, argued that an obsession with sensual matters would be inherited, leading to a decline in the race. Indeed, even the lawfully married could not be too careful about the spirit in which they approached sexuality:

> It is an established physiological fact that the character of off-
> spring is influenced by the mental as well as the physical condi-
> tions of the parents at the moment of the performance of the
> generative act. In view of this fact, how many parents can regard
> the precocious — or even mature — manifestations of sexual
> depravity in their children without painful smitings of conscience
> at seeing the legitimate results of their own voluptuousness? (qtd.
> in Walters 152)

Many Victorian convictions about sexuality, such as the belief that masturbation could lead to idiocy, arose against the backdrop of racial degeneration.

The two themes — the sexual and the racial — were, of course, commonly intertwined, in that the "lesser" races were believed to be prone to sexual indulgence. Such a belief, a classic example of the projection of repressed desires onto the "Other," applied even to the Irish, with their extremely low birthrate, their late marriages, and their rigid social separation of the sexes in youth. Stephen's guilt and terror at his sexual self-indulgence arises from religious and ethical sources, but the imagery in which his unease expresses itself is rooted in degeneration theory. Stephen sees beasts all around him, and in despair sees himself also as an animal: "he rose and went to the window, clearing the thick scum from his mouth with his tongue and licking it from his lips. So he had sunk to the state of a beast that licks his chaps after meat" (p. 107). If Stephen is sometimes an animal, his friends are almost invariably so. Lynch is reptilian, Davin brutish, Temple gnomish. His erotic dreams are populated by "apelike creatures" (p. 110), perhaps recalling the "feeble creature like a monkey" who turns out to be a senile relative of his and who mistakes him for "Josephine" (pp. 71–72). In his hallucinatory vision following the sermon he sees "[g]oatish creatures with human faces, hornybrowed, . . . trailing their long tails behind them," one of which is clutching around his ribs a torn waistcoat (p. 128).

Perhaps the most vivid such example is the old "captain," the library attendant with monkey's eyes whose "blackish monkey-puckered face pursed its human mouth with gentle pleasure" (p. 202). Stephen immediately thinks of the rumor that the man is the product of an incestuous union (one of the surest routes to degeneration), and he elaborately envisions the seduction scene: a couple lie beside a pond slimed by swans and embrace "without joy or passion." Stephen notes that the man's hand is Davin's and is angry with himself at the thought. Perhaps a part of his anger expresses his unarticulated fear that the true Irish peasant race has incestuously bred itself backward along the evolutionary path. He does not want to see the peasantry as subhuman but does so despite himself, fearing that they are himself, or at least the paradoxically subhuman angel with whom he must wrestle. In his diary he notes dreaming of struggling with an ignorant old peasant with "red-rimmed horny eyes" (p. 223), recalling the "hornybrowed" (p. 128) Pan figures of his vision (as well as Jacob wrestling with his angel in Genesis 32).

Stephen hopes to be his race's savior, and oddly enough he expresses this hope in terms of a kind of Lamarckian spiritual eugenics: how, he asks, could he "cast his shadow over the imagination of their daughters, before their squires begat upon them, that they might breed a race less ignoble than their own?" (p. 211) And just as Stephen imagines an alternative future for his race, so he imagines alternative versions of its past. In his diary he notes a pair of dreams, in the first of which he visits a gallery "peopled by the images of fabulous kings" whose eyes are "darkened for the errors of men"; in the second he sees "strange figures" who are "not as tall as men" advancing from a cave, their faces "phosphorescent, with darker streaks" (p. 221). These silent creatures stare at him as if to ask him something. Is he the son of eternal kings, or the offspring of something subhuman? Or are the creatures, like H. G. Wells's degenerate Morlocks in *The Time Machine,* not his race's past but its future?

Clearly, Joyce's representation of Stephen is shot through with ambivalences, ambiguities, and contradictions with respect to race and, more generally, with respect to the young man's status. Is he a Milesian among Firbolgs, or a Firbolg himself? Are all the Irish a brutish race — as Goethe put it, like dogs always baying around some noble stag — or are they, as Davin believes, a noble alternative to the brutal English? Is Stephen in some sense an aristocrat, and if so, in what sense? From about the end of the first chapter, Stephen is continually judging his own superiority or inferiority to others, and his judgment vacillates wildly with his mood and experiences. But very seldom does he view himself as basically *like* his schoolmates. More often, he feels infinitely their superior or else far beneath them, but in either case he sees himself as different in kind. Certainly this is a matter of character, and certainly it has to do with his sense of uniqueness as an aspiring artist, but both Stephen's character and his sense of election are greatly dependent on social formations of the time. The particular form of Stephen's self-exaltation depends upon a complex of ideas and images at the turn of the century that derive from the patterns of degeneration and progressive evolution and that cluster around the term *genius*.

IV

The word *genius* did not begin to take on its modern sense of a uniquely talented man — the word was almost invariably reserved for males — until the eighteenth century (Battersby 2). But it was the Romantics who impressed the concept with their logic of exclusion, creating the genius not simply as a person with a greater talent than others but as a man different in kind from other men, and superior to them. As Christine Battersby explains, genius "had been transformed from a kind of talent into a superior type of being who walked a 'sublime' path between 'sanity' and 'madness,' between the 'monstrous' and the 'superhuman,'" and the focus had shifted toward the personality of the creative individual (103). Byron, the poet Stephen defends from his schoolfellows' mockery, was the most famous "type" of the genius. His unconventional life, his notorious affairs, and even the rumors of incest in his life all fed his legend. Even the Count of Monte Cristo, with all his sinister uniqueness, is seen by Parisian society as Byronic. On the other hand, in *On Heroes and Hero-Worship* (1840), the essayist Thomas Carlyle stressed the divine quality of the genius, the "most precious gift that Heaven can give to the Earth; a man of 'genius' as we call it; the Soul of Man actually sent down from the skies, with a God's-message to us" (38). At the least the genius was a sort of secular saint. Indeed, the poetic genius in particular was held up as being himself a sort of God; as early as the eighteenth century the Earl of Shaftesbury claimed in *Characteristics* that "a poet is indeed a second Maker; a just Prometheus under Jove" (93).

Thus Stephen's final goal, to become a "priest of the eternal imagination, transmuting the daily bread of experience into the radiant body of everliving life" (p. 196), merely restates in slightly less blasphemous terms the divine mission of the genius. The genius was the carrier of the *logos spermatikos,* the engendering "word" discussed by St. John and by the Stoics; much of the rhetoric surrounding the genius during the nineteenth century put equal emphasis on the sexual and the transcendent qualities of this extraordinary being. In his 1767 *Essay on Original Genius,* William Duff reported that the ardor of a genius makes him "particularly susceptible of the charms of the fair sex," but warned that the youthful genius might waste his powers in "dangerous passion" (qtd. in Battersby 79). Others took a less morally rigid view, arguing that the sexual athleticism of a figure like Balzac was simply another expression of his superhuman potency. In this light Stephen's sexual precociousness, whatever its personal cost to him, is but one more sign of his potential genius.

But perhaps the most bizarre transmutation of the genius figure resulted from its insertion into the myth of degeneration. Lombroso was responding to this strange linkage when he followed his book on criminal types with one on hereditary genius. Late in the nineteenth century a number of medical observers, inspired by the period's mania for finding physiological and biological correlates for "spiritual" qualities, underwrote the popular view that genius, rebelliousness, and madness were closely allied. Reversing the polarity of Max Nordau's judgments in his book *Degeneration,* they argued that the reason so many of the artistic and intellectual figures he discussed displayed "degenerate" qualities was because genius was itself a possible aspect of degeneration. In 1895 W. L. Babcock discussed the possible patterns of life for what he termed a biological "throwback":

> First, and most prominent in the order of frequency is an early death. Second, he may swell the criminal ranks. Third, he may become mentally deranged and ultimately find his way into a hospital for the insane. Fourth, and least frequently, he startles the world by an invention or discovery in science or by an original composition of great merit in art, music, or literature. He is then styled a genius. (qtd. in Becker 38–39)

This version of the genius, of course, is directly opposed to the more common variant in which he is the next evolutionary step in a vaguely Darwinian model.

The figure of the genius-degenerate does neatly capture a fundamental ambivalence about the superman figure that was to play itself out later in science-fiction treatments: a man sufficiently superior to ordinary mortals becomes not only a hope for the race (or the species) but a threat to it as well. Many of the genius figures of literary high modernism, such as Stephen or D. H. Lawrence's Rupert Birkin, are strongly ambivalent in their attitude to ordinary humanity. Even the Count of Monte Cristo, in good Faustian fashion, has purchased his remarkable abilities at the cost of his common humanity, and as Dumas's novel draws to a close he frequently agonizes over whether he has become a diabolic figure rather than the agent of providence. At least in the popular mind, these extremes tend to meet: the superman and the throwback, the genius and the degenerate are similar in that they owe little allegiance to the rest of humanity, that crowd whom the young Joyce called "the rabblement." Again, aspects of this pattern pervade *Portrait*. By the church's standards, Stephen is indeed a moral criminal. Around the time of his experience with the prostitute, he feels totally removed from the rest of mankind, and looks on it coldly. "He had known neither the pleasure of companionship with others nor the vigour of rude male health nor filial piety. Nothing stirred within his soul but a cold and cruel and loveless lust" (p. 94). Even his sanity is in question: we should realize that during the retreat sermon he literally hears voices and sees visions — visions even more compelling than those he sees in moments of inspiration.

In some respects, the Romantic genius figure only reached full flower at the end of the nineteenth century, when science and pseudo-science lent their authority to ideas of a superior being. As late as 1903 Joyce's famous contemporary, the Austrian writer Otto Weininger, twenty-three years old and the author of an influential study of genius, sought out the room in which Beethoven had died in order to commit suicide; he believed that it was better to die than to live with mere talent and convinced himself by racialist arguments that Jews like himself could not be geniuses. Perhaps without intending to do so, Francis Galton, the founder of modern eugenics and the cousin of Darwin, encouraged such a radical view in his study *Hereditary Genius* (1869). Galton's assumption, which he claims to defend logically, is that "high reputation is a pretty accurate test of high ability" in any field (2), and his thesis is that men of the most exceptional "natural gifts" more often than not are genetically related to others; he is particularly interested in "famous families" such as the Adamses in America and the Russells and Darwins in England.

It soon becomes clear, however, that Galton's ostensibly objective, scientific study is actually legitimizing an aristocracy. His tacit assumptions are made clear in his casual note that France would be a poor subject for study because "the Revolution and the guillotine made sad havoc among the progeny of her abler races" (4). As the phrase "abler races" makes explicit, Galton's approach is actually a microscopic version of a racialist and classist argument, and indeed his project occurred to him during an examination of the characteristics and abilities of various races. In his preface to the book's 1898 edition, Galton admits that he is concerned by "the striking effects of an evil inheritance" that are shown in "the yearly output by unfit parents of weakly children who are constitutionally incapable of growing up into serviceable citizens" (xx). On the other hand, it is now possible to breed a superior race:

> The improvement of the natural gifts of future generations of the human race is largely, though indirectly, under our control. . . . The processes of evolution are in constant and spontaneous activity, some pushing toward the bad, some towards the good. Our part is to watch for opportunities to intervene. (xxvi–xxvii)

By the turn of the century, such ideas were in the air even in Ireland and seemed all the more crucial because of widespread fears of racial degeneration. Because most scientists had been Lamarckian until well after the turn of the century, few people understood that Darwinian selection was an effective corrective to such minor instances of biological degeneration as actually occurred (and that these invariably happened among very primitive organisms). Even in 1921, the physician Samuel Holmes could announce that "everywhere the nemesis of degeneracy hangs threateningly over the organic world" (4–5). Yet this specter was not enough to rally people to Galton's eugenics program. Whatever millennial hope the idea of positive evolution held out was counterbalanced by a certain fear of the evolution of a "master race." Some observers wondered just who was to implement programs like Galton's, and on what basis. On a less conscious level, popular myths articulated deep fears of the superman. Dracula, for example, is firmly identified in the Irishman Bram Stoker's 1897 novel as a degenerate and criminal type; the character who realizes this makes formal, scholarly allusions to Lombroso and Nordau. Indeed, it is because they can identify him as a degenerate that the band of heroes is able to outsmart the vampire despite his superhuman powers. We can only wonder at the nineteenth-century faith in taxonomy that allows a creature who is dead and drinks blood to be subsumed so easily into a generally accepted physiological-psychological category.

Meanwhile, a more fundamental if less likely threat had been articulated in imaginative literature. Since about midcentury, increasingly alienated artists had been envisioning new and superior types of men, such as the poet Arthur Rimbaud's "assassins," who would have no truck with the bourgeois rabblement. In a well-known essay, Hugh Kenner pointed out the affinity between the innately superior figure of the dandy and aesthete, such as Yeats's Owen Aherne, and the "super-brain," whose most popular version was Sherlock Holmes; both these are reflected in Stephen Dedalus (158–78). Friedrich Nietzsche's *Übermensch* is the most famous of these conceptions, a superior creature who is beyond ordinary morality and is, by the Christian standards that Nietzsche deplored, a monster of egotism. In *Ulysses* Stephen's friend Mulligan, feeling his side, claims that his twelfth rib is gone, and exclaims, "I'm the *Übermensch*. [Stephen] and I, the super-men" (1:708–09). Mulligan is being facetious, but toward the climax of *Portrait*, when Stephen envisions the mysterious host who "call to me, their kinsman, making ready to go, shaking the wings of their exultant and terrible youth" (p. 223), he is fully serious.

"A man of genius," says Stephen in *Ulysses*, "makes no mistakes. His errors are volitional and are the portals of discovery" (9:228–29). Shortly afterward, he announces: "His own image to a man with that queer thing genius is the standard of all experience, material and moral" (9:432–33). One implication of these rather obscure pronouncements is that the genius makes his own rules and cannot fail — if he were to fail, he would be no genius. And if his "own image" is the "standard of all experience," then he is outside the Panopticon entirely. He cannot be identified and judged by "Them" because he is literally incomparable to those around him. He embodies the frightening superiority of H. G. Wells's *Invisible Man*. The genius, the superman, the aristocrat of art — all these are attempts to recenter the subject, the "I," in a world grown maddeningly regimented and restricted. For Stephen, his own transformation into some vaguely imagined winged being, an aesthete high above the multitude, is bound up mysteriously with the idea of escape; because he is Irish, he can briefly convince himself that in France they order these things better, or at least less. Later he will return, his wings clipped.

The interlocking cultural constructions of genius and degeneration,

I have tried to show, inform *Portrait,* and function as oppositional structures — "tactics," in de Certeau's terms — to the social Panopticon. Naturally, I have adopted a faintly parodic tone in discussing these constructions: we know better now than to invest our energies in such outmoded and scientifically invalid terms. And yet the occasion of this essay, and of the entire volume, is Joyce's "genius," which was first perversely recognized as a sort of degeneracy, as a glance at *Portrait*'s early reviews will show. Although I have tried to demonstrate ways in which genius and degeneracy pervade late-nineteenth-century writing as a whole, including literary, subliterary, and nonliterary works, the unacknowledged point of my demonstration has been, paradoxically, that this pervasiveness is significant because it exists also in Joyce. If our common humanity is a fundamental tenet of contemporary Western culture, it would seem that we are equally committed to a fascination with the uncommon strains that play within it, at a cost we do not usually recognize or assess.

WORKS CITED

Arnold, Matthew. *The Study of Celtic Literature.* Port Washington, NY and London: Kennikat, 1970.

Battersby, Christine. *Gender and Genius.* London: Woman's Press, 1989.

Becker, George. *The Mad Genius Controversy: A Study in the Sociology of Deviance.* London: Sage, 1978.

Benjamin, Walter. *Illuminations.* Trans. Harry Zohn. New York: Schocken, 1969.

Brasted, H. V. "Irish Nationalism and the British Empire in the Late Nineteenth Century." *Irish Culture and Nationalism, 1750–1950.* Ed. Oliver MacDonagh, et al. New York: St. Martin's, 1983. 83–103.

Carlyle, Thomas. *On Heroes, Hero-Worship, and the Heroic in History.* Ed. Michael K. Goldberg, Joel J. Brattin, and Mark Engel. Berkeley: U of California P, 1993.

Certeau, Michel de. *The Practice of Everyday Life.* Trans. Steven Randall. Berkeley: U of California P, 1988.

Costello, Peter. *James Joyce: The Years of Growth, 1882–1915.* London: Kyle Cathie, 1992.

Daly, Mary E. *Dublin: The Deposed Capital: A Social and Economic History 1860–1914.* Cork: Cork UP, 1984.

Deane, Seamus. *Celtic Revivals.* London: Faber, 1985.

Foucault, Michel. *Discipline and Punish: The Birth of the Prison*. Trans. Alan Sheridan. New York: Vintage, 1979.

Galton, Francis. *Hereditary Genius: An Inquiry into Its Laws and Consequences*. 1869. New York: St. Martin's, 1978.

Gilman, Sander, ed. *Degeneration: The Dark Side of Progress*. New York: Columbia UP, 1985.

Gobineau, Arthur, Comte de. *Essai sur l'inégalité des races humaines*. Paris: Belfond, 1967.

Harper, Margaret Mills. *The Aristocracy of Art in Joyce and Woolf*. Baton Rouge: Louisiana State UP, 1990.

Holmes, Samuel J. *The Trend of the Race: A Study of Present Tendencies in the Biological Development of Civilized Mankind*. New York: Harcourt, 1921.

Horkheimer, Max, and Theodor N. Adorno. "The Culture Industry: Enlightenment as Mass Deception." In *The Dialectic of Enlightenment*. New York: Continuum, 1985. 120–67.

Jackson, John Wyse, and Peter Costello. *John Stanislaus Joyce: The Voluminous Life and Genius of James Joyce's Father*. London: Fourth Estate, 1997.

Joyce, James. *Ulysses*. Ed. Hans Walter Gabler, et al. New York: Random, 1986.

Kenner, Hugh. *Dublin's Joyce*. Boston: Beacon, 1962.

Kershner, R. B. "Degeneration: The Explanatory Nightmare." *Georgia Review* 40 (Summer 1986): 416–44.

———. *Joyce, Bakhtin, and Popular Literature: Chronicles of Disorder*. Chapel Hill: U of North Carolina P, 1989.

Lombroso, Cesare. *L'homme criminel*. 2 volumes. Paris: F. Alcan, 1895.

Magnan, Jacques Joseph Valentin. *Les Dégénerés: Etat mental et syndromes épisodiques*. Paris: Rueff, 1895.

Mullin, Katherine. *James Joyce. Sexuality and Social Purity*. Cambridge: Cambridge UP, 2003.

Nordau, Max Simon. *Degeneration*. New York: Fertig, 1968.

O'Brien, Joseph V. *"Dear, Dirty Dublin": A City in Distress, 1899–1916*. Berkeley: U of California P, 1982.

Shaftesbury, Anthony Ashley Cooper, Third Earl of. *Characteristics of Man, Manners, Opinions, Times*. Ed. Lawrence E. Klein. Cambridge: Cambridge UP, 1999.

Shaw, George Bernard. *John Bull's Other Island, and Major Barbara*. New York: Brentano's, 1907.

Walters, Ronald G., ed. *Primers for Prudery: Sexual Advice to Victorian America*. Englewood Cliffs: Prentice, 1974.

Postcolonial Criticism
and
A Portrait of the Artist
as a Young Man

WHAT IS POSTCOLONIAL CRITICISM?

Postcolonial literature refers to a body of literature written by authors with roots in countries that were once colonies established by European nations, whereas *postcolonial theory* refers to a field of intellectual inquiry that explores and interrogates the situation of colonized peoples both during and after colonization. Postcolonial literature and theory are often, but not always, anti-imperialist in character.

As with poststructuralism, the prefix *post-* in *postcolonial* implies opposition as well as chronological sequence; that is, postcolonial not only denotes the period after a former colony has become independent but also typically connotes political and moral attitudes opposed to colonization. By extension, works produced during the colonial period can be anachronistically viewed as postcolonial in character if they express, even implicitly, resistance to colonialism and in some way project the potential for independence.

The term *postcolonial* is sometimes also extended to refer to situations that share material characteristics with postcolonial conditions but that do not actually involve a former colony. The situations of African Americans and of the Irish, who were long under English domination, are cases in point. Thus, both African American works and works by nonblack authors about slaves and their free descendants may include postcolonial perspectives and invite interpretations that draw on post-colonial theory. Moreover, critics applying postcolonial theory to works by writers ranging from Toni Morrison to William Faulkner tend to view the situation of African Americans as a result of domestic colonization that is historically tied to European empire building through the slave trade. Postcolonial readings of Irish literature have had to take into account Ireland's status as a colony in all but name — but one that, unlike colonies such as India, was near the center of the empire with regard not only to location but also race and language.

As a literary category, postcolonial literature has displaced and expanded narrower rubrics such as "Commonwealth literature" and "literature of the Third World" (which is usually subdivided into anglophone literature, francophone literature, and so forth). Postcolonial literature includes works by authors with cultural roots in South Asia, Africa, the Caribbean, and other places in which colonial independence movements arose and colonized peoples achieved autonomy in the past hundred years. Works by authors from so-called settler colonies with large white populations of European ancestry — such as Australia, New Zealand, Canada, and Ireland — are sometimes also included. (Note that a postcolonial author need not reside in the former colony and may well live in the capital of the former empire or in some other industrialized region.) In practice, most of the works currently studied by scholars of postcolonial literature and by postcolonial theorists are written in English; that is, they are addressed, either implicitly or explicitly, to an international audience of English speakers rather than to a national or regional audience that speaks a non-European language.

Critical readings of postcolonial literature regularly proceed under the overt influence of postcolonial theory, which raises and explores historical, cultural, political, and moral issues surrounding the establishment and disintegration of colonies and the empires they fueled. As an interdisciplinary field, postcolonial theory routinely crosses perceived boundaries between literary criticism, history, anthropology, and other subjects, in part because postcolonial theorists themselves analyze such a wide range of issues and in part because they believe that the strict division of knowledge into academic disciplines contributes to colonizing mindsets. Like its object of study, postcolonial theory is *in-between*, a word that some postcolonial theorists also routinely employ in their own analyses.

The most influential postcolonial theorists are Edward Said, Gayatri Chakravorty Spivak, and Homi K. Bhabha. Said, a politically active scholar of Palestinian descent who taught in the United States, laid the groundwork for the development of postcolonial theory in general, as well as specifically identifying and analyzing the process of orientalism, in his book *Orientalism* (1978). In this study, Said, who was influenced by French philosophical historian Michel Foucault, analyzed European discourses concerning the exotic, arguing that stereotypes systematically projected on peoples of the East contributed to establishing European domination and exploitation through colonization. Although *Orientalism* focuses on colonialist discourses, both Said and other postcolonial theorists have applied its insights in interpreting the aftermath of colonialism.

Spivak, an Indian scholar, has highlighted the ways in which factors such as gender and class complicate our understanding of colonial and postcolonial situations. In essays such as "Can the Subaltern Speak?" (1988), Spivak challenges postcolonial theory to address the silencing of women and other subaltern subjects not only by and in colonial discourses but also in postcolonial responses to those discourses. (*Subaltern*, a British military term that refers to a low-ranking, subordinate officer, is used in postcolonial theory to designate the colonized, whom Europeans considered to be subject races. Spivak also uses the term to refer to voiceless groups within colonies or former colonies, such as women, migrants, and the subproletariat, who are dominated by other groups inside the colonized culture.)

The issues Spivak raises concerning how agency — the ability to choose and to speak independently — can survive the impact of long-term hierarchical situations are central to the difficulties facing not only postcolonial theory but also individuals and groups in postcolonial contexts. Some of these difficulties have been addressed by the Subaltern Studies Group through the production of revisionary historical accounts of life as experienced by once-silent or silenced colonial subjects. Ranajit Guha's "The Prose of Counter-Insurgency" (1988), for example, provides a critical alternative to accepted historical narratives by contrasting official documents with personal ones, contemporary accounts with retrospective ones, and European views with indigenous ones.

Bhabha, another Indian scholar, has shown how colonized peoples have co-opted and transformed various elements of the colonizing culture, a process he refers to as *hybridity*. In his essay "Of Mimicry and Man: The Ambivalence of Colonial Discourse" (1987), he sketches the process by which colonized peoples turn the tables on the colonizing culture through imitation that produces a difference. In "Dissemi-Nation: Time, Narrative and the Margins of the Modern Nation" (1990), Bhabha himself mimics and transforms the title of poststructuralist theorist Jacques Derrida's *Dissemination* (1972). The concept of hybridity — which suggests a crossover or amalgamation that produces something unalterably new and independent and which characterizes a contradictory, in-between "location of culture" that enables the emergence of postcolonial nationhood and individual agency — has been widely embraced by postcolonial theorists.

Hybridity also has implications akin to the biological, cultural, and linguistic connotations of *creolization,* a term used by Caribbean writer Edward Kamau Brathwaite in *The Development of Creole Society in Jamaica 1770–1820* (1971). Both *hybridity* and *creolization* attempt to give name to the coexistence of seemingly incompatible elements, a coexistence that frequently characterizes postcolonial societies and writing. The terms are not, however, synonymous, since *creolization* evokes more historical and regional specificity than does *hybridity.*

Important antecedents of postcolonial theorists include writers from former colonies, such as Brathwaite, Chinua Achebe, Aimé Césaire, and Frantz Fanon, who have reflected as critics both on their societies and on the predicament of postcolonial intellectuals, especially in relation to the history of colonialism. For example, in "An Image of Africa" (1977), Achebe, a Nigerian writer, perceives racism and condescension in Joseph Conrad's representation of the Belgian Congo in *Heart of Darkness* (1899), a book he considers "offensive and deplorable." Césaire, who experienced colonial life in the Caribbean and who founded the pan-national "Negritude" movement, writes vividly about the barbarism of the colonizer in *Discours sur le colonialism* (*Discourse on Colonialism*) (1950). Fanon, a French-trained psychiatrist from Martinique who practiced in the French colony of Algeria during the war for independence and who was the foremost precursor of postcolonial theory, wrote a series of essays (based on his experiences) commenting on the problems and needs of colonized peoples and advocating independence movements. Of particular importance are the essays collected in *Les damnés de la terre.* (*The Wretched of the Earth*) (1961), including "Spontaneity," which addresses spontaneous violence and national consciousness, and "On National Culture," which describes the native intellectual's role in the stages by which a postcolonial national identity — and by implication the intellectual's own identity — can develop.

Postcolonial theory has also been influenced by poststructuralist approaches including deconstruction, though it diverges from poststructuralism in its attention to history and politics. Deconstruction's challenge to hierarchical, binary oppositions has provided postcolonial

theory with conceptual strategies for undermining the ostensible difference between center and margins that is frequently at work in the relationship of the colonizing culture to the colonized. Insofar as
postcolonial theorists such as Spivak and Bhabha have focused on such
abstract argumentation derived from European tradition, however,
they have come under fire from other postcolonial theorists. For
example, in *Beyond Postcolonial Theory* (1998), Epifanio San Juan, Jr., a
scholar of Philippine descent who teaches in the United States, takes to
task postcolonial theorists whom he considers too abstract and insufficiently committed to effective political action.

Because of diverse historical, geographical, linguistic, and intellectual factors, postcolonial literature and postcolonial theory are still
developing as categories of writing. Neither looks the same as it did
around 1990, when the terms first gained wide currency. Matters such
as the character and effects of diaspora — the dispersion of peoples
from their homelands — have only begun to be explored. Moreover,
postcolonial theorists have begun to study the differences among various postcolonial experiences. Postcolonial situations vary widely, in part
because of the idiosyncratic character of the many European countries
that had imperial ambitions and in part because of the global dispersion
of their colonies. Postcolonial theorists have also recognized that the
cultural location of the writer — whether author, theorist, historian, or
literary critic — also makes a difference. The writer's angle of vision
varies (as does the reader's), depending on factors such as gender, class,
and cultural roots, whether in a former colony, in Europe, or in the
United States.

To date, postcolonial literature and theory have been strongly influenced by theorists primarily concerned with the Middle East and the
Indian subcontinent. Many of their insights and concepts regarding
postcolonial writing cannot, however, be transferred to other regions
without significant revision due to sharp regional and historical differences. Accordingly, it is likely that African, Caribbean, Hispanic, and
Irish voices, among others, will increasingly give postcolonial literature
and theory new inflections.

In the essay that follows — "Nationalism, Celticism, and Cosmopolitanism in *A Portrait*"— Vincent J. Cheng, in his own words,
"quarries" Joyce's novel "for its detailed representations and illustrations of the theoretical and ideological issues of nationalism and Irishness" (p. 389 in this volume). Cheng begins his study by revealing the
extent to which "the image of the Irishman as a barbarian" (p. 389) was

prevalent in nineteenth-century England. "The racial comparison most frequently and insistently made," according to Cheng, "was with 'negroes,' especially with Bushmen and Hottentots, generally perceived as the lowest rungs on the scale of human races, just above the apes" (p. 390). (Citing L. P. Curtis's 1971 book *Apes and Angels: The Irishman in Victorian Caricature,* Cheng explains that, as they came to view and represent Irishmen as apes, the English "reserved the designation of angels for themselves, frequently punning on angels, Angles, and Anglo-Saxons.") It is little wonder that, "when the Irish turned to political activism and agitation in their demands for Home Rule" (p. 391), periodicals including *Punch* began to picture Ireland's disaffected Celtic peasants as dangerous gorillas or — in Charles Kingsley's words — "white chimpanzees."

Joyce was cognizant of this offensive tradition of caricature, revealing "his pained awareness of such derogatory stereotyping in *Stephen Hero,* when Madden . . . speaks of those 'old stale libels — the drunken Irishman, the baboon-faced Irishman that we see in *Punch*'" (p. 390). In *Portrait,* of course, Stephen Dedalus not only wishes to shatter what Cheng calls the "binary pattern" (p. 393) involving English angels and Irish apes but, ultimately, to escape all constraining "nets" that "deny him personal autonomy and personal home rule" (pp. 393–94). These include the nets of: (1) nationalism (and, more specifically, the "pressures to participate in the . . . popular Celtic fervor for the Fatherland"); (2) religion (Cheng writes that Joyce, like Stephen, "viewed religion as inseparable from the politics of nationalism and empire in Ireland"); and (3) the "'native' Gaelic tongue" advocated by the Celticist movement but that was "no more native nor natural (nor familiar/familial) to Stephen than English" (pp. 394–95).

In a marvelously insightful passage, Cheng writes: "Stephen recognizes that the emphasis on Irish language and culture is a misdirected nostalgia for a glorious Celtic past and purity which may have never really existed" (p. 398). Instead, it may have been a "reaction," a product of "the oppressed group within a binary logic and structure imposed by the oppressors. . . . [N]o more real than the vaunted Anglo-Saxon racial purity erected by the other side," Cheng maintains, the "Celticist logic is a binarity" that seeks to "deny/demean anything English and glorify everything Irish" (p. 398). As a result of Stephen's eventual, evolved understanding, he "in the end chooses to look linguistically and politically beyond the English/Irish binary opposition toward Europe and toward a more internationalist and cosmopolitist perspective based on multiplicity and difference" (p. 394).

In the final pages of his essay, Cheng doubles back to consider another set of nets that Stephen contends with in the course of his putative maturation. He argues that even Joyce's depictions of women and female sexuality (not to mention his representations of Stephen's ambivalence toward both) are linked to the binary opposition Anglo/ Celtic, as well as to the separate and distinct allure of continental cosmopolitanism. Cheng points out that, whereas to Davin the invitation to spend the night with a lonely, bare-breasted, probably pregnant farm girl was a "sexual and adulterous overture" (p. 402), to Stephen it triggers her transformation, in his imagination, into "a type of her race and his own" (p. 165).

In Cheng's words, she becomes at once the "symbolic embodiment" of Celtic identity and a "warning" regarding the "Mother Ireland" who "nurse[s] her native/natal sons to maturity" (p. 403). For once the young woman has been symbolically transmogrified, her "sexual invitation" comes to "suggest" the "implied threat of symbolic incest — and the consequent need for flight, once the young bird is ready to fly the nest" (p. 403). In other words, her very image warns of the need to "reject the maternal (and the nation which she symbolizes) in order to experience the larger, less provincial world outside the maternal farmhouse (in Stephen's case, cosmopolitan Paris)" (p. 403). Cheng takes care, during this discussion, not to equate Joyce with Stephen; nonetheless, he does point out that Joyce, like Stephen, was a "pacifist and a cosmopolitanist" (p. 404) with an "internationalist political agenda" (p. 405), one that Joyce was more fully able to present through the character of Leopold Bloom in *Ulysses*.

"Nationalism, Celticism, and Cosmopolitanism in *A Portrait*" typifies postcolonial criticism insofar as it explores the condition of people living in a colonized place by studying their representation in a work of literature written by an author with deep roots in that place. Like most critical readings of postcolonial literature, the essay proceeds under the overt influence of postcolonial theory, which combines literary analysis with anthropological insights as it raises and explores historical, cultural, and moral issues arising out of the acts of oppression and resistance arising out of the colonial situation. Unlike the colonized people represented in most postcolonial literature — and studied by most critics applying postcolonial theory — the colonized Irish were of the same race and spoke the same language as the colonizing English. And yet, as Cheng reveals, the English colonizers, in fact, created a myth of racial difference — even as the colonized Irish set out to create, through the resurrection of Gaelic, a linguistic difference.

Much as Edward Said did in *Orientalism,* Cheng examines the way in which colonial power controls by stereotyping its colonized subjects. Drawing on deconstructive insights, he shows these stereotypes to rest on spuriously constructed binary oppositions (e.g., angel/ape). And, in the manner of Gayatri Chakravorty Spivak and other feminist postcolonial theorists, he suggests ways in which gender is implicated in the stereotyping process. (Stephen associates "woman" and "Ireland," thereby turning each into a suffocating mother figure to be spurned in the pursuit of masculine adventure/fulfillment.) Finally, although Joyce and his protagonist, Stephen, may seem unlike the authors and heroes of much postcolonial literature insofar as they would escape the nets that would define them as being in the insurrectionist camp of the colonized, there is a way in which they strive to amalgamate elements from both sides of the cultural divide, in the process sidestepping binary oppositions like English/Irish to produce, in their lives as well as their art, something new, cosmopolitan, and different.

POSTCOLONIAL CRITICISM:
A SELECTED BIBLIOGRAPHY

Postcolonial Literature and Theory:
General Accounts, Historic and Influential Texts

Ashcroft, Bill, et al., eds. *The Empire Writes Back: Theory and Practice in Postcolonial Literatures.* New York: Routledge, 1989.

Centre for Contemporary Cultural Studies. *The Empire Strikes Back.* London: Hutchinson, 1982.

Césaire, Aimé. *Discours sur le colonialisme (Discourse on Colonialism).* Paris: Réclame, 1950.

Chow, Rey. *Writing Diaspora: Tactics of Intervention in Contemporary Cultural Studies.* Bloomington: Indiana UP, 1993.

Derrida, Jacques. *Dissemination.* Trans. Barbara Johnson. Chicago: U of Chicago P, 1981. Trans. of *La Dissemination.* Paris: Editions du Seuil, 1972.

Fanon, Frantz. *Les Damnés de la terre (The Wretched of the Earth).* 1961. Préface de Jean-Paul Sartre. Paris: Editions la découverte, 1985.

————. *Peau noire, masques blancs (Black Skin/White Masks).* Trans. Charles Lam Markmann. New York: Grove, 1967.

JanMohamed, Abdul, and David Lloyd, eds. *The Nature and Context of Minority Discourse*. New York: Oxford UP, 1991.

Kaplan, Amy, and Donald E. Pease, eds. *Cultures of United States Imperialism*. Durham: Duke UP, 1983.

Neocolonialism. Special issue of *Oxford Literary Review* 13 (1991).

Poovey, Mary. *Uneven Developments*. Chicago: U of Chicago P, 1988.

Young, Robert. *White Mythologies: Writing, History, and the West*. London: Routledge, 1990.

Works by Homi K. Bhabha, Edward Said, and Gayatri Chakravorty Spivak

Bhabha, Homi K. "DissemiNation: Time, Narrative, and the Margins of the Modern Nation." *Nation and Narration*. New York: Routledge, 1990. 291–322.

———. *The Location of Culture*. New York: Routledge, 1994.

———. "Of Mimicry and Man: The Ambivalence of Colonial Discourse," *The Location of Culture*. New York: Routledge, 1994. 85–92.

———, ed. *Nation and Narration*. New York: Routledge, 1990.

———. "Postcolonial Criticism." *Redrawing the Boundaries: The Transformation of English and American Literary Studies*. Ed. Stephen Greenblatt and Giles Gunn. New York: MLA, 1992. 437–65.

Said, Edward. *After the Last Sky: Palestinian Lives*. New York: Pantheon, 1986.

———. *Culture and Imperialism*. New York: Knopf, 1993.

———. *Orientalism*. New York: Pantheon, 1978.

———. *The World, the Text, and the Critic*. Cambridge: Harvard UP, 1983.

Spivak, Gayatri Chakravorty. "Can the Subaltern Speak?" *Marxism and the Interpretation of Culture*. Ed. Cary Nelson and Larry Grossberg. Urbana: U of Illinois P, 1988. 271–313.

———. *In Other Worlds: Essays in Cultural Politics*. New York: Methuen, 1987.

———. *Outside in the Teaching Machine*. New York: Routledge, 1993.

———. *The Spivak Reader: Selected Works of Gayatri Chakravorty Spivak*. Ed. Donna Landry and Gerald MacLean. New York: Routledge, 1996.

———. "Three Women's Texts and a Critique of Imperialism."
Critical Inquiry 12.1 (1985): 243–61. Rpt. in *"Race," Writing,
and Difference.* Ed. Henry Louis Gates, Jr. Chicago: U of Chicago
P, 1986.

African, Creole, and African American Studies

Achebe, Chinua. "An Image of Africa." *Massachusetts Review* 18
(1977): 782–94. Reprinted in *Joseph Conrad: Third World
Perspectives.* Ed. Robert D. Hammer. Washington, D.C.: Three
Continents, 1990.

Baker, Houston. *Blues, Ideology, and Afro-American Literature: A
Vernacular Theory.* Chicago: U of Chicago P, 1984.

———. *The Journey Back: Issues in Black Literature and Criticism.*
Chicago: U of Chicago P, 1980.

Brathwaite, Edward Kamau. *The Development of Creole Society in
Jamaica, 1770–1820.* Oxford: Clarendon, 1971.

Gates, Henry Louis, Jr. *Black Literature and Literary Theory.* New
York: Methuen, 1984.

———, ed. *"Race," Writing, and Difference.* Chicago: U of Chicago
P, 1986.

Gayle, Addison. *The Black Aesthetic.* Garden City: Doubleday, 1971.

———. *The Way of the New World: The Black Novel in America.*
Garden City: Doubleday, 1975.

Ngugi wa Thiong'o. *Decolonising the Mind: The Politics of Language
in African Literature.* London: J. Currey; Portsmouth, NH:
Heinemann, 1986.

Stepto, Robert B. *From Behind the Veil: A Study of Afro-American
Narrative.* Urbana: U of Illinois P, 1979.

Postcolonial Theory and Criticism with a Feminist Emphasis

Anzaldúa, Gloria. *Borderlands = La Frontera: The New Mestiza.* San
Francisco: Spinsters/Aunt Lute, 1987.

Jayawardena, Kumari. *Feminism and Nationalism in the Third World.*
New Delhi: Kali for Women; London: Zed Books; Totowa, NJ:
Biblio Distribution Center, 1986.

Mohanty, Chandra Talpade, et al., eds. *Third World Women and the
Politics of Feminism.* Bloomington: Indiana UP, 1991.

Sharpe, Jenny. *Allegories of Empire: The Figure of the Woman in the
Colonial Text.* Minneapolis: U of Minnesota P, 1993.

Subaltern Studies

Guha, Ranajit. *Subaltern Studies: Writings on South Asia History and Society,* 8 vols. New Dehli: Oxford UP, 1982–1994.

———. "On Some Aspects of the Historiography of Colonial India." *Subaltern Studies: Writings on South Asia History and Society I.* 1–8.

———. "The Prose of Counter-Insurgency." *Subaltern Studies: Writings on South Asia History and Society II.* 1–40.

Postcolonial Studies of British Imperialism and Its Literature

Arata, Stephen D. *Fictions of Loss in the Victorian Fin de Siècle.* Cambridge: Cambridge UP, 1996. 107–32.

Brantlinger, Patrick. *Rule of Darkness: British Literature and Imperialism, 1830–1914.* Ithaca: Cornell UP, 1988.

New Subjects, New Voices

Pines, Jim, and Paul Willeman, eds. *Question of Third Cinema.* London: BFI, 1989.

San Juan, E. (Epifanio), Jr. *Beyond Postcolonial Theory.* New York: St. Martin's, 1998.

Postcolonial Criticism of *A Portrait*

Cheng, Vincent. *Joyce, Race, and Empire.* Cambridge: Cambridge UP, 1995.

Eide, Marian. "The Woman of the Ballyhoura Hills: James Joyce and the Politics of Creativity." *Twentieth-Century Literature* 44 (Winter 1998): 377–93.

Nolan, Emer. *James Joyce and Nationalism.* London: Routledge, 1995.

Thompson, Spurgeon. "Returning the Gaze: Culture and the Politics of Surveillance in Ireland." *International Journal of English Studies* 2 (2002): 95–107.

Wollaeger, Mark. "Joyce in the Postcolonial Tropics." *James Joyce Quarterly* 39 (Fall 2001): 69–92.

A POSTCOLONIAL PERSPECTIVE

VINCENT J. CHENG

Nationalism, Celticism, and Cosmopolitanism in *A Portrait*

A Portrait of the Artist as a Young Man (published 1916) features at its center a young man discovering his artistic vocation, Stephen Dedalus. *A Portrait* (and its earlier manuscript draft, *Stephen Hero*) contains numerous fictional characters, often based closely on real persons in Joyce's acquaintance. This essay quarries *A Portrait* for its detailed representations and illustrations of the theoretical and ideological issues of nationalism and Irishness. For fundamental to *A Portrait* (as well as to *Stephen Hero)* are the depictions of the Irish Nationalist movement popular in Joyce's youth — as exemplified by the Daniels household that young Stephen frequents and by his companions at University College Dublin — and of Stephen's responses to the fervent Celticism that marked much of the movement, within the binary dialectics of Irishness and Englishness.

RACIALIZED IRISHNESS

The image of the Irishman as a barbarian was a consolidated tradition (the "wild Irish") in England and Scotland by the nineteenth century. In 1797 the Scottish historian John Pinkerton had written that the Irish Celts were "savages, have been savages since the world began, and will be forever savages; mere radical savages, not yet advanced even to a state of barbarism" (Curtis, *Apes* 95). As L. P. Curtis notes, "Adjectives like 'savage' and 'wild' recur" in descriptions of the Irish; "In an age when the manners and mores of primitive tribes were being studied with greater care, the Irish had to endure comparisons with aboriginal peoples in Africa, the antipodes, and the Orient" (*Anglo-Saxons* 58) — peoples such as the Chinese, Hottentots, Maoris, Aborigines, Sudanese, and other supposedly "barbarian" peoples (*Apes* 2). Charles Darwin himself, in his chapter on the extinction of races in *Descent of Man* (544–45), had compared New Zealand's Maoris with Irish peasants. One particular tradition since the discovery of the New World was to compare the Irish to Native American Indians in terms of their relative primitiveness and savagery — a habit traced and analyzed by Luke Gibbons in his essay on "Race Against Time: Racial Discourse and Irish History"; for example, in 1839 Gustave de Beaumont, having been to the New World, visited Ireland and found that the Irish peasants lived in even greater poverty and squalor than the noble savages of America (Gibbons 98).

In 1880, two years before Joyce's birth, the Belgian political economist and essayist Gustave de Molinari reported that English newspapers "allow no occasion to escape them of treating the Irish as an inferior race — as a kind of white negroes [sic] — and a glance at *Punch* is sufficient to show the difference they establish between the plump and robust personification of John Bull and the wretched figure of lean and bony Pat" (qtd. in Curtis, *Apes* 1). This observation about the Irish as "white negroes" suggests the prevalent English attitude and discursive formation concerning the Irish: the racial comparison most frequently and insistently made about the Irish during the latter half of the nineteenth century was with "negroes," especially with Bushmen and Hottentots, generally perceived as the lowest rungs on the scale of human races, just barely above the apes. In a scientific discourse about race propelled by respected scientists and theorists such as Cuvier, Gobineau, and Nott, notions of Aryan superiority seemed incontestable, and were supported by "scientific" evidence arising from cranial measurements and other such questionable practices. In stereotyping the Irish, the English resorted to arguing that the Celtic race was closer to Bushmen and Hottentots on the human tree or ladder.

For example, John Beddoe, president of the Royal Anthropological Institute, Fellow of the Royal Society, Fellow of the Royal College of Physicians, and respected author of *The Races of Britain* (1885), believed that hair and eye color were keys to ethnic and racial identity, and he developed a specious formula he called the "index of nigrescence," which supposedly quantified the amount of melanin in skin, eyes, and hair — in the process assuming that one end of the nigrescence scale was clearly preferable to the other. He used this index of nigrescence to "prove" that the Irish were darker and more Negroid than the English. As Curtis relates: "Just how white-skinned were Irishmen? Who were the so-called 'black Irish,' and where did they come from? How close was a prognathous and nigrescent Celt to a Negro? Such questions were implicit and at times explicit in Beddoe's work; and the implicit answer was that not all men in the British Isles were equally white or equal" (*Anglo-Saxons* 72). Speculating on the African genesis of what he called "Africanoid" Celts, Beddoe's index of nigrescence provided the scientific justification for English racial hatred of the Irish as an inferior race. It was but the logical next step in such racist/ethnocentric reasoning to consider the Irish as subhuman apes.

This in fact had already been happening; by the 1860s the popular image of the Irishman in both popular cartoons and in written discourse was an anthropoid ape. L. P. Curtis's *Apes and Angels: The Irishman in Victorian Caricature* (1971) convincingly documents how Victorian cartoons and illustrations transformed "peasant Paddy into an ape-man or simianized Caliban . . . by the 1860s and 1870s, when for various reasons it became necessary for a number of Victorians to assign Irishmen to a place closer to the apes than the angels" (2). The English, of course, reserved the designation of angels for themselves, frequently punning on angels, Angles, and Anglo-Saxons. Joyce comments ironically on such contrasts and puns when, in *Exiles*, Richard Rowan asks Robert Hand if he found Richard's son to be a child or an angel, and Robert answers, "Neither an angel nor an Anglo-Saxon" (81). Earlier, in *Stephen Hero*, Joyce had problematized the possibility of either race being angelic by having Stephen Daedalus respond to a question by Madden thus:

> [Madden:] — You want our peasants to *ape* the gross materialism of the Yorkshire peasant?
> [Stephen:] — One would imagine the country was inhabited by *cherubim*. (54, my emphases)

The timing of this culturally created image (of Irish apes) was again not accidental, for it was when the Irish turned to political activism and agitation in their demands for Home Rule that *Punch* and other periodicals began to "picture the Irish political outrage-mongering peasant as a cross between a garrotter and a gorilla" (Curtis, *Apes* 31). Furthermore, the choice of the ape to represent a derogatory bestiality now politically convenient to assign to the Irish was most likely suggested by the coincidence of Fenian agitation with the debate over Darwin's *Origin of Species*, and fueled by the specters Fenianism conjured up for the English, such as mob rule, "Rome rule," republicanism, anarchism, and revolution against the empire.

Bolstered by such scientific, anthropological reasoning as Beddoe's nigrescent and "Africanoid" Celts and Daniel Mackintosh's data claiming that the heads of Irish people were characterized by absent chins, receding foreheads, large mouths, thick lips, melanous and prognathous features, etc., it was inevitable that Anglo-Saxonist racism would turn the "white Negro" into a simian Celt. As Curtis argues:

> The price paid by Irishmen for increasing political activity and agrarian protest was the substition of epithets like Caliban, Frankenstein, Yahoo and gorilla for Paddy. . . . By the 1860s no respectable reader of comic weeklies — and most of their readers were respectable — could possibly mistake the simous nose, long upper lip, huge projecting mouth, and jutting lower jaw as well as sloping forehead for any other category of undesirable or dangerous human being than that known as Irish. (*Apes* 22, 29)

The simianization of the Irish was part of the larger racialized discourse behind the Irish Question, and was not just limited to the visual media of cartoon and caricature. An 1860 visit to Sligo provoked a troubled Charles Kingsley to write:

> I am haunted by the human chimpanzees I saw along that hundred miles of horrible country. I don't believe they are our fault. I believe . . . that they are happier, better, more comfortably fed and lodged under our rule than they ever were. But to see white chimpanzees is dreadful; if they were black, one would not feel it so much, but their skins, except where tanned by exposure, are as white as ours. (see Gibbons 95 and Curtis, *Anglo-Saxons* 84)

Historian James Anthony Froude had already, in 1845, described the people in Catholic Ireland as "more like tribes of squalid apes than human beings" (Curtis, *Anglo-Saxons* 85); Anglo-Irish novelist Edith Somerville could now replicate the hegemonic demotion of Irish Catholics to apes in her fiction, referring to "The Wild Irish — as who, in later days, should say The Gorillas" (Curtis, *Apes* ix). And *Punch* could depict characters such as "Mr. MacSimius," a hirsute Irishman, saying: "Well, Oi don't profess to be a particularly cultivated man meself; but at laste me progenitors were all educated in the hoigher branches!" (Curtis, *Apes* 57)

But the most prevalent manifestations of the equation of the Irish Celt with an ape appeared in the popular cartoons of the day, in English periodicals such as *Punch* and *Judy,* in which any character with a prognathous jaw and simian features was readily recognized as representing an Irishman without any need for further identification. Joyce reveals his pained awareness of such derogatory stereotyping in *Stephen Hero,* when Madden (Davin in *Portrait*) speaks of those "old stale libels — the drunken Irishman, the baboon-faced Irishman that we see in *Punch*" (64). Two of the cartoons reproduced in the "Cultural Documents" section, taken from L. P. Curtis's *Apes and Angels,* illustrate Madden's point. The first depicts Anarchy as an Irish agitator with repellent features evoking simianness (see the figures on pages 237 and 238). The second and most striking example shows Paddy and Bridget, as the essentialized Irish pair, portrayed as living in their native habitat, a shanty. The rather Wakean title of "The King of A-Shantee" connects the Irish Celt with the African Ashanti, and Paddy's clearly apelike features imply that he may be the "missing link" in the evolution between the lower species of apes and Africans.

This, then, was the context of "race"— of racialized discourse and racial *idées reçues* — at the end of the nineteenth century: a discourse racialized along a binary axis that posited the English "race" as one pole (the positive) and the Irish as the other (the negative), in which "Irish" was defined as everything not desirably "English." Thus, the conception of an essentialized and racialized Irishness *depended,* for its very definition and formulation, on the English ideal of Englishness, a national ego-ideal. Furthermore, given the dependency of Irishness (as a racial concept) on the English-Irish opposition, any discussion of the Irish "race" inevitably carried with it the weight and associations of empire (and its corollaries, the Irish Question and Home Rule).

For this binary pattern is a trap that essentializes and limits representation to precisely its own terms, terms one must play by if one accepts the binary oppositions. In other words, if you try to prove that you aren't what "they" say you are, you are judging/arguing by the same rules/categories "they" are and so you end up reifying/maintaining those categories in place as functional realities; for example, if you try to prove that you are more angel than ape, that you aren't a Hottentot or Maori, then you are only reinforcing and reinscribing the terms of a hierarchy that places angels (and Anglos) at the top and "Negroes" and Orientals near the bottom. As Joyce has Madden point out in *Stephen Hero,* the Irish Celt has been labeled/libeled as "the baboon-faced Irishman that we see in *Punch*" (64). How can one break this pattern and represent oneself and one's own "race"–and create the conscience of one's race?

STEPHEN DEDALUS AND IMPERIAL AUTHORITIES

For the young Stephen Dedalus of *Stephen Hero* and *A Portrait,* the various and constraining structures of authority and institutional power are imperial in that they have empire over him, they deny him personal

autonomy and personal home rule. What he is concerned with most, by
the end of both texts, is the development of his personal liberty and
artistic freedom; any force that would constrict such development is
suspect, including the Nationalist movement: "The programme of the
patriots filled him with very reasonable doubts; its articles could obtain
no intellectual assent from him. He knew, moreover, that concordance
with it would mean for him a submission of everything else in its interest. . . . He refused therefore to set out for any task if he had first to
prejudice his success by oaths to his patria" (*Stephen Hero* 76–77).

In *Portrait* Stephen declares his *non serviam* against the "nets"
that would entrap him and which together constitute the institutions
of hegemonic authority over him: "nationality, language, religion"
(p. 182 in this volume) — along with their familial corollaries, collaborating in "Home Rule" issues in every sense of the word "home."
Nationality includes not only "patria" and the nightmare of Irish history that have created a colonized Ireland enslaved to England, but also
the consequent pressures to participate in the current popular Celticist fervor for the Fatherland — a movement whose familial presence
began with Stephen's own father, the Parnellite whose tears shed over
the Chief moved young Stephen at the Christmas dinner in Bray early
in the novel, and who continued to berate "the Bantry gang" (which
included Tim Healy) even near the end of the novel (p. 203). Religion includes not only the Roman Catholic Church whose "fathers"
ruled over Stephen's education and career, but their familial counterparts in the devout Dante and in his mother who wishes him to make
his Easter duty. And language includes not only the language of the
English oppressors which Stephen uses but always with an outsider's
consciousness —

> How different are the words *home, Christ, ale, master* on [the
> Englishman's] lips than on mine! I cannot speak or write these
> words without unrest of spirit. His language, so familiar and so
> foreign, will always be for me an acquired speech. I have not made
> or accepted its words. My voice holds them at bay. My soul frets in
> the shadow of his language. (p. 170)

— but also the "native" Gaelic tongue that the Celticist movement ad-
vocates but that is no more native nor natural (nor familiar/familial) to
Stephen than English. Rather, Stephen in the end chooses to look linguistically and politically beyond the English/Irish binary opposition
toward Europe and toward a more internationalist and cosmopolitist
perspective based on multiplicity and difference.

It is important to keep in mind that Joyce viewed religion as inseparable from the politics of nationalism and empire in Ireland. For Stephen, too, religion is a very major element within the hegemonic powers of institutional authority that would hold sway and empire over him — not only because of the church's direct role in Irish politics (as in the Parnell affair) and in betraying the Irish cause, as delineated angrily by Mr. Casey at the Christmas dinner:

> — Didn't the bishops of Ireland betray us in the time of the union when bishop Lanigan presented an address of loyalty to the Marquess Cornwallis? Didn't the bishops and priests sell the aspirations of this country in 1829 in return for catholic emancipation? Didn't they denounce the fenian movement from the pulpit and in the confessionsbox? And didn't they dishonour the ashes of Terence Bellew MacManus? (p. 47)

— but also because the church represents for Stephen a generalized authority and empire over his mind and person. He explains his refusal to do his Easter duty thus: "I fear . . . the chemical action which would be set up in my soul by a false homage to a symbol behind which are massed twenty centuries of authority and veneration" (p. 215; Cranly's subsequent question about whether Stephen would have done the same "in the penal days" serves to remind the reader of the intricate connections between imperial English rule and religion, since the longstanding penal code was used to subjugate Catholics only). As Stephen says in *Stephen Hero* (53), "The Roman, not the Sassenach, was for him the tyrant of the islanders." His responses to Irish Nationalism have been in part shaped by its hand-in-glove collusion with Catholicism under the auspices of a generalized "authority and veneration" from which Stephen wishes to declare his independence; thinking of his fellow students seduced by Irish Nationalism, Stephen remarks that they "respected spiritual and temporal authorities, the spiritual authorities of Catholicism and patriotism, and the temporal authorities of the hierarchy and the government. The memory of Terence MacManus was not less revered by them than the memory of Cardinal Cullen" (*Stephen Hero* 173). The hegemonic structures of hierarchy exist as much in religious institutions as in the secular world, as Stephen remarks about the Jesuit monastery he visits: "The toy life which the Jesuits permit these docile young men to live is what I call a stationary march" (*Stephen Hero* 187).

In fact, Stephen thinks of the church precisely in terms of militaristic and imperial rule (as in "stationary march"): "He spurned from before him the stale maxims of the Jesuits and he swore an oath that they should never establish over him an ascendancy" (*Stephen Hero* 38); to an Irish reader the word "ascendancy" could not but suggest the Protestant Ascendancy over Catholic Ireland, suggesting a similarity between the English political tyranny over the Irish body and the Catholic spiritual tyranny over the Irish soul. The specific spiritual tyranny Stephen is subjected to in *Stephen Hero* is the censorship of his paper on Ibsen — censorship by Dr. Dillon, the President of the College, who as a figure of hierarchical tyranny and suppression, is appropriately both an Englishman and a Catholic priest. To Stephen, the Jesuit monastery resembles the militaristic mentality associated with conquest and empire: "He recognised at once the martial mind of the Irish Church in the style of this ecclesiastical barracks" (*Stephen Hero* 73).

This ecclesiastical militarism of the soldiers of God was, of course, also literally implicated in the spread of European empires and foreign colonies. Stephen recalls hearing "his godfather explain to a more rustic proprietor the nature of the work done by the missionary fathers in civilising the Chinese people. He [Stephen's godfather] sustained the propositions that the Church is also the chief repository of secular culture. . . . He saw in the pride of the Church the only refuge of men against a threatening democracy and said that Aquinas had anticipated all the discoveries of the modern world" (*Stephen Hero* 241). The militaristic role of "conquest" by the church is made even more explicit by the rector in *Portrait*, urging the boys (during the religious retreat in Chapter III) to consider a missionary vocation by invoking the college's patron Saint Francis Xavier, who had been

> sent by saint Ignatius to preach to the Indians. He is called, as you know, the apostle of the Indies. He went from country to country in the east, from Africa to India, from India to Japan, baptising the people. . . . He wished then to go to China to win still more souls for God but he died of fever on the island of Sancian. A great saint, saint Francis Xavier! A great soldier of God! . . . Ten thousand souls won for God in a single month! That is a true conqueror. (p. 104)

The "apostle of the Indies" here, as a "great soldier" and "true conqueror" "winning" over country after country, is hardly to be distinguished in his activities from Napoleon in Egypt or Wellington in India — and thus the Jesuit Belvedere College begins to meld into the playing fields of Eton.

The collusion between imperialism and religion in the conquest of foreign colonies and their subsequent economic exploitation (*India mittit ebur,* as Stephen later recalls [p. 161], India sends ivory; as Frantz Fanon [102] pointed out, "Europe is literally the creation of the Third World") is also suggested in the story of Dante, the religious zealot Mrs. Riordan. During the Christmas dinner scene we learn that Stephen "had heard his father say that she was a spoiled nun and that she had come out of the convent in the Alleghanies when her brother had got the money from the savages for the trinkets and the chainies" (p. 44). As Ellmann points out, the real Dante Conway in Joyce's childhood similarly "had been on the verge of becoming a nun in America when her brother, who had made a fortune out of trading with African natives, died and left her 30,000 pounds" (24). In other words, Dante's sanctimonious religiosity and high moral tone are belied by her complicity — one shared by the missionary sects in foreign colonies — with colonial exploitation (*India mittit ebur*) and the African trade, which have funded her freedom and social position.

CELTICISM AND COSMOPOLITANISM

The church's role in encouraging Irish Nationalism also makes Stephen suspicious. In both *Stephen Hero* and *Portrait,* Stephen experiences the call of Celticism, a "voice [that] had bidden him be true to his country and help to raise up her fallen language and tradition" (p. 85). In the nationalistic Daniels household and at University College, this Celticist voice hails Stephen and makes its appeal, in simultaneity with the priestly pressure hailing him with a religious calling; both voices pitch interpellated "vocations" that he distrusts. ("He himself was the greatest sceptic concerning the perfervid enthusiasms of the patriots" [*Stephen Hero* 204].) The depiction of Mr. Hughes, the teacher of the Irish language class, is Joyce's portrait of the Celticist enthusiast:

> He spoke in a high-pitched voice with a cutting Northern accent. He never lost an opportunity of sneering at seoninism ["West Britonism," derived from Seon/John, esp. John Bull] and at those who would not learn their native tongue. He said that Beurla [English] was the language of commerce and Irish the speech of the soul. . . . He scoffed very much at Trinity College and the Irish Parliamentary party. He could not regard as patriots men who had taken oaths of allegiance to the Queen of England and he could not regard as a national university an institution which did not express the religious convictions of the majority of the

Irish people. . . . Hughes, who was the son of a Nationalist solici-
tor in Armagh, was a law-student at the King's Inns. (*Stephen
Hero* 59–60)

Stephen's own response and critique of Nationalism is in part colored by the role of the church. To begin with, Stephen argues that the
priests are disingenuous in their encouragement of Gaelicist practices,
encouraging a nostalgia for lost origins, as a means by which to solidify
the faith and their control over the believers: "— Do you not see, said
Stephen, that they encourage the study of Irish that their flocks may be
more safely protected from the wolves of disbelief; they consider it is an
opportunity to withdraw the people into a past of literal, implicit faith?"
(*Stephen Hero* 54). Stephen recognizes that the emphasis on Irish language and culture is a misdirected nostalgia for a glorious Celtic past
and purity that may have never really existed, based on the reaction of
the oppressed group within a binary logic and structure imposed by the
oppressors; this pure Celtic glory and Firbolg/Milesian origin is no
more real than the vaunted Anglo-Saxon racial purity erected by the
other side. Nevertheless, the Celticist logic is a binarity that seeks to
deny/demean anything English and glorify everything Irish — as in
Hughes's essentializing characterizations of English/Beurla as "the
language of commerce and Irish [as] the speech of the soul."

The result of such binary logic is a romantic sentimentalization of
all things Celtic and a consequent chauvinistic blindness to the specific
permutations of actual conditions and social realities. In *Portrait*,
Stephen recalls the hostile Nationalistic audience's boos and catcalls
during the infamous debut of Yeats's *The Countess Cathleen* at the
Abbey Theatre: "A libel on Ireland!" "Made in Germany!" "Blasphemy!" "We never sold our faith!" "No Irish woman ever did it!" "We
want no amateur atheists." "We want no budding buddhists" (p. 201).
Joyce, who *was* an amateur atheist and Buddhist sympathizer (more on
that later), was himself in the audience and, unlike the hissers and boo-
ers, "clapped vigorously" (Ellmann 68–69) — refusing to see the world
only through shamrock-tinted glasses that would deny any possibility of
Irish immorality or even imperfection.

When in *Stephen Hero* Stephen's friend Madden (Davin in *Portrait*), the ardent Nationalist peasant, tells him that "— We want an
Irish Ireland" and then asks: "— And don't you think that every Irishman worthy of the name should be able to speak his native tongue? . . .
and don't you think that we as a race have a right to be free?" (*Stephen
Hero* 54, 56) — Stephen's response refuses to be lured by the circular

logic of the binarity: "— It seems to me you do not care what banality a man expresses so long as he expresses it in Irish." When Madden argues that "I do not entirely agree with your modern notions. We want to have nothing of this English civilisation. . . . You want our peasants to ape the gross materialism of the Yorkshire peasant?"— Stephen refuses to engage in the essentializing of either culture as apes or angels: "— One would imagine the country was inhabited by cherubim" (*Stephen Hero* 54). Rather than get sucked into a mirrored binarity, Stephen is willing to acknowledge the cultural relativism implicit in different cultures and multiple perspectives, as he later tells Cranly: "What we symbolise in black the Chinaman may symbolise in yellow: each has his own tradition. Greek beauty laughs at Coptic beauty and the American Indian derides them both" (*Stephen Hero* 212; in *Portrait* [p. 186] he reiterates that "The Greek, the Turk, the Chinese, the Copt, the Hottentot . . . all admire a different type of female beauty").

Stephen's young Nationalist friend Madden/Davin (based on Joyce's friend George Clancy), however, is trapped inside the powerful, binary logic of Celticism. Davin is the character in Joyce's works who perhaps most closely embodies the Celtic Revival's (and "Irish Ireland"'s) notion of the authentic Irish Celt — Davin, the peasant *ingenu* with "the rude Firbolg mind," "the young peasant [who] worshipped the sorrowful legend of Ireland," and whose "nurse had taught him Irish and shaped his rude imagination by the broken lights of Irish myth . . . [with] the attitude of a dullwitted loyal serf"; as a result, "Whatsoever of thought or of feeling came to him from England or by way of English culture his mind stood armed against in obedience to a password: and of the world that lay beyond England he knew only the foreign legion of France in which he spoke of serving" (p. 163). In effect, such a closed system is trapped within the oscillation of an English/Irish dialectic, in which everything is still defined around Englishness.

Stephen at one point thinks of Davin affectionately as a "rude Firbolg mind" with a "delight in rude bodily skill — for Davin had sat at the feet of Michael Cusack, the Gael" (p. 162). Davin is an athlete and a sports enthusiast, disciple of Michael Cusack, the real-life founder of the Gaelic Athletic Association (and model for the xenophobic "Citizen" in *Ulysses*), whose championing of Irish sport was a central force in the Celticist movement. At the Irish language classes in *Stephen Hero*, Cusack, "A very stout black-bearded citizen . . . was a constant figure at these meetings" (*Stephen Hero* 61), along with Madden/Davin "who was the captain of a club of hurleyplayers" as well as Arthur Griffith, "the editor of the weekly journal of the irreconcilable party" (*The United Irishman*). Stephen, who is not an athlete, perceives some relation between the movement's emphasis on sport/play and its liberationist ethos: "The liberty they desired for themselves was mainly a liberty of costume and vocabulary. . . . here he saw people playing at being free" (*Stephen Hero* 62). Stephen cites as an example the case of Hungary, a nation which the Celticists glorify as a "long-suffering minority, entitled by every right of race and justice to a separate freedom," but which has managed to emancipate itself; "In emulation of that achievement bodies of young Gaels conflicted murderously in the Phoenix Park with whacking hurley-sticks" (*Stephen Hero* 62). Stephen's ironic observation to Madden/Davin about such emulative play: "— I suppose these hurley matches and walking tours are preparations for the great event." Hurley, or hurling, the Irish Nationalist sport (and a game still associated with both Irish Nationalism and the Irish language), is a rough and brutal sport with similarities to football, rugby, hockey, and lacrosse. In *Portrait*, Stephen, after first quoting ironically from the Fenian drill book ("— Long pace, fianna! Right incline, fianna! Fianna, by numbers, salute, one, two!"), then comments to Davin/Madden about the relations between Fenian drills, revolutions, and hurley: "— When you make the next rebellion with hurleysticks . . . and want the indispensable informer, tell me. I can find you a few in this college" (pp. 180–81).

Stephen goes on to deride the Nationalist zealot Hughes, the law student with the barrister father: "— One of these days he will be a barrister, a Q.C., perhaps a judge — and yet he sneers at the Parliamentary Party because they take an oath of allegiance. . . . I do not quite follow the distinction you make between administering English law and administering English bullets: there is the same oath of allegiance for both professions." When Madden suggests that "Better be a barrister than a redcoat," the pacifist Stephen reminds him of the militaristic nature of hurley clubs: "— You consider the profession of arms a disreputable one. Why then have you Sarsfield Clubs, Hugh O'Neill Clubs, Red Hugh Clubs?" (*Stephen Hero* 63; all named after legendary Irish warriors). The logic of a Celtic xenophobia constructed as a mirror image of English racial/national chauvinism results in such mirror images of aggressive, martial behavior (as was so even, say, with the York and Lancaster "teams" that Stephen's class in Clongowes had been divided into). As an older Stephen would again reflect later in *Ulysses*, listening to the bellicose sounds of the schoolboys' hockey game in "Nestor," there is a direct correlation between war/combat and the playing fields of Eton or Clongowes: "Jousts. Time shocked rebounds, shock by shock. Jousts, slush and uproar of battles, the frozen deathspew of the slain, a shout of spearspikes baited with men's bloodied guts" (2.316–8).

As Stephen later notes, "Renan's Jesus is a trifle Buddhistic but the fierce eaters and drinkers of the western world would never worship such a figure. Blood will have blood" (*Stephen Hero* 190). These words of Stephen's bring to mind Joyce's review in 1903 of a book about Buddhism, in which his sympathy with Buddhist methods of nonaggression and pacifism is clear. After pointing out that "Five things are the five supreme evils for [Buddhists] — fire, water, storms, robbers, and rulers" (note that water, storms, and rulers are things that Stephen fears, too), Joyce goes on to characterize Western values as bellicose and bloodthirsty by contrast: "Our civilization, bequeathed to us by fierce adventurers, eaters of meat and hunters, is so full of hurry and combat, so busy about many things which perhaps are of no importance, that it cannot but see something feeble in a civilization which smiles as it refuses to make the battlefield the test of excellence" (*Critical* 94). There is an echo in these thoughts of Stephen, whose only "arms" will be silence, exile, and cunning, and of Joyce, who would — even through two world wars — steadily refuse to grant the battlefield any validity as a test of worth.

The narrowness of some versions of Celticist logic — based on the closed system of a binary, mirrored English/Irish dialectic — results in a narrow-minded provincialism that Joyce depicts in *Stephen Hero* and *Portrait* as part of Stephen's critique of Celticist Nationalism. When Stephen's mother admits to never having heard of Ibsen, Stephen takes the occasion to point out that "in Ireland people don't know much about what is going on out in Europe" (*Stephen Hero* 84). When the President of the College, as the Censor, tries to suppress Stephen's paper on Ibsen, he admits (when questioned by Stephen) to never having read a word of Ibsen (*Stephen Hero* 93). And the general response to Stephen's paper, when he does deliver it, is that it is "a reproduction of the decadent literary opinions of exhausted European capitals" (*Stephen Hero* 102). Hughes's response to the paper is emblematic:

> He declared in ringing Northern accents that the moral welfare of the Irish people was menaced by such theories. They wanted no foreign filth. Mr Daedalus might read what authors he liked, of course, but the Irish people had their own glorious literature where they could always find fresh ideals to spur them on to new

patriotic endeavours. Mr Daedalus was himself a renegade from
the Nationalist ranks: he professed cosmopolitism. But a man that
was of all countries was of no country — you must have a nation
before you have art. (*Stephen Hero* 103)

Stephen would certainly have agreed with part of Hughes's assessment,
since, like Joyce, he was indeed a renegade from the Nationalist ranks
and a professed cosmopolitist; for Joyce, it was in fact desirable to be of
all countries rather than of a single country, to put art before nation
rather than to render art subservient to nation as "The cracked looking-
glass of a servant" (*Ulysses* 1.146). Responses like Hughes's, refusing to
acknowledge other, more internationalist and cosmopolitan perspectives in favor of a narrow nationalistic one, are only a willed version of
the provincialness of the Celtic enthusiast, exemplified here by both
Hughes and Stephen's friend Davin/Madden.

Davin tells Stephen the story of one evening in which he had to
walk home alone at night through the countryside, stopping at a lonely
farmhouse to ask for a glass of water:

> After a while a young woman opened the door and brought me
> out a big mug of milk. She was half undressed as if she was going
> to bed . . . and I thought by her figure and by something in the
> look of her eyes that she must be carrying a child. She kept me in
> talk a long while at the door and I thought it strange because her
> breast and her shoulders were bare. She asked me was I tired and
> would I like to stop the night there . . . *Come in and stay the night
> here. You've no call to be frightened. There's no one in it but our-
> selves.* (pp. 164–65)

To Davin, the moment is a troubling one ("I thanked her and went on
my way again, all in a fever") because of its sexual and adulterous overture. But to Stephen this peasant woman in her doorway becomes not
so much an adulterous seducer as "a type of her race and his own," a
symbolic embodiment — like the old milkwoman in the "Telemachus"
episode of *Ulysses* — of Ireland, within the "discourse" of authentic
Celtic peasant identity. What both of these women — the figure at the
door, and the old milkwoman in *Ulysses* — offer to young Irishmen
(Davin, Stephen, Buck) is *milk,* the maternal and natal bodily nourishment most closely parallel to the sacral qualities of Irish "race" and
"soil" (as in "racy of the soil," the epigraph of *The Nation* newspaper).
Indeed, the sexuality of this bare-breasted woman at the door offering
Davin milk and looking as if she were pregnant is clearly tempered by
the maternal, and the milk she offers thus carries with it the suggestive-

ness of breast milk from the woman herself, from Mother Ireland, the poor old woman and silk of the kine. If Mother Ireland is to nurse her native/natal sons to maturity, the sexual invitation also suggests the implied threat of symbolic incest — and the consequent need for flight, once the young bird is ready to fly the nest. We see compacted here, in this small vignette of Davin's, one of the central tensions in the *Bildungsroman* and especially the *Kunstlerroman* (as in, say, D. H. Lawrence's *Sons and Lovers* or Joyce's *A Portrait*), in which the relationship between the young sensitive boy and his mother is both nourishing and finally incestuously suffocating, resulting in the need to flee the nest and reject the maternal (and the nation she symbolizes) in order to experience the larger, less provincial world outside the maternal farmhouse (in Stephen's case, cosmopolitan Paris).

The fear of sexuality and immorality that drives Davin leads him further to be troubled by a story that Stephen had in turn told him, about the latter's encounters with Dublin prostitutes: "— I'm a simple person, said Davin. You know that. When you told me that night in Harcourt Street those things about your private life, honest to God, Stevie, I was not able to eat my dinner. I was quite bad. I was awake a long time that night" (p. 181). No doubt Davin would have been even more troubled had he known that Stephen would soon (in *Ulysses*) frequent the whorehouses of that cosmopolitan Babylon, Paris. This fear (within a Nationalist discourse about peasant purity and Celtic authenticity) of the urbane, the sophisticated, the modern, and the consequently degenerate is encapsulated in the final pages of *A Portrait* by the story of the old man in the west:

> 14 *April:* John Alphonsus Mulrennan has just returned from the west of Ireland. (European and Asiatic papers please copy.) He told us he met an old man there in a mountain cabin. Old man had red eyes and short pipe. Old man spoke Irish. Mulrennan spoke Irish. Then old man and Mulrennan spoke English. Mulrennan spoke to him about universe and stars. Old man sat, listened, smoked, spat. Then said:
> — Ah, there must be terrible queer creatures at the latter end of the world. (p. 223)

These apocalyptic "terrible queer creatures" of modernity in the larger universe beyond one's rural enclave, incomprehensible to the peasant mind, suggest the fears and threat to a national discourse of authenticity represented by the cosmopolitan world of Paris, the Moulin Rouge, and the Bohemian Latin Quarter, the very world Stephen desires to inhabit. Such a discourse of national anxiety can only conceive of the urbanity and hybridity of the international as "terrible queer creatures," immoral and degenerate.

Stephen, as an artist seeking to create the "uncreated conscience" of the Irish race, realizes that it is with this old man, the old peasant in the West speaking Gaelic, the personified figure of Irish provincial narrowness and the avatar of "authentic" Irish identity, that he must battle in seeking a spiritual liberation for Ireland that looks toward a wider, internationalist perspective: "I fear him. I fear his redrimmed horny eyes. It is with him I must struggle all through this night till day come" (p. 223). For as yet Ireland was only what Stephen calls "the afterthought of Europe" (*Stephen Hero* 53; in Joyce's own notes on the corresponding manuscript page appear the words "Ireland — an afterthought of Europe"), physically and spiritually "at the farthest remove from the centre of European culture, marooned on an island in the ocean" (*Stephen Hero* 194); and Ireland needs to become a part of Europe, to "take her place among the nations of the earth" (with an echo of Robert Emmet's dying words), not existing only in relation to England: as Joyce had articulated it, "a bilingual, republican, self-centred, and enterprising island with its own commercial fleet, and its own consuls in every port of the world" (*Critical* 173). When Madden/Davin suggests to Stephen that the Irish have nothing to gain from the English literature and language, Stephen reminds him that "English is the medium for the Continent" (*Stephen Hero* 54). As Robert Hand would say to Richard Rowan in *Exiles:* "If Ireland is to become a new Ireland she must first become European. And that is what you are here for, Richard. Some day we shall have to choose between England and Europe" (51). Choosing Europe and the internationalist perspective of a world community would allow Joyce and Ireland to break free from the binary operations of a closed system of English/Irish, Saxon/Celtic opposition, in which the rules have already been constructed always to favor the first of the two terms in each set of oppositions.

STEPHEN DEDALUS AND THE "SPIRITUAL LIBERATION OF MY COUNTRY"

While Stephen appears to be, like Joyce, a pacifist and a cosmopolitist, it is also clear in these two texts that Stephen is not quite Joyce, but a "young man" with ideas and with rather arrogant pretensions to being an artist. This is starkly clearer in *Stephen Hero* than in *Portrait,* for the earlier work contains frequent qualifications (not yet revised/ refined out of existence) of Stephen as a "perturbed young Celt" (*Stephen Hero* 40) with an "ineradicable egoism" (*Stephen Hero* 34) and a self-important need for the "flavour of the heroic" (*Stephen Hero* 29), and so on. A pacifist who refuses to sign the czar's petition for universal peace, Stephen (like the younger Joyce) is prone to couch his serious arguments in arrogance and egotism: "I care nothing for these principles of nationalism. . . . My own mind is more interesting to me than the entire country" (*Stephen Hero* 247–48).

The limitations of Stephen's attitudes toward his country are also tested by Joyce in these two texts by his two Nationalist friends, the characters Madden/Davin and MacCann ("McCann" in *Stephen Hero*), both of whom are treated relatively affectionately in the texts. For example, Madden tells Stephen accusingly that "No West-Briton could speak worse of his countrymen" (*Stephen Hero* 64). Especially probing are the conversations between Stephen and McCann, "a serious young feminist" (*Stephen Hero* 39) modeled directly on Francis Skeffington, whom Joyce had called the cleverest man in University College, after himself (Ellmann 63).

In *Portrait* the seemingly good-natured MacCann speaks quite frankly to Stephen: "Dedalus, you're an antisocial being, wrapped up in yourself. I'm not. I'm a democrat: and I'll work and act for social liberty and equality among all classes and sexes in the United States of the Europe of the future" (p. 160). While Joyce shared Stephen's distrust of Irish Nationalism, Joyce might well have also agreed with Mac-Cann's assessment of Stephen; and "equality among all classes and sexes in the United States of the Europe of the future" is not that different from the internationalist political agenda that Joyce would develop in the less demagogic medium of his subsequent fiction (and in his own beliefs), an agenda that would be presented in *Ulysses* through the utopian visions of Leopold Bloom. MacCann's blend of political idealism and pragmatism, while derided by Stephen, is an activist version of at least some of the pacifist and internationalist views that Joyce would try to promote through his fiction, especially *Ulysses* and *Finnegans Wake:*

> MacCann began to speak with fluent energy of the Csar's rescript, of Stead, of general disarmament, arbitration in cases of international disputes, of the signs of the times, of the new humanity and the new gospel of life which would make it the business of the community to secure as cheaply as possible the greatest possible happiness of the greatest possible number. . . .
> — Three cheers for universal brotherhood! (p. 176)

In *Ulysses* Leopold Bloom's pacifist/utopian visions of a universal brotherhood will be even more comically parodied and mocked than MacCann's are here by Stephen, without necessarily being rendered any less genuine or powerful.

MacCann jibes back at Stephen: "Minor poets, I suppose, are above such trivial questions as the question of universal peace" (p. 177); even if Stephen was, Joyce was certainly not above such questions, for he would deal with the question of universal peace in his fiction for the rest of his life. But MacCann proceeds to comment good-naturedly: "— Dedalus, . . . I believe you're a good fellow but you have yet to learn the dignity of altruism and the responsibility of the human individual" (p. 178; also *Stephen Hero* 52). This observation is not that different from Stephen's mother's prayer at the end of *Portrait* that he "may learn . . . what the heart is and what it feels" (p. 223), a wish that Stephen takes seriously enough that he will later struggle over his mother's words and meaning throughout *Ulysses*. It is something that Joyce may well have expected the reader to agree with, too.

Likewise, the much simpler-minded Nationalist Davin/Madden, whom Stephen treats most affectionately among his university companions, urges Stephen to "Try to be one of us. . . . In your heart you are an Irishman but your pride is too powerful" (p. 181) — another observation that the reader (and Joyce himself) might wish to agree with. Speaking of Irish patriots like Tone and Parnell (who were, after all, heroes of Stephen and of Joyce, too), Davin observes that "They died for their ideals, Stevie. . . . Our day will come yet, believe me" (p. 182). The poignant irony of Davin's comment — in a quite different retrospective coloring — must have given Joyce pause in later life: for, as with Tone and Parnell, their day would indeed come to die for their ideals. Among Joyce's patriot friends, both MacCann and Davin/Madden would become Irish martyrs: MacCann/Skeffington would be killed by the British in the Easter Rebellion (1916, the same year *Portrait* was published), and George Clancy (Davin/Madden), after becoming mayor of Limerick, would be murdered in his own house and in front of his family by the English Black and Tans (pp. 9–10). As Joyce had predicted, the hurleystick rebellions would prove no match for British military power, giving birth instead only to Yeats's "terrible beauty."

In Chapter V of *Portrait*, Stephen's rejection of Irish Nationalism and his decision to go abroad to Europe are paralleled by his simultaneous rejection of "E. C.," the young lady whom he is nevertheless very clearly attracted to. The connections between this personal/romantic denial and his artistic/political stance are suggested more clearly in the earlier *Stephen Hero,* where "Emma Clery" is depicted (and named) much more fully. Stephen first meets Emma at the nationalistic Daniels household (based on the Sheehy family in Joyce's own youth):

> A dark full-figured girl was standing before him. . . . he found out that she was studying in the same college with the Miss Daniels and that she always signed her name in Irish. She said Stephen should learn Irish too and join the League. A young man of the company . . . spoke with her across Stephen addressing her familiarly by her Irish name. Stephen therefore spoke very formally and always addressed her as "Miss Clery." She seemed on her part to include him in the general scheme of her nationalising charm.
> (*Stephen Hero* 46)

As the dark temptress whose "nationalising charm" invites him to "learn Irish too and join the League," Emma is here portrayed much more clearly than in *Portrait* as a feminine embodiment of Irish Nationalism, whose feminine lures clearly attract Stephen (who goes on immediately to enroll in a Gaelic class). Her position as an emblem of the Irish Nationalist cause, hailing Stephen to her/its side, clarifies an important dimension to her role as the "Temptress" of the Villanelle and to the (otherwise murky and misogynistic) reasons behind Stephen's portrayal of her in *Portrait*'s Chapter V as the dark embodiment of the "batlike race" of Ireland that Stephen needs to reject and leave behind.

Thus, Emma's interests in Stephen as a Nationalist convert also connect her with the West of Ireland (and with the Celticist enthusiasm of Miss Ivors in "The Dead"), as he learns at one point that "Emma had gone away to the Isles of Aran with a Gaelic party" (*Stephen Hero* 162). In *Portrait* Stephen recalls Davin's story about his long walk back after a hurling match (in the countryside near Limerick) when "there was a mass meeting that same day over in Castletownroche" (p. 164) (presumably a Land League agitation meeting); and then that half-dressed peasant woman in a lonely farmhouse along the road offered Davin a glass of milk and invited him to stay the night with her. Stephen goes on to think of this woman as "a type of her race and his own, a batlike soul waking to the consciousness of itself in darkness and secrecy and loneliness and, through the eyes and voice and gesture of a woman without guile, calling the stranger to her bed" (p. 165). At that moment Stephen is accosted by a young girl trying to sell him flowers: "He left her quickly, fearing that her intimacy might turn to gibing and wishing to be out of the way before she offered her ware to another, a tourist from England or a student of Trinity" (p. 165). Interestingly, the images of these three figures — Emma, the half-dressed woman offering Davin milk, and the flowergirl — combine in Chapter V with the old milkwoman in the first episode of *Ulysses* into a feminized embodiment, for Stephen, of Ireland and her provincialness. The flowergirl will instead sell her wares to "a tourist from England or a student of Trinity," just as the old milkwoman will play up to Haines and Mulligan, an English tourist and a Trinity medical student, her imperialist and shoneen exploiters, and not recognize in Stephen the true conscience of her race: "She bows her old head to a voice that speaks to her loudly. . . . me she slights" (*Ulysses* 1.418–19). So also the half-dressed peasant woman offers her milk and her self to strangers. Stephen thinks of Emma similarly as a representation of Ireland, unable to recognize in him (rather than in the Celticist enthusiasts) her own personal alternative and liberation — and so it is she who finally embodies for Stephen the seductive, bloodsucking, batlike soul of Ireland and its race:

> perhaps the secret of her race lay behind those dark eyes. . . . a batlike soul waking to the consciousness of itself . . . [with] a priested peasant, with a brother a policeman in Dublin. . . . To him she would unveil her soul's shy nakedness, to one who was but schooled in the discharging of a formal rite rather than to him, a priest of eternal imagination, transmuting the daily bread of experience into the radiant body of everliving life. (p. 196)

Emma's familiarity with the young priest (Father Moran) and with her policeman brother suggests to Stephen an emblematic collusion of the Irish race with the religious and secular institutions that constitute the authorities and hierarchies that oppress it (and him); as Ireland embodied, she seems to him more willing to unveil her body and sell her soul to those authorities and strangers who would exploit her, rather than to recognize in Stephen the artist/priest of her imagination seeking to liberate her — favoring, like the flowergirl or old milkwoman, her exploiters rather than her artists. To Stephen, justly or not, Emma *is* Hibernia (he is of course misogyinistically essentializing Irish womanhood with the pejorative image of a "batlike soul"); significantly, while Stephen desires her, he feels that he must scorn and leave her. In such a context and in view of Stephen's mythopoetic mentality, his rejection of Emma (after imaginatively functioning her as the seductive lure of Ireland and Irish Nationalism) seems somewhat more comprehensible; his leaving Ireland for Europe not only parallels his rejection of Emma, but in a sense they are the very same act, since she has grown to represent for Stephen the very Irish Nationalist mindset he must put aside.

Thinking of Emma as someone who "could love some clean athlete who washed himself every morning to the waist and had black hair on his chest" (p. 207), but who would not love a scruffy but independent young artist, Stephen arrogantly wonders how he might be able to liberate the conscience of the Irish race: "How could he hit their conscience or how cast his shadow over the imaginations of their daughters, before their squires begat upon them, that they might breed a race less ignoble than their own?" (pp. 210–11). While Stephen's "ineradicable egoism" might declare its *non serviam* in arrogant ways, the novel portrays Stephen as trying to learn how to liberate Ireland in a new and different way, trying to be an Irish patriot through other means than a provincial Nationalism and armed rebellion, through his art and a revolution of the word.

Indeed, we learn that Stephen's artistic calling had its first roots in the politics of national liberation. Immediately after the highly charged political discussion at the Christmas dinner scene, culminating in Mr. Casey's and Simon Dedalus's tears over "Poor Parnell! . . . My dead king!" (p. 48), young Stephen, we learn, had tried to write his first poem: "sitting at his table in Bray the morning after the discussion at the Christmas dinnertable, trying to write a poem about Parnell on the back of one of his father's second moiety notices" (pp. 73–74; Joyce himself had as a young boy written a first poem about Parnell, titled "Et Tu, Healy"). Similarly, his understandings of politics (p. 29: "He wondered if they were arguing at home about that. That was called politics") were conceived in concert with his aesthetic appreciation of visual beauty: colors were associated with both beauty and political factions: maroon and green for Davitt and Parnell; York and Lancaster as symbolized by white and red roses. Stephen, significantly, is on the York side of his Clongowes class — that is, on the Irish side (the Irish had backed York against Lancaster); but he wonders: "White roses and red roses: those were beautiful colours to think of. . . . But you could not have a green rose. But perhaps somewhere in the world you could" (p. 25). Young Stephen's aesthetic musings here have suggestive political implications — since red and white are the colors of England, can one even have a "green rose" "perhaps somewhere in the world"?— in terms of the very possibility of Irish nationhood within the world community, independent of the colors of England.

As a young, fledgling artist, Stephen passes his leisure time "in the company of subversive writers whose gibes and violence of speech set up a ferment in his brain" (p. 80). Joyce provides Stephen — in the latter's growing sense of himself as a revolutionary of the word, searching for national liberation through the conscience of his race — with a personal lineage of Irish patriots very much like Joyce's own. Not only is Stephen's father a former disciple of Parnell's who bequeaths his nationalistic fervor to his son (recall not only the Christmas dinner but memories such as Simon taking Stephen to the laying of a stone memorial to Wolfe Tone on Grafton Street [p. 165]), but Mr. Casey (based on the Joyce family friend John Kelly) is a patriot who got "three cramped fingers making a birthday present for Queen Victoria" (p. 38). As Ellmann explains: "Kelly was in prison several times for Land League agitation, and John Joyce regularly invited him to recuperate from imprisonment . . . at the house in Bray. In jail three fingers of his left hand had become permanently cramped from picking oakum, and he would tell the children that they had become so while he was making a birthday present for Queen Victoria" (23n.). Stephen himself is descended from a line of patriots: "his father had told him that . . . his granduncle had presented an address to the liberator there fifty years before" (p. 36); Joyce's own granduncle was John O'Connell, father of William O'Connell ("Uncle Charles" in *Portrait*), and a distant relative of Daniel O'Connell, the Liberator who fought to repeal the Act of Union. On his own side of the family, Simon Dedalus can point to the portrait of his grandfather on the wall: "Do you see that old chap up there, John? . . . He was a good Irishman when there was no money in the job. He was condemned to death as a whiteboy" (pp. 46–47). Ellmann confirms that there was such a personage in the Joyce family, part of the "ancient tribe of the Joyces" (*Critical* 197): "The great-grandfather bequeathed a zeal for nationalism . . . in the life of the writer. As a young man this Ur-James Joyce joined the 'Whiteboys,' or Catholic agitators against landlords, and was condemned to death, though the sentence was not carried out" (Ellmann 10).

In *Exiles*, the Irish journalist Robert Hand considers Richard Rowan — an exiled Irish writer based on Joyce himself — a patriot and calls him "The descendant of Archibald Hamilton Rowan" (53), although Richard himself denies the lineage. In *Portrait*, young Stephen at Clongowes had "wondered from which window Hamilton Rowan had thrown his hat on the haha" (p. 23). The Irish patriot Hamilton Rowan was a friend of Wolfe Tone who had escaped to Clongowes Castle after being convicted in 1794 for sedition: "He shut its door just as the soldiers were shooting, so that their bullets entered the door;

then he threw his hat on the haha [a sunken hedge or wall] as a decoy, and let himself through a secret door into a tower room. His pursuers were fooled, thinking he had left, and he was able afterwards to make good his escape to France" (Ellmann 29). While, like Richard Rowan, Stephen is not related to Hamilton Rowan, his first youthful success at defying oppressive authority is linked to Rowan's own heroism at Clongowes, for, as he courageously walks toward the rector's quarters after the unjust pandybatting by Father Dolan, we are told that "He came out on the landing above the entrance hall and looked about him. That was where Hamilton Rowan had passed and the marks of the soldiers' slugs were there" (p. 62) — allying Stephen's own fledgling act of resistance against injustice with the marks of heroic, patriotic resistance to imperial tyranny and authority.

By the time he is at University College, Stephen has realized that national zeal and heroism for him would take place not through physical combat but in a different arena of revolutionary activism, that of spiritual and artistic liberation: as he tells Madden in *Stephen Hero* about his paper on Ibsen (titled significantly "Art and Life"), "This is the first of my explosives" (*Stephen Hero* 81). Stephen — whose weapons are neither bombs nor hurleysticks, but the arms of his literary art (silence, exile, and most of all cunning) — certainly runs the risk of an apolitical aestheticism (such as Joyce has been accused of) in his concerns with an Aristotelian/Thomistic aesthetic theory based on "nominal definitions, essential definitions" (p. 160), as he chooses to turn away from the political discussion with Davin (in which he has rejected Ireland as "the old sow that eats her farrow" [p. 182]) to matters of aesthetics with Lynch, to the definitions and logocentrism of an essentialist *claritas*: "Aristotle has not defined pity and terror. I have" (p. 183). But at least Stephen, in doing so, is aware that, in his attempt to fashion a spiritual liberation for his "race," he must get out of the Celticist vicious cycle, in which a provincial Ireland is narrowly locked in an inescapable struggle with England within a closed binary system:

> *3 April:* Met Davin at the cigar shop. . . . He was in a black sweater and had a hurleystick. Asked me was it true I was going away and why. Told him the shortest way to Tara was *via* Holyhead. (p. 221)

Stephen's cryptic response to Davin's question suggests his conviction that the road to Irish freedom (the traditional Irish seat at Tara) was to be found not through the hurleystick of Irish Nationalism carried by Davin, but via Holyhead, the closest port outside Ireland on the way to the Continent. It is there that Stephen hopes to "discover the mode of life or of art whereby [his] spirit could express itself in unfettered freedom" (p. 217) — so as "to forge in the smithy of my soul the uncreated conscience of my race" (p. 224).

WORKS CITED

Curtis, L. P., Jr. *Anglo-Saxons and Celts: A Study of Anti-Irish Prejudice in Victorian England*. Bridgeport: University of Bridgeport, 1968.

———. *Apes and Angels: The Irishman in Victorian Caricature*. Washington, D.C.: Smithsonian, 1971.

Darwin, Charles. *The Descent of Man and Selection in Relation to Sex*. London: John Murray, 1882.

Ellmann, Richard. *James Joyce*. First edition. Oxford: Oxford UP, 1959.

Fanon, Frantz. *The Wretched of the Earth*. Trans. Constance Farrington. New York: Grove Weidenfeld, 1968.

Gibbons, Luke. "Race Against Time: Racial Discourse and Irish History." *Oxford Literary Review* 13: 1–2 (1991): 95–117. Special issue on *Neocolonialism*. Ed. Robert Young.

Joyce, James. *The Critical Writings of James Joyce*. Ed. Ellsworth Mason and Richard Ellmann. New York: Viking, 1964.

———. *Finnegans Wake*. New York: Viking, 1939.

———. *Exiles: A Play in Three Acts*. New York: Viking, 1951.

———. *Stephen Hero*. Ed. John J. Slocum and Herbert Cahoon. Norfolk, CT: New Directions, 1959.

———. *Ulysses*. Ed. Hans Walter Gabler, et al. New York: Vintage, 1986.

Combining Perspectives on *A Portrait of the Artist as a Young Man*

So far, this volume's emphasis has been on mapping the boundaries of particular contemporary critical approaches and traditions. In presenting this final essay, "Walking in Dublin" by Cheryl Herr, the emphasis is reversed, for the intention is to demonstrate the permeability of such approaches, traditions, and boundaries. The goal is to show how supposedly diverse critical assumptions and traditions can mix, merge, and metamorphose. To put it more plainly, Herr's essay allows us to see how a critic can draw on the insights of *several* approaches (in effect, combining perspectives) to present a view of a work unavailable from any one window, any single critical perspective.

Herr discusses Joyce's fiction in terms of characters "whose paths intersect" on Dublin streets and even of "the paths themselves as they are simultaneously encountered and created by Dubliners" (p. 416 in this volume). In *Portrait*, she argues, "the streets of Dublin and the practice of walking in the city not only constantly transform Stephen's sense of the world but also materially shape his emergent Being-in-the-world" (p. 416). (This is a "hyphenated Heideggerian locution" Herr uses to point to "the way in which ourselves and our surroundings are aspects of activities that make up a specific world" [p. 416].)

Focusing on the "interaction of body and street in Joyce's Dublin," Herr seeks to "bring forward the phenomenology of the everyday practice of walking in the city" (p. 417). At the same time, she shows how "[t]hinking about *Portrait* through cultural studies, colonial and post-colonial theory, feminism, and psychoanaly[tic criticism]"— the five critical approaches introduced earlier in this volume — "helps us to appreciate the complexity of Joyce's project as well as its grounding in everyday practical activity" (p. 417).

Indeed, even before she gets around to Jacques Lacan's theories regarding human identity or feminist readings of *Portrait,* Herr invokes studies of "urban walking" made by Walter Benjamin and Michel de Certeau, two of the theorists whose writings underpin contemporary Marxist and cultural criticism. Particularly useful to Herr is de Certeau's investigation of the way "ordinary social practices — from telling stories to riding a train"— both shape human subjectivity and create "possibilities for ordinary practitioners of the everyday to resist total dominance by instrumental social regimes" (pp. 417–18). The latter opportunities emerge because, in de Certeau's words, "activities" such as "moving about, speaking, reading, shopping, and cooking . . . corre-spond to the characteristics of tactical ruses and surprises: clever tricks of the 'weak' within the order established by the 'strong'" (p. 418).

De Certeau's writings are particularly useful to Herr because "[t]he street-level behaviors that fascinate de Certeau — the practical grap-plings with social materiality — are the same sort of everyday actions that Joyce keenly interrogates from the beginning of Stephen's story to the end" (p. 418). The very beginning of *Portrait,* Herr reminds us, involves a "moocow" meeting "a nicens little boy named baby tuckoo" on the road where Betty Byrne "sells lemon platt." ("Even in this mini-mal rendering," Herr writes, "the story has a protagonist, . . . potential transactions [greeting the moocow, procuring lemon platt, or per-haps just saying hello to Betty Byrne]), and a path to connect them" [p. 418].) And "[a]lmost from the beginning of *Portrait,* Stephen's surname is an issue for him" (p. 420) — a mythical name that connects Stephen's very identity with the idea and creation of a labyrinth.

As a metaphor, many critics have noted, the labyrinth provides a way of understanding the novel's narrative. But it also, as Diane For-tuna has argued, suggests what the narrative's protagonist actually *does* — namely, walk, in circumlocutious fashion, down country and suburban lanes, school corridors, and urban streets winding among brothels. But whereas, in Fortuna's view (quoting Herr), "the farther that Stephen notionally flies from the streets of Dublin, the more likely he is to be freed," Herr takes the position that the "labyrinth comes into being only as someone walks through it" (p. 422). Thus, whereas "Fortuna argues that the narrative aim is to secure Stephen's freedom by way of his flight to Paris," Herr's view is that "Stephen can never extricate his Being-in-the-world from the roads that he travels" (p. 422).

Herr proceeds by moving deftly from an engagement with Fortuna to one with Joseph Valente, a postcolonial critic who views Joyce's Ireland as both "a colony and a space that contested its colonization" (p. 423). (We might say, figuratively speaking, that Joyce's Ireland is a "walker" whose subjectivity is oppressed by the external environment and, at the same time, a "subject" whose walking practices amount to acts of resistance.) Indeed, by the time she reaches her conclusion, Herr manages to engage two of the other authors (Suzette Henke and Sheldon Brivic) whose viewpoints (feminist and psychoanalytic, respectively) are represented earlier in this volume. But it is less important, here, to follow Herr's unfolding argument, with its complex blend of critical influences and approaches, than it is to indicate in advance the high quality of analysis that Herr is able to achieve by orchestrating voices from different traditions, by effectively combining approaches to a text that is, itself, a rich mix of viewpoints, voices, texts, and traditions.

Ross C Murfin

COMBINING PERSPECTIVES

CHERYL HERR

Walking in Dublin

BEING-IN-THE-WORLD

For Joyce scholars, one of the most enduring connections between continental theorizing and Joycean narrative has been the exploration of walking in the city. Whether we turn to *Dubliners, Portrait,* or *Ulysses,* we discover Joyce's characters strolling around their conurbation, often wandering the streets for lack of anything else to do, following the lead of the mitching boys in "An Encounter" and of the opportunistic duo of "Two Gallants." In *Ulysses,* Leopold Bloom spends his day somewhere between purposeful movement and aimless wandering. Given that Bloom's profession of advertising concerns the look of the urban environment, it is both convenient and appropriate that Bloom spends his working day pounding the pavement and musing about what he encounters: as Bloom knows, all kinds of places are good for ads precisely because people move past those places while walking in the city. While he ponders the advertising nexus (street, hoarding, and passerby), Bloom walks to the National Library; he pops into the museum to see whether goddesses have been given anatomically correct anuses and to avoid Blazes Boylan; he meets and greets the blind stripling, Mina Purefoy, Dennis Breen, and the citizens of Dublin who crisscross the urban landscape in a seemingly endless encounter with and within Dublin's infrastructure. Like all of Joyce's earlier writing, *Ulysses* has often been seen as the story of those whose paths intersect, but it can also be approached as the story of the paths themselves as they are simultaneously encountered and created by Dubliners (she who walks a path in some sense constructs that path as she goes), represented by Joyce, and engaged with by the reader.

Suspended between the short walks that make up *Dubliners* and the extended peregrinations of *Ulysses, Portrait* finds Stephen Dedalus restlessly searching the streets both to encounter reality and to encounter what he can of himself. As a very young child, of course, Stephen occupies the highly controlled and mostly interior environments of home or school. But as Stephen grows older he increasingly ventures into the messy contingency of Dublin at the turn of the century. Pedestrian Stephen discovers the contradictions structuring his society, the mediations that mark his identity, and the challenges to artistic agency posed by urban modernity.

In short, the streets of Dublin and the practice of walking in the city not only constantly transform Stephen's sense of the world but also materially shape his emergent Being-in-the-world. This hyphenated Heideggerian locution denotes the mutuality of embodiment and embeddedness; it indicates the way in which ourselves and our surroundings are aspects of activities that make up a specific world. Heidegger wanted to grasp and describe the everyday routines that coordinate body and environment in a given cultural setting, that elude the naive belief that the subject is *here* and the object is *there*, cleanly differentiated and primarily available to mental representation. Hubert Dreyfus, whose reading of Heidegger turns on the concept of "immersed coping," puts it this way: "Heidegger does not deny that we sometimes experience ourselves as conscious subjects" possessed of "states such as desires, beliefs, perceptions, intentions, etc., but he thinks of this as a

derivative and intermittent condition that presupposes a more fundamental way of Being-in-the-world that cannot be understood in subject/
object terms" (5). This way of Being-in-the-world is not something
obscure or unfamiliar: it simply consists in our everyday, unreflective
abilities, abilities we employ in getting on with others and making use
of ordinary things. Being-in-the-world finds a ready image in the ordinary Dubliner out for a stroll.

This essay takes us down some of the paths that Stephen travels in
Portrait. My aim is to focus on the interaction of body and street in
Joyce's Dublin; that is, I want to bring forward the phenomenology of
the everyday practice of walking in the city. As Stephen Dedalus draws
his way of being from the world around him and also produces glimpses
of that world for the reader, the everyday dialectic between the street
and the self is brought forward. Never contented with just one task,
however multidimensional, Joyce weaves many concerns and themes
into his study of practical activity. The language of *Portrait* thus leads a
reader from contemplating the materiality of the urban street to reaching out toward many schools of contemporary theory. Thinking about
Portrait through cultural studies, colonial and postcolonial theory, feminism, and psychoanalysis helps us to appreciate the complexity of Joyce's
project as well as its grounding in everyday practical activity. In the
essay that follows, I refer to the myth of Daedalus, to early-twentieth-
century archaeology, to Ireland's colonial history, to Jacques Lacan's
views on human identity, and to feminist commentaries on *Portrait*.
Following a Joycean path through these linked critical and theoretical
spaces will help us to encounter what we might call Being-in-Joyceworld.[1]

WALKING IN THE CITY

The act of urban walking has long been a focus of attention in studies of modernity. While some scholars find inspiration in Walter Benjamin's interrogation of the flâneur, others invoke this field by asking
their students to read Michel de Certeau's classic essay, "Walking in the
City." His discussion of ordinary social practices — from telling stories
to riding a train — explores the pressure of environments on subjectivity

---

[1]My use of the term "Being-in-Joyceworld" refers to Heidegger's "Being-in-the-
world." Murray Beja uses the term "Joyceworld" in his essay "Joyceworld: Dublin and
Dubliners."

as well as the possibilities for ordinary practitioners of the everyday to resist total dominance by instrumental social regimes.

Clearly influenced by Heidegger, de Certeau is fascinated that individuals not only carry out the tasks assigned by their cultures but also make their worlds and secure their places in those worlds through all manner of improvisational activity. He explains, "Dwelling, moving about, speaking, reading, shopping, and cooking are activities that seem to correspond to the characteristics of tactical ruses and surprises: clever tricks of the 'weak' within the order established by the 'strong,' an art of putting one over on the adversary on his own turf, hunter's tricks, maneuverable, polymorph mobilities, jubilant, poetic, and warlike discoveries" (40). The city walker is always, according to de Certeau, a potential "poacher." In "Walking in the City," de Certeau moves deftly from the viewpoint of the city planner to the lived, ground-level experience of passersby. The "ensemble of possibilities" that the walker actualizes (de Certeau 98) in his pedestrian practices creates place and person in one never-ending gesture.

The street-level behaviors that fascinate de Certeau — the practical grapplings with social materiality — are the same sort of everyday actions that Joyce keenly interrogates from the beginning of Stephen's story to the end. Just as a child's introduction to the concept of a street often begins with a bedtime story, so *Portrait* famously opens with the textual traces of the story that Simon Dedalus tells his son, a story about moving along a roadway: "there was a moocow coming down along the road" where he meets "a nicens little boy named baby tuckoo" (p. 20 in this volume). Betty Byrne lives on this road and sells lemon platt there. Even in this minimal rendering, the story has a protagonist (perhaps two of them), potential transactions (greeting the moocow, procuring lemon platt, or perhaps just saying hello to Betty Byrne), and a path to connect them. As we shall see, the father's fairy tale may signal, at some level, Stephen's separation from the mother and entry into what Jacques Lacan calls the Symbolic Order — an order in which practices are as important as language. The story certainly communicates a way of being in the world in which roads are navigated and transactions undertaken.

Storied byways pave the path toward engagement with the world. The topography of Stephen's remembered Clongowes school days includes a "main avenue of limes" (p. 35) that suggests an altogether more peaceful education than the one Stephen experiences there. Still, such bucolic spaces of transit punctuate Stephen's childhood; they mark the stages of his engagement with the world and with a scripted way of being. Joyce lets us glimpse the period when Uncle Charles takes Stephen on errands around Blackrock. Sometimes Stephen, his father, and Uncle Charles take ten-mile constitutionals along roads leading out into the further suburbs. Closer to home, Stephen joins Aubrey Mills and his "gang of adventurers" as they maraud the avenue and ride in the milk car to Carrickmines. The streets of Stephen's world enable everyday purchases as well as childhood games as marauding becomes an option in addition to taking a quiet stroll. And Stephen steadily learns, as most children do, to take part in the daily street activities that prepare him for more complicated and contradictory adventures.

If we stay on them long enough, suburban roads turn into city streets. The idyllic period gives way before the Dedalus family's steadily declining fortunes. As Simon Dedalus becomes more impoverished and comes under increasing political attack, he moves his family from "the comfort and revery of Blackrock" to "the gloomy foggy city" (p. 70), from leafy avenues to sullen streets. Stephen's earliest days in Dublin, fraught as they are with Simon's political and economic problems, nonetheless energize and stimulate him in new ways. Being on the streets means learning new games. An often quoted passage bears repeating here:

> Dublin was a new and complex sensation. Uncle Charles had grown so witless that he could no longer be sent out on errands and the disorder in settling in the new house left Stephen freer than he had been in Blackrock. In the beginning, he contented himself with circling timidly round the neighbouring square or, at most, going half way down one of the side streets: but when he had made a skeleton map of the city in his mind he followed boldly one of its central lines until he reached the customhouse. (p. 70)

The final sentence carries a telling textual ambiguity: does Stephen make a mental map of the city, or is he making a map of "the city in his mind"? Surely both meanings must be entertained. Stephen constructs his map before he knows the city's many parts: his making sense of his path is precisely part of his coming to be within the urban world. Moving down a road toward Betty Byrne's shop or pacing the school's avenue of lime trees or even playing in a lane with local children suggests movement along a single, simple trajectory. Walking into the city, with its more complicated urban infrastructure, with its circular roads, side streets, and multiple intersections, Stephen clearly builds on skills learned during walks with his father and Uncle Charles. The roads that he has traveled have etched themselves into his brain: his skeleton map is indelibly part of his physical comportment. His travels soon involve not just following the roadway but also choosing one direction over another. As Stephen quickly learns, such choices sometimes take a person more and more deeply into a labyrinth.

NAVIGATING LABYRINTHS

Almost from the beginning of *Portrait,* Stephen's surname is an issue for him, for his acquaintances, and for the reader. Of course, much has been written about Joyce's fictional deployment of the myth of Daedalus. For me, the most impressive essay on this subject remains Diane Fortuna's "The Labyrinth as Controlling Image in Joyce's *A Portrait of the Artist as a Young Man,*" because Fortuna brings forward the cultural contexts that surely shaped Joyce's choices. Fortuna begins by focusing on Stephen's last name and Nasty Roche's jeering inquiry about it. She explains, "The name is like a Latin word, *daedalus,* from the Greek *daidalos,* 'skillfully or cunningly wrought,' a word derived from the name of the Greek mythic artist, Daedalus, inventor of dolls, axes, plumb lines, and masts of ships and the architect of the labyrinth built for the Cretan king, Minos" (120). Fortuna narrates the interlocking stories of Minos, Pasiphae, the Minotaur, Daedalus, Icarus, Theseus, and Ariadne, fables that join the master builder's entrapment of Pasiphae's bestial offspring with Minos' revenge on Daedalus for enabling his queen's lustful procreation, with the winged escape that took Icarus to his doom, and with Ariadne's facilitating of Theseus' flight from his sacrifice to the devouring Minotaur.

From these mythic outlines, now familiar to all of Joyce's serious readers, Fortuna turns to the "why" of Joyce's choice of myth. She briefs the reader on the classical studies of Joyce's school days, and she brings forward the archaeological inquiries of Joyce's era, noting that during the first decade of the twentieth century,

> efforts to document the validity of myth and a separate but not unrelated exploration in Crete coincided to keep one myth in particular — that of Daedalus and the labyrinth — constantly before the public. Before 1900, little more was known about labyrinths and their function than had been known to the ancient world.

After 1900, the literature derived from the exploration at Knossos and interpretations supplementing those findings is astounding both in its detail and its sheer volume. (123)

In particular, celebrated British anthropologist Arthur Evans's discovery of Minos' palace in April 1900, reported in the London *Times,* captured the public imagination at a time when Joyce was studying at University College. Not only was the myth demonstrated to be in some sense historically verifiable, but a host of writers popularized Evans's findings.

Fortuna's interpretation closely follows that of these cultural commentators, who often furthered noted British social anthropologist James Frazer's interest in the origins of initiation rituals. These materials, claims Fortuna, led Joyce to begin associating himself with an alter ego (not just a character) whom he called Stephen Daedalus (126). Having established the cultural connections between the discovery of Minos' palace and the explosion of writing about initiation rites, Fortuna builds a persuasive interpretation of *Portrait* as an "intricate initiation" of its protagonist (134). Fortuna notes that the earliest Joyce critics (she cites Harry Levin and Dorothy Van Ghent) commented on Stephen's "continual walking" and recognized a "labyrinthine" quality to the narrative. But she chides them for missing the circularity of Stephen's movements:

> Stephen not only walks, he creeps along the fringe of the line, files in and out of winding corridors, circles, ascends, descends, runs round the park track, makes rounds with the milkman, takes turns riding the tractable mare around the field, circles nearer and nearer to the quarter of the brothels, feels his mind wind itself in and out of curious questions, circles about his own center of spiritual energy, notes with dismay . . . that Jesuits do much cycling and that Clongowes was where Jesuits walked round the cycle track, and attends a physics lecture on theories of coils, winding ellipses, and ellipsoids. (135)

Clearly, this circling echoes on many levels the specificity of the spiral labyrinth on Crete: the movements are not randomly mazelike but purposefully concentric. Moving into the spiral structure, Stephen finds the hellish, bestial center in Chapter III, after which he begins to extricate his body and his identity from the pattern holding him in thrall. Fortuna demonstrates that the reimagining of *Stephen Hero* as *Portrait* involved extending the labyrinth image until it became the structure of the later work. According to this reading, the farther that Stephen notionally flies from the streets of Dublin, the more likely he is to be freed. Rather than taking the view that the labyrinth comes into being only as someone walks through it (that the labyrinth and the walker are aspects of a single practice that demands our interrogation as such), Fortuna argues that the narrative aim is to secure Stephen's freedom by way of his flight to Paris. My view would be rather that Stephen can never extricate his Being-in-the-world from the roads that he travels.

METRO-COLONIAL MIGRATIONS

Fortuna's conclusions remind us that the excavation of buried cultural contexts is an ongoing process for both critic and reader. Joyce's obsessive gathering of encyclopedic details for his writing allows the reader to sustain a lengthy engagement with the interpretive process. However compellingly one generation of scholars presents its findings, the following generation of Joyceans has always found more layers to probe, more relations to draw together. Thus it is no surprise that we can say more about both the myth and the history to which *Portrait* directs us. In particular, we might want to supplement Fortuna's view of Stephen's situation with the approach to walking presented by Joseph Valente in his 1998 essay "Between Resistance and Complicity: Metro-Colonial Tactics in Joyce's *Dubliners*."

Valente wants to understand not Minos but modernity by bringing the cultural philosophy of de Certeau to bear on Joyce's short stories. Reacting to a late-twentieth-century critical designation of Joyce as a subaltern writer (he cites the work of Emer Nolan, Enda Duffy, and Vincent Cheng in this regard), Valente turns to de Certeau's distinction between "tactics" and "strategy." The latter refers to techniques for control of a place; those techniques both produce and are produced by the panoptical purview of the colonizer, the powerful, the "metropolitan." In contrast, tactics are defined as the default mechanisms of the disfranchised as they make their way through the places of power. As we noted earlier, de Certeau wants to understand how individuals living under hegemonic rule can opportunistically "poach" power and use it to their own advantage. Valente's intervention regarding this well-known dichotomy is to demonstrate how Joyce presents a complicated ("doubly inscribed") subject position for his Dubliners as they move through the city.

What the reader discovers is that Joyce's characters embody the "ambiguous status" of Ireland within the British empire (Valente 325). Insofar as Joyce's Ireland was both a colony and a space that contested its colonization, Valente argues that imperial strategies coexisted both spatially and performatively with Irish "ethnonationalism." The stories in *Dubliners,* Valente maintains, show the tensions of a "doubly/divisively inscribed interspace" (327). Valente calls this condition "metro-colonialism," and on this reading Stephen Dedalus is himself a border-phenomenon, a metro-colonial. Far from endorsing Fortuna's optimistic sense that a very special Dubliner might be able to extricate himself from the labyrinth of his culturally inscribed identity, Valente claims:

A profoundly ambivalent ethnonational identification . . . constitutes the enabling and galvanizing condition of Joyce's insight into the problem of tactics. The hybridity that functions as a crippling social and even ontological insecurity at the level of the narrative, driving the character in circles of frustration, affords stylistic and perspectival mobility at the level of narration, allowing Joyce to identify, and no less importantly, disidentify with the conditions of his own personal and artistic development. (328)

The payoff, then, is both narrative and autobiographical.

Although Valente addresses Joyce's short stories rather than *Portrait,* and although he writes less about actual walking than he does about local practices such as standing drinks in the pub (all in the service of displacing a clear-cut strategy-versus-tactics discrimination in *Dubliners*), we can transpose his argument about de Certeau into the register given to us in *Portrait.* We can thus follow de Certeau's own study of "walking in the city" while thinking about Stephen Dedalus as a wanderer in a maze, as an initiate traversing a labyrinth, and as a metro-colonial moving through territory that both alienates and attracts, finding his way with the attitude of the potential poacher.

Some of Stephen's most enjoyable walks in the city occur in relation to his winning a school prize. At the end of Chapter II, Stephen and his family are in the heart of Dublin at the Bank of Ireland, now as then located "in the house of commons of the old Irish parliament" (p. 95). Famously, the building erected in 1729 to house the Irish Parliament was forcibly restructured after the 1800 removal of the government to London. The interior layout was, by decree, altered so that the building would no longer accommodate a parliamentary gathering. This imposing Georgian structure carries the story not just of the exercise of

British imperialism over Irish self-determination but also of the preceding Irish uprising in 1798. The material remains of an oppressive regime eloquently express the political history of Dublin. Simon Dedalus reads this architectural signature and articulates it for his son: "God help us! he said piously, to think of the men of those times, Stephen, Hely Hutchinson and Flood and Henry Grattan and Charles Kendal Bushe, and the noblemen we now have, leaders of the Irish people at home and abroad. Why, by God, they wouldn't be seen dead in a tenacre field with them" (p. 95).

Glowing in the joy of receiving his prize money, Stephen would rather escort his family through the city streets than ponder the injustices of the past. He buys a triumphal dinner, pays for theatre parties, and liberally avails himself of his new purchasing power: "Great parcels of groceries and delicacies and dried fruits arrived from the city" (p. 96). Prize-winning Stephen is much less interested in his nation's history than he is in walking about the city spending money — acting the role of the franchised and respectable burgher.

In a Georgian city like Dublin, the built environment constantly announces its colonial origins. Leinster House, the National Museum, the National Library, the Bank of Ireland, University College, Dublin Castle — these and other architectural gems proclaim the power of the state apparatus, the importance of class status, the hegemonic control of economic transactions. As Stephen moves between city center and his own family's increasingly shabby dwellings, he comes to understand the nature of social power and wants to know more about the world around him. Stephen's wanderings indicate not only his growing awareness of desire but also his belief that he can find what he needs by moving through the city. The lack of a singular place and a satisfying identity propel him forward in the constitutive ritual of walking toward the boundaries of the city. His moving encounters suggest that the internal splittings and doublings of the metro-colonial subject continually emerge from and are shaped by the material structures of city and suburb.

When the prize money runs out, we are told that the "breakwater of order and elegance" that Stephen has tried to fashion gives way, and "the tides within him" (p. 97) come forward to threaten his youth and piety. That is, when shopping is no longer an option, when legitimate expenditures are out of the question, Stephen drifts toward the outer edges of ordered urban experience: he begins to probe those boundaries, to notice whether and how others poach on the system, and to explore a less administered way of being. He still entertains the concept of flying away, even though his embodied and embedded experience suggests that his fate is otherwise.

LIQUIDATING LACK

Joyce's Dubliners construct their world by entering the city's maze and seeking, often aimlessly, a meaning that eludes them. Very often that gnomonic meaning is coded as feminine. Consider Stephen's attempt to understand his puzzling experience with E—— C——. After the party at Harold's Cross, Stephen and E—— C—— move down the "glassy road" to the "last tram" (p. 72), where horses and a conductor fill out the quiet suburban scene. When he later writes a poem about this event, Stephen purifies the experience so that "all those elements which he deemed common and insignificant fell out of the scene. There remained no trace of the tram itself nor of the trammen nor of the horses" (p. 74). In this etherealized scene, Stephen attempts to constitute himself and E—— C—— as nearly disembodied energies bathed in moonlight. His daydream reality is grappling with "the city in his mind" to recover the pre-urban Stephen, a Stephen in whom hormonally driven attractions to girls were unknown. Stephen would like to regain the purity of his devotion to the notional Mercedes living in "a small whitewashed house" on "the road that led to the mountains" (p. 67).

Stephen's body will have it otherwise, and that same body carries itself ever more deeply into the contradictory fabric of the city. It is on these streets that Stephen physically defends Byron's poetry against bullying schoolboys and where he strides wildly toward the morgue and the "rank heavy air" of the "dark cobbled laneway" next to it (p. 87). He cannot let go of his maturing sense of physical desire; he cannot withdraw from the material, disturbing, compelling, and contradictory space that has become inseparable from his ever-emergent map of himself.

When maturing Stephen experiences his inner tides, he discovers an aspect of the lack referenced in Jacques Lacan's famous "n+1" formulation. In "Of Structure as an Inmixing of an Otherness Prerequisite to Any Subject Whatever," Lacan argues that the structure of the psyche emerges out of the attempt to liquidate the lack signed by the mother on the entry into the Symbolic Order. That attempt is basically an act of addition: the plus-one is that toward which we move, by way of the nets of language, in the vain hope of finding or completing ourselves.

As a way of pressing further into the uncharted terrain of his Being-in-the-world, Stephen begins to retrace his earliest steps. Without knowing it, he is looking for the moocow and Betty Byrne; he is looking for Mercedes; he is looking for E—— C——. His search drives him through the mazelike streets, moaning to himself like the Minotaur. The narrative states that Stephen "continued to wander up and down day after day as if he really sought someone that eluded him" (p. 70). The earlier walk down the road and the casual construction of an internal city map adapt to the rhythm of Stephen's inner tides, themselves seeking their outward confirmation in a girl who will, notionally, liquidate Stephen's lack. On the way, he discovers Dublin's prostitutes and their shadowy environment. Thus, his search amounts to the pursuit of illegitimacy, the possibility for poaching, a walk on the wild side.

When Stephen's growing desire turns to what he views as uncontrollable lust, he abandons home and family for a newly minted version of the movement toward Mercedes or E—— C—— in which he traverses "dark slimy streets," "narrow and dirty streets," "the quarter of the jews" (p. 98). We read that Stephen "stood still in the middle of the roadway" (p. 98) when he finds the prostitute in pink who first leads him to bed. Chapter II ends with his urban-specific sin. Transgression follows him into Chapter III, which begins with Stephen's anticipation of another nightly return to "the squalid quarter of the brothels," where his "devious course" and constant "circling" would find their goal. Joyce's prose conveys the sense that Stephen knows his way around and that Stephen's sensibility has now been irrevocably marked as a function of the city's forbidden but readily available pleasures.

Here, Joyce again brings forward the force of Stephen's last name. As in *Ulysses,* where the Circe episode reveals the heart of the city and the recesses of the psyche to constitute the same space, so in Chapter III of *Portrait* Joyce asserts the Daedalus myth in all of its complicated way-finding registers. Walking in the city, where commodities both victual and sexual vie with the material structures of colonial oppression, begins to activate the mythic narrative and cultural contexts that Joyce brings into his thinking about Dublin.

When the school retreat frightens Stephen into repentance, he again ranges widely in the streets that frame his pain. He wanders in an imagined "black cold void waste" (p. 130). When he comes to himself — achieves consciousness of his phenomenological condition — we read, "The squalid scene composed itself around him; the common accents, the burning gasjets in the shops, odours of fish and spirits and wet sawdust, moving men and women. An old woman was about to cross the street, an oilcan in her hand. He bent down and asked her was there a chapel near" (p. 130). The old woman gives Stephen directions: the urban fabric in which Stephen is embodied and embedded contains not only the stridency of his sin but also the location of his spiritual release. Guided by the old woman, surely a version of the mother whose absence inaugurates identity, desire, and movement, Stephen has confessed and been absolved, and his relief is entirely apparent: "The muddy streets were gay" (p. 134).

Chapter IV finds Stephen living not on the streets but in "devotional areas": his scheduled meditations and planned privations seem to take place either indoors or in an outside world so vague as to recall his early poem about the evening by the tram in Harold's Cross. His reveries turn on the image of himself as a "young and silentmannered priest" (p. 144) whose personal movements and gestures take place in a purely imaginary space, where "the fantastic fabrics of his mind" temporarily hold sway before being dispersed as easily as the tide "dissolves the sandbuilt turrets of children" (p. 146). This telling image of sand castles by the sea presides over the scene in which Stephen strolls through the streets pondering whether to become a priest. As he passes "the jesuit house in Gardiner street," Stephen realizes that his path actually leads not to a room in that building but through "a hamshaped encampment of poor cottages" (pp. 147–48) from which his family was shortly to remove toward deeper penury. The impoverished way of being evinced differently by both cottages and brothels draws Stephen much more profoundly than the trendy shops of Grafton Street.

Stephen's search reminds us that the final three paragraphs of de Certeau's "Walking in the City" pointedly link spatial practices to childhood experience. De Certeau invokes Heidegger's idea of "Being-there" as a function of "moving into something different" (109). Classic childhood games act out the separation from the mother that allows the child to inaugurate his identity. The structure of the event is spatial; the result is the ability to be-there without the mother. By this logic, walking in the city means always seeking the lost mother who composes the texture of one's embodied experience. In Joyce's text, Stephen is preoccupied by his search for some sort of mother substitute, for the Ariadne whose thread promises escape from the labyrinth.

For the purposes of Joyce's narrative, Stephen's lack becomes, at least temporarily, the place plenitudinously occupied by the bird-girl, caught up as she is in the border between land and water, symbol and substance — the list can be extended as far as a reader chooses. The girl by the sea strikes Stephen as being-outside-the-city. In her recalcitrant multiplicity, she seems temporarily to exceed Stephen's contradictory, practice-based interdependence with the functionally rationalized environments that he moves through.

Essays in this volume by Suzette Henke and Sheldon Brivic both address the dynamics of Stephen's problems with women. Brivic states:

> On the beach, Stephen tells himself that he has risen from the repressive "grave of boyhood" and that he will create out of freedom. . . . He uses the birdlike girl he sees to project his new freedom of seeing reality without idealizing or condemning it. . . . [but] Stephen's myth of transcendence is not an escape from his neurosis but a product of it, and his parental attachments and anxieties return in the fifth chapter. (pp. 292–93)

Henke is even harder on Stephen. She finds his extreme narcissism expressed through his reaction to the girl by the sea: "He glorifies the wading girl as angelic muse but never actually joins her in the teeming ocean waters" (p. 329). Stephen mortally fears water, which symbolizes the "fluidity of female desire. . . . Woman proves to be the blind spot in Stephen's poetic discourse" (p. 330).

One of the joys of reading *Portrait* is that readers constantly discover new stories within its textual complexity. While Stephen certainly has problems with girls, is clearly both neurotic and narcissistic, and has a strong tendency to wrap his desire in suffocating verbiage, it must also be admitted that he does not give up his search. The forward movement, the striding through streets and byways, the sometimes frantic mobility that brings Stephen into being constitutes both self and world. By this line of reasoning, the bird-girl becomes not an end in herself but a primary emblem for Stephen's active search, for his moving encounters with the mother/girl/woman on the road who either beckons or shows him the way, for his own imagined flight beyond the labyrinth, and for the phenomenological connection between what his mind has mapped and what remains to be encountered for the first or for the millionth time.

WORKS CITED

Beja, Murray. "Joyceworld: Dublin and *Dubliners.*" *El Dublín de James Joyce.* Ed. Juan Insúa. Sevilla: Centre de Cultura Contemporánea, 1995. 242–45.

Benjamin, Walter. "The Flâneur." *Charles Baudelaire: A Lyric Poet in the Era of High Capitalism.* Trans. Harry Zohn. London and New York: Verso, 1989. 35–66.

de Certeau, Michel. "Walking in the City." *The Practice of Everyday Life.* Trans. Steven Rendall. Berkeley: U of California P, 1984. 91–110.

Dreyfus, Hubert. *Being-in-the-World: A Commentary on Heidegger's "Being and Time," Division I.* Cambridge: MIT P, 1991.

Fortuna, Diane. "The Labyrinth as Controlling Image in Joyce's *A Portrait of the Artist as a Young Man.*" *Bulletin of the New York Public Library* 76 (1972): 120–81.

Lacan, Jacques. "Of Structure as an Inmixing of an Otherness Prerequisite to Any Subject Whatever." *The Structuralist Controversy.* Ed. R. Macksey and E. Donato. Baltimore: Johns Hopkins UP, 1970. 186–200.

Valente, Joseph. "Between Resistance and Complicity: Metro-Colonial Tactics in Joyce's *Dubliners.*" *Narrative* 6 (1998): 325–40.

Glossary of Critical
and Theoretical Terms

ABSENCE The idea, advanced by French theorist Jacques Derrida, that authors are not present in texts and that meaning arises in the absence of any authority guaranteeing the correctness of any one interpretation.

See **Presence and Absence** for a more complete discussion.

AFFECTIVE FALLACY *See* **New Criticism; Reader-Response Criticism.**

BASE *See* **Marxist Criticism.**

CANON A term used since the fourth century to refer to those books of the Bible that the Christian church accepts as being Holy Scripture — that is, divinely inspired. Books outside the canon (noncanonical books) are referred to as *apocryphal. Canon* has also been used to refer to the Saints Canon, the group of people officially recognized by the Catholic Church as saints. More recently, it has been employed to refer to the body of works generally attributed by scholars to a particular author (for example, the Shakespearean canon is currently believed to consist of thirty-seven plays that scholars feel can be definitively attributed to him). Works sometimes attributed to an author, but whose authorship is disputed or otherwise uncertain, are called apocryphal. *Canon* may also refer more generally to those literary works that are "privileged," or given special status, by a culture. Works we tend to think of as classics or as "Great Books"— texts that are repeatedly reprinted in anthologies of literature — may be said to constitute the canon.

Note: The following definitions are adapted and/or abridged versions of ones found in *The Bedford Glossary of Critical and Literary Terms* by Ross C Murfin and Supryia M. Ray.

Contemporary **Marxist, feminist,** minority, and **postcolonial** critics have argued that, for political reasons, many excellent works never enter the canon. Canonized works, they claim, are those that reflect — and respect — the culture's dominant ideology or perform some socially acceptable or even necessary form of "cultural work." Attempts have been made to broaden or redefine the canon by discovering valuable texts, or versions of texts, that were repressed or ignored for political reasons. These have been published both in traditional and in nontraditional anthologies. The most outspoken critics of the canon, especially certain critics practicing **cultural criticism,** have called into question the whole concept of canon or "canonicity." Privileging no form of artistic expression, these critics treat cartoons, comics, and soap operas with the same cogency and respect they accord novels, poems, and plays.

CHICAGO SCHOOL Originally a group of literary critics associated with the University of Chicago; other critics who have followed in their footsteps have also been referred to as Chicago School critics or, more simply, as Chicago Critics. In 1952, the original group of Chicago Critics collectively published a landmark book entitled *Critics and Criticism,* which outlined their thinking about both practical criticism (a type of literary criticism) and the general history of criticism.

Chicago School critics typically examine works on an individual basis (as do practical critics and objective critics). They view the text in terms of its form, or shaping principle, and the way in which that form is articulated in the work's structure. They also, however, consider the relationship between individual works and broadly defined categories of works, or **genres.** Because they combine a historical interest in schools of criticism and literary genres with a practical or objective focus on the internal structure and relations of elements within individual works, the Chicago School critics are sometimes said to be **Neo-Aristotelian** critics. The approach of the Chicago critics has also been called formalist insofar as it involves analyzing works on an individual basis; it is important to note, however, that the Chicago critics' interest in historical matters is decidedly not formalist. Influential Chicago critics include such figures as R. S. Crane, Elder Olson, and Wayne Booth.

CULTURAL CRITICISM, CULTURAL STUDIES *See* "What Is Cultural Criticism?" pp. 337–51.

DECONSTRUCTION Deconstruction involves the close reading of **texts** in order to demonstrate that any given text has irreconcilably contradictory meanings, rather than being a unified, logical whole. As J. Hillis Miller, the preeminent American deconstructor, has explained in an essay entitled "Stevens' Rock and Criticism as Cure" (1976), "Deconstruction is not a dismantling of the structure of a text, but a demonstration that it has already dismantled itself. Its apparently solid ground is no rock but thin air."

Deconstruction was both created and has been profoundly influenced by the French philosopher of language Jacques Derrida. Derrida, who coined the term *deconstruction,* argues that in Western culture, people tend to think and express their thoughts in terms of *binary oppositions.* Something is white but not black, masculine and therefore not feminine, a cause rather than an effect. Other common and mutually exclusive pairs include beginning/end, conscious/unconscious, **presence/absence,** and speech/writing. Derrida suggests these oppositions are hierarchies in miniature, containing one term that Western culture views as positive or superior and another considered negative or inferior, even if only slightly so. Through deconstruction, Derrida aims to erase the boundary between binary oppositions — and to do so in such a way that the hierarchy implied by the oppositions is thrown into question.

Although its ultimate aim may be to criticize Western logic, deconstruction arose as a response to **structuralism** and to **formalism.** Structuralists believed that all elements of human culture, including literature, may be understood as parts of a system of signs. Derrida did not believe that structuralists could explain the laws governing human signification and thus provide the key to understanding the form and meaning of everything from an African village to Greek myth to a literary text. He also rejected the structuralist belief that texts have identifiable "centers" of meaning, a belief structuralists shared with formalists.

Formalist critics, such as the **New Critics,** assume that a work of literature is a freestanding, self-contained object whose meaning can be found in the complex network of relations between its parts (allusions, images, rhythms, sounds, etc.). Deconstructors, by contrast, see works in terms of their *undecidability.* They reject the formalist view that a work of literary art is demonstrably unified from beginning to end, in one certain way, or that it is organized around a single center that ultimately can be identified. As a result, deconstructors see texts as more radically heterogeneous than do formalists. Formalists ultimately make sense of the ambiguities they find in a given text, arguing that every ambiguity serves a definite, meaningful — and demonstrable — literary function. Undecidability, by contrast, is never reduced, let alone mastered. Though a deconstructive reading can reveal the incompatible possibilities generated by the text, it is impossible for the reader to decide among them.

DIALECTIC Originally developed by Greek philosophers, mainly Socrates and Plato (in *The Republic* and *Phaedrus* [c. 360 B.C.]), a form and method of logical argumentation that typically addresses conflicting ideas or positions. When used in the plural, dialectics refer to any mode of argumentation that attempts to resolve the contradictions between opposing ideas.

The German philosopher G. W. F. Hegel described dialectic as a process whereby a *thesis,* when countered by an *antithesis,* leads to the *synthesis* of a new idea. Karl Marx and Friedrich Engels, adapting Hegel's idealist theory, used the phrase *dialectical materialism* to discuss the way in which a revolutionary class war might lead to the synthesis of a new socioeconomic order.

In literary criticism, *dialectic* typically refers to the oppositional ideas and/or mediatory reasoning that pervade and unify a given work or group of works. Critics may thus speak of the dialectic of head and heart (reason and passion) in William Shakespeare's plays. The American **Marxist critic** Fredric Jameson has coined the phrase "dialectical criticism" to refer to a Marxist critical approach that synthesizes **structuralist** and **poststructuralist** methodologies.

DIALOGIC *See* **Discourse.**

DISCOURSE Used specifically, (1) the thoughts, statements, or dialogue of individuals, especially of characters in a literary work; (2) the words in, or text of, a **narrative** as opposed to its story line; or (3) a "strand" within a given narrative that argues a certain point or defends a given value system. Discourse of the first type is sometimes categorized as *direct* or *indirect*. Direct discourse relates the thoughts and utterances of individuals and literary characters to the reader unfiltered by a third-person narrator. ("Take me home this instant!" she insisted.) Indirect discourse (also referred to as free indirect discourse) is more impersonal, involving the reportage of thoughts, statements, or dialogue by a third-person narrator. (She told him to take her home immediately.)

More generally, *discourse* refers to the language in which a subject or area of knowledge is discussed or a certain kind of business is transacted. Human knowledge is collected and structured in discourses. Theology and medicine are defined by their discourses, as are politics, sexuality, and literary criticism.

Contemporary literary critics have maintained that society is generally made up of a number of different discourses or *discourse communities,* one or more of which may be dominant or serve the dominant ideology. Each discourse has its own vocabulary, concepts, and rules — knowledge of which constitutes power. The psychoanalyst and **psychoanalytic critic** Jacques Lacan has treated the unconscious as a form of discourse, the patterns of which are repeated in literature. **Cultural critics,** following Soviet critic Mikhail Bakhtin, use the word *dialogic* to discuss the dialogue between discourses that takes place within language or, more specifically, a literary text. Some **poststructuralists** have used *discourse* in lieu of **text** to refer to any verbal structure whether literary or not.

FEMINIST CRITICISM *See* "What Is Feminist Criticism?" pp. 299–307.

FIGURE, FIGURE OF SPEECH *See* **Trope.**

FORMALISM A general term covering several similar types of literary criticism that arose in the 1920s and 1930s, flourished during the 1940s and 1950s, and are still in evidence today. Formalists see the literary work as an object in its own right. Thus, they tend to devote their attention to its intrinsic nature, concentrating their analyses on the interplay and relationships between the text's essential verbal elements. They study the form of the work (as opposed to its content), although form to a formalist can connote anything from **genre** (for example, one may speak of "the sonnet form") to grammatical or rhetorical structure to the "emotional imperative" that engenders the work's (more mechanical) structure. No matter which connotation of form pertains, however, formalists seek to be objective in their analysis, focusing on the work itself and eschewing external considerations. They pay particular attention to literary devices used in the work and to the patterns these devices establish.

Formalism developed largely in reaction to the practice of interpreting literary **texts** by relating them to "extrinsic" issues, such as the historical circumstances and politics of the era in which the work was written, its philosophical or theological milieu, or the experiences and frame of mind of its author. Although the term *formalism* was coined by critics to disparage the movement, it is now used simply as a descriptive term.

Formalists have generally suggested that everyday language, which serves simply to communicate information, is stale and unimaginative. They argue that "literariness" has the capacity to overturn common and expected patterns (of grammar, of story line), thereby rejuvenating language. Such novel uses of language supposedly enable readers to experience not only language but also the world in an entirely new way.

A number of schools of criticism have adopted a formalist orientation, or at least make use of formalist concepts. The **New Criticism,** an American approach to literature that reached its height in the 1940s and 1950s, is perhaps the most famous type of formalism. But Russian formalism was the first major formalist movement; after the Stalinist regime suppressed it in the early 1930s, the Prague Linguistic Circle adopted its analytical methods. The **Chicago School** has also been classified as formalist insofar as the Chicago critics examined and analyzed works on an individual basis; their interest in historical material, on the other hand, was clearly not formalist.

Another sort of formalism, namely **Neo-Aristotelian criticism**, coexisted (but often quarreled) with the New Criticism. Centered at the University of Chicago, and practiced by such critics as R. S. Crane, Wayne Booth, and Sheldon Sacks, Neo-Aristotelian criticism derived from Aristotle's *Poetics* an appreciation for plot and the belief that, in a successful novel, plot and such other elements of fiction as characters, themes, and language would cohere to form an integrated work. The "structural" analysis of the Chicago School came into conflict, first, with the "textural" analysis of the New Critics and, later, with the theories of **reader-response** and **deconstructive** critics, who, in variously insisting on the indeterminacy of the literary text, opposed what they saw as authoritarian in the Neo-Aristotelian method.

GAPS When used by **reader-response critics** familiar with the theories of Wolfgang Iser, the term refers to "blanks" in **texts** that must be filled in by readers. A gap may be said to exist whenever and wherever a reader perceives something to be missing between words, sentences, paragraphs, stanzas, or chapters. Readers respond to gaps actively and creatively, explaining apparent inconsistencies in point of view, accounting for jumps in chronology, speculatively supplying information missing from plots, and resolving problems or issues left ambiguous or "indeterminate" in the text.

Reader-response critics sometimes speak as if a gap actually exists in a text; a gap, of course, is to some extent a product of readers' perceptions. One reader may find a given text to be riddled with gaps while another reader may view that text as comparatively consistent and complete; different readers may find different gaps in the same text. Furthermore, they may fill in the gaps they find in different ways, which is why, a reader-response critic might argue, works are interpreted in different ways.

Although the concept of the gap has been used mainly by reader-response critics, it has also been used by critics taking other theoretical approaches. Practitioners of **deconstruction** might use *gap* when explaining that every text contains opposing and even contradictory discourses that cannot be reconciled. **Marxist critics** have used the term gap to speak of everything from the gap that opens up between economic **base** and cultural **superstructure** to two kinds of conflicts or contradictions found in literary texts. The first of these conflicts or contradictions, they would argue, results from the fact that even realistic texts reflect an **ideology**, within which there are inevitably subjects and attitudes that cannot be represented or even recognized. As a result, readers at the edge or outside of that ideology perceive that something is missing. The second kind of conflict or contradiction within a text results from the fact that works do more than reflect ideology; they are also fictions that, consciously or unconsciously, distance themselves from that ideology.

GAY AND LESBIAN CRITICISM Sometimes referred to as *queer theory,* an approach to literature currently viewed as a form of **gender criticism.** *See* **Gender Criticism.**

GENDER CRITICISM A type of literary criticism that focuses on — and critiques — gender as it is commonly conceived, seeking to expose its insufficiency as a categorizing device. Gender critics reject the view that gender is something natural or innate, arguing instead that gender is a social construct, a learned behavior, a product of culture and its institutions. **Gay and lesbian criticism** is generally viewed as a major emphasis within gender criticism, although not all gay and lesbian critics would so categorize their work.

Many commentators have argued that feminist criticism is also a type of gender criticism, despite the fact that feminist criticism arose as an approach to literary criticism in the 1970s, whereas gender criticism appeared on the critical scene a decade later. Gender critics have drawn heavily upon feminist theory and practice even as they have attacked many feminist concepts and claims.

Many gender critics hold "constructionist" views and take issue with those feminists who urge an "essentialist" approach. Stated simply, the word *essentialist* refers to the view that women are essentially — that is, naturally — different from men. The most essentialist feminists write as if no amount of enculturation could alter female nature, female difference. *Constructionist,* by contrast, refers to the view that most of the differences between men and women are characteristics not of the male and female sex (nature) but, rather, of the masculine and feminine genders (nurture). Constructionist gender critics vehemently disagree with those feminists who emphasize the female body, its sexual difference, and the manifold implications of that difference, especially those French feminist critics who argue that the female body gives rise to a special feminine language, writing, and style. Unlike these essentialist feminists, constructionist gender critics would attribute differences in language, writing, and style to cultural influences, not to sexual differences between female and male bodies.

Following the lead of French philosophical historian Michel Foucault, gay and lesbian cultural critics associated with so-called *queer theory* have argued that the heterosexual/homosexual distinction is as much a cultural construct as is the masculine/feminine dichotomy. These critics have been especially critical of heterosexuality as a norm, arguing that it is an enforced corollary and consequence of a "sex/gender system" which presupposes that men are masculine, that masculinity carries with it an attraction to women, and that it is therefore unnatural for men to be attracted to other men. Gay and lesbian writings have produced compelling, if controversial, reinterpretations of works by authors as diverse as Herman Melville, Emily Dickinson, Henry James, Virginia Woolf, and Toni Morrison.

Gay and lesbian critics are not the only gender critics who have critiqued masculinity. An unprecedented number of gender theorists have analyzed masculinity as a complex construct which produces and reproduces a constellation of behaviors and goals such as performance and conquest, many of them destructive and injurious to women. The construct of masculinity has been studied in works by Stephen Crane, T. S. Eliot, F. Scott Fitzgerald, and Nathaniel Hawthorne.

GENRE From the French *genre* for "kind" or "type," the classification of literary works on the basis of their content, form, or technique. The term also refers to individual classifications. For centuries works have been grouped and associated according to a number of classificatory schemes and distinctions, such as prose/poem/fiction/drama/lyric, and the traditional classical divisions: comedy/tragedy/lyric/pastoral/epic/satire. More recently, Northrop Frye has suggested that all literary works may be grouped with one of four sets of archetypal myths that are in turn associated with the four seasons; for Frye, the four main genre classifications are comedy (spring), romance (summer), tragedy (fall), and satire (winter). Many more specific genre categories exist as well, such as autobiography, the essay, the Gothic novel, the picaresque novel, the sentimental novel. Current usage is thus broad enough to permit varieties of a given genre (such as the novel) as well as the novel in general to be legitimately denoted by the term *genre*.

Traditional thinking about genre has been revised and even roundly criticized by contemporary critics. For example, the prose/poem dichotomy has been largely discarded in favor of a lyric/drama/fiction (or narrative) scheme. The more general idea that works of imaginative literature can be solidly and satisfactorily classified according to set, specific categories has also come under attack in recent times.

HEGEMONY Most commonly, one nation's dominance or dominant influence over another. The term was adopted (and adapted) by the Italian **Marxist critic** Antonio Gramsci to refer to the process of consensus formation and to the pervasive system of assumptions, meanings, and values — the web of **ideologies**, in other words — that shape the way things look, what they mean, and therefore what reality is for the majority of people within a given culture. Although Gramsci viewed hegemony as being powerful and persuasive, he did not believe that extant systems were immune to change; rather, he encouraged people to resist prevailing ideologies, to form a new consensus, and thereby to alter hegemony.

Hegemony is a term commonly used by **cultural critics** as well as by Marxist critics.

IDEOLOGY A set of beliefs underlying the customs, habits, and practices common to a given social group. To members of that group, the beliefs seem obviously true, natural, and even universally applicable. They may seem just as obviously arbitrary, idiosyncratic, and even false to those who adhere to another ideology. Within a society, several ideologies may coexist; one or more of these may be dominant.

Ideologies may be forcefully imposed or willingly subscribed to. Their component beliefs may be held consciously or unconsciously. In either case, they come to form what Johanna M. Smith has called "the unexamined ground of our experience." Ideology governs our perceptions, judgments, and prejudices — our sense of what is acceptable, normal, and deviant. Ideology may cause a revolution; it may also allow discrimination and even exploitation.

Ideologies are of special interest to politically oriented critics of literature because of the way in which authors reflect or resist prevailing views in their texts. Some **Marxist critics** have argued that literary texts reflect and reproduce the ideologies that produced them; most, however, have shown how ideologies are riven with contradictions that works of literature manage to expose and widen. Other Marxist critics have focused on the way in which texts themselves are characterized by gaps, conflicts, and contradictions between their ideological and anti-ideological functions.

Fredric Jameson, an American Marxist critic, argues that all thought is ideological, but that ideological thought that knows itself as such stands the chance of seeing through and transcending ideology.

Not all of the politically oriented critics interested in ideology have been Marxists. Certain non-Marxist **feminist critics** have addressed the question of ideology by seeking to expose (and thereby call into question) the patriarchal ideology mirrored or inscribed in works written by men — even men who have sought to counter sexism and break down sexual stereotypes. **New historicists** have been interested in demonstrating the ideological underpinnings not only of literary representations but also of our interpretations of them.

IMAGINARY ORDER *See* **Psychological Criticism and Psychoanalytic Criticism.**

IMPLIED READER *See* **Reader-Response Criticism.**

INTENTIONAL FALLACY *See* **New Criticism.**

INTERTEXTUALITY The condition of interconnectedness among texts, or the concept that any text is an amalgam of others, either because it exhibits signs of influence or because its language inevitably contains common points of reference with other texts through such things as allusion, quotation, genre, stylistic features, and even revisions. The critic Julia Kristeva, who popularized and is often credited with coining this term, views any given work as part of a larger fabric of literary **discourse**, part of a continuum including the future as well as the past. Other critics have argued for an even broader use and understanding of the term *intertextuality,* maintaining that literary history per se is too narrow a context within which to read and understand a literary text. When understood this way, *intertextuality* could be used by a **new historicist** or **cultural critic** to refer to the significant interconnectedness between a literary text and contemporary, nonliterary discussions of the issues represented in the literary text. Or it could be used by a **poststructuralist** to suggest that a work of literature can only be recognized and read within a vast field of signs and **tropes** that is like a text and that makes any single text self-contradictory and **undecidable.**

MARXIST CRITICISM A type of criticism in which literary works are viewed as the product of work and whose practitioners emphasize the role of class and ideology as they reflect, propagate, and even challenge the prevailing social order. Rather than viewing texts as repositories for hidden meanings, Marxist critics view texts as material products to be understood in broadly historical terms. In short, literary works are viewed as a product of work (and hence of the realm of production and consumption we call economics).

Marxism began with Karl Marx, the nineteenth-century German philosopher best known for writing *Das Kapital* (*Capital*) (1867), the seminal work of the communist movement. Marx was also the first Marxist literary critic, writing critical essays in the 1830s on writers such as Johann Wolfgang von Goethe and William Shakespeare. Even after Marx met Friedrich Engels in 1843 and began collaborating on overtly political works such as *The German Ideology* (1846) and *The Communist Manifesto* (1848), he maintained a keen interest in literature. In *The German Ideology,* Marx and Engels discussed the relationship between the arts, politics, and basic economic reality in terms of a general social theory. Economics, they argued, provides the *base,* or infrastructure, of society, from which a *superstructure* consisting of law, politics, philosophy, religion, and art emerges.

The revolution anticipated by Marx and Engels did not occur in their century, let alone in their lifetime. When it did occur, in 1917, it did so in a place unimagined by either theorist: Russia, a country long ruled by despotic czars but also enlightened by the works of powerful novelists and playwrights including Anton Chekhov, Alexander Pushkin, Leo Tolstoy, and Fyodor Dostoyevsky. Russia produced revolutionaries such as Vladimir Lenin, who shared not only Marx's interest in literature but also his belief in its ultimate importance. Leon Trotsky, Lenin's comrade in revolution, took a strong interest in literary matters as well, publishing a book called *Literature and Revolution* (1924) that is still viewed as a classic of Marxist literary criticism.

Of those critics active in the USSR after the expulsion of Trotsky and the triumph of Stalin, two stand out: Mikhail Bakhtin and Georg Lukács. Bakhtin viewed language — especially literary texts — in terms of discourses and **dialogues.** A novel written in a society in flux, for instance, might include an official, legitimate discourse, as well as one infiltrated by challenging comments. Lukács, a Hungarian who converted to Marxism in 1919, appreciated prerevolutionary, realistic novels that broadly reflected cultural "totalities" and were populated with characters representing human "types" of the author's place and time.

Perhaps because Lukács was the best of the Soviet communists writing Marxist criticism in the 1930s and 1940s, non-Soviet Marxists tended to develop their ideas by publicly opposing his. In Germany, dramatist and critic Bertolt Brecht criticized Lukács for his attempt to enshrine realism at the expense not only of the other "isms" but also of poetry and drama, which Lukács had largely ignored. Walter Benjamin praised new art forms ushered in by the age of mechanical reproduction, and Theodor Adorno attacked Lukács for his dogmatic rejection of nonrealist modern literature and for his elevation of content over form.

In addition to opposing Lukács and his overly constrictive **canon,** non-Soviet Marxists took advantage of insights generated by non-Marxist critical theories being developed in post–World War II Europe. Lucien Goldmann, a Romanian critic living in Paris, combined structuralist principles with Marx's base-superstructure model in order to show how economics determines the mental structures of social groups, which are reflected in literary texts. Goldmann rejected the idea of individual human genius, choosing instead to see works as the "collective" products of "trans-individual" mental structures. French Marxist Louis Althusser drew on the ideas of the **psychoanalytic** theorist Jacques Lacan and the Italian communist Antonio Gramsci, who discussed the relationship between ideology and **hegemony**, the pervasive system of assumptions and values that shapes the perception of reality for people in a given culture. Althusser's followers included Pierre Macherey, who in *A Theory of Literary Production* (1966) developed Althusser's concept of the relationship between literature and ideology; Terry Eagleton, who proposes an elaborate theory about how history enters texts, which in turn may alter history; and

Fredric Jameson, who has argued that form is "but the working out" of content "in the realm of superstructure."

METAPHOR A **figure of speech** (more specifically a **trope**) that associates two unlike things; the representation of one thing by another. The image (or activity or concept) used to represent or "figure" something else is known as the **vehicle** of the metaphor; the thing represented is called the **tenor**. For instance, in the sentence "That child is a mouse," the child is the tenor, whereas the mouse is the vehicle. The image of a mouse is being used to represent the child, perhaps to emphasize his or her timidity.

Metaphor should be distinguished from **simile**, another figure of speech with which it is sometimes confused. Similes compare two unlike things by using a connective word such as *like* or *as*. Metaphors use no connective word to make their comparison. Furthermore, critics ranging from Aristotle to I. A. Richards have argued that metaphors equate the vehicle with the tenor instead of simply comparing the two.

This identification of vehicle and tenor can provide much additional meaning. For instance, instead of saying, "Last night I read a book," we might say, "Last night I plowed through a book." "Plowed through" (or the activity of plowing) is the vehicle of our metaphor; "read" (or the act of reading) is the tenor, the thing being figured. (As this example shows, neither vehicle nor tenor need be a noun; metaphors may employ other parts of speech.) The increment in meaning through metaphor is fairly obvious. Our audience knows not only *that* we read but also *how* we read, because to read a book in the way that a plow rips through earth is surely to read in a relentless, unreflective way. Note that in the sentence above, a new metaphor — "rips through"— has been used to explain an old one. This serves (which is a metaphor) as an example of just how thick (another metaphor) language is with metaphors!

Metaphors may be classified as *direct* or *implied*. A direct metaphor, such as "That child is a mouse" (or "He is such a doormat!"), specifies both tenor and vehicle. An implied metaphor, by contrast, mentions only the vehicle; the tenor is implied by the context of the sentence or passage. For instance, in the sentence "Last night I plowed through a book" (or "She sliced through traffic"), the tenor — the act of reading (or driving) — can be inferred.

Traditionally, metaphor has been viewed as the principal trope. Other figures of speech include simile, **symbol**, personification, allegory, **metonymy**, synecdoche, and conceit. **Deconstructors** have questioned the distinction between metaphor and metonymy.

METONYMY A **figure of speech** (more specifically a **trope**), in which one thing is represented by another that is commonly and often physically associated with it. To refer to a writer's handwriting as his or her "hand" is to use a metonymic figure.

Like other figures of speech (such as **metaphor**), metonymy involves the replacement of one word or phrase by another; thus, a monarch might be referred to as "the crown." As narrowly defined by certain contemporary critics, particularly those associated with **deconstruction**, the **vehicle** of a metonym is arbitrarily, not intrinsically, associated with the **tenor**. (There is no special, intrinsic likeness between a crown and a monarch; it's just that crowns traditionally sit on monarchs' heads and not on the heads of university professors.)

More broadly, metonym and metonymy have been used by recent critics to refer to a wide range of figures. **Structuralists** such as Roman Jakobson, who emphasized the difference between metonymy and metaphor, have recently been challenged by deconstructors, who have further argued that *all* figuration is arbitrary. Deconstructors such as Paul de Man and J. Hillis Miller have questioned the "privilege" granted to metaphor and the metaphor/metonymy distinction or "opposition," suggesting instead that all metaphors are really metonyms.

MODERNISM *See* **Postmodernism.**

NARRATIVE A story or a telling of a story, or an account of a situation or events. Narratives may be fictional or true; they may be written in prose or verse. Some critics use the term even more generally; Brook Thomas, a **new historicist**, has critiqued "narratives of human history that neglect the role human labor has played."

NARRATOLOGY The analysis of the **structural** components of a **narrative**, the way in which those components interrelate, and the relationship between this complex of elements and the narrative's basic story line. Narratology incorporates techniques developed by other critics, most notably Russian **formalists** and French **structuralists**, applying in addition numerous traditional methods of analyzing narrative fiction (for instance, those methods outlined in the "Showing as Telling" chapter of Wayne Booth's *The Rhetoric of Fiction* [1961]). Narratologists treat narratives as explicitly, intentionally, and meticulously constructed systems rather than as simple or natural vehicles for an author's representation of life. They seek to analyze and explain how authors transform a chronologically organized story line into a literary plot. (Story is the raw material from which plot is selectively arranged and constructed.)

Narratologists pay particular attention to such elements as point of view; the relations among story, teller, and audience; and the levels and types of **discourse** used in narratives. Certain narratologists concentrate on the question of whether any narrative can actually be neutral (like a clear pane of glass through which some subject is objectively seen) and on how the practices of a given culture influence the shape, content, and impact of "historical" narratives. Mieke Bal's *Narratology: Introduction to the Theory of Narrative* (1980) is a standard introduction to the narratological approach.

NEO-ARISTOTELIAN CRITICISM *See* **Chicago School, Formalism.**

NEW CRITICISM, THE A type of **formalist** literary criticism that reached its height during the 1940s and 1950s, and that received its name from John Crowe Ransom's 1941 book *The New Criticism*. New Critics treat a work of literary art as if it were a self-contained, self-referential object. Rather than basing their interpretations of a **text** on the reader's response, the author's stated intentions, or parallels between the text and historical contexts (such as the author's life), New Critics perform a close reading of the text, concentrating on the internal relationships that give it its own distinctive character or form. New Critics emphasize that the structure of a work should not be divorced from meaning, viewing the two as constituting a quasi-organic unity. Special attention is paid to repetition, particularly of images or symbols, but also of sound effects and rhythms in poetry. New critics especially appreciate the use of literary devices, such as irony and paradox, to achieve a balance or reconciliation between dissimilar, even conflicting, elements in a text.

Because of the importance placed on close textual analysis and the stress on the text as a carefully crafted, orderly object containing observable formal patterns, the New Criticism has sometimes been called an "objective" approach to literature. New Critics are more likely than certain other critics to believe and say that the meaning of a text can be known objectively. For instance, **reader-response critics** see meaning as a function either of each reader's experience or of the norms that govern a particular interpretive community, and **deconstructors** argue that texts mean opposite things at the same time.

The foundations of the New Criticism were laid in books and essays written during the 1920s and 1930s by I. A. Richards (*Practical Criticism* [1929]), William Empson (*Seven Types of Ambiguity* [1930]), and T. S. Eliot ("The Function of Criticism" [1933]). The approach was significantly developed later, however, by a group of American poets and critics, including R. P. Blackmur, Cleanth Brooks, John Crowe Ransom, Allen Tate, Robert Penn Warren, and William K. Wimsatt. Although we associate the New Criticism with certain principles and terms (such as the *affective fallacy* — the notion that the reader's response is relevant to the meaning of a work — and the *intentional fallacy* — the notion that the author's intention determines the work's meaning), the New Critics were trying to make a cultural statement rather than to establish a critical dogma. Generally Southern, religious, and culturally conservative, they advocated the inherent value of literary works (particularly of literary works regarded as beautiful art objects) because they were sick of the growing ugliness of modern life and contemporary events. Some recent theorists even link the rising popularity after World War II of the New Criticism (and other types of formalist literary criticism such as the **Chicago School**) to American isolationism. These critics tend to view the formalist tendency to isolate literature from biography and history as symptomatic of American fatigue with wider involvements. Whatever the source of the New Criticism's popularity (or the reason for its eventual decline), its practitioners and the textbooks they wrote were so influential in American academia that the approach became standard in college and even high school curricula through the 1960s and well into the 1970s.

NEW HISTORICISM, THE A type of literary criticism that developed during the 1980s, largely in reaction to the text-only approach pursued by **formalist New Critics** and the critics who challenged the New Criticism in the 1970s. New historicists, like formalists and their critics, acknowledge the importance of the literary **text**, but they also analyze the text with an eye to history. In this respect, the new historicism is not "new"; the majority of critics between 1920 and 1950 focused on a work's historical content and based their interpretations on the interplay between the text and historical contexts (such as the author's life or intentions in writing the work).

In other respects, however, the new historicism differs from the historical criticism of the 1930s and 1940s. It is informed by the **poststructuralist** and **reader-response theory** of the 1970s, as well as by the thinking of **feminist**, **cultural**, and **Marxist** critics whose work was also "new" in the 1980s. They are less fact- and event-oriented than historical critics used to be, perhaps because they have come to wonder whether the truth about what really happened can ever be purely and objectively known. They are less likely to see history as linear and progressive, as something developing toward the present, and they are also less likely to think of it in terms of specific eras, each with a definite, persistent, and consistent zeitgeist (spirit of the times). Hence, they are unlikely to suggest that a literary text has a single or easily identifiable historical context.

New historicist critics also tend to define the discipline of history more broadly than did their predecessors. They view history as a social science like anthropology and sociology, whereas older historicists tended to view history as literature's "background" and the social sciences as being properly historical. They have erased the line dividing historical and literary materials, showing not only that the production of one of William Shakespeare's historical plays was both a political act and a historical event, but also that the coronation of Elizabeth I was carried out with the same care for staging and symbol lavished on works of dramatic art.

New historicists remind us that it is treacherous to reconstruct the past as it really was — rather than as we have been conditioned by our own place and time to believe that it was. And they know that the job is impossible for those who are unaware of that difficulty, insensitive to the bent or bias of their own historical vantage point. Hence, when new historicist critics describe a historical change, they are highly conscious of (and even likely to discuss) the theory of historical change that informs their account.

Many new historicists have acknowledged a profound indebtedness to the writings of Michel Foucault. A French philosophical historian, Foucault brought together incidents and phenomena from areas normally seen as unconnected, encouraging new historicists and new cultural historicists to redefine the boundaries of historical inquiry. Like the philosopher Friedrich Nietzsche, Foucault refused to see history as an evolutionary process, a continuous development from cause to effect, from past to present toward *the end,* a moment of definite closure, a day of judgment. No historical event, according to Foucault, has a single cause; rather, each event is tied into a vast web of economic, social, and political factors. Like Karl Marx, Foucault saw history in terms of power, but, unlike Marx, he viewed power not simply as a repressive force or a tool of conspiracy but rather as a complex of forces that produces what happens. Not even a tyrannical aristocrat simply wields power, for the aristocrat is himself empowered by discourses and practices that constitute power.

Not all new historicist critics owe their greatest debt to Foucault. Some, like Stephen Greenblatt, have been most nearly influenced by the British cultural critic Raymond Williams, and others, like Brook Thomas, have been more influenced by German Marxist Walter Benjamin. Still others — Jerome McGann, for example — have followed the lead of Soviet critic Mikhail Bakhtin, who viewed literary works in terms of polyphonic **discourses** and dialogues between the official, legitimate voices of a society and other, more challenging or critical voices echoing popular culture.

POSTCOLONIAL CRITICISM, POSTCOLONIAL STUDIES *See* "What Is Postcolonial Criticism?" pp. 378–85.

POSTMODERNISM A term referring to certain radically experimental works of literature and art produced after World War II. *Postmodernism* is distinguished from *modernism,* which generally refers to the revolution in art and literature that occurred during the period 1910–1930, particularly following the disillusioning experience of World War I. The postmodern era, with its potential for mass destruction and its shocking history of genocide, has evoked a continuing disillusionment similar to that widely experienced during the modern period. Much of postmodernist writing reveals and highlights the alienation of individuals and the meaninglessness of human existence. Post-modernists frequently stress that humans desperately (and ultimately unsuc-cessfully) cling to illusions of security to conceal and forget the void on which their lives are perched.

Not surprisingly, postmodernists have shared with their modernist precur-sors the goal of breaking away from traditions (including certain modernist tra-ditions, which, over time, had become institutionalized and conventional to some degree) through experimentation with new literary devices, forms, and styles. While preserving the spirit and even some of the themes of modernist lit-erature (such as the alienation of humanity and historical discontinuity), post-modernists have rejected the order that a number of modernists attempted to instill in their work through patterns of allusion, symbol, and myth. They have also taken some of the meanings and methods found in modernist works to extremes that most modernists would have deplored. For instance, whereas modernists such as T. S. Eliot perceived the world as fragmented and repre-sented that fragmentation through poetic language, many also viewed art as a potentially integrating, restorative force, a hedge against the cacophony and chaos that postmodernist works often imitate (or even celebrate) but do not attempt to counter or correct.

Because postmodernist works frequently combine aspects of diverse **gen-res**, they can be difficult to classify — at least according to traditional schemes of classification. Postmodernists, revolting against a certain modernist tendency toward elitist "high art," have also generally made a concerted effort to appeal to popular culture. Cartoons, music, "pop art," and television have thus become acceptable and even common media for postmodernist artistic expres-sion. Postmodernist literary developments include such genres as the Absurd, the antinovel, concrete poetry, and other forms of avant-garde poetry written in free verse and challenging the **ideological** assumptions of contemporary soci-ety. What postmodernist theater, fiction, and poetry have in common is the view (explicit or implicit) that literary language is its own reality, not a means of representing reality.

Postmodernist critical schools include **deconstruction**, whose practitioners explore the **undecidability** of texts, and **cultural criticism**, which erases the boundary between "high" and "low" culture. The foremost theorist of post-modernism is Jean-François Lyotard, best known for his book *La Condition Postmoderne* (*The Postmodern Condition*) (1979).

POSTSTRUCTURALISM The general attempt to contest and subvert **structuralism** and to formulate new theories regarding interpretation and meaning, initiated particularly by **deconstructors** but also associated with cer-tain aspects and practitioners of **psychoanalytic, Marxist, cultural, feminist,** and **gender criticism.** Poststructuralism, which arose in the late 1960s, includes such a wide variety of perspectives that no unified poststructuralist theory can be identified. Rather, poststructuralists are distinguished from other contemporary critics by their opposition to structuralism and by certain concepts they embrace.

Structuralists typically believe that meaning(s) in a text, as well as the meaning of a text, can be determined with reference to the system of signification — the "codes" and conventions that governed the text's production and that operate in its reception. Poststructuralists reject the possibility of such "determinate" knowledge. They believe that signification is an interminable and intricate web of associations that continually defers a determinate assessment of meaning. The numerous possible meanings of any word lead to contradictions and ultimately to the dissemination of meaning itself. Thus, poststructuralists contend that texts contradict not only structuralist accounts of them but also themselves.

To elaborate, poststructuralists have suggested that structuralism rests on a number of distinctions — between signifier and signified, self and language (or **text**), texts and other texts, and text and world — that are overly simplistic, if not patently inaccurate, and they have made a concerted effort to discredit these oppositions. For instance, poststructuralists have viewed the self as the subject, as well as the user, of language, claiming that although we may speak through and shape language, it also shapes and speaks through us. In addition, poststructuralists have demonstrated that in the grand scheme of signification, all "signifieds" are also signifiers, for each word exists in a complex web of language and has such a variety of denotations and connotations that no one meaning can be said to be final, stable, and invulnerable to reconsideration and substitution. Signification is unstable and indeterminate, and thus so is meaning. Poststructuralists, who have generally followed their structuralist predecessors in rejecting the traditional concept of the literary "work" (as the work of an individual and purposeful author) in favor of the impersonal "text," have gone structuralists one better by treating texts as "intertexts": crisscrossed strands within the infinitely larger text called language, that weblike system of denotation, connotation, and signification in which the individual text is inscribed and read and through which its myriad possible meanings are ascribed and assigned. (Poststructuralist **psychoanalytic critic** Julia Kristeva coined the term **intertextuality** to refer to the fact that a text is a "mosaic" of preexisting texts whose meanings it reworks and transforms.)

Although poststructuralism has drawn from numerous critical perspectives developed in Europe and in North America, it relies most heavily on the work of French theorists, especially Jacques Derrida, Kristeva, Jacques Lacan, Michel Foucault, and Roland Barthes. Derrida's 1966 paper "Structure, Sign and Play in the Discourse of the Human Sciences" inaugurated poststructuralism as a coherent challenge to structuralism. Derrida rejected the structuralist presupposition that texts (or other structures) have self-referential centers that govern their language (or signifying system) without being in any way determined, governed, co-opted, or problematized by that language (or signifying system). Having rejected the structuralist concept of a self-referential center, Derrida also rejected its corollary: that a text's meaning is thereby rendered determinable (capable of being determined) as well as determinate (fixed and reliably correct). Lacan, Kristeva, Foucault, and Barthes have all, in diverse ways, arrived at similarly "antifoundational" conclusions, positing that no foundation or "center" exists that can ensure correct interpretation.

Poststructuralism continues to flourish today. In fact, one might reasonably say that poststructuralism serves as the overall paradigm for many of the most prominent contemporary critical perspectives. Approaches ranging from **reader-response criticism** to **the new historicism** assume the "antifoundationalist" bias of poststructuralism. Many approaches also incorporate the poststructuralist position that texts do not have clear and definite meanings, an argument pushed to the extreme by those poststructuralists identified with deconstruction. But unlike deconstructors, who argue that the process of signification itself produces irreconcilable contradictions, contemporary critics oriented toward other poststructuralist approaches (**discourse** analysis or Lacanian psychoanalytic theory, for instance) maintain that texts do have real meanings underlying their apparent or "manifest" meanings (which often contradict or cancel out one another). These underlying meanings have been distorted, disguised, or repressed for psychological or **ideological** reasons but can be discovered through poststructuralist ways of reading.

PRESENCE AND ABSENCE Words given a special literary application by French theorist of **deconstruction** Jacques Derrida when he used them to make a distinction between speech and writing. An individual speaking words must actually be present at the time they are heard, Derrida pointed out, whereas an individual writing words is absent at the time they are read. Derrida, who associates presence with *logos* (the creating spoken Word of a present God who "In the beginning" said, "Let there be light"), argued that the Western concept of language is **logocentric.** That is, it is grounded in "the metaphysics of presence," the belief that any linguistic system has a basic foundation (what Derrida terms an "ultimate referent"), making possible an identifiable and correct meaning or meanings for any potential statement that can be made within that system. Far from supporting this common Western view of language as logocentric, however, Derrida argues that presence is not an "ultimate referent" and that it does not guarantee determinable (capable of being determined) — much less determinate (fixed and reliably correct) — meaning. Derrida in fact calls into question the "privileging" of speech and presence over writing and absence in Western thought.

PSYCHOLOGICAL CRITICISM AND PSYCHOANALYTIC CRITICISM *See* "What Is Psychoanalytic Criticism?" pp. 261–72.

QUEER THEORY *See* **Gay and Lesbian Criticism, Gender Criticism.**

READER-RESPONSE CRITICISM A critical approach encompassing various approaches to literature that explore and seek to explain the diversity (and often divergence) of readers' responses to literary works.

Louise Rosenblatt is often credited with pioneering the approaches in *Literature as Exploration* (1938). In a 1969 essay entitled "Towards a Transactional Theory of Reading," she summed up her position as follows: "a poem is what the reader lives through under the guidance of the text and experiences as relevant to the text." Recognizing that many critics would reject this definition, Rosenblatt wrote: "The idea that a *poem* presupposes a *reader* actively involved with a *text* is particularly shocking to those seeking to emphasize the objectivity of their interpretations." Rosenblatt implicitly and generally refers to formalists (the most influential of whom are the **New Critics**) when she speaks of supposedly objective interpreters shocked by the notion that a *"poem"* is cooperatively produced by a *"reader"* and a *"text."* Formalists spoke of "the poem itself," the "concrete work of art," the "real poem." They had no interest in what a work of literature makes a reader "live through." In fact, in *The Verbal Icon* (1954), William K. Wimsatt and Monroe C. Beardsley used the term **affective fallacy** to define as erroneous the very idea that a reader's response is relevant to the meaning of a literary work.

Stanley Fish, whose early work is seen by some as marking the true beginning of contemporary reader-response criticism, also took issue with the tenets of formalism. In "Literature in the Reader: Affective Stylistics" (1970), he argued that any school of criticism that sees a literary work as an object, claiming to describe what it is and never what it does, misconstrues the very essence of literature and reading. Literature exists and signifies when it is read, Fish suggests, and its force is an affective force. Furthermore, reading is a temporal process, not a spatial one as formalists assume when they step back and survey the literary work as if it were an object spread out before them. The German critic Wolfgang Iser has described that process in his books *The Implied Reader: Patterns of Communication in Prose Fiction from Bunyan to Beckett* (1974) and *The Act of Reading: A Theory of Aesthetic Response* (1976). Iser argues that texts contain **gaps** (or blanks) that powerfully affect the reader, who must explain them, connect what they separate, and create in his or her mind aspects of a work that aren't *in* the text but that the text incites.

With the redefinition of literature as something that only exists meaningfully in the mind of the reader, with the redefinition of the literary work as a catalyst of mental events, comes a redefinition of the reader. No longer is the reader the passive recipient of those ideas that an author has planted in a text. "The reader is *active*," Rosenblatt had insisted. Fish makes the same point in "Literature in the Reader": "reading is . . . something you *do*." Iser, in focusing critical interest on the gaps in texts, on the blanks that readers have to fill in, similarly redefines the reader as an active maker of meaning. Other reader-response critics define the reader differently. Wayne Booth uses the phrase *the implied reader* to mean the reader "created by the work." Like Booth, Iser employs the term *the implied reader,* but he also uses *the educated reader* when he refers to what Fish calls the "intended reader."

Since the mid-1970s, reader-response criticism has evolved into a variety of new forms. Subjectivists like David Bleich, Norman Holland, and Robert Crosman have viewed the reader's response not as one "guided" by the text but rather as one motivated by deep-seated, personal, psychological needs. Holland has suggested that, when we read, we find our own "identity theme" in the text using "the literary work to symbolize and finally to replicate ourselves. We work out through the text our own characteristic patterns of desire." Even Fish has moved away from reader-response criticism as he had initially helped define it, focusing on "interpretive strategies" held in common by "interpretive communities"— such as the one comprised by American college students reading a novel as a class assignment.

Fish's shift in focus is in many ways typical of changes that have taken place within the field of reader-response criticism — a field that, because of those changes, is increasingly being referred to as *reader-oriented criticism.* Recent reader-oriented critics, responding to Fish's emphasis on interpretive communities and also to the historically oriented perception theory of Hans Robert

Jauss, have studied the way a given reading public's "horizons of expectations" change over time. Many of these contemporary critics view themselves as reader-oriented critics and as practitioners of some other critical approach as well. Certain **feminist** and **gender critics** with an interest in reader response have asked whether there is such a thing as "reading like a woman." Reading-oriented **new historicists** have looked at the way in which racism affects and is affected by reading and, more generally, the way in which politics can affect reading practices and outcomes. **Gay and lesbian critics,** such as Wayne Koestenbaum, have argued that sexualities have been similarly constructed within and by social **discourses** and that there may even be a homosexual way of reading.

REAL, THE *See* **Psychological Criticism and Psychoanalytic Criticism.**

SEMIOLOGY Another word for **semiotics**, created by Swiss linguist Ferdinand de Saussure in his 1915 book *Course in General Linguistics.*

SEMIOTICS A term coined by Charles Sanders Peirce to refer to the study of signs, sign systems, and the way meaning is derived from them. **Structuralist** anthropologists, psychoanalysts, and literary critics developed semiotics during the decades following 1950, but much of the pioneering work had been done at the turn of the century by Peirce and by the founder of modern linguistics, Ferdinand de Saussure.

To a semiotician, a sign is not simply a direct means of communication, such as a stop sign or a restaurant sign or language itself. Rather, signs encompass body language (crossed arms, slouching), ways of greeting and parting (handshakes, hugs, waves), artifacts, and even articles of clothing. A sign is anything that conveys information to others who understand it based upon a system of codes and conventions that they have consciously learned or unconsciously internalized as members of a certain culture. Semioticians have often used concepts derived specifically from linguistics, which focuses on language, to analyze all types of signs.

Although Saussure viewed linguistics as a division of semiotics (semiotics, after all, involves the study of all signs, not just linguistic ones), much semiotic theory rests on Saussure's linguistic terms, concepts, and distinctions. Semioticians subscribe to Saussure's basic concept of the linguistic sign as containing a *signifier* (a linguistic "sound image" used to represent some more abstract concept) and *signified* (the abstract concept being represented). They have also found generally useful his notion that the relationship between signifiers and signified is arbitrary; that is, no intrinsic or natural relationship exists between them, and meanings we derive from signifiers are grounded in the differences among signifiers themselves. Particularly useful are Saussure's concept of the *phoneme* (the smallest basic speech sound or unit of pronunciation) and his idea that phonemes exist in two kinds of relationships: diachronic and synchronic.

A phoneme has a diachronic, or "horizontal," relationship with those other phonemes that precede and follow it (as the words appear, left to right, on this page) in a particular usage, utterance, or **narrative** — what Saussure called *parole* (French for "word"). A phoneme has a synchronic, or "vertical," relationship with the entire system of language within which individual usages, utterances, or narratives have meaning — what Saussure called *langue* (French for "tongue," as in "native tongue," meaning language). *An* means what it means in English because those of us who speak the language are plugged in to the same system (think of it as a computer network where different individuals access the same information in the same way at a given time). A principal tenet of semiotics is that signs, like words, are not significant in themselves, but instead have meaning only in relation to other signs and the entire system of signs, or *langue*. Meaning is not inherent in the signs themselves, but is derived from the differences among signs.

Given that semiotic theory underlies structuralism, it is not surprising that many semioticians have taken a broad, structuralist approach to signs, studying a variety of phenomena ranging from rites of passage to methods of preparing and consuming food to understand the cultural codes and conventions they reveal. Because of the broad-based applicability of semiotics, furthermore, structuralist anthropologists such as Claude Lévi-Strauss, literary critics such as Roland Barthes, and **psychoanalytic theorists** such as Jacques Lacan and Julia Kristeva have made use of semiotic theories and practices. Kristeva, who is generally considered a pioneer of feminism (although she eschews the feminist label), has argued that there is such a thing as *feminine language* and that it is semiotic, not **symbolic** in nature. She thus employs both terms in an unusual way, using *semiotic* to refer to language that is rhythmic, unifying, and fluid, and *symbolic* to refer to the more rigid associations redefined in the Western canon. The affinity between semiotics and structuralist literary criticism derives from the emphasis placed on *langue*, or system. Structuralist critics were reacting against formalists and their method of focusing on individual words as if meanings did not depend on anything external to the text.

See also **Symbolic Order; Structuralism.**

SIMILE *See* **Metaphor; Trope.**

STRUCTURALISM A theory of humankind whose proponents attempted to show systematically, even scientifically, that all elements of human culture, including literature, may be understood as parts of a system of **signs.** Critic Robert Scholes has described structuralism as a reaction to " 'modernist' alienation and despair."

European structuralists such as Roman Jakobson, Claude Lévi-Strauss, and Roland Barthes (before his shift toward poststructuralism) attempted to develop a **semiology**, or **semiotics** (science of signs). Barthes, among others, sought to recover literature and even language from the isolation in which they had been studied and to show that the laws that govern them govern all signs, from road signs to articles of clothing.

Structuralism was heavily influenced by linguistics, especially by the pioneering work of linguist Ferdinand de Saussure. Particularly useful to structuralists were Saussure's concept of the *phoneme* (the smallest basic speech sound or unit of pronunciation) and his idea that phonemes exist in two kinds of relationships: diachronic and synchronic. A phoneme has a diachronic, or "horizontal," relationship with those other phonemes that precede and follow it (as the words appear, left to right, on this page) in a particular usage, utterance, or narrative — what Saussure called *parole* (French for "word"). A phoneme has a synchronic, or "vertical," relationship with the entire system of language within which individual usages, utterances, or narratives have meaning — what Saussure called *langue* (French for "tongue," as in "native tongue," meaning language). *An* means what it means in English because those of us who speak the language are plugged in to the same system (think of it as a computer network where different individuals can access the same information in the same way at a given time).

Following Saussure, Lévi-Strauss, an anthropologist, studied hundreds of myths, breaking them into their smallest meaningful units, which he called "mythemes." Removing each from its diachronic relations with other mythemes in a single myth (such as the myth of Oedipus and his mother), he vertically aligned those mythemes that he found to be homologous (structurally correspondent). He then studied the relationships within as well as between vertically aligned columns, in an attempt to understand scientifically, through ratios and proportions, those thoughts and processes that humankind has shared, both at one particular time and across time. Whether Lévi-Strauss was studying the structure of myths or the structure of villages, he looked for recurring, common elements that transcended the differences within and among cultures.

Structuralists followed Saussure in preferring to think about the overriding *langue* or language of myth, in which each mytheme and mytheme-constituted myth fits meaningfully, rather than about isolated individual *paroles,* or narratives. Structuralists also followed Saussure's lead in believing that sign systems must be understood in terms of binary oppositions (a proposition later disputed by poststructuralist Jacques Derrida). In analyzing myths and texts to find basic structures, structuralists found that opposite terms modulate until they are finally resolved or reconciled by some intermediary third term. Thus a structuralist reading of Milton's *Paradise Lost* (1667) might show that the war between God and the rebellious angels becomes a rift between God and sinful, fallen man, a rift that is healed by the Son of God, the mediating third term.

Although structuralism was largely a European phenomenon in its origin and development, it was influenced by American thinkers as well. Noam Chomsky, for instance, who powerfully influenced structuralism through works such as *Reflections on Language* (1975), identified and distinguished between "surface structures" and "deep structures" in language and linguistic literatures, including texts.

SYMBOL Something that, although it is of interest in its own right, stands for or suggests something larger and more complex — often an idea or a range of interrelated ideas, attitudes, and practices.

Within a given culture, some things are understood to be symbols: the flag of the United States is an obvious example, as are the five intertwined Olympic rings. More subtle cultural symbols might be the river as a symbol of time and the journey as a symbol of life and its manifold experiences. Instead of appropriating symbols generally used and understood within their culture, writers often create their own symbols by setting up a complex but identifiable web of associations in their works. As a result, one object, image, person, place, or action suggests others, and may ultimately suggest a range of ideas.

A symbol may thus be defined as a **metaphor** in which the **vehicle** — the image, activity, or concept used to represent something else — represents many related things (or **tenors**), or is broadly suggestive. The urn in Keats's "Ode on a Grecian Urn" (1820) suggests many interrelated concepts, including art, truth, beauty, and timelessness.

Symbols have been of particular interest to **formalists**, who study how meanings emerge from the complex, patterned relationships among images in a work, and **psychoanalytic critics**, who are interested in how individual authors and the larger culture both disguise and reveal unconscious fears and desires through symbols. Recently, French **feminist critics** have also focused on the symbolic. They have suggested that, as wide-ranging as it seems, symbolic language is ultimately rigid and restrictive. They favor **semiotic** language and writing — writing that neither opposes nor hierarchically ranks qualities or elements of reality nor symbolizes one thing but not another in terms of a third — contending that semiotic language is at once more fluid, rhythmic, unifying, and feminine.

SYMBOLIC ORDER *See* **Psychological Criticism and Psychoanalytic Criticism; Symbol.**

TENOR *See* **Metaphor; Metonymy; Symbol.**

TEXT From the Latin *texere*, meaning "to weave," a term that may be defined in a number of ways. Some critics restrict its use to the written word, although they may apply the term to objects ranging from a poem to the words in a book to a book itself to a biblical passage used in a sermon to a written transcript of an oral statement or interview. Other critics include nonwritten material in the designation text, as long as that material has been isolated for analysis.

French **structuralist** critics took issue with the traditional view of literary compositions as "works" with a form intentionally imposed by the author and a meaning identifiable through analysis of the author's use of language. These critics argued that literary compositions are texts rather than works, texts being the product of a social institution they called *écriture* (writing). By identifying compositions as texts rather than works, structuralists denied them the personalized character attributed to works wrought by a particular, unique author. Structuralists believed not only that a text was essentially impersonal, the confluence of certain preexisting attributes of the social institution of writing, but that any interpretation of the text should result from an impersonal *lecture* (reading). This *lecture* included reading with an active awareness of how the linguistic system functions.

The French writer and theorist Roland Barthes, a structuralist who later turned toward **poststructuralism**, distinguished text from *work* in a different way, characterizing a text as open and a work as closed. According to Barthes, works are bounded entities, conventionally classified in the canon, whereas texts engage readers in an ongoing relationship of interpretation and reinterpretation. Barthes further divided texts into two categories: *lisible* (readerly) and *scriptible* (writerly). Texts that are *lisible* depend more heavily on convention, making their interpretation easier and more predictable. Texts that are *scriptible* are generally experimental, flouting or seriously modifying traditional rules. Such texts cannot be interpreted according to standard conventions.

TROPE One of the two major divisions of **figures of speech** (the other being *rhetorical figures*). Trope comes from a word that literally means "turning"; to trope (with figures of speech) is, figuratively speaking, to turn or twist some word or phrase to make it mean something else. **Metaphor, metonymy, simile,** personification, and synecdoche are sometimes referred to as the principal tropes.

UNDECIDABILITY *See* **Deconstruction.**

VEHICLE *See* **Metaphor, Metonymy, Symbol.**

About the Contributors

THE VOLUME EDITOR

R. Brandon Kershner is Alumni Professor of English at the University of Florida, where he teaches twentieth-century literature, cultural studies, and poetry writing. In addition to numerous articles, he has published: *Dylan Thomas: The Poet and His Critics* (1977) and *Joyce, Bakhtin, and Popular Literature* (1989); the latter won the 1990 American Conference for Irish Studies award as the best work of literary criticism in the field. He has also authored *The Twentieth-Century Novel: An Introduction,* from Bedford Books (1997) and edited *Joyce and Popular Culture* (1990) and *Cultural Studies of James Joyce* (2003). He is a member of the Board of Advisory Editors of the *James Joyce Quarterly* and a past Trustee of the International James Joyce Foundation (1999–2004).

THE TEXTUAL EDITOR

Chester G. Anderson, Professor Emeritus of English at the University of Minnesota Celtic Studies program, edited the corrected text of Joyce's *Portrait* in 1964 and the Viking Critical Edition of *Portrait* ("Text, Criticism, and Notes") in 1968. He is the author of *James Joyce* *and His World* (1968) and of the chapter "Joyce's Verses" in the 1984 *Companion to Joyce Studies,* edited by Zack R. Bowen and James F. Carens.

THE CRITICS

Sheldon Brivic is a professor of English at Temple University where he specializes in modern British literature and psychoanalytic criticism. He has published *Joyce between Freud and Jung* (1980), *Joyce the Creator* (1985), and *The Veil of Signs: Joyce, Lacan, and Perception* (1991). His most recent book is *Joyce's Waking Women: An Introduction to "Finnegans Wake"* (1995). He currently serves on the editorial boards of the *James Joyce Quarterly* and *Journal of Modern Literature.*

Suzette Henke is Morton Professor of Literary Studies at the University of Louisville. She is the author of *Joyce's Moraculous Sindbook: A Study of "Ulysses"* (1978), coeditor of *Women in Joyce* (1982), author of *James Joyce and the Politics of Desire* (1990), and author of *Shattered Subjects: Trauma and Testimony in Women's Life-Writing* (2000). She has published articles on Virginia Woolf, Anais Nin, Dorothy Richardson, Linda Brent, Janet Frame, and others; and she is currently working on a collection of essays that examines the literature of modernity in the context of a psychoanalytic and poststructuralist paradigm.

Cheryl Herr is a professor of English at the University of Iowa, where she teaches post–1950 British and Irish culture. After spending 1992 in the Irish Republic and Northern Ireland as a Guggenheim Fellow she published two books — *Critical Regionalism and Cultural Studies: From Ireland to the American Midwest* (1996) and *The Field* (2002), the latter as part of the "Ireland into Film" series. She is also the author of *Joyce's Anatomy of Culture* (1986) and editor of *For the Land They Loved: Irish Political Melodramas, 1890–1925.* She has served as a trustee for the International James Joyce Foundation and is an Advisory Editor for the *James Joyce Quarterly.*

Vincent J. Cheng is Shirley Sutton Thomas Professor and director of the Tanner Humanities Center at the University of Utah, where he teaches twentieth-century literature, British literature, and ethnic studies. Among his scholarly articles and books are *Shakespeare and Joyce: A Study of "Finnegans Wake"* (1984) and *Joyce, Race, and Empire* (1995).

The former was the winner of the Choice Outstanding Book Award, and the latter the winner of the Phi Kappa Phi Book Award. Most recently he published *Inauthentic: The Anxiety over Culture and Identity* (2004), which deals with the struggle of identity in a multicultural society.

THE SERIES EDITOR

Ross C Murfin, general editor of *Case Studies in Contemporary Criticism*, is provost and vice president of academic affairs at Southern Methodist University. He has taught at the University of Miami, Yale University, and the University of Virginia, and has published scholarly studies of Joseph Conrad, Thomas Hardy, and D. H. Lawrence. With Supryia M. Ray, he is the author of *The Bedford Glossary of Critical and Literary Terms*.

(continued from p. iv)

"Nationalism, Celticism, and Cosmopolitanism in *A Portrait*" by Vincent J. Cheng. Parts of this essay were adapted, with permission, from the book by Vincent J. Cheng, *Joyce, Race, and Empire* (Cambridge: Cambridge UP, 1995; copyright © 1995 by Cambridge University Press) and from the essay by Vincent Cheng, "Terrible Queer Creatures": Joyce, Cosmopolitanism, and the Inauthentic Irishman," in *James Joyce and the Fabrication of an Irish Identity*, ed. Michael Patrick Gillespie, special volume of *European Joyce Studies* (Amsterdam: Rodopi, 2001), pp. 11–38; copyright © Rodopi 2001.

"Stephen Dedalus and Women: A Feminist Reading of *Portrait*" by Suzette Henke is a substantially revised version of an essay that appeared in *Women in Joyce*, ed. Suzette Henke and Elaine Unkeless (Urbana: U of Illinois P, 1982; © 1982 by the Board of Trustees of the University of Illinois) and *James Joyce and the Politics of Desire* by Suzette A. Henke (New York and London: Routledge, 1990; copyright © 1990 by Routledge, Chapman, and Hall, Inc.)